BIG EASY

THE COMPLETE SERIES

MARI CARR

BLANK CANVAS
BIG EASY, BOOK 1

Disillusioned by divorce, Jennifer's about to discover her wild side, starting with a tattoo from Caliph. And continuing with submission, spankings, wax play...all under the skilled hands of her wickedly sexy tattoo master.

CHAPTER ONE

Jennifer O'Neal released a long sigh as she stared at the front door of Midnight Ink. What the hell was she doing here? She wasn't this kind of person. Was she? The kind who called in sick to work to get a tattoo? The type who wore a tube-top in public? The sort who allowed some stranger to cover her back in ink?

No. She wasn't.

And that was the problem.

Marcus' voice drifted back to her.

I'm bored. Day after day of the same thing, Jennifer. I wake up every morning thinking there's gotta be more to life than this.

At the time, the words—when paired with *I've met someone else*—had cut through her like a machete. She'd been maimed, mortally wounded, devastated.

There was security in familiarity and after seventeen years of marriage, she and Marcus were about as familiar as it got. Their lives had fallen into a very comfortable routine. Maybe they didn't talk as much as they had in the early days of their relationship, maybe they didn't set the sheets on fire, but that didn't mean she didn't love him. For her, trading passion and excitement for a safe, reliable future with the man who had become her best friend had been worth it.

Marcus hadn't felt the same.

Which left her here. In front of a tattoo shop in the middle of Canal Street on a Tuesday morning taking advantage of a "New Beginnings" sale.

This was a mistake. She started to turn around, but before she could take the first step, the front door opened and a bell jangled, drawing her from her thoughts.

"Jennifer?"

She nodded mutely as she stared at Caliph, the artist she'd met with briefly the day after New Year's when they'd sat down to design her tattoo.

He was another reason she'd found it so difficult to return. He was the exact description of every man her mother had ever warned her to stay the hell away from. Tall and rough-looking, with a shaved head and muscular arms covered in bright tattoos, he was intimidating and overwhelming with an air of danger that made her stomach feel funny things that had nothing to do with fear and everything to do with sex. Which was weird because she hadn't felt those kinds of stirrings in a few years. Jesus. Maybe it was closer to a decade.

Caliph grinned when it became obvious she wasn't going to speak. "I thought that was you. Reconsidering?"

She started to shake her head no, then stopped and shrugged. "I don't know."

He stepped to the side and gestured toward the shop. "Wanna come in and talk about it? No pressure. You won't be the first person to change their mind and I promise it won't hurt my feelings if you do. Tattoos are forever, so it's smart to be completely positive."

"Okay."

She managed to take the steps required, pausing only briefly once she was next to him. The man had her by at least a foot and a hundred pounds. He was massive.

"Good girl," he murmured with a genuine smile as he placed his hand on her lower back and gently directed her inside the older building. She tried to repress the shiver his soft touch provoked. "Let's grab a cup of coffee, then we'll snag some seats in the reception area. I haven't hit my quota of caffeine for the day, so your cold feet are coming in handy. Giving me a chance to polish off another cup or three."

Another artist looked over at them as they walked past and pointed to Caliph with narrowed eyes. "You finish that pot again without making another one and I'll kick your ass."

"That might actually be a threat if you had a hope in hell of beating me in a fight, Shep. But, of course, you don't," Caliph teased.

Jennifer eyed the other artist, taking in his equally impressive height and the wicked scar on his brow. She wasn't sure she shared Caliph's confidence. Then she studied Caliph's Mr. Universe-sized physique and suspected if nothing else, it would be one hell of a fight.

The receptionist—Sassy—looked up from her seat behind the front desk as Caliph and Shep were talking. The last time Jennifer had visited Midnight Ink, the streak in Sassy's hair had been hot pink. Today, it was a vivid red that brought out that same color in the tattooed roses on her full sleeves. "Wow. If that isn't the pot calling the kettle black. Shep, you're one to talk about leaving the pot empty. I'm starting to think I'm the only one in the place who knows how to work the machine."

Shep grinned at her. "But your coffee is the best, Sassy."

Sassy shot him a dirty look. "Don't even try that line on me. You're the king of bullshit and I know it. I'm heading out to run a couple of errands, so you two are on your own for a while. Rosie is coming in later this afternoon. Y'all need anything?"

Caliph and Shep both said no.

"You good, Jennifer?"

Jennifer nodded, surprised the receptionist remembered her name. She'd only been in the shop once before and even that visit had been brief. "I'm fine. Thanks."

Sassy stopped at the front door and gave her an encouraging grin. "You're in good hands, baby doll. Caliph is one of the best." With that, she left.

"You want some coffee?" Caliph offered when they reached the pot. "Sassy really does make the best brew in the state of Louisiana."

She shook her head. She was already too keyed up, on edge. Coffee would only make that condition worse.

Caliph poured himself a cup and winked as he put the now-empty pot back. Then he led her back to the reception area, waiting until she sat down. He grabbed the seat next to her, chuckling. "You'd think after six years of being my best friend, Shep would know better than to tell me what to do. I'm just ornery enough to always do the opposite."

She laughed lightly at his joke. Then Jennifer was struck by how wrong the stereotypes about tattooed guys in leather were in regards to Caliph. How many women would walk by him on the street and feel genuine fear? Hell, she probably would have felt the same way prior to meeting him. She would have reached into her purse to wrap her hand around the can of pepper spray, not relaxing her white-knuckled grip on it until Caliph was well out of sight.

That realization made her feel guilty.

Caliph stretched out his legs, filling their tiny corner.

She grinned.

"What?" he asked.

"You're huge. It's like you take up every spare inch of space and then some."

He laughed, clearly not offended by her observation. "Yeah. Hit my growth spurt at fourteen. Spent the next four years turning down the high school football coach who begged me to play. Jesus, the guy tried everything from bribery to threats. I think he even cried once. He couldn't understand why a kid my size would spend his afternoons in the art room, drawing stupid pictures, rather than on the gridiron."

"Looks like you had the last laugh. You've made a career of art."

Caliph leaned forward. "You don't know the half of it. Fate is a bitch with a wicked sense of humor and I think she likes me. Few years ago, that coach showed up here and I gave him his first tat. He's been back three times since for more ink."

"Bet he's glad you spent the time honing your skills now."

"Yeah, but the truth is nobody was surprised when I started doing tattoos. Been drawing pictures since the cradle, according to my mom."

Jennifer had looked through a portfolio of his work. It was beautiful, a lot of his artwork simple and colorful. It was the main reason she'd selected him to do her tattoo. Midnight Ink was known as one of the best shops in New Orleans, with a reputation for cleanliness and incredible designs.

"Must be nice to have a job where you can put your talents to work."

He nodded. "It is. What do you do, Jennifer?"

"I'm the manager of Le Chateau Bayonne."

Caliph's eyebrows rose. "Hey, that's a classy hotel. Man, I'd love to see the inside of that place. Heard about the European décor. I know a guy who stayed there once. Super pricy apparently, but he said it was the best bed he's ever slept in."

Jennifer was flattered by his comment, even as she considered the hotel's typical clientele. Caliph hadn't exaggerated. The nightly room rates were more than she paid in one month's rent for her crappy apartment.

After the divorce, she and Marcus had sold their three-bedroom home, neither of them able to afford the mortgage on their own, let alone buy the other person out. So, she'd been uprooted from her nice, friendly neighborhood and thrust back into the world of paying rent on a lousy, too-tiny apartment in a less than desirable part of town.

In some ways, it rubbed against the grain to spend her days surrounded by people for whom money wasn't a concern while she was constantly counting her pennies, sticking to a budget. Her salary was okay—pretty good by most standards—but it was tough adjusting to living on one paycheck after years of sharing the load with Marcus and his teaching pay.

"It really is beautiful inside—French doors, gabled windows, wrought iron balconies. If you ever want a tour of the hotel, just let me know."

Caliph's face lit up. "Seriously? Because yeah, I wouldn't mind seeing it."

Jennifer was happy to have something cool to offer. Caliph was fascinating to her on about a million different levels, which made her feel like the Queen of Dullsville.

Then she realized her stomach was no longer twisted in knots and her fears over getting the tattoo fell away. Caliph had promised not to pressure her and he hadn't. Hell, he hadn't even mentioned the ink. He'd simply sat down and talked to her until her nervousness faded away.

"I'd like to get the tattoo," she said quietly.

"Hell yeah, that's my girl. Come on." He offered a hand to help her rise, then led her to his corner of the shop, the wooden floors creaking along the way. Jennifer studied each station they passed as a means of distraction. Brightly colored Mardi Gras beads adorned one, while Caliph's was much simpler. Sparse actually. Just an old family photo sat in a frame next to his equipment.

"Did you eat breakfast like I said?" Caliph asked.

She nodded. The toast she'd consumed had tasted like sawdust, but she'd choked it down.

"Pretty blouse. Take it off."

She'd covered the tube top she'd bought especially for today with a blouse. She'd had to force herself to keep the top four buttons open because she didn't want to look like a complete prude in front of Caliph.

She could have walked down the street in just the tube top as it was unseasonably warm. You had to love January in New Orleans. The temperature could be fifty degrees one day and eighty the next. For the past few days, they'd been riding in the upper seventies with blue skies and full sunshine that made it feel even hotter.

Despite the gorgeous weather, it had been uncomfortable for her to walk out of her apartment, sans bra, in the revealing outfit. She wasn't exactly lacking in the breast department and the only time she took off her double D bra was in the privacy of her own home.

She tugged the blouse off, folding and placing it on a nearby chair, sighing softly as she acknowledged the blouse was far from pretty and much closer to plain. The best description for her wardrobe was conservative. She did a mental eye roll. That was being nice. The truth was her clothing—like her—was boring.

God, why couldn't she shake that word from her vocabulary? Marcus had walked out on her almost a year earlier. It was time to let it go.

It was actually the arrival of the final divorce papers in the mail shortly before Christmas—*happy holidays to me,* she thought sardonically—that had jarred her out of her numb state and convinced her she needed to do something unpredictable and adventurous. When New Year's Eve arrived, she'd decided —with the help of a bottle of Pinot Grigio—this would be the year she sorted her shit out. She was going to break free of her same old routine and force herself to try different things.

Unfortunately, so far, the wildest thing she'd conjured up was getting this tattoo. She was so lame.

She glanced at the table before her.

"You're going to lie on your stomach, Jen. I need to sit down to work. I'm steadier that way."

She blushed as she crawled onto the table. She wasn't sure why, but the position made her feel vulnerable. Maybe it was because her dirty mind had invented too many fantasies the past two weeks about her getting horizontal with the gentle giant currently looming over her.

Then she considered how he'd shortened her name, calling her Jen. It was something only her family and closest friends did and it made her feel more at ease.

He didn't speak again as he put her into the position he wanted, lowering her tube top a wee bit as he lightly touched and cleaned her skin. She'd elected to have the tattoo put on her upper back, near her right shoulder. That way it would be hidden beneath her clothing. The owner of the hotel didn't have a policy about managers and tattoos, but that was probably because she seemed like the person least likely to ever get one. Even so, she didn't want to test the theory. She needed her job.

Then she recalled her wardrobe once more. With the exception of when she went swimming, this tat would probably *never* see the light of day. Bare skin wasn't part of her repertoire.

Neither of them spoke as he sprayed liquid soap to the spot and transferred the image on her skin. Jennifer took the time to study his face as he concentrated on his work, his warm hands gently smoothing the paper over her skin. It occurred to her she didn't have a clue how old he was. His face was tanned; his jaw covered with dark stubble that indicated he probably hadn't shaved this morning. There were laugh lines around his eyes she had the irresistible urge to run her fingertips over. The man could be anywhere between twenty-five and forty.

His fingers felt like magic, firing up some hot buttons that had lain dormant for far too long. She struggled to pull air into her lungs.

Caliph must have mistaken her arousal for nervousness. "Relax, beauty. You don't want to tense your muscles like that. The reality of this is it's going to hurt, but if you could loosen up a little, it'll be easier for you."

"Okay," she whispered, closing her eyes and cursing her suddenly tight throat, afraid of how she'd react to the pain. She wanted this damn tattoo. She really did. So why was she acting like a scared mouse? Why couldn't she summon even an ounce of bravery? Caliph probably thought she was a wuss.

He leaned closer. "Jen. Look at me."

She opened her eyes, trying not to reveal what his close proximity did to her. Mercifully, her position facedown on the table hid the fact her nipples had just gone hard, but it was more difficult to shield her flushing face and accelerated breathing.

He stroked her cheek gently with one finger. She pressed her legs together, trying to calm her arousal. Her pussy clenched hungrily and her panties were definitely damp.

"I'm finished with the sketch. Now comes the hard part. If it starts to be too much, tell me to stop and I will."

"Should I have a safe word?" She'd meant the words as a risqué joke, amazed she'd found the balls for off-color humor, but something about Caliph made her think *Dom*.

After her husband walked out, Jennifer had turned to books—reading voraciously for hours each night after work. Her love for historical romances soon drifted toward the erotic genre when the sweet, closed-door love scenes stopped doing it for her. She'd gone through a shifter phase, then a ménage one. These days she couldn't get enough of BDSM stories.

Caliph's gaze darkened and Jennifer reconsidered her previous assessment about his gentle personality. This man was no puppy dog. He was pure Pit Bull. Foolishly, that discovery didn't make her want to run. It only ramped up her desires even more.

"I was just kidding," she hastily added. "Very bad joke."

Caliph didn't reply, didn't let her off the hook easily. She fought the desire to stand and walk out of the shop. What on earth had possessed her to make such an inappropriate comment to a virtual stranger? She'd always considered common sense one of her better traits. Where the hell had that gone?

Finally, a slight smile tipped his lips. "You're an interesting woman, Jen. I like that."

Interesting? It was on the tip of her tongue to correct his misapprehension. He'd just caught her on a good day.

"You ready?" he asked.

She nodded once, then braced herself for the first pierce of the needle.

He'd warned her about the pain, but holy shit!

"Ohmigod! Jesus Christ! Fuck me!"

Caliph chuckled. "If you insist."

It took a second for the haze of pain to clear enough for her to understand his joke.

She glared at him. "That hurt."

"Never said it wouldn't. You wanna go on?"

No. She didn't. But as Caliph said, fate was a wicked bitch

and she chose that moment to arrive and bless Jennifer with courage. Or was it pride?

"Yes," she replied through gritted teeth.

Once again, he murmured his standard good girl, the compliment inciting an unfamiliar warmth inside her.

The tattoo gun fired up again, provoking another long stream of curse words to fly from her lips. Caliph grinned, but he didn't stop this time.

For several moments, he worked in silence as Jennifer tried to adapt to the pain. The initial hurt had started to wane and soon she learned to regulate her breathing as she anticipated his moves. Before too long, the buzz of the gun turned to white noise and she actually became drowsy.

Caliph must have sensed when she'd finally managed to relax because he broke the silence, his question rousing her just before she drifted off.

"Why a daisy?"

She jerked slightly and he apologized softly.

"Sorry. Were you falling asleep?"

She shook her head, lying so he wouldn't feel bad. "No."

He repeated the question. "Why a daisy tattoo?"

Jennifer considered her response, wishing he hadn't asked. The real reason was too personal, too revealing, too damn girly. She didn't want to know what Caliph would think if she told him the truth.

"It's my favorite flower." That much was true. Maybe that would be enough of a reason for him.

Unfortunately the man was too astute. "You don't have to tell me if you don't want to."

She frowned, feeling an odd need to protest his dismissal. "It really is my favorite."

"I'm sure it is. How old are you?"

She tried to understand his bizarre switch in subjects. "I'm going to be forty in August."

He smiled. "You know, most women would have said thirty-nine rather than confess to hitting the big four-oh so soon."

She considered the truth of that. "Forty is coming whether I admit it or not."

Her answer pleased him. She could see it in his expression. It increased the warmth inside her, leaving her confused about why his happiness left her feeling so content, gratified.

"Glad to hear you're not one of those women who has issues with age."

Jennifer winced slightly when his needle poked a sore spot. Suddenly she was glad for the distraction of conversation. "Nope. No sense fighting the inevitable. Besides I'm sort of looking forward to getting the hell out of my thirties." She'd spent most of that decade with Marcus and look how well that turned out. She'd started this year determined to make some changes, so why not start with a new number in front of her age?

"Good for you." Caliph picked up something from his tray, but Jennifer averted her eyes. There was a big difference between knowing there was a needle jabbing into her skin and seeing said needle. "Which leads me back to my original question. Why a daisy?"

She tried to dodge answering with an inquiry of her own. "Why did you want to know how old I was?"

His eyes never left the site of the tattoo. She found his intense concentration sexy as hell.

Jesus, lock the hormones away, Jennifer. Pretty soon you'll start drooling.

"It's not unusual for women to get a tattoo when those big birthdays start looming, but for most of them, I think it's a way to pretend the clock isn't ticking. It's their attempt to turn back time. You don't seem to care about age, so clearly that's not the impetus for this tat."

Impetus? Tattoo artist armchair psychiatry. "Where did you go to school?" She didn't specify high school or college on the off chance she was wrong and she'd somehow offend him.

"ULM."

Nope, not wrong. College grad. She tried to school her features, but she didn't fool him.

He chuckled. "Surprised to find out your tattoo artist has a bachelor's degree?"

She shook her head as more of the stereotypes fell away. God. Was she really so narrow-minded?

"It's okay, Jen. Tattoo artists aren't obligated to get a degree in art. That requirement came from my mother. She'd preached about the importance of a college education from the day I was born until I graduated from high school and nothing short of a zombie apocalypse was going to be a good enough excuse not to further my education."

"She sounds scary. And awesome."

He stopped working for a moment to capture her gaze. "You're right. She's both. But enough of that. You keep changing the subject. If you don't want to tell me what the daisy represents, just say 'fuck off'."

Even with his permission, she'd never say that to him. Probably because part of her was afraid he would and she didn't like the thought of him leaving.

She shook that thought out of her head instantly. She was just getting a tattoo from the guy, not dating him.

"I don't understand why you keep insisting there's some deep meaning behind it. Can't I just like a flower?"

"You've left this soft, pale skin untouched for thirty-nine years. You don't strike me as the impulsive type. I'd be willing to bet you're a planner, a list maker. Someone who thinks before they act. You're also intelligent and sensitive. There's a story behind the daisy."

His astute observations left her speechless. He was right. She'd spent countless hours pouring over images of tattoos as she considered what was right for her. When she'd seen the delicate rendering of the daisy with several of its petals lightly drifting down, it had spoken to her, felt right.

"My husband left me for another woman last year." She hadn't intended to speak the words aloud. In fact, she could count on one hand the number of times she'd actually admitted to Marcus' desertion. A few close friends knew the truth. As for the rest of her acquaintances, she'd used the tried and true *we just drifted apart* lie.

"What a jackass."

Caliph had muttered his reply, but his vehemence caught her off-guard. She giggled.

"Don't move," he instructed, lifting the tattoo gun away.

She apologized as she struggled to compose herself again.

"Thanks. Jackass fits," she said after he'd resumed his work.

"Don't thank me. I'm just stating a fact."

More warmth. More happiness. So much in fact, she wondered if there was some narcotic in the ink that was drugging her senses, serving as an aphrodisiac.

"I've spent the last year trying to figure out what I did wrong."

Caliph turned off the gun, frowning. "*He* had the affair and you think *you* did something wrong?"

"People who are happily married don't stray."

"Maybe not, but fucking someone else is a surefire way *not* to fix the marriage."

His strong opinions made her curious. "Have you ever been married?"

He released a long sigh. "No, Jen, I haven't. Marriage isn't really something I aspire to. But that doesn't mean I don't understand. I've had a couple long-term relationships go south. Maybe there weren't wedding rings on our fingers, but I was committed just the same."

"I'm saying this badly. Marcus and I were together for seventeen years. Long enough for me to start becoming complacent, maybe even a little lazy. In the future, I won't take my relationships for granted."

"I get that, but I don't like that you're blaming yourself."

"My ex was an asshole. The way he chose to leave was cowardly and wrong. I'm not denying that, but it would be very shallow and shortsighted of me to pretend it was all his fault. Takes two to tango."

"That still doesn't explain the tat."

"I've spent the past year feeling like complete dog shit."

Caliph chuckled at her description; his eyes were brimming with compassion.

"I got my divorce papers just before the holidays and they sort of woke me up. Jerked me out of my depression."

"Doesn't sound like a bad thing."

She released a long breath, wondering why she found it so easy to talk to Caliph. "It wasn't. I spent the last year dwelling on the negative, feeling sorry for myself. This year, I'm going for the positive. That's where the daisy comes in."

Caliph's brow creased. "How?"

She smiled when she considered her reason. "It's going to be my reminder that we don't get just one shot at happiness in life. Marcus loved me. Then he loved me not."

Caliph pressed a soft finger to a spot on her back. Though she couldn't see it, she suspected it was one of the petals that had fallen from the flower.

"There are a lot more petals on that flower." Maybe it

would sound silly to Caliph, but to her the reason for getting this tattoo made sense. "I have a lot more chances to find my happily ever after."

"You think you need a man to be happy?"

She shook her head. "No. Not at all." She'd heard the same argument from her girlfriends for months. They were full of well-meaning advice, telling her to take time for herself, enjoy life on her own. Hell, she was pretty sure half the married ones were jealous of her single state, wishing for their own freedom.

"I don't have to be in a relationship to feel good about myself. I got knocked down a peg when Marcus left and I've been trying to find my balance since then. I'm still a bit wobbly, but I'm getting there. Being in love has nothing to do with that."

Caliph looked like he might argue, but she cut him off.

"I've spent the last year living on my own. Can I do it? Yeah, sure. I just don't want to. I loved being married and I looked forward to growing old with someone. It's not something I need, Caliph. It's just something I want. A man to talk to about my day, to eat dinner with, to fight over the remote with. His side of the bed, my side. Twice the laundry and dishes. Sharing the bills, splitting dessert in a restaurant. The good and the bad. I miss it."

He smiled at her. "You might be the first person on earth to actually make marriage sound good to me."

She laughed. "So you're really not a fan of marriage at all?"

He shrugged. "Not sure I've ever considered it one way or the other. I've always been pretty happy with my status quo."

Jennifer felt a twinge of envy. She hadn't enjoyed much about her life for the past year. No, it was more than that. If she was being honest, she'd been just as miserable and bored in her marriage to Marcus as her ex had been with her. Only she'd been too afraid—or was it lazy?—to do anything about it.

"Well, I'm certainly not looking to get married again right

away. That's a plan for some distant future. For now, I'm hoping to find a way to shed some of my inhibitions and have fun. I started the year vowing I would go wild. Unfortunately, I sort of suck at it."

Caliph tilted his head and studied her face. He had a way of looking at her that made her feel like he could see straight through her. "Think of it like this, Jen. You're a blank canvas. Beautiful, clean, white. The colors are all there inside you. You just need to set them free."

She swallowed heavily as she glanced at her shoulder. She couldn't see the pretty shades of her tattoo yet, but she knew they were there.

Today she'd taken the first step and grabbed a new beginning. The heaviness that had weighed her down for so long lifted and a spark of joy flared.

Colors.

Set free.

Yeah.

CHAPTER TWO

Caliph leaned back and admired his work. After Jennifer explained the daisy, their conversation slowly faded away as he lost himself in the art. He'd taken his time with this tat, putting special care into every single line. The design was simple, honest, elegant. It reminded him of the woman lying in front of him, the beauty who was going to wear his art for the rest of her life.

He was always flattered, even a little humbled, by the people who put so much faith in his abilities that they allowed him to draw on their skin with permanent ink. It was a gift countless clients had given him even though he'd never admitted such to them.

Jennifer was different from the usual Midnight Ink clientele. She didn't want the tattoo to hide past scars. Many people—male and female—used body art to conceal terrible wounds, physical and emotional. Caliph understood their reasons, felt their pain, and always prayed his art would somehow help them find peace again.

Neither was she trying to draw attention to herself, to

appear tough or in-your-face or cool, which, sadly, seemed to be the reason for getting a tat amongst a lot of the younger clients. Caliph suspected Jennifer spent most of her time trying to blend into the background. Which meant her trip to his chair had taken a great deal of courage on her part.

No. Jennifer wasn't trying to hide from her pain or make a big flashy statement. Instead she was incorporating her past failures into the picture, including them as a part of the canvas in an effort to make her stronger, smarter.

He thought about her ex-husband. He had the insane urge to find the asshole and beat him to a pulp for the way he'd damaged Jennifer's self-esteem. It was clear she was a compassionate woman and it pissed him off to see her feeling badly about herself. While she put up a tough front, pain still lingered in her eyes. Her trusting nature as well as her faith in herself had been shaken. Hard.

"You like jazz?" he asked.

She grinned. "Isn't that sort of a prerequisite for living in New Orleans?"

Caliph chuckled. "I know plenty of people who hate it. Tasteless bastards. You ever heard of the Jazz Parlor?"

"In the French Quarter?"

"Yeah. There's a guy playing there Friday night, Jeremy 'Trombone' Lionel."

"Let me guess. He plays the trombone."

Caliph rolled his eyes. "He's one of the best I've ever heard. You wanna go?"

"With you?" Jennifer winced as soon as the question passed her lips. It was an endearing expression that he was starting to become accustomed to. Her mouth seemed to kick in before her brain at times, treating him to her real thoughts. It was refreshing, nice. With Jennifer, you got what you saw. That wasn't true of most women and he found he preferred the unfiltered view.

"Sassy is coming and my brother, Justin, too. So you don't have to worry about me putting the moves on you." For a second he thought he saw a flash of disappointment in her pretty blue eyes. The look encouraged him to add, "Much."

Her smile reflected pure, genuine happiness and Caliph struggled to catch his breath. Something strange stirred in his gut. It was like he'd been sucker punched, but he didn't feel like hitting back.

"I'd love to go. Thank you for the invitation. Should I just meet you here? Friday night?"

He nodded slowly, pleased by her quick response. She didn't employ any of those female games where she had to pretend to think about it so as not to appear too anxious. Jennifer didn't even try to hide the fact she was excited. "Yeah. Eight o'clock work for you?"

"Yep. It sure does." She was still lying on the table, though he'd put the tattoo gun down, his work finished. She bit her lower lip nervously. "Can I look at it now?"

Caliph had been purposely stalling. Not that he thought the tattoo looked bad. In his opinion, it was some of his best work. Knowing what the flower represented to Jennifer had encouraged him to enhance the original drawing, making sure the image would allow her to find that strength and love she was seeking.

"Of course you can." He placed a firm hand on her arm, not mistaking the slight shudder his touch provoked. It wasn't the first time he'd felt her tremble under his fingers. At first, he'd blamed it on fear—he was used to women's frightened responses to him, he was no pretty boy and he knew it—but Jennifer's trusting eyes and flushed face made him wonder if her response was based on something far different.

His stomach clenched again and this time he recognized the cause. Lust. Pure. Unbridled. His cock thickened slightly despite his attempts to will it away with deep, steadying breaths.

Jennifer sat up slowly, hastily tugging up her tube top. Her modesty was cute. It made Caliph want to peel her clothing away slowly, revealing one creamy inch of skin at a time. Her body was sumptuous, though he suspected she probably considered herself fat. Society had done a real number on women with curves in the last fifty years, trying to convince them that stick figures were desirable. Fuck that. As far as he was concerned, Jennifer's generous hourglass was the standard for true feminine beauty.

She followed as he led her to the large mirror hanging against the back wall. He placed a handheld mirror in her hands, watching nervously as she studied the reflection.

"You didn't bleed very much. I have an A and D ointment here that I'll put on before I cover it. Sassy has flyers on her desk that will give you instructions for aftercare. I want you to follow them to the letter." Caliph stuck his hands in the back pockets of his jeans and forced himself to stop rambling. Her silence made him nervous. Christ. He never got this worked up over a client's reaction to a tat. According to Shep, he had more than his fair share of cockiness when it came to his work. Unfortunately that confidence was on shaky ground at the moment.

Finally, he couldn't stand it anymore. "Jen?"

She looked at him—that was when he noticed the tears in her eyes. Oh hell, did she hate it? He'd seen clients cry before, overwhelmed by their first tattoo. But he couldn't stand the thought that maybe she was genuinely upset.

He took the mirror from her and placed it on the counter,

then he grasped her hands and gave them a squeeze. "Aw, hell, honey. I'm sorry."

She shook her head. "No. Don't be. It's just—"

"You were nervous about the tat. Second-guessing your decision. I should have told you to go home and sleep on it."

"No." Her grip on his hands tightened. "I love it."

He studied her face, trying to decide if she was lying just to assuage his guilty conscience. As always, he saw nothing but honesty in her gaze. "You do?"

She gave him a wobbly smile, her tears overflowing. "Oh my God, yes. It's even better than I imagined. It's perfect."

Caliph rubbed his jaw, relief suffusing him. "Damn, girl. You scared the shit out of me."

Jennifer laughed, then picked up the mirror once more, taking even longer to admire her new look. The pleasure in her eyes warmed him.

Shep walked over to join them, studying the tat. "Nice work, Cal. That's a beaut."

Caliph nodded, barely acknowledging Shep's compliment. He was more interested in watching Jennifer.

Then he heard Shep mutter something like "aw jeez, here we go" and Caliph's attention turned back to his friend. "What?"

Shep rolled his eyes at Caliph's confusion, then looked at Jennifer. "Congratulations. It's a great tattoo."

Jennifer smiled widely. "Thanks."

Shep returned to his chair as Caliph led Jennifer back to his. Obviously Caliph hadn't managed to mask his attraction to Jennifer from his friend. One of the dangers of working with the same people for so long. The artists in the shop spent too much damn time together. Sometimes it was nice to have such fierce friends at his back, but most of the time it was a pain in the ass. Shep was definitely going to give him shit for this, tease him about getting the hots for the quiet, conservative hotel manager.

Caliph picked up a tube of ointment and turned Jennifer away from him. As he squeezed some onto a stick, he felt her quiver and he had to resist the impulse to lean forward and place a kiss on the back of her slim neck. He spread the lotion onto her skin.

While he worked, he briefly ran through a mental list of reasons why he shouldn't start an affair with Jennifer.

For one thing, the pain from her divorce was present and though she had a good attitude in regards to moving on, she still had a ways to go. Besides, he wasn't looking for a relationship and certainly didn't want to end up hurting her like her ex had.

They were also different people. Jennifer was clearly conservative, reserved. He wasn't sure how she'd respond to his impulsiveness, his tendency to live in the moment. Jennifer didn't strike him as someone who'd find that an easy thing to deal with even for the short-term.

He also wasn't sure what she'd make of their age difference —he was thirty-two to her nearly forty. While she didn't seem hung up on the numbers, Caliph didn't know how she'd feel about sleeping with a younger man. Then, he dismissed that thought as unimportant.

Because there was one way in which she was definitely wrong for him. She may have been married for seventeen years, but he had no doubt her adventures in the bedroom didn't extend much beyond missionary. Compared to him, she was an innocent.

Caliph couldn't remember the last time he'd had missionary sex. His desires ran along a much different path. He pictured taking Jennifer to the Bastille, a local sex club. He liked the idea of exposing her to that world to see if his suspicions about her sexually submissive nature were true. Her blushes and trembles when he touched her, the way her eyes lowered whenever he asked her to do something, the tiny ways she deferred to him, all combined together in such a way that had him longing to tie her to his bed and fuck her senseless.

Then he imagined Jennifer taking one look at the dark, intimidating sex club with its St. Andrew's crosses and wooden posts with eyebolts and chains. She'd most likely scream as she ran from the room.

Or would she?

Her mention of a safe word earlier threw him. Made him wonder.

And want.

He covered her tattoo with plastic wrap, then he reached for the blouse she'd worn to the shop. He helped put it on, pleased when she turned to face him, allowing him to button it for her.

His excuses for avoiding sex with her fled the instant her pretty blue eyes met his. Jennifer may have been hurt by her ex, but the asshole's cruelty hadn't killed her spirit. The same desire he felt was reflected in her face. Jesus. She wanted him.

"Thanks," she said softly when he'd fastened the last button.

He didn't release the material. He heard Shep talking to his client, a regular, neither man paying attention to them. Sassy had returned from running errands an hour ago and was in the back room. No one else was working yet, the other artists choosing to work later shifts.

Jennifer held his gaze. "Caliph?" she whispered when the silence continued a beat too long.

"How wild do you want to go?"

She frowned, then gave him a rueful grin. "I love my tattoo more than I can say, but I'm definitely not ready for another."

He shook his head. "That's not what I mean." He lowered his voice. "I'm attracted to you, Jen."

She licked her lips, the action a perfect blend of nervousness and arousal. Caliph's cock thickened even more.

"I want you too." Her admission came out more air than tone, but he heard it, let the beauty of it soak deep.

"Friday night, after the jazz club." He didn't say more. He didn't need to. Jennifer was already nodding.

"Okay. I'd like that."

"So would I."

Then her brow furrowed. That didn't take long. Less than five seconds in and she was already reconsidering.

"Tell me what you're thinking," he prodded.

"I've never had a one-night stand."

Caliph was touched by her honesty, but bothered by it as well. That list of reasons he should have stayed away rained down on him again. Women like her didn't do casual sex, but he was pretty damn sure that was all he had to give her. He hadn't lied about his disinterest in marriage. "Jennifer—"

He started to offer her an out, but she cut him off.

"No. I'm not saying that's a bad thing. It's actually a really good thing. I might be putting the pieces back together, Caliph, but the truth of it is, I'm still pretty broken. At this point in my life, I have basically nothing, but sex to give you. Besides, something tells me you'd be a great guy to go wild with."

He grinned. "I'm glad you have such faith in my abilities. I'll do my best not to disappoint you."

She laughed. "I'm not worried."

Caliph knew he should take her agreement to sleep with him and run with it, but he couldn't lie to her when she looked at him with those gorgeous, trusting eyes. She needed to know exactly what she was agreeing to.

"Maybe you should be. Because, Jen, you *will* need a safe word Friday night."

Her cheeks flushed a pretty pink, but she held her ground. His respect for her went up several more notches.

"Does it make me sound completely twisted if I say that's the hottest thing anyone's ever said to me?"

He barked out a laugh and shook his head. "You're a fascinating woman, Jen. And I can't wait to paint on your canvas some more."

CHAPTER THREE

Jennifer leaned back in her chair and wished the soft, mellow music would work its magic on her. As it was, she was a bundle of nerves and pent-up hormones. Ever since Caliph issued his invitation to the club—and everything that would come after—she'd found it impossible to think about anything else. Her work was suffering. She hadn't slept more than a few hours each night and the woman who never missed a meal was suddenly living on only a couple of bites here and there.

In a word, she was a mess.

Caliph reached under the table and placed a firm hand on her knee to still her rapidly bouncing leg.

She glanced at him. "Sorry," she whispered.

When they'd entered the club, Caliph had escorted her to a table along a side wall. He'd wasted no time pulling his chair as close to hers as possible. Sassy had come with them, but within minutes of arriving, she'd run into other friends. Jennifer glanced over to the bar and saw the vivacious woman laughing and talking. Jennifer wished she felt even half as carefree at the moment.

Caliph squeezed her knee gently. "Relax, Jen."

It was on the tip of her tongue to tell him that was easier said than done, but before she could speak, a man approached their table.

"There you are. Sorry I'm late, Cal. Fucking work is insane right now. We landed three big clients, so I'm in deadline hell." The man plopped into a chair across from them. "Hey. You must be Jennifer. I'm Justin."

Jennifer took the man's outstretched hand and shook it. "Nice to meet you."

Caliph pushed the extra Guinness he'd ordered toward his brother. "Here. Had the waitress bring this over when you texted to say you were on your way. Figured you could use a cold one."

Justin smiled and muttered a quick word of thanks before taking a drink.

Jennifer was struck by how different the men were. Where Caliph was a huge, hulking figure with his smooth, shaved head, tattooed skin and tight black T-shirt, Justin was long, lean and clean-cut with an expensive hairstyle, conservative shirt and new jeans. Caliph was linebacker to his brother's point guard, and besides their height, she was hard-pressed to find one physical similarity between them.

Caliph must have noticed her attempt. "Don't bother trying. Justin's my half-brother and, according to our mom, he's the spitting image of his old man, while I'm the mirror image of mine."

Justin chuckled. "Pisses her off too. Says it's not fair that none of her kids got even a speck of her good looks."

They all laughed.

"I can't decide if I want to meet your mother or not. She seems like a force to be reckoned with," Jennifer joked.

Caliph put his arm around her shoulder, the close proximity doing funny things to her libido. Jennifer struggled to keep cool, but had no doubt her flushed face was giving her away to both men at the table. "Don't worry, Jen. I'd protect you from her."

Justin snorted. "Yeah right. Just admit you're afraid of her too. Hell, we all are. When Meg Lewis says move, you better believe everybody in the house goes into motion."

"Everybody? You have other brothers and sisters?" As she asked the question, she realized how little she really knew about Caliph. This was only the third time she'd even seen the man and she'd agreed to have sex with him. Responsible Jennifer would never have dreamed of jumping into bed with a stranger, yet the decision to sleep with Caliph had been surprisingly easy. And it occurred to her that most of her nervousness wasn't based on fear, but anticipation.

"My mom had four kids, Justin's the oldest, then me, then our brother Jett. Chloe is the only girl and the baby."

"Which means she's spoiled rotten," Justin added.

Jennifer could tell from their expressions both men adored their kid sister.

Caliph ran his finger along the nape of her neck and Jennifer resisted the urge to shudder...and purr. "But the family is actually bigger than that."

Justin took a swig of beer and put the glass back down. "Mom has taken in a lot of foster kids over the years. She was a social worker before she got married. After she started having kids, she quit her job."

"Her workdays were unbelievably long and she didn't want to be away from us for so many hours every day," Caliph continued. "Of course, she also couldn't stand the thought of other kids out there who needed a safe place to stay."

"Over the years, we've had six foster brothers and sisters live with us, off and on, depending on how much the system wanted to fuck with them." Justin's tone didn't mask his disgust and Caliph's expression proved he felt the same way.

She could imagine how hard it would be to bring a child into your home only to have the courts yank them back out to return them somewhere less safe. Jennifer smiled sympathetically. "Your mom sounds great. What about your dad...or sorry, dads?"

Justin chuckled. "I was an oops during my parents' senior year at college. They never got married, but I know my dad. He's still around. Papa Lewis is the one she married."

"My dad was a boxer before he started working on oil rigs. He wasn't home much. Used to joke that was why my mom kept taking in strays. To keep from getting lonely."

"As if you could get lonely in that house," Justin added.

Caliph's eyes dimmed. "Dad had a massive heart attack a few years ago and died."

Jennifer took Caliph's hands. "Oh. I'm so sorry."

Caliph squeezed her fingers lightly, clearly appreciating her words. "It's okay, but thanks."

Justin's cell beeped and he glanced at the screen, his eyes going wide with excitement. "Hot damn."

Caliph shook his head in feigned disapproval. "Let me guess. Ned?"

Justin gave his brother a shit-eating grin. "Yep. Turns out my partner may have an interesting, er, prospect for us tonight. You guys care if I shove off early?"

Caliph pointed to Justin's glass. "You're leaving money for that beer. I'm getting sick of covering your bar tabs whenever you get a better offer."

Justin threw a ten-dollar bill on the table with a laugh. "Nice to meet you, Jennifer."

"You too," she said as he walked away. She turned to look at Caliph. "Prospect?"

Caliph hesitated for a moment. Finally, he answered. "My brother and his marketing partner, Ned, are best friends. They like to share."

The light went on. "Women?"

He nodded. "Yeah." He studied her face as she fought to school her features. She certainly didn't want to look like a judgmental prude when the truth was the whole idea made her hot.

"Oh. Well, that's cool."

Caliph laughed. "Glad you think so."

His words ran over her like ice water and for the first time since she'd agreed to sleep with him, panic set in. "I mean, I don't, I didn't—"

Caliph took her hands in his once more. "Relax, Jen. Tonight is just you and me. Threesomes are Justin's kink. Not mine."

"What are yours?" The question fell out before she could think better of it, but she didn't bother to take it back. Despite her undeniable horniness, she hadn't taken complete leave of her senses. Probably best to put all their cards on the table now.

"Bondage. Domination. Spanking. Wax play. Anal."

He rattled off his grocery list of sex acts with such ease Jennifer struggled to catch her breath. "Oh. Is that all?"

Caliph laughed at her joke, shaking his head. "You're adorable." He wrapped his arm around her shoulder and pulled her closer. His size became even more apparent as she was engulfed in sheer muscle. "Tonight's not about my kinks, Jen. You wanted to go wild. Tell me how."

She licked her suddenly dry lips. She'd read about—fantasized over—everything he'd mentioned. But there was safety in fiction. Caliph was offering to make her dreams a reality and that scared the shit out of her. "I sort of thought I was pushing the envelope by having sex with a virtual stranger. Starting to think I might be out of my league."

Caliph ran the back of one finger along her cheek in a way that should have been endearing, but was the equivalent of throwing gasoline on a flame. Her pussy clenched. "Your league is just fine. Tell me where you see tonight going."

She considered his list. "I don't know you well enough to let you tie me up and render me helpless."

Caliph grinned. "Good girl. You're right. You don't."

He accepted her admission too easily and she was concerned he'd misunderstood. "But...that doesn't mean I don't want it. I mean...I would...eventually."

Heat suffused her face. God. Caliph had invited her out tonight—only offered her one evening. She hadn't meant to insinuate she wanted more.

He cupped her cheeks in his hands, forcing her to look at him. "I love your expressions."

She frowned. "What do you—"

"You're a very easy woman to read, Jen. I want tonight to go well. And if it does, we can talk about seeing each other again. There's nothing to say a one-night stand can't run over into two. You seem to be a very sensual woman with some fantasies that need exploring. Let's just roll with it. Don't shield your words or hide your feelings from me because they aren't going to scare me away."

Jennifer wasn't sure how to respond. She'd come here tonight fully prepared for a one-night stand. Truthfully that seemed like the most she could handle. She'd never mastered casual sex. Ever since she'd lost her virginity in eleventh grade, she'd had a tendency to lead with her heart. If she let tonight trickle into more, wouldn't she be setting herself up for heartache?

After nursing a broken heart for the better part of last year, she wasn't sure she was ready to open herself up for more hurt.

"Uh oh. You're thinking too much." He stood, throwing money on the table. "Come on, gorgeous. I'm taking you back to my place and fucking you until you forget your name."

She rose slowly, then hesitated for a moment. She hadn't lied earlier about what made this night seem wild, even if it felt tame compared to Caliph's sexual proclivities. Essentially, they really were strangers. She didn't even know where he lived. This was stupid and reckless.

Caliph held out his hand. "Give me your phone."

"Why?" Even as she asked the question, she handed it over.

"Who's your best friend?"

"Beth."

He turned it on and clicked on her list of contacts before handing it back to her. "Send a text to Beth. Tell her where you're going and give her my address."

"Okay." Apparently Jennifer wasn't the only one with common sense. Caliph read her concerns and he'd found a way to alleviate the fear. She tapped out the address he gave, promising to check in, and then she hit send. No doubt Beth would be beating on her apartment door first thing tomorrow morning, excitedly demanding details and a complete recap of the evening.

"Better?" he asked.

She nodded.

"You still wanna come home with me?"

She smiled and released a long, slow breath. "So damn much."

Caliph stopped by the bar to make sure Sassy had a ride home. They'd decided to leave her car at Midnight Ink and ride to the club together. He assured her that her car would be fine at the tattoo shop overnight, so he drove her to his house. The trip was surprisingly relaxing as they talked about anything and everything—her family, his work at the shop, their mutual love of jazz. When they reached his house, Caliph turned the car off, but neither of them bothered to get out. They just kept talking.

Though they'd only known each other a short time, Jennifer felt like she'd shared more of herself with Caliph in just one evening than she had with Marcus during the last few years of their marriage.

Finally, Caliph glanced at his phone, his eyebrows rising. "Damn. Where did that time go?" Nearly two hours had passed, but to Jennifer it felt like the blink of an eye.

"I have no idea, but Caliph..." Her nervousness had evaporated somewhere in the midst of their long talk, and now, when faced with the prospect of going inside, she felt nothing but overwhelming desire and need.

He'd said her expressions gave her away. Apparently he hadn't lied. Caliph's eyes darkened with honest-to-God hunger. It took her breath away. No one had ever looked at her with such unbridled lust.

"I don't think I'm going to make it inside," she whispered, assaulted by an arousal so painful and beautiful she wasn't sure she could walk without coming.

"Oh fuck yeah." Caliph was out of the car and opening her door between one blink of the eye and the next. He reached down to help her out, wrapping her in his huge embrace. She recalled building a tent as a child, tying the corners of a big blanket to the four posts of her bed. She'd huddle beneath it in the darkness, soaking up the warmth and security of her snug hiding spot. Caliph's hug reminded her of that place, bringing back sensations of being safe and happy.

Neither of them spoke when he loosened his grip, taking her hand to lead her into his small house. It reminded her of the man—simple, straightforward. His yard was neatly trimmed, the porch clean, freshly painted. When he opened the door and turned on the light, she admired the cozy warmth of his home. Family portraits covered the wall of his living room.

"Want a tour?" he offered.

She shook her head. There would be time for that later. Maybe. "No." She let that one word tell him exactly what she wanted.

Caliph tightened his grip on her hand and tugged her down a narrow hallway and straight into his bedroom.

"Take off your clothes."

The quick demand would have freaked out old Jennifer, but the woman Caliph was helping her discover was beyond modesty.

She unbuttoned her blouse, shrugging it over her shoulders without hesitance. Caliph didn't join her in disrobing. Instead he ate her alive with his eyes, and amazingly, he appeared to like what he saw. Marcus had pointed out the fact that she'd let herself go, that she'd gained a few pounds, as yet another reason he'd wanted out. She shoved that memory away. The bastard had no place here tonight. She wasn't going to let him cast his miserable shadow on one minute of this.

Jennifer toed off her shoes, then unzipped her skirt. Her actions slowed. Despite her attempts to hold on to her newfound confidence, she found it wavering.

Caliph stepped closer. "You're beautiful. Perfect. Take off the skirt."

She reacted without thought—as the skirt, her panties, and even her bra fell away with ease—until she stood before him completely naked. Jennifer resisted the urge to close her eyes, to hide before she could see his response. She wasn't thin and she sure as hell wasn't young.

"Turn around," Caliph demanded.

Since entering the room, she'd noticed the change in his demeanor. Her gentle giant had disappeared, replaced by this commanding, sexy-as-sin man. Every order he issued sent shivers of excitement down her spine.

Jennifer spun a half turn, then paused, letting him look his fill. Facing away from him gave her the freedom to relax, to stop working overtime to shield her expressions. She scrunched her eyes closed tightly and prayed.

Please don't let him be disgusted like Marcus. Please.

She jerked slightly when Caliph's hands landed on her shoulders. "Dammit, Jen. Stop that."

Her eyelids flew open and that was when she noticed the mirror in front of her. So much for playing it cool.

She captured his gaze in the reflection, forced herself to face what she'd been afraid to see.

"What were you thinking about?"

She didn't bother to lie. "Marcus. He didn't care for my looks."

His fingers stroked her shoulders, drawing circles on her skin. "He doesn't have any place here. He was an idiot and a fool. His loss. My gain."

She smiled, swallowing hard against the lump in her throat, fighting to hold back the tears threatening to fall. God. She'd told him she was broken. Falling apart and crying like a baby in his arms would only drive that point home.

She wouldn't do it. Jennifer took a deep breath, then turned around to face him. "Do I get to see you naked?"

He cupped her cheeks and placed a soft kiss on her lips. Their first kiss. Like everything about him, it washed away her preconceived notions of how a man who looked like

Caliph would kiss. It was soft and warm, nothing scary or rough.

"Go sit on the bed."

More commands. When she considered their conversations —few though there had been—she realized almost everything he'd ever asked of her had been worded as a demand, rather than a request. And yet that didn't bother her. Didn't send her hackles up like it would whenever Marcus tried to tell her what to do.

In fact, Caliph's orders made her hot, made her melt inside. She walked over to his bed, sitting on the edge to watch as he treated her to her own private striptease.

Once Caliph removed his shirt, Jennifer was able to finally see the whole picture of his tattoos, rather than the half peeks she'd glimpsed at the shop and tonight.

"Wow," she whispered, rising from the bed. She walked over, compelled to add touch to sight. She ran her fingers over every beautiful work of art on his chest, his arms. Stepping around him, she stroked the large tree that covered his back, her eyes discovering the clever way he'd incorporated the names of his brothers and sisters into the branches and leaves. It reinforced what she'd learned at the jazz club earlier. Family was very important to him. That thought touched her.

Her grandmother had always told her when she was younger to look at how a man treated his mother because that offered a clue about how he would treat his wife. Figures that pearl of wisdom reappeared now—two decades too late. Marcus barely spoke to his mother. Then she considered what a shame it was that Caliph didn't believe in marriage. Given his undeniable love for his mother, she suspected he'd shower a wife in adoration.

"You've gone quiet back there." Caliph's deep voice drew her from her thoughts.

"Just admiring the artwork. It's amazing."

He turned to look at her, smiling. "I was worried it might be a bit too much for you."

She shook her head. For old Jennifer, yeah. The image of so much ink would have intimidated and freaked her out a bit. Triggered all those stupid stereotypes she suddenly hated. Now she wasn't sure she'd ever seen anything more beautiful. "Not at all."

"Good. Then I'm going for broke." He slid off his shoes, unzipped his jeans and dropped them to the floor. Caliph went commando.

Her gaze drifted lower. Her subconscious acknowledged the tats on his legs, but Caliph's fully erect cock overshadowed them.

"Whoa."

Caliph chuckled, taking her hand and wrapping it around his thick girth. He kept his grip on hers as he guided her strokes along his hard flesh.

"How long has it been?"

She searched for an answer, trying to calculate months... and then years. Finally, she said, "Too long."

"Don't move." He stepped away from her, quickly pulling a drop cloth from under his bed. She watched as he stripped away the soft comforter, replacing it with the cloth.

"Are we painting or something?" she asked.

He looked over his shoulder at her and winked. "Oh yeah. Art class is about to begin." He returned to her and kissed her briefly once more.

"Go lie on the bed. On your back."

Moment of truth. Thank God.

She assumed the position, expecting Caliph to join her, to crawl over her body and give her exactly what she'd been longing for.

Instead, he walked away from the bed, dragging a box from the closet.

She started to ask what he was doing, but something about his demeanor told her to remain silent. Again, she was struck by his dominance, his complete control over his body and tonight's adventure. He was clearly ready to roll if his hard-on was anything to go by.

Jennifer was very familiar with the wham-bam-thank-you-ma'am style of sex. It had been Marcus' forte, but Caliph didn't appear to be in a hurry to do the deed. Instead, he was drawing out the experience, ramping up her desires with anticipation. It was a deadly concept. And freaking hot.

After years of lackluster, predictable sex, the appeal of not knowing what was going to happen was cranking up her arousal, making it hard for her not to find her clit with her own fingers to grant herself some measure of relief.

Caliph approached the bed. "I said I wouldn't tie you up and I won't. But I need you to lie perfectly still, Jen. Keep your arms and legs where I put them without moving. Can you do that?"

She had no idea, but she damn well intended to try. She nodded.

"Your safe word is daisy."

It was perfect. He'd picked the one word that would remind her she was in control. That she was strong.

"Daisy," she repeated, blinking once more against the tears forming. God. She wasn't sad, wasn't scared, yet she felt the uncontrollable urge to crawl into a ball and cry her heart out. What was wrong with her? She was exactly where she wanted to be, doing something she'd never dreamed she'd have the courage to try.

Hello basket case.

Caliph reached into the box and pulled out a candle. She

ran through his list of kinks. Wax play. She'd read about it. Knew the hot wax would hurt, but that pain could morph into something even hotter inside. She wanted to experience it and she had no doubt Caliph could make it good for her.

He didn't pause in his preparations as he removed several different colored candles from the box, then a lighter. He set them up on his nightstand, lighting each one. Once he was ready, he tossed the empty box in a corner and turned back to her.

He leaned over the bed, one of his knees landing on the mattress by her hip. Lifting her arms, he placed her hands beside her head on the pillow. The position was one of pure surrender. Her heart raced as fear, anticipation, and need all morphed together until it took every ounce of strength in her body not to pull Caliph on top of her and force him inside her.

"I'm not sure I can do this."

Caliph frowned, concern in his dark brown eyes. "If it's too much, too painful—"

"No, it's not that. I'm so fucking horny. I don't think I can wait."

His face cleared, replaced with a grin so genuine and mischievous, she knew she'd just sealed her own fate. Caliph was going to drag this out, there was no denying it. He'd play with her until she begged and even then, she suspected he wouldn't give in.

"You're not going to take it easy on me, are you?" she asked.

He shook his head as he moved lower on the mattress. "No." He grasped her knees and pulled her legs apart. "I'm not."

She glanced down and saw her ankles were lined up perfectly with the bottom posts on his bed. Part of her was sorry she'd taken bondage off the table. If it turned out tonight was all she got, she'd regret missing out on that experience.

Maybe a compromise.

"Could you tie just my legs?" With her hands free, she could still escape the bonds, though she knew she wouldn't try.

Caliph studied her face, not bothering to hide his pleasure at her request. "Are you sure?"

She nodded. "Please."

He reached toward the foot of the bed, pulling up straps that had been tucked beneath the mattress.

"Seriously?" she asked when she realized the ties were already secured to the poles.

"Never claimed to be a choirboy."

She let her gaze travel over his chest and erection. "Believe me, that thought never entered my mind."

He tickled the bottom of her feet as he strapped her ankles to the bed. She was grateful for the reason to giggle, otherwise sheer panic would have taken over.

Once she was tied in place, he crawled over her body, remaining above her on all fours. "Okay?"

"Yeah."

"Say your word and the straps come off."

She shook her head. "No. I don't want to say it. I trust you."

He gave her a crooked grin, then bent to kiss her. This time, the kid gloves came off. His lips pressed against hers roughly, his tongue seeking entrance to her mouth. She opened and returned the kiss.

Twice she started to lift her hands from the pillow, wanting to wrap them around his neck, to hold him tight to her. Both times, Caliph issued a warning growl. The deep timbre of his voice made her wet and hot and achy. The kiss was intense. Primal. Passionate.

He broke off the connection to kneel on the bed, reaching for a bottle of mineral oil. He squirted some on his hands, then began to rub it into her skin. The sexy massage did little to relax her. Instead, it had the opposite effect, firing off a whole new set of needs. Every part of her body was awake, alert, aware. Aroused. She felt as if she was coming unhinged as her pussy clenched continually, seeking penetration.

After several minutes—that seemed like years—he lifted his hands. "Ready to get started?"

She snorted. "Dear God. What have we been doing the past half hour?"

"Preliminaries. Prepping the area. Getting ready to add the design, then the color."

Tattoo-speak. Before her turn in his chair on Tuesday, she wouldn't have understood the allusion. "So now what? You draw?"

He nodded. "Yep. Time for some art."

He rose from the bed, strode across the room to turn off the overhead light, then returned and lifted one of the lit candles. "How much do you know about wax play?"

"Next to nothing."

He looked at her face and she wondered what he saw there. "You want a brief lesson? Wanna know about the wax, temperatures, stuff like that?"

"Nope. Don't give a shit. For the first time in my life, I think I'd prefer experience over education."

"Yeah. That sealed it. Your one-night stand just became a weekend. You up for it?"

She laughed quietly. "Guess it all depends on how you stick the landing."

"Is that right?" Caliph cut her laugh short when he tilted the candle, allowing a large splash of wax to hit her nipple.

"Fuck." She lifted her hands, intent on wiping the painful substance away, but Caliph narrowed his eyes in warning.

Slowly, she forced them back to the pillow. "I think it would be easier if my hands were bound too."

Caliph moved the candle over to her other breast. Jennifer sucked in a deep breath and held it, preparing herself. His second splash of hot liquid hit its mark as well, coating her nipple in white. She clenched her fists, but kept her hands in place.

"I would have thought you'd realized I'm not going for easy, Jen. This weekend is all about pushing your limits, driving you wild."

It was poised on the tip of her tongue to call him a bastard when he placed another large splash of the red-hot liquid on her stomach.

And as usual, he read the thought. "Careful, gorgeous. It's never a good idea to taunt a man who's bigger than you."

He put the white candle back on his nightstand and picked up a blue one. After that, all conversation died as Jennifer gave herself up to the moment.

Each splash of wax burned, scorching a path through her skin straight to her pussy. She clenched her inner muscles, though they remained empty, aching. Caliph ignored her pleas, her cries, her demand that he "put down those goddamn candles and fuck me."

Jennifer lost all sense of time, of place. The dark room, illuminated only by candles, allowed her to disappear into the shadows. After spending the past year standing in a glaring light that forced her to see and acknowledge every flaw and shortcoming, the black night was a blessed relief.

Here, she was sheltered, safe.

She started to anticipate and look forward to each splash, every sting. Her eyelids drifted closed and her begging turned to just one word. His name.

"Caliph. Caliph. Caliph."

Jennifer wasn't sure how long she'd lain on his bed after Caliph stopped painting her body with wax. When she opened her eyes, she was surprised to discover he'd turned on his bedside lamp.

It took several moments for her gaze to focus, for her vision to clear enough to find him. He was sitting on the side of the bed, looking at her body.

When he realized she was looking at him, he smiled. "You're beautiful."

Jennifer lifted her head to glance down. She gasped as she took in his artwork. Her body was a kaleidoscope of texture, shape, and form.

He'd set her colors free.

CHAPTER FOUR

Caliph took his time cleaning the wax from Jennifer's soft skin. He'd indulged in wax play with several women over the years, but none of them had ever responded so naturally, so intensely as Jennifer. She'd accepted his dominance—handing herself over to him, allowing him to take her somewhere she'd never gone before. Her trust was awakening places in him he didn't know existed.

He'd covered her with mineral oil in order to make the clean up easier. Once the last of the wax was stripped from her body, he placed the blunt knife he'd been using on the nightstand.

Jennifer's eyes were closed, not in exhaustion, but bliss. Her chest rose and fell rapidly and her nipples were tight, hard little cherries begging him to take a bite. He let his hand drift lower, watching her face closely as he dragged his fingers along the slit between her legs from anus to clit.

She gasped, her gaze finding his. She was wet, hot, the scent of her arousal increasing his own hunger.

"I want you, Jen."

She lifted one shoulder, the gesture so innocent and honest it hit him like a wrecking ball. "I'm yours."

He tried to ignore the incredible impact those words had on him. "How far are you willing to go?"

Her eyes blinked rapidly, her brow creased as she considered his question. Then, she smiled. "I'm going to be forty soon, Caliph. I've wasted decades of my life, settling for good enough instead of reaching for something amazing. I'm tired of coloring inside the lines. I want an explosion, an adventure. Hell, I'd even settle for a red-hot mess. I guess what I'm saying is I want as much as you're willing to give me."

Caliph felt lightheaded as he considered her offer. "Be very sure, Jen. If you're serious about this, I'm not going to hold back. I'll make demands that I will expect to be obeyed."

Her face flushed, but there was no mistaking it for nervousness. Right before his eyes, the flower bloomed, the petals opening. She wasn't scared. She was in.

"Daisy." He felt compelled to remind her one last time. "That's the only word that will end this. Not no or ouch or even stop."

"Daisy," she repeated. "I'll remember."

Caliph reached down and released the straps on her ankles. Jennifer made a soft mew of disappointment that made him chuckle. "Don't worry. We'll use those again. Later. Right now..."

He reached for her hand, drawing her up until she was sitting in front of him on the bed. Jennifer used her freedom to press her legs together, not because of modesty, but as a means of seeking relief. He allowed her the brief attempt, perfectly aware it wouldn't help much. She'd been riding the edge of an orgasm for nearly an hour. He longed to say to hell with everything, push her to her back and fuck her until they both went blind with pleasure.

And while that was clearly what she wanted, it wasn't even close to what she needed.

He grasped her hand and tugged gently until she was standing beside the bed.

He took a few minutes to clean up, removing the drop cloth and putting the comforter back on the bed. Then he sat on the edge.

"Kneel here." Caliph threw a pillow on the floor and put her in the position he wanted, Jennifer on her knees between his legs. "Leave your hands on your thighs. Don't move them."

Gripping his cock, he ran his hand along the hard flesh as Jennifer watched. She licked her lips and started to move toward him, but he stopped her with a firm grip on her long brown hair. She gasped at his tight hold.

"Just watch, Jen. Don't do anything I don't tell you to do."

Her breathing became more erratic, but she didn't try to pull away. "Okay."

He continued to stroke his cock, letting her see how hard he liked it, how fast, what places were more sensitive than others. Jennifer was a serious student, her expressive blue eyes observing everything he did.

"Open your mouth."

She obeyed instantly and he was struck by the fact she didn't lift her hands or try to move closer. She simply did as he asked. Caliph touched her lips with the head of his cock, but made no attempt to push inside her mouth.

"Let me feel your tongue."

Again, she gave him what he asked for. Her licks were timid at first, quick swipes, but soon she became more adventurous, taking longer tastes, teasing the opening to his cock with the tip of her tongue. He fought to regulate his own breathing as she treated his dick like an ice cream cone she simply couldn't get enough of.

After several minutes, Caliph used his fist in her hair to tug her away. Jennifer's eyes closed and she moaned softly. She was definitely getting off on his roughness, on his control. It drove the Dom inside him crazy. He wasn't sure he'd ever met such a natural—yet untried—submissive. Every alpha nerve in his body was clamoring to take her, teach her, make her his own.

He shook off the thought. Jennifer wasn't looking for more than the weekend and she wasn't ready for what he was considering.

Shit, he hadn't thought he was looking for a more serious relationship prior to tonight. He was happy with his bachelor status. Or he had been.

Now...

Jennifer moved slightly and he realized she was frowning.

"I'm sorry. Did I do something wrong?"

He shook his head. Her tone of voice, laced with fear of failure, pissed him off. Her fucking ex had a lot to answer for. "No, Jen. You did everything right. I needed a second to get control or this was going to be over too damn quick."

Her face lit up. "Really?"

He rolled his eyes at the disbelief in her question. "Yes. Really. New rule, Jen. No more talking."

She narrowed her eyes briefly.

"You don't like that rule?" he asked.

"What if I have questions?"

He resisted the urge to laugh. She was inquisitive, a newbie to all the things he wanted to expose her to. "Make a list in your head. We'll do a Q and A afterwards."

She giggled, but didn't complain. "Okay."

"Now open that mouth and come here." This time he didn't stop with just the head. He pushed deeper, going slowly to give her time to adjust to his size. He figured he wasn't much bigger than the average guy, but Jennifer clearly wasn't accustomed to giving blowjobs. She struggled a bit.

Once half his cock was in, he paused. "Take more."

Her brow creased, but she made the attempt.

Caliph cupped her cheeks, running his thumbs along the soft skin there. "Open your throat and take me all the way in."

She resisted when he pushed against the back of her throat. His grip on her face tightened.

"You can do it, Jen. Just relax and try."

He thrust in several times more, watching as Jennifer fought to give him what he wanted. Finally, on the sixth attempt, something gave way and his cock slid deeper.

Her eyes widened, first with surprise, then with obvious delight. If Caliph had been able to offer praise, he would have. As it was, it was taking all his powers of concentration not to come too quickly. Now that Jennifer had mastered the technique, she was putting it to good use. Her head bobbed along his flesh, taking him deeper, swallowing at just the right time. Her hands had moved to grip his thighs and she was using them as leverage to help her move even faster.

Jesus. He'd been holding her face as a means of control before, but now he needed his hands there just to fucking hold on.

Twice, three more times, she took him in and Caliph gave up the battle. A deep groan rumbled through his chest as he came. Jennifer was ready, swallowing his come as spots formed behind his eyes.

"Mother of God," he said through gritted teeth. When the last drop had been squeezed out, he tried to pull back, but Jennifer followed him, holding his now-flaccid cock in her mouth as she rested her head against his thigh.

Caliph ran his hands through her long tresses gently as he lightly massaged her scalp.

Then he cupped her cheek and pushed her face away from his cock. She looked up at him and smiled. He started to return the grin, then he noticed her hands were still on his thighs.

"You moved your hands."

Jennifer seemed confused for a few seconds before her memory kicked in. "I forgot."

He frowned, though he was far from angry. She'd just offered him the perfect opportunity to expand their play. "And it appears you forgot that you aren't supposed to speak either."

Jennifer bit her lip, but the excited flush in her cheeks urged him to go on. He'd long ago learned that many women craved the dangerous bad boy. Caliph had no problem playing that role because it allowed him to indulge his own desire to dominate. And punish.

"Stand up, Jen."

She rose, her movements a bit wobbly. Caliph placed a firm hand on her elbow to help.

"I think it's time you learn what happens to subs who don't do as they're told."

She blinked rapidly. "Subs?"

His jaw tightened and she winced, aware she'd spoken out of turn once again. He gripped her wrist and tugged until she lay facedown over his lap.

Jennifer fought briefly against the position, her body going into flight mode before her brain could catch up. He placed a firm hand on her upper back, pressing down, while his other kept her legs from thrashing. Then he paused for a full minute, letting her adjust to the situation and waiting to see if she would say the safe word.

When it became clear she wasn't going to speak, he moved his hand from her legs and began to stroke her bare ass. She jerked at the initial touch, clearly expecting him to strike rather than caress.

"Do you understand why you're being punished?"

Silence met his question.

"You can answer my question, Jen. In fact, I expect you to respond when I ask you something."

"Yes. I know why."

"Tell me."

She shivered slightly. "I disobeyed your orders. Three times."

"That's right. You did." He lifted his hand and brought it down against her ass. Jennifer's response was exactly as he'd anticipated. She reared up, intent on escape. He kept one hand on her back, preventing it. He spanked her several more times, the rhythm of the blows varying in placement and strength. He didn't pause. Jennifer knew how to stop him—her word was there to protect her if she needed it.

Apparently she didn't. Her hands found his right shin, gripping it tightly as he continued her punishment. After a dozen or so swats, he pushed her legs open, running his fingers along her slit.

Jennifer moaned. She was hot, wet and so fucking aroused. He'd kept her on the verge of a climax for nearly two hours.

She tried to push closer to his fingers, seeking more.

"You want to come, Jen?"

"Please," she whispered.

Caliph pushed two fingers inside her pussy, the simple touch triggering an avalanche.

Jennifer reared up roughly as she cried out. "Oh God. Harder."

Caliph continued to move until she stiffened, her body trembling with her orgasm.

He had glimpsed Jennifer's submissiveness in the shop. When combined with her bruised self-esteem, it had tugged at his heart, triggered a need in him to reach out to hold her.

He longed to expose her desires, to show Jennifer the beauty to be found in giving herself to a man completely, while trying to bolster her confidence. Caliph was pissed off at her ex for the number he'd worked on her and he hoped he never ran into the man on the street. His plan had been to give her one night to discover who she was and exactly how much she had to offer.

What he hadn't expected was to find the perfect complement to his own desires. She was the yin to his yang, the medium to his technique.

But Jennifer wasn't looking for a relationship. She'd said so herself. And he believed her. Understood that she truly needed time to find herself.

Even as he thought the words, he wanted to rage against the cliché.

She began to tremble and he heard her soft sniffle. He lifted her, drawing her onto his lap. Caliph felt a splash of wetness on his skin.

"Jen?"

She burrowed deeper against his chest, obviously ashamed of her tears.

"Hey." Caliph lifted her face until he could see her pretty blue eyes. "Don't hide from me."

"I d-don't know why I'm c-crying. You must think I'm insane."

He frowned. "No. I think you're a beautiful woman who just experienced something new and pretty fucking intense. It's going to take you a little while to find your footing again. Just hold tight to me, okay? I won't let you fall."

Her grip around his neck tightened, her tears flowing more freely now. He placed soft kisses on the top of her head, whispering "shh" over and over until her trembling stopped and her breathing slowed. Her response to his spanking was normal.

She was new to the experience and though there was genuine submissiveness at her core, it was natural for her to be confused by her response and her feelings about the act, as they were likely in direct opposition to everything she'd ever been raised to believe about being an independent woman.

"Feel better?"

She nodded. "I didn't expect—" She paused and he sensed she was searching for a way to explain.

"You loved it."

It wasn't a question. Her responses to him were incredible, open, honest. Just like the woman in his arms.

"So much," she whispered.

"You want more?"

"God yes."

Caliph's cock had begun to thicken during the spanking. There was something wholly arousing about watching a woman's beautiful ass turn red under his hand. But Jennifer's request, her desire for something stronger, fed his needs.

He pushed her onto her stomach on the bed, lifting her hips until her knees found support on the edge of the mattress. He stood behind her, stroking her ass for only a moment.

Caliph reached for the nightstand and donned a condom. "How hard do you want it, Jen?"

She shuddered, her body quivering in response. Obviously the spanking had awakened something inside her. Pain turned her on.

"Please, Caliph. I need—"

Her tone told him all he needed to know. Before she could finish her request, he was there, shoving in to the hilt in one strong, deep blow.

Jennifer screamed as her inner muscles clenched around his cock. Caliph didn't give way, didn't ease up. Instead he pummeled faster.

Her first orgasm hit hard and fast, but he wasn't finished yet. He couldn't give up the heaven he found inside her body. She didn't shy away from his strength, from his rough claiming. Instead, she added to the pressure, her fists gripping the bedspread as she shoved back in time with his thrusts forward.

Caliph's vision blurred as his balls drew tight. Usually he had more self-control than this. He tried to draw in a deep breath, fighting against the desire to come. It was all happening too fast.

Jennifer needed—deserved—so much more. He forced himself to slow his pace.

"No." Jennifer sensed his retreat, so she doubled her efforts, pushing against him more roughly.

He gripped her hips, attempting to hold her still. She didn't give up the struggle to take control.

"Jen. Stop." His voice was deep, stern. Demanding.

She responded to it instantly.

"Caliph," she whispered. "Please."

Her soft plea was almost his undoing. Almost.

Then he shook his head. She was topping from the bottom. He'd never let a sub get away with that. Ever.

He slapped her ass, two hard blows to remind her who was in charge.

The effort was wasted on his sexy lover. Rather than subdue her, it fired her libido even more.

She lifted her ass higher. "Again. Do it again."

He stifled the laugh clamoring for release. His submissive was going to be fun to tame. Caliph pulled out and stepped away from the bed.

Jennifer lifted her head, looking over her shoulder. She started to speak, but he shook his head once, the only warning he intended to give her.

She closed her mouth and waited, though he could see how difficult the effort was.

"Roll over onto your back. Open your legs and hold them that way until I tell you otherwise."

It was time to test some limits. Jennifer had come to his bed with the desire to expand her sexual experiences. While there was no denying she enjoyed the blowjob and doggie style, neither were likely new for her. She'd responded strongly to the unknown—the wax play and the spanking—and he was anxious to introduce her to more.

Jennifer slowly spread her legs, gripping them below the knee. He could tell she was uneasy with being on display. Despite all they'd already done, lying still while exposing her most private places was going to force her to overcome her issues with self-esteem.

Caliph didn't bother to mask his perusal of her body. He let his gaze slide over every sensuous curve. He wondered if she'd be willing to pose for him some time. Let him draw her. Her body was art incarnate—a beautiful study.

Once he'd looked his fill, he decided to up the ante.

"Touch yourself."

CHAPTER FIVE

Heat suffused Jennifer's body at the idea of masturbating in front of Caliph. Just when she thought he couldn't surprise—or arouse—her any more, he'd lay down his next challenge and she'd struggle to catch her breath, to summon her nerve.

He was a contradiction from the word go. She'd noticed that in the shop. Tonight, he'd fluctuated from tender lover to demanding Dom, constantly keeping her on her toes, struggling to keep up.

She'd come here with only a cursory knowledge of what it meant to be submissive to a man. While the concept never failed to inflame her whenever she read an erotic novel, there was a huge difference between fantasy and reality. She truly longed to play the submissive role, but she'd spent a lifetime trying to prove herself as a strong woman—even within her marriage—so she was struggling to make her head and her body agree.

Caliph didn't move as he waited for her to obey. She wasn't sure why touching herself as he watched felt harder than all the rest. He'd pushed some difficult limits tonight, but this one was the toughest. Which seemed ridiculous.

She started to move her hand toward her pussy, her eyes closing automatically. Maybe if she tried to forget he was there...

The mattress shifted and she opened her eyelids to find Caliph leaning over her. He lifted her head to place a pillow beneath it.

"Keep your eyes open and on my face. Don't look away."

Her jaw tensed. Damn man stripped all her defenses away. She scowled, but remained silent. He'd taken away her right to speak, but he'd also revealed his ability to read her expressions. She'd use that to her advantage.

His eyes narrowed. "Are you sure you want to test me, Jen?"

The question was laced with just enough sensual threat to send even more juices to her pussy. Maybe he should have left the drop cloth on the bed. If he kept playing with her like this, she'd drown them both in her arousal.

She smoothed out her features, aiming for a repentant look. She wasn't sure she'd pulled it off, but her contrition must have been enough because Caliph moved away, standing at the edge of the bed once more. His cock was hard as a rock, looking almost painful. He hadn't bothered to remove the condom. How could he deny himself something he so obviously needed?

"Time to stop stalling. Touch yourself. I want to see how you make yourself come."

She frowned again, but this time her response wasn't based on annoyance. She was worried. The truth was she'd never brought herself to climax with just her hands. Jennifer was the proud owner of an array of toys—sex aides she needed to provoke the response he was demanding now.

He crossed his arms, letting his impatience show.

Jennifer forced her gaze to remain on his face as she lightly stroked her clit. The touch was more powerful than she'd expected and she jerked slightly, shocked by the impact.

"Shit," she muttered, quickly pressing her lips together and hoping he hadn't heard her slip-up.

Of course, he had.

Caliph reached beneath her, gripping her ass in his large hands. It was still sore from his previous punishment, but he didn't let that stop him. He squeezed, adding pressure until she winced.

"That's the last reminder you're going to get, Jen. No talking. Period. Next time you say something without permission, I'm getting out my belt."

She blinked rapidly. He wouldn't dare. Would he?

Yeah. Part of her was fairly certain that was exactly what he'd do. She pursed her lips tightly, not willing to push him further.

He released her ass, then gestured for her to continue. She ran her fingers over her clit again, building up the speed and pressure quickly. While she'd come earlier, that orgasm was a distant memory now. It certainly hadn't done much to douse the desires still coursing through her veins.

Unfortunately, too many things were working against her. She couldn't relax with Caliph watching. She couldn't stop thinking—about every stupid freaking thing. Was this turning him on? Did her stomach look fat in this position? How bad did her hair look? Every insecurity pushed its way to the forefront until she became numb to her actions.

God, how long would he make her try before he realized she simply couldn't come this way? Her fingers weren't enough to push her over the edge, especially not with an audience.

After a few moments, Caliph's hand landed on hers, halting her motions.

Finally.

She started to lower her legs, but he shook his head.

"You ready to take this seriously?"

She frowned. "What do you—" She paused. Did that count as a question he wanted answered?

He lifted one eyebrow and waited for her to respond. "Well?"

"What do you mean?"

"What were you thinking about just now, Jen?"

She blushed, unwilling to tell him for fear he'd realized how close to unhinged she really was.

"Were you thinking about me? About giving me what I'd asked for? Something I wanted?"

She licked her lips. Shit. She hadn't been thinking about him at all. Not really. She'd been more concerned with her own hang-ups. Her own reasons why she couldn't do what he'd requested.

She shook her head. "No."

His fingers tightened. Her hand was still pressed to her clit but his strong grip prevented her from withdrawing it. "Why not?"

Caliph kept forcing her to expose herself. She'd expected tonight to just be about sex, a brief foray into BDSM. She hadn't anticipated sharing more than her body. That much she'd been ready to give.

The rest?

Not so much.

"Caliph..." Her words dried up. "I'm sorry."

Her apology seemed to anger him and while she'd witnessed several of his stern looks, she'd never seen him truly angry. "Don't. Don't say that to me. I'm not your ex. I don't look at you and see flaws. Jesus. Stop worrying about stuff that doesn't matter and start concentrating on what's right."

As he spoke, he began to push her fingers against her clit once more. "This is right, Jen. What's going on between us is good. Hell, it's better than good, it's off-the-charts, fucking amazing."

He took control of her hand, molding it as if it was made of clay and he was sculpting a sex toy for her. He grasped two of her fingers, pressing them inside her pussy. She was overwhelmed by the heat, the moisture, the tight clenching and the sparks.

Oh my God.

It was electric.

Caliph determined the depth, the speed. "Add another finger."

She reacted without thought. Instead, she let him be her guide. His eyes never left hers and she let herself see—really see—what he felt. Something hard and cold melted inside her. The depression she'd allowed to fester and grow faded away.

He thought she was beautiful.

This is right, he'd said, and for the first time she let herself acknowledge that fact. Accept it.

He slowly released her hand, but she didn't hesitate, didn't give up the incredible rhythm he'd introduced. She thrust her fingers deeper as she added her thumb to the dance. Once, twice she drew it along her clit, fighting to keep her eyes open and on his. He wasn't hiding from her and she wanted to offer him the same. The pressure built, her hand moving on autopilot as she gave free reign to every astounding sensation.

Nothing mattered but this place, this moment. This man.

He wanted to see her come and it was a gift she was dying to give him.

She thrust one last time and flew away. Her back arched as she cried out loudly. She sensed Caliph moving, felt the bed dip. She was in the midst of her climax when his strong arms spread her legs farther apart. She screamed as he pushed his cock inside her, the powerful force, the beauty of being filled by him drove her to come again. Or was this still the original orgasm?

All she knew was she never wanted it to end.

Caliph didn't take her gently. His hard thrusts offered no reprieve, no time for rest or recovery.

She reached up, grasping his upper arms, needing to touch him. When that contact proved too little, she tried to pull him closer.

He dropped down to his elbows, his forearms lying next to her sides, his firm hands gripping her shoulders to hold her still.

Her ability to think deserted her as Jennifer gave herself over to the tactile, the emotions. She wanted to kiss him, so she did.

Caliph missed a beat when she clasped his face in her hands and pulled his lips to hers. Then he took over, his tongue mimicking the motions of his cock. He was claiming every part of her and she was glad to put the reins in his hands. The past year had been exhausting.

Now, tonight, Caliph was bearing the heavy load. It was the most wonderful thing anyone had ever done for her.

She wrapped her legs around his waist and tilted her hips higher, encouraging him to go deeper. He took the invitation.

Sweat slid along her brow as the temperature in the room increased.

Caliph released her lips, his breathing hot and heavy against her cheek. "Come with me, Jen."

She didn't have the strength to tell him she was already there. Her body stiffened as her orgasm crashed through her once more.

Caliph lowered his head to her shoulder, groaning. His motions slowed as he thrust inside her as deeply as he could go before holding there, his body jerking with his own climax.

Neither of them moved for several minutes. Caliph simply held himself above her as they slowly drifted back to earth.

Then, he pushed himself to her side, removing the condom and tossing it into a trashcan before tugging until her back was pressed against his chest, spoon-fashion.

His arm loosely wrapped around her, his hand covering one of her breasts in a way that was nothing less than familiar, possessive. Lovely.

She was the first to break the silence, not based on nerves—though she wasn't foolish enough to think they wouldn't return—but because she was riding a high. Giddy.

"You okay back there?"

He chuckled softly. "I think so. That was one hell of a ride, Jen."

She grinned, pleased by the gruff sound of his voice. It betrayed how exhausted he was. She liked the idea of wearing him out. That had certainly never happened before with any other man.

"It was incredible. I'm not sure I've ever experienced anything like that. I mean I've read lots of books about BDSM, but damn, there's a huge difference between imagining and doing. I didn't realize how intense it was going to be. I guess you're used to this sort of thing, but I have to admit...I didn't have a clue sex could be so, so..." She sighed. "I don't think anyone's invented a word to describe what I just felt."

Caliph placed a soft kiss on her shoulder. "Maybe we should think of one. Or we could just forget the vocabulary and do it all over again."

She laughed, twisting until she faced him. Despite his height and sheer muscle mass, their bodies fit. Perfectly. "Again? Really?" She ran her hand along his flaccid cock, surprised when it stirred and began to thicken. Caliph's stamina was off the charts. Her nipples budded in response.

Caliph noticed. He bent his head, sucking one of the tight buds into his mouth roughly. She groaned, silently hoping he'd repeat the action on the other nipple.

"Again," Caliph said. "Again and again."

Jennifer grinned, then she gasped.

Then she learned the true meaning of again.

All night long.

CHAPTER SIX

Caliph felt the heat of the sun on his bare skin, but didn't bother to open his eyes to acknowledge it was morning. He tightened his hold on Jennifer instead, enjoying the feeling of her hair tickling his chin, her hot breath caressing his chest. It wasn't uncommon for him to have sleepovers with lovers. Morning sex was one of his favorite things.

His lips tipped upward, the grin emerging as he recalled the previous night. Jennifer had been more than a pleasant surprise. She'd actually blown his misconceptions about her conservative nature out of the water. It seemed amazing to him that he'd considered—even for one second—that she was too innocent to accept his desires.

One night in and he began to wonder if he'd be able to keep up with her. He had thrown her into the deep end right out of the gate and while she'd struggled a bit to adapt, in the end, she'd taken to his demands, his darker desires, as if she'd been part of the lifestyle forever.

He'd invited her to stay for the weekend and he hoped she'd take him up on that offer.

Unfortunately, the morning-after glow he was experiencing clearly wasn't present for Jennifer.

"I think maybe I should head home," she said softly.

Caliph shook his head. "Nope."

He didn't bother to open his eyes. Even so, he could feel her smile against his chest. "Caliph—"

She intended to argue, but he wasn't in the mood to listen. He tilted her face up to his with his fingers. "I want the whole weekend, Jen. I'm not ready to let this go yet. There's still so much for us to explore. Besides, your car is parked at Midnight Ink, so you don't have any way to leave."

He placed a soft kiss on her forehead when she scowled at him.

"So basically I'm your prisoner?" Her tone told him exactly how much she didn't mind that.

"Yep. You're all mine for the rest of the day and tonight. Maybe tomorrow too. I'll have to see how my cock is holding up by then."

She laughed. "So does this kidnapping come complete with bondage? Because I fully intend to be a very naughty captive."

Jesus. He'd thought he'd woken up with a hard-on, but her sexy taunt proved him wrong. His cock thickened even more. He rolled forward, climbing over Jennifer until she was caged beneath him. Grasping her wrists, he pulled her hands above her head, keeping a firm grip on them, letting her feel what it would mean to be helpless, at his mercy. "You sure you want me to tie you up?"

He'd paused several times last night, giving her a chance to adjust to his demands and to use her safe word if necessary. She'd never uttered it. Never given any indication she wanted to. Those kid gloves came off today.

Jennifer's breathing accelerated, her generous breasts rising and falling, almost distracting him from his question.

He pressed her hands against the pillow harder. "Answer me."

She nodded instantly. He'd noticed her responses came quicker the more demanding he became.

"Say it out loud."

"Yes." Her reply was a whisper, betraying exactly how much she wanted what he was offering. He didn't hesitate. Instead, he reached above her, searching for the straps already secured to the headboard. She gave him that same amused smile she'd offered last night when she discovered he had straps attached to his foot posts.

"Were you ever a Boy Scout?"

He got her joke instantly. "Nope, but that doesn't mean I don't know how to prepare for the really important events."

Her grin faded when he tied the first hand, tightening it until she couldn't move her arm at all. Last night, he'd left the bonds on her ankles relatively loose, introducing her to the sensation.

He didn't feel the need to do that again. Caliph wanted to push her further. Holding on to her free hand, he attached it as well until both wrists were bound directly above her head.

Caliph rose from the bed, walking to the foot of the mattress. Reaching forward, he grasped her ankles, tugging her entire body lower on the bed until her arms were stretched to the max. Then he hooked her ankles to the corner posts, leaving her legs open to him.

He admired his work as Jennifer flushed slightly. How many times would she blush before she became comfortable with his scrutiny?

She had definitely learned many of last night's lessons well. Rather than try to look away or hide from him, her gaze remained steadily on his while he studied her body. He'd decorated her skin with a different sort of art last night. Her lips were puffy and red from his kisses and there were several love bites around her neck and on her breasts. There were some small bruises on her thighs, left there when he'd held her open, fucking her roughly. He knelt between her outstretched legs and ran his fingers over them.

Jen lifted her head, watching. "They don't hurt."

He captured her gaze as he moved his hand higher. Using the tip of one finger, he ran it along her slit, studying her face for a reaction. She was wet, ready for him. He was quickly becoming spoiled by her continual arousal. Nothing he did seemed to faze her, scare her. It was as if he'd molded his dream lover from clay and some magic had brought Jennifer to life and to his bed.

"Sore?"

As always, he was treated to her complete honesty. "A little. But I don't care."

He gave her a crooked grin. "I do."

She frowned. "You aren't going to stop, are you?"

He shook his head. "I probably should, but I can't. I'm too greedy when it comes to you."

She smiled. "Good. Now...will you please hurry up? I think I might be dying of horniness."

Caliph had never let any of his previous lovers—the submissive ones—speak to him so cheekily, but he loved her humor, her shy demands. This felt a lot less like a scene and more like a relationship.

As soon as the word crossed his mind, he realized the truth of it. He'd entered this bedroom with Jen, intent on exposing her wild side and introducing her to BDSM. And, of course, in return, he'd get to spend a sex-filled night with a hot woman.

Somewhere along the line, the desire to simply get laid had morphed into something more. Something better. Unexpected.

And not entirely wanted.

While he wasn't opposed to long-term relationships, he'd always preferred an unencumbered life. One where he didn't have to answer to anyone.

"Caliph?"

Shit. He'd gone quiet too long. Time to snap out of it. Get this weekend back on course. He lifted his hand and slapped the inside of Jennifer's thigh.

She gasped.

"I need to explain the concept of topping from the bottom to you."

Jennifer bit her lip guiltily. "No, you don't. I've read about that in my dirty books. I know what it is."

Caliph slapped the other thigh, adding more bite, knowing exactly how to make it sting. "And yet you keep doing it."

"I can't help it." Her eyes darkened with lust. He'd noticed last night that her body responded as much to pain as to pleasure. Then she made him an offer he couldn't refuse. "Make me remember."

He took a deep breath, trying to keep calm as the Dom inside him emerged fully. God, she was a flirty little thing, every word she spoke provocative. Challenging.

"I'm going to gag you."

Jennifer exhaled sharply and started to speak.

"No. No talking, Jen. Hold up two fingers on your left hand."

She obeyed instantly.

"That's your safe word while the gag is in. If you want me to stop, hold up those two fingers. Understand?"

She nodded.

He walked to the corner of his bedroom, grabbing a bag.

After Jennifer left Midnight Ink on Tuesday, he'd gone to the sex shop over his lunch break and picked up a few items. As the week passed, he'd returned to the store two more times as he fantasized even more ways he wanted to take her. He'd acquired quite a kinky collection and he was looking forward to using every single toy on her.

Last night, she'd distracted him from those plans, seducing him in ways he hadn't anticipated. Today, he intended to make up for lost time.

He pulled out the ball gag, then perused the other items in the bag. Fuck it. He picked up the entire package and returned to the bed with it. They'd use it all eventually.

Caliph bent over the side of the bed, lifting her head slightly to put the gag in her mouth, then securing it in place. She struggled against it initially and he glanced toward her hands. No signal.

"This morning's lesson is about obedience."

She blinked rapidly at the sound of his deep voice, then a line formed in her brow, warning him she would put up some resistance. With former lovers, he would have been annoyed by that look of defiance, expecting total submission from his bedmates. But with Jennifer, he looked forward to the challenge she represented.

He pushed the thought away. The damn woman was still getting under his skin and she couldn't even speak.

Grabbing the bag from the bed, he walked to the bathroom, opening all the packages, washing the array of toys he'd purchased. Jennifer wasn't going to know what hit her.

Returning to the room, he plucked the bullet vibrator from the pile and pushed it into Jennifer's pussy. No fanfare, no preparation—he already knew she was wet. He just pressed the toy in.

"You aren't allowed to come unless I give you permission."

Her eyes narrowed and he had no doubt she'd have disagreed if she could speak. He gave her a superior smile, then flipped the switch on the remote to high.

Jennifer jerked roughly, beautifully restrained by the straps on her wrists and ankles. She cried out, the sound muffled by the gag. He didn't lower the speed on the vibrator and made no move to touch her at all.

Instead he watched her struggle, trying to decide if she was fighting the orgasm or working to achieve it. With his rebellious lover, it could be either.

She hadn't fully embraced the concept of submission yet, though he knew the traits were there as well as her desire to accept them. It would take time for her to learn what it truly meant to give herself to him, to bend her will to his. She'd been on her own for nearly a year and she'd spent that time fighting to find her own strength, to make it through life without a man. It wasn't going to be easy for her to now release her grip on what she clearly viewed as progress and hand the control over to him.

He'd have to find a way to prove to her the power in this situation was hers.

He looked at her hands once more, searching for the sign. She may be fighting the sensations provoked by the vibrator, but she sure as hell didn't want to give up the war. Her hands remained firmly clenched into tight fists.

Jennifer's breathing increased and she moaned. The labored sound gave her away. Caliph turned off the remote.

Her expression reflected pure murder. Yep. She'd definitely been ready to come and, given her anger, it appeared she hadn't intended to hold back.

Caliph climbed onto the bed, hovering over her on his hands and knees. "Bad girl."

She shook her head, trying to dislodge the gag, but her hands remained closed.

"You've just sealed your fate, Jen. If you'd behaved, I wouldn't have left you hanging for very long. Now the clock is set. You're not going to come for the next two hours."

She made a sound of protest.

"Keep it up and I'll make it three."

She huffed, but fell silent. Her eyes still promised retribution.

"You need to learn to school those expressions, Jennifer. Dirty looks are as bad as speaking without permission. Shoot any more of those daggers at me and I'll punish you."

Her reaction to the word *punish* went through him like an aphrodisiac. She wanted it. There was no denying that when her nipples budded and her eyes went soft.

"There are different types of punishment. Some you will enjoy, others you won't. Don't provoke my temper or you're going to learn that difference the hard way. That spanking last night had very little to do with correcting bad behavior. I did it primarily for your pleasure. If you continue to disobey me, I'm going to reprimand you in a way that brings you no satisfaction. Do you understand?"

She nodded slowly. Her arousal was beginning to wane, allowing uncertainty and confusion to creep in.

Caliph turned the vibrator on once more, only this time he set it on low.

Jennifer's eyes drifted closed, but her calmer response told him this sensation wasn't enough for her. She tried to lift her hips toward him, but the straps held her almost completely immobile. She shuddered, clearly needing more stimulation.

He wasn't going to give it to her. Not yet. She was his for the next two hours and he intended to use that time to his advantage.

Bending his head, he sucked one of her nipples into his mouth. Jennifer groaned, arching her neck with delight. He'd been pleased to discover how sensitive her breasts were. Perhaps later, he'd bring her to orgasm simply with breast play, but for now, he had another plan.

Moving his head from one nipple to the other, he sucked and nipped at them until they were large, red, tight. Then he retrieved the clamps he'd bought. Jennifer's face told him instantly they were entering new territory. That knowledge excited him, fed his own arousal.

He placed a clamp on her left nipple as Jennifer's back bowed upward, sharp, harsh breaths escaping her nose as he tightened it. He used her breathing to let him know when the pain crossed from good to bad, then he dialed the screw back a notch.

Caliph repeated the process on her other nipple, then pushed up to kneel between her legs and admire his work. Thirty minutes had passed.

"I'm going to take the gag out, but you're still not allowed to speak."

Her face was calmer now, her expressive eyes silent for once. Caliph recognized the look. She'd stopped listening to her conscience, moving beyond the logical, embracing the visceral. He unhooked the gag and removed it. Gently he wiped her lips and lightly massaged her jaw.

Unable to resist, he bent down to kiss her. Kissing had never been a big part of any scene for him, but there was something about Jennifer that made him want to coddle her as much as he wanted to dominate. It was slightly unnerving, but—like her—he was finished thinking about this. From this moment on, he simply wanted to give in to his desires.

Jennifer returned his kiss, her tongue stroking his. When he pulled away, her face lifted, trying to keep him close. If her hands had been free, he had no doubt she would have latched onto his neck to hold his lips to hers.

She wanted him—really wanted him.

In the past, he'd indulged in casual affairs. No woman had ever acted as if he was vital to her. They'd just taken their own pleasures and moved on.

Before this weekend, Caliph would never have admitted to enjoying a woman who needed him so much, but Jennifer's subtle *stay with me* overtures touched him. Turned him on.

She narrowed her eyes when he picked up the remote to the vibrator once more. Then he watched her suck in a deep breath and hold it to prepare herself. He pushed it up a notch to medium, holding the high speed in reserve. Her body tensed in her effort to stave off her orgasm. Caliph was impressed by her willingness to satisfy him, to give him what he wanted.

"And now things get serious."

She frowned, but didn't reply. Didn't even attempt to.

Leaving the bed, he walked to her feet and untied the straps. He massaged her ankles for a few moments, then told her to bend her knees, leaving her legs open.

She obeyed. Caliph wondered if she'd accept the next position as easily. He removed the straps from the bottom of the bed and attached them to eyehooks higher on the opposite sides of his headboard.

She watched his movements in silence, but he could read the concern—and doubt—on her face.

Once the bindings were in place, he knelt on the bed and lifted her legs, keeping a firm grip on her ankles. He tugged them upward until she was bent in half. Then he bound them with her legs straight above her head.

"Does that hurt?"

She shook her head.

"Good." He ran his hand over her bare ass, enjoying exactly how much this position left her vulnerable. Open.

He cupped her breasts and gave a firm squeeze to the fleshy mounds. It increased the pressure to the clamps. Jennifer's eyes closed and she groaned blissfully. The sound must have shocked her, causing her to panic. She looked at him to gauge his reaction.

Caliph chuckled. "I said you can't speak. Those cute little sex sounds are definitely allowed. In fact..."

He ran his fingers along her slit, enjoying her soft whimper. A glance at the clock confirmed an hour had passed. His cock was rock-hard and reading him the riot act for holding off. Caliph wrapped his fist around his erection and slowly stroked the sensitive flesh as Jennifer watched.

She licked her lips and, for a moment, he was tempted to move over her and push his cock into her wet, hot mouth. He resisted the urge. This scene was meant to push her limits, test her ability to obey his demands no matter what. There was still work to do.

Reaching back into the bag of toys, he retrieved a tube of lubrication and a butt plug. She'd confessed last night she'd never indulged in anal play, but her tone when she mentioned it told him her curiosity outweighed her fears. That seemed to be true for most of her desires. Jennifer had yet to balk at a single thing he'd suggested or tried.

Taking the cap off the tube, he squeezed some onto his finger, then rubbed it around her anus. She wiggled slightly, but didn't try to move away. She also didn't say her safe word. Caliph realized he'd stopped listening for it. The previous night, the word was never far from his mind as he'd expected it to pop out at any time. Today, they'd turned a corner. He'd learned to read her responses, to know what she genuinely liked.

He added more lube to his finger, pressing it inside her ass. Jennifer's breathing had regulated, but with this new sensation, it sped up, became louder. He worked the lubricant into her ass, adding more and more. Then one finger became two and two became three. He initiated her to the act slowly, giving her tight, virgin muscles time to adjust to the unfamiliar invasion.

Jennifer's moans became louder as he finger-fucked her ass, adding speed and strength to each thrust. His balls drew tight. What would he give to pull his hand away and fuck her there with his cock?

Someday. Soon.

Then he wondered if she'd give him another night, another weekend. His initial desire for a one-night stand had been rejected as true greediness took over. He wanted more. A lot more.

Her panting breaths alerted him to how close she was to coming. He withdrew. Time wasn't up. She growled, the sound reflecting anger more than arousal. He lifted his hand and swatted her ass in warning. Jennifer lifted her bottom as much as the straps would allow, silently begging for more. He indulged her request, mainly because there was nothing he loved more than spanking her ass, watching it turn red under his hand. He placed several more blows to her bottom as Jennifer's back arched and her cries grew louder.

Christ. She was in danger of coming merely from a spanking. Once again, Caliph stopped. She shuddered roughly as she attempted to fight back her desire to come.

The game was far from over. Lifting the butt plug, he coated it with lubrication, then slowly pressed it into her ass. Jennifer's eyes drifted closed as she whispered his name. He didn't chastise her for speaking without permission. She was drifting into subspace—he could read it in her face, in her responses.

He wondered if his next action would drag her back or push her further into her state of bliss. He hoped the latter.

Once the plug was in place, he leaned forward and reached for a clamp. He briefly considered warning her about the pain to come, but didn't want to ruin the moment with words. She was floating and if his suspicions about her need for pain proved true, this would only add to the experience.

He removed the clamp.

Jennifer jerked. "Oh my God."

Caliph had anticipated the response, her shock when she felt that initial jolt of pain. He was there, waiting for her. He put his lips over her sore nipple, caressing it with soft strokes of his tongue and gentle sucks until she calmed down.

She stiffened in preparation when he moved to tug the second clamp free. He repeated the same ministrations, helping to turn the pain into something more pleasurable. He took his time, acknowledging how easy it would be to spend hours playing with her breasts. They were full and sensitive.

Then he felt her stir. He lifted his head and found her eyes on his. He knew what she wanted, but the selfish man inside wanted to hear it from her lips.

"Say it," he prompted.

"Please," she whispered. "I need you."

Heaven to his ears. He didn't bother to look at the clock. It was close enough. Reaching above her head, he released her ankles, then her hands. He removed the bullet, tossing it aside.

"Wrap your legs around my waist and hold on, love."

She followed his command, gasping when he placed his cock at her opening. The plug was still in her ass, but he didn't plan to remove it. It would only heighten the pleasure. Then he paused.

"Shit. Condom."

He started to reach for the nightstand, but she halted him. "Do you have to use one?"

He frowned. "I'm clean, Jen, but—"

"So am I. And I'm on birth control."

He blew out a long, hard breath. He'd never taken a woman without a condom. Not once. In his entire life. Neither one of his previous long-term girlfriends had been able to take the Pill without getting sick, so he had been in charge of taking the necessary precautions.

"You're sure?" he asked.

She nodded. "Come inside me."

There was a double meaning to her request. And both offers were too good to pass up.

Caliph pushed in slowly, his chest constricting as he forgot how to breathe. He wasn't sure he'd ever felt anything so powerful, so freaking amazing.

As much as he tried to savor the moment, to prolong the beauty of it, his measured pace didn't help. Jennifer had been riding the razor's edge too long. She shook beneath him and he realized she was still trying to hold off. He pressed in to the hilt, leaned down and kissed her lightly on the cheek. "Come for me, Jen."

He started to move, just a slight withdrawal before pushing deeper. It was all she needed. Her body stiffened as she released a loud, keening cry. Her inner muscles clamped down on his aching cock and she dragged her fingernails down his bare back—leaving some serious artwork of her own on his skin.

Caliph closed his eyes and fought to regulate his breathing. He didn't want this to end too soon. He rode out the storm of her powerful orgasm, then—when calmness began to descend once more—he thrust harder, choosing his favorite rhythm, speed.

Jennifer wrapped her legs tighter around him, spurring him

on, accepting his rough claiming. When her pussy clenched again, he realized she was on the verge of yet another orgasm. He'd never be able to resist coming this time.

Jennifer trembled with the second orgasm and Caliph joined her, giving in to his own pleasure. The impact of his climax would have knocked him down had he been standing. Jet after jet of come exploded from him, each pulse sending electricity up and down his spine.

What a weekend.

As soon as he was able to move—his strength had deserted him—he fell to her side, pleased when Jennifer rolled, curling against his chest, soft and warm as a newborn kitten. She was asleep within seconds. He wouldn't be far behind. Caliph tucked her closer with an arm around her shoulders, enjoying the feel of her next to him. For the first time, it felt like someone belonged here. With him. In his bed.

Jennifer fit.

He'd told her she was a blank canvas, that her future was hers to design, to color. But now he wondered if he hadn't been a bit blank himself. The colorful life he thought he'd been living suddenly felt bland, a whole lot of off-white and gray. In a few short days, Jennifer had added shocking reds, cool blues and vivid purples, opening his eyes to opportunities he'd never considered.

His eyes drifted closed, a heavy warmth coursing through him.

Then he contemplated what happened when the weekend came to a close and the contentment started to wane as reality crashed around him.

The next move wasn't his to make.

It was hers.

CHAPTER SEVEN

Jennifer tightened her grip around Caliph's waist as the motorcycle sped up. She'd spotted the Harley in Caliph's driveway as they had walked toward his car and admitted she'd never ridden on one. He had taken her admission as something akin to a mortal sin, thrown a helmet on her head and now they were headed to Midnight Ink to retrieve her car.

Sunday had arrived and the weekend was officially over.

They had spent most of the day—and two nights—before in his bed and had only woken up a couple hours earlier, after which they'd showered together. She had joked that they both looked as if they'd been ridden hard and put away wet, after she complained about her stiff muscles and he winced when he tried to put a shirt on over the deep scratches she'd left on his back.

Breakfast had been a quiet affair, both of them talking about a whole bunch of nothing. Truth was Jennifer hadn't known what to say, so she'd filled the silence with nonsense about the weather and past Mardi Gras parties.

She'd been both relieved and disappointed when they'd

hopped on the motorcycle because it didn't give them an opportunity to talk on the way to the shop.

Caliph took the long way to Midnight Ink, treating her to a quick ride on Pontchartrain Expressway so he could rev up the motor and gain some serious speed. She clung tighter to his waist, enjoying the roar of the engine, the vibrations, the sense of flying. Just when she thought Caliph couldn't make this weekend any more amazing, he found a way to take her breath away once more. She'd been in a constant state of exhilaration and it was addictive.

As he pulled up to the tattoo shop, her heart began to race. The idea of not seeing him again was extremely unappealing. For a split second, she even considered signing on for another tattoo just to prolong their association, but she quickly dismissed that idea with a soft laugh.

Caliph dismounted the bike, then helped her off. She handed him the helmet.

"What did you think of the ride?"

She knew he was asking about the spin on the motorcycle, but her sex-soaked mind went straight back to the bedroom. "It was incredible." There...that covered it all.

Caliph was obviously pleased by her response. "I'm glad you enjoyed it. I was afraid I'd scare you."

"Never." She'd never spoken a truer word. Then her mouth went dry. This was it. "Well..."

Jennifer's brain failed as she sought for something to say. Some way to tell him what this weekend had meant to her. And to ask for more.

She'd never do that. It wasn't in her chemical makeup to be so assertive. At work, she could make her wishes known clearly and without hesitance, but when it came to grasping anything for herself, she floundered like a fish out of water. Hell, when Marcus told her he was having an affair and asked for the divorce, she'd merely nodded. It wasn't until he'd packed up all his stuff and left the house that she found the raging words she wished she'd said.

And as far as this affair with Caliph was concerned, she knew what she wanted, but she didn't feel confident enough to say it aloud only to have him reject her. She'd ridden the rejection train before and, quite frankly, it sucked.

Unfortunately, Caliph had taken her on adventures her sex-starved, fairly vivid imagination hadn't even thought to conjure up. He hadn't just ruined her for other men. He'd made sure she wouldn't be able to escape into her books anymore without wishing she were the heroine and he the hero in every story. So much for fictional therapy.

"I had a really great time." The inane words were nearly accompanied by a wince, but she managed to school her features just in time.

Caliph nodded slowly. "So did I. You're an incredible woman, Jen."

She wasn't feeling very incredible right now. In fact, all she felt was pure terror. So she instituted the standard quick escape. "Well, I guess I'll see you around."

She backed up her lame farewell with the most ridiculous platonic hug in history. God, she gave her distant cousin, the one she only saw every third year at the family reunions, a more familiar embrace.

Caliph was frowning when she stepped away, but she couldn't summon enough courage to do more than lift her hand in a lighthearted wave before she turned and all but sprinted to her car.

By the time she'd buckled herself into the driver's seat and found the nerve to turn around and look back toward the shop, Caliph had entered the building.

She fell forward as she lightly pounded her forehead on the steering wheel.

"Stupid fucking girl," she muttered, completely disgusted with herself.

What the hell had she done?

The answer resounded in her head like a cathedral bell. She'd reverted to character. The Jennifer who'd arrived at Caliph's house on Friday night had returned with a vengeance, running like a scared mouse at the first sign of rejection.

God, she was an idiot.

She hated that woman. The one who'd sat quietly and let her husband of seventeen years break her heart and walk away without one word of anger. The one who'd wasted a year of her life mourning over a man who didn't deserve her.

The one who'd just let the coolest, hottest, kindest man she'd ever met go without telling him exactly how wonderful he was.

If she could manage the position, she felt the overwhelming desire to get out of the car and kick her own ass.

No. Screw this. This life. This eternal hell.

She wanted more and, by God, she was going for it.

Before she could think of any reason why it was a bad idea, she was out of her car and standing at the door to Midnight Ink. She pushed the door open with way more force than she should have, the bell above it making her jump as it jingled.

While her arrival seemed unnervingly showy to her, it didn't appear to have caught anyone's notice.

"Caliph," she said, louder than she'd intended. The only other person in the shop was a woman Jennifer hadn't seen before. She assumed this was Rosie, the female tattoo artist Caliph had mentioned.

Caliph glanced up. He'd been standing next to his chair, staring into his cup of coffee like a zombie.

"Jen?"

"I don't, I mean, I was hoping…" God, she sounded like a complete tool.

"Say it."

His tone was one of pure command, the sound reminding her of everything that had passed between them. It spoke to her on some level she'd never acknowledged or noticed prior to this weekend with him. And it left her so damn hot, she felt as if she could burst into flames.

"I want to see you again."

She could feel the other woman staring at her, but Jennifer pushed through her embarrassment, her nervousness. She'd spent two days and only a handful of hours prior to the weekend with Caliph, yet he'd done more to help her find her feet, her strength than months' worth of conversations with well-meaning friends after her divorce. "I'd really like to go out with you again."

She held his gaze and let her words stand, willing to take this risk. If he told her he wasn't interested, she would be hurt. But she wouldn't fall apart. She wasn't the fragile woman Marcus had left nearly a year ago. She'd proven she could pick up the pieces and move on. There was a big difference between needing a man in your life and wanting one.

And she wanted this one…for as long as it lasted. If that wasn't forever, then so be it. There were plenty of other fish in the sea, petals on her daisy. One day, she'd find the one who would love her for who she was, who would make her happy. And even if she didn't, she intended to live a life without regrets.

Caliph grinned. "I'd like to keep seeing you too."

"You would?" Damn insecure Jennifer crept out at the most annoying times.

Caliph didn't seem to mind. He laughed. "Yeah. I would.

In fact, I'd like to nail down our next date right now. Make this decision official before you try to run away again. You realize that was the worst morning-after goodbye in history, right?"

She laughed, relief flowing through her like a hot shower on a cold winter's night. "Yeah. My brain wasn't fully functioning back there. Luckily it caught up to my stupid mouth before I drove away."

He walked over to her. "So what about that date?"

"I'm free next weekend."

He shook his head. "Too far away. Dinner. Tomorrow night."

Jennifer didn't even need to consider her schedule. She'd make it work. "Deal. I'll cook for you at my place to make up for being such a jackass."

Caliph grasped her hand and pulled her closer. "Food is a good way to apologize, but I can think of a better one."

"Dirty bastard."

He wrapped his arm around her and pinched her ass as she giggled. "Don't remember hearing any complaints when I had you tied to my bed yesterday."

Jennifer had forgotten they weren't alone until she heard the woman at the next station laugh.

"TMI," the other woman joked.

Caliph chuckled, then did the introductions. "Jen, this is Rosie. Rosie, this is Jennifer."

Like Sassy, Rosie was sporting some fun colored streaks in her hair, not to mention some serious ink on her arms and collarbone. For a moment, Jennifer considered asking Rosie where she got her hair done. She wouldn't mind adding a bit of color—maybe purple—to her own long tresses.

Rosie gave her a quick up-and-down glance. "So this is the daisy tattoo girl."

Jennifer looked at Caliph curiously.

Rosie answered her unspoken question. "He was a maniac last week, waiting—not very patiently—to see you again on Friday. Glad to see you two had a good time."

"We did."

Rosie studied Caliph's face. "And I'm glad to hear you're willing to see him again tomorrow. Something tells me he's not going to get you out of his system for quite a while."

Jennifer laughed, flattered to hear he had been looking forward to their date as much as her. "I hope not."

Her quick response appeared to have won Rosie's approval. The pretty tattoo artist looked at Caliph. "Well done, my friend."

The bell jangled over the door as a handsome, hulking blond man entered.

"Hello, sweetheart."

Rosie's face lit up as she walked away from them without a second glance.

Caliph leaned closer to whisper in her ear. "That's Finn. I haven't been the only maniac around here lately. Finn seems to make the rest of us mortals disappear in Rosie's world."

Jennifer understood the feeling. Whenever she was with Caliph, it felt as if they were the only two people on the planet.

"You in a hurry?" Caliph asked her.

She shook her head. One of the best parts of her job was that she—as senior hotel manager—got the weekends off.

"Good. Come here."

Caliph grasped her hand and tugged her through a door that led to a storage area in the back. He threw the lock on the door.

"What are you—"

Her question was cut off when Caliph grabbed her, kissing her so passionately her head spun. The embrace could have lasted for minutes or months for all Jennifer knew.

When he finally released her, he looked at her with stern, serious eyes. "I should punish you for that stunt you pulled in the parking lot. I thought you were really leaving."

"I thought I was too."

"What stopped you?"

"I'm tired of being a doormat." The words flew out without thought and she realized they weren't entirely correct. "I can't keep standing on the sidelines of my own life like some uninterested observer. I felt more alive this past weekend than I have in years. God, maybe even decades. It was a good feeling."

The laugh lines beside his eyes became more pronounced as she spoke. His smile grew wider.

"We're complete opposites, Caliph, and maybe this fling is just going to be that. A fling. But for now, it's exactly what I need."

Caliph tilted his head and studied her face. "I'm cool with riding this out, seeing where it takes us. The weekend wasn't enough for me, Jen. I want more of you."

Her stomach fluttered at his admission—with anticipation and desire. "I can't imagine there's much of me left to claim. You explored a hell of a lot of uncharted territory this weekend."

He laughed. "Oh, trust me, love. We haven't even touched the tip of the iceberg."

She made a face, pretending to be worried, which made him laugh louder.

"In fact," he said as he reached out and grasped her waist, pulling her hips against his, "I think we should seal this dating deal with a kiss."

"Just a kiss?" she asked when his lips were a mere breath away from hers.

"We'll start with that. Then see where it leads." He ran his hands over her ass, squeezing them firmly. "After all, there's nothing I love more than covering this pretty canvas of yours with color."

She rubbed her cheek against his, savoring the sensation of her soft to his rough. "Pervert," she whispered.

Caliph laughed. "Definitely. But you're kinky, so that makes us even."

Jennifer turned at the same time as Caliph, their lips finding each other's, though neither of them sought to turn the touch into a kiss. "Caliph?"

"Hmm?"

"Have you ever had sex back here?"

He chuckled. "Nope."

"Wanna do something really wicked?"

He laughed, then tugged on her hair with just enough force to get her engine revving. "I might have a few things we could try, kinky girl. Take off your clothes."

CRASH POINT
BIG EASY, BOOK 2

Fate brought Blake, the bad boy Chloe gave her body and heart, back into her life. He betrayed her trust, broke her heart, and stole from her family. Her fury still rages a decade later—so why does she want him more than ever?

Blake never stopped wanting Chloe. Through years of bad choices, Chloe was his light, leading him away from a life of crime to turn him into a better man. Now, Blake's back. And ready to show her some bad boys can be good. Very, very good.

CHAPTER ONE

"I know, Mama. Yeah...Yeah...Mmmhmm."

Blake Mills leaned against the doorframe of the studio. He watched the petite blonde—who had her back turned to him—set up her camera equipment while balancing her cell phone between her shoulder and cheek. Her head was fully tilted to the right, yet she worked with ease.

"I understand how important this fundraiser is, Mama. I'm just not all that jazzed about taking a bunch of beefcake pictures of some brainless mimbos with more muscles than sense."

Blake stifled the urge to clear his throat, slightly offended by the photographer's insult, but he let it slide, unwilling to let her know he was there. He'd never been referred to as a male bimbo before. Even so, he was fairly certain he'd find a way to make her eat those words. He might not be the smartest guy on the planet, but he wasn't an airhead with a penis either.

The woman sighed heavily, continuing to speak. It occurred to him there was something vaguely familiar about her voice.

For now, he held his tongue, intent on enjoying the view as she bent over to retrieve something from her camera bag, her firm, perfect ass pointed in his direction. She wore skintight jeans that accentuated the bottom half of her generous hourglass just right.

"Fine," she said in reply to something her mother had said. "I won't insult the models. At least not to their faces. But I'm reserving the right to make fun of them at Sunday dinner. I can't believe that last guy was able to squeeze his ego through the front door."

Ah, Blake thought, her annoyance started to make sense. The last guy had been a tool. He sympathized with the pretty woman. He'd been roped into this charity calendar bullshit too. Sounded like neither he, nor the photographer, were here willingly.

She stood up with her back still to him as she snapped her camera onto the tripod. It was clear her mother was giving her an earful by the short, cutoff replies the photographer was making.

"Yeah, but…"

"I know that. All I'm…"

"Alright, I can…"

Finally the woman pulled her cell away from her ear and mimicked the action of throttling it. Blake lost his ability to remain silent. He chuckled.

The photographer turned to face him and he sucked in an astonished breath.

Fuck.

Chloe Lewis.

For the briefest of moments, he hoped she wouldn't recognize him. After all, ten years had passed.

That wish was squashed instantly.

Her eyes narrowed when she saw him. "I have to go, Mama." She didn't even wait for her mother to say goodbye. Instead, she clicked the end button and slid the cell into her back jeans pocket. It was on the tip of his tongue to express surprise that she could squeeze anything else into the tight denim, but he was starting this conversation on thin ice as it was. No need to make it worse. Though there had always been something about Chloe that had him longing to tease her...just so he could hear her loud, joyful laughter. He'd never met anyone before or since who could laugh with such unrestrained, utter delight.

It was the first thing that had drawn him to her all those years ago. Chloe had trapped him in her tractor beam within minutes of their initial introduction and held him there for months—the best summer of his life. There was no denying the two of them had set off fireworks together—in and out of the bedroom. He'd never understood the word *tumultuous* until that summer. Perhaps enough time had passed that Chloe would forgive him and they could let bygones be bygones.

Chloe's eyes flashed fire.

Nope. No bygones.

"Hey, Chloe. Good to see you."

It was clearly the wrong opening. "Fuck you, Blake."

He deserved that. Even so, his pride—the same pride that had screwed things up between them so many years ago—surfaced. "I'm game if you are."

"That's it. Last straw. I'm not doing this. My mother can find someone else to take these damn pictures." She turned away from him, reaching for her phone, intent on calling her mother back.

He walked across the room and wrapped his hand around her wrist to stop her. "Wait."

She whirled on him, her temper blowing fast and hot. It took all the strength in his body not to grin. A smile when she was in the midst of an explosion was tantamount to committing suicide. Chloe may be small, but her boxer of a father and three older brothers had taught her well when it came to self-defense. Hell, it might be more accurate to say they'd given her brilliant lessons in all-out offensive attacks.

"Don't touch me."

Blake didn't remove his hand. Maybe the term *mimbo* did work for him. He'd never been accused of being too bright. Trying to keep hold of this miniature raging bull proved that. "Don't quit because of me."

She struggled to escape, but he merely tightened his grip. His body had shifted into overdrive the second he'd gotten close enough to smell her floral perfume and feel the undeniable heat that rose up every time the two of them got within a few feet of each other.

He could tell Chloe felt it as well. Her chest rose and fell rapidly and her face was flushed. Their brief scuffle hadn't produced either side effect. It was the same for him. Two minutes with her and he was on fire, his cock hard enough to pound nails in concrete.

When it became obvious he wasn't going to release her, she froze, her body rigid with fury...and arousal. Even after all these years, he knew her well enough to recognize both.

"The committee is going to have to find another photographer. I've hit my limit on manhandling for the day."

It was the only thing she could have said that would have prompted him to loosen his grip. He dropped her hand. "What do you mean manhandling?"

She closed her eyes as if praying for patience. Blake had provoked that response in her no less than a million times in the past. And as always, it hit him like the world's most powerful aphrodisiac. He still drove her crazy. For some reason, that idea turned him on even more.

"How the hell did you get involved in this calendar, Blake? I can't imagine the committee actually thought it was a good idea to include some punk-ass biker as part of the collection." Then her gaze sharpened. "Did my mom call you to do this?"

He shook his head quickly. "Of course not." He hadn't seen Mama Lewis in nearly a decade. The same day he'd hopped on his motorcycle and driven away from Chloe without a word. He'd been a fool. Chloe had been adorable, cute at nineteen. At twenty-nine, she was a fucking knockout.

"I doubt your mom even knows I'm involved. I drew the short straw this morning down at the precinct. My captain's wife is on the committee and decided the NOPD needed to be represented. Captain Rogers isn't exactly known for being organized. He forgot to round someone up until today when his wife showed up and read him the riot act for it. Next thing I know, I'm on my way here."

Chloe's brows furrowed in confusion. "NOPD? Precinct?" Then she erupted in laughter...and it was just as Blake had remembered. Loud. Infectious. "Dear God, please tell me they didn't let you join the police force."

He smiled. "Detective Mills, at your service. Just got promoted to the Special Victims Unit last fall."

She shook her head, her mirth dying as she realized he was telling her the truth. Chloe was allowed her shock. There was a big part of him that still couldn't believe he'd joined the force. For most of his life, he'd half-expected his future to include time spent behind bars, not escorting others there.

"You're joking."

"Nope. Wanna see my handcuffs?" He winked at her wickedly, letting her know exactly how he'd use them on her.

She scowled. "It's not possible. There's no way—"

"I'm a cop, Chloe." He whipped out his badge and flashed it at her.

She reached into her back pocket to retrieve her cell phone. "It doesn't matter. I'm still calling my mother. Surely there has to be someone who can—"

"Take pictures as good as you? Not likely, CJ Lewis."

Shock registered on her face when he used her pen name. Chloe had made a name for herself in the world of photography, having published a collection of her work called *The Face of New Orleans*. Blake had spotted it in the window of a bookstore and bought it instantly. He couldn't begin to count the hours he'd poured over the pictures, amazed by her talent and her eye for hidden beauty. She'd captured the people of New Orleans perfectly, bringing their hometown to life in vivid color.

"How did you know that was me?"

He ran his finger along her cheek, trying not to let her see how much it hurt him when she winced and pulled away. What was he expecting? He'd broken her heart. "I always knew you'd find success with your photographs, Chloe Jeannette. You were too talented not to." He also knew she'd been named after both her grandmothers.

"You remembered my middle name?"

He nodded. It was strange how much he recalled about Chloe. There were times when Blake thought he recalled her life story better than his own. At nineteen, he'd hung on her every word, certain she was the most beautiful, fascinating girl he'd ever met. Now, he was finding the woman she'd become just as enthralling.

"Chloe, this is an important project and you know it. The money raised is going to a good cause. Besides, do you really want to call Mama Lewis and tell her you're bailing? You think that would be a fun phone call?"

Chloe shuddered. "She doesn't know *you're* here, that you're involved. I might actually get a bye based on that."

His grin grew, causing her frown to deepen. "Your mom always liked me."

"Liked. As in past tense. Then you stole her favorite wedding gift, cleaned out her wallet and made me cry. I suspect she'd be in the front of the line, even before my brothers, to kick your ass."

Blake was sure she was right. And that thought hurt. He'd always adored Chloe's mother. She was the only mom in history who hadn't taken one look at his ripped-up jeans, leather jacket and bad attitude, then issued an order for him to get the hell away from her daughter. Instead, she'd invited him in for Sunday dinner, engaged him in conversation and seen something of value inside him that Blake couldn't see himself at the time.

Then he'd betrayed Mama Lewis' belief that he'd do the right thing, rejected Chloe and run off like a thief in the night.

No. Not *like*. Literally a thief. He'd stolen two hundred dollars from Mama Lewis' purse and a silver serving platter.

"I'm sorry, Chloe."

She studied his face for several quiet moments. He didn't bother to hide. He wanted her to see, to read the sincerity in his words. His life was overflowing with regrets, but stealing from Chloe's family and leaving her ranked at the very top of the list.

"Maybe you are. But you're not forgiven." Her words were hard, final.

And not at all surprising. Because he'd stolen more from Chloe than just some money. He'd taken her virginity and her young girl's love and trust and he'd trampled all over it.

"I'll tell my captain to find someone else from the NOPD to pose for the calendar. You're more valuable to the project than I am."

She nodded. "Fine."

He took one last look at her, wondering how long—if ever—it would be until their paths crossed again. Would he have to wait months? Years? Longer? He'd thought of her more than he cared to admit over the past decade—her face often the last one he saw when he closed his eyes at night. He'd always wondered if she was happy, if she'd married or fallen in love, had kids. A quick glance at her bare ring finger answered the marriage question.

The idea of never seeing her again was more painful than he would have imagined. "Goodbye, Chloe."

He turned to leave, but his exit was cut short when Captain Rogers' wife appeared with two other women in tow. "Oh, Detective Mills, I'm so glad we caught you and Chloe before you started. My friends and I were just heading out for lunch and I wanted them to meet you." She turned to the women with her, briefly introducing them as fellow committee members. "I was absolutely delighted when you volunteered for this project."

"Short straw, huh?" Chloe muttered.

"I was afraid my husband was going to have to recruit someone unwilling. Heaven only knows how that would have turned out." Mrs. Rogers turned to Chloe, beaming. "Didn't I send you a wonderful subject? And I have no doubt his bio for the calendar will be the most impressive one. After all, he received the Medal of Valor when he saved two people from a burning building and his work with juveniles has been truly inspiring. Speaking of bios," Mrs. Rogers pulled several sheets of paper from her purse. "Here's Blake's bio, along with two others. I told your mother I'd drop them off to you today."

Blake didn't turn to look at Chloe. He hated being the center of attention. He'd done his job, nothing more. To hear

Mrs. Rogers going on and on about his accomplishments like he was some sort of freaking superhero made him uncomfortable.

"I didn't do anything more than any other officer on the force would have done." He hoped that answer would be enough to kill the subject. It wasn't.

Mrs. Rogers was on a roll. "Plus he was instrumental in shutting down a major drug ring. My husband said it was the first time in all his years he felt a spark of hope for our local kids. Blake ensured there would be a lot fewer dealers on the playgrounds. All of this and he's only been on the force for five years."

Taking down that drug ring was one of the hardest things he'd ever done in his life—because it had involved him arresting his own father. That was one of the lowest moments in Blake's life, and to hear Mrs. Rogers discussing it as an accolade made him sick to his stomach.

"Actually, Mrs. Rogers, I'm afraid I'm not going to be able to—"

"Take the pictures today," Chloe interjected. "Detective Mills and I were just discussing some possible locales."

Blake turned to look at Chloe. She'd just threatened to walk off the project if he was involved. Now it sounded as if she was volunteering to make the job even harder. Locales?

Mrs. Rogers frowned, confused. "I was under the impression all the photographs would be shot here in your studio."

"That was the original plan, but after talking to the detective, it occurred to me that the photos would be more interesting if they were taken in a variety of locations and included something that reflected each man's interests."

Blake nodded, not about to miss this opportunity to spend more time with Chloe. "I'm into motorcycles, so we were thinking of riding out to Lake Pontchartrain and snapping some shots. Or we even discussed the possibility of taking River Road and posing at the plantations."

Chloe scowled, but didn't contradict him. The two of them had spent hours flying up and down the highways on his bike when they were younger. The plantations on River Road and the lake had been their favorite destinations. Blake had only gotten his motorcycle—an ancient Harley he'd seen an ad for in the classifieds—that summer. Chloe had been shocked to discover he'd never seen anything outside of the city limits, so she'd made it her mission to expose him to all the beautiful places he'd missed. In a few months, she'd done a great job of opening his eyes to the world just outside the city.

Mrs. Rogers clapped her hands together. "Oh! This sounds wonderful. Even better than we'd hoped. Well then, don't let us distract you from your work. I can't wait to see the end result."

With that, Mrs. Rogers and her friends left in a flurry of excited chatter.

Blake crossed his arms. "I thought you wanted me out."

"I did, but how could I explain wanting to kick out such an icon of the police force?"

"I was going to take the fall. Tell them I wasn't comfortable taking my shirt off for the picture."

Chloe snorted. "Yeah. I'm sure they would have believed that."

He grinned. "Are you saying I'm immodest?"

"I spent an entire summer with you and I can recall you wearing a shirt less than a handful of times. Usually at my mother's Sunday dinners and only then because she said you had to."

Blake rolled his eyes at her exaggeration, though when he considered it, she had a good point. That summer had been hot as hell and they'd spent most of it on his motorcycle, traveling an hour to the Gulf Coast beaches. Or riding beside the

Mississippi. Or walking along the French Quarter. Or wrapped up in each other's arms. "I can come up with another reason to bail."

She shook her head. "No. I'm a professional and it's no big deal. I'll snap a few pictures, then you and I can go our separate ways again."

"In other words, you're afraid of your mother and Mrs. Rogers."

She shot him a dirty look, then said, "Yeah. I've decided you're the lesser of two evils."

He chuckled, then stepped closer, enjoying the way she held his gaze as he leaned down. "I fully intend to change your mind about that."

Blake had to give Chloe credit. The woman never backed down from any challenge. "I'm not worried."

Before he could think better of it, Blake closed the distance between them, placing a quick, hard kiss on her lips.

It was just as he'd remembered—only better. Chloe's lips were soft and she tasted so damn sweet—like peppermint and chocolate and sunshine all rolled up into one.

He'd spent most of his younger life around jaded, hard women who smelled of booze and cigarettes. However, since joining the police force, his dating life had dwindled down to nothing. Blake had been more celibate than a monk the past year or so. He hadn't minded that state until he'd seen her again.

He broke the union before Chloe had a chance to reject him...or knee him in the balls.

He tapped her nose playfully. "You should be. I'll call you later about the photo shoot."

Blake made his escape quickly before Chloe changed her mind about his participation in the project. He'd been ready to accept her dismissal and walk away. Until that kiss.

Now...well, now...he was driving without brakes. And the crash was imminent.

He grinned as he walked back out into the sunshine, grabbing his helmet and pulling it on.

He straddled his Harley and fired up the engine.

Crashing never sounded so exciting.

CHAPTER TWO

"Earth to Chloe. Pass the potatoes, pipsqueak."

Chloe gave her brother Jett a dirty look, but passed the bowl of scalloped potatoes as she did so.

Jett dipped out a healthy portion before handing the bowl to their foster brother, Zac.

Jett looked at her and shook his head. "Damn, girl. Where the hell are you today? I asked you three times to hand me those before you even heard me saying your name."

She shrugged. She'd been floundering around, lost in her own thoughts since running into Blake again at the studio on Thursday. Seeing him had brought up a whole bunch of feelings—sadness, regret, anger—as well as an unbearable mountain of lust. He'd been her first and, while she'd never admit as much to the asshole, there was some truth to that line about him ruining her for all other men. While she'd taken her fair share of lovers, Blake had always been the yardstick she'd compared them to and none had measured up. Not even close.

Which pissed her off even more because hell would freeze over before Blake Mills touched her again, and she didn't care if that meant taking responsibility for every single one of her own orgasms from now until the end of time.

"Chloe!" This time it was Justin yelling her name.

"What?" She didn't bother to hide the irritation in her tone. Her annoying brothers could see she was distracted. Why didn't they just leave her alone?

"What's wrong?"

"For the last time, nothing."

Her mother tilted her head, studying her face. "This is about Blake, isn't it?"

The head of every sibling at the table flew up.

"Blake Mills?" Caliph asked.

She closed her eyes, wishing she were anywhere else right now. Seeing her first love had thrown her for a loop. There was no way she was ready to undergo the Spanish Inquisition about that unexpected reunion with her family. "He's one of the models for the Blessing House calendar." The Blessing House provided temporary housing for homeless families. Her mother had served on the board for years, organizing fundraiser after benefit auction after bake sale to keep the House open and solvent.

This year, the fundraising committee had decided to take a page from the book of other large cities, putting together a sexy calendar as a fun way to raise money. The calendar, "Hot Hunks in the Big Easy," was gathering a lot of attention, and given her mom's successful track record, was certain to make a slew of cash for the Blessing House.

Justin looked at Mama. "You're putting thugs in the calendar?"

Chloe grinned, appreciating his appalled tone. It was nice to know her brothers always had her back.

"No. We're not. Agnes Rogers found him. Apparently, Blake is a detective with the NOPD these days. She called me a couple of days ago to say the police department would be well represented."

"The hell you say," Jett proclaimed. "How hard up is the city for law enforcement? They're hiring crooks now?"

"Who is Blake Mills?" Caliph's girlfriend, Jennifer, asked. Jen and Caliph had started dating a few months earlier. Since then, she'd become a staple at the family's Sunday dinners. Chloe adored the woman and hoped she and Caliph would stick.

"Chloe's first boyfriend," Caliph answered. "A real badass and every father's worst nightmare when it comes to the guy you don't want your daughter dating."

"He wasn't that bad," Mama said. "I swear that poor boy's reputation has grown more despicable with every telling. Next thing I know, y'all will be swearing he was a serial killer and responsible for every hurricane to ever hit New Orleans."

Chloe sighed. Mama had never wavered in her belief that there was some good buried deep inside Blake. Right after she'd gotten off the phone with Mrs. Rogers, Mama had called Chloe to make sure she was okay with taking pictures of Blake. Chloe had assured her mother it wouldn't be any big deal, but she'd never managed to pull the wool over Mama's eyes and obviously she hadn't fooled her this time either.

Of course, since learning he'd joined the police force, her mother acted as if her faith in Blake had at last been proven true.

"We broke up when he stole money from Mama and took the silver serving platter my grandmother had given my parents as a wedding gift."

Jennifer winced. "Yikes. Doesn't sound like a very nice guy. And you say he's a cop now?"

Chloe nodded. "Yeah. And he's posing for the calendar."

Jennifer reached over and squeezed her hand gently. "That

can't be easy for you. I know I wouldn't want to have to work with my ex on anything. Ever." Jennifer's ex-husband had left her for another woman. That painful event had led to her meeting Caliph. In an attempt to reinvent herself, Jennifer had shown up at Midnight Ink and gotten her first tattoo from Caliph. Since then, Chloe had watched her older brother fall head over heels in love with the woman. It was sweet. Even if it did reinforce the loneliness that had plagued Chloe lately.

She would be thirty on her next birthday, and while that age wasn't bothering her, it forced her to recognize some things she'd been ignoring. Like the fact she wanted kids. A slew of them like her mother had. Chloe absolutely adored her big family and she dreamed of having her own. But to do so, she had to get serious about dating and finding the man she wanted to marry. She'd put off doing that for too long, focusing instead on building a clientele for her photography studio and putting her book together.

"It'll be okay, Jennifer. I really only have to see him one more time. I'll snap a few pictures and walk away. No harm, no foul."

A quick glance at her mother's face proved her lie wasn't convincing the one person she really wanted to believe her.

Before she could reassure Mama she was speaking the truth, the doorbell rang.

"Chloe's the closest," Jett pointed out, not bothering to put his fork down as Zac snickered.

She rolled her eyes. They may all be adults, but there was something about returning to this house each Sunday that seemed to bring out the child each of them held on to. "Lazy jackass."

Jett gave her a shit-eating grin as she rose to answer the door while they all continued eating.

She barely paid attention as she swung open the front door.

It wasn't unusual for neighbors or friends to stop by on Sunday, as they knew the entire family would be there. Mama always made enough to feed an Army and as such, there was plenty of room at the large table for one or two or twelve drop-ins.

Chloe wasn't aware that her mouth had flown open until Blake placed his hand on her chin to push it closed.

"What the hell are you doing here?"

Blake smiled. "Mama Lewis invited me."

Chloe shook her head. "That's Mrs. Lewis to you and she wouldn't do that."

"Chloe," her mother called out from the dining room. "Invite him in."

Chloe closed her eyes, hoping that by blocking out Blake's cocky face, he'd simply vanish. When she opened them to find him still standing in the doorway, she muttered, "I'm going to kill her."

Blake chuckled. "If you do that, I'll have to pull out my handcuffs and arrest you."

She was tempted to slam the door in his face, then reconsidered as a wide smile crossed her face. Maybe this wasn't such a bad thing after all.

Blake's lowered brows betrayed his sudden suspicion at her quick change in demeanor. "You like the idea of handcuffs?" He grinned, his dirty mind kicking in.

"No, perv, I don't." She was lying, but she wasn't about to admit her libido had suddenly jerked into gear at the thought. "You realize you're about to willingly walk into the lion's den, right? My brothers will tear you limb from limb."

Unfortunately her threat didn't faze the infuriating man. "I'm banking on your mother to protect me. But just in case," he patted his hip, drawing her attention to his holster, "I'm packing."

There was no way she could convince him to leave and

time was up anyway. If she stalled much longer, her brothers' curiosity would win out and they'd all manage to make their way to the front door, lazy jackasses or not. She stepped aside, allowing Blake to enter.

He glanced around the entryway, looking fondly at the photographs and furniture. "It's exactly the way I remember it."

"Everyone is in the dining room and my food is getting cold." Her tone was short and annoyed, but she didn't feel like playing nice. He didn't deserve it. He'd hurt her worse than anyone in her life and while that wound had been inflicted nearly a decade earlier, it ached as if it had happened only yesterday.

She hated that she'd let him get so deep inside her he still had the power to cause her pain.

Blake waited for her to lead the way. She kept her eyes on her mother as they entered the room together. She didn't have to look at her brothers to see how pissed off they were.

Jett stood, his stance pure aggression. "What are you doing here?"

"I invited him," Mama replied, as if bringing the man who'd stolen from their family into their home was the most natural thing in the world. Of course, for their mother, it was. Her capacity for forgiveness was limitless.

Chloe could only assume that attribute skipped a generation because God knew she couldn't find it in herself right now.

Her mother rose, then gestured to an empty chair next to her as she grabbed a plate from the sideboard. "Help yourself, Blake."

He smiled his thanks as he took a seat. "I apologize for being late. Wound up pulling some overtime after the midnight shift. Lots of idiots on the street last night. Took me a few extra hours to finish the paperwork."

Chloe reclaimed her seat, grateful that Justin sat between her and Blake.

Blake kept his attention on her mother, pointedly ignoring the glares he was receiving from everyone else at the table. "I was sorry to hear about Papa Lewis."

Mama smiled gratefully. "Thank you, Blake. We all miss him something terrible."

That was an understatement, but Chloe didn't say anything. Though her father had passed away three years ago, sometimes it felt as if he was just away, working on the oil rig and that he'd be back, crashing through the front door with that loud bellow of his, telling all his kids to get their asses downstairs so he could hug them. Her father had been a giant of a man—Caliph and Jett had gotten his stature—but as gentle as a butterfly.

"And what is your father up to these days, Blake?" her mother asked.

Blake fell silent for only a moment, then gave her a rueful smile. "He's up to twelve months served on a twenty-year stint in prison."

"Oh, I see."

Blake shrugged. "Not surprised, are you?"

Mama shook her head. "Not really, but I *am* sorry."

"Don't be." Blake's voice was harder than Chloe had ever heard it. "I'm the one who put him there."

"You put your own father in jail?" Jennifer asked.

Blake looked at Jennifer, clearly waiting for an introduction. Caliph quickly did so. "This is my girlfriend, Jen."

Blake smiled. "Nice to meet you, and yeah, I did. He was selling drugs at some of the local schools. And not just marijuana, but ecstasy and heroin. I think there are a lot of people better off with him in jail."

Chloe put her fork down, unable to swallow through the

lump that had grown in her throat. She knew Blake's childhood hadn't been easy, but he'd never shared many details about it with her. She hadn't known him at all until the summer he'd gotten a job at the sub place near the community college she attended. They'd both gone to different public schools, growing up on opposite ends of the city.

"I'm sorry, too," Chloe said softly. Blake caught her gaze, his eyes reflecting too many emotions to register—sadness, regret, anger, remorse. She looked away rather than face them. She'd seen all those things when they first met as well.

Maybe she was more like her mother than she realized—inexplicably drawn to people in pain, in need of rescue. Though Blake sure as hell hadn't let her save him. She doubted that would change now and she refused to be pulled back into Blake's life.

Jett broke the silence. "Guess the police force is a more interesting job than Sid's Sub Shop. Isn't that where you used to work?"

Blake nodded. "Yeah. Met Chloe there. She used to do homework between classes at the table in the corner." He faced her once more. "You still put down those Italian subs like you're never going to eat again?"

Her brothers chuckled. She flashed them all dirty looks until they sobered up.

Blake may be older, but the bad boy was still there, lurking beneath his skin. She could see it in his face as he gave her a crooked grin.

It was the same smile that had captured her attention back in college. She'd taken one look at the bad boy behind the shop counter and fallen hard. A lot of people had tried to warn her away from him, telling her stories about how he stole beer and cigarettes from convenience stores, drove his motorcycle like he had a death wish and vandalized buildings. Blake had never denied the stories, but he'd never gotten caught either.

It hadn't mattered to her at the time because when he was with her, he had been sweet and funny. Her badass biker boyfriend. Given her goodie-goodie status, it had felt scandalous to be with someone with a reputation and wonderful to be so adored by him. She'd always hoped she had helped him be a better person, while he taught her how to be just a little bit wicked. Whatever they'd done for each other, there had never been a doubt in her mind that Blake had loved her.

Until he disappeared. Then she'd spent months—years—wondering what had been real and what had been lies. In the end, she'd felt used and stupid. And so angry.

"It was wonderful of you to volunteer to participate in the calendar." Her mom looked genuinely pleased and almost grateful.

Why was Chloe the only person who remembered the past?

Chloe snorted at her mother's praise, drawing everyone's attention to her. "He drew the short straw."

Blake grinned, while Mama looked confused. "Short straw?"

Blake leaned back in his chair, looking far too comfortable and at home. "It's a good cause. I don't mind helping out."

Caliph rolled his eyes. "I'm sure you don't. As I recall, you don't have a bit of trouble strutting around with your shirt off."

Chloe gave Blake a superior smile, grateful for Caliph's snide comment. Finally. She'd warned him about her brothers' anger and though it would cost her in good karma, it felt good to watch them give Blake shit.

Blake crossed his arms, drawing too much attention to the muscles bulging beneath his t-shirt. "I figure those of us who haven't let ourselves go owe it to those who have to step forward. By the way, I don't remember seeing your name on the list of models, Caliph."

Caliph's eyes darkened as Jennifer slowly wrapped her hand around his wrist. Chloe was trying to decide if the touch was a warning or Jennifer's way of holding Caliph in his seat.

"I'm still trying to convince my sons to participate. We have two slots open." Mama gave Caliph a hopeful glance.

"I told you, Mama, I don't think the older members of your group would embrace the idea of a guy covered in tattoos."

Jennifer shook her head as if the argument was a familiar one. "I told him that only *every* woman who bought the calendar would be into that, but he's stubborn."

Caliph gave Jennifer a sweet kiss on the cheek. "Not every woman in the world is as open-minded as you, Jen. There are plenty out there who still turn up their noses when they see my ink. Besides, I have no desire to make a jackass of myself, posing like some king of *GQ*."

Mama looked from Caliph to Justin, but he cut her off at the pass. "Don't look at me. I already suckered Ned into doing it. You only need one marketing exec." Ned Kinnaman was Justin's partner at their advertising firm and one of the sexiest men Chloe had ever met. She was actually a bit nervous about photographing Ned. He literally oozed sex and sin.

Justin laughed when he spotted Chloe's flushed cheeks. "See," he pointed at her, making her blush even more. "That's what Ned's going to bring to the calendar. I've done my part."

Chloe scowled at her brother for embarrassing her, then she caught a glimpse of jealousy in Blake's gaze. Revenge reared its beautiful head.

"I'm not going to lie, Justin," she said as she fanned herself. "I'm really looking forward to Ned's day to pose. He's February, and I'm envisioning putting him on my bed with red silk sheets, completely naked, except for a box of chocolates covering his—"

"I think we get the gist," Justin said, cutting her off and pretending to shudder. "We don't need to hear the dirty details about your photo shoots with all those sexy bachelors. Good thing you're single. You can have some fun as you work." He winked at her, careful to make sure Blake couldn't see his face.

Chloe loved her oldest brother and his nose for mischief. She had absolutely no intention of posing Ned that way and Justin knew it, but that didn't mean he wouldn't help her get a few digs in at Blake.

"I didn't realize the photos were going to be risqué," Blake said.

Mama frowned. "Neither did I."

Oops. Chloe would have to tell her mom she was joking before she left today or she was liable to receive concerned phone calls from every woman on the fundraising committee tonight.

The rest of the meal passed much more easily than Chloe would have expected. Conversation turned to innocuous things as Justin described his latest project and Caliph and Jennifer talked about the long weekend trip they'd planned to take to Key West. Blake was a polite guest, answering questions about his work and complimenting her mother's cooking.

Once dessert and coffee had been consumed, the family began to rise. Jett and Justin made their goodbyes, both claiming to have other plans, while Zac, Jennifer and Caliph went to the living room to watch TV. Her mother was tidying the kitchen, which left Chloe alone with Blake.

Blake peered toward the kitchen door. "Let me pop into the kitchen to thank your mom and then I'm going to head out."

Chloe nodded as Blake disappeared into the kitchen. She walked to the front door to wait, anxious to see the frustrating man on his way. Her insides felt like churned butter and she was tempted to move Blake's photo shoot forward, simply so she could get it over with.

She cheered herself up with a mental pep talk. She'd meet him at Lake Pontchartrain—she had no intention of ever getting on his motorcycle again—take the pictures, then turn around and walk away. This time, it was Blake who was going to see taillights. The whole thing shouldn't take more than three or four hours. Surely she could survive that much more time in his presence.

"That's a deep thought."

She was startled by his voice, jumping slightly when she realized Blake was standing right next to her.

She put her hand on the doorknob, ready to get him the hell out of her mother's house, but paused. "Should I pat you down to make sure you aren't sneaking off with something?"

She felt horrible the moment the words crossed her lips, but there was something about seeing Blake again that was bringing out the worst in her. She didn't consider herself a bitter person by nature, but for days, all she'd been able to summon was cold, hard anger. Well, that...and lust.

Blake took her comment in stride, lifting his arms. "You won't hear any complaints from me. Take your time on that area below the waist. Lots of pockets down there."

She blew out an exasperated breath, though she was able to admit she'd walked right into that one. "Don't be such a pig."

"Hey, you're the one who offered. I've never looked a gift horse in the mouth. Should I turn around?" He spun, lifting his hands to the wall. The position sent her eyes straight to his ass, which he wiggled for her amusement.

One brief burst of laughter escaped before she could shut it down. Damn him. "Turn around and get out, you idiot."

"I love your laughter."

Chloe tried to ignore the tug his soft comment evoked. It had always been there between them—this electrical current that flowed hot and powerful, tying them together in ways Chloe could never understand...or fight. It was always sparks, heat, energy and painful need.

"Walk outside with me."

Blake had her hand in his before she could refuse. It appeared his take-no-prisoners attitude was still there as well. She'd followed his lead when she was nineteen because she was young and inexperienced. If he still thought she was that same silly girl who would come merely because he beckoned, he was destined for disappointment. She tried to pull her hand away, but his grip tightened.

They participated in a mini tug-of-war all the way to his motorcycle. Once they were there, he reached for a helmet. "Hop on."

She laughed at his audacity. "No."

"Get on the bike, Chloe. You need to get away for a little while. I can see it in your face. When is the last time you escaped, letting wind and the road take over until you forgot everything and everyone?"

Ten years ago.

She didn't say it aloud, but something in Blake's expression told him he knew the answer. "I'm not getting on the motorcycle with you. Not now. Not ever again."

"Yes, you will."

She narrowed her eyes. "Blake—"

"Our photo shoot, remember? We're taking the Harley to the lake."

"I have too much equipment. I'll follow you there in my car." She was pleased to see she'd stumped him with that. Clearly he hadn't taken that into account.

Blake leaned against his motorcycle casually. "So what are your plans for the week?"

She shook her head at his audacity. "None of your business."

He lifted one shoulder at her dismissal. "Maybe. Maybe not. You taking pictures of the manhandler?"

Chloe felt an uneasy flutter in her stomach. Blake Mills on a mission was never a good thing. He had the tenacity of a pit bull when he wanted something. She'd always blamed that on the fact he'd basically had to raise himself, given his father's disinterest in his son and his lack of mother.

"Again, none of your business."

"Give me your phone."

"Why?"

Before she could stop him, Blake had one arm wrapped around her waist, the other diving into her back pocket. She placed her hands on his chest, intent on pushing him away, but the man was solid muscle, his chest rock hard. Once her phone was in his hand, he released her and took a step back. It bugged her that she hadn't been able to break free on her own.

He clicked the cell on, taking her to task for her lack of a passcode. He went to the contacts page and, as she watched, added his name and phone number.

"I'm deleting that."

"No. You're not. At least not until all of the calendar pictures have been taken. You're going to be alone with these guys and, while your mom and the committee might trust their characters, I'd feel better if you had my number handy. You feel threatened, even just a little, you call me. Okay?"

"I can take care of myself."

"Oh yeah?" Blake turned her phone off, grasping her once more. "Prove it."

"What?"

He slid her phone into her back pocket, taking advantage of the opportunity to run his fingers over her ass. She tried to shove him away, but she'd have had more luck moving a mountain.

"Break free from my hold and I'll delete the number myself." His arms tightened around her.

Chloe's mind whirled over all the self-defense moves her brothers had taught her when she became a teenager and got boobs. The more her body developed, the more intensive their training. "I don't want to hurt you." She put as much bravado into her tone as possible.

Blake laughed. "Of course you do."

She noticed he'd positioned himself so that his balls were protected and her bent arms were trapped against his chest. She marveled at how familiar, yet different Blake's body was. He'd always been tough as a young man, his body lean and fit, but now...

Chloe couldn't help but wonder what drove Blake to work out so much. Why did he need to be so damn strong? Blake had only shared skeletal notes of his childhood with her, never giving details. All she'd had to go on was his scant information, usually shared by accident, and her gut feelings. Yet, she'd always viewed him as a wounded beast, striking out at the world as a means of defense. Chloe had also thought she was safe from his swing, assumed she was different.

She'd learned the hard way how wrong she was.

"Don't, Blake."

His arms loosened slightly. "Don't what?"

"Don't set your sights on this. On us. It's not gonna happen."

He didn't move, continuing to hold her close. All of his attention, all of his focus homed in on her. She'd been the center of his universe for three glorious months. She remembered how special and wonderful that had been. Even so, it wasn't worth the inevitable pain that followed. She wouldn't play the fool for him again.

"I get it, Chloe. I'm sure you think I don't, but I do. If I were a better man, I'd accept that I hurt you, that you have every right in the world not to trust me and I'd keep my distance. You didn't deserve what I did to you and I'm not real sure how to make up for that. Maybe I can't. But the thing is, I'm going to try because I'm *not* a good man. I'm a selfish bastard. And I want you. I never stopped wanting you."

Chloe's lungs seized as she struggled for air. There was determination written on every line of his face, but more frightening than that was the hunger in his eyes. She'd seen it before —in the faces of the foster kids her mother had taken in over the years. The kids had always looked like they were starving to death, like they would do whatever it took to get a bite of bread. Chloe knew that hunger wasn't literal. What those kids—like Blake—wanted more than anything was love. Unconditional love.

"I can't give you what you want. Not the forgiveness. Not the understanding. And not the..." She couldn't say the word *love* to him. Couldn't let that single syllable out in his presence. "I'm not the girl I used to be." She wasn't sweet, trusting, or gullible anymore. He'd squashed those characteristics out of her, stomped on them until they simply vanished.

Blake released her waist. She had only a split second of freedom before he took her face in his hands. She wanted to shove him away, but she was rooted to the spot. "Yes. You are. You're still that girl and a hell of a lot more. But I'm more too. And I want a chance to prove that to you."

She started to shake her head, but Blake's grip tightened. "Blake—"

Her denial was cut off with a kiss. The second his lips

touched hers, she was transported back in time. Their first kiss had been right here, in almost this exact same spot. They'd spent weeks circling around each other at the sub shop, her flirting while he made completely inappropriate but entirely hot sexual innuendoes. Then one afternoon, he'd offered her a ride on his motorcycle and she'd accepted. They had ridden around the city for nearly an hour as Chloe clung to his leather jacket and breathed in the humid Louisiana air. They'd stopped at the French Quarter, walking along the crowded streets until dusk, talking about everything and nothing. When he'd pulled up in front of her house that night, Blake had gotten off the Harley, taken her face in his hands and kissed her.

It had felt just like this—exciting, scary, overwhelming, powerful. And then—like now—Chloe had been helpless to do anything other than accept.

Helpless.

The word jarred, going through her like nails on a chalkboard.

She placed her hands on his shoulders and pushed. Blake clearly hadn't anticipated her refusal as he stepped back, slightly off balance at her rough shove.

"I'm going inside."

He smiled. "Running away isn't going to save you."

Her pride piqued. "I'm not running. I'm finished with the conversation. I'll text you later this week once I've found a place to take your photo for the calendar. We'll get it over with and then, this," she waved her hand between them, "is over. Again." She stressed the last word, letting it punctuate her sentence like an angry accusation.

Of course, Blake didn't acknowledge anything she'd said. "We'll see." Then straddled his bike, put his helmet on, fired up the engine and pulled away.

Chloe balled her hand into a fist, wishing she had something—anything—to punch. Blake infuriated her, pissed her off, left her struggling to keep her wits.

She released a loud "argh!" then muttered every bad name she could think of as she returned to the house. The front door had only just closed behind her when she heard her mother calling out for her to come to the kitchen.

She sighed. The kitchen window faced the front yard, which meant her mother had no doubt witnessed the entire scene with Blake. Great. Her Sunday just kept getting better and better.

"Did you need help with something?" Chloe asked, half-heartedly hoping for a reprieve. She didn't get it.

Her mother was sitting at the small kitchen table, sipping a cup of coffee and looking wearier than Chloe had ever seen her.

Mama shook her head, then pointed to the chair across from her.

Chloe decided to take the bull by the horns. There was no purpose to beating around the bush. "I guess you saw Blake kiss me."

Her mother didn't reply at first. "Actually, no. I didn't. I didn't think it was my place to spy."

Chloe bit her lip, wondering if there was any physical way to kick her own ass. "It didn't mean anything."

Her mother smiled, though the expression certainly didn't depict happiness. "Aren't you tired, Chloe?"

Chloe was. Exhausted. But she couldn't understand how her mother knew that. "What do you mean?"

"Anger takes a lot of energy to maintain. You've been holding on to your Blake fury for nearly a decade now. Doesn't that leave you drained?"

Chloe swallowed heavily. Truthfully, until running into Blake this week, she thought she'd let go of all those old hurts. If someone would have asked, Chloe would have laughed and sworn she didn't have any feelings for the man one way or the other. This past week had proven that belief false. She was harboring more pain and rage than she'd thought possible. And her mom was right. It was wearing her out...dragging her down.

"I was just surprised to see him again. It sort of knocked me back to a bad time. But it'll pass soon."

"No. It won't. None of this is going to go away until you forgive him."

Chloe's temper sparked. "Forgive him? God, Mama. At some point, you're going to have to stop being a doormat, stop letting people take advantage of your kindness."

"I don't think it makes me weak to try to find the good inside people. That's not being a doormat. It's being compassionate."

"And look what that compassion got you. Blake stole two hundred dollars from your purse. That was our grocery money for the week. Maybe you don't remember how tight times were back then, but I do. We barely made it until payday at the end of the month."

Her mother reached into the pocket of her apron and pulled out a wad of money, tossing it onto the table between them.

"What's that?" Chloe asked.

"Blake just gave it to me. Five hundred dollars. To replace the money he stole and to make restitution for the platter."

"That doesn't cover it. Grandma Jeannette's platter was a family heirloom—irreplaceable. It was the only thing that survived the fire that destroyed everything your family owned. You were just sixteen and you lost everything. Everything except that platter. Maybe you think three hundred covers it, but I don't."

Mama sighed. "Chloe, you're not mad about the money or the platter."

Chloe wanted to deny it, but couldn't. In some ways, it was easier to maintain her fury over tangible things. That was simpler to explain to her mother. To herself. If she delved deeper, she'd have to admit to things she couldn't find the words to express.

"He said he loved me. Then he left without a word. Just disappeared for ten years. I guess in some ways he did me a favor. He taught me not to be such a sucker, not to believe everything someone tells me."

"Have you ever considered there might have been a good reason for his departure? Have you asked him why he left?"

Chloe shook her head. She wasn't interested in exploring ancient history. "It doesn't matter now."

Mama reached across the table and took her hand. "Of course it does. As long as this is hurting you, the reasons matter. It's time to swallow your pride, Chloe, time to put aside your anger and get some answers. Otherwise, I'm afraid you're destined to be tired for a very, very long time and I couldn't stand to see that."

"I'm sorry I called you a doormat. I didn't mean it."

Her mother grinned. "I know. Now...about this plan to have Ned posing nude..."

Chloe laughed, then spent the next hour reassuring her mother she and Justin were joking and that the calendar would be perfectly respectable.

CHAPTER THREE

Blake leaned against the wall of the building, watching the front door of the Blue Note. Chloe was inside the bar, taking photographs of one of New Orleans' most talented and lusted-over jazz musicians. He wanted to pretend he was here to simply keep an eye on her. After all, one of the men posing for the calendar had apparently tried to manhandle her, and while he knew Chloe was perfectly capable of taking care of herself, he figured it wouldn't hurt to be close by...just in case.

Unfortunately, he knew the truth. He was so jealous, he could hardly see straight.

He'd never been a possessive lover with any other woman in his life. The only one to ever evoke that emotion had been Chloe. He reached into his wallet and pulled out a tattered picture. He'd carried the photograph around with him for a decade—clinging to it like a lifeline through some of the darkest times of his life.

The image of Chloe, riding his back, piggyback-style, as the two of them mugged for the camera never failed to help him find his way. Though she wouldn't believe it, Chloe had helped him become the man he was today. She'd fallen in love with a boy who'd always thought himself unlovable. After all, his father declared him worthless on a daily basis and his mother had split when he was just six months old. From the day he'd been born, no one had ever looked at him the way Chloe had. Like he hung the moon. Like he was a hero. Like his life mattered.

So...whenever he got lost or started down the wrong path, he'd pull out this picture and clean up his act, find a better direction. He wouldn't be where he was today without her. Until he'd seen her again last week, he'd been content to maintain his distance because that was safer. For both of them.

He had considered looking her up the second his feet hit the pavement of New Orleans almost six years earlier. After he left her, Blake had spent four years on the road, the first couple with his father. Sometimes they traveled alone, other times, they would ride with a motorcycle gang. He'd done a lot of things he wasn't proud of during that time—petty thievery, vandalism, smoking pot and drinking heavily. He'd even participated in several fight clubs as a means of making money. He'd beaten up a few of his opponents badly, the images of their bloody faces haunting him too many nights.

However, he'd walked away from it all the night his father and a few of his friends cornered a waitress in a bar parking lot where they had all spent hours getting wasted. Blake had sat with them, nursing the same whiskey, fed up with his life. He'd spent hours watching his father as the realization he was turning into his old man dawned hard. Looking at himself in the mirror behind the counter, he saw the same hard eyes, tight lines by his mouth and haggard expression. It was as if someone had dumped a cooler full of ice water over his head, forcing him to wake up, covering him with a freezing cold numbness that almost made his teeth chatter.

When his father threw the struggling waitress onto the hood of a car and started to lift her skirt, the other men holding her down and tearing off her clothes, his dead soul came to life. He didn't remember grabbing his father or pulling him away from the woman. There were only brief flashes of recollection in his memory. Of him pounding his old man into the asphalt. Of him beating the shit out of the other three men. Of the crying woman running away—her eyes reflecting absolute fear even though he'd just saved her. He didn't blame her for being afraid. He could only imagine what he'd looked like in that moment. Too many years' worth of rage had found their way to his fists and he was a man out of control.

In the end, all he recalled was standing in the middle of a dark parking lot with four unconscious men and the sound of sirens in the distance. He'd hopped on his bike and never looked back.

"Blake? What are you doing here?"

Blake blinked, forcing himself to the present, shocked to find Chloe standing in front of him. How the hell had she left the bar and walked all the way across the street without him noticing? So much for this stakeout.

Chloe looked completely annoyed. And a bit nervous.

He grinned. He could work with that. "I just got off duty, so I thought I'd take a little walk."

She rolled her eyes. "Not much of a walk. I could see you from the front window of the Blue Note. You've been holding up this wall for the last twenty minutes. How did you even know I was going to be here?"

"I'm a detective."

She smirked. "My mother told you."

He chuckled. "Yeah. I just wanted to make sure you were okay."

She sighed. "I'm perfectly capable of fending a guy off if he oversteps, despite my failed attempts with you."

He knew that, but he suspected she'd prefer thinking he was just concerned for her safety rather than the fact he was so jealous he couldn't see straight, so he let the lie stand. "Are you finished for the day?"

She shrugged. "I'm finished as far as working with Mr. January is concerned. Now I'm heading back to my studio to download the photos, find the best and tweak it."

"Have time for lunch?"

She hesitated, but didn't instantly refuse. Blake took that as a sign of progress. Before she could answer one way or the other, he pointed down Bourbon Street. "What do you say we grab some crawfish beignets at Bayou Burger?"

Chloe crinkled her nose. "Please tell me you don't still eat those."

Blake wrapped his arm around her shoulder, gently directing her toward the restaurant. Chloe fell into step easily beside him.

"Gotta say, Chloe, I'm sorry to hear you're still a finicky eater."

She scoffed. "The fact that I don't cover every meal in hot sauce does not mean I'm picky. Quite the opposite, actually. It means I prefer to taste my food. You should try it some time."

He laughed, the two of them trading barbs about their eating habits all the way to Bayou Burger. It wasn't until they were seated and their drinks ordered that Blake could lean back and relax without worrying she'd change her mind and run.

"It was good to see your family again on Sunday, but I'm not sure who Zac is."

Chloe took a sip from her water glass. "He's my foster

brother. You wouldn't have met him. He came to live with us the summer after you..." She paused.

There was no point pretending. "After I left," he finished for her.

She nodded. "He and his younger brother, Noah, were removed from their home when their mother was arrested for prostitution and drugs. Zac was fifteen and Noah was only twelve. Before they came to stay with us, they'd been living in a house with no running water and eating whatever they could steal from dumpsters behind restaurants."

The story sounded familiar. Blake had done a bit of fine garbage dining himself when he was younger, but Chloe didn't know that. He'd never told her anything about his childhood because at the time, Blake had worried she would either dump him or worse, pity him. There were times he wished he could go back and kick his nineteen-year-old self's ass for being such a prideful idiot.

Listening to her tell Zac's story, he didn't hear sympathy as much as anger toward the boys' mother.

"How long did they stay with you?"

Chloe sighed. "Two years the first time. Then the court—in its less-than-infinite wisdom—gave them back to their mother. Their lives returned to more of the same, only worse. Their mother kept smoking crack and sleeping with men for drug money. One of the guys—a customer—beat Zac up one night. It was really bad. Noah was scared so he ran to a neighbor's house and called my mom. She phoned the police, then all three of my brothers. They got to the house just before the cops and found Zac in a bloody heap on the floor."

"Jesus." Blake couldn't imagine how hard it would have been for those young boys to spend two years in the loving, safe Lewis home, only to have to give that up to return to the slum. Then he recalled the few times he'd found security in his young life. Every single time, he'd willingly given it up and gone back to the hell that was life with his dad.

"Mama said she'd never been so scared in her life. She thought Zac was dead. Anyway, Caliph stayed with Zac, while Jett and Justin helped Mama and Noah pack up all their belongings."

"What about Zac and Noah's mother?"

"She'd been passed out in her bedroom. Didn't even realize anything had happened to Zac. She came out in the hall and started screaming at my mother because she thought she was stealing her sons. She told them to get out, to leave her boys alone. Justin said Mama looked that woman straight in the eye and told her she should be ashamed of herself."

Blake fiddled with his fork, chuckling. "Did it work?"

Chloe grinned. "What do you think? Mama's good at guilt trips. It's pretty much the way I was raised. She only had to look at me with that *I'm so disappointed* face and I'd crumble like a house of cards."

Blake laughed. "I remember that. She used that look on me a couple times. It's powerful."

"Justin said the lectures we'd gotten as kids were small potatoes compared to the speech she gave Zac and Noah's mom. He said he was nearly in tears and begging for forgiveness himself and he hadn't done anything wrong. Their mom fell apart when she saw Zac lying on the floor and she asked my mother to take her boys, to give them a chance to grow up safe and healthy. They've been ours ever since."

"What happened to their mom? Did she straighten her act out?"

Chloe shook her head sadly. "She's still alive. I know Zac goes to see her every now and then, takes her some food and medicine, but no. There wasn't a happy ending. She's still addicted. You know how that goes."

Blake knew only too well. "Yeah, I do."

"Did you really arrest your dad?"

He nodded. He'd been expecting the question ever since he stupidly made that comment at Sunday dinner. "I did."

"That couldn't have been easy."

Blake shrugged as he recalled the near-rape in the bar parking lot. In some ways, putting his dad in prison had been a hell of a lot simpler than he would have thought. "My dad and I had parted ways several years before the arrest. He'd been a criminal, on some level, for my entire life. Stealing, drunk driving arrests, drugs—selling and using—assault, you name it, it was on his rap sheet."

"Why didn't you ever tell me that when we were dating?"

Blake wasn't pleased with his answer, but it was the only one he had. "Pride."

She frowned. "What?"

He released a long breath. "You weren't like any other girl I'd ever dated, Chloe. You didn't come from the same place I did. When I was with you, I could pretend I wasn't that guy."

"What guy?"

"My life wasn't all that different from Zac and Noah's. Only I was dealing with a drunk dad instead of a strung-out mother."

"I wish..."

Chloe's whisper faded away, leaving Blake to fill in the blank. What did she wish? That she'd known? That Mama Lewis had shown up in the middle of the night and dragged *him* out of hell? That he hadn't been such a prideful, puffed-up idiot?

He smiled. "There are a lot of things I wish too. But none of that matters. I've done a lot of things I regret, Chloe, but I can't let my mind linger on that too long. Everything that's happened has made me the man I am today."

She studied his face in silence, glancing away briefly. Then her eyes lifted to his once more. They were shuttered, closed and he knew she was finished with this conversation.

The waiter brought their meals and they allowed the conversation to drift to safer realms. Chloe talked about her experiences putting together her book and he shared some of his more humorous arrest stories just so he could hear Chloe's laughter.

Once he'd paid the bill, he took her hand, offering to walk her back to her place. She didn't refuse.

When they arrived, she invited him inside, giving him a tour. The studio apartment was a large, wide-open space, filled with sunlight and color. It suited Chloe perfectly. Near the front door, she'd set up her portrait area with lighting and backdrops, tripods and cameras. Then, they walked farther into the room to her living area. A plush couch and ottoman flanked by two recliners all faced the large-screen television.

Blake whistled. "Damn. Man cave."

She laughed. "Yeah. My brothers and I are huge hockey fans and I was tired of all of us trying to cram ourselves into Jett's shoebox apartment on game nights."

"Why not go to Justin's? Didn't he mention something on Sunday about his house?"

Chloe nodded. "Yeah, but he lives too far out of town. The trek there and back in a cab is a pain. And Caliph's work schedule changes all the time."

"So you put a hockey haven in your apartment."

She grinned. "Yep. Between October and April, you can find at least a couple Lewises here almost every night, depending on the match-ups."

"Sounds like fun. I'm a Maple Leaf fan myself."

Chloe looked horrified. "Dear God. I didn't think anyone

rooted for Toronto unless they were forced to because they lived there. You must be a glutton for punishment."

He narrowed his eyes. "They aren't that bad."

She shuddered, clearly enjoying the opportunity to push his buttons. "Yeah, well, they aren't that good, either."

"You and I are going to make a wager once the season starts back up."

"What makes you think you're still going to be around come October?"

Blake reached for her before she could read his intent. He tugged her body flush against his until he could feel her hot breath on his face. "I'm going to be here."

She opened her mouth to chastise him, but there was only one way he'd accept her tongue-lashing and that was literally. He kissed her, holding tightly—partly out of fear she'd try to stop him and partly because there was no way he could resist the feeling of her body pressed against his. The last decade melted away—all the pain, anger and loneliness fading until there was nothing left, but this moment. And them.

Chloe wrapped her hands around his neck, the action lifting her breasts higher against his chest, capturing his attention. Keeping one arm around her waist, he brought his left hand up to cup her breast.

Chloe's lips left his as she released a sharp, excited breath. Blake increased the pressure of this touch, squeezing, kneading. Neither of them sought to continue the kiss. Instead, Blake placed his lips to her forehead as Chloe panted softly, her quiet mews encouraging him. He ran his hands under her shirt, savoring the softness of her skin. He stroked his way around her waist, up her sides until he found the breast he'd just left. He smiled when he felt her lacy bra, the texture reminding him of the first time he'd ventured under Chloe's shirt. Her breasts were slightly smaller then.

However, Chloe's response was just the same. Her breathing was heavy, her body so hot, he wondered how she wasn't burning his fingers. Her hips—now, like then—ground against his, taunting his cock, driving him insane with need.

When he was younger, he'd insisted they were made for each other. Chloe would laugh and tease him, claiming it was the girl's job to be the silly romantic, not the guy's. However, after years spent trying to find warmth in the arms of too many women, he realized it hadn't been a foolish dream. It was the truth.

Blake ran his hands along the top of her bra, enjoying the slight shudder his touch provoked. Then he dipped his fingers beneath the lace, delving deeper until he found what he was searching for.

"God!" Chloe jerked when he lightly pinched her nipple, but his arm was still wrapped around her back and it kept her from escaping. Not that she was trying to. She plunged her hands into his hair, gripping it so tightly it stung. He didn't care. He relished the pain, loved feeling her passion, her need. It made him feel less alone.

He pinched her nipple again, firmer this time. Chloe's hips thrust against his and he wished there weren't so many damn clothes between them.

That thought prompted action. He reached for the button on her jeans, delighted when Chloe mimicked the motion on his pants.

"I want you, Chloe," he whispered, needing to make sure she understood. If they took their pants off, he was lying her down on the couch and taking her.

"Hurry up."

Her words hit him like the loud bang of a starter pistol. The only sounds in the room were those of the rushed flurry of hands as they unzipped and tugged down their jeans, of shoes hitting the floor, of a foil condom wrapper crinkling and Chloe's soft cry when Blake lay her down on the couch and came over her. He pushed his cock deep inside her with one hard thrust.

It wasn't until he was completely buried that they paused, both of them panting, air being sucked in and blown out loudly. Blake rested on his elbows above her, studying her flushed face, her closed eyes.

"Chloe. Look at me."

Her eyelids flittered open, her vision clearly fuzzy. He waited until her focus returned. He saw the moment it happened because a crease formed in her brow. They'd acted on impulse, neither of them considering the consequences of what they were doing until now.

Blake's heart raced and his jaw clenched as he resisted the overwhelming need to thrust, to pound, to fuck.

"I won't be another regret."

She frowned. "What?"

"I know you regret what happened between us all those years ago and I wish there was some way I could go back in time and change what I did, but I can't. I can't undo the hurt, Chloe. Can't fix the mistakes."

"Blake—"

"But I'm telling you right now, I can't be another regret in your life. If that's what this is going to be, say so and I'll stop."

She didn't speak for several tense moments. Blake held his tongue, gave her time to decide while silently praying he'd have the strength to leave her if that was what she asked.

Finally, she cupped his cheek in her hand. "I don't want you to stop."

It was all he needed to hear. He lifted his hips until his cock was just barely inside her, then slid in again. She wrapped her legs around his hips as his thrusts grew harder, went deeper.

Chloe worked free the buttons on his shirt, not bothering to remove it. She simply slid her hands beneath the cotton, her nails scratching their way along the muscles of his shoulders and back. She'd left her mark the first time he'd taken her too.

Chloe may have been the virgin when they succumbed to this passion ten years earlier, but she'd been the one to teach him. About burning, heart-pounding lust. About craving. About giving and taking and what it truly meant to be hungry. He may have spent too many nights with an empty belly as a child, but until Chloe, he'd never suffered genuine hunger.

And he'd never experienced sex mixed with love until her. Hell, he hadn't felt it since.

Not until now.

Chloe's hips lifted to meet his and her soft groans told him exactly how close she was. He reached down, intent on drawing more than just one orgasm from her. He'd spent years dreaming of having her under him once again. He wasn't going to waste the opportunity.

He pressed her clit firmly, loving the wild, unrestrained response it provoked. Chloe's back arched as she released a loud cry. He thought he'd loved the sound of her laughter, but that music was a far second place. Blake waited a few seconds as Chloe trembled, her climax running its course. Then he fired the trigger again. He stroked her clit as he increased the speed of his thrusts.

Chloe gasped, shaking her head. "I can't. Not again. Too much."

He kissed her roughly, cutting off her refusal. He knew her too well to be fooled by such a lie. They'd spent a summer in each other's arms. He remembered exactly how many times she could come in a night and they weren't even close to that number yet.

His kiss combined with his finger on her clit and his cock

pounding inside her hot pussy pushed her over the edge a second time. This time, he didn't stop moving, working instead to draw the sensations out, prolonging the pleasure for her.

As the orgasm subsided, Chloe's arms left his shoulders, dropping heavily to the couch cushions beside her. Her eyes were closed—her face the perfect blend of exhaustion and bliss.

"We're not finished."

She blinked rapidly, forcing her gaze to his. "I'm out of shape. It's been a few months since..."

Blake laughed. "It's been almost two years for me. So get your second wind. There's no way I'm letting this end so fast."

"Years?" Her skeptical expression was flattering...and slightly insulting.

He narrowed his eyes. "Yeah. Just so we're clear on this, I'm not some sex-craved pervert sleeping in a different bed every night. I do have standards."

Chloe shook her head in mock disappointment, laughing softly. "Damn. Such a shame. What happened to the horny, gets-hard-when-a-strong-wind-blows bad boy I fell in love with all those years ago?"

He knew she meant her words as a joke, but all he could focus on was the reminder that she used to love him. He'd thrown that away because of pride and stubbornness. "A week ago, I would have said he was gone, but now..."

Blake punctuated the pause with a quick, hard thrust. Chloe gasped, her arousal firing hot once more.

She tightened her legs around his waist. "Do that again."

He tilted his head, considering. He'd never taken the submissive role in the bedroom and he didn't intend to now. He held still as Chloe worked hard, trying to force him to move. She lifted her hips as much as her position underneath him would allow. When that failed, she dug her heels into his back, trying to push him as low as she could.

When all her attempts proved fruitless, she stopped moving and gave him a dirty look. "You joined the police force and yet, you still suck at following commands."

He chuckled, kissing her lightly on the cheek. A decade apart hadn't changed one thing. It still felt as if Chloe knew him better than he knew himself. "I'm a model detective. But doing my job there and doing it here are two entirely different things. Put your hands above your head."

"Why?"

He lifted one eyebrow, letting his impatient look answer the question. She lifted her arms, resting her hands in a position of surrender. It turned him on. A fact that wasn't lost on Chloe as his cock twitched and grew even harder.

She sighed. "Liar." The word wasn't spoken with malice or accusation, but he was confused by the name. Then she added, "You are still a very bad boy."

He grinned, pleased, then bent his head to take one of her nipples into his mouth. They hadn't shed a damn piece of clothing besides their pants—something he would rectify the next time—so he added extra pressure, sucking harder, making sure she felt his touch through her blouse and bra.

Her back arched as she attempted to keep his mouth there. He added his teeth to the game, nipping lightly at first, then digging deeper.

She cried out, not in pain, but in true pleasure.

He lifted his head. "And you're still trying to pretend you're a good girl."

She cupped his face with one of her hands, intent on pushing him back to her breast. Blake gripped her wrist firmly, pressing it against the couch cushion above her head. "Don't move your hands or I'll tie you up. I have my handcuffs with me."

Her pussy clenched tightly against his cock. Blake fought to restrain a groan, stars forming behind his eyelids. Chloe had liked it rough; her sexual needs a mirror image of his. At nineteen, he'd chalked it up to her innocence, believing her desires were fueled by genuine curiosity. Now he knew it was more than that. Not all women were created equal.

Blake pushed off his elbows, grasping Chloe's wrists in his hands, forcing them into the cushion. The power play, the show of strength had Chloe's eyes drifting closed, her body shuddering with need.

"Please, Blake." Her voice was soft. He knew what she was asking for.

He withdrew from her body until just the tip of his cock remained and then he shoved in hard, going as deep as their bodies would allow. Chloe didn't shy away from his almost brutal thrusting. Instead, she added her own fuel to the flames, joining the rhythm, driving her hips up as he came down. The only sound in the room was that of their mingled cries and the slapping noise of skin on skin. Blake's grip on her wrists slipped a bit as both of them started to perspire, the temperature in the studio rising to rival that of the sun.

Neither of them stopped for air or for rest. Instead they kept fighting for climax, two bodies slamming together in a selfish search for completion. Chloe came first...and second. Two orgasms, one right on the heels of the other. She groaned loudly, trembling, but when Blake refused to give way, to stop, she quickly recovered, rejoining the race.

When he finally approached his end, Blake released one of her wrists, letting his fingers drift along her body to her clit. He wanted to feel her coming around him again as he found his own pleasure.

Chloe jerked when he touched the swollen, sensitive nub. "I can't," she cried.

He stroked her clit faster. "Yes, you can. You're going to come with me, Chloe. You and me. Together."

She gasped and he felt the familiar fluttering of her pussy. She was almost there. Thank God. Blake was seconds away from falling over the cliff himself. Chloe pushed him off. Her inner muscles clenched, squeezing his cock almost painfully. He dropped to his elbows as he came, jet after jet of come filling the condom.

"God." The word felt as if it was ripped from his chest. Every muscle in his body tensed in beautiful agony. How much time had passed since he'd been this affected by sex? He knew the answer to that.

Ten years ago.

Chloe lay beneath Blake, refusing to open her eyes. She'd told him she wouldn't regret it.

But she'd lied. And not for the reasons he might think.

Chloe had done some serious introspection since the conversation with her mother. She'd comprehended the wisdom in her mama's advice. Chloe needed closure where Blake was concerned.

She'd had her heart broken by him when she was young, inexperienced, foolish. As a result, she'd held on to that pain, harbored it, made it larger than it should have been. She was an adult now, a woman, and she was no stranger to love affairs or casual sex.

Chloe believed if she slept with him just once more, she'd realize she had built him up to some mythological proportions that were inaccurate. A brief, one-time fling with Blake would prove to her that he was a man just like any other and she'd be able to let go of her sex-god beliefs and move the hell on.

So much for that idea.

"Closing your eyes isn't going to make me disappear." Blake's smug voice proved he knew she was trying to hide from the consequences of her actions.

She didn't open her eyes. "Maybe you'll think I fell asleep and leave peacefully."

He kissed her cheek. She wished that friendly, platonic buss didn't feel so freaking good. "I'm not leaving."

He was still buried inside her, his body covering hers in such a warm shelter, she found it hard to remember why this was wrong.

Chloe released a long breath, then let her gaze find his. He was more handsome now than he'd been at nineteen. Though he'd never had a boyish look, not even when he was younger, some of the hard lines around his mouth and eyes had softened.

"You don't look as pissed off at the world as you used to."

Blake chuckled, unoffended by her remark. "People don't annoy me as much these days."

She needed to get away from him—put some distance between them before she said or did something else completely stupid. Chloe lightly pressed on his shoulders, surprised when he gave way easily. He sat, helping her up as well. He made no move to stop her when she rose and began to tug on her jeans. Mercifully, they'd limited the disrobing to just the waist down.

Blake stood as well, walking to her kitchenette to throw the condom away before tugging his own pants on. Because of the open floor plan of her apartment, the only area of the place closed off by walls was the bathroom. She had placed a large Chinese screen at the foot of her bed to give the illusion of a bedroom and to hide the fact she had a tendency to leave her dirty clothes lying in a heap on the floor.

She followed him to the kitchen, feeling some of her confidence return now that she was dressed again. Chloe opened the fridge and pulled out a couple of bottles of water. She tossed one to Blake, suddenly aware that he hadn't bothered to button his jeans or shirt back up. They both hung open in a way that was far too sexy for her peace of mind.

She reached up to her hair. She'd started the day with a loose ponytail, but most of it had escaped the elastic band. She felt around, trying to find the band, intent on repairing the mess.

Blake took a long swig of water then crossed the room, taking her in his arms. He reached up and tugged her hands down. "Leave it. You look tousled and sexy."

"Blake." She needed distance.

"What do you say for the encore we take all our clothes off and try to make it to your bed?"

She scowled. Cocky, arrogant asshole. "Actually, you can take the rest of that water to go. I have work to do. Thanks for the trip down memory lane. It was fun."

Chloe hoped she'd infused just the right amount of dismissal and hell-will-freeze-over-before-we-fuck-again into her tone.

Apparently she had because Blake's brows furrowed. "You think that was a one-night stand?"

"It might be more accurate to say it was a one-afternoon stand."

Blake shook his head. "Think again."

He hadn't released her. Instead, he'd tightened his grip, letting her feel just how much he wasn't finished with her yet. How in the hell could he be hard again already? Then she considered the foolishness of her thought. This was Blake. The more things changed, the more they stayed the same. He'd always been ready to roll when it came to sex.

She wanted to hate his alpha power plays, wanted to be pissed off by them. And in a lot of ways, she was. Unfortunately, they also triggered some latent desire to be completely dominated by him. Not in everyday life—that would drive her nuts and force her to cut his penis off.

But in the bedroom...sexually...God yes.

Before she could respond, the door to her apartment slid open. Justin and Ned walked in. Chloe tried to push Blake away, but he held fast.

"Let go of me," she muttered when she caught her older brother's dark look.

"You heard her," Justin said, his fists clenched. Great. Nothing like adding embarrassment to mistake.

She'd been wrong to think she could open the door a crack for Blake and not expect him to push it wide and walk in.

Justin's gaze took in her messy hair and Blake's open shirt, his scowl growing. It was far too obvious what had taken place here.

Time for distraction. She shrugged out of Blake's arms, flushing hotly when he reached down to zip up his jeans, not bothering to hide the action from her brother and his business partner. "What are you doing here, Justin?"

"You and Ned have an appointment to discuss the calendar, remember? We had a work meeting on this side of town, so I rode with him, figured I'd chill on your couch while the two of you worked out a plan for Ned's pose."

Ned grinned, obviously sensing her desire to diffuse the volatile situation. "He was planning to be a pain in the ass, making me regret volunteering to do this damn thing. If it had been anyone other than Mama Lewis asking, I would have said no."

Chloe smiled gratefully. "I'm sorry. I forgot about the meeting. Give me a second to..." To what? What was she supposed to do now? Blake didn't look like he was going to go peacefully.

Justin crossed his arms, letting her know he was going to

watch her every move. She shot him a dirty look, then turned to Blake.

"I really do need to get back to work."

"What are you doing for dinner tomorrow night?"

She rolled her eyes. He was like a dog with a bone. "Listen, Blake. We tried the relationship thing once and it failed…miserably."

"We were kids, Chloe. That hardly counts as a serious attempt."

He was right, but that didn't mean the way things ended hadn't hurt. A lot. "I'm nothing like the girl I used to be."

"So we'll go out for dinner, get reacquainted."

"Looks like you already did that," Justin muttered.

She turned around. "Dammit, Justin. Mind your own business."

Blake buttoned his shirt. He leaned closer, keeping his ultimatum quiet enough only she could hear it. "I'll go as soon as you agree to dinner."

"That's blackmail," she whispered.

He didn't reply. Just gave her that wicked, bad-boy grin that always got her into trouble.

"Fine. But just dinner. Nothing else—not a movie or dancing or coffee at my place afterwards. And I'm meeting you at the restaurant. No riding together."

Blake looked like he might argue, but she raised her hand to cut him off. "Those are my conditions. Take it or leave it."

"Fine. I'll call you later with the details."

She shook her head. "Just text me." Until she gathered her wits about her, she wasn't about to get roped into another conversation with him. Texting was safer.

Blake nodded, then kissed her, the touch too fucking familiar and sexy when his tongue brushed hers.

She half-heartedly pushed at his shoulders. She was about

to get the mother of all ass-chewings from her brother. Of course, that was a given. So...she might as well get her money's worth. She felt Blake's brief spark of surprise when her tongue entered his mouth and she gave his ass a quick squeeze before she stepped away.

"Goodbye, Blake," she said, proud of the strength in her voice.

He grinned. "I'll talk to you later."

Justin didn't bother to step out of the way as Blake left. The two men faced each other like adversaries on the battlefield and for a moment, Chloe thought she might have let her guard down prematurely.

Then Blake stepped around her brother, leaving without another word. Chloe released a long breath when Blake slid the door closed behind him.

"Does somebody want to confirm that's who I think it is?" Ned asked.

Ned Stevens had been Justin's best friend since their freshman year in college. They were assigned as dorm roommates and they'd been inseparable ever since. In truth, Ned had become a member of the family, another damn overprotective brother. Just what Chloe needed.

"My old boyfriend, Blake," she answered, realizing the simplicity of the answer would never satisfy either man.

"Are you sure he's not a current one?" Ned asked with a wicked grin.

"What the hell was that, Chloe?" Justin threw his hands up in disbelief. She didn't blame him. She'd been pretty cold to Blake at Sunday dinner. Now, forty-eight hours later, she was boinking the guy on her couch.

"I don't know what that was."

"The guy's a thief," Justin added.

"He gave Mama the money back on Sunday." Chloe wasn't

sure why she was saying that as if it forgave all. She certainly hadn't felt that way two days ago.

"Oh. Did he tell you why he took it and ran off?"

Chloe shook her head. "No. I didn't ask."

"Why not?"

She couldn't explain why she hadn't asked Blake. Not even to herself. The question had been on the tip of her tongue every single time she'd seen him since his return, but something always caused the words to get lodged in her throat. "What difference would it make, Justin? We know he did it. Can you think of a good reason why he would steal Mama's money and disappear without a trace for nearly a decade?"

Justin considered the question briefly, and then shook his head. "No, I can't. Which is why I don't understand your reason for playing hide the salami with the guy again."

She blew out an annoyed breath. "Don't be such a juvenile."

Her brother grinned, used to her admonishing him for his colorful, somewhat vulgar nicknames for sex. Justin wrapped his arm around her shoulder, pulling her close and placing a sweet kiss on her forehead. "Just be careful, pipsqueak. Maybe the guy has changed. But maybe he hasn't. Keep your eyes open this time. Okay?"

She nodded. Eyes open was her initial intent. Then Blake had fucked her into a state of delicious delirium and she'd allowed it to blind her once more.

"So, tell Ned all about this idea you had for him, a bed, a box of chocolates and no clothes."

Ned crossed his arms and scowled. "I told you, Justin, I'm not doing that."

Justin's face reflected pure mischief as he ignored his friend's complaint. "And listen, Chloe, don't waste a bunch of money on the big heart-shaped box. A small sampler will be more than enough to cover his—"

Justin didn't get to finish his joke as Ned punched him in the arm.

Chloe laughed, grateful for their timely interruption and the welcome distraction. She spent the next hour plotting with Ned over possible locales and poses, while Justin cracked jokes at both of their expenses and made a general nuisance of himself.

It was exactly what she needed.

For now, it was her turn to escape.

CHAPTER FOUR

Chloe had postponed her dinner date with Blake, putting him off for four straight nights. She hadn't intended to skip out on him, but she'd been knocked down by a killer case of the flu. The illness had put her in bed for two days before she graduated to resting on the couch for two more. As a result, she was days behind on her shooting schedule and scrambling to make up for it.

Blake had offered several times to take care of her, but she'd refused, claiming she didn't want him to catch what she had. Even so, that hadn't stopped him from making little deliveries outside her apartment door. One day, he'd left flowers, the next a quart of homemade chicken soup. Two days ago, she'd found an erotic romance novel. Inside Blake had written an inscription, telling her he hoped it would inspire her for the next time they went out. All it had done was leave her hot and bothered. And she'd been too worn out to use her vibrator to nip the problem in the bud. She'd read him the riot act for that after he called to see if she'd gotten his gift. Asshole had just chuckled and told her to hurry up and get better.

Chloe ran a comb through her damp hair and sighed. She'd gotten a shower first thing this morning, hoping it would wake her up and give her some sort of energy. She was tired of being...well...tired.

She dragged herself to the kitchen counter, fired up the coffeepot, then sat down to look at her calendar. If the models could be a bit flexible with their schedules, perhaps she could double up on shoots and still hit the publishing company's deadline. She hated missing deadlines and refused to see the fundraiser lose even a single dollar due to her illness.

She picked up her cell and for the next hour, rearranged everything until she managed to fit in every single model. While Chloe was laid up in bed, her mother had managed to find guys for the last two months, so they had a full year's worth of hotness ready to roll. All Chloe had to do now was dash from one end of New Orleans to the other every day, then spend her nights choosing the best photo for each month and enhancing it.

She looked at her schedule. Eleven photo shoots and twelve portraits to touch up in less than two weeks. She was screwed.

Her phone rang. She glanced at the number and sighed. Her last model. Blake was the only man who hadn't answered when she'd called. "Hey, Blake."

"Back in the land of the living?"

He'd called her every day since their impromptu hook-up on Tuesday afternoon. It was strange how easily they'd fallen into familiar patterns. Blake called her as soon as he got off duty and then again before bedtime. Their conversations had only touched on safe subjects—like their jobs, the weather, sports—but they'd become the highlight of each day for her.

She hadn't questioned him about his disappearing act ten years earlier and they never addressed what his return in her life meant.

"Yeah," she replied. "I'm back and sort of wishing I could crawl under the covers and hide again. There's no way I'm going to hit this calendar deadline."

Blake didn't sound concerned. "Of course you can. I'm around if you need help."

"Uh, thanks, but no thanks. I tried to give you some photography lessons a long time ago. All you managed to master was dark and blurry."

Blake chuckled. "That was before I got my iPhone 8. Now I take great pictures."

Chloe groaned.

"Besides, I wasn't offering to take the photographs, just to lug your equipment, help you set up the shoots, stuff like that."

"And you're doing this all out of the goodness of your heart and not because you want to play chaperone while I'm taking pictures of the shirtless, hot guys, right?"

"Absolutely." His tone was pure innocence, but she knew him better than that.

"Forget it. You'd just clam jam me." She restrained her giggle at the silence that followed her comment, then he gave into curiosity.

"I give," he said. "What the hell is a clam jam?"

"Female equivalent of a cock block."

Blake snorted with laughter. "God. There is something seriously twisted and wrong with you. I blame it on all those brothers you grew up with."

She leaned back in her chair, propping her feet up on the one across from her. She was smiling and happy for the first time in days. In less than five minutes, Blake had found a way to make the stress she was feeling over her work vanish and the tension in her shoulders subsided.

"So I see I missed your call. You putting off our date again?"

She had called him for that reason. "Yeah, I'm sorry. I'm wicked busy."

"I understand."

"Hey listen, I need to try to find a time to do your photo shoot. Are you still determined to take the pictures on your Harley by the lake?"

"Yep. And you're riding with me."

"I told you, Blake, my equipment—"

"Downsize it as much as you can. I borrowed a big-ass motorcycle bag from a friend of mine. We can put your cameras and stuff in there."

"What if it rains? My equipment costs—"

He cut her off. "It's waterproof."

"Why do you want me to get on that bike again so badly?"

"Why are you so resistant?"

Chloe wasn't sure how to answer. They'd spent that entire summer so long ago on his motorcycle. It was the last time she'd felt carefree, wild, over-the-moon happy. He'd also driven off into the sunset on that motorcycle. While it wasn't logical, it was easier to forgive Blake, the cop, the man who didn't exist all those years ago, and hold on to her anger toward his bad-boy biker persona.

"I just don't think they're safe."

Blake snorted at her obvious lie. "What day did you leave open for me?"

"Let me see. I'm popping over to Justin's office this afternoon to take the pictures of Ned."

"No box of chocolates in bed?"

Chloe thought she detected the slightest trace of relief in Blake's voice. "He wouldn't go for that. The most he would agree to was an open shirt with a tie hanging around his neck. We thought it would look cool if he was sitting at the head of a conference table. Set it up for today because none of the employees will be in the office since it's a Saturday."

"Sounds very tasteful."

No doubt she and Justin had given him a bad impression of what the calendar was about. Truth was all the pictures would be PG with none of the men exposing more than their chests and arms. Her musician had been sitting sideways on his piano bench, shirtless, in a vest and simple black pants as he toyed with a couple of keys. While she'd selected the shot she wanted to use, she'd come down with the flu before she could tweak the print.

"It's going to be a classy calendar."

"Of mimbos," he added.

She frowned, then a light went on. "You were eavesdropping on my phone call with Mama that first day."

"Yep."

She grinned wickedly. "Well, if you're expecting me to take it back or revise my opinion, I won't."

Blake chuckled. "You will. Eventually. I'll make sure of it."

His deeply spoken threat was laced with just a hint of sexual malice. Chloe grew wet and warm at the thought of it. She pressed her legs together, suddenly annoyed at the way Blake could turn her into a raving sex maniac in mere seconds.

"In fact, what are you wearing right now?"

Chloe wanted to ignore his question, but that damn dirty book he'd given her had fired up some needs she really wanted taken care off. She hadn't bothered to get dressed after her shower, just donning her robe.

She decided to play hard to get. "Why do you want to know?"

"Tell me, Chloe."

"Just a robe."

"Nothing under it?"

She shook her head, trying to ignore how hot his questions were making her. "Nothing."

"Slip it open, but keep it on."

Chloe rested her phone between her shoulder and head as she untied the belt around her robe.

She heard Blake chuckle softly. "There's this feature on cells called speakerphone. Turn it on and put your phone down where you can still hear me. You're going to need both hands."

"Blake," she started.

"Just do it."

"Where are you?" she asked, suddenly worried about him initiating phone sex with her in the middle of the precinct.

"I'm at home. On my couch. Just got off-duty."

She turned the speakerphone on and placed the cell on the table. "Okay."

"Where are you in your apartment?"

"My kitchen table."

"Nice. I want you to do what I tell you. Follow my instructions completely. If I suspect you're cheating, I'll come over there, toss you over my knee, and paint your ass red with my hand until you learn to obey."

The feminist part of her was outraged and tempted to hang up on him, but, at the moment, her libido was currently making all decisions.

Blake appeared to have interpreted her silence correctly. "We both want the same thing right now." His voice sounded more distant. Apparently he'd put her on speakerphone as well.

"What are you doing now?" she asked.

"Unzipping my jeans."

She licked her lips, sorry she hadn't suggested postponing her meeting with Ned and inviting Blake over.

Before she could make the offer, Blake took charge. "Cup your breasts. Lift them up and squeeze them."

Chloe dragged her hands along her stomach, surprised by the sudden sensitivity of her skin. How could Blake get her to this point with no more than a few words? She held her breasts, her nipples budded, ready.

"Squeeze them hard. There's no point in denying you don't like your pleasure laced with pain."

Her face flushed, the response caused by embarrassment and need. She'd tried to hide her darker kinks from other lovers, always feeling slightly strange for her desires. She'd never had to do that with Blake. He'd just seen what she wanted and given it to her. No questions, no qualms. Hell, most of the time it seemed as if he wanted it even more than she did. Something she didn't think possible.

She applied the pressure to her breasts, pinching her nipples roughly. Her breathing grew heavier.

"Are you touching your nipples?" he asked.

"Yes," she whispered.

"Pinch them hard. Let me hear that pretty whimper of yours."

She tightened her fingers, suddenly self-conscious of her sounds.

Blake's voice when he spoke again, seemed breathless. "You can take more pain. Stop holding back."

She gave in to the desire, pinching her nipples harder than she'd ever dared. The sharp sting sent zings of pure pulsing arousal straight to her pussy. She pressed her legs together to capture the heat and moisture.

"Are you wet, Chloe?"

"God." She felt lightheaded with need. "Yes."

"I'm so hard right now. My hand is wrapped around my cock, but it's not the same as being inside you."

"Come over." The invitation was out before she could consider why she shouldn't issue it.

"I can't. You have to go to work soon. We're just going to have to let this be enough for now."

This was nowhere near enough. Chloe fought to restrain her brief flash of temper, a disposition her mother said she'd inherited from Papa Lewis. Like her father, she was prone to impatience and while their tempers ran hot, they usually only blazed hot for a moment before they were able to rein it back in. "Dammit, Blake."

"Shh. It's time to get serious. Keep one hand on your breast, while you drop the other lower. I want you to tell me how hot and wet your pussy is for me."

She obeyed his request, opening her legs. She drew her fingers along the seam, gasping at the sensations provoked by that simple touch. "Oh," she cried.

"You sound so sexy, Chloe. God, baby, you have no idea what you're doing to me. The head of my cock is seeping come and my balls are tight. We're going to have to move fast. I'm not sure how much longer I can hold off."

The gruffness of his voice told her he was telling the truth. Chloe wasn't worried. It wouldn't take much to push her over at this point.

"Rub your clit. Push your fingers against it hard and fast."

Chloe did as he asked. She groaned then released her breast, using her free hand to grasp the edge of the kitchen table. She needed something to hold on to, to keep her grounded.

"My cock is going to explode. Are you close?"

"Yes," she hissed, her fingers familiar with this motion. She was no stranger to masturbation and she knew all too well how to get herself off. Even so, this was way faster and so much hotter than anything she'd ever done. Knowing Blake was on the other end of the phone, imagining his hand stroking his own cock, his head thrown back against his couch with his eyes closed. It was as if he was sitting right in front of her, each of them performing their shows in person.

"Push two fingers into that hot cunt. Shove them in deep and fast."

Chloe knew what would happen if she did that. Her climax would be inevitable.

"Do it. Now, Chloe."

She pressed her fingers deep, thrusting them, pretending it was Blake's cock that was pounding inside her.

"Add another finger, baby. Make it bigger, thicker."

She obeyed, not bothering to slow her rhythm. She released the table and added her other hand to the game, fingering her clit, touching that one spot...that one place that made her...

She cried out loudly. "Oh my God. Blake." Chloe doubled over, her head flying toward her lap as her orgasm racked her frame. It was potent, powerful. Overwhelming.

She could tell from Blake's rough grunts that he was with her. She closed her eyes, letting herself see the jets of come erupting from his cock, landing on his shirt as the stroking of his hand slowed.

For several long moments, the phone line was quiet except for the soft sound of Blake's breathing. He was obviously listening to the same thing from her.

"You still there, baby?"

She grinned, dragging her fingers from her body, struggling to sit upright once more. "I'm going to need another shower."

He chuckled. "Wish I was there to scrub your back."

"That's all you'd scrub?"

"You ready to go again? So soon?"

She groaned at the thought. If he were here, she'd definitely give it the college try, but the truth was she was zapped. While the flu had passed, she suspected she was still a few days away from full-strength. "No. Unfortunately, I'm not."

He seemed to understand. "I'll take a rain check for the shower."

Damn man kept making these grand assumptions about their future. Granted, her actions weren't helping to dissuade him. Even so, she still had too much pride for her own good.

"You may be waiting a damn long time to collect on that. I'm still not planning to see you after the photo shoot."

Blake wasn't deterred. "You will. So when are we meeting to take the pictures?"

She glanced at the clock. She really did need to shower and dress then gather up her stuff for the shoot with Ned. She was in serious danger of being late. "What does tomorrow look like?" She hadn't scheduled anything for Sunday, pretending it was so she wouldn't miss Sunday dinner. Now that she was asking, she knew it was because she'd intended to give Sunday to him.

"I'm on-duty."

Chloe tried to ignore her disappointment.

"But I'm off next Sunday."

So it would be another whole week before she saw him again. Silently, she chastised herself. What was wrong with her? She was supposed to be over Blake Mills, not counting the minutes until she saw him again.

She tried to chalk up her weakness to the flu. Clearly she was still sick and not thinking clearly. "How about next Sunday afternoon after dinner at Mama's then? We're usually finished eating by two, so we'll have a few hours of good light."

"Is that an invitation to dinner?" he asked.

"Are you sure you really want to push your luck and step into the lion's den again?"

"Mama Lewis will protect me. She likes me."

Chloe wanted to deny that, but he was right. Her mother

had always had a soft spot for Blake. Chloe blamed it on her Mama's tendency to root for the underdog.

"You know the drill. Table is loaded with food by noon. Get there by then or we're starting without you."

Chloe clicked off without saying goodbye, hoping that would make it clear she didn't want to see him between now and then. She rolled her eyes.

Sure you don't.

There was no way to ignore how excited she was about next Sunday.

BY THE FOLLOWING FRIDAY, Chloe was regretting agreeing to help out with her mother's damn calendar even more than before. If she never saw another shirtless, beefcake, prima donna asshole again in her life, it would be too soon. With the exception of Ned—whose photo shoot was a blast—and a lovely pediatrician, the last five guys had run the gamut from God's gift to women to more demanding than J. Lo on tour.

Today's shoot was the one she'd been dreading the most. With good reason. The manhandler had arrived in full-force.

Javier Ramsey was one of New Orleans' premiere chefs, his restaurant in the French Quarter winning national acclaim from all the critics and making it a local hotspot whenever the rich and famous came to town. Reservations for dinner were booked months in advance.

Now Chloe was beginning to understand why he was so talented. It appeared he had at least a dozen extra hands, all of them managing to touch her constantly, and while his supposedly glancing blows hadn't crossed the line to inappropriateness yet, he was getting damn close.

Chloe reached up to adjust the lighting once more. Even though she'd told Javier to stand still so she could get it right, the man was behind her in an instant. He placed one hand on her hip as the other met hers on the light. His bare chest pressed against her back and she stifled the urge to curse. Their close proximity drew her attention to his erect cock.

Great. This wasn't going to end well.

Javier had elected to wear just an apron, and while she knew he had boxers on beneath it, they wouldn't appear in the picture. It was the most risqué portrait she'd done thus far and she was a little bit worried about her mother's response when she saw it. Of course, none of that would matter if Mr. Hands didn't stand still long enough for her to snap his picture.

"Javier," she said, her temper beginning to pique despite her attempt to remain calm. She'd been trying to set things up for nearly forty-five minutes, but Javier kept changing his mind about his pose. It was mid-morning and she wondered how long he could continue to stall before he'd have to give in and let her take the damn picture. The restaurant was opening in a few hours.

During their initial meeting, he'd sat too close to her on her couch as they'd discussed their ideas for the calendar. He had asked her out, but she'd refused. Then he'd played the French card, kissing her on both cheeks as he left. That wouldn't have bothered her if he hadn't lingered on the second kiss and placed it a bit to close to her earlobe, adding a bit of hot breath to the touch.

The guy squicked her out. Majorly. He'd called a few times since then, but she'd sent him straight to voicemail.

"I don't want you to burn yourself," he murmured, his lips too close to her ear for comfort.

She tried to take a step away, but he tightened his grip on her hip.

"I really need you to stand over there so I can make sure the direction is correct."

"You are a very beautiful woman, Chloe."

She sighed and wondered how much it would piss her mother off if she brought her heel down on Javier's foot and crushed all of his toes. Given his behavior, she suspected her mother would encourage it. However, she recalled the fundraiser committee's glee when the famous chef had agreed to participate. They'd been thrilled, claiming his presence alone would sell tons of calendars.

"Thank you," she replied through gritted teeth. "I think the lighting is fine now. You can take your place." She didn't give a shit if his whole face was in shadow. She was snapping a few shots and getting the hell out of here.

Javier didn't appear anxious to move away, but mercifully, his sous chef arrived, an Amazonian woman named Elise whom Chloe had liked the moment they'd met. Javier released her and moved back to his place by the chopping board.

"What do you want?" he barked at his assistant, clearly annoyed by the interruption.

The woman must have been accustomed to his rude manner. "If we're going to serve the *tarte au pistou* tonight, I need to begin preparing the ingredients before the rest of the staff arrives."

"We're not finished yet. You'll have to wait. Go away."

Elise seemed unfazed by her boss's anger. She walked over to Chloe. "How much longer will you be?" While her question was innocuous, the concerned look on Elise's face proved the woman was really wondering if she was okay.

Chloe tried to decide if there was any way she could finish her job without making a scene. Perhaps Elise could help. She handed the woman her phone and spoke quietly, hoping Javier couldn't overhear. "Do you mind clicking on my contacts, calling Blake Mills and telling him that I'm running late for our meeting. Tell him it would save time if he could meet me here."

"Of course." Elise gave her a subtle wink—all too aware that Chloe was calling in the cavalry—and took the phone out into the main restaurant.

Blake was at work and they didn't have any meeting scheduled. Hopefully he'd catch the drift that Chloe needed help and he'd come over. She wasn't all that worried about Javier trying something. Chloe was more than capable of fending off an overzealous womanizer. The problem was Javier wasn't responding to her verbal warnings. All she had left was her right hook. If she pulled that out, he'd withdraw his agreement to participate.

Chloe sucked at peaceful resolutions. She'd grown up in a houseful of boys. All disputes were handled quickly and efficiently...physically. While her brothers had never lifted a hand to hurt her when they were all kids, that hadn't kept them from wrestling or tickling her into submission in order to get a toy or the last dessert.

Javier started to walk back toward her, but Chloe threw her hand up to halt him. "No, don't move. The lighting is perfect and I don't want to lose my shot."

The spotlight was nowhere near right, but it was close enough. Javier seemed to struggle for a reason to approach her. Failing that, he returned to his original place. She adjusted the camera lens, tweaking the focus and the aperture. She also awaited the inevitable. They'd gotten this far in the process three times before and each time, Javier had declared the pose wrong for some asinine reason or another. The only thing giving her hope was that the man was beginning to run out of places in the kitchen to stand.

Sure enough, just as she bent to click a shot, Javier threw up his hands. "This feels too awkward. I would never stand like this while cooking."

Chloe took a deep breath and counted to ten before speaking. "You aren't cooking. You're posing for a calendar. The idea of this shot isn't to show you working, but to capture you in your workplace. You're the one who chose to take the picture in the kitchen. Trust me. This pose is the best. Now hold still."

She plastered a fake smile on her face and decided if the asshole wanted to continue to bitch, he'd have to do so while she snapped away. She started clicking despite Javier's refusal to pose properly. If the bastard thought he was going to blow this shoot and drag her back here again for another attempt, he was sorely mistaken. She'd give money out of her own pocket to send in another photographer. She knew a couple of large, no-nonsense male colleagues who would be only too happy to do her a favor.

Chloe pretended Javier was doing a great job, even though she could see from his tight expression he was trying to come up with a way to stall. "Those are great. Now, what if you pick up one of the kitchen utensils? Grab that silver bowl. Maybe you'd feel better using props."

Javier hesitated, but Chloe kept snapping. Maybe the gods would take mercy on her and one of the shots would actually look good.

"Perhaps you could show me what you mean."

It was a deliberate attempt to draw her closer. Chloe wasn't biting. "You're the cooking expert. I'm just the photographer. I'm going to switch lenses. Just find a way that feels comfortable and natural." Chloe bent to grab the lens, intent on making the change as quickly as possible.

When she looked at him once more, Javier was grinning, his pose perfect. Hallelujah. The guy must have caught her hint. She focused and started to snap.

She'd only taken a few pictures when Javier turned around, pretending to reach for a pan hanging from a rack behind him.

Chloe took two more pictures before her finger caught up with her brain.

"Where the hell are your boxers?"

Javier glanced over his shoulder, his slimy smile wide. "You said comfortable and natural."

"That's not what I meant." Chloe's head was beginning to pound, her patience officially gone.

"It would be easier if you came over here and posed me the way you wanted."

Chloe opened her mouth to inform the idiot the only way this would be easier was if he had a fucking brain, but at that moment, she was saved.

"Hey, Chloe. Whoa," Blake said, stopping mid-step. "Thought this calendar was PG."

Elise hovered just behind Blake. She giggled when she caught sight of her boss's bare ass.

"This is a closed photo shoot," Javier said furiously as he turned back around, the apron mercifully covering something Chloe *really* didn't want to see.

"I'm going to go adjust the menu. There's no way we're going to get the tarts made today." Before she left, Elise glanced at Blake, then gave Chloe an impressed look that said she approved of the cavalry.

Blake walked over to Chloe and gave her a quick kiss on the cheek. "I'm going to stick around. I'm Chloe's assistant."

Javier's face went red with frustration and fury. "I'm not comfortable working with another man in the room."

"I can see why," Blake murmured.

Chloe wavered between laughing hysterically and crying her eyes out. She'd been running a hundred miles an hour since recovering from the flu. Now she was starting to think a relapse of the illness would be a welcome respite.

"Have your assistant wait outside." Javier drew out the word *assistant* to prove he wasn't buying Blake's lie.

Blake tucked a stray hair behind her ear before cupping her cheeks in his hands. The action was one of pure possessiveness. He didn't speak as he studied her face. She wasn't sure what he saw there. Probably because there were too many things to see. Chloe was tired, frustrated and, if she was being completely honest, somewhat amused by Javier's ridiculous antics now that Blake was here and she felt safe.

Mercifully, Blake didn't pick a fight with Javier. Instead, he made it clear that Chloe was spoken for.

Even though technically, she wasn't.

"Take your pictures, Chloe. I'll be right outside. How much longer do you need?"

Chloe glanced at Javier and saw the man's narrowed eyes. The chef didn't like discovering she wasn't available.

Even though technically, she was.

"Five minutes." It would be a miracle if she got a useable shot in that amount of time, but she didn't trust herself alone with the asshat chef for one second longer than that.

"There's no way we can finish in five—"

Blake cut off Javier's complaint. "I'll be back here in five minutes to help you pack up your stuff."

"But—" Javier blustered.

Blake tugged his phone out of his back pocket. "I'll make a few calls while I wait."

"Thanks, Blake."

Blake walked out of the kitchen, but from the clomping of his boots, she could tell he hadn't taken two steps into the other room before he stopped.

"Is that your boyfriend?" Javier asked. "I thought you said you weren't seeing anyone."

Foolishly, she had made that comment at their first meeting. She could only assume that was what had triggered open season on Chloe for the guy.

She glanced over her shoulder, certain Blake had remained within listening distance. She'd love to lie and say he was her boyfriend, simply to get the octopus off her back. But, knowing Blake, he'd find some way to make her repay him for that deceit. Probably with sex.

And with that thought, her libido reared its ugly head, assuring her it was a price it was more than willing to pay. It figured the one man who turned her into a raving sex maniac was also the one who'd broken her heart...and her trust.

Chloe simply nodded in response to Javier's question. Maybe that would cool his engines and Blake would be none-the-wiser about her pretending he was her boyfriend.

"Yes what? Yes, you're seeing him or yes, you aren't seeing anyone?"

"Javier, I don't see why my personal life has any bearing on this photo shoot. I'm here to take your picture for this calendar and that's it. Now, if you would just put your boxers back on and pick up that whisk, I could—"

Javier was across the room in three long strides. He grasped her shoulders tightly, tugging her against his chest. When he spoke, his voice was quiet enough that Chloe knew he understood how close Blake was as well. "You must know how much I want you, Chloe."

"Let go of me, Javier. I'm really, *really* not interested."

The chef paused and Chloe got the sense he was confused.

"Hasn't anyone ever said no to you before?" she asked.

He chuckled, the sound husky and deep. "Don't be ridiculous. Of course not."

His answer—so completely cocky—made her laugh. Javier released her, joining in her mirth.

She placed her hands in her front pockets. "Wow. You really are something."

"And yet, you're not interested?"

She shook her head. "Sorry."

"Not nearly as much as I am. Your boyfriend is a very lucky man."

For the first time, Chloe could see why other women would be attracted to the chef. After all, he was rich and famous, and attractive in a tall, boyishly handsome way. He rubbed elbows with Hollywood elite as well as international royalty. And he could cook.

However, none of that was even remotely appealing to her. Her ideal man had dark hair and crystal-blue eyes with a muscular body that wouldn't stop. He had a charming smile, wicked wit and a tattoo on his upper left arm.

She made herself stop listing attributes. She was describing Blake. Dammit.

"Our time appears to be running out. Shall we try to get in a good shot before your *assistant* returns?"

Chloe nodded, relieved when Javier tugged his boxers on—though he kept his back turned toward her—making a show of it. Then he turned on the charm for the camera, posing as if he'd walked straight off the pages of *GQ*. Of all her models thus far, Javier was the most natural, knowing how to highlight his gorgeous features to perfection.

Chloe had only snapped about two dozen shots when Blake returned, but she wasn't worried. She could probably fill the entire calendar with just the last few pictures of Javier and the thing would sell.

Blake didn't speak immediately. Chloe wondered if he could sense the tide had turned. She flipped through the images on her viewfinder and, satisfied with the results, she looked at Javier and smiled. "All set."

Javier reached for his pants and shirt as Blake helped her pack up all of her equipment. Given the end result, she felt guilty for calling him. Though she suspected Javier wouldn't have backed off if he hadn't seen Blake in the flesh. And really, if the chef had touched her one more time, there was no force on earth that would have kept her from cold-cocking the guy. Then Blake would have been called in anyway...to arrest her for assault.

"Sorry for bothering you when you were on duty."

Blake folded the legs on her tripod. "No problem. I actually wasn't far from here, working on a case. I'd just finished interviewing a witness and was heading back to the precinct to type up the report. Your timing was perfect."

Blake had told her a little bit about the details of his job. She wondered how he could stand to spend so much of his day dealing with anger and sadness and pain. He investigated cases involving domestic violence, child abuse and rape.

Javier walked over to say goodbye when they finished packing up. He gave Chloe two platonic kisses on the cheek, then—to her dismay—told Blake he was a very lucky man. Blake didn't bother to correct him. Instead, he gave her a wink that told her she was in his debt.

That didn't bug her as much as she might have expected.

Chloe retrieved her cell phone from Elise, thanked her for her help and she and Blake stepped out into the bright sunshine together.

"What's next on your list for today?" Blake asked as he placed her bags in the trunk of her car.

"I'm taking pictures of Caliph. At the tattoo parlor."

Blake chuckled. "Sounds like your mom wore him down."

"I think it was actually a tag-team effort. Jennifer was fairly convincing too."

"Guess I don't have to worry about your safety with your

brother around. That's a shame. I was enjoying being your bodyguard."

"I shouldn't have called you, but I was dangerously close to pulverizing that guy, which would have pissed my mother off. I thought maybe if you showed up and I pretended that you were..." She wasn't sure why it was hard for her to say "boyfriend" to him, but for some reason, it felt wrong.

"Your boyfriend," he finished for her.

She nodded. "I thought that would make him back off and it worked. So I owe you one."

Blake reached for her. Chloe didn't bother stepping away. Not when she wanted him to hold her. She was beginning to crave his kisses more than chocolate and that was saying something. "I think I like having you in my debt."

She narrowed her eyes. "I wouldn't call this a debt. Just one friend owing another a favor. A very small favor."

Blake placed his lips against her cheek, the touch more caress than kiss. His breath was warm against her skin, sexy and sweet, all at the same time. "When can I collect my favor?"

Her eyes had drifted closed, but now she opened them, her gaze taking in the busy street behind them.

What was she doing? Blake Mills had stolen from her family, broken her heart, left without a trace for years and now she was letting him walk right back into her life without so much as a hi or bye. She was letting her body make the decisions—choosing sex over common sense.

She took a step away. Blake looked as if he'd try to pull her back, so she added another step, more distance. "I can't do this again."

"Do what?"

She pointed to herself, then him. "This. Us. I've been down this road before and it didn't end well."

"I'm not the same man I was when I was nineteen years old, Chloe."

"Why did you leave?" The words fell out unbidden, unwanted. Chloe hadn't meant to ask because she didn't want to know. In her mind, there was no reason good enough for him to do what he'd done. None.

Blake ran a hand through his dark hair. In the sunlight, it was so black it shimmered like water. It betrayed the Italian heritage on his mother's side, which was actually the only thing Chloe knew about Blake's mother apart from the fact she hadn't been around when he grew up.

"I was wondering when you were going to ask me that."

"Forget it. It doesn't matter."

Blake frowned. "Of course it does." Before he could say anything more, Blake's cell phone beeped. He read the screen and sighed. "I have to go. Domestic dispute. The neighbor just called it in."

She nodded. "Okay. I'm late for my shoot with Caliph anyway."

"I want to talk about this, Chloe."

She walked toward the driver's side door and opened it. "I meant what I said. You and I are ancient history, Blake. I think it would be best if we just left all of this in the past and got back to life as normal."

"I'm not going to do that."

She gave him a sad smile. "I wasn't asking."

Blake's eyes darkened with a determination that told her she wouldn't win this fight. "I'll be at Mama Lewis's house on Sunday for dinner."

Fuck. The photo shoot. "I have a friend who is a photographer. She's really—"

"No. You're taking the pictures."

"Blake. Please. Why can't you just let this go?"

He walked toward her, cornering her. "I made a mistake, Chloe. Shit, I've fucked up a million times. But if I let you walk away right now, without explaining, without fighting for you, it'll be the biggest mistake of my life."

He took advantage of the fact her mouth had fallen open. Blake's lips landed on hers, kissing her roughly, telling her in no uncertain terms that *this* was nowhere near over.

CHAPTER FIVE

Blake loaded Chloe's equipment into the motorcycle bag he'd borrowed from a friend as she watched, quiet and tense. She'd been the same way all through her family's Sunday dinner. Her mother had even remarked on her silence, but Chloe simply dismissed it, saying she hadn't slept well the night before.

Blake had followed her to her apartment on his Harley, refusing to budge when Chloe insisted she could drive herself to the lake. They were evenly matched on stubbornness, so Blake pulled out the "you owe me one" card, forcing her to give in.

He turned to find her on the sidewalk, her arms crossed stiffly. Blake tapped her on the nose, hoping the playful gesture would help her loosen up. "You're not facing the firing squad here. We're just going for a ride on my Harley, taking some pictures and having a little talk."

Her shoulders slumped slightly as she released a sigh. "Fine. You're right. Today's conversation is about ten years overdue. Let's get this over with."

Blake swallowed heavily as he considered what he'd say. They'd only dated for three months all those years ago. When he thought of it that way, it blew him away. Those ninety days had had a huge impact on his life.

Problem was he'd been a jackass when he was younger, too embarrassed by his home life to come clean to his pretty little girlfriend. He'd painted a picture of some badass guy who went through life with no regard for following rules or obeying authority figures. It was easier to pretend he didn't care what anyone thought of him than admit to Chloe how much he wanted her to look at him and see someone who was worthy of her love and respect.

He placed a helmet on Chloe's head, helping her with the strap before putting on his own. Then he threw his leg over the bike and gestured for her to hop on. The second her thighs rested against his, Blake felt himself transported back to the first time they'd ridden together. He'd watched her and her friends studying in the back corner of the sub shop where he worked for several weeks, his gaze constantly drawn to her bright blue eyes and her loud, infectious laugh.

Most of the time, Blake lived in a rundown apartment on the wrong side of town. That was whenever his dad didn't drink the rent money. During bad times, they crashed on the dirty floors of neighbors or even on the street. There weren't too many happy people in his world and Blake felt as if he were constantly wading through a sea of misery.

Chloe was the complete opposite of all that. She was light and sunshine and fresh air and laughter—all rolled into one beautiful package.

Blake fired up the engine on his Harley, loving the way Chloe leaned into him, pressing her breasts against his back. He weaved his way carefully through city traffic, glad when they hit Interstate 10. Blake pointed the nose of the bike toward the west and pulled back on the throttle.

Blake was never more at peace than when he was on his motorcycle. Sometimes it felt as if the roar of the engine was the only thing that could drown out his bad memories. He'd recognized that the first time he straddled a Harley. The feeling of peace the bike gave him hadn't waned since.

Chloe's grip tightened around his waist, but he didn't give way, didn't slow down. He knew her, knew she loved this feeling of flying as much as he did. It was another way they were alike, in synch. Sometimes it amazed him how many similarities he and Chloe shared, given their completely different upbringings.

For nearly an hour, it was just the two of them, soaking up the sunshine and the silence while letting the wind blow all the hurt away. Blake didn't pretend that pain wouldn't resurface, that the next few hours wouldn't be difficult. He'd never talked about his past or his father. Ever. But complete honesty was the only chance he had at possibly regaining Chloe's trust. And maybe even her love.

He'd bare his soul to the world if it meant getting her back.

Once they turned on Old 51 Highway, the traffic all but disappeared and soon, they arrived. Blake parked in such a way that Chloe could capture him and the bike with the picturesque view in the background.

She studied his choice and nodded approvingly. "This will work."

She removed the helmet and started to retrieve her equipment from the bag. Glancing up at the sky, then back at him, she gestured toward the sun. "We'll have to work fast in order to take advantage of the light."

He helped her set up the tripod, then moved the bike a couple inches this way or that as she tried to line up the perfect shot. Once she had the position she wanted, she pointed to his shirt. "Some guys have taken their shirts off completely, others have just unbuttoned them and left them hanging open. The musician wore an open vest with his jeans. It's up to you. Whatever your comfortable with."

Blake stripped off his shirt without hesitation. With his chest bare, the badge he'd hung from his jeans showed better. They'd discussed whether or not he should wear his gun belt, but decided against it.

Chloe rolled her eyes at his quick disrobing.

"You didn't really expect me to be shy, did you?"

She shook her head, then bent down to fiddle with her camera. Blake was unnerved by her continued silence. Apart from discussing the photo shoot, she hadn't engaged in any real conversation. He'd let her get away with that until their work was finished. After that, all bets were off.

She snapped a couple of shots she called testers then nodded approvingly at whatever she saw in the viewfinder. "The crash point on this setup is amazing."

"Crash point?"

"Sorry. Photography slang. It's just an expression someone used in one of my classes once that stuck with me. Basically, it has to do with symmetry and the rule of thirds. You are the crash point. Everything in this image draws the viewer's eye to you."

She didn't bother to explain further. Instead, he stood, turning this way and that as Chloe worked her magic with the camera. He was no stranger to being her model. He'd posed for countless pictures that summer so long ago. She had been enrolled in her first photography class and was obsessed with applying everything she'd learned, dragging him along any time she needed a model.

Then he considered her term. *They* were at a crash point.

Everything that had happened in their pasts had put them on this course, until now...all that was left was this moment and the truth.

Blake tried to put all that away, focusing on Chloe's instructions, letting her call the shots. He teased her about it, saying he'd never noticed her dominatrix tendencies. She pretended to crack a whip, then continued to take pictures.

All too soon, she decided she'd captured exactly what she needed. She appeared pleased, but that look passed quickly, replaced by one of reticence, nervousness.

Once they'd finished packing all the equipment away, Blake locked the bag, securing it to the bike.

"Walk with me." He held out his hand.

Chloe hesitated and he feared she'd refuse. He raised his eyebrows, silently pleading with her to give him a chance to explain.

She sighed. "Okay."

She accepted his proffered hand and they walked along the shore, listening to the sound of the water repetitively slapping against the bank. It was quiet for a Sunday afternoon in May. The weatherman had forecasted a late-day shower, so Blake could only assume the threat of impending weather had kept most people away.

He led her to a private spot then gestured at the grass. "Wanna sit down for a while?"

She nodded and plopped down on the soft ground. He joined her and they looked out over the lake.

Crash point, Blake thought once more. It was time. "You asked me why I left. I didn't have a chance to answer."

Chloe turned her head, looking back the way they'd come. He'd become very good at reading body language during his years on the force. Every fiber of Chloe wanted to run, to escape. But—in typical fashion—his brave woman resisted the urge. She faced him once more.

"So tell me."

"You are the most beautiful woman I've ever met, Chloe."

She rolled her eyes, clearly thinking he intended to charm his way out of answering.

"I mean it. When you grow up the way I did, well, let's just say, I wasn't all that familiar with women who smiled and laughed and were so genuinely honest."

A crease formed in Chloe's brow. "You never told me about your childhood. You just said you lived with your dad."

He nodded. "Do you know why I volunteered to pose for this calendar?"

She gave him an impish grin. "Because you drew the short straw?"

"I spent one Christmas in the Blessing House. A social worker found me and my dad living on the street. It was one of those rare, cold-ass winters in New Orleans. She told us about the house, said we could go there for the holiday. My dad told the woman to mind her own business. Actually, I think his exact words were 'Fuck off, bitch' but she didn't listen to him. She just handed me a flyer with the address to the house. Promised me I'd be warm and there'd even be presents."

"How old were you?"

Now that he'd opened the vault to his past, Blake found too many memories coming at him too fast. Maybe that was good. He could keep the emotions at bay because there wasn't time to process them. "Eleven. After she left, my dad fell into a bottle of whiskey and passed out. It was cold as shit that night. So, I covered my old man up with my blanket and walked nearly two miles in the dark until I found the address of the Blessing House. I'd been lied to by nearly every adult I'd ever met, so when I knocked on the door, I was more than ready to run in case it was a trap."

"A trap?"

He shrugged. "My dad wasn't the most law-abiding citizen. He'd taught me at a young age to always be on the lookout for the law."

"He told you the police were the bad guys?"

Blake nodded.

"And yet you joined the force."

He grinned sadly. "It seemed like the best way to stick it to my old man. The guy was a fucking asshole in case you haven't figured that out yet."

Chloe didn't reply. His words had come out too bitter, too strong. Most folks would have accepted that at face value. She didn't. "He was still your dad."

"I know. I spent one night in the Blessing House, watching all the other kids—some with folks, some without—and in the morning, there was a present for me and I got a holiday meal."

"Sounds nicer than the street."

Blake lifted one shoulder. "I guess. I didn't stick around. I left the toy I'd gotten—some plastic fire truck—stole a bunch of food from the kitchen and a couple of blankets and took off."

"You went to find your dad."

Blake picked up a blade of grass, pressing it between his thumb and forefinger. "Yeah. I got worried about him being hungry."

Blake looked out over the lake. He hated trudging up all this old shit. It didn't change anything. His jaw tensed as he fought to beat back the anger. After several deep breaths, he was able to center himself again.

Chloe didn't seek to fill the silence with questions. She let him find his way through the story at his own pace. He appreciated that she didn't push him for more.

"I always took care of him. He was an alcoholic. He couldn't hold down a job for more than a few days at a time."

"So you became the caregiver."

He nodded. "Yeah. I guess so."

"It was the same for Zac and Noah. They kept the house as clean as they could while their mom was strung out. Zac made sure Noah did his homework, got something for dinner, put him in bed at a reasonable hour. Parents shouldn't do that to their kids."

Blake turned to face her. He'd avoided looking at her for fear of seeing pity in her eyes. There were a lot of things he could take from her, but sympathy wasn't one. What he saw instead was anger. Strangely that helped. Made Blake feel like they were on the same page. "I'm not making excuses for what I did, Chloe. I'm not playing the poor pitiful me card. My dad was a lousy excuse for a person, but the choices I made were mine. Right or wrong, I can't blame him for what I did. All I can do is hope to make you understand why I stole the money, why I left."

She reached out and took his hand in hers, giving it an encouraging squeeze. "So tell me about that night."

"We'd told your mother we were going to the movies, but we actually snuck into that old shed behind your girlfriend's house."

Chloe laughed. "Her family was on vacation. You brought those sleeping bags and threw them on the floor. You'd bought a rose and scattered the petals on them. I thought it was all completely romantic."

He was glad she remembered that part of the night with fondness. "We were pretty damn horny most of the time."

"God," she joked. "That's a mild word for it. We were ravenous, insatiable. We couldn't walk three steps without touching and we couldn't touch without it sparking something hotter."

"I remember. We did it in two public restrooms, the back-seat of your brother's car, no less than half a dozen times around this lake and God only knows where else."

"We were young. For me, sex was new. Sometimes, when I looked at you, it was almost painful how much I wanted you."

He understood that. He'd felt the same way back then. Hell, he'd felt that way since bumping into her two weeks ago. He went to bed every night with a physical ache caused by longing.

"You had to be home by midnight, but we were a little late."

Chloe nodded. "We were a lot late. I used the hidden key under the mat in the backyard, thinking I could sneak in through the back door in the kitchen.

"But Mama Lewis was sitting there, waiting for you. I was surprised that she didn't yell at us. Whenever I pissed my dad off, the whole neighborhood knew. He'd cuss me up one side and down the other, then finish it off with a punch or two."

Chloe winced. "My mother never hit me or my brothers. And she said yelling was never a good way to express an opinion."

"Yeah. She just looked at us and said she was disappointed. She explained how worried she'd been that we'd been in an accident. How much it would kill her to lose you. I swear I felt way worse after that conversation than I ever did when my dad yelled at me."

"Punishment through guilt and disappointment," Chloe said. "I totally intend to use it with my kids. It's very effective."

They laughed together quietly. Then Chloe sobered up. "You came back that night. You knew where we hid the key."

Blake nodded. "When I got back to my apartment, the neighbor was waiting for me. Said my dad had been arrested for getting into a fight. I figured he'd gotten drunk and punched some guy at a bar. It had happened before and the cops just made him sleep it off in the drunk tank, then sent him home the next day. The neighbor said this time was different. He said my dad was in real trouble and he needed money for bail. I dug through all my hiding spots, but I could only come up with about fifty bucks. I didn't have anyone else to ask."

"You didn't ask." There was no tone of accusation, just the statement of fact. He hadn't asked. He'd simply taken.

Blake blew out a long breath, then decided fuck it. He'd gone this far. It was time to say it all. "You're right. I didn't. I got back to your place. All the lights were out. Everybody was asleep. I used the key and I swear to you, I was going to sneak up to your room to see if you could loan me money, but..."

"But?" she prompted.

"I'd have to tell you why I needed it and I didn't want you to know my dad was a drunk loser in jail."

"Why not?"

"I was embarrassed. You were the best thing that had ever happened to me and the entire time we dated, I knew I didn't deserve you."

Chloe scowled. "That's bullshit."

He gave her a crooked grin. "I was a stupid nineteen-year-old kid. I'm not saying I was the sharpest tool in the shed. All I had going for me was my Harley, a lousy dead-end job in a sub shop and my pride. None of those things seemed like enough to keep a girl like you interested. I was in love with you, Chloe, and terrified of fucking everything up. Which I did anyway."

"So you walked into the house..." she began.

"Your mother's purse was on the kitchen table. Stealing wasn't exactly a new thing for me. I rifled through her wallet and found a couple hundred bucks. I was about to leave when I remembered the silver platter in the hutch in the dining room and I grabbed it too. And then I ran. You know, I've been wondering. How did you all know it was me who took the money?"

"You'd tucked some of those rose petals in your pocket before we left the shed. A few of them must have fallen out. I wouldn't have thought anything about it because you'd been in the kitchen when Mama found us sneaking in. But there were a couple by the hutch as well."

"Guess it's a good thing I became a cop. I clearly suck at covering my tracks as a thief."

Chloe smiled at his joke. "What happened after you left?"

"All hell broke loose."

"What do you mean?"

"I waited for the pawn shop to open the next morning. Took in your mom's platter and got a few hundred bucks for it. Then I went to the police station and bailed my dad out. I was stressing out over how I was going to find the money to buy the platter back. It was worth more than I realized. Anyway, my dad was in deep shit with some shady guys. He'd agreed to deliver some package, but he didn't."

"What was in the package?"

"Drugs. Never figured out if he sold them himself or had one hell of a party, but the package was gone and the guys wanted it or the money it would have brought in sales. They confronted my dad in the parking lot of a bar. Gave him a pretty good beat down. They took off when the cops showed up, but not before they told Dad he had twenty-four hours to produce the drugs or the money."

"Why was he arrested?"

Blake snorted, the sound betraying a bitterness he didn't like to show. "Even bloodied, my dad was a mean drunk. He took a swing at one of the cops. When they ran his name through the system, they found out he had some outstanding warrants. The second I sprung him from jail, he started making plans."

"What kind of plans?"

A rumble of thunder distracted them. Blake looked up at the sky. Afternoon was quickly turning to dusk and dark clouds were forming. Apparently the weathermen had been right. A storm was coming. They'd need to head back to the bike soon or risk getting wet. As it was, Blake wasn't sure they'd make it to the city before the rain started falling.

"Can we finish this at your place?"

Chloe looked up as well. He got the sense she wanted to finish what they'd started, but even she could see that wasn't going to happen here. "Sure."

Her tone gave him no hint to her feelings. Blake stood then offered her a hand. He didn't release it as they started walking back to his Harley. She didn't try to pull away. It gave him hope.

The ride back to Chloe's place felt less peaceful than the trip to the lake. For one thing, Blake couldn't put the bad memories away. Dredging up the past bothered him more than he'd expected. For years, he'd felt on top of his game, certain he'd kicked all the crap from his childhood to the curb. Clearly, he hadn't.

Secondly, the rain hadn't held off. They'd just made it to the city limits when the sky opened up. By the time they reached Chloe's apartment, they were drenched from head to toe. He halfway expected her to tell him to take a hike. The afternoon by the lake had taken its toll and now they were cold and wet.

Instead, she pulled off her helmet, laughing as she lifted her face to the rain. "That was incredible. I couldn't decide if I was having fun or scared out of my wits. How could you see the road? That was a deluge."

He looked at her, raindrops sliding down her rosy cheeks, and felt like a two-ton truck had hit him. He grasped her face in his hands and, heedless of the storm that continued to pound down on them, he kissed her.

Chloe didn't resist. She simply wrapped her arms around his neck and kissed him back. Their tongues tangled as he ran his fingers through her hair. She pressed her chest closer to his, sharing her body warmth. He had no idea how long they stood on the city sidewalk, letting the rain pummel them as they kissed, but Blake could have stayed there forever.

Finally, common sense reared and he took a step back. "I know I said that motorcycle bag is waterproof, but we probably shouldn't tempt fate. You've got some expensive equipment in there."

She nodded as he unhooked the bag and threw the strap over his shoulder. She carried their helmets, leading the way upstairs to her apartment.

"You can put that bag over there." She pointed to the corner of her studio. "I'll go grab some towels from the bathroom."

Blake set the bag down then hovered by the door. He was dripping all over her hardwood floors.

Chloe was back within seconds with an armload of fluffy towels. "Why are you standing there?"

He gestured at the puddle forming around his feet. "Didn't want to ruin your floor."

Chloe shrugged. "It's just water. It'll dry. Here." She held out a towel.

He crossed the room and took it from her. He ran it over his hair and face, then started undoing the buttons of his shirt. Chloe watched, making no move to stop him. Once he'd shrugged the clinging cotton off, she was there, rubbing all the water away with a towel.

When she finished, Blake reached for the hem of her t-shirt and tugged it over her head. Then he dried her as well. She sucked in a soft breath when he reached around her, unhooking her bra and adding it to the pile of wet clothing at their feet. He took his time, drying her breasts, loving the way her cold nipples budded even more at his touch.

Chloe reached for the button on his jeans and slowly slid the zipper down. He toed off his boots, chuckling as Chloe cursed in her struggles to strip the wet denim away. She followed the stubborn material down, kneeling before him as she gestured for him to lift one foot, then the other. She peeled off his socks as well.

She made no attempt to rise. "Still go commando, I see."

He cupped her face in his palm, forcing her to look at him. "You're beautiful."

She gave him a wicked grin. "You're just trying to sweet talk me into giving you a blowjob."

He laughed. "Well, since you're down there anyway, it seems like a shame to—" His jest was cut short when Chloe grasped his cock, taking the head into her mouth without hesitation.

His hands flew to her hair. "Jesus, Chloe. I was kidding."

She didn't release him, just sucked him harder, deeper. Blake struggled to catch up. He'd been emotionally done in when they'd left the lake, then stressed out as he'd tried to get them home safely on the motorcycle during the storm. Now he was standing in Chloe's apartment, her lips wrapped around his cock, and his brain was scrambled, fried.

She cupped his balls in one palm, her other wrapped around the base. He recalled the first time she'd given him a blowjob. She'd dragged him into the back storeroom of the sub shop one night after closing and shocked him by asking him to teach her how to suck his dick.

Given the way she was driving him to the peak right now, he'd say she'd learned her lesson well. Increasing her speed, she took him deeper and deeper into her mouth with each pass. The head of his cock brushed the back of her throat. He tightened his grip on her hair, trembling slightly when she groaned, the vibrations adding another dimension to the blowjob.

"Chloe."

She looked up at him, her expression the perfect blend of mischief and dare. She'd turned the tables on him, grasping control, and now she was challenging him to take it back. If he hadn't been so mentally exhausted he would have called her to task immediately, pulling her over his knees.

Somehow she'd known. Known what he needed to make it through the next part. And she'd given it freely.

He tugged her hair more roughly than before. Chloe moaned again, her eyes closing in bliss. Her desire fueled his, gave him back the strength that had been waning. It wasn't time for this. Not yet. There was still more to say.

He pushed her mouth away. Chloe frowned and started to protest, but he put a firm finger beneath her chin, forcing her face up. "No. Not this way."

Blake lifted her slowly then placed his lips on hers. For several moments, they simply kissed. Then he moved, resting his forehead against hers. She shivered and he realized she was still wearing her wet jeans.

"Take off your pants. We need to get you dry and warm."

Chloe moved away only a few steps, slipping her own jeans off as Blake watched. She didn't have a shy bone in her body—never had—so her disrobing became part seduction. She turned her back to him before sliding the denim over her hips. She tugged her panties down at the same time, so when she bent forward to draw the material over her feet, he was treated to a bird's-eye view of her perfect ass.

Before he could think better of it, he reached over and slapped it. Chloe gasped—the sound more surprise than pain—then she grasped her ankles. "Do that again."

He considered making her beg. They had only started to explore their sexual kinks when he'd stolen that money and left town. Even so, he had recognized Chloe's desire for pain, her love of rough play and her need to be dominated. He'd spent too many lonely nights, jacking off in bed as he imagined all the ways he would have taken her if life hadn't thrown them the curveball.

Now, all those fantasies came rushing to the surface. He would make them a reality. But first...

He grasped her gently by the elbow and helped her up. She turned, confusion briefly flashing across her face before she understood.

"I'm sorry, Blake. I..."

He tugged her into his arms, holding her tightly. "I get the same way around you. I lose all sense of control. I just need to try to make things right between us before we let this go any further."

She nodded. "I agree."

He led her to the couch and they sat down together side by side. Chloe tugged an afghan from the ottoman and spread it out over top of them. It was cozy and warm.

"You said your dad was making plans after you bailed him out. To do what?"

"He was in big trouble with the drug pushers. We went back to our place and he started packing up our stuff. Within half an hour, we were back on the street. I'd worked at that crummy sub shop for nearly three years after school, saving enough money to buy my motorcycle. My dad went out that afternoon and stole one. By noon, we were on the highway, speeding away from New Orleans."

"Just like that?"

Blake rubbed the back of his neck. He'd spent countless hours trying to figure out why the hell he'd followed his father so easily, why he hadn't fought to stay. "I'd stolen from your mother, Chloe. I couldn't figure out a way to make that right."

"You could've explained it to me, Blake."

He lifted one shoulder. "I know. But my dad..."

"He couldn't stay in New Orleans. And you couldn't leave him."

"That was the biggest mistake I made that day. I chose to stay with the wrong person."

Chloe fell silent. Blake wasn't sure what else to say. At this point, the ball was in her court. Either she would forgive him. Or she wouldn't.

"You've been back in New Orleans for almost six years?"

He nodded.

"Did you come back to town with your dad?"

"No. My dad and I split ways about two years after we left." Blake didn't tell her about the near-rape or the fight. That was a story he'd take to his grave. "I'd been on the force nearly three years before I realized he'd come back to New Orleans too. Got a call when I was on duty. Drunk and disorderly. I walked into the bar in my uniform and sure enough, there he sat."

"That must have been an uncomfortable reunion."

Blake snorted. "You can't even imagine."

"Did you arrest him?"

Blake shook his head. "No. I drove him back to his place. Crazy asshole was actually proud of me for joining the force."

"Really?" Chloe asked. "I thought he hated cops."

"He's a twisted bastard. He believed he could use my position to cover up his crimes."

Chloe winced. "Wow."

"I pretended he could."

Her eyebrows rose. "What? Why?"

Blake had never admitted his reasons before. He wondered if Chloe would change her mind about him if she learned exactly how manipulative he was. "Entrapment. I set up a mini-sting with my captain. Pretended to be in cahoots with my father while gaining information about a local drug ring. I knew my dad hadn't changed his ways and I figured he'd be useful. He was."

"That couldn't have been easy for you."

Blake leaned his head against the back of the couch. "You'd be surprised."

She scowled. "Don't. Stop playing the tough guy. You put your dad in jail. And even if he was an asshole, he was the only parent you'd ever had."

Blake wrapped an arm around her shoulders, pulling her head to his chest. "The world is simpler when you look at it in black and white. If you start adding color into the equation..."

"Is that why you've never called me?"

Blake wasn't sure how to respond, so he stalled. "What?"

"You've been back in New Orleans for years. You saw my book. You knew I was still here. Why didn't you call me?"

She sounded so genuinely hurt, it made Blake's chest ache. "I didn't think you'd forgive me."

She lifted her head. "You were wrong."

He gave her a tentative grin, hope blossoming. "So you do forgive me?"

She shook her head.

His brow creased. "You don't?" For a moment, he felt lost. If she couldn't understand his reasons for stealing the money, everything they once had was truly lost.

"It doesn't matter if I forgive you, Blake. I'm pretty sure I stopped being mad at you the second my mother said you paid her the money back. I wouldn't have had sex with you otherwise."

He felt the urge to laugh, but his gut told him something was still wrong.

Chloe cupped his cheek in her hand. "It's not *my* forgiveness that matters. You have to forgive yourself, Blake. You stayed away because you were trying to do penance, right?"

Her words hit him like a ton of bricks. Had he done that? Had he let guilt for his actions stop him from searching for her, for happiness? For love? "I'm not sure what to say."

Chloe gave him a wicked grin that told him exactly how much of a fool he'd been to stay away. "You could always start with 'You're right'."

He chuckled. "I'm pretty sure I'd be smart to use those words sparingly."

She gave him a light punch on the arm. "Blake."

"You're right, Chloe. I've been letting guilt guide my decisions. I was wrong to do that."

Chloe leaned closer and kissed him, showing him with actions rather than words that all truly was forgiven between them. It was a gift Blake had never let himself hope for.

For the first time in six years, he felt like he'd truly come home.

CHAPTER SIX

Blake reached for her, pulling her onto his lap. He had obviously reached the same realization she had. The time for talking was over. One main benefit of the rain was it had helped them shed the clothes early on. Blake was naked, his skin warm against hers.

He kissed her gently at first. An apology. Chloe accepted it, offering her own in return. She was sorry for doubting him. For failing to believe in the man she'd known he was. Both of them had let pride and the exaggerated emotions of youth—the ones that believe every problem is insurmountable and the worst thing that could ever happen—take control.

Chloe met Blake's tongue halfway, letting the passion of the kiss build as she turned. Straddling his body, her knees on the cushions by his ass, she relished the hardness of his cock as it brushed her pussy, her stomach.

She'd spent too many years settling for lackluster sex. Chloe could see now she was to blame for those passionless affairs. Sex was way hotter when you were in love.

Love.

She broke the connection of their lips. She was wrong. There was still one more thing left to say.

Blake scowled at her retreat, clearly not finished. He started to pull her face back to his, but she resisted. "Chloe?"

"I love you."

His smile grew so wide, Chloe couldn't help but return it. "Say it again."

She lifted one eyebrow. "I think I'd be smart to use those words sparingly at first."

Blake laughed, shifting her until the head of his cock rested at the opening of her body. "I'll make it worth your while."

She glanced down, intent on taking her prize, with or without his permission. She started to slide down, but Blake's grip on her waist tightened, holding her in place. Dammit. She kept forgetting how strong he was.

When her gaze met his again, she saw something almost like sorrow in his eyes. "Blake?"

"I'm going to be greedy for a while, Chloe. I can't help it. I want too much from you."

She understood the sentiment. She shared it. "We'll be gluttons together. I love you. I love you so much it hurts. And if you ever try to leave me again, I will hunt you down to the end of the earth and I'll—"

Blake cut off her threat with a kiss. "Never gonna happen, but you know...there are laws against threatening a police officer."

She returned his kiss with interest, nipping his lower lip. "Oh yeah? Handcuff-worthy laws?"

Blake chuckled. "Definitely."

He loosened his grip on her waist, using his hands to guide her, drawing her body down onto his cock. Both of them gasped once he was fully seated. Her position on top left her wide open and able to take him deeper. It still didn't feel like enough.

She lifted up a few inches then slid back down slowly, savoring Blake's pained expression, his quick intake of air.

He gave her a warning look. "Are you really sure you want to play the control game, Chloe?"

She recognized the threat. She'd been trying to force his hand ever since they'd walked into the apartment, daring him to take charge.

Regardless of the danger, it was a challenge she couldn't refuse. After so many years apart, she felt the need to test him, to see if he was still the dominant lover she remembered. Craved.

However, she needed him to understand that she had changed. While she still wanted to submit to him, she wasn't the weak, inexperienced little girl he'd taken all those years ago. She wouldn't bend to his will easily. She intended to make him work for it.

Chloe rose once more, returning even slower, taking the time to tighten her inner muscles. Blake felt it. The stiffness of his posture told her that while he may appreciate her efforts, he was determined to come out on top.

She repeated her seductive slide a third time, adding her breasts to the game as she leaned forward, rubbing them against his face.

Blake's tenuous grip on control slipped a bit as his hands found her ass, his fingers digging into the flesh there. She expected him to try to seize power. After all, it was clear he needed her to move faster, harder. She wanted that too.

Unfortunately, the damn man was too astute. She should have known better than to play with a cop and his instincts. His grip on her ass loosened, though he didn't move them away. Instead, he reached farther around her, his fingers slipping into the crease.

She gasped when he parted the twin globes, dragging one

finger lower.

Their sexual experiences ten years earlier had been cut short. Chloe had always wished there had been more time for them to explore their kinkier desires. Now, at last, there was.

"Who's in charge, Chloe?" His voice was deep, dark, tinged with a hint of menace.

She wasn't afraid. She smiled and continued her painfully slow glide up and down his cock. "I'm not sure."

He leaned closer, his teeth capturing one of her nipples. She gasped when he started to press down. She felt Blake's gaze on her face. One of the reasons she felt safe exploring these games with him was because she knew he would never let it go too far. He read her face, protected her...even from herself. Her hands tightened on his shoulders and he released her.

"Do you want to reconsider your answer?"

She bit her lip, pretending to think. Then she shook her head.

"Good girl."

She didn't understand his pleasure until he lifted her off his cock, twisted her quickly, and tossed her facedown over his lap. Before she could even consider escaping, his hand struck her bare ass three times. Chloe gripped Blake's calf, torn between halting the spanking and begging for more. It hurt more than she'd expected, but not so much that she couldn't feel her arousal sparking, flaring.

Blake stroked the heated flesh, his fingers surprisingly gentle after his hard blows. Then he repeated the motions, striking her ass three more times before caressing the skin again.

Her stomach clenched in anticipation when he raised his hand, her body readying itself for more. He paused. She knew the game. He wanted her to ask for it, to beg. She lifted her head, glancing at him over her shoulder.

"Who's in charge, Chloe?"

She narrowed her eyes, not ready to give in yet. She let her silence answer the question.

Blake grinned at her stubbornness, clearly enjoying the struggle for power. He lifted her from his lap—much to her dismay—pulling her up until she straddled his lap once more.

He guided his cock to her pussy, using a strong grip on her waist to press himself inside her. Fully seated, he held her in place, refusing to let her move.

"Are you on the Pill?"

She nodded.

"Are you okay with not using the condom?"

"Yes."

His strong hands held her down despite her attempts to move. She needed friction, thrusting, anything. Her pussy clenched against his cock, seeking more, but Blake held steady.

"Blake," she snapped, her temper firing. "Fuck me. Now."

He leaned toward her, nipping her earlobe in warning. "That's not a very nice way to ask. Who's in charge, Chloe?"

She continued her struggle, wiggling her hips as much as his hands would allow...which wasn't anywhere near enough.

"Hand the reins over to me and I'll give you everything you want."

It was the most tempting offer she'd ever received in her life. Given her rather powerful personality, she'd only managed to attract men who expected her to control every aspect of her life—professionally, personally...and sexually. She was damn tired of being on top.

Still, her pride made it hard for her to give in so easily. Even if she was cutting off her nose to spite her face. It was on the tip of her tongue to tell him what he wanted to hear, but Blake must have decided her time was up.

He lifted her off his cock then grasped her hand in his. He

tugged her to her bed, where he pulled back the covers and tossed her into the middle of the mattress. She started to sit, but he held his hand up, halting her.

"Don't move. Not one muscle. If you do, I'm going to demonstrate the difference between a spanking to stimulate and a spanking to punish. Understand?"

She nodded, the sadist in her really wanting to test that limit. Instead, she decided to let this game play out. She lay on the bed and watched as he rifled through her dresser. He found what he was seeking in the second drawer.

Chloe closed her eyes, fighting her growing arousal when he came back to the bed, scarves in hand. He used one to bind her wrists together then he tied them outstretched above her to the headboard. She wiggled, trying to loosen the knot, but Blake knew his stuff.

She startled, her gaze flying to his face when his hands pressed her legs apart and he knelt between them. She read his intent as he looked down at her pussy. He looked a bit like a man surveying the all-you-can-eat bar. She giggled.

Blake paused, his mouth quirking up at the corners. "You find bondage funny?"

She shook her head. "Not really. I'm excited and edgy. My mind is whirling a million miles a minute, thinking about ridiculous things. I'm a nervous giggler."

"Maybe I should try to distract you." With that, he bent down, his tongue finding her clit on the first stroke.

Her hips reared up, but Blake's hands were there, holding her against the mattress. Though he hadn't restrained her feet, Chloe didn't pretend that she wasn't truly helpless. Blake had complete control of her body, his own personal plaything. That idea didn't frighten her at all. It made her even hotter.

Blake ran his tongue along her slit from ass to clit and back again. She felt consumed, possessed. Chloe closed her eyes, but that didn't stop her from feeling Blake's head shake.

"No, Chloe. Open your eyes. Watch me."

She obeyed. The command forced her to see as well as feel. It was a potent combination. Most men viewed this act as a chore. Blake clearly did not. He pressed his tongue inside her pussy and she bit her lip, fighting not to come so quickly. She was trying to play hard to get, but that game would only work if she didn't have an orgasm every time Blake looked in her direction.

Then she wondered why she was resisting. Blake was a very generous lover, never stopping when she'd come just once. She released a long breath and gave herself over to the magic of his lips, tongue and fingers. She was seconds away from complete bliss when Blake pulled away.

She frowned. "Wait."

"Who's in charge, Chloe?"

Damn him. He had her over a barrel and he knew it. She didn't bother to protest. This game was over before it started. "You are."

He smiled, the expression transforming his entire face. He was so handsome he took her breath away. The tight lines around his mouth, the haunted look in his eyes had faded. She suspected it would take some time before they vanished for good. Maybe they never would. Given Blake's painful childhood, perhaps he'd never totally escape the bad memories. But she sure as hell intended to distract him for the next fifty years or so.

"Remember you said that." He spoke lightly enough, but there was something behind the warning that triggered alarm bells.

"Okay."

"You're not to come without permission."

And that was the sound of the other shoe falling. He gave her a wicked wink then resumed his place between her legs, driving her arousal higher and higher, while offering no reprieve.

She was trembling and panting, begging, but Blake ignored her. His tongue wiggled against her clit as he drove three fingers inside her, deep and hard. Just when she knew she'd fail, he withdrew, giving her time to recover before starting the same glorious torture over. And over. When he dragged one wet finger lower, pressing it just inside her anus, she felt a tear slide down her cheek.

"Blake. Please."

Chloe wasn't sure what he heard in her voice, but he lifted his head. "Come, baby."

With that, he pushed the finger at her ass in all the way while pressing his tongue inside her pussy. She thrashed and cried out loudly as her body exploded into a million bright, shiny pieces.

The moment she came down, Blake was there. He untied her arms then thrust his cock in with one strong push. She was back up in an instant, her body reacting to his hard fucking as if she hadn't just had the most incredible orgasm in the history of sex.

She wrapped her arms around his neck and her legs about his waist. She wasn't sure why she felt the need to cling to him. Maybe she was still harboring some fears of her own. She didn't believe he'd leave her again, but even as she thought it, she realized her heart wouldn't survive losing him.

"Love you," she whispered, the words coming out in a harsh pant as Blake drove into her like a man possessed.

How long would it take the two of them to feel confident that this time it would stick, it would last?

"I love you, Chloe. God, so much. So fucking much." As he

spoke, he stroked her clit, her hot button. He played her body like a violin. Her back arched as she screamed. Best of all, Blake was right there with her. He stiffened, jet after jet of come filling her.

Once they recovered, Blake fell to her side, his arm wrapped loosely around her waist. "Damn. I always thought I'd built our sexcapades up in my mind over the years. Made them bigger than they really were."

Chloe laughed, turning to face him. "I thought the same thing."

"It's actually better than I remembered. Off the charts. I swear I thought my cock was going to explode."

She moved her face closer, the two of them rubbing noses playfully. "We're quite a pair."

"Yeah. We sure are. I should warn you. I still have my fair share of pride. I'm just a bit better about keeping it contained."

She grinned, kissing him lightly. "Well, my temper is just as bad as ever and I'm not even trying to keep it under control. You're just gonna have to deal."

Blake ruffled her hair. "Yeah, I've noticed that. I'm not worried. I have a feeling we're going to be okay from this point on."

"I wouldn't say that."

"What do you mean?"

She lifted one shoulder. "We're going to have to break the news that we're dating again to my brothers."

Blake fell to his back and released a long breath. "Damn. We were so close to that happy ending."

She giggled, punching his shoulder. "Chicken shit. You can break it to them at Sunday dinner."

Blake rolled toward her, pulling her underneath him as he slid into her once more. "Okay. But I'm warning you right now. I'm bringing my gun."

FULL POSITION
BIG EASY, BOOK 3

Though Bella has crushed on Justin and Ned since her first day on the job, she's smart enough to know a ménage with her hot bosses is probably number one on the list of workplace no-nos. But a genius wouldn't say no to their exceptionally tempting offer — a no-holds-barred night of wicked fantasies at a local sex club.

Justin and Ned believe in propriety in the workplace, but falling for their sexy graphic artist has blurred the line between professional and personal. These Big Easy men might surprise their small-town girl with their bedroom habits. But the biggest shock could come the morning after...when Bella discovers what they really want.

CHAPTER ONE

"So basically I'm finished with men."

Justin Lewis rolled his eyes. "Of course you are."

Bella leaned closer, her face completely earnest. "I mean it. You guys are part of an entire gender of fucksticks. I'm done."

Ned snorted. "Until next week, when your hormones get the better of you."

Bella gave Ned a dirty look. "For your information, when that happens I turn to my boyfriend, Roger. He's reliable, efficient and he doesn't talk."

Justin took a swig of Dixie beer. "Giving your rabbit a name doesn't make it a boyfriend, Bells. It's still just a vibrator."

"Yes, but it's the deluxe model. No expense spared. And thanks to my cushy job with you guys, I can afford the best."

Bella Carper had worked at Lewis and Kinnaman Marketing since graduating from college with her graphics art degree six years earlier. Justin's best friend and business partner, Ned Kinnaman, had taken one look at her portfolio and known she was destined to be one of their artists. Since then, they'd helped mold her craft, while giving her the creative freedom to try new things. She'd lived up to every professional expectation they'd had and more.

Ned rolled his eyes. "I'm glad to hear you're investing your income so wisely."

Justin laughed at their easy, off-color banter. He hadn't anticipated that Bella would become a friend as well as an employee. He'd never really had many female friends. Not in high school or even after. He figured his sisters didn't count. He'd chalked that deficit up to a personality thing. He was too much of a guy—prone to heavy drinking, cussing fluently during televised sports and flirting rampantly with any pretty woman who entered his dance space.

And, of course, he blamed Ned too. Ned tended to intimidate women, which wasn't entirely surprising. At six foot four and two-twenty, Ned cast a rather large shadow. Add in his dominant personality and his far-too-serious nature and women tended to give both men a wide berth.

Well, most women.

The exceptions were the submissives at Extreme Connections, the private sex club he and Ned belonged to. Those women actually sought them out. Of course, that had everything to do with sex and nothing to do with friendship.

"So what was wrong with this last guy? Phillip?" Ned asked.

"Patrick," she corrected. "And do you mean apart from the fact he was a complete male chauvinist pig, annoying and a know-it-all? I wouldn't mind so much, but now I have to find a new personal trainer."

Ned failed to suppress his *I told you so* grin. "He never should have started an affair with you. It was completely unprofessional."

Bella flipped her hair over her shoulder. "You and your

damn professionalism. He was hot, and I'm pretty sure I won him over with my incredible stamina and flexibility. He just couldn't resist my lunges and burpees."

She and Ned laughed at her joke, but for some reason, Justin was finding it difficult to play along with their irreverent, off-color banter tonight. While Bella's sarcastic wit was as firmly in place as her smile, her pretty green eyes gave her away. She was sad.

Justin realized that look had been there a lot the past few months. "Regardless of your pretzel-like physique, I'm glad you got away from Patrick. I didn't trust that guy."

Bella's eyes widened a bit, betraying her surprise at his confession. Justin rarely commented or expressed an opinion on her love life. "If you want the truth, he was meek as a kitten in bed. All those sleek, hard muscles turned to mush between the sheets. Kept wanting me to take the lead, get on top, blah blah blah. Boring." She blinked a couple times as if realizing what she'd just said then winced. "God, I'm the queen of TMI tonight—vibrators and boring lovers. I must be drunker than I thought."

Off-color humor wasn't uncommon between them and none of them were exactly shy about discussing the whens and whos of their sexual affairs. However, Bella had never revealed quite so many details about the during. Justin put his beer bottle down. "Wait. Back up the bus. Are you trying to tell me you prefer to play the bottom?"

Bella's brows creased and Ned flashed Justin a warning look. Unfortunately, it was too late. "Play the bottom?"

Justin tried to cover up his mistake. "I meant be on the bottom."

Bella tilted her head, curiosity radiating. However, before she could question Justin, Ned intervened.

"I think you're smart to take a break from dating for a while.

Gives you a chance to reevaluate what you want in a relationship. Maybe you're going for the wrong type of guy."

"The problem isn't knowing what I want. I know exactly what kind of man I'm looking for. Unfortunately, my fantasy guy doesn't exist in reality."

Ned waved the waitress over and asked for another round, even though Justin suspected Bella had been ready to wrap things up and call it a night. Now that she'd mentioned her fantasies, it appeared his friend's curiosity had been piqued.

What *did* Bella want in a man? Justin knew Ned had always cast her in the role of a Domme. Not that Bella would know that. As a result, his friend had dismissed her as a compatible sex partner. Actually, Ned would never let himself consider Bella in a sexual way because of work, which made Justin wonder if his friend had clung to that Domme excuse as a way to make it easier to stay away from her.

The truth was, Bella was quite beautiful. Her light-brown hair hung in long waves and had just a few touches of blonde highlights that glittered whenever she was outside. Her green eyes were tipped with dark lashes and incredibly expressive. Justin loved to watch them widen whenever she told a funny or exciting story. She also talked with her hands. It was rare to hear words coming out of Bella's mouth without her hands waving around in front of her. Ned often warned her she'd take flight one of these days if she didn't stop flapping so hard. She'd always laugh, but never attempted to still her hands.

All of those things had been apparent about her right from the beginning. What Justin had only started to notice lately was her body.

They had a very loose dress code at work, so he seldom saw her in anything other than jeans, t-shirts and her standard ponytail at work. However, about a year ago, Ned had been knocked down with a killer case of the flu the morning of a big presentation. Bella had created the logo, so Justin asked her to help him make the bid. She'd shown up in a short skirt, silk blouse and sexy heels that nearly had him falling to his knees in front of her, ready to beg for mercy—or whatever else she was willing to give him. Her outfit had actually been perfectly professional, but it had taken Justin's dirty mind to places it had no business going.

The problem was, he and Ned had never revealed any details about their private affairs to Bella either. Instead, they'd sort of taken her under their wing like an adored kid sister, sheltering her from what small-town-girl Bella would likely consider extreme sexual practices. He suspected in her eyes, they were just her easygoing, laidback playboy bosses, kings of vanilla sex with lots of women.

If she knew the truth...

Well, Justin didn't want to consider what she'd think of that because it would tempt him. He'd been fantasizing about her too much lately as it was. Way too much. Then, six months ago, something else happened. Something that turned the tide for him for good. It was a stupid thing really, but it had burrowed in Justin's brain and driven him crazy ever since.

She'd come to Sunday dinner at his mother's house. Over the years, she had become a regular there, usually managing to make an appearance once a month. On that Sunday, Ned, Justin and his brothers—Caliph, Jett, Noah and Zac—had gone to the living room to watch football, while Bella remained in the dining room with his sister Chloe and Caliph's girlfriend, Jennifer. They'd all been sitting there, drinking wine, talking about girl stuff, but when Justin passed through to grab the next round of beers from the kitchen, he heard Bella talking about wanting children. The image of her pregnant flashed in his mind—and in that instant, Justin realized he was actually jealous of the future father. So jealous he couldn't see straight.

He'd never met a woman who made him consider marriage or babies. But since then, he'd grown more and more convinced Bella was meant to be his wife, the mother of his children.

However, Ned was determined that they keep their professional and personal lives separate, so Justin played along, despite how much that was starting to rub against the grain. At some point, he was going to have to come clean, going to have to tell his friend about his infatuation for Bella.

When the waitress headed back to the bar, Ned turned to Bella. "Why don't you describe your fantasy man to us? Maybe Justin and I know him. We could set you up."

Even as his friend spoke, Justin knew there were no men of his acquaintance he would consider good enough for Bella.

Justin grinned when she hesitated, spying a way to explore that complaint she'd made about her ex earlier. "Yeah, Bells. Give us every dirty detail."

Bella tilted her head. "Are you asking for personality traits or sexual positions?"

Justin gestured to Ned. "I suspect *he* means personality, but I don't think that will help you much. If this past lover bored you so much in bed, maybe we need to start with sex and work our way back from there."

Ned gave him a dirty look, obviously thinking he was crossing a line, but Justin ignored it. Mainly because there was a shortage of blood in his brain. His cock had decided it was time to join the party about an hour earlier. He was sporting one hell of a woody and it was damn uncomfortable. His jeans weren't exactly loose.

Bella shook her head. "I'm not about to feed your twisted fantasies, Justin."

Justin leaned closer to her, reaching across the table to grasp her wrist as she went for her beer. The tight grip halted her movement—and drove the most beautiful flush to her cheeks. She didn't try to release herself, though Justin's sudden hold had definitely confused her.

Actually, Justin didn't think it was the grip that confused her. It was her reaction to it. It made him wonder if she understood her needs at all.

"Tell us what you like in bed, Bella." Justin was usually the most affable man on the planet, and he only ever used this deep tone when they were playing at the club.

"Justin." Ned's voice was quiet, but the caution was apparent. They were Bella's bosses and she was their most valuable employee. Ned had just given Bella shit for starting an affair with her trainer, calling it unprofessional.

Jesus, the line Justin wanted to cross with her would blow that out of the water.

His grip on Bella's wrist was unrelenting. Her eyes narrowed briefly before she licked her lips. "I want what any girl wants. For a man to sweep me off my feet."

Justin knew plenty of women who didn't want that. Mistresses at the club who preferred men who licked their boots and bent over to please them. Of course, now that he thought about it, perhaps that *was* their equivalent of being swept off their feet. "Do you mean you like a man who takes charge of the date, picks you up, pays?"

She nodded.

"What else?"

For a moment, he didn't think she'd reply. Then she took a deep breath and told Justin exactly what he'd been waiting to hear. "I want a guy who isn't shy about taking what he wants in the bedroom without constantly asking permission—to kiss me, to take off my shirt, to touch me. It gets really tedious and throws me completely out of the moment. I swear, the last couple of guys I slept with were totally macho until we hit the mattress. Next thing I know, I'm lying next to passive puppy dogs, waiting for *me* to make all the moves. Did someone tell you guys in sex ed. that women want to take the lead all the time? That females are only attracted to men who just lie there?"

Justin chuckled. "I must have skipped school the day they taught that lesson."

Bella gave him a *sure you did* look. "Right. Of course. I'm pretty sure that's what all men think."

Ned groaned. Bella had thrown down a challenge, something Justin had never been able to resist, and his friend knew it.

Justin tightened his grip. "Do you need proof?"

For the first time, Bella sought to escape his hold. Justin hesitated for just a moment before common sense kicked in and he released her.

"Hell no." Her strong voice was betrayed by her eyes, which darted around the room, looking anywhere except at them.

Justin's lighthearted chuckle slowly returned things at the table to normal. Bella flashed him a look, pretending to be annoyed at his teasing. "Very funny." Her tone told him she wasn't angry, but the flush on her cheeks proved she was definitely feeling something else that was making her hot.

Ned sighed. Justin had managed to break the sexual tension.

For now.

Justin had been best friends with Ned since college. They'd shared a dorm room, then an apartment and, after graduation, the running of their marketing business. And more lovers than Justin could count. They'd stumbled upon the concept of a threesome during their freshmen year in college, when a senior girl set her sights on both of them at a frat party. She'd taken them upstairs to an empty bedroom and opened their eyes to a world neither of them had ever wanted to walk away from. While they occasionally took lovers separately, they preferred sharing women.

Secretly, Justin hoped it would always be that way, but he wasn't sure how to broach the subject with too-serious Ned. Despite his kinks in the bedroom, Ned tended to view the rest of the world through conservative eyes. He believed in professionalism and—Justin feared—traditional marriages, though they'd never discussed that.

They were thirty-seven, and his friend had recently started talking about his plans for the future. Like Justin, Ned's goals included finding a woman, settling down and starting a family. The only thing was, Justin didn't know where he fit into that equation, so he'd kept quiet about what—actually, *who*—he wanted to include in his future.

Awkwardness aside, Justin wasn't finished with this conversation. Now that they'd opened the door, he was ready to walk in. "You realize you've basically given us nothing to go on, Bells."

"Of course I have," she insisted.

Justin shook his head. "You want a guy to take charge in the bedroom. That could mean anything from taking the top in missionary style, to tying you to the bed and playing with you until you come twenty times."

Bella's eyes widened slightly. "Oh wow. Um...yeah...I think I'd like that second thing."

Despite how unwise this discussion was, there was something so refreshingly innocent about Bella that Justin found difficult to resist.

In the past, he'd enjoyed the company of experienced submissives, understanding Ned's need to control a woman. Justin usually went along for the ride because he possessed more than his fair share of dominance as well. It was a fun way to pass the evening, but there was no challenge with the lovers they'd chosen. There were no emotions either. It was purely physical. Lately, Justin felt unsatisfied at the end of an evening and he always left the club wanting more.

One glance at Ned revealed his friend was suddenly starting to notice what Justin had been seeing for months. Ned's gaze sharpened on Bella's expression. Justin could imagine what his friend was reading in her light blush and the way she kept licking her lips. It wouldn't take Ned long to recognize the truth.

Then Ned surprised him by entering the conversation. "Bondage is just one example of taking charge, Bella. The man could also order you to take off your clothes, and then punish you if you don't comply."

"Punish me?" Her question came out as a whisper that had Ned leaning closer as he responded.

"He would tug down your pants, pull you over his lap and spank you. Either with his hand or a belt."

Bella fell silent for just a moment before her feminist side found her voice again. "Hell would freeze over before I gave a man that much control."

Her assertion was powerful, but her body betrayed her. Her nipples were poking through her t-shirt and she shifted in her seat, pressing her legs together. Most men would have heard the words and taken them at face value, but Justin had learned a long time ago that the most interesting information was shared through a different sort of language.

Justin reached out despite his better judgment and ran a finger along her arm. "You should never say never, Bells."

Just like that, the tension returned. Justin's cock was erect, aching. It was time to rein things in or this was going to take a hard left down a street he feared neither Ned nor Bella had any intention of taking...at least not tonight. Justin intended to change their minds on that. Soon.

Bella must have recognized the danger. She pasted on a carefree smile that didn't fool any of them and reached for her purse. "Well, I'm tired. My bosses are slave drivers and I have a big project to work on tomorrow. I guess I should call it a night."

Justin watched something come to life in Ned's eyes.

"Slave drivers?" Ned's voice was deep, with a rough timbre that sent the subs at the club to their knees before he finished giving the command. "Is that what this feels like to you, Bella? We give the orders and you obey?"

"You're the bosses. Of course I do what you tell me."

Ned leaned closer. "I didn't tell you to work this weekend."

Bella's joke about working through the weekend had clearly revealed something that should have been obvious to both of them. Suddenly, everything Bella did at work took on a new meaning.

She was a diligent worker, always jumping to do whatever Ned or Justin asked. Usually, Bella moved quickly to please them. One of them might ask her to create a new logo or to enhance the color of a design and she'd immediately switch over to that project with no question or complaint about having other work to do.

Bella leaned away from Ned, a dangerous move. "I know, but I just thought you'd like it if I got a jump on—"

Ned reached out, grasping Bella's arm, halting her retreat. "We don't expect you to give up your weekends simply to please us."

Bella squirmed in her chair again. For a moment, Justin imagined he could feel the heat radiating from her body, could smell her arousal. Her breathing grew more rapid.

"I like to make you happy," she confessed, her words coming out no louder than a whisper.

Justin had tried to dismiss what seemed her submissive reactions as wishful thinking, but after listening to her tonight, he knew he was right. Her submissiveness was instinctual, though he was certain Bella didn't recognize or comprehend it. Hell, he hadn't even noticed it because she buried it deep beneath a powerful, indomitable spirit. She was spunky, opinionated and bold. He couldn't believe it had taken this many years for him to wake up and see the writing on the wall.

No doubt Bella viewed her actions as a strong work ethic. But to Justin, her natural responses to his demands felt heady, horny, heavenly.

However, there were still too many obstacles to overcome, too many barriers standing in their way. The main one was sitting across the table, suddenly shooting daggers at him. Apparently Ned wasn't happy about the knowledge he'd just acquired.

He would refuse to consider taking their relationship to the next level. And given the angry look on Ned's face, Justin suspected he was going to spend the next few hours enduring a lecture from his friend on just why they couldn't seduce their beautiful Bella.

Ned returned her smile. "You do make us happy. Don't work too hard this weekend, Bella."

She lifted one shoulder casually. "It's no big deal. It's not like I have anything else going on. I'll see you guys on Monday." She waved as they both said goodbye. Ned watched her walk completely out of the bar before he turned to glare at Justin.

"Forget it. Forget everything that happened at this table," Ned warned.

Justin didn't respond. Instead, he picked up his beer and

took a long swig. Finally, he leaned back in his chair and shook his head. "No. I don't think I will."

Ned rubbed his eyes wearily. "She's our best employee, Justin. I just finished telling her how unprofessional it was of her trainer to start an affair with her. That's child's play on the concept of unethical conduct compared to what you're thinking of doing."

"Not really."

Ned didn't respond immediately. Justin wondered briefly if his friend was planning to define a few words for him. Ned was one of the shrewdest, most intelligent men he'd ever met. He didn't speak without thinking. And his expression told Justin he was definitely plotting one hell of a response.

He briefly debated warning Ned to save his breath. After all, his friend should know by now that Justin never approached things from a normal point of view.

Ned often remarked that Justin's unconventional upbringing had left him with an eccentric view of how life should be lived. Justin always took that comment as a compliment, though he suspected Ned didn't intend it as such.

To state it baldly, Justin had been an accident. His mother had gotten pregnant with him during her senior year of college, after which, his sperm donor dad disappeared. For a few years, Mama had raised him on her own. Until she met and married his stepfather. Ralph Lewis, a former boxer, had been a giant of a man, gruff and uneducated, and he'd taken Justin in and raised him as his own.

His mother, a former social worker, had taken in countless foster children over the years. Justin had so many brothers and sisters, his mother had started putting up two Christmas trees each year because there weren't enough boughs on one tree to hang all the homemade ornaments.

Papa Lewis had worked on an oilrig, absent from the family

home for months at a time. He'd passed away from a massive heart attack several years earlier, and Justin missed him profoundly.

Ned sighed heavily, exhaustion rife in his voice. "Justin, I'm serious. Whatever it is you're thinking, you need to stop now. We're not seducing Bella."

"You're right."

Justin's quick agreement had clearly not set his friend's mind at ease when Ned asked, "I am?"

Justin nodded. "We're *not* seducing her. We're marrying her."

CHAPTER TWO

You're out of your mind." Ned paced around the office on Monday morning as Justin leaned back in his chair and propped his size-twelve tennis shoes up on the cluttered surface of his desk.

Ned wasn't sure how his partner could do his job in such chaos, preferring to work in his own neat, well-organized space down the hall. Justin's office always looked as if someone had just dropped a bomb on it.

"It's time to think outside the box, Ned. Stop looking at the world through conventional eyes and consider what I'm proposing."

"I've been thinking about it. All damn weekend. What you're proposing is crazy."

"Is it?" Justin gave him a long, steady, assessing stare that caused Ned to stop in his tracks and truly consider his friend's unorthodox suggestion once again. Justin had spent nearly two hours on Friday night laying out the mother of all life plans for Ned, insisting that the two of them would never be satisfied in traditional marriages, never be happy as "one man and one woman."

Ned didn't want to admit to the part of him that knew Justin was right. He'd taken women to his bed without Justin, but the experience always paled in comparison, left him almost bored. However, it was a far cry from the occasional night of threesome sex to a committed ménage relationship.

Even so, when Ned saw his future, imagined his life twenty years from now, Justin was there. He was a part of it. That was the thought that had played out in his mind pretty much nonstop all weekend. That and the realization that Bella was the perfect woman to complete the triad.

Ned didn't reply to Justin's question and the silence in the room continued for several minutes. Ned had thought of little else since Friday night when Justin first suggested his idea.

To his best friend's credit, Justin didn't fill the quiet with chatter or keep trying to persuade him. Instead, he let Ned put the pieces together for himself. And as more and more of them fell into place, Ned found himself longing for exactly what Justin was suggesting. The answer was completely out of the realm of normalcy, and yet it felt perfect.

Then he realized his opinion really didn't matter as reality laced with fear reared its ugly head. "Bella will never agree to it."

Justin clearly didn't agree. "Finish thinking it through. Stop looking at this from your perspective and try to see it from hers."

Ned dropped down into the chair across from Justin and considered the past six years. He'd convinced himself that Bella had captured his attention with her talent as a graphic artist and she'd earned his friendship because of her quick wit and straight-shooting, no-nonsense approach to life.

But now he realized it wasn't those things that had

captured and held his attention at all. The blinders had fallen away, opening him up to a weekend spent fantasizing too much about their pretty young artist. She was a submissive, and she'd been obeying him in very subtle, sexy ways for years. That idea had kept his cock hard for days. He'd jacked off more times than he could count since Friday—his dick was actually sore— and he'd slept precious little.

Justin's idea of claiming her, seducing her, trying to win her heart, had driven him nearly insane with lust and longing. Ned liked to consider himself a practical, reasonable man, but nothing about Bella felt rational. He'd been walking around since that damn happy hour like a man holding on to a live wire. He knew he should let go, but he was addicted to the shock, the current. He needed more.

Then he'd run into her this morning—literally—when he had stepped off the elevator. Her fresh, floral perfume and the slight pink hue that touched her cheeks had sent him from soft to erect in an instant. The way she lowered her eyes for just a split second—she'd obviously done a bit of fantasizing this weekend too—when he apologized for bumping into her made him long to touch her in extremely inappropriate ways.

Ned had never felt such a powerful lure to anyone before. Typically he was able to control the Dominant lurking beneath the surface, keeping the beast contained until nights when he could unleash him in the sex club...with true subs who longed for his commands.

But it wasn't simply his physical needs driving this over- whelming attraction. Bella was intelligent, determined to succeed and funny. Her sense of humor rivaled Justin's and the three of them had spent many late nights at work as she and Justin traded cutting, witty barbs.

Bella wasn't a doormat. She wasn't weak or easily controlled. While she may have submissive qualities, she wouldn't accept them. In fact, he suspected she'd wage quite a battle against them, which poked the beast even more.

For the first time since meeting her, Ned struggled to remember Bella's place in his life. She was an employee, a friend, not a sub or a lover. Friday night, Justin had turned on a light, blinding Ned and making it impossible for him to find the switch to turn it off.

"I'm amazed we didn't notice her submissiveness right from the start." Justin pulled his feet off the desk, leaning his elbows on the surface. "She was all but smacking us in the face with it."

Justin confessed he'd recognized what was lurking beneath the surface about six months earlier, but he'd dismissed it. Ned had to hand it to Justin. His friend had hidden his feelings well.

"She doesn't know she's a submissive."

Justin shrugged. "Maybe not, but it's still there. It would only take a Dom—or two—to expose her to all that she's missing. Not understanding something about yourself doesn't mean it's not who you are. You should know that. How many years did you struggle with your stronger sexual urges before you discovered BDSM, before you realized exactly what was missing for you in the bedroom?"

Too many years. Ned had been raised in a very conservative, religious home. As such, he'd never even heard of bondage or sadomasochism or Doms and subs until Justin found a sex club on the outskirts of the college campus during their senior year. While they'd indulged in countless threesomes prior to that, Ned had never realized how much more was out there. Justin had dragged Ned there one night and in three hot, eye-opening hours, Ned's entire life changed.

Justin was right. Not understanding his urges hadn't made him less Dominant. It had only confused and frustrated him. It was clear Bella was feeling the same way. After all, hadn't she confessed as much at happy hour? She knew something was missing, but she didn't know what.

"I'm not disagreeing with you about Bella's submissive nature. We both know it's there. And I'd love nothing more than to expose her to everything she's missing, but Justin, she works for us. We're her bosses."

Justin waved his hand, dismissing Ned's argument as unimportant. "That's a lame excuse and you know it."

"Not to her. Or to me. She uprooted herself and moved at least half a dozen states away from her family to work for us. She's worked overtime in her personal life to switch from the mentality of small-town girl to the frenzy of the French Quarter. She won't risk losing this job. Not easily anyway. And I don't want to put her in that position."

Ned stood again, his circuit back and forth across the room starting anew. Walking usually helped him think, but right now, his thoughts were a jumble—desire and common sense working in direct opposition of each other.

"We're not going to fire her, even if things do go south. Which they won't."

Ned closed his eyes and shook his head. Justin lived his life in a perpetual state of optimism. It was refreshing...and annoying as hell.

"Goddammit, Justin. There are a million ways what you're suggesting could fail. If we do decide to go through with this—"

"*When* we decide to go through with it," Justin interjected.

Ned released a long sigh. "If or when, I think we need to be able to answer all of Bella's concerns—logically, practically. We can't just look at her and say, 'We won't fire you.'"

Justin pulled a sheet of paper from the mountain of crap on his desk. Ned tried not to marvel over how easily his friend had put his hands on exactly what he was looking for. "Here."

Ned glanced at the paper, his eyes widening. "A contract? For sex? You're out of your fucking mind."

Justin was undaunted. "Just consider what it's saying. We'll ask Bella to give us one night to experiment. It's totally risk-free."

"I'm not giving her that goddamn piece of paper to sign. Besides, I thought you were thinking lifetime, not one-night stand."

Justin shrugged. "I'll admit I'm struggling with how to get this ball rolling. I think once we start, once she understands what we're offering and how perfectly the three of us fit together, she'll be all-in. But, like you said, that first step is tricky. Thought the contract would ease the burden."

Ned rolled his eyes, letting the expression answer the obvious. Bella wasn't the type of woman who would agree to sleep with someone—two someones—in such a businesslike, emotionless way. While she didn't have a problem with casual affairs, Ned knew her well enough to know she probably didn't sleep with someone on the first date. She was the type of woman who would want to get to know her potential lovers well before taking the leap.

Ned rubbed his brow, trying to ward off the coming headache. "You realize we're asking for too much. Even if she would consent to sleeping with the boss, we're not asking her to take just one, but both of us. Then, on top of that, we want her to bend to our will in the bedroom—and beyond. *And,* just when we've dropped those bombs, we add the *forever* caveat at the end. It's preposterous."

"I disagree. Besides, we're not going to walk out there to her cubicle and propose. That's a little too impulsive...even for me."

Ned had always chastised his friend for being impetuous, for failing to consider all the angles before jumping in with both feet. Of course, he also realized that was one of the reasons their friendship—and business—had flourished. They were polar opposites, but Justin's spontaneity and Ned's conservativeness seemed to blend in such a way that it could only be described as the sweet spot.

"Well, I'm glad to hear you've retained enough of your wits to make that call."

Justin chuckled. "It's not easy. My fucking cock has been rock hard since Friday night. Considered calling you to see if you wanted to hit the club to blow off some steam, but then I realized I didn't want to have sex with anyone except Bella."

Ned sympathized. The same had been true for him. "That doesn't change anything. We still have too many problems to overcome."

Justin's brows gathered. He was obviously deep in thought over their predicament.

Ned's mind was churning as well over the trouble they'd somehow borrowed without even asking for it. He took a strange comfort from Justin's expression, from his friend's determination. Justin had a stubborn streak a mile wide. When he saw something he wanted, Justin plowed forward.

Problem was, he rarely stopped to look left or right before barreling straight across the four-lane highway—and that was what concerned Ned the most.

"I'm not sure we have as many issues as you think."

Ned sighed heavily. "Bella's submissiveness is buried in a mountain of practicality. You don't really expect her to simply jump into something so extreme and unorthodox as a committed ménage, do you?"

Justin picked up a pen, tapping it rapidly on the surface of his desk. "Actually I do. Because I think she's experiencing the same conundrum as us."

"Meaning?"

"She's attracted to both of us and can't figure out a way to choose. We'd be taking that problem off the table."

Ned considered that, tried to reconcile Justin's assertion with past evidence. It was amazing how clear everything was now that his eyes were wide open. There had been countless tells in the past. The way Bella would touch each of them, nothing inappropriate, of course, but it wasn't unusual for her to reach out and lay her hand on theirs whenever they were laughing or worried about something.

And neither he nor Justin had been shy about returning those casual touches—offering a friendly hug whenever she got dumped or placing an arm around her shoulders whenever she created something truly amazing on the computer.

Then Ned spoke the one thing that concerned him the most. "I don't want to scare her, Justin. I don't want to freak her out so much that she goes away."

Justin rose slowly. Something in Ned's tone must have alerted Justin that he was weakening, that he was actually considering this idea. Ned was afraid he didn't have any choice. Now that he was aware of his feelings for Bella, he knew himself—and Justin—well enough to know nothing would stop them. Not pragmatism or common sense or even fear.

"We won't, Ned. We'll plan it out. Take it slow. This will work. I really believe that."

Justin's confidence went a long way toward soothing Ned's nerves. In fact, he felt a spark of hope emerging.

"It has to work, Justin, because failure isn't something I can even consider at this point. I want her too badly."

Justin released a short, almost sad snort. "Join the club."

CHAPTER THREE

"I need a favor, but I don't want you to judge me when I ask."

Justin looked up from his desk as Bella hovered in the doorway to his office. "I'm from New Orleans, Bells. I think it's safe to say I'm as jaded as they come. Nothing you say will shock or appall me."

Bella stepped into her boss's office and closed the door behind her. She'd decided to approach Justin with her question as opposed to Ned for the very reason he'd just stated. Justin rolled with the punches and took everything in stride. He was easy to talk to and really funny. There was something totally attractive about a man who could make a girl laugh. Plus, he'd said something last Friday night at happy hour that made her think he could definitely provide the information she needed.

While Ned was a really cool boss, he was definitely more serious than his party-guy business partner. Plus there were simply too many times Bella went tongue-tied around Ned. He was quieter, more mysterious and sometimes, when he looked at her, she felt the overwhelming urge to rip off all her clothes and kneel in front of him.

Which was equal parts disturbing and weird and...well...hot.

Whenever she was around Justin or Ned, her nipples tightened and her face flushed. It had actually been like that from the beginning and she'd worked hard to overcome her racy desires. She was proud of her efforts—or had been. Her attraction to the two of them had gotten worse over the past few months—or hell, maybe even the last year. She wasn't exactly sure when she'd lost control of this annoying schoolgirl crush on her bosses, but it was really starting to piss her off. She knew better.

She had thought she'd done a great job hiding her feelings. Bella actually prided herself on her poker face, but she feared she'd let it slip last Friday. As a result, she'd spent the past three days at work dodging Ned and Justin, while searching for some way to rein in her raging hormones. Unfortunately, they weren't going anywhere. If anything, her body was in a constant state of sex-starved need. It was becoming painful.

However, she needed their help and time had run out. Bella took a deep breath and plowed forward with her request. "My girlfriend, Missy, is coming to visit tomorrow. We went to high school together and I introduced her to Tim, the new guy from accounting. They've sort of made this online love connection so now she's traveling here for a face-to-face meeting."

"Wow. Someone else managed to break free from the hold of Carlisle, Pennsylvania? I didn't think anyone besides you ever *willingly* left that Mecca of the East Coast."

"Very funny. You know, you really should visit there before you make fun of it." Bella didn't bother to hide how enamored she was of her hometown, frequently declaring it one of the best places on earth. Maybe to people who'd been raised in the

Big Easy, like Ned and Justin, her little Podunk town looked boring by comparison, but she loved where she'd come from and she wasn't going to pretend otherwise.

Justin picked up a pen, tapping it on the desk in his usual way. "So Missy and Tim are checking each other to make sure neither of them is hooking up with a catfish. Cool. So what's the favor, Bells?"

Bella tried to ignore how gorgeous Justin looked in his royal blue polo shirt. It matched the color of his eyes almost perfectly. Of course, he'd look a hell of a lot hotter without it... and the jeans, now that she thought about it.

Stop it, you horny slut!

She glanced away quickly, afraid Justin would recognize the lust in her gaze. She really needed to find a way to get over these feelings. She had her dream job in the French Quarter and she didn't want to screw that up. Of course, that didn't stop her from indulging in some of the raciest fantasies ever dreamt up by a horny woman every single night. Justin would probably be amused—and Ned concerned about her professionalism—if he realized all the incredibly wicked things the three of them had done together in her dreams over the past year or so. Dreams that had only grown hotter since their conversation at happy hour last week.

"This is Missy's first trip to New Orleans and she's sort of, well, she was hoping, um..."

"Spit it out," Justin prodded.

"If things work out with Tim, she was hoping to go to a sex club with him." Bella felt flames licking her cheeks and could only imagine how red her face was.

Justin, true to form, simply grinned. "Damn. Didn't see that coming."

"Missy was always the wild one in school. There's nothing she wouldn't try. Apparently she and Tim have been sexting some pretty hot things and she's hoping they could explore some of that while she's here. Problem is, Tim only moved to the area about six months ago and he doesn't know of any sex clubs, and I sure as hell don't, so I thought maybe you…"

"You figured I was just the sexual deviant to help you out."

That was exactly what she'd thought. Especially after his talk of bondage. "I never said that. It's just that you grew up here. So…"

Justin stood, his expression proving he was enjoying this conversation and her discomfort a great deal. Reaching on top of the filing cabinet, he pulled down a box, rifling through a stack of business cards. "Here," he said, handing her one. "Extreme Connections. There's a big event happening this Saturday. Perfect timing for your friend's visit."

"An event? How do you know that?"

Justin took a step closer to her. "I'm a member."

"Oh." *Shit.* Any chance she had at reining in her overactive fantasies about Justin was officially blown out of the water. Not only would she be dreaming of him tying her to his bed, she was suddenly imagining him in black leather pants.

How freaking hot would that be? She resisted the urge to fan herself. After all, the AC kept the office a perfectly cool sixty-five degrees.

"So you'll all come Saturday night?"

Bella shook her head. "Oh no. Not me. I'm just going to send Missy with Tim."

Justin studied her face. "You have no interest in seeing the club?"

She started to shake her head again, but Justin raised his hand. "Bear in mind, you're a terrible liar, Bells."

She blew out a long sigh. "Fine. I'll admit I'm curious, but I think in this situation, three might be a crowd."

"You won't be the third wheel. Meet me there at nine. Tim

and Missy can go do the nasty in whatever kinky way strikes their fancy and I'll give you a tour of the place."

Bella's heart stuttered, skipped a beat as she considered his offer. "That would be..."

"Awkward."

The deep voice from the doorway distracted her and she turned around just in time to watch Ned come into the office. Bella glanced at his handsome face quickly before her eyes drifted lower. The response was instinctual, instantaneous, annoying. She'd never had trouble maintaining eye contact with Ned before he'd planted that damn seed about punishment, but now his overwhelming presence had her deferring to him in ways she couldn't control or understand.

Justin chuckled. "I feel confident the word she was looking for was 'awesome.'"

Ned sat in a chair in front of Justin's desk, stretching his legs out before him. Both men were tall and well built, with dark hair and slight southern drawls that made her panties melt. They were both about a decade older than her, each in their mid-thirties.

And to make matters worse for her libido, they had a casual dress code at Lewis and Kinnaman, which meant most everyone in the office worked in jeans, including them. As she studied Ned in his faded Levi's, she tried to decide if there was anything hotter than a sexy guy in blue jeans.

Justin and Ned had never made her feel too young, accepting her as a valuable employee at work and then including her in their Friday happy hours, offering her genuine friendship.

However, now, when she considered Justin's membership to a sex club, she realized exactly how inexperienced and small-town she must seem.

"Don't worry, Bella. I'll join you and Justin on your tour of the club. Keep things from becoming uncomfortable."

Ned actually thought taking a tour of a sex club with *both* of them would make things easier? Her pussy went wet just thinking about what they were proposing. How the hell was she supposed to walk around watching people engage in all sorts of provocative sex acts and manage to hide her attraction to not just one, but both of them?

"I'm not sure—"

Justin leaned on the desk. "It's a private club, Bells. The only way Tim and Missy can get in is if I put their names on the guest list."

"And you won't do that if I don't come?"

Justin winked. "Don't make it sound like blackmail."

She crossed her arms, hoping the action would conceal her suddenly taut nipples. "Why not? That's exactly what it is."

Justin's gaze traveled south and she realized she'd actually drawn attention to what she was trying to hide. "I know you. You're dying to see that club. I'm just helping to ease your conscience by taking the decision out of your hands. If you have no choice, you don't have to feel like a dirty girl for wanting to go."

Sometimes it sucked having observant bosses. While they never manipulated her, Ned and Justin seemed to understand what made her tick. She wasn't sure if she should be touched by how well they knew her or terrified by the fact they seemed to be able to see straight to the heart of her.

They had her back against the wall, which never failed to make her want to come out swinging. Even if they were giving her what she wanted. "Fine. I'll come along with Missy and Tim. But only for a quick tour. No touchy. No sucky. No fucky. At least for me. I'm just watching. You two can do whatever you want after I leave."

Justin walked toward her, placing his arm around her shoulders. "It's a sex club, Bells. No limits, no holds barred."

"But I don't want—"

Justin placed his finger on her lips. "Shhh. Bad liar, remember?"

She was tempted to open her lips and bite his finger. Or better yet, suck it into her mouth and show him exactly what she wanted to do to him.

Instead, she took a step away as he released her.

"Saturday at nine," she repeated, stupidly trying to fill the silence in a room that suddenly felt too sexually charged.

She backed toward the door and was almost home free when Ned said, "Oh, and Bella, wear something sexy."

CHAPTER FOUR

ed stood in the foyer of Extreme Connections and glanced at his watch again. "It's ten after nine. Think they chickened out?"

Justin shook his head. "I hope not. I've had a hard-on for three straight days, thinking about how tonight will play out. If Bella doesn't show up in the next half-hour, there's no way in hell I'm going to be able to keep myself from driving to her place and taking her there."

Ned agreed. "Yeah. I'm good with that plan."

Justin grinned at him. "It's about time you got onboard."

Ned shot his best friend a dirty look. "Bella's different, Justin. You know that. If we don't take things slowly and ease her into what we want, she'll be on the first plane to Pennsylvania two seconds after we issue our proposal."

Ned's feelings for Bella had turned from an employer/employee relationship he'd managed to maintain for six years to cock-burning lust about two minutes after Justin pointed out her submissiveness to him at happy hour. Since then, there was something about the way she looked at him with those innocent green eyes that had him aching for her. The fact that Justin felt exactly the same way only made those desires burn hotter.

Now that the game was about to change, the Dom Ned kept under wraps was unrestrained. He was finished waiting.

He glanced at Justin, noticing for the first time the special pains his friend had taken with his appearance tonight. He wore new black jeans and it looked like he'd gotten a haircut.

Justin was struggling to remain composed, but Ned could sense the same nervous energy radiating from his friend that he felt.

While the concept of a threesome was familiar territory for them, Bella didn't fit the same mold as the lovers who'd preceded her. Those other women came to them because they liked the idea of an illicit one-night affair and desired the forbidden pleasure to be found in indulging in a ménage for a single evening. No one had ever wanted more than the solo adventure, Justin and Ned included.

Tonight, they would have to proceed with caution and care. Neither of them would be satisfied with a one-night stand with Bella. When he looked at her, Ned saw a future. Justin saw the same. That added even more pressure to an already tenuous situation.

Bella had begun to provoke some deeper needs that Ned had managed to control for most of his adult life. However with her, he found it impossible to curb the Dom who sought to claim his sub permanently. BDSM had always been a part-time lifestyle for him, something he indulged in on weekends at the club. Suddenly he was envisioning Bella at work and at home, submitting to him, belonging to him.

And Justin.

They'd share her.

Ned could barely remember a time when Justin wasn't in his life. Now that they'd decided to take this incredible step toward grasping something unique, special, amazing, Ned was anxious to begin.

And Bella was late.

Justin sighed, then straightened. "Hey. There they are."

Ned glanced toward the door. His cock had been riding at half-mast all day in anticipation of tonight. As he watched Bella walk into the club in her shimmery blouse and mini-skirt, he gave up trying to hold back. He'd simply have to spend the rest of the night trying to walk around with a tent pole in his pants.

"You're late," Ned said, kicking himself when Bella gave him a guilty look.

"I'm sorry." She tugged at her skirt, clearly feeling conspicuous in her sexy attire. Ordinarily Bella was the queen of conservative, living in jeans and t-shirts that did little to accentuate her firm, full breasts and tiny waist. Once she was theirs, they were buying her a new wardrobe. One that showed off her assets. "We got lost."

Justin gave her an exasperated look. "You've lived here for six years, Bells." Bella's severely lacking sense of direction had been a source of entertainment for them ever since she'd moved to New Orleans.

"I know, but all these damn streets look the same to me." She turned to her friend. "Justin, Ned, I'd like you to meet my friend, Missy."

Given the way Missy was currently wrapped around Tim, Ned assumed the online love affair was translating very well to real life. He and Justin shook her hand in greeting and said hello to Tim.

Then Justin gestured behind him. "Should we start the tour?"

Missy and Tim followed eagerly, while Ned noticed Bella's reticence. He hung back with her. He and Justin agreed they would tag team at first, take turns approaching her, so as not to overwhelm her.

"Cold feet?"

She shrugged. "I guess. A little. Not sure exactly what to expect."

"Just stay close. If you have questions, ask. If you're uncomfortable, say the word and we'll move on." He grasped her hand, squeezing it for encouragement as they proceeded to the bar area. Ned felt it tremble slightly, so he tightened his grip and held on. Justin had started the tour with the most innocuous area of the club. Even so, Bella's eyes widened as she took in the scantily clad men and women seated at the tables and bumping and grinding on the dance floor.

Ned turned to look at her. "What do you know about sex clubs?"

She glanced around the room. "I know there's usually someone in charge and someone who follows orders."

He was amused by her layman's terms. "Dominant and submissive."

"Right." She let her gaze travel over his clothing, taking in the dark jeans and tight black t-shirt. "I think it's a safe bet that you and Justin fall into the 'Dominant' category."

He was pleased she didn't seem intimidated by that idea. "We like to be the boss—in and out of the bedroom."

She licked her lips when he mentioned 'bedroom,' the sexy gesture driving even more blood to his already too-thick cock. "You're good when it comes to taking charge."

He chuckled. "I suppose you've noticed that at work."

"So it's the same when you're here?"

He lifted one shoulder casually. "The same, yet very different."

Her eyes lowered, her voice softer when she spoke. "So

when you're with a woman, you prefer to have her on her knees? Calling you Master?"

Ned swallowed heavily. He'd never been in a serious, committed relationship with a submissive, never gone to that level with a woman, though he'd dreamed of it. He wasn't sure how to respond. God knew he didn't want to scare her off this early in the evening.

She glanced up at his silence, studying his face closely. Sometimes he got the sense Bella could see beneath the façade he showed others.

"I'm sorry," she said quickly. "That was an incredibly personal question. Forget it."

She was letting him off the hook. Was it because she didn't want to know the answer? Or because she already did?

If only she really knew what kind of control he hoped to wield over her.

"Where do you think you fall in this world? Dom or sub?" Ned knew the answer, but he wondered if Bella did.

She shrugged casually. "I don't think I'm either."

"I see."

"Like I said at happy hour, my past experiences have been pretty boring compared to what goes on here. Pretty straightforward sex."

"Vanilla."

"Yeah. Lame."

The sadness in her tone as she revealed more and more of herself shook him to the core. His determination to claim her pounded through his veins. "It's time for you to learn who you are in the bedroom, Bella. Here. Tonight."

Bella didn't accept his offer outright. Ned wasn't even sure she realized it *was* one. Instead she looked around the room, scrutinizing everything going on. "I think I'd like to see what goes on in a club like this. I sort of hate being…" She seemed to search for the word.

"Disappointed?" he asked.

"I was going to say bored with sex, but your word fits better. I've been thinking lately that maybe I'm the one to blame for my lackluster sex life."

He frowned. "What do you mean?"

"I keep blaming the guys, but it all boils down to something else. I'm the common denominator in all my affairs. I mean… what if I'm just really bad at sex?" She added a soft laugh to the end of her question, attempting to minimize it, to act as if it wasn't a genuine concern. Ned knew better.

He struggled for control, fought against the urge to push her against the nearest wall and prove to her exactly how wrong she was. "Perhaps it's time to put that misapprehension to rest."

Her eyes crinkled when she smiled, a mischievous gleam appearing as she glanced back toward the dance floor. "You might be right. Maybe it's time to try something a little wilder. And it certainly looks like there are plenty of available men around here willing to indulge me."

He was pleased by her sudden enthusiasm, not bothering to correct her false impression of how this evening would end. He'd kill any man besides Justin who tried to touch her. She was beautiful and she was going to be his.

"Then we'll work on expanding your horizons tonight. Why don't we start simple? Dominant. Submissive. I suspect you have a preference even if you don't realize what it is right now. Should we test it?"

She didn't reply at first. He could tell she was tempted, but Bella was his employee. The wheels in her brain were working overtime to figure out if she should answer such a personal question. No doubt she would consider opening up to her boss, telling him so many secrets about herself, foolish and dangerous. Plus her inexperience in this realm was becoming more and more apparent. It could make it difficult for her to accept just how wild and wicked he and Justin hoped to make her tonight.

And every night after.

"How can you test something like that?"

"Unbutton your blouse."

"What?"

With a dark look, he let her know her question displeased him. Ned had no intention of shielding her from exactly who he was. What he would expect from her. "I don't ask twice, Bella. Unbutton your blouse."

She stood motionless. He didn't pressure her to move faster. She needed time to process exactly what was going on, what was about to happen.

When her fingers began unfastening her buttons, he thought he'd died and gone to heaven.

Justin was standing near the bar, chatting casually with Missy and Tim, but Ned wasn't fooled for a minute. His partner was watching every single moment of this interlude with Bella.

Once she'd finished unfastening her blouse, she held the material shut in front of her and looked at him with flaming cheeks and heavy eyelids. She was embarrassed. And aroused.

"Open it. Let me see those pretty tits of yours."

She wanted to refuse, he could see it in her face.

He narrowed his eyes and shook his head, warning her not to say no.

She responded to the look, pulling her blouse apart, letting him look his fill at her lacy black bra and the way it showcased her beautiful breasts. He was going to spend hours tonight playing with those. "Perfect," he whispered.

She closed her eyes, seeming to recall she was standing in

the middle of a public place with her shirt open. She hastily pulled the silk together once more.

Ned reached over and fastened one button. Just one. In the middle. "Leave it like that."

"But—"

"Just like that, Bella."

Justin and the others approached them once more. "Should we venture on? It sounds like Missy and Tim would be interested in visiting the Whipping Post."

Unlike Bella, Missy was certainly not innocent. And Ned would bet a million dollars she wasn't the submissive in her relationship with Tim. Ned had little doubt which of Bella's friends would be feeling the end of a whip tonight and who would be administering the blows.

He also noticed that Bella winced at the name of the room. Good. Neither he nor Justin was into extreme pain. While they weren't averse to a spanking—Justin especially liked that act—whips and chains didn't interest them much. If Bella wanted it, they would give it to her, but he was glad to see they seemed to be well suited as far as that particular kink was concerned. It was just another clue that proved how perfect Bella was for them.

Ned suspected Justin would enjoy rubbing in that he was right about this for a very long time. However, Ned was too happy to care. His friend deserved the bragging rights.

He reclaimed her hand as Justin led the way deeper into the club. When they entered the room, Bella hesitated by the door. The scene being enacted on center stage was particularly powerful. A Dominatrix had her sub strapped to a St. Andrew's cross and she was using a bullwhip on him. His bare back was covered in lines, vivid red welts rising under the bright spotlights.

Bella froze. Ned wrapped a protective arm around her.

Justin, also noticing her unease, said something to Missy and Tim. Missy waved to Bella, walking farther into the room with her new beau.

"Do you and Missy need to plan a place to meet up later?" Ned asked.

Bella shook her head. "We already figured that out. She and Tim are going to take a cab back to his place when they're finished here, so I'll just drive myself home after the tour."

Ned was pleased to learn they had Bella all to themselves for the entire evening.

Justin joined them. "Your friends want to stay in this room. The Dominatrix onstage offers lessons after the performance. Missy was very interested in learning."

Bella shrugged. "I told you she was the wild one."

Ned studied her face. "I don't know about that. You didn't hesitate to unbutton your blouse for me."

"By the way, you owe me a peek." Justin gestured for her to open her shirt. Bella didn't resist, though her eyes were definitely troubled. While he and Justin had come here tonight with an agenda, poor Bella was blindsided. At some point, they'd have to fill her in on all of their intentions.

However, they agreed their unusual proposal might come easier after they'd shown her exactly why this relationship would work. Actions spoke louder than words.

They would teach her everything, open her eyes to a whole new world. While she may be innocent in the ways of BDSM, there was a streak of adventure and a healthy dose of courage inside her. After all, she'd left the security of her hometown to move half a country away to a new city—one known for sin—to accept their job offer.

She'd come to this sex club tonight with very little knowledge of what to expect. She was also beginning to respond more quickly to their commands, her movements telling Ned that while her mind may not be onboard just yet, her body longed for the pleasure he and Justin could introduce her to.

Justin tucked a finger under her chin. "Look at me, Bells."

She gazed up at him.

"You're gorgeous."

She smiled at the compliment. "So are you."

"Should we get out of this room?" Ned suggested.

Bella took one last look toward the stage. "I can't believe Missy actually finds this hot. It looks and sounds painful."

Justin refastened the same button on her shirt, then wrapped his arm around her shoulders. "Some pain is good. Maybe you'll let us show you that tonight."

"Us?" she murmured.

Ned shook his head covertly, so Justin didn't reply to her question. Just left it hovering in the air, unanswered.

She'd discover the truth soon enough.

CHAPTER FIVE

Justin led them to the Voyeurs room, anxious to get the evening started. Ned had warned him they needed to take things slowly, but proceeding with caution had never been Justin's style. When he saw something he wanted, he went for it. The restraint he'd shown the past six months as he'd tiptoed around his newfound attraction for Bella had taken a toll.

Now that they'd laid out a game plan and decided on a course, Justin was all systems go.

Ned was worried about Bella's conservative upbringing, her sexual inexperience and her need to obey society's strictures. Entering a Dominant/submissive ménage a trois with her bosses would certainly test every single one of those limits and then some.

Even so, Justin knew they could make this relationship work. And now that they were all here together, there was no way he could hold back his enthusiasm.

The Voyeurs room appeared to be more Bella's speed. It was a large, dark auditorium with tables and chairs scattered around a stage. Because it was so dimly lit, it encouraged people to not only enjoy the show, but to play in relative privacy as well.

Justin pulled out a chair for Bella, who thanked him as she sat. She was more subdued than usual. The two of them were both rather loud people, who loved to tell stories, drink a little too much and laugh often. Tonight she seemed to be struggling to find her sea legs. He could only imagine what she was thinking. He had to give her credit. For a small-town girl, she was holding her own in a hardcore New Orleans sex club.

Justin suspected she had no idea how lovely she was with her shirt only loosely held together by a single button, her long brown hair hanging down, wavy over her shoulders. He longed to press a kiss to her slim neck, then nibble his way down to her gorgeous tits. He'd only had a peek, but it was enough to make him long for a better view and hours to pay them the attention they deserved.

Instead, he resisted the impulse and claimed the chair to her left, while Ned took the one to her right. They both moved their seats closer to hers.

She looked at Justin, then Ned, acknowledging she was surrounded, caged in. "Okay. I give. What's going on?"

Justin took a strand of her hair in his hand, enjoying the soft texture of it, the sweet scent of strawberries assaulting his senses. The smell was so Bella. It reminded him of long summer days filled with sunshine and picnics. "We're playing, Bells. Getting into the spirit of the club. Going with the flow."

"I thought tonight was just going to be a tour."

Ned ran his finger along the top of Bella's open shirt, letting his finger slip lower, stroking her cleavage. "Consider it the grand tour, complete with demonstrations."

"Demonstrations?"

Justin playfully tugged on her hair. "We want it all, Bells."

She blinked rapidly, trying to digest what they were saying. Then practical Bella made it to shore. "We?"

"You, me, Ned. A bedroom. A few thousand sex acts—some of them illegal in various states."

Ned rolled his eyes at Justin's attempt to lighten the request, but Justin forged on. "You can't deny you want that too, can you?"

Bella didn't reply immediately. Instead, a crease formed in her brow as she contemplated his offer. In the end, common sense reigned supreme. "I'm not sure that's such a good idea. I'm pretty sure kinky threesome sex with your bosses ranks right up there as number one on the no-nos for workplace behavior."

Ned chuckled. "I'm sure it does. But we're not stopping."

She frowned at Ned's easy dismissal of her concern. "Do you two do this often?"

Justin understood the seriousness of her question, but he tried to make light of it. "Seduce employees?"

She bit her lower lip nervously and Justin cursed his wayward tongue. She was obviously terrified about losing her job and that concern was real. While he and Ned knew their intentions were good, in Bella's mind, she was risking her liveli-hood, her "dream job," as she called it.

"No, Bells. We don't seduce our employees. Ever." Justin wanted to stress that to her, didn't want her to think this was just a game they played.

"But you've shared women before?"

Justin wouldn't lie to convince her to stay with them. "We have. Quite often." However, while he and Ned had partici-pated in threesome sex, that wasn't all they wanted from Bella. "But it will be different with you."

She gave him a smirk. "Yeah, right. I bet you say that to all the girls."

Ned leaned forward. "No. We don't."

Bella swallowed heavily, clearly sorry. "I didn't mean to insinuate that you were playing me."

Ned didn't give way. "You weren't insinuating that at all. You said it very directly."

"You're right. I did. I'm sorry. You guys are kind of throwing me for a loop here. If this has something to do with me insulting you at the bar last week..."

Justin laughed. "You did throw down a challenge, Bells."

She narrowed her eyes, however, he continued speaking, "But that's not why we're here tonight."

They'd come here to capture Bella's heart, to convince her they wanted a shot at a lifetime with her. Her inexperience with threesomes and BDSM didn't change that fact at all. If anything, it made tonight even more special. They would be her firsts. Her only. Justin looked at Ned and knew his friend felt the same way. Ned gave him a subtle nod.

"What are you offering?"

Justin ran his finger along her cheek. "We want the chance to prove to you that not all guys are narcissistic bastards. We want to show you what it means to be the center of someone's universe."

She laughed, though Justin suspected it was forced. They'd knocked Bella for a loop and she was struggling to keep up. "So break it down for me. I'm full position?"

Justin rolled his eyes, shaking his head. "Really? You want to make this about marketing?"

She shrugged. "I'm way out of my element right now. You've gotta give me something I can understand."

Justin ran his hand through her hair. "Fine. Yeah. You're in prime position. The top dog of all ads. Our eyes are only on you."

"Why?" she asked.

Ned reached for Bella's hand. "Because we want you. Badly."

Justin leaned closer, pressing his lips against Bella's cheek. "And you want us. It's in your eyes every time you've looked at us this week. Let's explore that. Give ourselves the chance to indulge in every wicked fantasy the three of us have ever had."

Temptation was rife in her expression. "You might be surprised how many fantasies I've had about this. I'm not sure we could scratch the surface in one night."

Justin was thrilled by her bravery, her spunk. She'd been tossed off-balance by the newness of the club, their touches, their unusual request, but the real Bella was finally starting to reappear. "I like the sound of that. I don't see anything wrong with taking as much time as we need."

"Oh, no." Bella shook her head. "I shouldn't have said that. The truth is I'm not sure even one night is a good idea, but my brain sort of deserted me at the front door. I want what you're suggesting."

Justin's cock twitched, thickened. Christ. How would he be able to control his baser desires enough to be gentle with her? "I'm only going to ask this one time, Bells. Are you sure you want to do this? Because you have to understand, we don't take turns, hopping in and out of the bed. We'll both be there with you...the whole time. Mostly at the same time."

Her expression was clear of doubt, her eyes twinkling with excitement. "If you think that's going to scare me away, it's not. I've never been surer of anything. But no more than this one night. A whole evening of the wickedest fantasies the French Quarter has ever seen. Then tomorrow, we walk away. No strings attached."

"No." Ned started to argue, but Bella held her hand up to stop him.

"Please. Just give me tonight. And then it goes in the vault.

We take a vow of silence and come Monday, it'll be business as usual. Okay? It's the only way I'll agree to this."

Ned scowled and Justin found it difficult to lie. This wasn't going to end tonight.

Their silence must have drifted on too long because Bella started to stand. "Maybe I should leave. Go home now."

Damn woman had them over a barrel.

"Fine," Justin blurted. "One night. Every fantasy we can squeeze in. But we're reserving the right to try to change your mind."

She laughed. "You can try. But I won't."

Ned clearly wasn't happy with the bargain they'd struck. "I don't agree."

Bella glanced at Ned, confusion and surprise in her features. "I don't understand. I've never known either of you to embark on long-term affairs."

"You're not a stranger, Bella. You're our friend. We care about you. You deserve a hell of a lot more than a one-night stand."

Bella smiled. "Oh, Ned. That's really sweet. But you'll just have to trust me when I say I don't mind. I promise you this won't change anything between us."

Ned ran a frustrated hand through his hair and Justin held his breath, praying his friend didn't ruin things. Tonight would change everything, but now wasn't the time to discuss that.

Bella looked over her shoulder toward the exit, clearly intent on leaving. She wasn't going to give in.

"Fuck," Ned muttered. "Have it your way. Take off your panties."

Bella jerked at his command. "Ned—"

"You've only given us one night, Bella. I don't intend to waste a second of it. Take off your panties and hand them to me. Now."

Bella glanced around the room.

Justin cupped her cheek. "Look at us. Don't worry about anything except what we tell you to do."

She squirmed uneasily, but then she subtly reached beneath her short skirt, tugging her panties down. She used the table as a shield as much as possible. Justin had to fight to restrain a grin. They'd have her reserve broken before the night was over. There was nothing they'd allow her to hide from them.

She balled the material in her fist, then tried to hand it to Ned discreetly under the table. He took them, stroking the soft silk. "So wet, Bella."

"Is she?" Justin felt the same sense of urgency Ned was experiencing. If they had only one night to convince her to stay with them, then they didn't have a moment to waste.

Justin placed his hand on her knee, amused when she jumped slightly. "Nervous, Bells?"

She blew out a breath. "I'm struggling to keep up. I don't... I've never...this isn't really my scene."

Justin kissed her lightly on the cheek. "We'll take care of you. Though if you'd prefer to leave the club, we can go—"

"No!" She shook her head. "I want to stay here." She glanced around the room once more. "I like it."

Justin looked at Ned, her words further confirmation that Bella was made for them. She may be an innocent, but there were sexy kinks lingering beneath her soft skin. Justin couldn't wait to expose them, expand on them. "Do you know what a safe word is?"

"Yes. Missy mentioned it in the car on the way over here."

"Yours is Pennsylvania. If we do anything you don't like, just say that word and we'll stop. Talk things out. Okay?"

"Pennsylvania," she repeated. "I love it."

She was irrepressible, adorable.

"Open your legs. I want to see exactly how wet you are." Justin tugged on her knee as he issued the command, then felt Ned's hand on the other. Her thighs parted easily as her skirt inched higher. She tried to tug it down, but Ned caught her wrist, his voice deep, stern.

"Leave it."

"Ned," she whispered, uncertainty creeping in again. There was a difference between talking and doing. They'd test her limits tonight, push her completely out of her comfort zone.

Justin leaned closer, trying to set her mind at ease. Ned was always too intense, his need to control a woman coming out stronger, darker. While Justin didn't think Bella was balking, she was still a novice and probably not completely confident in her decision to pursue this adventure. "Trust us, Bells. We'll never hurt you."

Her expression cleared, showing him just how much faith she had in them. It twisted Justin's insides, made him warm, happy.

She touched his face gently. "I do trust you. Completely. I wouldn't be here otherwise."

Unable to resist any longer, Justin ran his hand along the inside of her leg. He sat close enough to hear her sharp intake of breath. The heat of her pussy hit him before his fingers reached their goal. Their girl was on fire.

Then he hit pay dirt. Bella's eyes closed as he stroked his finger along her slit. She was heat and moisture and sex incarnate.

Ned leaned closer. "Don't close your eyes, Bella. Look at what's happening on that stage."

Bella lifted her eyelids slowly and he watched her struggle to focus. Justin studied her face and realized when she recognized what was happening in the performance.

"She misbehaved," Ned whispered as Justin circled her clit.

Bella bit her lip so tightly, he worried she'd split the skin and draw blood.

Ned continued to talk about the show onstage. "Her teacher is angry with her. He's punishing her."

The actor onstage—the professor—had bent his naughty schoolgirl over his desk and taken out a ruler. The scene was an old, familiar one, but Justin could tell from Bella's responses it was speaking to some hidden desires. Did she like the idea of being punished by an authority figure?

She slid down on her chair—just a little, but enough—to allow Justin better access to her pussy. He didn't accept her invitation, determined to crank the heat even higher. While the silent actions of her body told him she wanted a stronger touch, he wouldn't give in until she was pleading, begging. He dragged his finger over her clit once more, making the touch lighter this time.

She groaned softly.

"We'll punish you the same way the next time you're late to work."

Bella's gaze jerked to Ned's face. No doubt she wanted to reiterate the time limit she'd placed on this encounter, but neither of them was in the mood to continue that pretense. Justin pressed on her clit again, distracting her before moving lower to circle the entrance to her pussy.

Bella's breathing became more labored. Between Justin's touches and Ned's dirty promises, she appeared to be losing her grip, relinquishing control of her inhibitions.

"We'll pull you into my office, bend you over the desk, lift your skirt and yank down your panties."

"I don't wear skirts to work," Bella whispered, though it was clear she was turned-on by Ned's story.

"You will from now on. We're changing the dress code for you."

She looked as if she would argue, so Justin went for more distraction, pressing the tip of his finger into her wet pussy.

She closed her eyes, her expression betraying how much she loved this. She gave herself up to the moment.

"I'll pull a ruler out of my desk drawer and Justin and I will take turns spanking you. I want to see that sexy ass of yours blush as prettily as your cheeks are right now."

Justin pressed his finger deeper, realizing Ned's fantasy wasn't just working against Bella. His cock was so stiff it hurt. The tight clench of her pussy didn't help. She felt like heaven.

Ned added more fuel to the fire building in her body. "Once we've finished punishing you, we'll take turns fucking you from behind. You're going to spend hours with our cocks inside you from now on, beauty."

"Just tonight."

Justin added another finger to her heat. She gasped, then spread her legs wider, every bit of reserve gone as she silently told him she wanted more. Her hips began thrusting toward him as she sought more stimulation.

Ned ran his hand through her hair, turning her to face him. "You're going to come on Justin's fingers, Bella. Right now."

Bella blinked rapidly and started to shake her head as she recalled where they were. "There are too many people around."

Ned's eyes darkened and his hand tightened in her hair. "You'll do exactly what I say. You've agreed to be ours for the night. Obeying our commands is part of that."

"What about what I want?"

Justin loved her feistiness. While Bella had definite submissive qualities, she wasn't weak. That was one of the reasons she was such a valuable employee. She wasn't a yes-man and she had no qualms telling them when they were wrong. She was bright, with a good eye for design, and she wasn't shy about expressing her opinions. It helped that she had the talent to back them up. Some of her marketing creations had been works of art.

Unfortunately, she didn't understand the boundary she was crossing with Ned. While Justin enjoyed the games associated with BDSM, he didn't take the roles as seriously as Ned. Justin liked issuing dirty demands, tying a woman up, taking her to the limit and beyond, but there was a difference between being dominant and being a Dominant.

For Ned, the need to be in charge ran much deeper. It wasn't role-playing for him. It was who he was.

"Careful, Bella-love," Ned warned. "We're indulging fantasies. Mine is that you'll be my submissive. That you'll do everything I ask. Without question or comment."

Bella's brow creased, but her pussy muscles contracted strongly around Justin's fingers at the thought. Oh yeah, she was more than willing to bend to their commands.

Justin realized as she shook her head that she was about to deny what she wanted. Her body betrayed her next words as an outright lie. "I didn't agree to that."

Ned smiled, his cocky expression unconcerned. He looked at Justin. "Her words say no, but I suspect her pussy is telling you the truth. Does she want it?"

Justin nodded. "Badly."

Ned tugged her head back slightly and again, Bella's body responded as more moisture flowed. "You're ours, Bella."

She struggled to argue, but Justin added a third finger, stretching her tight pussy as he ran his thumb over her clit. In the back of his mind, he tried to tell himself to slow down. Then Bella trembled when he thrust them deeper. She lifted her hips to meet him, to add even more power to the thrusts. "God, yes."

"You can't deny you love this," Justin murmured. "Your

pussy is burning my fingers, clamping down with every warning Ned issues. You want this, Bells. Admit it."

Justin didn't relax his motions, pushing her higher as Ned continued to hold her head still with tight fingers in her hair. Then Ned used his free hand to cup one of her breasts.

Bella tried to fight their hold, to resist their unrelenting demands. Justin could see it in the pained expression on her face. She was waging an inner battle—trying to maintain that good-girl façade, trying to hold on to that ideal that told her women didn't let men fondle them to orgasm in public, that succumbing to their commands would make her weak.

None of it was true, but a lifetime of ingrained beliefs was difficult to break. Bella was giving it a valiant effort, but in the end, primal, basic desires beat out years of suppressing what she really wanted.

Ned squeezed her breast, building the pressure as Justin stroked her clit faster.

"Come," Ned whispered.

She splintered in their arms, her climax causing her to jerk roughly. However, she managed to retain a slight grip on her control, remaining almost silent—except for one harsh exhalation of breath.

Justin resented that quietness. He wanted her cries, her screams.

Soon.

The next time she came, he'd make damn sure Bella released all the restraints. That she gave them everything.

Then they'd ask for more.

CHAPTER SIX

"Should we move this party to somewhere more private?" Ned suggested.

Bella knew they were members of this club. And given the way they'd just brought her to climax in a room full of people, she'd guess their experiences in this realm were vast.

Which made the fact they wanted her even more incredible, heady, exciting. Ned and Justin had come here tonight to seduce and share her. That idea terrified and thrilled her at the same time. While she'd never considered herself the type to submit to anyone, she was finding it incredibly difficult to resist.

Suddenly she understood that odd need she'd felt to kneel before Ned. Something about him right now made her want to obey, to give herself to him completely. To put herself in their very capable hands and claim every bit of pleasure she could ring from this night.

"Where should we go?" she asked.

"I've reserved a private room for us here in the club."

Justin's response confirmed her suspicions that everything happening had been premeditated.

"You knew we were going to do this?"

Justin shrugged. "Let's just say Ned and I were hopeful. And ready to be very persuasive if necessary."

She shivered as Justin slowly withdrew his fingers from her. There was a lot to be said for their powers of persuasion.

Ned rose, and then offered his hand. She took it, marveling at the strength and confidence in his grip. It occurred to her that if she were alone with Ned, her fears would most likely get the better of her. While his intensity was sexy as hell, it also scared her a bit. Having Justin there tempered the fear, broke some of the hardcore sexual tension and made her feel as if she were standing on steadier ground.

Yet another way her bosses made an amazing team.

They walked through several darkened corridors, leaving behind the thumping bass of the dance floor, the crack of whips and cries of pain and pleasure—each sound adding to the magic of this surreal night.

Finally they entered a less crowded, much quieter area. The hallway here was more ornate, losing some of the seedy look of the rooms they'd just left. For a moment, she could almost pretend they'd entered some five-star hotel.

Ned turned to look at her. "If you need sweet from us, if your expectations for a ménage are different than this, we can go somewhere else, give you what you—"

She cut him off. "I don't want sweet. Or soft. Or gentle. I just want you. Both of you."

She'd given herself one night to be with them. While she didn't doubt they'd restrain their darker natures to offer her the most magical night she could ask for, they would be holding back what they really wanted from her. And she would hate it.

Justin placed his hand on her lower back, forcing her to look at him. "Bells, I know you said only one night, but we could go for two. Take tonight to teach you about the beauty of making love with three. Then come back here next weekend to unleash all our freaky fantasies."

She was already tempting fate. Any more than tonight would spell disaster for her. Bella was struggling to keep a lock on her heart, to hold her feelings for these men at bay. Adding another night in their arms—especially a romantic one—would break her. Destroy her. Better to stick to the fantasies of the flesh, the kinkier the better. If kisses and soft words came into play, she was a goner. "No. Tonight only. Here. Wild and unrestrained. What did you say at the office, Justin? No holds barred?"

"As you wish." Ned led her to one of the doors, produced a key and unlocked it. Bella realized the hallway was as far as the resemblance to a fancy-schmancy hotel went.

She stepped into the bedroom, wondering what sort of wicked wonderland she'd entered. The room was beautifully adorned with rich colors and lit by dozens of candles. However, that was it for normalcy. In contrast, the furniture and decor looked like something out of a madman's dungeon as her gaze took in the St. Andrew's cross, various padded benches—God only knew what they were for—restraints on the four-poster bed, an open chest of sex toys, and wall full of whips, chains and ropes.

"Holy shit," she whispered.

Justin stroked her arm seductively. "Think we can cover the freaky fantasy basics with this?"

She closed her mouth when she realized it was hanging open. She was speechless and scared spitless and so turned-on, she wondered if simply walking across the room would provoke another orgasm.

"We'll start slow." Ned placed a comforting hand on her back and guided her farther into the room. She heard the door close and the lock flipped.

"Hey, Bells."

She found Justin studying her face, concern in his eyes. "You remember your safe word, right?"

"Pennsylvania."

He gave her a comforting grin. "Good girl."

"Feeling brave?" Ned asked.

She smiled. "I've made it this far, so I think it's safe to say I'm either the most courageous woman on Earth or certifiable."

"You're incredible. Never doubt that, Bella-love." Ned pressed on her back, guiding her to a stripper pole set up near the foot of the large bed. "Dance for us."

She blushed at the thought, not certain she'd have the nerve. Though she loved to dance and the idea of giving her handsome bosses a provocative show was definitely tempting. After all, she'd come to this room knowing they'd make some seriously tough requests. And truthfully, this didn't feel all that difficult. The idea of giving something back to Ned and Justin appealed to her a great deal.

Music began to play as Ned fiddled with an iPod on the nightstand. He adjusted the volume on a seductive song, then came back with two chairs. He and Justin sat down, observing her patiently, neither pushing. They would make their requests. Then the decision was in her hands. The safe word protected her, gave her an out.

She didn't need or want it.

She was reminded of Ned's fantasy and something sparked, came to life inside her. She *would* submit to them. Give them everything they requested. Because she wanted to. Desperately. More than she wanted her next breath.

Suddenly it wasn't a question of whether or not she should dance. That decision had been taken from her as she allowed her submissive side to escape.

Rather than upset her, it felt as if she'd truly been set free.

By relinquishing control of her own free will, she could explore and do and experience things she'd never have the courage to try on her own. Every fantasy she'd ever entertained was being brought to life by the two men who'd started out as her bosses, and then become her friends. Tonight, they'd add lovers to the list. Even if only briefly.

"As you dance, take off your blouse, bra and skirt. Leave the stockings and heels on."

She gave Ned a seductive grin as he issued his order, enjoying the glimmer of shock that entered his expression. Clearly he'd expected her to put up a fight, to resist.

No. No way. She'd come too far to turn back. Not that she would anyway. She'd dreamed of being with these men, separately and together. Whether this was the best decision or biggest mistake of her life was tomorrow's concern.

For now, she was going to live in the moment.

Bella reached up, gripping the bar above her head, then took a slow spin, letting the music soak into her soul, allowing her body to find the rhythm of the sexy beat.

She closed her eyes and acted on instinct, feeling her way through her first experience as a stripper. It was hotter than she would have imagined. Her skin burned and tingled and her clothing felt too constricting. She longed to bare herself to Ned and Justin.

Reaching up, she popped the button on her blouse, enjoying the collective intake of breath she heard from her audience of two.

Slowly she allowed the silky material to glide over her arms, the gentle brush of slickness against skin adding even more fuel to her own arousal. Then she stepped away from the pole and dropped the shirt over Ned's shoulder. His hungry gaze encouraged her to continue, to push the temperature even higher.

Returning to the pole, she straddled it, arching her back, moving her hips in time with the music several times, losing herself to the power of the movement, to the spellbound stares of her soon-to-be lovers.

Then she stood upright once more. Turning her back to her men, she unfastened her bra and let the straps slide down one at a time while holding the cups in place. Glancing over her shoulder, she gave them a teasing smile, thrilled by their rapt attention. She dropped the bra to the floor before reaching for the pole once more and spinning to face them.

Justin's groan warmed her, made her even more daring. Slipping the zipper on her skirt lower, she shimmied the tight material over her hips torturously slow, keeping her gaze on their faces. Inch by inch, she revealed herself to them, her pussy already naked thanks to the fact Ned had claimed her panties at the table.

Once the skirt hit the floor, she kicked it off then turned to face the pole. Bella bent forward, swaying her hips and giving them a bird's eye view of her ass.

She didn't have time to consider what her big ending would be when Ned's voice broke through the music.

"Come here."

His deep, commanding tone sent shivers of anticipation along her spine. Bella didn't hesitate. Once she stood directly in front of him, she stopped and awaited his next order. Her obedience wasn't lost on him as he slowly perused her body. Then he patted his thighs.

"Lap dance."

She giggled, loving the opportunity to finally get up close and personal. So far she hadn't had a chance to explore their bodies. Her fingers itched to touch Ned's skin, to stroke his muscles, to taste the light sheen of sweat she could see at his temple.

Bella opened her legs, straddling Ned's lap. His hands came to her waist, where he grasped her lightly for only a moment before tugging her down completely. She placed her hands on his shoulders, still gyrating in time with the music as he stroked her sides. His fingers were wreaking havoc on her system, making her long for so much more.

Her pussy ached to be filled when he lifted his hands and gripped her breasts in his large, firm palms. Nothing about Ned was gentle or easy. His rough touches, his stern, hungry expressions let her know he'd be denied nothing.

Not that he needed to worry. She sure as hell didn't intend to turn down a single thing he offered. He awakened wicked places inside her she didn't know existed.

"Open my pants, Bella."

Her fingers were at the fastening to his slacks before he'd finished speaking her name. She needed with a passion so overwhelming, so devastating, nothing short of slamming down on his cock would satisfy it.

Sliding the zipper down, she licked her lips as she uncovered her prize. Holy mother. Ned's dick was long. Thick. Her pussy clenched with eager expectation and the slightest bit of trepidation.

Oh yeah. This might actually hurt.

Ned seemed to read her concern. "We'll go slow, Bella."

Something shiny captured her attention and she turned to see Justin standing next to her. He handed her a condom. "Put it on him."

Justin's pants were open as well and she closed her eyes, fighting back a wave of lightheadedness. Justin was equally well endowed. What the hell had she signed on for?

She took the condom and slid it over Ned's erect flesh as Justin stroked himself. Personal space didn't seem to be a concern for either man, neither bristling at their oh-so-close proximity. She loved that there were no boundaries between them.

Ned clasped her hips, lifting her slightly until his cock nudged her wet slit. "You decide the pace. Determine how much you can take. Slide down. Nice and easy. Once you're all the way in, you're going to open that pretty mouth and suck Justin's cock while you ride mine."

She wondered what it said about her to be so turned-on by Ned's dirty demands. She'd told them she longed for a man to take charge in the bedroom. They were answering that plea. And then some.

Ned helped guide her descent, paying careful attention to her facial expressions and slight gasps when his thick dick stretched her. She suddenly understood the concept of being ruined for all other men. Despite the brief tinges of pain, this was the most beautiful moment of her life. Bella prayed for time to slow, needing tonight to last long enough that she could memorize every glorious second. She had no doubt she would relive this experience over and over.

The journey took time. Justin whispered beautiful compliments and stroked her hair. Then, finally, she was seated to the hilt. They all froze.

"Damn." Her voice broke on the last word, even as she fought to hide her feelings, but the moment was so perfect, she couldn't keep her emotions contained.

Ned cupped her face affectionately. After his stern looks and tone, the kind gesture was almost her undoing. If she wasn't careful, her crush on these men was going to blossom into full-blown love. Her heart couldn't take much more.

"You're amazing, Bella."

She hoped he couldn't see the tears forming in her eyes.

"Ready for more?"

She nodded eagerly, prompting Justin to grasp her hair in his hand. "Thank God. Come here, Bells."

He leaned forward and kissed her—the touch full of heat and passion. She rejoiced in its power and sheer hungry need. They weren't treating her with kid gloves. They knew what they wanted and they were claiming it. She was so glad it was she who provoked them to such desire. Bella broke the kiss first, stroking Justin's close-trimmed beard. She loved the texture of it.

"I think you promised me a ride," she said to Ned. Then she looked back at Justin. "And you owe me a taste."

She twisted slightly as Justin placed the head of his cock against her lips. Mere inches separated Ned and Justin. Again, she was taken aback by their genuine ease with this nearness.

"Open your mouth, Bella. Let me see you suck that cock in." Ned watched intently as Justin began to thrust into her mouth, shallowly at first, then driving deeper. She fought against the urge to gag when the mushroom-shaped head brushed her throat.

Ned's fingers tightened on her thighs. "Relax. Let him go deeper."

She struggled while Justin patiently continued to tempt her past what she thought she could handle.

Then, suddenly, she did it. Opened her throat and swallowed Justin deep.

"Fuck." Justin's fingers tightened in her hair, her scalp prickling as he used it to pull her closer. "So good, Bells. God. Perfect."

Justin found his pace, directing her as he fucked her mouth. She'd only adjusted to his motions when Ned's hands wrapped around her waist, lifting her off his cock slightly.

After several awkward attempts, they found their rhythm

as Bella bounced on Ned's dick while Justin thrust into her mouth.

Too many sensations raked over her as she was inundated by pleasure laced with slight twinges of pain. Ned stretched her pussy deliciously as Justin tugged her hair. The dual sensations sent shards of electricity straight to all her erogenous zones. They were taking over her body, making demands she had no choice but surrender to.

After a lifetime of mediocre, so-so, meaningless affairs, Bella felt adored, cherished.

Powerful.

Justin's and Ned's actions told her they needed her every bit as much as she needed them. It was an intoxicating realization.

Justin was the first to fall, jets of come splashing against the back of her throat. Bella swallowed deeply.

As Justin withdrew from her mouth, Ned was there. Ready for more.

Apparently he had been holding back. His hands tightened as he lifted and dropped her more roughly on his cock, each entry touching places that had never known the stroke of a man. Bella dug her nails into the muscles of his shoulders, resentful of the shirt that still covered him as her orgasm started.

Before she could give herself over to it fully, Justin stepped behind her, cupping her ass. He added his strength to the fucking, using his grip to pound her faster on Ned's cock.

She screamed as the impact of her climax magnified, morphed, grew. When Justin pressed a fingertip into her anus, she was well and truly lost. Her body writhed, out of control as wave after wave of pleasure flowed through her.

It was only as Justin lifted her limp frame from Ned's lap that she realized her other lover had come as well. She had been so overwhelmed by her own orgasm, she'd lost track of her surroundings.

Justin carried her to the bed and gently laid her down on the soft duvet as Ned followed, grabbing a washcloth from a bowl of water on a nearby dresser. Together they gently cleaned her body, wiping away any remaining traces of their lovemaking, while carefully massaging away any lingering pain.

Bella closed her eyes, touched by their kindness, their care. So much for holding on to her heart.

She was falling fast.

This night was going to end far too quickly.

CHAPTER SEVEN

Justin watched Bella's breathing soften as she fell into a light sleep. They would give her a few minutes to rest and recover. Then they'd rouse her, even though Justin suspected she could sleep the remainder of the night if they allowed it.

They couldn't. She'd insisted on the time limit. They needed to take advantage of every second. Needed to use each moment to wrap her tighter to them, tie her up with lust in the hopes that binding would keep her close enough to eventually let them capture her heart as well.

Ned lay down next to her, facing her, resting his hand on one of Bella's breasts. Justin followed suit, understanding his friend's inability to resist touching her.

"Well?" Justin whispered.

"Don't you think it's a bit soon to try to claim the *I told you so*? After all, we haven't succeeded in our goal yet."

"We will." Justin wouldn't rest until Bella belonged to them completely—sexually, emotionally, even legally, once they figured out those logistics. While he lusted after her body, he felt an even bigger pull to her smiles, her intelligence and creativity, her beautiful spirit. His life was a brighter place with her in it. The love he saw reflected in Ned's eyes as he gazed at their sleeping beauty told him it was the same for his friend.

"She was remarkable." Ned's tone mirrored exactly how Justin felt. Seeing her dance and watching her respond to their touches had stirred more than his cock. She was made for them.

Ned glanced at the clock on the bedside table. "Time is slipping away from us."

Justin understood the urgency. "Wake her up."

Ned bent forward, kissing Bella softly. It occurred to Justin they hadn't spent much of the night paying homage to her lips. They'd have to make up for that. Bella was made for kisses. Lots of them.

She stirred slowly, her lips moving to meld with Ned's before her eyelids lifted.

"Sorry, Bells," Justin said. "But you've put us on a clock that's ticking too fast. We haven't scratched the surface of our fantasies yet."

"I can't imagine anything more incredible than what we've already done."

Ned shook his head. "Then I'm disappointed. You're one of the most creative artists I've ever met. Surely you can think of something wilder. More wicked." His face softened. "Are you tired?"

She shrugged lightly. "A little. Not enough to stop. Justin's right. We need to take advantage of the few hours we have left."

Ned scowled at her stubbornness, but he didn't call her out or try to correct her misapprehension. She'd find out soon enough that things weren't going to end at dawn. There would be no locking this night—or their future—in some damn vault.

Ned gestured to the room. "Look around, Bella. Point to a

piece of furniture and let us draw you a picture of how much more there really is. With our hands."

Justin kissed her shoulder. "And our mouths."

Ned grasped Bella's hand and guided it lower. "And our cocks."

Her eyes widened. "Already?"

Justin wrapped her free hand around his thick erection as well. "You inspire us."

Bella pressed her legs together, prompting Justin to push between them to drag his finger along her slit. Sure enough, she was wet and warm.

"I see you're ready for more, too," he teased.

Ned pulled her to a seated position on the bed.

"Point to something, Bella."

She studied all the sex furnishings, her gaze sliding around the room slowly.

Justin expected her to ask what some of the pieces were for. After all, she was a novice when it came to BDSM games. Surely she would struggle to figure out the purpose of some of the benches.

Or maybe not.

Justin's cock nearly doubled in size when she pointed to the spanking bench. Goddammit. She'd landed on his favorite. How many times had he dreamed of tying Bella facedown over a bench just like this, spanking her until she begged him to fuck her? Taking her pussy, her ass.

"You know the purpose of that bench?" Justin wanted to make sure she understood exactly what she was asking for.

"You'll spank me. Like Ned said in the Voyeurs room."

Justin hadn't just imagined it. She really *did* like the idea of being punished. He stood rapidly, unable to resist making her fantasy a reality. "Good pick."

He tugged her from the bed as she giggled at his haste. Ned

shook his head at Justin's impatience, but shadowed them across the room.

She followed Justin's lead as he guided her into position and secured the restraints. She offered no resistance. Simply let him put her where he wanted.

Then Justin stepped back to admire his work. The sight of Bella bent over the bench, her wrists chained to the front legs while her ankles were fastened spread eagle to the back legs was almost more than he could stand. She still wore her stockings, though he'd encouraged her to toe off her heels.

There wasn't a doubt in Justin's mind that a slight breeze could set him off and make him come at this point. He'd wanted this fantasy for too long.

Bella's firm, bare ass taunted him. Unable to resist, he laid his palm against it sharply. She gasped and her flesh turned pink. The color prompted a need for more. Justin continued to spank her, changing the rhythm, the pace and placement, so Bella would never know when or where to expect it. For several minutes, he worked her over until her ass glowed red.

Bella didn't cry, didn't ask him to stop. She never uttered her safe word, though part of Justin kept waiting to hear it. She'd asked them to give it all to her. They'd offered sweet and she'd refused. Her honesty and courage deserved the same. He would give her all of himself, without holding back. He'd started the night unwilling to lie, and apart from allowing her to believe this was a one-night stand, he'd managed to remain true to that goal.

Soon Bella panted, begging him to fuck her, the juices of her arousal gleaming on her inner thighs. While the idea of whips and chains frightened her, she certainly didn't have a problem with his hand spanking her ass. Thank God.

Through it all, Ned had been a quiet observer, allowing Justin the space and time to indulge his favorite kink.

"Please," Bella cried. "Fuck me. I need you."

Ned ran his hand along her cheek, forcing her to face him. "That's right, Bella. Beg us. Demand. Plead. Let Justin hear how much you need him."

"Ned. Justin." Her voice broke on their names, the tone telling him she still needed them, that they'd left some desires unsatisfied.

Justin didn't give in. "Not yet."

"Dammit!" she cried, prompting Justin to place another slap on her ass.

Then Ned pulled something from his pocket. Justin grinned as his friend put the blindfold over Bella's beautiful green eyes.

"There's something deeply erotic about losing one or more of your senses," Ned whispered. "You won't know which of us is touching you or what's coming next. We can do anything to you and you won't be able to anticipate it, to steel yourself for it or prepare."

Bella shivered at Ned's dark taunt, but Justin knew her body's responses well enough to know it wasn't fear driving the reaction. She loved being bound, blind, at their mercy. As they uncovered more and more of her layers, it was becoming obvious her desires were as kinky as theirs.

Justin was pleased with Ned's game. He lightly stroked Bella's ass as she jerked in surprise at the unexpectedly soft touch.

Ned joined him, each of them taking turns touching various parts of her body. Justin pinched her left nipple as Ned lightly bit her earlobe. Justin tickled the bottom of her foot as Ned wiggled his finger around her anus. Every stroke and caress fed her arousal, her pleas growing louder, more vehement. For nearly thirty minutes, they played, explored, tested her limits for pain. Found her hot spots.

Bella shook her head when they continued to tease, refusing to give her what she needed most. "No more. Please let me come. I can't take it anymore."

Justin nuzzled his nose against her cheek. "No, Bells. You're ours. That means we control your body. And your orgasms. You're not going to come without permission."

Ned crossed the room, studying the array of toys available before coming back with a vibrator. "And just so you know. We're going to put your self-control to the test."

He punctuated that threat by pressing just a bit of the vibrator into her pussy.

Bella tensed when she felt it. "Oh my God. Please. Don't. I won't be able to stop myself. I'm too close."

Ned froze, the toy only lodged a couple inches deep. "You will stop yourself or we'll tie you to the bed and torment you to the edge of climax all night. Do you understand? We'll play with you for hours, but never let you come."

"Please, Ned! It hurts!"

Justin clasped her cheeks in his hands and lifted her face, tugging the blindfold from her eyes. "Try, Bells. For us."

He kissed her, pressing his tongue into her mouth as Ned pushed the vibrator all the way into her pussy. Justin heard the soft vibrations as Ned switched the toy on. Bella went rigid as she fought to restrain her climax. She hadn't lied. She was so close. Justin could only imagine how difficult her battle to contain her orgasm was.

He was struggling himself, forcing himself to remain apart when every fiber of his being was telling him to pull that vibrator out and replace it with his dick. He still hadn't fucked her yet. She wasn't the only one in agony.

"Five minutes," Justin whispered. "Resist it for five minutes, and then we'll let you come for hours on end if you want."

She closed her eyes tightly and the tear that slid along her face was nearly Justin's undoing.

He knew why Ned had started this game. Knew Ned wanted to see how deep her submission ran. How far they could push her.

Justin tried to distract her with kisses and encouraging words, while Ned pushed every sexual hot button he could find, making Bella work overtime to obey.

Finally, the five minutes were up.

"Come, Bella," Ned said, as he turned the vibrator to high.

Bella screamed as she came, her back arching as much as the restraints would allow.

Justin stared at her in amazement, wondering if he'd ever seen anyone come so beautifully undone.

Before she fully recovered, he gave in to his own overpowering needs, slipping on a condom, tossing the vibrator aside, then shoving into her pussy in one deep thrust.

The movement triggered another orgasm in Bella. Justin bit the inside of his mouth, hoping the pain would allow him to control his own desire to come. He thrust again. Just once. Bella's pussy contracted on his cock so tightly, he knew his struggles were pointless.

Fuck it. He'd waited too long to get into her body. This was only the first time. Not the last. He'd have years to perfect his act, to stretch out the time between penetration and completion.

This time, he wasn't going to fight it.

Justin pumped inside her roughly as the bench and the restraints held her in place for his hard fucking.

Bella came once more and Justin followed her, gripping her hips as his dick exploded, filling the condom with come.

Bella shuddered when he pulled out, and then groaned, her arousal reignited when Ned took his place, pounding inside her and drawing orgasm after orgasm out of their lovely girl.

Justin released her from the bindings shortly after she and Ned came together in one last explosion. Then he carried her to the bed, crawling in next to her and embracing her. She was asleep before her head hit the pillow, the sweet scent of her hair soaking into his senses, lulling him into a peaceful slumber as well.

She was softness, sunshine, sin and sex all rolled into one.

A man could get used to this.

CHAPTER EIGHT

"Bella?"

Ned whispered her name, trying to push down his guilt at disturbing her again. Worn out from their earlier adventures, she was in a very deep sleep.

Justin stirred when Ned repeated her name. He glanced at the clock. "Three a.m.?"

"She's indulged our desires, obeying my commands, submitting to you on the spanking bench. Now I think it's time we find out exactly what it is she wants from us. I get the sense she's not being completely honest about her own fantasies."

Justin rose slowly onto his elbow. "I have to admit I'm curious to know myself. She blushes every time she admits to dreaming about us."

"Knowing Bella, it won't be tame. I had no idea just how strong her wild streak ran." Ned stroked a soft hand over her stomach but Bella didn't respond. "She actually told me in the bar earlier that she thought she wasn't good at sex."

"You're kidding? How could she think that? She's amazing." Justin drew his fingers through the light smattering of hair over her pussy. Again, nothing.

Ned narrowed his eyes at her lack of response. She was sound asleep. Even so... "I wonder." He leaned closer, adopting a deep, stern voice. "Bella. Wake up. Justin and I want you. Now."

Her eyes opened as she blinked rapidly, looking around the dim room. Ned's chest constricted at her quick response. Bella's submissiveness drove more blood to his already thick erection.

"Is it morning?" she asked.

Justin shook his head. "Nearly. We have time for one more fantasy. Yours."

She swallowed heavily, looking at them nervously. "Mine?"

Ned frowned. What the hell did she want? And did she seriously think there was anything they would deny her? "Yes. Yours."

"You've already given me more than I've ever dreamed."

Justin picked up on her reticence as well. "You said you've imagined us together. Tell us how, Bells?"

She licked her lips, betraying her anxiety. "Just like tonight."

Justin narrowed his eyes. "Don't lie to us. You're not good at it. Tell us what you want."

Ned was surprised by the vehemence in Justin's tone. His best friend was a difficult man to anger. Obviously Justin didn't like the idea that Bella—who'd given herself so freely to them all night—was suddenly holding something back.

She glanced at Ned, though if she was expecting him to save her, she was destined for disappointment. "I suspect your ass is still sore from your earlier spanking. However, if you're looking for more punishment, I'm happy to oblige." His words were a bluff, but they did the trick.

"Okay. Fine. But I'm just asking a hypothetical question. I'm not expecting anything from you."

She'd sparked Ned's curiosity. "Tell us what you want."

"I couldn't help but notice all night that the two of you don't seem to mind being close. Physically, I mean."

She was right. They weren't squeamish about personal space. Her comment opened a door, so Ned stepped through, hoping his response would help her understand what they wanted. And why it would work. "I don't have a problem with Justin being naked and in the same bed as me. As long as there's a beautiful woman between us. We're best friends, Bella. We share. Everything."

His ready answer seemed to surprise her. "Have you ever fucked a woman at the same time?"

"Yes," Justin whispered.

She considered that for a few minutes. "So, you'll take me that way too?"

Ned closed his eyes, praying for the strength to give her the right answer. Blazing desires aside, he and Justin needed to act with prudence. "Bella. What you're asking for is..."

His words drifted away as he struggled to explain. It was intense, hardcore, and potentially painful, despite how much they might try to prepare her for it.

"Ned. In my fantasy," she said, her voice so low, Ned had to lean forward to hear her, "I want a true ménage. I want both of you inside me."

"Have you ever had anal sex, Bella?" Ned asked.

She shook her head, proving what he already suspected. "I've never trusted anyone enough to take me that way."

She simply wasn't physically ready for what she asked for. And it fell to them to protect her.

Ned moved between her legs, lifting them until her ankles rested flat on the mattress by her hips. Her knees dangled outward, leaving her wide open for his perusal. "So I take it you liked Justin's finger here." He reached down to stroke his fingertip along her anus.

She gasped when he pressed in to the second knuckle. He wouldn't venture farther—not without lube—but he wanted her to feel the pinch, to recognize the pain that would be associated with this act when they filled her ass. To add another cock to her pussy would be more than she was capable of. Which was why they had been stupid to agree to one night. Some fantasies took time. More than they had if they couldn't convince her to allow this affair to continue.

Ned felt a spark of electricity zip along his spine at the thought of claiming her the way she requested. He wanted it. Badly. But it simply wasn't happening tonight.

However, there was one last portal to breach. He wiggled his finger.

"Do you want us to fuck you here? To steal this little piece of virginity and stretch out this pretty ass? Make you ours in every way possible?"

Her eyes drifted closed, but if she thought to shield her desire, her need for what Ned was offering, she failed.

Justin reached over and gripped her breast firmly, squeezing and pinching the nipple until she began to squirm. Her reaction to pleasure-pain was magic. They had put her through her paces and she'd merely become more aroused in response. She was the perfect complement to them.

"We can't give you what you want, Bella."

Her eyes opened, landing on Ned's face. "You said you would."

He pressed his finger deeper, the dryness making it a rough entry. She winced. "We'll fuck your ass, but nothing more. What you want takes time, preparation. Give us another night."

"Or better yet, give us forever. Fuck this pretense, Bells." Justin's patience had clearly been stretched to the hilt. The band had broken and the walls were tumbling down on all of them.

"Forever?" She laughed nervously. "That's a hell of a jump. From one-night stand to forever?"

Justin didn't laugh, didn't bother to pretend he'd misspoken his true desires.

Bella's brow creased as realization dawned. She shook her head. "What you're asking for is impossible."

Ned had believed the same thing, but he didn't feel that way anymore. "No. It's not."

"I need my job. Tonight has probably already put that at risk. We have to stop now before this goes too far. Before one of us gets hurt."

The pain in her eyes told him that hurting was already inevitable. His gaze no doubt reflected the same agony. If she continued to fight them, to refuse to give this relationship a chance, then all of them would pay the price.

"Get me the lube, Justin."

Her eyes widened as she looked at Ned. "So you'll give me my fantasy? *Just* the fantasy?"

He shook his head. "No. I wouldn't hurt you that way for all the money in the world. But this night isn't over yet. There are still a couple hours until dawn. Until then, I intend to show you exactly why this will work. Why we're fucking perfect for each other."

A sad laugh escaped. "Perfect fucking doesn't translate to forever."

Ned scowled. "That's not what I said."

"We're more than that, Bells," Justin insisted. "And you know it."

Ned took the lube Justin handed to him, uncapping the

bottle and squirting a healthy dollop into her ass. She squirmed.

"Cold?" Ned asked.

She nodded.

"Then let's heat it up." He pressed one of his fingers in to the hilt, not bothering to go slow. She'd pushed him to the edge of a cliff. Left him straining to regain his balance. His control.

Bella closed her eyes briefly.

"No. Open them, Bella-love. Watch. See what you do to me."

Her gaze connected with his as he worked another finger in next to the first. Her breathing began to come faster, harder, as he unleashed the Dom who longed to claim his sub. With each thrust, with the addition of a third finger, she adjusted, accepted, yielded to his will.

Once her ass was stretched, he looked at Justin. "She's ready for you."

Justin's tight expression told him he was barely holding on to his own overwrought emotions. The night was running out and still Bella fought them, denied them.

Justin tugged on a condom, taking Ned's place between her legs as Ned stretched out next to her on the mattress.

When Justin lifted her ankles to his shoulders and placed his cock at her tight opening, Ned was there, his lips upon her breast, sucking her tight nipple in. Hard. Hungry. He reached down to stroke his cock, feeling the intense desire to mark Bella with his come.

Justin gave up his own shackles, thrusting into Bella's virgin ass with one slow, steady slide, taking his time as he buried himself deep.

Bella screamed when he was seated to the hilt, her cry a perfect blend of pain and bliss. Justin paused for only a second before finding his rhythm, his pace. In typical fashion, their

Bella was a quick study. Soon she was lifting her hips to welcome Justin's return to her body. Her fingers tugged tightly at Ned's hair as she held his head to her breast.

"Harder," she demanded. "God, give me more. Give me all of it."

Ned tightened the suction on her nipple as Justin drove into her body more roughly. Ned released her breast, rising on his knees to watch. With one hand, he tugged on his cock. Then he reached lower to stroke her clit with a firm touch.

She exploded, splintered. Flew apart.

Ned observed that exact moment when she lost herself in the sensations. He'd never seen a more beautiful sight. Then he tightened his grip and gave in to his own climax, jet after jet of come painting her stomach and breasts.

Justin followed them quickly, his body jerking. When he pulled out, he fell to Bella's side gasping for breath, covered in a light sheen of sweat.

"Stay with us, Bella," Ned whispered as he wrapped her in his embrace.

He felt her shake her head against his shoulder. "I can't."

"Why not?" Justin asked. "Tonight should have shown you exactly how good this is. It works."

"For now, Justin. But what happens when the newness, the novelty wears off? A threesome is a fun fantasy, but it's hardly something you see in reality. I told you both before we started. It can only be one night. Any more than that and…"

Her words drifted away but Ned could fill in the blanks. He saw the emotions warring on her face. She was fighting with everything she had to keep this casual. But Bella wasn't made for detached flings. In her mind, she clearly thought she could handle one night, could keep the deeper feelings away. Maybe she genuinely believed that.

Ned knew she was wrong.

CHAPTER NINE

Bella glanced through the peephole in her apartment door and groaned. She'd snuck out of the sex club shortly before dawn, neither man waking as she quietly dressed and then got the hell out of Dodge.

She'd managed to take a very long hot shower and a half-hour catnap on the couch, but it looked as though time had run out. She hadn't expected either man to take her escape well, but she had needed some space and a few minutes to sort herself out. It would have been far too easy to stay in that bed, to wake up with Ned and Justin and let them convince her to keep going. That would have been wrong.

With some distance, she could see now just how much she had put at risk last night. She'd been a fool to start. So it was time to stiffen her backbone and think with her brain, not her hormones.

She'd fallen into the submissive role, letting them take the lead because it had felt so incredible to live out the fantasy, but she wasn't that person in real life. She was *this* person. The woman cowering behind a locked door.

Ugh.

She threw back the deadbolt and opened the door.

Justin gave her a smile that was too fucking charming for her sanity. "You left without saying goodbye."

"Sorry. Didn't realize that was standard operating procedure after a three-way in a sex club. I'll tuck that information away for the next time I participate in a ménage." She hoped her light, casual tone would put them back on familiar ground. She was desperate for things to return to normal.

Ned didn't reply, but his dark gaze shot through her like a laser and it took all the strength she had not to fall to her knees and apologize.

Jesus. Get them out of here. Now.

"Is there something else you needed? Besides the proper farewell?"

Ned's scowl deepened, so she turned her attention to Justin. Maybe she'd pull this off more convincingly if she just ignored Ned. As it was, he had some tractor-beam that pulled at a part of her she wasn't sure she could keep locked down.

Justin ran a gentle finger along her arm. "We wanted to make sure you were okay, Bells. Last night was pretty intense."

She tried to smile but the attempt was wobbly at best, so she bit her lower lip and waved his concern away. "Oh, I'm fine. Had a nice hot shower and a nap already. Now I just need to whip up some lunch and I can settle down in front of my computer this afternoon to work on that graphic for—"

"You're coming to lunch with us," Justin said before she could lie any more about her plans for the day.

Truth was, the second they left, she planned to drag herself to bed to cry a little. She'd been so sure she could hold her emotions at bay, but that had been total stupidity on her part. She'd worked with these men for nearly six years and if she were being completely honest, she'd been halfway in love with them before she even walked into the club. Last night had sort of sealed that deal. Which left her way fucked up.

She started to shake her head, but Ned took a step closer. She retreated without considering her actions...or his response. He took another step. And so did she. Before she knew it, both men were in her house and the front door was closed.

This was bad. Very bad.

"You're going to come to lunch with us, Bella."

She narrowed her eyes at Ned's deep-voiced command. If she couldn't find a way to resist it, she was in deep shit. "The statute of limitations on ordering me around ran out at dawn."

Ned chuckled, though there was no mirth in the sound. "You think so?"

She didn't want to admit—even to herself—how freaking wet her panties were at that second. Ned had her number. And he knew it.

"I know so."

Fortunately, Justin stepped in, breaking up their battle of wills. Thank God. Bella harbored no illusions she'd ever win that war against Ned.

"We need to go or we're going to be late."

She frowned. "For what?"

"Sunday dinner at my mom's house. You promised her you'd come this week."

The word "shit" came out on a sigh, prompting Justin to tease her. "I'm telling my mother you said that."

Bella gave him a dirty look. "Don't you dare. You know it has nothing to do with her."

Justin was grinning. "Which is your way of saying you don't want to be with us. That hurts, Bells."

His tone, his affable face and carefree posture, almost made Bella feel as if everything was going to be okay between them. Almost.

Then she made the mistake of looking at Ned, whose expression radiated pure hunger, and once again she felt like a deer being stalked by a tiger. Worst part of it was, she was tempted to bare her throat to him and say, "Have at it."

Last night had surpassed every dirty fantasy she'd ever had. Which was actually depressing because she didn't have a doubt in her mind that any sex she had in the future would pale in comparison.

"I don't suppose you would be willing to tell Mama Lewis I have a headache? I actually do feel one starting to—"

"No," Ned interjected. "We're not lying to Justin's mother for you."

She wasn't sure she could do what they were asking. "I need more time."

For the first time since he'd entered her house, Ned's eyes softened. Mercifully, he didn't ask her to explain. As always, he understood exactly what she was saying. "It's just dinner, Bella. We'll be surrounded by Justin's insane family. I think the distraction is what you need, more than time alone."

He was right...to a point. "Can we pretend like last night never happened?" It was a stupid request. Every second of the evening was chiseled into her brain like ancient hieroglyphics. The memory would last for centuries.

He shook his head and she respected his honesty, even though she had really hoped for a lie. "No. We can't. So we're going to have to find a way to carry on from here."

"Okay." For a moment, it seemed as if Ned understood her struggle and shared it. Maybe there was a chance they could return to life as normal.

Then he ruined it. "It would all be much simpler if you'd stop being so stubborn and give in to what we all know is right."

Justin moved closer, cupping her cheek with his large palm. "Last night was the best night of my life."

She didn't doubt that his words were sincere. Which made this so much more difficult. "Mine too. That's why I need more time."

Justin shook his head. "You think time is going to make you forget, make it easier for you to walk away. It's not."

Bella was terrified he was right. She fought for something to say, some argument to make them leave, but she was running on empty—tired, hungry and confused.

"Come on, Bells. It's just lunch. Everyone will be happy to see you."

She reached for her purse. They weren't leaving the house without her, that much was clear. "Fine."

Mama Lewis always found a way to make Bella feel better. She could still recall the first time she'd been invited to Sunday dinner at the Lewis house. She had lived in New Orleans for about six months and apart from making a few friends at work, she felt very much like a fish out of water in the big city.

She'd gone in to work on a Saturday, simply because she couldn't stand the idea of spending two whole days holed up in her lonely apartment. Justin had found her there when he'd stopped by to retrieve a file he'd forgotten. They'd struck up a conversation then, to Bella's horror, she'd actually started to cry as she talked about missing home and her family. Justin had offered his family as a surrogate. Next thing she knew, she was sitting at the huge table in the Lewis' dining room the following day, laughing at his brothers' antics, discussing fashion with his sister and getting the recipe for gumbo from his mother.

Since then, she'd gone back for dinner at least one Sunday a month and her homesickness had never returned.

Bella followed them out of the apartment and claimed the backseat of Justin's car, anxious to maintain at least some distance between them. She was grateful that neither man felt the need to fill the silence with mindless chatter.

When they pulled up to Mama Lewis' house, Bella took a deep breath, praying she could get through the next few hours easily.

Ned opened the car door and reached out to help her. It occurred to her, he'd done the same thing every time they'd ever gone anywhere together. The difference this time was, he didn't release her hand. She tried to tug it away but he kept a tight grip. She shot him a warning look but he simply ignored her.

Justin didn't bother to ring the bell or knock. As always, he just walked in. He called out to his mother and the three of them ventured into the dining room together. Several members of the family were carrying bowls of food to the table. Their timing had been perfect.

Justin gestured to them. "Brought Bella and Ned along with me this week."

Mama Lewis came over to Bella, offering one of her famous bear hugs. No one hugged better than Justin's mom. Bella returned it, clinging just a second longer than she should have. When Mama Lewis released her, she studied Bella's face, her astute gaze taking in more than Bella meant to show. She'd failed at masking her stress, which pretty much ensured Mama Lewis would find a way to pull her aside today to see what was wrong.

Now Bella would have to figure out some fake story to tell the lovely woman about why she was tense or she'd have to dodge Mama Lewis all afternoon, making sure the two of them were never alone. Neither option seemed achievable. Ned and Justin were right. She was a terrible liar. And Mama Lewis was tenacious when she wanted to know something.

They grabbed plates from the sideboard, then took seats at the long table as everyone began passing the bowls full of scrumptious food. Justin and Ned had managed to bully Bella into the chair between them, even though she'd been determined to nab the one next to Justin's sister, Chloe.

The Lewis family was never at a loss for something to say. The conversation wove its way from Caliph, telling the hilarious story of a woman who'd come into Midnight Ink to have a bad tattoo covered up, to Chloe's boyfriend Blake, talking about three drunks he'd arrested on Bourbon Street for indecent exposure. Justin's foster brothers, Zac and Noah started taking bets on who would win the hockey game. It was loud and chaotic and Bella loved every minute of it.

"Oh hey, congrats on the bestseller list, Jett," Ned said. "Justin was saying you hit pretty high."

Justin's youngest brother, Jett, grinned widely. "Yep. Nabbed the number two spot this time."

Jett had made a name for himself as a crime writer. His stories followed the exploits of a police detective who worked with a psychic to solve murder mysteries. They were set in New Orleans and critics had begun to call him the next James Patterson.

"Dani would have been proud. She always said you were going to hit the big leagues with your stories," Justin said.

Jett shook his head. "Doubtful. I think it's more likely she would have given me that unimpressed look and asked why I hadn't hit number one."

Everyone laughed, though Bella could see sadness in Jett's eyes when their foster sister's name was mentioned. According to Justin, Jett and Dani had been about the same age when she came to live with the family and they'd become best friends. She had lived with the Lewises for three years before the court ruled that she could return home. Dani had disappeared shortly after leaving them—a runaway—and they hadn't seen her since.

"Well, I am very impressed," Mama Lewis said.

The distraction provided by such good company would have done the trick, would have helped Bella relax, if not for Ned and Justin. Somehow they had managed to find ways to continually touch her throughout the meal, sometimes covertly, sometimes not.

Ned had placed his hand on her knee, his fingers lightly stroking the skin revealed by her short skirt within moments of sitting down. Several times, Justin had reached over to tuck a stray strand of hair behind her ear, and once he'd even leaned close under the pretense of whispering in her ear, only to nip the lobe with his teeth.

Then Ned put his arm across the back of her chair halfway through the meal, his fingers drifting every now and then to caress the nape of her neck—the bastard had discovered that erogenous zone last night and now he was using the knowledge against her.

Bella's eyes darted to Mama Lewis, who was observing every touch with great interest. Bella felt her face grow hot under the scrutiny and she was just starting to plot Ned's and Justin's murders when the meal ended. If she had any hope of making an escape, it was now.

"That was a wonderful dinner, Mama Lewis," Bella said. "Do you mind if I don't stay for dessert? I have a mountain of laundry waiting for me at home."

Ned and Justin looked as if they planned to override her request, but Mama Lewis saved her as she rose from the table. "I don't mind at all. Why don't you come into the kitchen with me and I'll wrap up a piece of cake for you for later?"

Fuck.

"Oh, that's okay. I'm trying to watch my weight," Bella called out, but Mama Lewis had already left the room.

Caliph's girlfriend, Jennifer, gave her an incredulous look.

"You're kidding, right? You have the metabolism of a humming-bird. I've never seen anyone eat like you do and stay so thin."

She blew out a long sigh. "Yeah. I know, but I'm almost thirty. I have a feeling that will start to catch up with me eventually."

Justin chuckled. "Almost thirty? Bells, you're twenty-seven. And you don't have to worry about your weight. You're gorgeous." He punctuated his compliment with a quick kiss that no one in the house missed.

She shot him a dirty look, muttering under her breath. "What the hell are you doing?"

Bella was too afraid to look around the table. She didn't need to. She could feel the sudden change in the air—the curiosity radiating from Justin's family. He'd just opened them up to a slew of unnecessary questions.

Justin didn't even pretend to look guilty. "Grab me a piece of cake while you're in the kitchen getting the third degree from my mom, okay?"

"I hate you."

Justin laughed. "No, you don't."

She started to argue the point, but Mama Lewis called her name from the kitchen. "Bella?"

"What am I supposed to say?"

Ned placed his arm around her shoulders to pull her closer. "Tell her you're our girlfriend."

She glared at him. "Hell will freeze over first."

Silence fell over the table and Bella knew Justin's family was hanging on their every word.

"Before you say that to Mama Lewis or before you admit it to yourself?" Justin asked.

Bella shook herself loose from Ned. "Still hate you. Both of you."

She could hear everyone chuckling as she walked to the

kitchen, her blood boiling. She'd told Ned and Justin what she'd wanted from last night's adventure and they were disregarding it. Pushing her feelings aside as if they didn't matter.

She wasn't sure what they had hoped to accomplish by dragging her to Sunday dinner, but she suspected they weren't going to like the end result. She was so pissed she'd managed to ward off her confusion, her aching heart. They'd actually made it easy for her.

Mama Lewis was slicing the cake, but she stopped when Bella stormed in.

"My son has always had a talent for getting under someone's skin and pushing their buttons with that constant playfulness of his."

"That's an understatement," Bella agreed. "Between Justin's teasing and Ned barking orders, I can't believe someone hasn't murdered them in their sleep by now."

"By someone, I assume you mean one of their lovers."

Bella sucked in a sharp breath. Mama Lewis knew?

Apparently she did, because Justin's mother didn't wait for her to answer. "Yes, Bella. I know about Justin and Ned's need to share women."

"And you're okay with that?" It was a stupid question. Bella had yet to discover anything that shook the steadfast Mama Lewis. Bella could only assume that during Mama Lewis' years as a social worker then throughout the past few decades as she took in countless foster children, there was very little the woman hadn't seen.

"It's not my place to judge what makes them happy."

"He's your son. Of course it's your place to judge him."

Mama Lewis snorted with amusement. "He's a thirty-seven-year-old man. If he were younger, perhaps I'd chalk it up to youthful experimentation. As it stands, I think it's safe to say Justin knows who he is and what he wants from life."

"But..." It had been on the tip of Bella's tongue to insist a ménage a trois wasn't normal, but she realized that may sound like an insult and hypocrisy. Especially considering how much Bella had loved her role in last night's threesome.

"But nothing, Bella. I can see you're struggling with Ned and Justin's attention. And you haven't asked for my advice, but I'm old and opinionated, so you're going to get it anyway."

Bella loved Justin's mother.

"Thoreau once said, 'Live the life you imagined.' I read that in college and it's always stuck with me. You know I was still single when I got pregnant with Justin?"

Bella had heard about Justin's childhood. The man had always been very forthcoming about it. It was one of the things she admired most about Justin. He was an open book.

"My parents strongly suggested that I give Justin up for adoption. After all, I was just beginning my senior year at college and I wasn't married. My mother thought it would make my life simpler if I started it unencumbered. She insisted there were thousands of couples who wanted a child and who were better prepared to raise my son. I've been around long enough to know she was probably right. I've worked with people going through the adoption process and I've seen the absolute desperation in their faces because what they want more than anything on earth is a child to love."

"But you didn't give him up."

Mama Lewis shook her head. "It would have made life easier, but it wouldn't have made it happier. That boy means everything to me. All my children do. So I faced the social stigma attached to single motherhood and forged on in spite of it. Because when I imagined my life, I knew that what I wanted above everything else was to be Justin's mom. And Caliph's. And Chloe's. And Jett's, Zac's, Noah's, Dani's and..."

Bella waved in surrender. "I get the point. You keep going

with that list and we could be here awhile."

Mama Lewis reached out for her hand. "Think about what you want from life, Bella. Then make it happen. Don't worry about what anyone else will say or think. Their opinions don't matter."

"It's not that easy."

"Of course it's not," Mama Lewis said. "But I suspect we never truly appreciate or value the things we get easily. The things we have to work for? Those are the real treasures."

Bella saw the wisdom in Mama Lewis' words, but she found it difficult to apply to her situation. It would actually be quite easy to walk into that dining room and fall into Justin's and Ned's arms. The tough part was everything else.

Mama Lewis handed her three pieces of cake, covered in Saran Wrap. "Here. For you and the boys. For later."

Bella thanked her for the cake and the advice. When she returned to the dining room, she found Justin and Ned waiting for her. The rest of the family had headed to the living room to watch a hockey game. She could hear Jett and Caliph yelling at the TV already.

"Sorry to make you leave. Did you want to stay for the game?"

Justin shook his head. "No." He winked. "I didn't get much sleep last night. I'm thinking my recliner and a four- or five-hour nap sounds pretty good right now."

"You okay?" Ned asked.

She spied the genuine concern in his eyes. "Just tired."

"Let's put it all away for now. We can talk about it later."

Bella smiled. "Okay. I'd like that." Maybe later she'd have her head screwed on straight, her future figured out.

Live the life you imagined.

It was good advice, but Bella didn't have the courage to go—or even admit—exactly where her imagination was leading her.

CHAPTER TEN

Justin studied the ad in front of him, his eyes failing to see the work. A week had passed since he and Ned had staked their claim on Bella at Extreme Connections, exposing her darker desires and trying to capture her heart.

Unfortunately the stubborn woman was clinging tight to her vow that their night together would remain just a memory, something to keep them warm on the lonely evenings they'd spent apart since then.

This week had been brutal. His senses had become too attuned to her—the subtle scent of her shampoo, the soft brush of her arm against his when she reached for something, the sound of her voice drifting down the hall. All of that and a million other little things were working against him, driving him to a state of utter pain. He'd spent most of the week working with a hard-on, forced to relieve the pressure with his own hand several times a day in his private bathroom. He wasn't used to being denied, to having heaven presented to him, then withdrawn.

"Fuck it. I'm done. Being romantic isn't working."

Justin glanced up to find Ned standing in his doorway. He knew exactly what Ned was alluding to. Justin had—foolishly— suggested that maybe they just needed to give Bella some time to see they were sincere in their intentions. So they had set out to woo her. They'd sent her flowers every single day and issued invitations to dinners, movies, plays. She'd resisted it all, insisting the fantasy was over. Nothing they said had convinced her to consider dating them.

"What do you suggest?" Justin asked as Ned walked in and shut the door behind him.

"It's open season on Bella."

Justin chuckled, though nothing about their situation felt humorous. "Sounds ominous."

"She's sticking to her guns, determined we're all better off if we keep our relationship professional. And I understand her concerns, I really do. But I swear to God, if she rattles off those reasons why we can't make a permanent threesome one more time, my head's going to explode."

Justin couldn't hold back his cocky expression. "You realize her list is pretty much identical to the same arguments you gave me when I first suggested the ménage."

Ned scowled, clearly unhappy to be reminded that he'd offered the same resistance Bella was giving them now, though Justin had to admit her list was growing longer and more adamant by the day. Bella claimed it was inappropriate for her to date her bosses—no surprise there. She also said society would shun them for their unorthodox relationship. She worried what their families and friends would say. She'd stressed how much she needed her job and if things went south, she'd be broke as well as broken-hearted.

Ned paced the floor. "It nearly killed me to sit next to her at that meeting this morning and not touch her."

Justin understood Ned's pain. "Maybe you're right. Maybe it is time to change our tactics."

Ned stopped walking and looked at him. "What are you thinking?"

Justin picked up his phone and dialed Bella's extension. He ignored the wary tone in her voice when she said hello. "Bella. Could you come to my office please?"

Bella started to offer an excuse, claiming she was under the wire on the Express campaign.

Justin cut her off. "It will only take a minute."

She sighed then agreed. Ned gave him a curious look, but answered the door when Bella knocked just a few moments later.

She hesitated at the doorway when she realized Ned was also in the office.

"Come on in, Bells." Justin rose from his desk, walking around it to stand closer to her. Ned closed and locked the door, his actions not lost on Bella, who instantly stiffened as if preparing for an attack.

"We thought we'd let you know we intend to change your mind about dating us." Justin leaned on his desk, trying to assume a casual pose in hopes of setting her at ease.

"You've been trying to change my mind for the past week. I told you, I'm not—"

Ned stepped behind her, dragging her hands behind her back.

Bella's body reacted instantly, her nipples budding, her breathing quickening. One look at Ned's face told Justin his friend hadn't missed her response.

Bella instantly went into fight or flight mode, trying to break his grip. "Let me go."

Ned refused. "You know your safe word."

She didn't say it, a fact that wasn't lost on either man.

Instead, she said, "You're breaking the rules. It was only supposed to be one night of fantasies. We agreed."

Justin shook his head. "No. *You* agreed. Ned and I said we would try to change your mind."

Ned released her hands only to change his hold. He wrapped his arms around her waist, and then placed a soft kiss on the side of her neck.

Justin watched as her eyelids slowly slid down. She was responding to Ned's touch just as she had at Extreme Connections. Words had failed to break down the walls she'd built against them. So they'd simply have to employ dirtier—hotter—tactics.

"You're not playing fair," she whispered.

"I can't, Bella-love." Ned's voice betrayed exactly how intense his need for her was.

Bella turned to look at Ned then faced Justin once more. He saw the surprise in her gaze. Clearly she hadn't realized how difficult her continual refusals had been on them.

Bella's face softened. "Please try to understand."

Justin shook his head. He couldn't. Couldn't comprehend why she was denying them all something that was obviously so right. "I can't."

Ned kissed her neck again, his hands rising to cup her breasts. Bella didn't seek to move them or stop his touches.

They'd reminded her of the safe word. God help them if she used it. They would release her if she did, but Justin suspected it would kill both of them to walk away from her.

"What we have doesn't fit in one night, Bells. Can't you see that? It's bigger than a fantasy."

Ned didn't seek to join the conversation. Instead he let Justin do the talking as he demonstrated exactly what they planned to do. He tackled the button and zipper on her pants then tugged her jeans to her ankles.

Her breathing was labored, loud in the quiet room. Justin recognized the fear laced with the excitement. She wanted this. And she didn't want it.

He crooked his finger at her once Ned removed her pants and panties completely. "Come here."

She shook her head. Her chest rose and fell rapidly, drawing his attention to her turgid nipples. There was no denying she wanted what they were offering. If only they could find a way to convince her, to help her overcome her fears.

"Say the word or come here, Bells." Justin didn't employ the Dom tone often, but she was pushing him past the point of no return. His restraint was in tatters, his heart aching.

She took the three steps required to join him. Justin acted quickly, pressing her facedown over the desk.

She gasped.

Justin stroked her bare bottom. "What did we say about the dress code for you?"

Bella tried to rise, but Justin kept a firm grip on her upper back, holding her to the surface. He smacked her ass, just once, but with enough force to make sure she felt it.

"I'm not wearing skirts."

It was a brazen thing to say, a direct challenge to their authority.

"Then you'll be punished every day." Justin didn't hesitate to put action to his words. He spanked her, peppering her ass as Bella lifted up on her toes, meeting him blow for blow, silently asking for more.

Ned claimed the other side and watched. After a half-dozen or so smacks, Justin paused.

"Open your legs," Ned demanded.

Bella complied instantly. She was squirming on the desk, quietly whispering the words "please" and "more."

Ned ran his fingers along her slit, holding them up to show

Justin the juices coating them. Then he gestured for Justin to continue.

Justin spanked her three, four times more as Bella's pleading became louder. She was on the edge of an orgasm. Ned stroked her once more from clit to ass. Using the moisture he'd collected, he pressed two fingertips inside her anus, just to the first knuckle.

"Yes," Bella hissed.

Ned's jaw was tight, his body tense with need. Justin recognized it because he felt it, shared that pain.

"Please, I need..." She didn't finish her request. Her fear still wouldn't allow her to give in.

And though it was the hardest thing he'd ever done, Justin refused her. He walked across the room and retrieved her jeans. Then, to her astonishment, he put them on her, leaving her—and them—unfulfilled.

"Agree to be with us, Bells, and I'll let you come. I'll give you so many orgasms, you'll pass out."

Bella stood before them, stunned, unsatisfied, and speechless for only a few seconds. Then, the damn stubborn woman dug deep and found the strength to pull herself together. She shook her head, said, "no thanks," and walked out.

CHAPTER ELEVEN

Two weeks in hell passed. Ned and Justin had continued their sensual games, cornering Bella, constantly asking her to reconsider her stance, to agree to be with them. When she refused, they added more fuel to the fire, touching, teasing, and tormenting her to the brink of orgasm before pulling away and begging her to come back to their bed for good.

Bella never failed to walk away.

On Wednesday afternoon, Ned had introduced her to the butt plug, filling her ass and telling her she would wear it several hours a day at work. At five o'clock for the past two days, they'd taken the plug out and promised to give her the fantasy they'd refused her, but again she'd said no.

No matter how many times they pushed her to the limit, Bella found the ability to walk away despite the undeniable arousal they saw in her heavy-lidded eyes, in the flush on her cheeks.

And every time she escaped, she left two aroused and aching men frustrated and reeling in her wake.

Now it was Friday afternoon and nothing but another long, painful weekend loomed in Justin's future.

Ned came into his office with Bella at five. Justin stared at her, wondering if he'd have the power to continue the game. His cock had been rock hard for the past two hours just thinking about closing time, when he'd see her again.

"Everyone else is gone for the day." Ned closed and locked the door. "Go over to Justin's desk, Bella. Bend over and lift your skirt."

She'd worn a skirt this past Tuesday, thinking that by complying with their demand, they'd leave her alone. That was when Ned bought the plug.

Ned had said the same thing the past two days before they removed their plug. Each day, their beautiful submissive girl had obeyed without question.

Today, she didn't move. "I can't do this anymore. Pennsylvania." Her voice quivered. Justin's heart ached at the sound.

Ned stepped closer to her, cupping her cheek in his hand. "Please, Bella. God, baby. Can't you see what this is doing to us? All of us?"

She tried to look away, shaking her head, but Ned held her gaze. "Dammit. Justin and I want to spend our lives with you. This isn't a game to us. And yes, there are risks. There are going to be people who will never understand or accept it, but you know what? Fuck them. I swear to you right now that I will never hurt you. I'll protect you from the narrow-minded pricks of the world."

She winced. "I think maybe I've been the narrow-minded prick lately."

Ned shook his head. "No. You're being logical and practical. But love doesn't work under those parameters. Besides, I know what we're asking for is a bit unconventional."

She snorted, a soft smile crossing her lips. "A bit?"

Justin crossed the room. For the first time in weeks, he felt hopeful. They were talking. It encouraged him. "It's a lot unconventional. But it's not wrong. I love you, Bells. Can you at least give us time to prove this will work?"

Bella reached up to swipe a tear away. "I thought I could do one night. That I could hold on to my heart, but I realize now, I wasn't holding on to it to begin with. I've been in love with both of you for a very long time."

Ned kissed her softly. "Take a chance on us?"

She nodded. "I don't have a choice. I'm not strong enough to keep walking away. These past two weeks have been brutal. You guys do *not* play nice. Holy crap. My vibrator's been getting a hell of a workout."

Ned frowned. "You've been giving yourself orgasms? Without our permission?"

Bella narrowed her eyes. "Don't play big-bad Dom with me, Ned. You were the one lighting the fire then walking away."

Ned looked as if he would argue the point, but Justin figured they had plenty of time to work out the dynamics of their relationship later.

Right now, he was too happy. He needed to touch her. Justin wrapped her in his embrace. "We're good together, Bells. The three of us make an awesome team. At work. In bed. Everywhere."

She gave him a sultry grin. "Maybe so. But I do have one condition. One thing you have to agree to or I'm leaving for good."

From the heated look on her face, Justin suspected her demand wouldn't be difficult. Hell, knowing their wicked girl, he was looking forward to giving in. Immediately, if possible. "What is it?"

"I'll only date you guys if you fulfill my fantasy. You owe

me. You left me hanging and you've made the past two weeks sheer sexual hell."

Ned gave her a haughty look, rife with warning. "So the submissive is making the demands now? Topping from the bottom?"

She gave Ned a look that promised serious retribution if they left her high and dry again. "Take off your clothes. Both of you."

"Thought you were sick of taking charge in the bedroom," Justin said, even as he reached for the buttons on his shirt. Right now, he didn't care if their beauty donned leather and start swinging a whip. He'd follow her anywhere if it meant sealing the deal on a real future.

"Are you refusing?" she asked in an overconfident tone.

Justin shook his head.

Ned was slower to start, but then he followed suit too. Bella watched them patiently, not bothering to remove her own clothing. It was clear she felt entitled to get back a little of her own after the sexual torment they'd subjected her to.

Justin felt compelled to point out she only had herself to blame for their current states, but at this moment, he didn't care. Bella had confessed her feelings. She loved them. She was willing to take this risk.

Once they were both naked, Ned lifted his hand. "It's your show, Bella-love. What next?"

She walked over to Ned and pressed a soft kiss on his cheek. "I'm yours. For now. For as long as you'll have me." She knelt in front of Ned. "Master."

Ned swallowed heavily. Justin was blown away by the naked emotion on his friend's face. While Justin was an open book and tended to wear his heart on his sleeve, Ned kept tight control over his feelings. To see the love, fascination, and joy written there overwhelmed Justin.

Ned smiled, blinking rapidly, and Justin wondered if his friend was fighting back tears. A first.

Then Ned found his footing. "I love you," he whispered.

Justin couldn't continue to watch the scene unfold without moving closer. He took the two steps necessary, and then helped Bella to her feet once more.

She smiled at him, her face completely clear of the confusion, the sadness that had been too predominant there the past few months.

He gave her a teasing grin. "Where's my nickname? Don't you want to call me master too?"

She laughed. "Oh God. Seriously?"

He hugged her tightly. "I'm kidding, Bells. You can just call me what you've always called me."

She gave him a mischievous wink. "Got it. Asshole it is."

He lifted her up, spinning her around wildly as she giggled.

Ned crossed his arms, shaking his head while pretending to be annoyed by Justin's over-the-top silliness. "You look ridiculous and if you're not careful, you're going to injure yourself. Roughhousing with a raging hard-on isn't exactly smart."

Ned's warning turned the tide instantly as Justin's happiness morphed into something hotter. He stopped moving and slowly released his grip, allowing Bella to slide sensuously down his bare body.

She licked her lips as she looked down. Once she was on her feet again, she continued the glide on her own, not stopping until she was on her knees, Justin's cock in her hand.

"God, Bells," he murmured when she took him into her mouth. He placed his hands on the sides of her head and started counting to one hundred in his head. One of these damn days he was going to build up some sort of stamina with her. As it was, two seconds in her presence had him ready to blow like Old Faithful.

She showed him no mercy, taking him to the back of her throat.

Ned walked closer, standing next to him. "Do you think I can get in on this?"

Bella smiled as she released Justin with a pop, turning her head toward Ned. Watching her suck on his best friend's cock was one of the horniest sights Justin had ever seen. Bella continued to play with them, stroking them both with her hands while moving her mouth from one cock to the next then back again.

Ned was the first to step away. "Not like this, Bella-love. You have a fantasy you want fulfilled. I think it's time."

Justin reached down, helping Bella to her feet. "I guess we're doing this here? You realize a bed would be more comfortable."

Ned gave him a rueful grin. "I can't wait that long."

"Neither can I," Bella added.

Justin laughed. "God. We're a threesome. Something tells me we're going to need to take a vacation somewhere for a month or two just to try to fuck some of this built-up sexual tension out. Otherwise, we're running a risk of public indecency."

Bella seemed to consider his suggestion, then said, "Might take me closer to six months to get it all out of my system."

Ned groaned. "Jesus. I'm up for that."

"Me too," Justin said.

Bella looked down at their cocks. "I'd say that much is obvious."

Ned reached around and swatted Bella's ass. "Bend over that desk, gorgeous. Let's get that plug out so we can fill you with something a little warmer."

Bella didn't refuse his request this time. Instead, she walked to Justin's desk and assumed the sexy position. Justin lifted her skirt, running his hand over her bare ass. He'd claimed her panties earlier in the day when he and Ned had placed the plug inside her. Knowing she was walking around with their toy in her ass and no panties had pretty much assured Justin's complete worthlessness as far as work concerns for the rest of the afternoon.

He gently worked the plug free as Bella pressed her head against the smooth surface of the desk, panting softly, pushing closer to him. She loved anal play.

"You okay, Bells?"

Her body betrayed her overwhelming need for more. "So fucking okay."

Ned ran his hand along her back, provoking a shiver. "Come here." He helped her stand, and then dragged her to the middle of the room. Ned looked at Justin and gestured to the couch by the wall. "Grab those cushions, Justin, and lay them on the floor."

Justin arranged the pillows, and then lowered himself to them, lying on his back. Ned tossed him a condom, which he put on as Ned undressed Bella.

Ned cupped Bella's cheek. "Ready?"

She nodded and turned to Justin.

He crooked his finger at her. "Hop on."

She giggled as she lowered herself over his hips, placing his cock at the opening to her pussy. She slid onto his erection slowly, both of them closing their eyes, trying to calm the undeniable need to come. Her inner muscles clenched him tightly and she groaned. God, she was as close as he was.

"You don't have to hold back, Bells. Come as much as you want."

She opened her eyes and smiled as she shook her head. "No. Not yet. I don't want to come until both of you are inside me."

Ned knelt behind her and Justin could see his friend had grabbed the lube from his desk drawer and donned his own condom. He placed his hand on Bella's shoulder, lightly pressing her forward.

Justin wrapped his arms around her waist, loving the feeling of her cheek pressed against his chest.

"I can hear your heart," she whispered.

Justin clutched her tighter.

She jerked slightly when Ned ran his hand over her ass. Then relaxed into Justin's hold again.

Justin felt Ned's finger penetrate her anus. "Jesus," he muttered.

Ever since Bella had told them about her fantasy at Extreme Connections, it was all the two of them could think about. They'd drowned their sorrows the night after Bella left them alone in the club and discussed it at length. Her dream, her trust in them to take her in such a way had worked its way into Justin's subconscious until there was little else he could think of. He'd spent weeks longing for this very moment.

Soon, one of Ned's fingers became two. Justin tried to hold still as Ned prepared her body to accept both of them, but it was difficult not to thrust against the pressure Ned was applying.

Finally, Ned withdrew his fingers and moved closer. Justin closed his eyes when he felt the head of Ned's cock penetrating Bella's tight ass.

Bella's breathing became shallow, came faster as Ned slowly pushed his way deeper.

"Fuck," Justin grunted when Ned was seated to the hilt. "Mother fucker, I've never felt anything so good. Bells, lift your head. Look at me."

Bella raised her face to his. Justin wanted to see her eyes, needed to know this was as good for her. One look told him all he needed to know.

He leaned forward to place a quick kiss on her lips. "You're so beautiful."

Then words gave way to motion, to magic, to perfection.

He and Ned found their rhythm, moving in tandem. It was a true melding of three bodies, three hearts.

Bella came twice before Ned and Justin gave in to their own overpowering climaxes. As the last drop erupted, Justin closed his eyes, trying to hold on to the moment. Bella lay atop him, her chest rising and falling rapidly.

"Can we stay here forever?" she asked.

Ned kissed her cheek. "Could make for an awkward scene when everyone comes back to work on Monday."

Justin ran his hand through her soft hair. "I vote for a second round. At my place. In a bed. This floor is hell on my back."

Ned withdrew, shaking his head. "Your back? My knees."

Bella giggled. "Funny. I feel just fine."

Justin tickled her, rolling with her until she lay beneath him, batting his hands away as she laughed louder. Unable to resist, he moved closer, kissing her.

"I love you." He'd never found those words easy to say. With Bella, they were hard to hold back.

She stroked his face. "I love you too. So much."

Ned picked up his clothes. "Should we head home then?"

Bella nodded, as Justin stood then reached down to help her up. They dressed in silence before Ned grasped Bella's hand, tugging her toward him for a hug. "So how did the reality stack up against the fantasy?"

She smiled, kissing him softly on the cheek. "No comparison. The two of you are my dream come true."

ROUGH DRAFT
BIG EASY, BOOK 4

Capture, bondage and fantasies fulfilled.

Bestselling crime novelist Jett has a wicked case of writer's block. His publisher's screaming "deadline", the fans are ready to riot, and Jett just wants to disappear. His friend Carissa suggests he get away, clear his head...get laid. And she has just the ticket. Literally. Two passes to an exclusive island paradise.

Jett convinces Carissa to go with him, and the resort is more than either of them bargained for—especially when the simple trip turns to murder. Thrust into a plot sinister enough to rival Jett's books, the couple embarks on a search for the killer. The most shocking revelation of all is their mutual attraction...and how much Jett and Carissa love working undercover.

CHAPTER ONE

"What are you doing here?"

Jett Lewis stopped just inside the door of the Royal Lunch, his favorite dive in all of New Orleans, but the bartender—and his best friend—Carissa was looking at him as if he'd just committed some unspeakable crime.

He tilted his head, confused by the hostility in her tone. "This is a bar and I want a drink. Those two things seemed to fit together."

Her scowl remained firmly in place. "It's Sunday."

He chuckled. "No shit."

She rolled her eyes, not amused. "You always go to your mother's house for dinner on Sunday."

Carissa wasn't behind the counter. In fact, she appeared to be on her way out. "You're not working today?" he asked, ignoring her previous comment.

He was purposely avoiding Sunday dinner at his mother's house, but he didn't want to get into that with Carissa. Truth was, he wanted exactly what he'd told her. A drink. Preferably a stiff one. And then maybe two or three or a dozen more after the first.

Carissa seemed flummoxed—something his self-assured, straight-shooting friend never was. "Um...no. I was going to run, um, a few errands."

Jett was fairly certain he'd never heard Carissa tell a lie until that moment. "Is that right?"

She narrowed her eyes as if annoyed, but swallowed heavily, her guilty behavior telling him she knew she'd been caught. "Yes." Her single-word response came just two beats too late.

"Where are you really going?"

She crossed her arms and blew out an exasperated breath. "What the hell are you doing here? You never come in on Sundays. Ever."

He ignored her question and glanced at Shawn, one of her part-time employees, manning the bar. "I'm having a drink."

Jett walked to his usual spot at the end of the counter and sat down. Raising his hand to catch Shawn's attention, he said, "Scotch on the rocks."

Shawn nodded and began pouring as Carissa audibly sighed from across the room. She pulled her cell out of her back pocket, typed something onto it then came over to join him.

"What about your errands?" he asked when she claimed the stool next to him.

"They can wait."

Jett grinned then picked up the drink Shawn placed in front of him, lifting it in a silent toast before taking a sip. The liquid gold slid down his throat, the heat it provided a welcome relief.

"Isn't it a bit early for Scotch?"

There was no judgment in Carissa's tone—she was a bartender, after all—so he just shook his head.

"Jett—" she started.

"I need this drink, Rissa. And then I need the one after this. And probably four or five more after that one."

"Oh. It's like that, is it?"

He grimaced. "Yeah. It's like that."

"Any special reason for getting shit-faced on a Sunday afternoon?"

Jett shrugged. He'd come to drink himself into oblivion, hoping to forget the reason that brought him here to begin with. Then he realized that was wrong.

He'd come here to talk to her.

He'd met Carissa Pierre seven years earlier, when he'd been a wannabe writer and stumbled into the bar. He had been laid off from his job as a reporter at the *New Orleans Sun*. The newspaper had decided to downsize just a year after he'd landed the job, and as a result, the last hired was the first fired. He'd tried to find another job, even working part time as a waiter to make ends meet, but short of relocating, he was out of options.

He'd been walking along Toulouse, wondering what the fuck he was supposed to do with his life when he'd spotted the bar with its name—Royal Lunch—written in neon. All he could think about was how he was "royally" screwed, so he'd walked in and claimed this very same spot at the bar. Carissa had been holding court behind the counter, chatting to a couple older guys who were clearly regulars. Something about her had reminded him of his foster sister Dani, and he'd felt instantly drawn to her.

When Jett had been a teenager, Dani was his confidante. He'd talk to her and she would find a way to make him feel better. When the court system decided she'd be better off with her abusive father than with his family, Dani had run away. He'd never seen her again, though he'd never stopped looking for her face in every crowd, hoping, praying that one day he'd find her. He hadn't realize how big the hole left in his life when Dani disappeared was until he'd found Carissa and she filled it.

"You remember the first time we met?"

If Carissa was taken aback by Jett's abrupt change of topic, she didn't let it show. That was one of the things Jett liked most about Carissa. She was steady as a rock. Which was funny considering he always put himself in relationships with women who were her polar opposite—high-maintenance, high-strung, high drama. Small wonder none of those relationships had lasted longer than a few months.

"I remember. You were crying in your beer over a job interview for some company that hadn't gone well."

He grinned. "I was hardly crying."

"That's true. You were actually pretty pissed off. They gave the job to one of the boss's nephews or something, right?"

"Yeah. They interviewed me just to make everything look like it was on the up and up, when they'd known all along who they were going to hire. Do you remember what you said to me?"

Carissa considered his question. "I think I asked you about the job. It sounded like some really horrible paper-pusher, fluorescent-lighting, cubicle kind of career."

"It was. You questioned if I really wanted to live like that. I said no. And then you asked me what my dream job was?"

She crooked her finger at Shawn, pointing to Jett's half-empty glass. "Set him up with another round." She lifted his Scotch and drank what was left. "You said you wanted to write a book."

"Yeah. And you said, 'so write one.'"

She smiled. "And you did."

Shawn brought him another drink in a fresh glass, taking the empty one away before walking back to the other end of the counter where a small TV was set up. The Angels were playing the Nationals. Shawn was clearly rooting for the Nats and unhappy that the new shortstop had missed a ground ball when he muttered, "You clumsy fuck. Go back to St. Louis."

Jett looked at Carissa. For the first time since walking into the bar, he realized she was actually sort of dressed up. While she still wore her usual ponytail, she'd replaced her standard black heavy-metal-band-of-the-day t-shirt and faded blue jeans for a pair of nice black pants and a pretty top. The outfit looked totally hot, even though he knew that wasn't her goal. He suspected she was going for respectable—and in truth, she'd accomplished that. It made him long to see her with her hair down. Something he'd never seen before.

He started to ask her about her appearance, then worried he'd kept her from going out on a date.

It was on the tip of his tongue to tell her she didn't have to keep him company, but he needed to be with her. His depression had hit an all-time low this morning and it had taken every bit of energy he possessed to get out of bed, pull on some clothes and walk here.

"Were you meeting someone?"

She hesitated then shook her head. Another fib. On a better day, it would have bothered him that she felt the need to lie. He'd always admired her honesty, but today he let it slide because she was where he needed her to be. He'd depended on her no-holds-barred honesty ever since their first meeting.

"You told me what I needed to hear that day. I mean, it was write a book or move away. There weren't any jobs around here for a fresh-out-of-college journalism major."

"Your mama was never going to let you leave town, Jett."

He snorted. "You're damn right about that."

The Lewis family had deep roots in New Orleans and the thought of leaving the Big Easy hadn't set well on Jett's shoulders either. He was very close to his siblings—foster and real—

and his mother. When he'd gone home after his first meeting with Carissa and told Mama he wanted to write a book, she'd merely nodded as if that had been the obvious answer all along. She'd loaned him two hundred dollars to buy a used laptop and told him to go write a bestseller.

The first novel hadn't hit any list, but it had caught the attention of an agent, who managed to sell it to a publisher. The story had only just earned out the advance, but it had done well enough for a debut book that the publisher bought the next in the series. That one barely squeaked onto the *New York Times* list, hitting at number twenty-five, but it was the money it brought in that made the difference. Jett was offered a lucrative three-book deal and the rest, as they say, was history.

He had a reputation as a quick, clean writer, a master of crime thrillers whose stories followed the exploits of a diamond-in-the-rough police detective. Patterson had Alex Cross, Berry had Cotton Malone and Jett had Riley James.

He'd added three or four Riley James novels to his backlist each year and luckily his readers continued to cry out for more.

Then the words had dried up.

The same ache that had resided in his chest for the past six months returned with a vengeance. He picked up the Scotch and drained the glass in one long swig.

Carissa frowned when he waved to Shawn, silently ordering another.

"You should have gone to your mother's house for dinner."

He gave her a sad smile. "I can't face that again, Rissa."

He didn't have to explain. Carissa was well aware of his writer's block, knew perfectly well why he was here with the intention of getting wasted.

The reason he'd opted to hang out at the Royal Lunch was because, unlike his well-meaning family, Carissa had never offered him advice on how to overcome the block or told him to be patient, that his words would return eventually. She didn't suggest meditation or relaxation techniques or send him emails with hyperlinks to articles about writer's block and how to beat it. She didn't dump him, like his last girlfriend, because he was "a real downer lately."

"They love you, Jett. That's what families do. They worry and fret and try to fix shit in your life when it's broken. They don't mean to annoy you."

He knew that. And if he weren't in the midst of the world's biggest and longest-running pity party, he'd appreciate their efforts to help.

Jett ran his finger along the rim of his glass. "I understand that. I do. I just needed a break from it today. I'll call my mother later to apologize for missing dinner."

Carissa nodded slowly. "You know, you've never asked me for advice about this."

He frowned. "You have advice?"

She raised one eyebrow as if to say *what do you think.* "Are you kidding me? I have an opinion on everything. You know that."

"But you've never said anything."

"Everyone's been offering their two cents' worth and it's pissing you off. I figured if you wanted to know what I thought, you'd ask."

"Would it hurt your feelings if I didn't ask?"

She chuckled. "Oh ye of little faith. I think you might like my answer."

He was sure it would be more of the same. He'd heard everything the past few months. There was nothing she could offer that would help. "Rissa—"

"And it won't really matter if my advice doesn't fix the problem because you'll still win."

Curiosity began to outweigh the self-assurance that told

him nothing was going to help at this point. With that truth crashing down on his head, he realized he had nothing left to lose. "Okay. What's your answer?"

She took an envelope out of her purse and slid it across the counter to him. "This."

He opened the expensive linen envelope, pulling out an ornate piece of parchment paper, the words written there in embossed gold. Tucked inside the letter were two tickets. "A trip?"

"Read the letter."

Jett scanned the details, his eyes widening.

Carissa was offering him an invitation to Eden?

"I don't understand."

"It's two tickets to paradise. Do you want me to break out into song? It includes airfare, the hotel room, all your meals and drinks. You need to get the fuck out of here, Jett. Clear your head and let go of all this anxiety. Grab that woman you're dating..." Carissa tapped her lips with one finger as if she were trying to remember something. "Dipshit...ditz...dingbat. God, what was her name again? Starts with a D."

Jett grinned, perfectly aware of Carissa's opinion of... "Darla. Her name is Darla."

"That's it. Tell her to pack a bag and the two of you can get the heck out of here for a while."

"I can't take this, Rissa. It's too much. This must have cost you a fortune."

She shook her head. "Didn't cost me a dime. I won the tickets."

"How?"

She pointed to the old radio on the shelf amidst the bottles of liquor. Whenever she manned the bar, she turned the TV off, opting to listen to music instead. "The bar phone rang last week.

It was one of those radio station contests that basically said, 'Give us the phrase that pays and you'll win.' It was actually the only radio station I listen to. So, I said 'K92.5 keeps the music alive' and the next thing I know, this envelope appeared in my mailbox. Pretty cool, huh? I've never won anything in my life."

He pushed the envelope across the counter to her. "It's your trip. I've heard you talk about Eden before. You said you'd love to go there and see it. Here's your chance. Grab that delivery guy you like to hook up with every now and then." He snapped his fingers as if thinking. "Um, jackass or jerk-off or something with a J."

She laughed. "Joshua. And hell no. He's okay for a one-night booty call when my vibrator's not cutting it, but there's no way we could keep that party going for a week. Our conversations begin and end with "You busy tonight" and "See you around sometime."

"So take another guy."

"And where am I supposed to conjure this fictional boyfriend from?"

He lifted one shoulder. "I don't know. Why don't you invite a girlfriend?"

Carissa rolled her eyes. "Look at the fine print, Jett. It's a romantic getaway. Oceanfront room with a Jacuzzi tub and king-sized bed, champagne and strawberries, the works. The room is called *The Lover's Retreat*. Besides, I don't really have any girlfriends. Sad as this may sound, you're sort of my best friend."

He feigned a wince. "Damn. Poor girl."

"I know, right? My life sucks."

He laughed at her teasing.

"Anyway," she continued, "the tickets have to be used next week. I could never find anyone to run the Royal Lunch for a whole week on such short notice. If you don't use them, they'll go to waste."

"I'd love to go to Eden, Rissa, but I'm afraid I'm sort of between lovers myself right now."

"Seriously?"

He nodded. "Darla dumped me a few nights ago."

"Oh. Is that why you're getting drunk?"

"Good God, no. I'd been trying to figure out how to break things off with her. She saved me the trouble. So, you see, that Lover's Retreat would be wasted on me too."

"Bummer."

"Yeah."

Carissa reached for his drink, taking another big swig. He didn't bother telling her to get her own drink. She didn't allow her employees to drink on the job, so she covertly hid her own alcohol consumption during work hours by taking sips from his. They'd been sharing drinks for years.

They sat in silence for a few minutes—neither seeking to fill the quiet with words. They simply passed the glass back and forth between them as Jett considered her generous offer. It was so like Carissa. On the surface, she appeared tough as nails, but once a person broke through the gruff exterior and earned her trust, there could be no better friend on the planet. He wasn't surprised by her willingness to give away something she really wanted if she thought it would make him happy.

Once the third drink was consumed, she reached out and touched his hand. "I still think you should go. Treat it like a writer's retreat. Get out of the city, clear your head of the bull-shit and start filling it with those damn serial killers you seem to love to terrorize the rest of us avid readers with."

It was a tempting offer. He'd read quite a bit about Eden over the past couple of years. Apparently an eccentric, reclu-sive billionaire had purchased the island, moved a castle there—

brick by brick—from Ireland and set it up as a tropical paradise. Located off the coast of Florida, it attracted the wealthy, the famous and those—probably like him—who just wanted to get the hell away from the world for a while.

What Jett suspected Carissa didn't realize was that Eden was also whispered about quite frequently in the BDSM community because of its well-known and popular dungeon, run by one of the most renowned masters in the world, Roan.

Jett's older brother, Justin, had introduced him to the BDSM lifestyle several years earlier when Jett was researching the sadomasochist set for a novel he was writing. He'd interviewed several prominent Doms—Roan included—taken a few lessons in bondage, studied the psychology behind the sex, and realized his interest had become less about work, taking a much more personal turn.

He'd joined a private club and started putting his new knowledge to use. While he didn't consider himself a lifestyle Dom, he couldn't deny how much he enjoyed "playing" with a sub, pushing a beautiful woman to her limits and sometimes beyond.

Justin's writer's block advice had actually involved Jett frequenting the club more often. His older brother was a firm believer in *sex cures all*. Justin had been a player for years, though recently he'd settled down with one woman, Bella, whom he shared with his best friend, Ned. Jett had wondered if Justin could make forever work in a committed ménage. So far, he had. Which thrilled the family because they all loved Bella and Ned.

"You could use the vacation as much as me, Rissa. When's the last time you got out of New Orleans?"

Carissa shrugged. "Never."

Jett frowned. "What?"

"I've never left New Orleans."

Jett wasn't sure how to respond. He and Carissa had been friends for years. How could he not have known this about her? "Seriously?"

She toyed with his glass, not bothering to look at him as she spoke. He got the impression she was embarrassed. "I've spent about ninety-nine percent of my life in this damn bar, Jett. It's not like this dump has made my family or me rich. Plus it's open from noon to four a.m. every single day of the week. That doesn't leave much time to play tourist anywhere else."

Her admission jelled with what he knew of Carissa's upbringing. It had taken him years of hanging out in the bar to get her to open up about herself. She'd inherited the Royal Lunch from her workaholic father, who—like Jett's own dad— had died of a massive heart attack while in his fifties. Carissa had shared that information with Jett when he'd been tying one on at the bar on the fifth anniversary of his father's death. He still missed his dad intensely. Papa Lewis had been larger-than-life and he'd seemed invincible to Jett. His father's passing had taught Jett a hard lesson about exactly how fleeting life was.

"You have to go to Eden, Rissa."

She shook her head and he suddenly realized why she was hesitant. How intimidating would it be for a girl who'd never left New Orleans to get on a plane and take off to some island in the middle of nowhere on her own?

However, regardless of her unease, Jett wanted Carissa to have the opportunity to see more of the world. Since becoming a full-time author, Jett had done quite a bit of jet setting around the world, for conferences, speaking engagements and book signings.

She gave him a look that told him she wouldn't be moved. "It's not going to happen. So take the tickets or they're going in the garbage. Even if I had someone to go with, I can't close the bar for a week and I have no one here to leave in charge."

Jett started to argue but Carissa's gaze left his, drifting out the front window to the street. She winced.

He turned to see what she was looking at.

"Um...listen, I'm sorry about this, Jett, but you sort of left me no choice."

There, waiting for the light to change so they could cross the street, was his family. All of them...plus the significant others.

He glanced at Carissa. "You ratted me out?"

"I *had* to. I was heading to your mother's house when you showed up."

"You were coming to Sunday dinner?"

Carissa nodded. "I called your mom to see if she thought you'd take the tickets. She loved the idea and then insisted I come to dinner to give them to you there. She said she'd make sure you didn't refuse. Mama Lewis thinks this trip could be the answer to overcoming your writer's block."

Jett wondered briefly if he could make a break for it, escape the coming onslaught by high-tailing it out the back door. That idea was dashed when the bell above the front door rang and the loud sound of his entire family—all talking at once—destroyed the peace that had reigned in the bar just moments before.

He turned to face his mother as she walked directly to him.

"You missed dinner."

He nodded. "I was going to call you later to explain."

Mama lifted her hand and patted his cheek. She'd used that gesture of affection for as long as he could remember. "It's time to turn the corner, son." Mama looked over at Carissa. "You told him about the trip?"

Carissa nodded, her expression wavering between amusement over his mother's arrival and guilt that she'd set him up for this. Jett narrowed his eyes, letting her know she wasn't off the hook.

The rest of his family seemed content to let Carissa and Mama handle things. Setting the Lewis clan free in a bar was equivalent to ringing the last bell before summer break in high school. Chaos ensued as they all bellied up to the counter, ordering Bloody Marys and Hurricanes and asking Shawn to turn up the volume on the baseball game.

"So you're going."

It wasn't a question. His mama had delivered an edict. Carissa snickered, fully aware there was only one person in the world he wouldn't say no to, and that was his mother. Carissa had taken the decision to accept or refuse the trip out of his hands the moment she'd called Mama.

Then Jett spied a way to get his revenge. "I'll go on one condition."

"And what would that be?" Mama didn't appear concerned. After all, there was pretty much nothing the woman couldn't accomplish when she put her mind to it. She'd raised four children of her own as well as countless foster kids. She was a force to be reckoned with and most people had learned it was much easier to just say yes from the get-go. Saved them time since Mama Lewis would continue pressing until she got her way.

Jett smiled at Carissa. "Rissa goes with me. She won the trip and I wouldn't feel right taking the tickets away from her. She's always wanted to go to Eden. Think she called it a 'dream trip' once." Jett continued to pile it on, making certain to cement Carissa's fate with his mother. "Besides, she's never taken a trip or even ventured out of New Orleans. This is an opportunity I can't deny her."

Mama turned to Carissa. "I think that's a wonderful idea! So it's all—"

"I can't go, Jett. I told you that. I can't afford to close the bar for a week and there's no one to—"

"Hey, Noah. What are you doing next week?" Jett asked his younger foster brother, cutting Carissa off mid-refusal.

Noah shrugged. "Thought I'd bum around as long as Mama Lewis will let me, then try to find some summer work. My next semester at the Culinary Institute doesn't start until September."

"How would you like to start that summer work now? Run the Royal Lunch for Rissa next week."

Noah rose from his stool at the bar and joined them. "Oh my God, man. Seriously? I'd love that!"

"Jett—" Carissa started.

"It's the perfect solution," Mama interjected. "Truth is Noah's only been home a few days and he's already driving me crazy. Plus, he's an incredible cook, Carissa. This would give him the opportunity to try out some of his recipes with your customers. It could be a win-win for both of you. And if it works out, maybe you'll consider keeping him on until he returns to school."

Jett walked over to a sign she'd posted in the window and pulled it down. He flashed the words Help Wanted at her. "Kills two birds with one stone."

Carissa closed her eyes, her expression proving she knew she'd been beaten. "Fine. Can you start tomorrow, Noah? The flight to Eden leaves next Saturday, so that will give me a week to show you the ropes around here and get you set up as far as the food orders and where to deposit the money."

Noah grinned, clearly thrilled to have landed a job that would include cooking and a cool boss. "I won't let you down, Carissa. I swear. I have a ton of ideas for some different po' boys you could add to the menu. And a new recipe for etouffee that's to die for. Might even try to pair some of your lunch specials with different drinks."

Noah's enthusiasm was infectious. Carissa laughed. "Okay, okay. That all sounds great. But keep in mind, this bar is pretty old school and known for its classic dive-like atmosphere. Don't get too fancy and everything will be fine."

"Deal." Noah returned to the bar, engaging Shawn in a conversation about what liquors they had on hand. Jett could practically see the wheels spinning in his foster brother's head.

Mama Lewis clasped his hand and squeezed. "I'm so pleased for both of you. And Jett, I know this trip is going to do the trick. I suspect the second your feet hit that sand, your words will come back to you."

Jett didn't reply. After six months of staring at a blank page on his laptop, he'd begun to lose faith. With the added pressure of a deadline looming, his agent and publisher screaming at him daily on the phone and fans continually asking "where's the next book?", he felt like a man with a noose around his neck.

"Now, I vote we shake things up this Sunday. What's the lunch special today, Carissa? And do you have enough to feed all of us?"

Carissa laughed. "It's gumbo. And there's plenty."

"Perfect. I'll just nip into the kitchen and help your poor cook dip it up." And with that, Mama Lewis disappeared into the back.

Jett winked at Carissa once they were alone again. "Gotcha," he joked.

"Awesome, Jett." Carissa's tone was pure sarcasm. "Did you forget the part about this trip being a lover's retreat? Jacuzzi. One room. *One* bed."

Jett enjoyed the slight flush that covered her cheeks as she stressed that they'd be essentially shacking up while on vacation. It provoked him to tease her even more. "I don't have a problem invoking a friends-with-benefits deal for the week."

She smirked. "I'm sure you don't, but no thanks. Hell will freeze over first. We're putting a line of pillows down the middle of the mattress. And there will be *no* crossing the barrier."

He chuckled, but agreed. Jett had been a bit annoyed about being backed into a corner on the trip, however, now that it was a reality, he found himself excited about the adventure. Carissa would be an easy traveling companion and the idea of sneaking away to explore Eden's dungeon each night appealed to him as well. Suddenly, he was imagining an entire week of beach, bondage and brainstorming ideas for his next book.

Mama was right. It was time to turn a corner.

CHAPTER TWO

Carissa stared at the puddle jumper in front of her and wondered how the hell Jett had managed to drag her from the safety of her tiny bar to this airport in Florida. They'd just finished driving twelve hours from New Orleans to Miami. Jett had offered to buy them tickets for flights from Louis Armstrong airport to this minuscule landing strip, but one flight was going to be scary enough. She didn't think she'd manage to work up the courage for two take-offs and two landings.

So they'd packed their suitcases in the car and left home at the ass crack of dawn. Hell, three a.m. couldn't even be considered dawn. They'd departed in the middle of the night, taking turns driving while the other caught catnaps. Around lunchtime, they were both wide awake and her excitement about the trip had grown as they talked about all the things they wanted to try while at Eden—everything from caviar to snorkeling, rock climbing to sunbathing with fruity drinks in hand. She dreamed of sexy cabana boys, while Jett joked about meeting an island babe, skipping the return flight home and living out his days as a native, wearing nothing but palm leaves for clothing.

As she studied the tin can that was apparently going to deliver her to paradise, she remembered the lesson her father had started teaching her from a very young age. All good things come with a price.

"This was a mistake," she muttered. She hadn't meant to voice her anxiety aloud. After all, she hadn't mentioned her fear of flying to Jett.

"No it wasn't," he said. "I was teasing about the friends-with-benefits thing, Carissa. We're just two pals going on a trip."

He'd misunderstood her anxiety. Mercifully. "When does the flight take off again?"

"Five o'clock."

Carissa checked her watch. They had less than an hour. She glanced around, hoping to spy a bar. Maybe she could curb her nervousness with a couple shots of tequila. That hope was dashed when a pretty dark-haired woman approached them.

"Are you Carissa Pierre and Jett Lewis?"

Jett nodded. "That's us."

The woman extended her hand. "I'm Joely, the pilot." As Jett accepted her handshake, she added, "I'm a big fan of your books, Mr. Lewis."

Jett smiled. "Please, call me Jett."

"You're the pilot?" Carissa didn't mean to speak so loudly or to put quite so much disbelief into her tone, but seriously? The woman looked like she should still be hanging out by the lockers in high school before first bell.

Joely didn't take offense. "I'm older than I look."

It was on the tip of Carissa's tongue to say "I doubt it," but she'd already been rude. It probably wasn't a good idea to piss off the woman who was going to hold Carissa's life in her hands in less than—Carissa glanced at her watch—thirty minutes.

"I'm going to throw up."

Her admission caught Jett's attention. "You're afraid of flying?"

Carissa didn't own much in life, but one thing she had in spades was pride. "No. I'm not." It was a lie, but she stiffened her spine, threw her shoulders back and delivered it with so much conviction she almost convinced herself her fear wasn't real.

Almost.

Jett narrowed his eyes, studying her face. She had one hell of a poker face, so she held her own.

Joely had lost interest in their conversation and was consulting her clipboard. "You two are my last flight today. There's a storm system moving in, supposed to hit Miami within the hour. How would you feel about leaving now?"

So much for the tequila. Jett quickly agreed, obviously delighted that they could begin their adventure sooner.

Her stomach roiled, but she followed the others, dragging her suitcase behind her, wishing she'd thought to bring Dramamine or a sleeping pill. Being unconscious for the next few hours would be a welcome respite.

Once their luggage was loaded onboard, Joely took her place in the pilot's chair and began fiddling with the controls. Mercifully, Jett had nabbed a window seat, saving her from having too good a view of their plummet back to earth when everything went terribly wrong.

Carissa's chest tightened, her lungs seizing as she found it difficult to breathe. She tried to focus on the back of Joely's chair, but her peripheral vision kept landing on all the buttons

Joely was pushing and then the sound of the plane's engine fired up loudly.

"Shit," she whispered, hoping the noise would drown out her panic.

It hadn't. Distracted from the scene outside, Jett's attention was drawn to her. She didn't bother to look his way. She was too embarrassed, perfectly aware that her astute best friend probably wasn't missing anything—not her labored breathing or her white-knuckle grip on the armrests or the way her knee was bouncing approximately seventy-two thousand times a second.

As if to confirm her fears, Jett's hand landed on her leg, halting her nervous habit.

"Look at me, Rissa."

She wanted to. She really did, but she didn't dare take her eyes off the back of Joely's chair for fear she'd catch sight of something she didn't want to see. The plane was in motion now.

Jett's hand cupped her chin, turning her to him. She squeezed her eyes shut to block out whatever might be happening outside his window.

They flew open when she felt Jett's lips on hers.

She tried to rear back, but Jett had anticipated her escape. His hand gripped the back of her neck, holding her in place as he tilted his head and deepened the kiss.

For several moments, Carissa wasn't sure what to do. This was Jett, a man she'd considered her best friend for years. They'd never kissed. It had never even occurred to her to do such a thing. It wasn't that she thought Jett was unattractive. It was simply that she wasn't attracted to him in that way.

Or, at least, she *hadn't* been. The man sure as hell knew how to kiss.

She followed his direction as his tongue swiped at her lower lip. She opened her mouth and let him in. His hand loosened when he sensed her acquiescence, moving to her cheek, his fingers lightly caressing her face.

God. Sexiest kiss ever.

Carissa lifted her arms to his shoulders, allowing herself to stroke his dark hair. Jett had been blessed with his mother's thick mane, as opposed to his brother Caliph, who kept his head completely shaved. Both looks were sexy, but she preferred the way Jett's hair fell over one eye when he let it grow just a touch too long.

She startled when Jett's hand left her face and drifted lower. Their lips parted for a split second as she gasped. Jett didn't allow her to pull away, following her retreat while leaving his rogue hand on her breast. His lips became harder, hungrier, as he cupped her sensitive flesh then used his wicked fingers to pinch her taut nipple.

She moaned, the sound swallowed by Jett's continued kiss. Days could have passed, for all the awareness Carissa had of her surroundings. All she knew was that by the time Jett gentled this touch and they broke apart, she was flushed, feverish and hornier than she'd ever been in her life.

"Feel better?"

She frowned. "What?"

Jett pointed toward the window. Carissa struggled to comprehend exactly what she was looking at. Then she realized. It was clouds. They were in the air.

"You were nervous. Thought you could use some distraction during the takeoff."

Joely's light laughter sounded from the front of the plane. "You can distract me anytime you want, Jett. That was freaking hot."

"You just focus on the road. Or the air or...whatever."

Carissa wasn't sure where she'd found the strength to speak. Jett had sort of unwittingly shoved her neck deep in quicksand. When she'd imagined this trip, in her fantasies, she'd always met some sexy stranger and the two of them had spent the week lounging by the pool and having sex in the ocean. To keep the fantasy neat and easy, Jett had met another woman and basically disappeared early on, clearing her way to find true love and orgasms at the hand of some as-of-yet unknown character.

Now, she was suddenly seeing him in the role of her paradise hero and it wasn't sitting very well. She had to find a way back to solid ground—literally and figuratively.

Carissa turned away from Jett, leaning back against the headrest and reclining the seat. She closed her eyes and pretended to be bored. "I'll give you an A for effort, though your technique could use some work."

Joely giggled. Carissa was pleased that it at least appeared like she was holding her own.

Jett leaned closer and lowered his voice, making sure only Carissa could hear him. "I plan to stick the landing."

Carissa tried to ignore the seductive threat. Rather than acknowledge his words, she kept her eyes firmly closed, feigning sleep. There was no way she was going to let Jett know that his tactics to distract her had worked perfectly. Instead of stressing out over the fact she could die at any moment in a fiery plane crash, she found herself reliving Jett's kiss over and over and counting down the seconds until he did it again.

Carissa had just begun to take notice of their descent when she felt Jett's hand on her jaw. And then he was there, kissing her, again. And it was even more magical than the first time.

The world vanished until she heard the plane's engine go silent and Joely laughed. "I'm finished watching the air. Can I have my distraction now?"

Jett released Carissa, grinning widely. He winked at Joely. "I'm afraid this one," he gestured to Carissa, "needs a lot of attention."

Jett and Joely chuckled while Carissa tried to decide if she was pissed off at his teasing, his cavalier attitude toward the most incredible kiss of her life or the fact he'd stopped kissing her. She decided to settle on all three.

"I wouldn't worry about me monopolizing any more of your time. Now that we're here, I fully intend to explore all my options. You've had your audition. I guess now you'll just have to wait to see if you get a callback."

Jett clasped Carissa's hand, helping her down the narrow stairs from the plane to the dock. In the past, she wouldn't have even noticed his touch, wouldn't have considered the strength in his hand, the roughness of his fingers. She wouldn't have considered all the ways those thick, large hands could touch her. Unfortunately, that was all she could think about now.

As they retrieved their luggage, she pulled her hand away from him, grateful for the opportunity to put some distance between them. She was tired from the long-ass day and stressed out from the flight. All she needed was a good night's sleep and tomorrow, she'd be back in fighting shape and Jett would be firmly back in the "just friends" zone.

Problem solved.

"Holy shit," Jett muttered, drawing her attention to their surroundings.

Every drop of anxiety vanished as she took her first good look at Eden.

"Jesus," she whispered.

The word *paradise* seemed a pale description for the lush beauty of the island. Palm trees lined the edge of a pristine white sandy beach. The crystal blue water was clear and as they walked down the dock, Carissa could see countless species of colorful fish.

On its own, the natural magnificence would have been impossible to beat, but the opulent castle nestled atop a hill just before them overshadowed all of that.

The sun was beginning to set, the gray of dusk shattered by the bright lights greeting them. For a moment, Carissa could almost believe she'd been transported back in time.

"I can't believe this place is real."

Jett didn't reply, so she turned to look at him. His gaze remained steadfast on the castle for a few moments more, and then he faced her.

"Thank you for bringing me here, Rissa."

His words were solemn, earnest. She smiled and shrugged. "Thank the radio station."

He shook his head, his eyes softening, reflecting some emotion that made Carissa nervous...in a good way. Butterflies fluttered in her stomach and her palms felt sweaty. She'd never done that typical schoolgirl crush routine when she was a teenager. Life working at her father's bar, surrounded by gruff, world-weary people who never tried to sugarcoat reality for her had taken away her ability to romanticize anything.

However, there was no denying she was falling head over heels into a fairytale fantasy right now. She took a deep breath and forced herself to look away.

Eden wasn't reality. New Orleans was. She needed to stay smart, keep her guard up, and maintain the status quo. Ten minutes on this island and she already knew leaving it would be one of the hardest things she'd ever do. She didn't need to add to that difficulty by indulging in dreams about something that could never survive on Toulouse Street.

Together, she and Jett climbed the stone steps leading to

the castle. A pretty young woman at the front desk greeted them, then a bellboy took them up to their room.

Carissa didn't think it was possible to top her first glimpse of the island and castle, but the room proved her wrong. She'd never seen such sensuous luxury. The first thing she noticed was a king-sized, four-poster, complete with a canopy and sheer drapes. The fancy bed made her think of that second Indiana Jones movie—the one she hated with the whiny blonde chick.

Through an open doorway, she spotted a bathroom that was larger than her entire apartment above the bar back home. French doors opened to a balcony overlooking the ocean—which was shimmering in the moonlight. A romantic table adorned with a fancy white tablecloth, fine china and lit candles sat near a large window.

The bellboy set their luggage down near the door, then pointed out several of the room's amenities, including the large Jacuzzi tub in the bathroom and the antique armoire that hid a state-of-the-art television and sound system. He also gave them a quick rundown of what he referred to as "special places" on the island he thought they might enjoy, including a small cove that was ideal for snorkeling, and the dungeon.

Carissa snuck a quick peek at Jett, curious to know his reaction to that information. She'd read about Eden's dungeon several years earlier and it was one of the things that had fascinated her about the island. The second she realized she'd be traveling here, Carissa had done some research on BDSM and indulged in a shopping trip. At some point, she planned to sneak away from Jett to explore that part of the castle.

It was unlikely she'd ever have the opportunity to take a trip like this again. As such, Carissa intended to take advantage of every adventure, including indulging her curiosity and interest in bondage. She was far too outspoken and opinionated to relinquish control of her life, but she definitely wouldn't mind trying out the submissive role for a week. Being dominated by a sexy stranger had always ranked high on her list of sexual fantasies. Eden was offering her a chance to experience it without risk or strings.

The bellboy pointed to the table. "Given your long journey, the master of the island thought perhaps you would prefer to dine en suite this evening."

Jett nodded approvingly. "I think that's a great idea."

Carissa agreed. The long day was beginning to catch up with her.

"I'll leave this with you, then." The bellboy handed Jett a menu. Jett reciprocated by handing the young man a tip and his thanks. Surprisingly, the bellboy refused the tip, claiming the master paid them very well.

Once they were alone in the room, Jett passed the menu to Carissa. "I'm going to grab a quick shower. You mind ordering?"

She shook her head. "Nope. What do you want?"

"Anything that mooed in a previous life."

Carissa laughed, perusing the list as Jett grabbed his shower bag from his suitcase and disappeared into the bathroom.

She ordered the largest steaks on the menu for both of them, added baked sweet potatoes and grilled asparagus, then decided to splurge, requesting Tiramisu for dessert and a bottle of red wine at the last minute.

She giggled as she listened to Jett singing "Layla" loudly in the shower, then she ventured out onto the balcony. Night was in full bloom, the moon shining so brightly, its reflection on the water almost gave the appearance of day. It was the most beautiful sight she'd ever seen.

"Quite a view."

She turned at the sound of Jett's voice and realized she'd been mistaken about that most beautiful sight. Jett beat the view hands down. He was shirtless, dressed only in jeans that hung low on his hips. His dark hair was wet. He hadn't bothered to shave again, so his jaw was covered with a five o'clock shadow that she longed to rub her cheek against. Then her hormones kicked in and she reconsidered—wishing she could feel that roughness on the skin of her inner thighs.

Her silence prompted Jett to take his gaze away from the scenery. He studied her face with a knowing grin.

Shit. The cocky man would have a field day if he realized how much he was turning her on. She searched for some smartass cut-down; some way to put them back in familiar territory, but no words came.

She was saved by a knock on the door. Hallelujah for room service.

A waiter delivered their food, setting it out on the table as Jett pulled on a clean t-shirt and complimented her for her choices. After the waiter left, they claimed their seats. Carissa's stomach growled and Jett laughed.

"It's been hours since those lame burritos at lunch." He picked up his fork. "I'm starving too."

They chatted as they ate, their conversation mixed with a continual chorus of "Oh my God, this is good" and "Can you believe this place is real?"

Once they finished eating, Jett stood and looked around the room. Carissa noticed when his gaze fell on the bed. Before they left, the idea of the two of them claiming opposite ends of the large mattress had felt a lot simpler. Faced with the reality they'd be sharing the bed and her sudden, unfamiliar attraction to Jett, Carissa realized the bed wasn't as big as she thought.

She felt Jett's attention turn to her and she wondered if he was struggling with the fallout from those kisses in the plane as well. Carissa didn't doubt he'd been sincere about trying to distract her...at first. But there was no denying that distraction had morphed to desire pretty damn quick.

"Tell you what," Jett said, breaking a silence that had gone on a few beats too long. "I'm going to take a walk around the castle, do a little reconnaissance work to see what our options are in terms of recreation. Why don't you get a shower and hit the sheets?"

He was giving her a chance to escape, to fall asleep without him in the bed. She wasn't as grateful for the kindness as she should be.

"Sounds good."

Jett headed for the door. "Don't wait up. I spotted the bar on our way to the room. I might check out the action there."

She nodded. "Okay. I'll see you in the morning then." She waved as the door closed behind him. And she missed him about three seconds after his departure.

She tried to shake some sense into herself, then blamed her temporary insanity on the Bermuda Triangle. Clearly there was something weird in the air on this island that was clouding her usual crystal-clear judgment.

She lifted her suitcase to the luggage rack, digging for her own bathroom bag. Her gaze landed on the outfit she'd packed to wear to the dungeon.

Suddenly exhaustion was replaced by adrenaline.

Grinning, she considered the next few hours. Jett had said he would be gone for a little while, which left her some time to do a bit of exploring on her own.

Time to find her sexy stranger and have some fun.

With any luck, her trip to the dungeon would end in a dalliance that would drive Jett Lewis and his gorgeous blue eyes out of her mind.

Gorgeous eyes.

Damn. Until a few hours ago, she wouldn't have even remembered his eyes *were* blue.

She peered back into the case and spotted the vibrator she'd foolishly thrown in at the last minute on a whim. She was pleased with her impulsiveness. At least with the toy, she had a plan B if the dungeon fantasy failed.

God. This was going to be a long week.

CHAPTER THREE

Jett stood in the main playroom, keeping to the shadows as he surveyed the crowd in the dungeon. He felt a bit guilty for lying to Carissa about his true plans when he'd left the room, but he wasn't sure how she would react if she knew about his interest in BDSM. He'd purposely avoided making eye contact with her when the bellboy mentioned the dungeon. When she didn't mention it over dinner, he assumed she was either indifferent or hadn't understood what the man was referring to.

He straightened the mask Roan, the dungeon master, had given him upon his arrival. Apparently tonight was some sort of theme party—Masquerade—and everyone was required to wear masks. The anonymity appealed to Jett as it added an extra layer of intrigue to the evening.

There were close to fifty people at the party. Roan explained there were quite a few staff members who were regulars, in addition to the guests at the hotel. Some of the latter were first-timers, but others apparently returned to the island often. There was a good mix of Doms and Dommes, as well as collared and available subs.

He understood why an invitation to Eden to play in the dungeon was so coveted. It was beautiful, everything done in red, black and chrome. The red-lacquer walls were decorated with large mirrors so people could watch themselves playing in the flickering light provided by sconces. The equipment was state-of-the-art, most of it designed by Roan himself.

Roan had remembered Jett from the phone interview he'd conducted of the man a few years earlier when he was researching his book. He'd welcomed Jett to the dungeon and given him a quick tour of the place. Now, Jett watched as Roan played with a gorgeous woman strapped to a giant St. Andrew's cross. A crowd had formed, watching as the master smacked her shapely bottom with a leather paddle, then paused to stroke the reddening skin when she moaned and arched into his touch. Then he started again, this time with a short leather flogger. Jett didn't doubt for a moment every female sub in the place was wishing she were tied to that cross.

Jett had spotted two possible women to play with as he'd toured the area with Roan—lovely, sweet subs who would help him work off some of this pent-up lust that had been steadily building since he and Carissa left New Orleans.

When he first escaped the hotel room, he'd actually considered doing exactly what he'd told Carissa—castle tour, beach walk, bar. There was a part of him that felt guilty for coming here. Which was ridiculous. He and Carissa weren't a couple so it wasn't as if he were cheating on her.

The problem was something had definitely shifted the moment he'd opened that fancy envelope she'd handed him in the Royal Lunch and he'd read the invitation to Eden. It was as if a veil had been lifted, his vision cleared. Despite his deep roots in New Orleans, he'd never set much stock in voodoo or magic. At least not until he'd read that letter. From that point on, there was one thing that seemed to shine brighter to him, that stood out like a beacon calling him home—and it was Carissa.

He'd told her that kiss in the plane was meant to distract her, but the truth was after all those hours together in the car, driving to Miami, his willpower was gone. He simply couldn't *not* kiss her for a second longer.

Jett had spoken to a couple of friends who'd traveled to Eden a year earlier. Both of them kept referring to the magic of the place, the way things that had always seemed cloudy were suddenly in focus—vibrant, crisp, sharp. The man said the trip to Eden had changed their lives completely and that they would never be the same, but Jett had dismissed his overzealous comment. He recalled thinking to himself that perhaps they'd smoked some sort of wacky island weed that had distorted their perspective and left them a little touched in the head.

But now...he felt it. He understood.

When she'd looked at the bed in their room after dinner, it had taken every ounce of strength he possessed not to push her down on the mattress and take her then and there. And the truly frightening part was he didn't think Carissa would have rejected him, wouldn't have said no.

Things had taken a weird turn somewhere and it left him wondering what the fuck he was supposed to do now.

He sighed.

He wasn't going to do anything. At least not in this dungeon tonight. And not with a stranger. Dammit.

The only woman he wanted was upstairs.

He pushed away from the wall, intent on leaving, when he spotted her.

Despite the mask, there was no mistaking Carissa's walk or the self-assured way she stood, almost daring everyone in the room to look at her.

Her posture and poise screamed Domme...yet her outfit was in direct opposition to her demeanor. She was dressed in a very short mini skirt, stockings and high heels. She wore a revealing, lacy black push-up bra that enhanced her curves and was covered by a sheer white blouse that she'd only buttoned halfway. She was displaying her assets perfectly.

However, the thing that caught and captured his attention the most was her hair. It was down, hanging loose and wavy. His fingers itched to touch, to tangle, to tug. She was sex incarnate and a quick glance around the room proved he wasn't the only Dom to notice.

He needed to act fast before the hounds descended.

Jett took slow, measured steps toward her, trying to decide his approach. It appeared Carissa had been keeping her own secrets in regards to this trip. She'd clearly packed that outfit knowing she'd be venturing to the dungeon. He grinned. This vacation just kept getting better and better.

He was only a few feet away when another Dom approached Carissa. The man had pushed his mask off and was leading a woman behind him on a leash. His submissive was crawling on her knees, her head bowed. Jett frowned as he watched the woman struggling to keep up with the Dom. Humiliation wasn't an unusual thing to observe in the clubs, though it didn't interest Jett.

He glanced around to see if the Dom's behavior was setting off any alarms, but Roan was still with his sub at the St. Andrew's cross. There were other dungeon masters around the perimeter of the room, their sashes clearly designating their role. None of them reacted to the Dom's actions, so clearly the play had been negotiated and agreed upon. Roan managed the dungeon very well—upholding the Safe, Sane and Consensual credo. He had explained during the tour that many of the visitors to Eden were new to the scene and they'd come to live out their fantasies. As such, he worked very hard to keep everyone safe.

The Dom stopped in front of Carissa.

"Get on your knees," he demanded.

Carissa's spine straightened. No doubt she knew her rights. The man wasn't her Dom and she certainly didn't have to obey him.

However, Jett had witnessed his wildcat tossing more than a few rowdy drunks out of her bar in his lifetime. He decided to step in and guide her through her fantasy. What worked in the Royal Lunch was not going to work in this dungeon.

Jett was behind her in less than two seconds. He wrapped his arms around her waist, gripping her tightly. "There you are, my love. Standing just as I told you to. You're such a pretty sub."

Carissa stiffened, but didn't try to escape his hold. She started to turn, but Jett grasped her hair, forcing her to face forward. He'd purposely deepened his voice, not wanting her to know it was him. She hadn't mentioned her interest in the dungeon or told Jett she was planning to leave their room, which indicated she'd come here looking for a dalliance with a stranger. He planned to give her that...sort of. She'd definitely be playing tonight. But she'd be doing it with him.

"This is your sub?" The other Dom studied him, suspicion on his face.

Jett tried to keep his fury toward the obnoxious man at bay, but it was difficult. He had no respect for men who were more bully than Dom. "She is."

"She's disrespectful. She didn't lower her eyes when I spoke and she didn't obey my command."

Jett didn't respond. Instead he leveled a stare at the man that would leave no sensible, intelligent person in doubt of his anger. It was lost on the idiot in front of him, who failed to back down.

"She doesn't have to respond to jackasses," Jett said at last.

"Who are you calling a jackass? Your sub is badly behaved. All I'm saying is I'd be more than happy to help you punish the bitch."

The man was clueless about dungeon etiquette. If he continued behaving this way, Roan would kick the man out on his ass.

Carissa pressed closer to Jett in an attempt to get away from the bastard. He held her tighter, his protective instincts on red-alert. "I don't intend to punish her."

The man leered at Carissa, viewing her like a juicy steak. "That's a shame. I'd like to see how she responds to the whip. Bet she takes it like a bitch in heat."

The man's comments and unsavory ogling sickened Jett. Carissa started to turn away, but Jett held her in place. It was important they keep up the appearance of Dom and sub, even though he wanted to pull her against his chest, shielding her from everyone in the room. She was his.

From now on, she would always be his.

But he needed to proceed with caution. And he needed to get them the hell away from this man before the asshole scared Carissa so badly she left.

"If you'll excuse us." Jett waited for the man to step aside.

He didn't.

"Is everything okay here?" Jett glanced over his shoulder to find Roan standing just behind him. "Master Gregory?"

Clearly another dungeon master had alerted Roan to the scene unfolding.

Gregory scowled, shooting a look at Jett that screamed

retribution. He started to drag the sub roughly, causing her to wince in pain. Roan stopped him. Reaching down, Roan helped the poor woman to her feet, lifting her mask to reveal blue eyes filled with tears. Jett could see blood welling from fresh scrapes on her knees from Gregory's strong pull.

Gregory blanched. "That was an accident."

Blood was a red flag in a place like this.

Roan looked at Jett, who still held Carissa in his arms. "I'll entrust the lovely Carissa to you." Obviously, Roan could tell how much Gregory's actions had upset her. "She's new to this scene." The words were a warning for Jett, but he didn't need them. All they did was confirm his suspicions. Carissa was a novice. The idea of teaching her the beauty of submission took his cock from half-mast to rock-hard instantly.

"I could have taught her a few things."

Gregory needed a lesson in keeping his mouth shut. Jett wished for the opportunity to teach the son of a bitch a thing or two about it. Gregory better hope they didn't run into each other on the beach.

Roan's eyes darkened and Jett realized any punishment he might mete out would pale in comparison to what Roan would deliver. Roan put a supportive arm around Gregory's sub, helping the limping woman walk to his office. Gregory followed behind, but not before he sent one last unsavory leer in Carissa's direction. "The island's not that big. We'll see each other again." The softly spoken words were laced with a threat, yet rather than scare Carissa, Jett felt that same stiffening of her spine that indicated she wasn't afraid. She wouldn't back down.

Gregory was picking on the wrong girl. Not only because Jett would kill any man who tried to hurt her, but because Carissa packed a powerful punch on her own.

"Thank you." She started to step away from him, but he

refused to relinquish his grip. She struggled slightly. "You can let go of me now."

"No."

His simple response seemed to confuse her. "I don't understand."

It was time to wipe away the unpleasant scene they'd just endured with seduction. "Why are you here, Carissa?"

She stopped trying to break free of his grip. She tried to turn her head once more, but Jett merely tightened his grip in her hair. The tug on her tresses had another, more sensual effect, however. Her voice was breathless when she asked, "What do you mean?"

"Roan said you were new. What brought you to the dungeon? What are you looking for?"

She laughed softly. "Shouldn't that be obvious? Sex."

"You're a beautiful woman. I hardly think it would be difficult for you to find a man to share your bed. You don't need this dungeon for that."

"You're right. I don't. I want more."

Jett loved her honesty. Loosening his grip, he stroked her hair lightly before closing his fingers again tightly. He applied more pressure, enjoying her heated response to the pain.

Carissa moaned quietly, then asked, "Who are you?"

"My name doesn't matter. You'll call me Sir."

She shivered at the title. Jett fought to restrain a grin.

"Answer my question, my love. Why are you here?"

She took her time, choosing her words carefully. Jett had always respected Carissa's cautious nature, the way she thought before speaking or acting.

"I want to see if...I think I might be..."

She struggled with the word. Jett wasn't surprised. Carissa was too independent to release her grip on the reins for long.

"Submissive?"

She released a breath. "Yes, but I think it will be hard for me to...I mean...I don't think I'll submit easily."

He chuckled. "I like a challenge."

Carissa stiffened at the sound of his laughter. "Do I know you?"

He'd nearly revealed himself. Until he convinced her he was the right man to indulge her fantasy, he couldn't let her know it was him. Carissa would never risk their friendship on what she would think was just sex. He deepened his voice once more. "No."

She didn't seem convinced, but mercifully she let it slide. "I can't let a man drag me around on a leash."

Jett grimaced. The asshole *had* scared her, given her a bad impression of what it meant to submit. "I don't drag women around."

"He was cruel to her."

Jett wanted to go find Gregory and beat the shit out of the man. "The only pain I give would bring you pleasure."

"Even if I did something wrong? I've never done this before. I don't know how—"

"I would like to teach you. How long are you staying at Eden?"

"A week."

"Give me the week. Promise to be my submissive and I'll show you exactly how incredible it can be to put yourself in the hands of a man whose only goal is to give you as many orgasms as you can stand."

She laughed. "Orgasms sound nice."

Carissa wasn't shy about asking for what she wanted. It was a refreshing change, given his last few girlfriends, who preferred to play games and make him guess what they wanted.

"Should we start your lessons?"

"Now?"

Carissa's courage was faltering in the face of making her fantasy a reality.

Jett lifted the hand wrapped around her waist to her breast. Cupping it, he pressed firmly, applying pressure until he heard her gasp.

"Now."

Carissa didn't protest or resist when Jett placed his hands on her hips and slowly pushed her forward.

"Where are we going?"

Jett didn't bother to respond, just continued to move them across the room. While there were many public areas where couples who enjoyed exhibitionism could play in front of an audience, Jett suspected Carissa wasn't ready for that. She was questioning her ability to submit, so he would have to guide her along the path slowly.

He had the perfect place in mind. He had spotted it when Roan had given him the tour. When they reached the private, curtained area, Jett directed her inside then bid her to kneel on the spanking bench. It was one of Roan's designs, with black leather padding covering the two levels. Carissa's knees would be cushioned on the lower bench, her upper body draped over the higher surface, which tilted slightly so that her head would be lower than her hips. It would leave her ass raised, vulnerable. There were straps attached to the four corners.

Carissa hesitated, studying the bench. He was pleased that, while she was excited and curious, her sense of self-preservation was firmly in place.

"Are you going to tie me up?"

"Do you want me to?"

She started to shrug, but he wasn't willing to let her off easy. This night would only succeed if she were honest about her desires, her needs.

"Yes or no."

"Yes, but—"

"But nothing. You said yes. Kneel."

She lowered herself to the padded bench, offering no resistance as he pressed on her back until her stomach was flat against the surface, her arms dangling toward the floor. Once she was crouched over the bench, he moved closer, brushing her ass with his crotch, letting her feel his erection.

Her hands hung loose, though she clenched her fingers tightly around the front legs of the bench. He considered using the straps to secure her, and then decided against it. Jett understood the psychology of BDSM well enough to realize there were other ways to make Carissa feel captured.

He bent over her, pressing his chest against her back, caging her beneath him. She tried to lift up—the response an instinctual one—to test her ability to escape. He prevented her movement, putting more of his weight on her.

Carissa stilled, but he felt the stiffness in her posture when he lifted the mask from her face.

"Relax," he whispered.

She snorted softly. "Yeah right."

"The correct response is 'Yes, Sir'."

Her right cheek rested against the leather and she licked her lips nervously. "Yes, Sir." He saw her struggling to use her peripheral vision to see his face, but the mask and near darkness of the curtained area protected his anonymity.

"I'm going to list some things. Your only responses are yes or no. Understand?"

She nodded. Then quickly added, "Yes...Sir"

Jett decided to start easy, tackling something they'd already discussed. "Bondage."

"Yes."

"Spanking."

"Yes."

Her answers were immediate, letting Jett know she had indeed been fantasizing about this.

"Flogger."

This time her response took longer.

"Yes?"

He heard the question in her voice, but he let it go.

"Exhibitionism."

"Yes."

"Anal."

"Shit," she muttered.

Jett tried not to laugh. "That's not an answer."

"Yes, dammit."

"Threesome." Jett wasn't sure why he'd added that to his list. It certainly wasn't something he'd ever seriously considered trying himself, even though his brother, Justin, found sharing the woman he loved hot. Carissa had remarked once how cool she thought Justin's relationship with Bella and Ned was. Jett hadn't thought much of it at the time, but now that he was looking at Carissa and thinking girlfriend, he wondered just how interested she was.

Carissa shook her head. "No. I don't think so. I'm not very good at sharing."

For a moment, Jett considered bending down to place a kiss on Carissa's cheek. However, he feared that would be too familiar, would give him away.

Instead, he continued his list. "Nipple clamps."

"Yes."

"Role play."

"This is kind of a long list. I'm only here for one week."

This time, he did chuckle. She was too adorable, too funny. She also didn't realize they had much longer than one week. Forever was starting to sound feasible.

"Answer my question or I'll spank you. You failed to respond correctly to most of these. Role play."

"Yes."

"Good girl. Now. Tell me your dirtiest fantasy."

She hesitated. "I...I—"

"This will only work if you're completely honest about what you want. As you said, our time is limited."

"Capture."

Though her response was short and succinct, it fired off a million kinky scenes in Jett's mind as he considered all the ways he'd like to capture her. Claim her. Take her.

He pressed his lips to her ear and whispered his own single word. "Yes."

With that, he pushed up, pulling her hands as he went, clasping them behind her back. "Your safe word is red. Say that and I'll stop whatever it is I'm doing and we'll talk about it. Understand?"

"Yes."

"Yes what?"

"Yes, Sir."

"Good." He'd taken a pair of handcuffs from the toy room after signing in with Roan. Pulling them from his back pocket, he slipped them around Carissa's wrists. She startled and started to rise, but he placed a firm hand on her upper back. "Don't move."

She'd obviously expected him to employ the straps on the bench. He liked keeping her off balance, always wondering what was coming next by not being predictable. She was captive to him and his desires.

He'd sensed her beginning to relax as they spoke. Jett had hoped that by talking a bit she would start to feel more comfortable. Now, with one click of the cuffs, he'd taken that comfort away, keeping her on her toes, wondering what would come next. The fear and excitement of the unknown would only continue to build her arousal.

The same held true for him. His cock was currently hard enough to pound nails in concrete. He was aching to touch her. To fuck her.

He had to keep reminding himself this was Carissa. His Carissa. The consequences of their actions tonight would be long reaching. Despite Carissa's belief she was indulging in some kinky play with a stranger, when he took the mask off, everything would change.

That thought gave him pause. He was taking the choice of leaving their friendship behind, to embark on something much more, out of Carissa's hands. He tried to summon up some guilt about it, but he couldn't. The magic of Eden was too powerful. He'd never been more certain about anything in his life. He wasn't going to let this moment, this chance for happiness, slip by simply because of Carissa's practicality. He'd show her there was something to be said for being impulsive.

Reaching lower, he lifted her skirt, groaning when he discovered her ass bare. "Dirty girl."

His words weren't an admonition, they were praise. He ran his hand over the smooth skin, enjoying the slight shudder his touch provoked.

Carissa wiggled her ass. A sexy invitation.

He tapped on the inside of her knees. "Open your legs."

She followed his command, spreading her thighs apart as much as the bench would allow. Jett ran his fingers along her wet slit.

Carissa gasped, squirmed, encouraged him without words to touch her again, to go deeper. She tried to press toward him, but he didn't give her what she wanted.

He dragged his fingers to her clit, lightly caressing the tiny button. It wasn't enough for her and she let him know. "Harder," she urged.

Jett took his hand away from her completely, letting her feel its absence for a few seconds before he swatted her ass firmly.

She gasped and tried to raise her chest. He pressed his hand to her upper back, holding her against the leather as he spanked her again.

"Wait. No." She continued to struggle.

Jett paused briefly, though he didn't lighten his grip. "The only word you're allowed to speak is red. Say that now or be quiet."

She stopped moving, her breathing faster, louder. For a moment, he feared he'd gone too far, too fast. Jett reached out and stroked her ass gently, hoping she'd understand that pleasure and pain could exist together.

"I..." Carissa's voice faltered. Jett silently willed her not to say the safe word.

Finally, she said, "I don't want you to stop."

He slowly released the breath he'd been holding. Carissa wouldn't give up on something she wanted so easily.

He rewarded her courage by running his fingers along her slit once more. This time he pushed two fingers into her opening to the first knuckle.

Seven years he'd been walking around with blinders on and now—within a single night—he'd found something he didn't even know he'd been looking for. He'd sure as hell turned a corner, but it wasn't on the street he'd been walking down. He wasn't sure it was even in the same state. Jett tried to remember if any moment in his life had ever felt this right, but nothing came to mind.

He pressed a bit deeper and it fired Carissa's arousal once more. She relaxed against the bench, her sigh one of bliss. She started to say, "Yes," but she cut the sound off, clearly recalling his admonition against speaking.

She'd said she would find submission difficult, but Jett was starting to think she was better at it than she realized.

He removed his fingers—drenched with her body's juices—and pressed them against her clit. This time, he gave her the pressure she wanted. He started with a slow caress against the sensitive nub, then built up the speed, following the cues of Carissa's body. Her hips were thrusting in time with his strokes—as much as her position would allow—and her moans grew louder.

Jett wanted to see her orgasm more than he wanted his next breath, but it was too soon. She was going to come apart at his touch—more than once tonight if he had his way—but he was going to make her work for it, earn it.

He stopped when he felt her reaching the brink. She groaned, then turned her head toward him. He knew her well enough to know she'd be pissed off. He silenced her with a hard slap on her ass.

This time, she didn't resist the pain, didn't seek to escape it. Jett continued to spank her, varying the placement. Some of his slaps were hard, others light. While she never knew what was coming, she started anticipating his hand, started lifting her hips toward him.

Just when they began to fall into a rhythm, he halted the spanking. Carissa moaned, but didn't bother to complain. She was a quick study.

He dipped his fingers into her pussy, driving two deep. Carissa jerked at the unexpected touch. Clearly she'd expected gentleness. He loved surprising her, keeping her on edge and always wondering.

He thrust the fingers in roughly a dozen times...just until he felt Carissa's inner muscles begin to flutter, to clench. He removed his hand once more, leaving her gasping and pleading.

"Damn you! Please."

She'd forgotten his command to remain silent, but he didn't punish her for it. There was nothing hotter on Earth than the sound of Carissa begging for him to fuck her.

Jett refused to give in, to let the evening end too soon. He repeated his sensuous torture—toying with her clit, spanking her ass, stroking the sensitive flesh, thrusting his fingers into her hot, wet pussy. Over and over, he drove her to the edge, never allowing her to fall into the white-hot bliss.

Carissa was out of control, writhing on the bench, gasping, crying, cursing. It was the most beautiful thing he'd ever seen.

Finally, he gave up his own restraint, unable to resist giving in to his own desires. He moved his hands away from her, unzipped his jeans, and placed the head of his cock at her opening.

Carissa tried to move toward him, tried to force him inside, but her range of mobility was too limited. Even so, he tightened his grip on her hips and held her still, not entering her.

He froze.

Jett wasn't sure what was holding him back. She wanted him and he wanted her.

Maybe that was the problem. He wanted Carissa, his best friend—but she wanted a stranger, not Jett. If she'd wanted him, she would have told him about her interest in the dungeon. She wouldn't have snuck away from the hotel room after he'd left.

He was going to take her. Jett had never been more certain of anything in his life.

But by God, she was going to know it was *him* before he did so.

He pulled away, then realized he hadn't bothered to put on

a condom. It hadn't even occurred to him, though he'd never had sex without one. He didn't want to put anything between him and Carissa, but that was another decision she needed to be a part of.

Carissa shook her head. "No, please. Don't stop."

Her quiet, anguished plea was almost his undoing.

Almost.

He dug the key to the cuffs out of his pocket and released her hands. Before she had time to register her freedom, he gripped her upper arm and lifted her. Then he helped her stand.

Jett's chest tightened, but he didn't let fear hold him back, stop him from doing what he knew was right. He couldn't take this decision away from her.

Her skirt fell back into place and he was somewhat shocked to realize that both of them were—more or less—fully dressed. He was also painfully aroused and teetering on the edge of losing all control. And the fact that Carissa was completely covered didn't change that. God help him when he got her clothes off.

She was unsteady, struggling to find her footing when he used his grip on her arm to turn her toward him. As she lifted her gaze to his face, he pulled off the mask.

Her eyes widened when she realized it was him. "Jett?"

He nodded. "I wanted you to see the man who's going to take you tonight, Rissa."

She shook her head slowly. Jett didn't think the response was a refusal as much as disbelief. She didn't speak. Instead her eyes traveled along his body, not stopping until she found his cock, still painfully erect and pointing directly at her. He didn't bother to hide it from her. He wanted her to understand exactly how much he desired her—not a stranger, not a faceless submissive. Just her.

When her eyes met his again, he read the confusion, then the resignation.

It was his turn to shake his head. "You're not going to say no."

Her gaze narrowed. "Excuse me?"

"This is going to happen, Rissa."

His beautiful, strong-willed friend reappeared with a vengeance, her haughty face scowling at him. The way she threw back her shoulders alerted him that she was about to unleash one hell of a Carissa-style put down. The angry look only sent more blood rushing to his filled-to-capacity cock.

"No, Jett. No way."

He reached for her wrist. Cupping her hand in his, he forced her fingers around his cock. "Feel that, Rissa. That's yours. From now on, it's only yours."

She kept her grip loose, fighting to free her hand from his grasp. "Don't say that. Don't even think it."

He applied more pressure to his hand, giving her no choice as he ran her palm up and down his aching flesh. "Yours," he repeated. "And not just for tonight or this week."

"Red."

He released her instantly, watching with regret as her hand fell back to her side. She was obviously surprised by his quick response.

A Dom always respected the safe word.

She took a step away and he allowed it. Carissa was a thinker. He couldn't force the issue or she'd shut down. She needed time to consider what he wanted.

She stepped to the right and he read the retreat on her face.

"You can leave for now. But remember what I said. Red only stops the play temporarily so that we can talk about it. This conversation isn't over."

She didn't bother to deny him. Carissa was sensible enough to recognize the truth, to understand what was inevitable.

She nodded once. Then left quickly. He watched her departure, making certain she made it out of the dungeon without being bothered. Then he slowly tucked his hard cock away carefully.

He was in for a long fucking night.

CARISSA WALKED ALONG THE BEACH. She'd left the dungeon nearly an hour earlier. It was close to two a.m., which meant twenty-four hours had passed since she'd seen a bed and sleep. She should be exhausted, but adrenaline kept her going.

When she'd first escaped Jett, she went straight outside to the ocean, her thoughts racing a million miles a minute, taking a thousand different twists and turns. Now, she was numb. And she was left with some hard facts to face.

Her best friend was a Dom and he wanted *her*.

After the initial freaking out died down, Carissa was forced to acknowledge another truth—she wanted him too. Which was stupid and impractical. It was a relationship that was destined for failure. She and Jett were too different. He was worldly and intelligent. He'd traveled to countless countries, dated exotic, interesting women, and grown up in a house filled with love and a family that cared about him deeply.

Meanwhile, she was the woman who'd spent her entire life behind the counter of a shitty bar in New Orleans, working her ass off in hopes of earning two seconds' worth of attention from a father who viewed her as nothing more than free labor. She couldn't spell to save her soul and the only books she'd ever read from cover to cover were Jett's, though she'd never admitted that to him.

When life had handed them lemons, Jett had taken his and turned them into a *New York Times* bestselling recipe for lemonade. She'd merely chopped hers up, stuck them on a sugar-rimmed glass of vodka and served them to a bunch of rednecks, frat boys on spring break, and drunk-ass tourists.

She needed to head back to the hotel, but she couldn't face the idea of returning to the room. Jett was expecting a conversation, probably one with answers. She had none.

Carissa sighed. This was ridiculous. She couldn't spend the rest of the week avoiding the room. She'd simply go back and tell him she needed some time to think. Maybe she could stall until they got off this island. Surely things would return to normal once they got back into the swing of their everyday lives in New Orleans and broke free of whatever freaky-deeky spell Eden had cast on them.

She turned toward the castle, deciding to walk along the tree line instead of the water's edge. She didn't feel like dodging waves in the dark or trudging through the fancy lobby with wet feet.

She was still a fair distance away when she saw something under one of the palm trees. It appeared to be someone reclined in a beach chair. Maybe this person was trying to avoid their hotel room as well.

Unfortunately, the moon cast weird, creepy shadows, making everything seem more menacing than it would be in bright sunshine. She approached the motionless person—a man she could see now—concerned by his utter stillness and his unusual position in the chair.

Then warning bells sounded and she realized it was pretty stupid of her to approach a stranger alone in the dark. She'd continue on to the castle and let the night clerk know there was someone out here.

She'd only taken a single step when the clouds covering the

moon dispersed and the beach brightened with more light. She looked at the body once more.

"Fuck," she whispered when a moonbeam shone down, allowing her to see the man more clearly.

He was dead.

CHAPTER FOUR

The man's body was bound to the lounge chair, his arms handcuffed to the frame above his head. His legs were sprawled open, hanging over the edges, his pants and shirt open. Blood covered his chest and legs, but that wasn't the most horrifying part as her gaze traveled to his face. It was contorted in pain, even after death

And stuffed in the man's mouth, was his penis.

Carissa started to scream, but a hand was placed over her mouth, cutting off the sound. She went into full-fight mode, driving her elbow back into the stomach of her attacker.

"Easy, Rissa," Jett said. "It's me. I've been looking everywhere for you."

She pulled his hand away from her mouth, wheeling on him. "You scared the fuck out of me, you jackass!"

He gestured toward the body. "You were a little preoccupied."

"Gee, ya think?"

Jett shushed her, his voice lowered. "I'm sorry I scared you, but I didn't want you to scream. The killer could still be around here."

Leave it to Jett to see a dead body and think completely rationally. "Writing those murder mysteries has left you twisted. That poor man has been killed!"

He grimaced. "Yeah. I see that. But I'd like to make sure we don't end up the same way."

She swallowed heavily and nodded. When she spoke again, she made sure to whisper. "I get that. I just...I've never seen..."

Jett wrapped her in his arms, holding her tight. She didn't bother to deny to herself how safe she felt there. "I know. It's okay."

Twisting slowly, she stayed close to him as she looked at the dead man once more. She steeled herself for what she would see, then recognition dawned.

"Jett. It's—"

"Gregory. It looks like he pissed someone off."

She nodded slowly. "From what I could tell, he pissed off everyone in the dungeon tonight. You and me included."

Jett tightened his grip on her, keeping his arms wrapped around her waist, her back pressed to his chest. "Yeah. But there's a difference between wanting to kick a man's ass for being a prick and *this*. Someone really had it in for the guy."

Carissa shivered, her body trembling roughly. "It got cold out, didn't it?"

"Shit. No. It's still warm. Come on. We need to report this, then get you a stiff drink and into bed. I think you're going into shock."

She tried to laugh. She wasn't the kind of woman to flip out over much of anything. "I'm f-fine." No doubt her reassurance would have sounded more convincing if her damn teeth hadn't started chattering.

Jett wrapped a strong arm around her and escorted her

back to the castle quickly. Once there, he led her to the front desk where he requested to see the manager.

"Is there something wrong?"

Jett nodded. "Yes, there is. It's vital that we talk to the person in charge." Carissa noticed he didn't tell the clerk about the dead body. Maybe he'd decided it would be better to report the murder to the manager.

The clerk studied them closely, taking in Jett's scowl and Carissa's trembling. Then he picked up the phone and quietly spoke to someone on the other end. Jett was surprised when the man instructed them to take the elevator to an office on the top floor. "The master of the island is expecting you."

Jett and Carissa got on the elevator, their movements almost mechanical. She was starting to feel like a zombie.

"Master of the island?" she whispered.

She and Jett had discussed the rumors surrounding the billionaire recluse who owned Eden. The man was a bit of a celebrity, despite the fact very few people had ever seen him. On the rare occasions he had been spotted, he was always wearing a mask that hid his face, which, of course, encouraged the tabloids to splatter the covers of their rags with fresh rounds of speculation regarding the man's appearance, his disdain for society and what skeletons he was hiding in his closet. Over the years, rumors had included everything from accusing the man of being a murderer on the run to a Russian spy to a recluse like Michael Jackson.

When they arrived at the door, Jett lifted his hand and knocked. A deep voice bid them to enter.

Carissa squinted in the dimly lit room. The curtains were drawn, keeping out any light that would have been provided by the moon. A single candle illuminated the large office, which meant they were essentially standing in the dark.

A rustling sound came from one of the corners and Carissa

could just make out the silhouette of a man sitting behind a desk.

"Is there a problem?"

Jett had taken Carissa's hand before they entered the room and he hadn't released it. She was grateful for it now when she heard the master's deep, gravelly voice.

Jett remained where he was rather than attempting to move closer.

"There's been a murder."

If they'd expected some sort of alarm or concern from the man, they would have been disappointed. "I see."

Carissa waited for him to ask more questions, but none came. She took a small step forward. "We met the man who was killed, tonight in the dungeon. I believe his name was Gregory. Someone tied him to a lounge chair, stabbed him, cut off his—" She stopped, embarrassed.

"Someone cut his cock off and stuffed it in his mouth," Jett finished for her.

Again, the master remained silent for several moments. Then he lifted the phone on his desk. "Roan? I need to see you in my office immediately."

Jett frowned. "Shouldn't you call the cops?"

The master didn't move. Carissa was tempted to take another step toward the desk, curious about the man, his face, his over-the-top need for complete privacy. Jett must have sensed her intention because he clasped her hand tighter and held her back.

"There isn't an official police force on the island. I have a security team who deals with any issues that arise. Sadly, the head of that team is stranded in Miami. A rather nasty storm front has moved in on the East Coast. It's halted air travel to and from the southern part of Florida and my man isn't able to get back. At least not for a day or two. Maybe more."

"But there's a murderer on the island!" Carissa was unnerved by the man's utter calm.

"That is unfortunate."

Carissa started to blast the man for his callous attitude, but before she could speak, there was a knock on the door.

"Enter," the master commanded.

Roan stepped into the office. Like Jett, he stopped just a few feet inside the door, not venturing any closer to the man behind the desk. "You wanted to see me?"

The master raised his hand to Jett, clearly indicating he wanted him to explain. Jett efficiently recapped their evening, telling Roan about Gregory's murder, where the body was, and the way the man had been killed.

"You know this man, Roan?" the master asked.

Roan nodded. "He's a guest on the island. Arrived today. I was leery about letting him play in the dungeon, but his father is a highly positioned foreign diplomat and he had proof of membership in an elite D.C. sex club. I let him in against my better judgment and had him escorted out an hour later. I suspected you'd called me up here because he had lodged a complaint. Didn't expect to hear he'd been murdered."

The master slowly tapped a pen on his desk, the light pounding the only sound in the silent room.

"Um, hello? A man has been killed. And even if he *was* a gigantic prick, it's a little more than 'unfortunate'." Carissa's tone was downright hostile, but she was annoyed by the utter lack of compassion in the room.

"I apologize if I seem cold, Ms. Pierre. However, it is imperative that we handle things carefully tonight. As I said, everyone on this island is essentially stranded here until the storm passes. I would prefer not to start a widespread panic should the guests realize there is a killer amongst them. Do you understand?"

Carissa nodded. "Of course I do."

"Roan, please have three of the security guards retrieve the body. Tell them to be careful when transporting it, so they don't compromise any of the evidence."

"Where should they move the body?" Roan asked.

"To the infirmary. I'll call Dr. Magdalene and inform her they'll be there shortly."

"I'll take care of it." Roan started to leave, but the master called him back.

"Roan. One moment. How many people saw you kick Gregory out of the club tonight?"

Roan considered the question. "There were three, maybe four members at the exit when I had my men escort him out."

"Did Gregory go quietly?"

Roan shook his head. "He was shouting, cursing, threatening to have me fired."

"Then you're a suspect."

Roan didn't seem surprised or bothered by that fact. "I suppose I am."

"I'll take care of that issue. You may leave."

Roan bowed his head before leaving them alone with the master once more.

Carissa shuddered slightly. She was starting to feel as if she were in the middle of a *Godfather* movie. She kept waiting for the master to peel off some Mission Impossible-style mask to reveal himself as Michael Corleone, ready to give someone the kiss of death.

She snorted, covering her mouth quickly. Unfortunately, it was too late, her brief laugh completely inappropriate for the situation. She looked over at Jett, who appeared confused, but amused, by her untimely giggle.

The master—mercifully—ignored the sound. "You are a crime writer, Mr. Lewis. Is that correct?"

Jett nodded. "Yes."

"I suspect you've conducted research on the criminal mind, studied the details surrounding murder scenes and the like to help you write your novels."

"I have."

The master stood, walking to the curtained window behind him. Carissa found herself hoping he would draw the heavy material back to allow some of the moonlight to hit his face. He didn't.

"I intend to hide the fact there's been a murder. When life goes on as normal tomorrow, when no crime is announced, the killer will realize we've covered it up. He will be suspicious of anyone who is a member of my staff and therefore on guard. You and Ms. Pierre said you met the victim in the dungeon tonight. It appears Gregory made quite a spectacle of himself there, so perhaps that would be a good place to launch an investigation. We need to sniff this man out."

"Why do you keep referring to the killer as a man? Gregory had his," Carissa hesitated, then said, "penis cut off and stuffed in his mouth. That feels like a crime of passion to me. The work of a woman scorned."

The master seemed to consider her assessment, but Jett shook his head. "Gregory was a large man. I can't imagine a woman would be able to overpower him and tie him up that way."

"Maybe she got him in the chair under the ruse of a sex game."

"Gregory is a Dom, Rissa. Unless you're suggesting he was a switch." Jett appeared to be wavering. "If that was the case..."

The master cleared his throat. "It's a theory worth investigating. Would you and Ms. Pierre be willing to do a bit of undercover work?"

Jett said, "we're not detectives," at the exact same time Carissa asked, "In the dungeon?"

Jett flashed her an exasperated look, but she ignored it. Carissa was oddly excited by the prospect of playing detective. She'd been reading Jett's novels for years and was a huge fan of murder mystery television shows.

Jett crossed his arms. "Listen, I would like to help, but—"

"We'll do it," Carissa replied before Jett could refuse.

"Rissa. I'm not about to put you in a dangerous situation. You saw the way that man was murdered. This isn't fiction. The threat is very real."

"How can you just stand by and let a killer go free? What if Gregory isn't his only intended victim? This murderer could have it out for anyone associated with BDSM or..." Carissa's tired mind was suddenly whirling again as she spied a way to distract Jett from his sudden, inexplicable interest in her. Maybe a murder investigation to knock out some of this intense, sexual tension between them.

Jett tried to reason with her, but she could have told him she was too far-gone for that. "If it were just me, Rissa, I'd be first in line to help, but—"

Carissa put her hands on her hips. "Don't you dare go all macho on me, Jett Lewis. I'm perfectly capable of taking care of myself and you know it. If you try to pull that chivalrous, protecting-the-little-woman bullshit on me, I swear to God, I'll smother you in your sleep tonight."

Jett narrowed his eyes, stepping closer. Carissa had to resist the urge to take a step back. He'd never used his size to intimidate her until this moment. And now that he was, she had to admit he was definitely scary when he was angry.

"You won't be able to smother me if I strap you to the bed and keep you there the rest of the week."

"You wouldn't dare!"

He tilted his head, his expression far too smug. "You were in the dungeon with me tonight, Rissa. I made it very clear there's nothing I'd like more than to tie you to my bed and have my wicked way with you. Don't worry, though. I'd make sure you weren't bored."

For the first time since she'd entered the room, she found the master of the island the lesser threat. She turned, searching for the man in the shadows. "I'll help you uncover the killer's identity. With or without Jett's help."

Before Jett could protest or contradict her, Carissa left the room. She'd spent the last couple of hours worrying about how to hold Jett at bay until they returned home and came to their senses. Jett had used kisses to distract her from her fear of flying. Now she was going to sidetrack him from his pursuit of her with a murder investigation.

"Dammit, Carissa. Wait."

She didn't have much of a choice. The elevator hadn't arrived.

"You're not going to change my mind about this, Jett."

Jett rubbed a hand over his jaw, dark circles under his eyes proving the lack of sleep was catching up to him as well. They were both running on empty. "Rissa—"

She leaned against the wall. "Can we table this conversation until tomorrow? I'm so sleepy."

Jett grinned tiredly. "Yeah. That's fine. But I'm not going to change my mind."

The elevator doors opened and they stepped inside, pushing the button for their floor.

"Neither am I. You need this, Jett."

Jett frowned. "What are you talking about?"

"Doing some undercover work on a murder investigation may be just the trick to get the wheels in your brain turning again. It'll put you back in the right frame of mind and jar loose whatever it is that's keeping you from writing."

"You think we should both put our lives in danger so that I can start writing again?"

She nodded. "Yep. That's exactly what I think. Let's face it, you haven't exactly been yourself lately. You're depressed, in a slump and nothing's helped. Not your family, not sex—don't even tell me you haven't tried to use that as a cure—or even this vacation."

"We haven't been here an entire day. Don't you think it's too soon to make that call, to declare this a failed venture?"

"Whatever. The point is you've been floundering, struggling to find your footing." Then another thought occurred to her. "I'm pretty sure it's this state of panic you've been in lately that has you thinking you're interested in me."

He frowned. "That's not true."

"Nothing has changed between us except the scenery. You're grasping for something, anything to make you forget your writer's block. I get that. And I'm actually sort of flattered. But you need to find another cure. Digging into a juicy murder investigation sounds like a much more effective way for a crime writer to break his mental block than lying around in the sun all day, pounding Coronas and Vodka Tonics and trying to get into my pants."

"You know, lots of famous authors have also been famous for their alcoholism. Hemingway, Poe—"

"I don't need the list."

"And you're wrong about you and me."

Carissa wasn't sure how to respond to the absolute assurance in his voice. So she held her tongue, stepped off the elevator and started walking toward their room. Once they were inside, Carissa found herself in the same place she'd been a few hours earlier. Staring at the bed she and Jett had to share.

"It's been the longest day in history, Rissa."

She laughed. "You're right. It has."

"So let's do what you suggested by the elevator. Table it all until tomorrow. Every single one of these issues is still going to be here when we wake up."

She gave him a rueful grin. "Could you be any less consoling? Whatever happened to 'nighty night, don't let the bed bugs bite'?"

"You find that more comforting?"

She grabbed her pajamas and headed toward the bathroom. She turned at the doorway. "Sweet dreams, Jett."

He tugged off his t-shirt and jeans as she fought like the devil to feign indifference. Once he was down to his boxer briefs, he gave her a wicked wink, climbed under the covers and claimed a spot closer to the middle than the edge. "Good night, Rissa."

He turned off the lamp on his side of the bed and sighed contentedly. Clearly he was going to be much better at this platonic sleeping together than she was.

Exhaustion was no match for her hormones.

"Shit," she muttered as she closed the bathroom door behind her and donned her PJs. She studied her tired face in the mirror. "Note to self, next time you fly off to paradise with your best friend, pack Dramamine, heavy duty sleeping pills, tequila and more than one vibrator."

CHAPTER FIVE

Carissa watched the sunrise cast yellow shadows across the ceiling above the bed. Her thirty-seventh glance at the clock told her it was only five minutes later than the last time she'd looked. She and Jett had fallen into bed around three a.m. She'd managed all of three hours of sleep before her eyes popped open—wide awake, her body overheated and her pussy clenching hungrily. She'd never been so horny in her life.

God. Her need was physically painful. She twisted and turned, but still couldn't find a position that alleviated the throbbing between her legs, the hunger for sex. To make matters worse, Jett was sleeping peacefully only a foot away from her, oblivious to her agony. It was his fault she was so hot and bothered. He'd set this fire in the dungeon, then left her to simmer.

Bastard.

She took several deep breaths, tried to count sheep, willed her body to calm the fuck down. None of it helped.

"Screw it," she muttered. She slowly climbed out of bed,

careful not to wake Jett. She could only imagine what he'd do if he woke up and discovered her in such a state. Actually, she didn't need to imagine. She had a pretty good idea of exactly how he'd handle it. And while it was more tempting than a chocolate ice cream cone on a hot summer's day, there was no way she could give in to what Jett wanted. She didn't mix sex and friendship.

Which was obviously why she didn't have a boyfriend, she thought, rolling her eyes at herself.

Regardless, if she couldn't do casual sex with Jett, couldn't give in to that friends-with-benefits offer of his, there was no way in hell she could go for what he'd proposed last night, which sounded less booty call and more relationship.

God. No way.

If she slept with him, she'd fall in love, and despite what he said, she wasn't sure that was really what Jett wanted. He was just in freak-out mode over the writer's block. Once he sorted that out, everything could go back to normal.

Reaching into her suitcase, she pulled out the vibrator she'd buried beneath her clothes and tiptoed into the bathroom. Given her current state, she wouldn't need more than a few minutes with her lovely toy. Then maybe she could get some sleep.

Shutting the bathroom door behind her, she was dismayed to find the lock broken. She'd have to call the front desk later to see about getting it fixed.

Carissa stripped off her pajama shorts and walked to the sink. She hadn't bothered to turn on the light. She knew her way around this particular area on her body very well in the dark. God knew she'd spent plenty of time perfecting the act of masturbation. That thought was depressing as hell, so she didn't bother to dwell on it.

Turning on the water to drown out the noise of her toy,

Carissa switched the vibrator on low, then placed it against her clit. She jerked roughly. She was hornier than she realized. Her pussy was hot and wet and ready for whatever relief she could provide.

She closed her eyes, letting the soft vibrations work their way deeper as she pushed the head of the toy inside. Her breathing became more labored as she started thrusting the vibrator—shallowly at first. She inched in incrementally with each retreat and return, teasing herself.

Carissa had only just pushed the toy home, lodging it deep, when the bathroom was flooded with light. She blinked against the sudden, blinding brightness, helpless when she felt Jett's arms surround her from behind.

The sound of running water ceased as he turned off the faucet. Then his large palm wrapped around her wrist, keeping the vibrator inside her.

"What are you doing?"

She squinted as her eyes began to adjust to the light. Finding his reflection in the mirror, she pointedly ignored her flushed face. Her cheeks were bright red—the perfect blend of embarrassment and arousal.

Carissa fought hard to regain control. Jett's arrival couldn't have come at a worst time. Her orgasm had been only a handful of thrusts away. Now she was teetering on the razor's edge of agonizing need and mortification.

She swallowed heavily, then cleared her throat. "I think that's pretty obvious." The response didn't sound as strong as she'd hoped, her voice weak, breathless, pained.

Carissa expected Jett to make a joke. It's certainly what the easy-going friend she'd always relied on would have done. This Jett didn't crack a smile. In fact, he looked downright pissed off.

Which left her unnerved. And fucking hot.

She closed her eyes in an attempt to stem the sudden flood of arousal his possessive stare provoked.

"You're right. It *is* obvious."

Carissa looked at him, confused by the almost hurt tone in his voice.

"Jett—" She started to apologize, even though she didn't understand what exactly she was sorry for.

His hand still engulfed her wrist, the muffled sound of her vibrator filling the silence in the room.

He released her. "Turn that thing off and take it out."

She lowered her eyes as she did as he commanded. She couldn't understand it, but somehow Jett's presence hadn't dimmed her hunger. If anything, she needed to come even more. Her pussy clenched against the plastic, resisting as she pulled the toy out. She gasped, the sound betraying how close she was.

Jett's gaze narrowed, but he made no move to stop her.

Carissa needed to get out of here, to get away from him. Unfortunately, there was nowhere to go. It was six a.m. and they were sharing this room. She supposed she could go hide in the lobby for a few hours, but what would that solve? It was the beginning of the vacation. She couldn't avoid Jett for the next six days.

Unless...she inquired at the front desk about another room.

She didn't have the money in her savings account to cover the cost and it would put a big dent in her credit card, but it would be worth it. She couldn't stay in this room and *not* have sex with Jett. Carissa just wasn't strong enough to resist whatever the hell this was.

She tried to hide the vibrator by her side, grateful she hadn't taken off her t-shirt. The material was long enough to cover most of her private parts. "I need to get out of here," she said, not bothering to look at Jett as she spoke.

She turned, intent on leaving.

Jett chuckled, the sound devoid of mirth, as he grabbed her upper arm. "You're not going anywhere."

He took the vibrator away, then used his grip to drag her back to the bedroom. Carissa put up a fight, resisting him. There was no way she was getting back in that bed. However, while Jett typically hid his muscular form under loose-fitting t-shirts, there was no denying he had her beat in the physical strength area.

Her struggles were useless. Jett continued to guide her to the bed with far too much ease. When they reached the side of the bed, he tossed the vibrator onto the nightstand, placed his hands on her shoulders and pushed her onto the mattress. She tried to bounce back up the moment her ass hit the sheets, but Jett was ready for her.

He placed one knee on the mattress as he propelled her downward, not stopping until she was flat on her back in the middle of the bed and he was straddling her.

Their position—her defenseless beneath him—fired up a fresh round of arousal that left her lightheaded, dizzy, out of control.

"Please." The word escaped her lips on a whisper, betraying her.

Rather than spur Jett to show mercy, it seemed to release something wilder, more demanding in him. He reached toward one of the posts of the bed. She blinked rapidly when she realized there were straps attached there.

"Where—"

"They were here when we arrived." Jett answered her question before she could answer it. "You didn't notice them?"

She shook her head. God only knew how she would have reacted if she had. Bondage had ranked number one on her list of sexual fantasies for as long as she could remember, but she'd never had the courage to try it. Mainly because she'd never been with a man she trusted enough.

She tried to free herself from Jett's relentless grip, but he didn't even bother to feign gentleness. She'd triggered something primitive with her actions, pissed him off with her masturbation. He wasn't going to set her loose until he was good and ready. And given the heated desire in his eyes, she'd guess that moment wasn't going to come any time soon.

So much for escaping.

Jett strapped a cuff around her left wrist. At that point, she stopped trying to fight. It was pointless. She wouldn't win. She didn't want to.

Jett restrained her right hand quickly. Carissa tested the strength of the straps. She knew good and well she couldn't get loose, but some part of her needed to know for sure.

Jett placed his hands on the pillow beneath her head, his knees straddling her hips, caging her in. She'd never felt so trapped, so helpless, so horny.

"Let's run through what happened here, so I'm sure I've understood this all correctly."

She licked her lips nervously. His voice was deep, laced with an anger she'd never heard from him.

"What do you mean?"

"You couldn't sleep?"

She shook her head. "No."

"Why not?"

She felt her face flush. He knew full well why not. "Jett—"

"Say it, Rissa. Tell me why you couldn't sleep."

She hesitated for a moment, then realized he wouldn't stop until he'd heard the truth. "I was horny, you jackass! Happy?"

His expression darkened, letting her know exactly how

unhappy he was. "So you decided to take care of that little issue on your own?"

She nodded.

"Where did you get the vibrator?"

She scowled. "It's mine. I brought it from home."

"You brought it from home? Even though you knew you'd be sharing this room with me?"

"I wasn't planning to have sex with you, Jett. I told you that."

"And you thought I'd just sleep through this nightly self-love fest of yours without comment?"

"I didn't realize you could hear me. Besides, I sort of imagined you'd find some woman to hook up with and disappear most nights." She gave him a sheepish grin, wishing she could find a way to make him relax. Humor had always worked in the past, so she gave it a try. "You're not a bad looking guy. I'm sure there are plenty of women here who would be more than happy to—"

"Were you in that dungeon with me? Did you hear a word I said?"

For the first time, Carissa felt her own anger spark. "I heard. And I refused. I said no to the friends-with-benefits thing back home and I sure as hell didn't agree to be your sub for the week. In case you failed to notice, I said the safe word."

Carissa tugged against the straps at her wrists, wishing for the first time she could free herself.

A change came over Jett's face, so suddenly it took Carissa a moment to understand it. His dark expression cleared and the laid-back Jett she'd been friends with for years reemerged. Or so she thought...until he spoke.

"You should have woken me up, Rissa. I could have helped you with your problem."

"I'm perfectly capable of taking care of it myself. As you

saw." Her words were spoken with more bravado than she felt. She hoped it would fool him, make him see her as off-limits.

Those hopes were dashed when he reached toward the nightstand and retrieved her vibrator. "There's a big difference between being capable and being truly pleasured."

Carissa tried to swallow, though her mouth had gone dry. Every drop of moisture appeared to travel to regions south. She pressed her legs together, the action not lost on Jett, who grinned, then slowly shook his head.

"No more of that." He shifted, tugging her legs apart so that he could kneel between them. The new position left her wide open. His for the taking.

"What are you doing?"

He tilted his head, one eyebrow raised. "Now who's missing the obvious?"

Before she could respond or offer her own smartass reply, he turned the vibrator on low and touched her clit. Carissa's hips thrust upwards and she cried out loudly. Funny how different that same touch had felt when *she* had been the one wielding the toy.

She shook her head, trying to clear out some of the fuzziness. "We have to talk about this. Think about this."

Jett chuckled. "No." He pressed the head of the vibrator to the opening of her body as Carissa tilted her hips, trying to drive the toy deeper. "We don't."

She sucked in several deep breaths, but the air didn't reach her lungs. Jett used his free hand to stroke her clit. He began to thrust the vibrator inside her, not bothering to go slowly as she had. Clearly he knew there was no reason to bother. She was soaking wet, on fire.

Jett could tell exactly what she needed and it wasn't a slow build. She was ready to be fucked. Past ready.

"Harder," she gasped when he managed to find her G-spot

on one deep thrust. She expected him to balk at her demand, but mercifully, he didn't. He turned the speed on the vibrator to high and gave her exactly what she'd asked for. The toy went deeper, faster. Jett mimicked the motion of the vibrator with his fingers on her clit, stroking in time, until she saw stars and her back arched.

She came loudly, calling out his name as she pulled roughly at the straps on her wrists, annoyed to have something holding her down. Without them, she would have flipped Jett beneath her, straddled his hips and fucked the hell out of him.

"Untie me." Her words came out harsh, furious.

He shook his head. "No."

She gritted her teeth as he continued to fuck her with the vibrator. Her orgasm had hit her like a freight train, waned for only a moment, and now a second was clawing beneath her skin. It was the most beautiful pain.

"God, Jett. Please! I need you. Need more. *Fuck me.*"

He didn't acknowledge her words, gave no clue he'd even heard her speak. Instead, he used the toy against her. Retreat, return. Retreat, return. Just when she thought she couldn't take another second, he threw more fuel on the fire.

Bending lower, Jett took her clit into his mouth and sucked. Hard. She splintered, shattered into a thousand pieces as she came once more. Tears streamed down her face as her body trembled, but Jett refused to offer a reprieve.

The vibrator became a relentless pounding inside her body, her pussy betraying her, clenching against it, demanding more.

Her skin was slick with sweat as she writhed beneath Jett. He nipped at her clit before pulling the toy out, replacing it with his tongue. His hot breath almost singed her sensitive flesh. He pressed his hands beneath her ass, his fingers digging in to hold her still for the assault of his mouth.

She struggled to breathe, unable to speak, captive to his demands. She was his willing hostage.

Then his hands slid inward, not stopping until the tips of his fingers found her anus. He stroked the virgin hole despite her cries. Jett pulled away briefly, his mouth leaving her pussy. She released an audible sigh of relief, but it was short-lived. Jett drove two fingers deep inside her, cupping her and finding her G-spot. She screamed. An actual scream, as he pushed her over the ledge a third time.

Carissa's life flashed before her eyes. This was it. She was going to die right here. Right now. Death by orgasm. And she wouldn't regret it a bit.

By now, she knew her climaxes meant nothing to Jett. He reacted to the latest as he had the previous two. Ignoring it. He replaced his fingers with his mouth once more, using his now-wet digits to explore new territory.

Lifting his head, he waited until she looked at him before saying, "Put your legs over my shoulders."

It was a simple request, but Carissa's legs felt as if they were filled with lead. Her strength had deserted her two orgasms ago.

Jett was amused by her inept attempts at following his command. He let her struggle for a few moments, then simply lifted them and put her legs where he wanted them. The new position left her completely vulnerable as Jett raised his chest higher. It didn't take her long to realize his goal when her ass left the mattress. He pressed the tip of one finger into her ass and wiggled it as he watched her face.

The Carissa she'd been an hour ago would have thrown up every shield she possessed to hide her reaction to his touch, but this woman was powerless. A stranger.

"You've never been taken here."

She didn't bother to lie. Carissa shook her head.

"It's mine."

His tone was pure possession. In another state of mind, she would have emasculated him for his arrogance. But that mind—like her strength—had fled.

No. It had been driven out...like the snakes from Ireland.

Jett had fucked her senseless with nothing more than his fingers, mouth and her vibrator. He had erased every trace of self-preservation she'd ever had. He'd recreated her. Made her into someone else. Someone she'd always wanted to be, but would never allow herself to accept.

A submissive.

She longed to be his. To please him.

Once the haze of sex cleared, Carissa knew that concept would scare her. Piss her off. But right now, it just felt right. Like she'd donned the softest pair of pajamas on the planet. She never wanted to take them off.

His finger delved deeper into her ass, pinching slightly. She didn't ask him to stop. She couldn't. She wanted this as much as he did.

Once his finger was fully lodged, he stopped. "You remember your safe word?"

She nodded.

"I let you use it to escape in the dungeon, Rissa. I won't do that again. It's not a get-out-of-jail-free card and it's not something I want you to use lightly. If you're in pain or seriously scared, say it and we'll stop and talk about it. You won't be allowed to say it and leave. Do you understand?"

"Yes."

He lifted one eyebrow until she hastily added, "Sir."

"Good girl."

Her mind told her the term of endearment was condescending. Insulting. So why did it make her feel so good?

Maybe because it was something she'd never heard growing up. She'd worked her ass off to be the diligent daughter, doing everything she knew to please her father, yet it always went unnoticed.

Jesus. Did this mean she had daddy issues?

Jett leaned down, his face close to hers. "What are you thinking about?"

"I'm trying to understand why I like this."

He kissed her softly on the cheek. "Do you need to know why?"

"If liking this means I'm sort of fucked up in the head or something...then yeah."

He chuckled. "You're not fucked up, Rissa. You're beautiful. Giving. Trusting. Intelligent."

She snorted at his list, but he didn't relent. Instead, he removed his finger, sitting up until his ass rested on his ankles. Once again, she was reminded of how much larger he was than her.

"So let me explain how this is going to go down."

He stroked her clit, then gave her a cocky grin that let her know he had her number. He knew exactly how to use her body against her.

"You seem to need some time to adjust to the new status quo. So we'll use this week to test out some new boundaries."

"What do you mean?"

"You're a submissive, Rissa, but you're struggling to accept that. Every night that we're on Eden, I'll be your Dom. I'm going to teach you exactly what it means to submit. I'm going to tie you up, spank you. I'll expose you to floggers and forced orgasms, exhibitionism, the cross. I'll give you every fantasy you've ever had and some you didn't even know existed."

Carissa bit her lip, trying to hide how much his words

thrilled her. "Why do I get the feeling this isn't your first BDSM rodeo?"

He laughed. "It's not. I'm a member of a club back home. When we return to New Orleans, I'll take you there."

She shook her head. "No. What we do here stays here. It can't go back home with us."

Jett narrowed his eyes. "That's what I'm talking about. You don't seem to understand. I'm going to use this week to expose you to a different side of yourself."

"What if I don't want that?" It was a stupid question. One they both knew was a total lie.

"You don't have a choice. You told the master of the island we'd go undercover to help him look for the murderer. To do that, we have to project the image of a committed couple."

"No we don't.

"Yes we do."

"I don't have to be your sub to go undercover, Jett. In fact it might be easier if we split up when we're there, so—"

"No. You'll be my sub or you won't go back to the dungeon at all."

She started to argue, but Jett reached under her shirt. He cupped her breast briefly, then pinched her nipple. The rough touch caused her to jerk and cry out in pain. It also sent a fresh round of arousal to her pussy.

"You don't want to test me on this, Rissa. Because I will win."

Asshole was right. "Fine. I'll be your submissive in the dungeon. But only as part of our cover and only until we catch the killer."

"No."

She waited for him to elaborate, but he didn't bother. Then her gaze landed on his cock—hard and testing the limits of the material of his briefs. She'd been so overwhelmed, she'd failed to think about him and *his* needs. She wasn't usually such a selfish lover.

Overcome with guilt, she pulled at the straps, trying to free herself. "Untie me, Jett. I want to touch you."

He didn't reach for the straps. Instead, he slipped his fingers under the waistband of his boxer briefs, sliding them down over his hips.

Carissa licked her lips as she caught sight of his erection. The skin was stretched taut. He was thick and long, the perfect example of what it meant to be well endowed.

"Please let me loose." Her fingers itched to wrap around him.

"No. There's one more thing you need to understand about this week. About us." As he spoke, he grasped his cock, stroking it slowly.

Carissa frowned, angry. That was her job. She wanted to be the one pleasing him.

Jett moved, lifting her t-shirt until her stomach and breasts were bared. Then he placed one hand by her head as the other continued to travel up and down his thick flesh. Every now and then, the head of his cock brushed against her stomach, leaving a drop of precome behind.

She thought his motions were merely foreplay, but when he started to stroke harder, faster, she realized he intended to come this way.

"No," she whispered. "Please. Let me. I need you."

Jett hesitated for just a moment, then he started to run his fist along his cock once more. "I need you too, Rissa. But I'm not going to take you, I'm not going to fuck you, until you recognize what's going on here. What I want from you."

His hand moved quicker until his eyes closed with something that looked almost like pain. She knew the feeling. Jett released a sharp, short cry as his climax erupted, his come landing on her stomach, painting her breasts. For several moments, neither of them spoke as Jett slowly recovered.

When he looked at her again, she studied his face, saw pain mixed with desire etched in the lines by his eyes and mouth. He released the straps, rubbing her shoulders as she lowered her arms. She knew what he was going to say, but she wasn't ready to hear it. Wasn't ready to admit it. "Wait, Jett. Don't—"

He forged on, talking over her. "This isn't about going undercover. It's not about fantasies or hooking up on holiday. I'm not in this for a week, Rissa. When I take you, it's going to be forever."

Fuck. He said it.

And now it was her turn to respond.

She closed her eyes, unable to face him as she told the lie. "I don't want that."

She felt his fingers under her chin, knew he wouldn't speak until she looked at him. Carissa lifted her eyelids.

"Of course you do. You're just scared. And stubborn." He bent and kissed her softly. It was the single most beautiful kiss of her life.

When he lifted his lips from hers, she felt his breath on her face as he said, "Lucky for you, I'm patient. And persistent."

"You're making a big mistake here."

He grinned and, finally, after hours of looking for him, her affable, lovable, safe best friend Jett, reappeared. "No, Rissa. For the first time in a long time, I'm getting something right. Now—" He stripped her t-shirt over her head and used it to wipe his come off her stomach. She didn't resist. Her head was spinning.

When he was finished, he turned her until she faced away from him, her gaze taking in the sun sparkling over the ocean through the French doors. He spooned her, wrapping his arm around her waist, tucking her close.

The word *paradise* drifted through her sleepy mind.

"Go to sleep, love," he whispered.

The last thing she remembered was Jett softly kissing the back of her head as her eyes drifted shut and the world disappeared for a little while.

CHAPTER SIX

Carissa stood by the counter at the Oceanside bar, waiting for the bartender to finish making a couple of pina coladas for an older couple seated across the way. She had slept until noon, then awoken to the sound of fingers tapping on a keyboard. Jett had set his laptop up on the table by the window, and she'd lain in bed watching as his fingers flew across the keys, beating out a steady pace.

Carissa was more than a little bit in awe of Jett's ability to put words together in such a way that they could transport her from her shitty little life in the Royal Lunch. He always found a way to take her to exciting places with people who were a hell of a lot more interesting than the usual bums who sat around her all day drinking Budweiser, bitching about the government and talking sports.

She'd stayed in bed for nearly half an hour watching him before he stopped to take a sip of coffee and turned around to look at her. He had a rather glazed-over look in his eyes and she wondered what he was seeing in those few seconds before his vision cleared and he realized she was awake.

He'd smiled and then crossed the room to sit on the mattress next to her. She didn't resist when he bent down to kiss her. She woke up slowly—worthless until she had at least three cups of coffee in her—so she let the wave of...whatever this was...carry her forward until she'd found herself in her bikini, lying in a lounger watching people frolic in the water.

For five hours this afternoon, she'd merely followed along behind Jett in a haze, accepting his sweet kisses and allowing him to hold her hand or place his hand on the small of her back whenever they walked. She'd taken it all in stride, not saying a word, simply because she didn't know what the hell *to* say.

Finally, a few minutes earlier, her brain caught up to her far-too-ready-for-round-two body and she'd started to freak out silently. She had asked Jett if he wanted a beer and then got the hell away from him.

Studying the blackboard on the counter, she searched for a drink that was strong enough to calm her nerves. Reading through the list, she chuckled at some of the names. She was tempted to ask for the ingredients in a few of them, then reconsidered. She could see the looks on her patrons' faces now if she started serving something called Jamaican Me Crazy or Goddammit Good at the Royal Lunch. On the whole, the people who drank at her bar had simple tastes, preferring beer or shots, nothing fancy and no silly names.

Then Carissa spotted it—Eden's Miracle Cure. She sure as hell needed a remedy right now and the drink had chocolate liqueur in it. Alcohol *and* chocolate? Yes please.

The bartender had just taken her order when a pretty dark-haired woman walked up and stood next to her, perusing the same drink list as Carissa.

"A chocolate drink?" the woman said softly.

Carissa laughed. "I just ordered it. I mean, how can it be bad?"

The other woman grinned. "I know, right?"

Carissa raised her hand to the bartender and asked him to make a second. "I'm Carissa."

"Lauren."

The two women shook hands, then grinned gleefully when the bartender set their drinks down in front of them. Tapping glasses in unspoken cheers, they each took a sip.

Carissa sighed, her tense shoulders finally relaxing as the smooth, sweet chocolate slid down her throat, leaving a trail of delicious heat in its wake. "Thank God," she muttered.

"That bad?" Lauren asked.

Carissa shrugged. "I'm here on a platonic vacation with my best friend. Problem is he wants to delete the platonic part and turn this week into forever."

"Wow."

"Yeah."

"And I gather you're not interested in him romantically?"

Carissa took another sip of her drink. "Truthfully, I...well... I mean..."

"Ah. So you are."

Carissa nodded. "Yeah. But he's never glanced my way once back home in the seven years we've been friends. I'm afraid it's the romantic atmosphere of this island that's got him all hot and bothered. What if I give in, then we go home and he realizes I'm not the woman of his dreams after all?"

"Do you really think that's what will happen?"

Did she? Carissa considered the question, and then realized she didn't doubt Jett's sincerity for a minute. "No," she begrudgingly admitted, "I don't."

Carissa watched as Lauren took another sip—gulp, actually —of her drink. "Looks like I'm not the only one freaking out."

Lauren gave her a rueful grin. "You're not. Do you believe in soul mates?"

Carissa didn't, but she wasn't sure how to respond as she watched Lauren take another gulp of her drink, then set it down.

Lauren saved her from having to answer. "I do. Or did. Or do."

"Which is it?" Carissa asked.

"I do." Lauren shrugged. "I'm here because the guy who I believe is my soul mate wants to reconnect."

"And that's a bad thing?"

"No. Well...maybe?" Lauren shook her head. "I don't know. Honestly. I'm so confused at this point. I mean, I've been in love with this guy for six years, but what if I've only been pining after a memory? Is that even possible? He seems to be too good to be real."

"Is it possible that it is real?"

Lauren quirked her lips and glanced behind her. "That's what scares me. I came here to say goodbye, but I find myself falling head over heels again, just like before." She finished the last of her drink and pushed the glass forward. "If my sisters were here, you know what they'd tell me?"

Carissa shook her head, somewhat relieved to discover she wasn't the only woman on Eden who was faced with a life-altering decision to make. It suddenly made Carissa feel a lot less lonely.

"They'd tell me to take a chance. To trust in love."

Carissa was a bit jealous of Lauren and her sisters. She was an only child. It would be nice to have a sister to confide in over stuff like this. "Sounds like good advice."

Lauren didn't seem to agree.

Carissa took another sip of her drink, then leaned closer to the sweet woman. "Tell you what. Pretend I'm one of your sisters. But instead of telling you to trust in love, I'm going to tell you to trust your heart."

Lauren smiled at Carissa. "Then I'm going to do the same. Trust your own heart and see what happens." Lauren pushed herself away from the bar. "Hopefully we'll run into one another again."

Carissa hoped the same thing as she waved goodbye. She was considering Lauren's advice and just about to order another drink when Jett appeared.

Jett gestured to her empty glass. "I wondered where you disappeared to."

"Sorry. I met a really nice woman. We sat and had a drink."

The bartender came over. "Would you like another Miracle Cure?"

Jett chuckled. "Miracle Cure, huh? I think I'm starting to understand. You'd been so mellow all afternoon, I thought we'd turned a corner. Have we entered the freaking-out stage of the day?"

Carissa shot Jett a dirty look. "Don't flatter yourself, hotshot."

Jett claimed the barstool next to her. "Set her up with another, please. And I'll have a Corona."

The bartender nodded as he turned to get their drinks.

Jett wrapped his arm around the back of Carissa's stool. Her mind went straight to the gutter as he leaned closer. He was shirtless, wearing nothing but a bathing suit and flip-flops. Before they'd traveled to Eden, Carissa had never seen Jett without a shirt on. He was well defined, with a decent six-pack and just a smattering of hair on his chest. His skin was tan and glistening with a light sheen of sweat after spending a couple of hours in the sun. In a word, he was hot—literally and figuratively.

Carissa was tempted to bend lower to swipe her tongue over one of his brown nipples. She shook the racy thought out of her head and searched for safer territory. "You never told me what you were writing this morning."

He shrugged. "A book."

She grinned widely. "Seriously?"

Jett's face morphed into one of pure delight. "Yep. I'm not sure what shook it loose, but I woke up this morning with an entire plot in my head. I couldn't fire the laptop up quick enough to start slamming down some notes."

"Thank God."

"No, thank *you*. I'd lost faith in myself, Rissa. For the last few weeks, I'd seriously considered giving up writing completely."

"You would hate that, Jett."

He chuckled. "I know. You didn't give up on me. Not once in six months. And more than that, you didn't give me shit for being such a pain in the ass."

Carissa feigned confusion. "Wait? You mean you were acting more miserable than usual? I had no idea. So...when can I read what you've written?"

Jett seemed to consider her request, then said, "When it's done."

She frowned. "I don't want to wait that long. You left me hanging in that last book. Does Riley get out of that burning building? Does he save his sister's baby?"

Jett grinned. "You'll just have to wait and see."

"You're a cruel man."

He wrapped his fingers around her ponytail and tugged her closer, placing a quick, hard kiss on her lips. Carissa marveled at how quickly Jett could switch gears, taking them out of the friend zone and onto lover's lane without blinking an eye.

When she fell silent, Jett tilted his head and studied her face. His sexy grip in her hair kept her from avoiding his gaze. "Why is this so tough for you to accept, Rissa?"

She closed her eyes, then moved forward, pressing her forehead against his. It wasn't hard for her to imagine sleeping with Jett at all. But when she tried to play the scene out beyond their time on Eden, when she tried to imagine a life with Jett back home, she struggled to find the happy ending.

Carissa would never have thought she'd set much stock by society's class structure, but the fact remained she was a bartender, a girl who'd barely squeaked by in high school. She was only ever described as intelligent in relation to having street smarts. She didn't have two pennies to rub together and before this week, she'd never ventured out of New Orleans. Hell, she'd never really wanted to travel. Her dreams were small because she'd learned a long time ago that they were a waste of time. Her feet were firmly set in reality and her world wasn't much bigger than the four walls of the Royal Lunch.

Jett lived on an entirely different plane. He never stopped reading, his nose forever buried in a book. He'd been away from New Orleans more than he'd been home the past few years. People sought his opinion on the judicial system, the government, military practices. He'd been asked to speak at countless engagements. Sometimes she'd overhear him talking about things she didn't even know existed. And if she was being honest, she hadn't bothered to learn more because it sort of bored her. Jett was handsome, successful, and worldly. She was simple.

And while she'd never suffered much in terms of self-esteem, she knew that the differences between them, such as their lack of common interests, were bound to become an issue somewhere down the line.

"Jett, you have a wonderful imagination, but the fact is you're a bit of a dreamer. You'd have to be in order to write such incredible stories. But you're going to have to understand that I can't think that way. I'm too practical. Which means I see something you can't."

He frowned. "What's that?"

"Not every story has a happily ever after."

Jett didn't respond immediately. Instead he released her hair, picked up his beer and took a long swig. She watched his face clear, his expression unconcerned, as they finished their drinks in silence.

Jett signed for the drinks, then reached over for her hand. She let him take it, confused by his easy acquiescence to her proclamation that things wouldn't work out between them.

"You ready to go?" he asked.

"Where?"

"Our room."

Carissa's pussy fluttered at the way he said *our* and the wicked gleam in his eye. She should have known better than to think Jett would give up without a fight.

"I might hang out here for a little while. Why don't you go on up without me?"

Jett chuckled, then tugged on her hand until she was forced to stand. "You can walk on your own or I can carry you. Preference?"

She scowled. "I'm happy here, Jett. There's nothing I want to do in the room."

He bent closer, taking her earlobe between his teeth and nipping sharply. "Liar."

Her nipples went on red alert, budding beneath her too-thin bikini top. Jett—the observant bastard—noticed immediately. "You don't play fair."

She was about to throw caution to the wind and follow Jett to the room—common sense be damned—when a man dressed in a lightweight white shirt emblazoned with the Eden crest approached them.

"Mr. Lewis. Ms. Pierre."

Jett took a step forward, slightly blocking Carissa from the stranger. She was touched by his protectiveness. He'd been shielding her in little ways all day—clearly not forgetting there was a killer on the island. Carissa felt the same tingle she'd experienced last night when Jett had bent her over the spanking bench in the dungeon. After a lifetime of taking care of herself, it was thrilling to have someone else claiming control.

"Yes?"

"I'm Mr. Sharpton, the manager of the hotel. The master of the island asked me to share this with you."

Jett took the file folder the manager proffered. "He said he hopes you'll find the information helpful." With that, Mr. Sharpton gave them a quick nod and left.

Carissa and Jett stepped away from the bar to a more secluded area where they couldn't be overheard. Opening the folder, Jett perused the papers inside, explaining it was the doctor's notes in regards to the way Gregory was murdered.

"So whoever killed him drugged him first?"

"It would appear so," Jett said in response to Carissa's question.

"That would have made it easier for a woman to bind Gregory to the chair. If he was incapacitated, he wouldn't have put up much of a fight."

Jett continued flipping through the details. "And after the killer had Gregory bound, he made sure the man suffered."

"How so?"

Jett grimaced as he read Dr. Magdalene's notes. "The penis was cut off first."

"Yikes. I was sort of hoping for Gregory's sake that had happened after he was dead."

"Me too." Jett turned to the last page. "The doctor said the amount of blood lost indicates the stab to the heart came later… much later."

"So this murderer was pissed off and determined to make Gregory suffer."

"It sounds like it." Jett studied a photograph.

"What's that?" Carissa asked.

Jett flipped through the small stack of pictures, showing them to Carissa. "The security team took pictures of the crime scene. Given the splatter pattern around the chair, the killer must have been covered in blood."

"How do you think he got back into the hotel without anyone seeing all that blood on his clothes?"

"I have no idea." Jett closed the file folder. "But you're not stepping foot in that dungeon tonight."

"Excuse me?"

Jett released a long sigh. "Rissa, please try to see reason. We're looking at a brutal killing. We have no idea what set this person off. We can't assume the killer had any personal relationship with Gregory at all. You said it yourself last night. What if it's someone who sees BDSM as an abomination and has it out for anyone who shows up at the dungeon?"

Carissa shook her head. "No. I was just grasping at straws. Besides, that scenario doesn't feel right to me. Whoever did this had a definite grudge against Gregory. It was personal."

"So let me go to the dungeon tonight alone. I'll ask a few questions, and then come back up to our room where we can discuss what I learn safely. We'll put the pieces together there."

"We can cover more ground if I come too, Jett. You can strike up conversations with the Doms, but let's face it, the subs aren't going to talk to you so openly. Unless you're intending to play with them, of course." Carissa tried to keep the jealousy out of her tone. But she failed miserably.

"I'm not playing with anyone but you, Rissa."

She rolled her eyes. "You have serious issues when it comes to listening."

Jett gripped her hips, pulling her lower body forward until his crotch—and erection—brushed against her. "You're right. I do. I'm much better at reading between the lines."

She tried to push away, but Jett's grip was tenacious. Finally, she simply gave in. It was easier. And her resistance when it came to Jett was perilously low. "I'm going with you tonight."

Jett studied her face. From his chagrined expression, he knew he wouldn't win. "Fine. But we're playing it my way. You'll go in as my collared sub. I don't want another man even looking at you."

"Jealous much?"

"Hell yeah. And determined to keep you safe. Any man in that place could be the killer, so you're going to give them all a wide berth. Understood?"

She nodded, her own unease growing. She'd volunteered them to go undercover for one very selfish reason last night. She had wanted a reason to return to the dungeon with him. One that didn't involve having to admit she was falling in love with Jett.

Now she realized there was no avoiding that inevitable outcome. So what she'd actually done was put them both in danger.

Unfortunately, even if she admitted the mistake, Jett was determined to investigate the crime. He'd talked of little else today as they'd lounged in the sand, watching the waves lick the shore.

His wheels were turning—analyzing all the clues and searching for motives. Jett's knack for problem solving was part of what made him such an amazing crime writer. He could see all the angles and twists. Carissa had never once managed to figure out who the killer was in one of his books.

"Come on, Rissa. Let's head back to the room. We can discuss our plan of attack for tonight."

She took the hand he offered, relieved that with crime on his mind, at least Jett was distracted from his previous intentions. Seduction seemed to be off the table this afternoon.

She'd dodged that bullet again.

For the moment.

CHAPTER SEVEN

Jett sat at a table in the dungeon, watching as Carissa crossed the room to get him a drink from the bar. There were two unattached subs sitting at the counter—one the woman they'd seen with Gregory the previous night. Carissa had insisted on going over to strike up a conversation with the woman and Jett couldn't come up with a good enough reason for her not to. Simply saying he didn't want her more than two feet away from him wasn't going to fly with his head-strong lady.

He shifted in his seat, trying to covertly adjust his cock in his tight jeans. He'd been rock hard ever since Carissa had stepped out of the bathroom an hour earlier in the outfit he'd purchased for her in the boutique downstairs. Roan had told him during the tour of the dungeon last night about the boutique's "back room," that specialized in fetish wear.

He'd dragged Carissa into the shop on their way back from the bar and picked out the sexy leather corset that zipped up the front, laced loosely down her back and framed her breasts perfectly. He'd thought she would balk when he finished the ensemble with a g-string, garters, black stockings and sexy fuck-me heels. Carissa hadn't blinked twice. Once they got this messy business of murder out of the way, the two of them were going to explore every single one of his little submissive's kinks.

Glancing around the room, he spotted several Doms looking in Carissa's direction. Fortunately, he'd been smart enough to add a collar to her outfit. Though BDSM was more play than lifestyle to him, he liked the idea of Carissa belonging to him more than he cared to admit.

His feelings for her had snuck up on him, taking him down like a ton of bricks falling on his head. In two days, he'd forgotten what it felt like to regard her as nothing more than a friend. He couldn't figure out how he'd felt such lukewarm affection for her for so long. He'd been a blind fool, but those days were over.

"She's quite beautiful."

Jett looked up, surprised to see another Dom standing next to his table. He was usually more aware of his surroundings, but with Carissa in the room, everything else seemed out of focus.

"Yes. She is."

The man gestured to a chair and Jett nodded. "Please. Join me. I'm Jett."

"Phillip," the man responded as he claimed the seat Carissa had vacated a few minutes earlier. "Jett, huh? That's an unusual name."

Jett had heard that a lot. "Yeah. I know. My mother wasn't big on family names. If she heard a name she liked, that was it."

Phillip chuckled. "Only other Jett I've ever heard of is that author. Writes pretty good crime novels."

"Jett Lewis."

"Yeah, that's it," Phillip said. "You a fan?"

Jett shrugged. "Sort of. I'm him."

Phillip reared back in his seat. "Is that right? How about that? I've read all your books. Haven't seen one lately though. You got anything new out?"

If he'd met this man two days ago, this conversation would have been a lot more painful. Today, however, he was a writer with a plot and the words were screaming to hit the page. "Not recently. But soon. I'm working on a story right now."

"I'll look forward to it."

Jett glanced in Carissa's direction to check on her.

Phillip followed his gaze. "I saw you and your lovely lady here last night. She wasn't collared."

Jett had been concerned someone would notice that fact. After all, Carissa had made quite an impression on the Doms last night. It wasn't surprising the man had recalled her unattached status, especially if he'd been interested.

"We traveled to Eden together. I wanted to solidify our relationship here."

"Very romantic."

Jett nodded. "Exactly." Then Jett decided to test the waters. "At least Gregory isn't here tonight to bother her again."

Phillip nodded and it struck Jett that there wasn't much the man had missed last night. "The night's still young. Gregory could always make an appearance later, although I'll admit I'm confused by Stella's presence here without him."

"Stella?"

Phillip nodded toward Carissa and the other woman at the bar. "Gregory's sub. She appears to be flying solo tonight. I can't imagine she's here with Gregory's permission. The guy is possessive as hell."

It struck Jett that Phillip knew more about Gregory and Stella than what a random stranger would notice at a glance. "Are you and Gregory friends?"

Phillip crossed his arms. "Not exactly." His tone said "not at all."

Jett tried to think of a way to keep the conversation going, but Phillip gave him a hand, explaining the acquaintance without further prodding. "My work takes me to D.C. quite often. I've crossed paths with Gregory a few times in a club there."

The look on Phillip's face told Jett the man wasn't fond of Gregory. "Small world. Guess you weren't expecting to run into him here as well. And it doesn't sound like you're happy about it."

Phillip scowled. "The BDSM community isn't that large."

Jett started to ask another question, but Phillip rose. "Congratulations to you and your sub. If you'll excuse me."

Phillip left hastily and his retreat made Jett suspicious. Of course, Jett had looked at everyone in the club tonight with an eye toward murder. Phillip hadn't done or said anything that made him a suspect apart from the fact he knew Gregory and didn't like him. Jett was certain most people who'd met Gregory weren't fond of the asshole.

"Jett?"

He looked up, surprised to realize Carissa had walked back across the room without him noticing. Some bodyguard he was. "Excuse me?"

She bit her lip. "I mean Sir."

He grinned and pointed to the chair next to him. Carissa was still a bit uneasy about her role in the dungeon. When they'd arrived, he'd told her that they may be undercover, but this place wasn't a game to him. She still hadn't accepted what he wanted from her, so instead he intended to show her. He'd instructed her to call him "Sir" while they were in the dungeon, explaining she would be his submissive within these walls.

She took the chair, then leaned closer. "I met Gregory's sub, Stella."

He nodded. "I noticed the two of you were chatting. Did you find anything out?"

Carissa shrugged. "Not really. I don't mean to sound cold, but Stella's not exactly the brightest bulb in the lamp."

Jett chuckled. "Did she mention Gregory?"

"Yeah. She's actually here looking for him. Said he was furious last night after Roan kicked him out of the club. Apparently the asshole blamed *her* for bleeding. She said he stormed off and she hasn't seen him since."

"And she wasn't alarmed enough to report him missing? We're on an island, for God's sake."

Carissa gave him an exasperated look. "She didn't seem to think his disappearance was all that unusual. I get the impression she views his absence as some sort of punishment."

"So she's here, sitting at the bar in the dungeon alone, dressed like that?" Jett turned to study Stella. Though she wasn't sending out any obvious signals, her mere presence and attire suggested she was looking for a Dom—any Dom. "I don't think Gregory and Stella have a clue how this community works."

Carissa grinned ruefully. "They're not exactly alone."

Jett turned his attention to her. He'd allowed her to come to the club under the ruse of participating in this investigation. Truthfully, he had an ulterior motive. One he intended to move on now.

"You look beautiful tonight, Carissa."

She stopped looking around the club, her gaze finding his as she flushed. He got the impression Carissa hadn't been paid a lot of compliments in her life. He planned to make up for lost time.

"Thanks. You know, you never call me Carissa unless you're pissed off at me. Or we're here."

He nodded, glad she'd picked up on the distinction. "I know."

She bit her lower lip. She was adorable when she was nervous.

"Stand up, Carissa. And turn around."

Carissa hesitated for only a moment before rising slowly. Jett wondered how he'd ever missed seeing this part of her. She'd always come off as hard as nails, the type to take no prisoners back home at the bar. Somehow he'd failed to see this softer side. The one that longed to give herself completely to someone she trusted.

Jett was honored she'd given that trust to him. Carissa stood with her back to him, her posture straight and sure. She may be out of her element, but she didn't let her unease show. Jett admired her confidence, the way she never backed down from a challenge.

Carissa didn't move as he let his gaze travel from the graceful curve of her neck, along her back and down to her shapely ass. The thong she wore revealed way more than it covered. She had a sexy body—one she'd kept hidden from him for years.

Jett stood and stepped closer. He let her feel the heat from his body against her back. He grasped her hips in his hands, tugging her until her ass brushed the front placket of his jeans. His cock was hard, aching. He'd told her he wouldn't take her until she agreed to a relationship. He didn't doubt he'd pay for that promise. Carissa wasn't going down easily. While she was willing to play with him here, she still viewed this time as a short-term escape from reality.

Something that wouldn't follow them back home.

She was wrong.

He wrapped his arms around her waist, his hands rising until he found her breasts. He dragged his fingertips along the tops before burrowing beneath the tight leather in search of her nipples.

"I want to show you off," he whispered, enjoying the way she shivered when his breath tickled her ear.

"Okay."

He kissed the side of her neck. "You aren't allowed to speak anymore. The rest of the evening is about feeling. Nothing more. The only word you're permitted to say is your safe word."

She nodded once, clearly wanting what he was offering.

Leaning closer, he found the front zipper to her corset. As he slid it downward a couple of inches, he said, "You're going to be tempted to say that word, Carissa."

She turned then, tilted her head to look at his face. He sensed she was seeking reassurance that it was still him. Still Jett, her friend. He didn't give her the comfort she sought. He'd lowered his mask, making sure she realized this wasn't the Jett she knew.

She frowned at the serious expression on his face. "Jett." Her voice was quiet, uncertain.

He scowled. "Not here, Carissa. Tonight I'm Sir. And I told you not to speak. You disobeyed me."

She licked lips he imagined had gone dry due to nervousness. He released her breasts and gripped her upper arm, leading her to one of the leather tables in the main room. It was in a fairly prominent spot, well-lit, visible to almost everyone around them. He'd offered her privacy last night, choosing to initiate her slowly and without the watchful eyes of others. Tonight would be different.

She started to bend over the table, but he tightened his hold on her arm. "Don't do anything I don't tell you to do."

She froze and he watched a myriad of expressions cross her

face—confusion, annoyance and a smattering of fear. He was stronger than her and he made sure she understood that through his tight grasp.

For a few seconds, they stood there in a mini face-off. Carissa was the first to relent, her body relaxing, the stiffness in her frame going softer. Then, she lowered her eyes.

Jett took in a deep breath, fighting for control. He'd never wanted anyone more than he wanted her.

He released her arm, and then reached for the zipper to her corset once more. Carissa glanced nervously around the room as he lowered it, revealing her breasts to anyone who cared to look in their direction.

"Keep your eyes on my face, Carissa. I'm the only person in this room who matters right now."

Her gaze flew back to his, her breathing more erratic.

The corset fell away easily once the zipper was undone. It was one of the reasons he'd picked it out. Given his eagerness to see her, he knew he'd never have the patience to fool around with tightly tied laces.

He placed the corset on a chair nearby as Carissa held still. The woman was a hundred and thirty pounds of pure courage.

Jett reached out to touch her breasts, cupping the firm flesh before pinching her nipples roughly. She winced at the quick, sharp pain. He leaned forward to kiss away the sting, enjoying the sound of her light sigh.

Jett suckled only a moment before he bit the distended nub. Carissa jerked slightly, her arms rising as if to push him away. He stood quickly and gave her a warning look. "Arms at your sides. You've already earned one punishment for speaking without permission. You don't want to add to that tally, Carissa. Trust me."

She lowered her hands, the fingers forming fists. Jett wondered if she'd throw a punch if he pushed her too far.

Carissa wasn't afraid to show her physical side, to use force if provoked. He'd actually intervened once at the Royal Lunch, pushing Carissa out of harm's way when she threw herself between two drunks picking a fight. He'd started to read her the riot act afterwards for putting herself in a dangerous position, but she'd cut his diatribe short, launching into one of her own, giving him hell for getting in her way.

She'd pinned her hair up earlier as she'd prepared for their trip to the dungeon. He'd tugged it loose before they left the room. If he had his way, she'd never put her thick tresses up in a ponytail again. He loved the way her brown wavy hair framed her face. She looked almost delicate with it down.

Jett returned his attention to her breasts, spending the next several moments treating her to a blend of pain and pleasure, his pinches followed by soothing licks, his light sucking replaced by teeth. He never picked a rhythm, didn't give her a chance to figure out what was coming next—the softness or the hurt. Carissa's chest rose and fell, her arousal becoming a tangible thing, expressed in flushes and moans and breathless whimpers.

One of the submissives working the floor passed nearby. Jett stopped her and requested a pair of nipple clamps, which the woman retrieved for him quickly. Carissa sucked in a pained gasp when Jett attached the first one to her taut nipple. Her mouth opened as if to speak. Jett narrowed his eyes in warning and she fell silent once more.

He attached the second, and then took a step back to admire his handiwork. Carissa's eyes were closed as she struggled to catch her breath. He watched her work through the pain, observed as she found a way to deal with it. Once she regained control, she lifted her eyelids and looked at him.

Jett witnessed something on her face he was certain he'd never seen there before.

Peace.

There was a chain between the two nipple clamps. Jett reached out to tug it. Carissa sucked in as he applied more pressure. "Do you like the clamps?"

She nodded, recalling his admonition that she not speak. He grinned. She was playing her role to perfection. Little did she know he hadn't even begun.

Stepping closer, he ran his finger along the edge of the collar he'd purchased at the boutique this afternoon. He'd remained in the shop after paying for Carissa's outfit, telling her he'd meet her in the room later. If she knew how much he'd paid for the chain around her neck, she'd likely flip out. He'd selected it for its simple beauty. It fit the woman wearing it. Carissa didn't need makeup or frills or flashy jewelry to enhance her looks. The thick silver necklace glittered against her light complexion. She'd gotten a bit of sun today, her normally pale color darkened with a pretty tan.

When she'd stepped out of the bathroom earlier, dressed in her sexy outfit, he'd bid her to turn around, then put the necklace on her. She'd smiled at him before going to look at it in the mirror, promising to return it to him once they'd finished playing their roles. He had no intention of ever taking it back.

"Touch me."

Carissa responded to his command like a sprinter to the starting gun. Apparently she'd been waiting for this request. She ran her hands over his chest, her fingers stroking the soft cotton of his t-shirt. He reached for her wrists, drawing her hands lower until she cupped his cock.

"Touch me here."

She slowly worked to free him from the confines of his jeans. Once the denim was unfastened, she reached inside. He'd eschewed the boxer briefs tonight, going commando. He would likely end the night chafed, but it would be worth it for these few minutes.

Carissa ran her fingers along the underside of his cock, then around the head. Her stroke was too soft. He wrapped his hand around hers, forcing her to grip him tighter.

"Do you feel how much I want you?"

She nodded once more.

"Soon, Carissa. Soon I'm going to bury my cock inside you. I'm going to take you hard all night long."

Her eyes drifted closed. "Now." The word escaped on a sigh, but Carissa's sudden wince told her she knew he'd heard her.

"That's two."

She didn't appear as worried about her punishment as she should be. That was because she only knew one side of him, had only ever seen Jett as an easy-going friend. She'd soon learn differently.

He guided her hand over his cock, increasing the pressure and the pace. Carissa licked her lips and for a moment, he was tempted to command her to her knees, to push his dick into her mouth, driving in until she swallowed his aching flesh. He needed relief, but he wasn't going to find it soon. Digging deep for control, Jett pulled her hand away. He tucked his cock back in his jeans and zipped up. It wasn't an easy task.

"You know what I want, Carissa. I won't fuck you until you admit it's what you want too."

She didn't reply though he found some solace in the obvious temptation in her eyes. She wanted to give in, but something was holding her back.

Time to up the ante.

"Hold your breath."

He didn't wait to see if she'd obeyed before he released the first nipple clamp.

She drew in a sharp, pained breath. "Oh my God."

Jett didn't rebuke her for talking. Instead, he bent forward to soothe the aching nub with his lips and tongue.

Then he repeated the process on her other nipple. She was new to clamps, so he kept her time in them short, allowing her to just feel the bite. Next time, he'd leave them on longer.

"Bend over the table, Carissa."

This time there was no hesitance in her movements as she stepped up to the end of the leather-padded table. He'd chosen it because it was the perfect height. She bent at the waist, groaning softly when her sore nipples hit the padding.

Jett reached into his pocket to tug out a blindfold. Carissa offered no resistance when he placed it over her eyes. He wasn't foolish enough to believe her easy acquiesce would last long. She was held tight in the throes of the fantasy, but there was a reality to this type of play that she had yet to experience... to feel.

He secured the cloth, making sure she couldn't see, then he used straps to bind her hands to the front legs of the table. Jett stepped behind her, running his hands over her ass. The G-string ran through the slit in her legs. It was damp from her arousal.

He gently stroked the soft skin of her ass, feeling her relax under his soothing massage. Then he lifted his hand and brought it down hard.

Carissa jerked and tried to rise. The straps held.

He didn't bother to pause or give her time to adjust. He continued to spank her, enjoying the flush and heat his hand provoked. Little did she know this spanking was just a warm-up, a prelude to the main event.

Carissa stopped struggling against her bondage. Like the previous night, she drifted away from the shock and pain quickly. She began to writhe, lifting up on her toes to meet him blow for blow.

Through it all, she managed to remain quiet, though Jett suspected she had plenty to say. Especially when he stopped the spanking and stepped away from her.

A quick glance around the room proved they'd attracted the attention of others. Phillip was standing against a wall near them, his gaze holding steady on Carissa. An uncharacteristic jolt of jealousy pierced. Jett had never felt so possessive of a sub.

Stella had left her spot at the bar and moved closer. She also seemed enthralled by the scene. Her eyes met his—just for a moment—before she lowered them. Jett was concerned by the complete lack of emotion there. Had Gregory abused her trust, taken his cruelty too far? The woman seemed lost, broken.

Carissa had stilled on the table and lifted her head. He'd only meant to give her a moment to compose herself before he continued, but he'd left her alone too long. He needed to put the murder out of his mind. Right now, this moment wasn't a ruse.

He walked to a shelf nearby and retrieved a short leather flogger. Her response when he'd suggested it had been hesitant, but her reaction to his spanking, the genuine pleasure she found in pain, led him to believe she simply wasn't aware of what he was offering.

When he returned to the table, he ran the tails of the flogger against her pink ass, giving her a warning about what was coming. She jolted at the foreign sensation. With the blindfold still in place, she couldn't see exactly what he was holding.

She wasn't resisting her bondage any longer. Her movements indicated she loved the feeling of being restrained, held tight. She didn't speak. Simply invited him to continue with some of the most beautiful body language he'd ever seen.

Jett lifted the flogger, slapping her ass with it lightly. He wanted to introduce her to the sensation, the impact, the sting.

She groaned, her ass rising, silently pleading for more.

Jett answered the unspoken request, swinging the flogger again—harder. Each time he lifted and brought it down, Carissa was there—ready, waiting. Her body trembled as sweat trickled from her hairline. Jett could sympathize. He was on fire, his cock throbbing in genuine pain.

He'd sworn he wouldn't take her until she was ready to commit to a relationship and he meant to keep that vow. God help him.

After he'd laid a dozen strokes on her ass, he tossed the flogger to the side. He stepped up to the table, his thighs brushing the backs of her legs. "Open," he commanded, his hands doing the work for her.

He ran his finger along her drenched slit. She moaned loudly. Jett could feel so many eyes on them. Carissa's natural, untutored responses had earned them an audience. Jett didn't care. At this moment, the only thing that mattered was her and her pleasure. He tugged the string of her thong aside and drove three fingers inside her pussy.

Carissa came undone. Her body jerked roughly against the table. Jett kept his hand in place as he leaned forward, covering her with his chest.

He thrust his fingers in and out no more than a handful of times as he pressed her against the table. She cried out loudly when her orgasm came, her inner muscles clenching tightly against his fingers.

He tugged off the blindfold. "Open your eyes," he whispered, when Carissa kept them pressed closed.

They opened slowly and she blinked several times before her vision cleared. She glanced at him over her shoulder.

Jett smiled and kissed her. "You were incredible."

She didn't return his smile, her face far too serious. "Please untie me."

Jett's brow creased as concern set in. Had he misread her responses? He rose without haste, releasing the straps on her wrists.

Carissa was off the table within seconds. She hadn't said the safe word, hadn't given him any indication that she was scared or hurt.

"Rissa—" he started, true worry gripping him.

She dropped to her knees before he could say another word. Her fingers hastily unfastened his pants, reaching inside to tug out his erection.

Jett placed his hands on her shoulders to push her away, but her lips found the head of his cock, sucking it in deeply on the first pass.

Honor be damned. There was no force in nature that could provoke Jett to call a halt as Carissa sucked harder.

His hands tangled in her hair and he used that grasp to increase the pace. Jett lost his tenuous grip on his control as he fucked Carissa's mouth. In another place, another state of mind, he would have taken more care.

But here, now, finesse and gentleness had been stamped out. Replaced by a clawing, ravenous hunger that could only be assuaged by demanding, almost cruel passion.

Carissa didn't resist, didn't pull away. She let him take her, encouraged him to claim more with her soft moans. She teased him with her teeth and begged him with her eyes.

Jett was lost. A goner.

His hand tightened in her hair as his cock exploded, sending jets of hot come down her throat. Carissa swallowed, didn't miss a single drop, holding him in her mouth even after he'd released her.

Jett stiffened his spine, fighting not to fall to his knees.

She'd sucked him dry. Neither of them moved for several moments as they worked to regain their strength. Carissa managed first. She slowly tried to rise from the floor on unsteady legs. Jett reached under her arms to help her stand.

They looked at each other, neither saying a word.

And then, she smiled.

Jett grinned, cupping her face with his hands. Bending forward, he kissed her. A slow, sensuous melding of lips before she pulled away, her face telling him the battle hadn't been won yet.

She was still resisting.

So he was changing tactics. If she wouldn't accept his words, he'd simply try to convince her with actions.

Jett was going to seduce his best friend.

CHAPTER EIGHT

Three days passed and the longer he was with her, the more Jett was convinced she was his kindred spirit—emotionally and physically.

Jett had launched an all-out assault on her with passion, driving her to orgasm after orgasm...with his fingers, his lips, her vibrator. He'd taken her a dozen different ways, but he'd never consummated the relationship, never made love to her the way he wanted to.

Though she'd played fair, stroking and sucking him to completion, she still held back, refused to give him what he knew they both wanted. It was frustrating, maddening, and the devil in him had to admit, hot as hell.

The hours since their arrival on Eden had flown by in a blur. Nonstop activity that meant nothing...and everything. They'd shared drinks by the pool with other guests as they tried to ferret out information. They'd gone for long swims in the ocean and taken long walks on the beach because Carissa insisted she needed to exercise after all the delicious food they'd gorged themselves on. They'd attended several of Eden's planned social events, in their attempts to discover the murderer.

In the midst of all of that, Jett's pent-up words had been released, and he spent several hours each day tapping away on his laptop while Carissa went shopping with Stella or explored the island on her own.

Each night they'd returned to the dungeon and Jett continued her instruction on the beauty of BDSM. The shared kinks and desires had broken something free, changed the easy relationship they'd always shared, adding a different, more heated dimension.

Both of them walked around like live wires, sparking at the slightest glancing brushes, electricity seeking an outlet, until Jett had no choice but to drag her to their room or find some out-of-the-way custodial closet where he'd tug down her pants and finger her until she came. Sometimes it was Carissa who broke first and Jett would be forced to remain stone-faced as she stroked his cock under the table in the restaurant or in the ocean. They couldn't keep their hands off each other.

The only thing that kept Jett from breaking his vow was Stella. She had attached herself to Carissa, constantly seeking them out during the day, planting herself beside Carissa for several hours.

Carissa had initially cultivated the association in an attempt to discover more about Gregory. The murder investigation was never far from their minds, both Jett and Carissa analyzing the information they had, sifting through the clues. They'd spent many afternoons tossing out suppositions, frustrated that their investigation hadn't yielded many results. They'd hit a brick wall.

Both of them agreed Phillip seemed to top their list in terms of motive. The Dom continued to come to the club each night, sitting in the corner nursing a drink while watching Stella. He never chose a sub to play with. Instead, he simply sat and observed.

However, as more time passed, Jett began to suspect that Carissa had a soft spot for Stella. Carissa was a sucker for a stray cat and Stella definitely fit that mold. The woman was a bit odd and Jett found himself growing more curious about her.

Carissa knew Jett was excited by his newly broken writer's block, so she would escape with Stella each afternoon in order to give him time to write. He appreciated her patience with him. Now that he'd found his voice again, Jett was afraid to let the momentum die. Carissa understood that and gave him the time he needed to keep the words flowing. He'd caught her trying to sneak peeks over his shoulder, but each time he teasingly told her she'd just have to wait to buy the book.

Throwing himself into his work was helping in another regard as well. He let the story harness some of his unending horniness and give him a brief respite from his pursuit of Carissa. He suspected it was his unrequited feelings for her that were molding the story. The rough draft hitting the pages was every bit as intense as his past books crime-wise, but this one was a bit different. A new, more erotic element had found its way into the story as well. Jett didn't have a clue if his readers would enjoy it, but personally, he thought it was shaping up to be the best book he'd ever written.

Jett lay on his back staring at the ceiling, listening to the water running as Carissa showered. It was Thursday night and he was worn out.

Carissa stepped out of the bathroom, wrapped in a terrycloth robe. She walked to the closet and started to pull out the mini-skirt she'd worn her first night in the dungeon. Clearly she expected them to repeat the same pattern as every other night, however, the dark circles under her eyes told him she was tired too. For a vacation, it had been a bit of a whirlwind.

"Put that away."

She turned. "What?"

"We're not going to the dungeon tonight."

"What about the investigation?"

"We're here on vacation, Rissa. Don't you think it's time we took a little time to focus on just us?"

She nodded. "I'd like that. You've sort of thrown me for a loop this week and I'm afraid I'm handling all of this very badly."

He chuckled. "What do you say we take a night off? Late dinner downstairs? Just friends?"

"I'd like that."

They needed to get out of the room. And away from the damn bed. Carissa put on a pretty sundress that fired his libido more than her mini-skirt. Or her bikini. Or the leather corset. Then it occurred to Jett that she could walk around in a feed sack and he'd still want her.

There was no way he could sit across the table from her and not want her. Despite offering to do the just friends thing, he knew that ship had sailed. He simply couldn't look at her without feeling a million different things that had nothing to do with platonic friendship.

He was in love with her. He was starting to think he'd been in love with her for years, but was too stupid and blind to realize it.

"I'm ready."

He smiled and offered her a friendly hand. By the time they'd been seated in the restaurant, Jett was starting to feel like he could breathe again. However he didn't hold out much hope that he'd make it through the night without reaching for her in their shared bed.

Jett ordered a bottle of wine and once it had been delivered, they sat quietly, listening to a man playing the piano. Jett was surprised by how relaxed he was, given the incredible tension he'd been suffering.

"Not exactly the vacation we'd planned, is it?" she asked after a few minutes of silent contemplation. The lines around her eyes and mouth had eased and he was glad he'd called for the temporary truce.

"No. I guess not. Although you did manage to help me break the writer's block. I'm not sure I'll ever be able to thank you enough for that, Rissa."

She smiled and shook her head, refusing to take credit for doing anything. He was used to her demurring and down-playing his compliments. "You would have figured it out on your own. You were born to be a writer, Jett. So what's the story about?"

He grinned. "Nope. No spoilers. You'll just have to wait until I'm finished."

She pouted prettily. "That's not fair. You've kept me in suspense for months over Riley's fate. What happens?"

In his last book, Jett had left the hero in a life or death situation, a stupid move on his part that had left his readers even more rabid than usual for the next story. He shrugged, enjoying the way her eyes narrowed in annoyance.

"You're a heartless bastard, you know that, right?"

Jett laughed. "I may have been told that a time or two or twenty in my life."

Carissa took another sip of her wine, then sighed. "I love this song."

Jett listened to the music. It was familiar and yet he couldn't quite place it. "Where have I heard this before?"

"It's the theme to *Forrest Gump*."

He nodded slowly. "Your favorite movie."

"Yep."

He and Carissa had spent one playful night at the Royal

Lunch reciting almost the entire movie with each other—her playing Jenny to his Forrest.

Jett leaned back. "Life is like a box of chocolates."

"And I sure wasn't expecting what I got this week."

She'd opened the door. Jett was glad. It was time to talk.

"Me either. But I'm not sorry about it, Rissa."

She toyed with the stem of her wineglass. "You know I love you, Jett."

They were the words he wanted to hear from her, but he understood the tone, the sentiment. She meant she loved him as a friend.

"This could be as easy as breathing. As far as I can see, we're compatible right down the line—sexually, emotionally, sarcastically."

Carissa rolled her eyes at his last comparison, then she threw him for a loop. "Are we? Really?"

It was clear she didn't think so.

He started to ask her where she thought they didn't match up when one of the resort employees walked up to their table. "Are you Jett Lewis?"

Jett nodded. "Yes."

"There's a call at the front desk from your mother."

Jett rose quickly.

Carissa stood as well. "Why wouldn't she call your cell?"

Jett shrugged. "My service has been spotty at best while we've been here. Maybe she couldn't get through."

"I hope everything is okay."

He silently prayed for the same thing, but he feared the worse. His mother wouldn't call him on vacation if it weren't an emergency. "I'll be right back."

"Okay."

He walked to the lobby, but he was stopped before he could reach the front desk.

"Jett."

He turned to find Stella standing next to him. "I'm sorry, Stella. I can't talk right now. There's a phone call for–"

"There's no call."

Jett frowned. "What do you mean?"

"I called the front desk and pretended to be your mother."

"Why would you do that?"

Stella looked around. She appeared to be terrified.

"I was trying to get you away from Carissa. I don't want her involved in this. It's dangerous."

Jett had thought Stella was a bit of an airhead as she contributed very little to any conversation they'd ever had—always distracted and laughing just a beat or two after he and Carissa, as if she hadn't gotten the joke. It appeared she was more intelligent than he'd given her credit for.

"What's dangerous?"

Stella bit her lip and glanced around the lobby again. "Do you think we could talk about this outside? I'm afraid I'm being watched."

Jett nodded, following Stella toward an employee's exit. They stepped out onto a small path that was overgrown with lush, green vegetation. There were two tracks that looked like they'd been made by the golf carts employees used to transport things all over the island. Two carts were parked next to them.

"Who do you think is watching you, Stella?"

She shrugged. "No one. I just wanted to get you alone."

Before Jett could respond, he felt something sharp pierce his arm. He tried to swat at the sting, thinking a mosquito had bitten him. However, he couldn't move and his vision went hazy. Black spots obscured his view. All he could see as his strength began to fail was Stella smiling, her face distorted with an unhinged glee, as she pushed him into the passenger seat of the golf cart.

It was her.

Stella was the killer.

And he was a dead man.

Carissa glanced around the lobby, expecting to find Jett there. When he hadn't returned to the table after ten minutes, she began to worry and decided to look for him. She inquired at the front desk, only to be told Jett hadn't shown up to his phone call and the person calling had hung up.

Panic began to set in.

"Carissa? Are you okay?"

Carissa bit back a curse as Phillip approached her. The man was at the top of the very short list of suspects she and Jett had managed to put together. If he'd done anything to Jett, Carissa would kill him.

"I was just looking for Jett."

Phillip scanned the lobby. "I haven't seen him."

"He probably just slipped back up to the room."

"You seem concerned. Do you want me to come with you?"

She shook her head and started toward the elevator. Unfortunately, Phillip began to follow.

"You really don't have to come with me, Phillip. I'm sure everything is fine."

"Where's Stella? I noticed the two of you seem to have become quite inseparable the past few days."

She wasn't sure how to respond. Every alarm in her brain was sounding loud and clear. "I haven't seen her tonight. Jett and I were enjoying a dinner together when he received a phone call from home. I'm sure everything is fine."

Phillip's expression darkened. "I don't think you should walk around the hotel alone, Carissa. People have a tendency to come up missing on Eden."

Carissa's blood began to run cold. No one had reported Gregory's disappearance and only a handful of people knew about the murder. The only way he could know Gregory was missing was if he'd committed the crime.

What if Phillip had lured Jett away in an attempt to separate them?

She decided to play dumb. "I have no idea what you're talking about. Actually if you want to help, maybe you could check the dungeon for me."

"Jett wouldn't go there without you."

It was clear Phillip had no intention of letting her out of his sight. Desperate times called for desperate measures.

Carissa reached for Phillip's arms. Her quick motions caught him off guard and he raised his hands to hers as she yelled loudly.

"Let me go!"

Several people in the lobby, including a security guard near the front entrance, began to approach them as Carissa held tight to Phillip, making it look like he was grabbing her.

Phillip tried to break her grasp as she continued to yell for help.

"What are you doing?" Phillip asked, obviously concerned.

The large security guard placed a firm hand on Phillip's shoulder, which he foolishly tried to shrug off.

Carissa released Phillip, then staggered away, holding her hand to her heart as if upset by the attack.

Another member of the security force arrived. Phillip proclaimed his innocence, insisting she had grabbed *him*. It was clear no one was buying Phillip's story as she pretended to cry. "He was trying to force me to his room."

Phillip scowled. "What? No, I wasn't."

Carissa slowly backed away, feigning genuine fear as the security guards dragged Phillip toward an office behind the front desk. "Please come with us, sir. We need to ask you a few questions."

One of the guards turned toward her. "Are you okay, Miss?"

She nodded. "Yes. Thank you so much for your help. I'm going to go back up to my room. I need to lie down."

The guard hauled Phillip behind closed doors. Carissa was about to head up to the room when she caught sight of the employee who'd come to tell Jett about the phone call.

She called out for the man, who stopped. "I'm looking for my date, Jett Lewis. You spoke to him in the restaurant."

The man nodded. "Yes."

"According to the clerk at the front desk, he never came to take the phone call."

The man shrugged. "Some lady pulled him aside as soon as we got to the lobby and they started talking."

"A woman?"

"Yeah. Pretty woman with long, straight dark hair."

Stella.

Suddenly, a light went on and Carissa knew they'd been duped. Fooled into believing Stella was some dim-witted, harmless woman when she'd actually been setting them up all this time.

"Did you see where they went?"

The man nodded and pointed to an employee exit at the side of the room. "Last time I saw them, they were headed over there."

Carissa didn't have a moment to lose. Stepping out onto the path, she took a second to catch her bearings, then her heart started to race. She was fairly certain this path would lead her to the spot where she'd found Gregory. That thought propelled her forward and Carissa sprinted through the woods.

She ran for several minutes, slowing down when she

spotted a light glowing in the distance. A flashlight dotted the darkness. The sky was fairly cloudy, the light of the moon continually appearing, then vanishing. When clouds covered the moon, the night swallowed her almost completely, making it difficult to stay on the path.

She moved toward the light, stopping when she heard a female voice. Creeping closer, Carissa silently kicked herself for taking off so heedlessly without going inside for help. Panic had set her in motion, but now that she was here, she realized she needed backup.

No one knew where she was. If she had a snowball's chance in hell of saving Jett, she'd have to do it on her own.

God. This was bad.

Taking cover behind a bushy tree about twenty feet away, she peered toward the flashlight, hoping Stella couldn't hear her panting breath—fear and the run had her gasping for air.

As a cloud moved away from the moon, Carissa was treated to her first glimpse of the clearing ahead.

Stella was talking as she secured something to a lounge chair. From Carissa's position, she could only see the back of the lounger. Leaning closer, she realized Stella was tying a hand to the arm of the chair.

It was Jett. It had to be. Given his stillness, she could only assume he was unconscious or—as Gregory had been —drugged.

Stella continued to speak, her singsong voice alerting Carissa to just how unhinged the woman was.

Carissa slowly tugged her cell phone out of her back pocket. She hesitated for a moment, uncertain if she should turn it on. What if Stella saw the glow of the screen and came to investigate?

Plus Carissa was fairly certain 9-1-1 didn't work on Eden

and she didn't have the number to the hotel plugged into her phone. What the hell was she supposed to do?

Tucking the phone away, too afraid of risking discovery, she started searching the area for a weapon. She didn't see Stella holding one, so maybe if she could find a big enough branch, Carissa could knock the woman out.

Unless Stella had a gun. Then it was Carissa who would be shit out of luck.

Carissa heard a groan and saw Jett begin to stir. It occurred to her that Stella had actually been waiting for Jett to wake up. The evil woman wanted her victim conscious.

Stella clapped as Jett began to struggle against the ropes binding his hands and legs to the chair. Stella knew her business. She'd definitely rendered Jett helpless.

Jett said something in a low voice. Carissa couldn't make out his words, but she could hear Stella's response.

"No. I'm not letting you go. You're hurting my best friend."

Carissa frowned. *Her?* Stella considered Carissa her best friend? They'd hung out for a few hours the past few days by the pool and perused a couple of hotel shops, while Carissa struggled to make conversation!

Jett responded, but again Carissa couldn't hear what he said.

Stella's smile faded, her expression morphing from insane to terrifying in two seconds flat. She lashed out, slapping Jett across the face. Hard.

Carissa struggled to remain where she was, every instinct pushing for her to kick the woman's ass. However, rushing in without a plan and with no idea of what she was up against was a sure way to fail.

She took a calming breath and tried to clear her mind. She needed a plan.

Jett continued to speak to Stella, no doubt attempting to keep her talking until the Calvary arrived.

Stella's tone was vicious as she answered whatever question Jett had asked. "Carissa is a nice girl and you're making her a bad one! Just like Master did to me."

Carissa found it interesting that Stella still referred to Gregory as her Master. Killing the man seemed to indicate the respect behind that title should have been long gone.

Jett's voice was louder, stronger now. The drug must have lost some of its potency. "I'm not forcing Carissa to do anything she's uncomfortable with."

Stella laughed loudly. "Yeah, right. That's what you all say. You tell us we want it, even when we don't. You force us to do whatever you command, no matter how painful or degrading or scary."

Carissa could almost feel sorry for Stella. Gregory had betrayed her trust.

"Why didn't you just leave, Stella?"

Stella actually seemed confused by Jett's question. "Because he was my Master."

Jett fell silent for a moment, but quickly spoke up when Stella opened the backpack at her feet and retrieved a wicked-looking knife.

"I'm not Gregory. I won't hurt Carissa."

Stella studied the knife, looking at it almost as one would a lover. Carissa clenched her hands into a fist, hoping to still the trembling that had begun the moment Stella retrieved the weapon.

It looked like time was running out. Carissa crouched down, desperately searching for something she could use as a weapon. It was too dark to see the ground clearly, so she was forced to feel around.

She was thrilled when she wrapped her hands around a

thick branch. Pulling it up slowly, she abruptly stilled when the leaves around her rustled from her movement.

A quick look confirmed Stella hadn't heard. Jett was still talking to her, trying to distract her.

"How did you manage to get back into the hotel without anyone seeing you after you killed Gregory? The doctor said he would have lost a lot of blood."

Stella seemed thrilled by the opportunity to brag about her previous crime. "I'll show you."

Slowly, Stella tugged her t-shirt over her head. She didn't wear a bra. Then she drew her shorts and panties over her hips, kicking off her flip-flops as she did so. Folding up the clothing carefully, she tucked it into her bag and tossed it several feet away from the chair. "The ocean makes a wonderful bathtub. Washes away all sin."

Carissa didn't have any more time. She tried to figure out the best way to approach. Stella stood facing the woods, so she'd see Carissa coming from at least fifteen feet away.

The only other way to enter the small copse was from the beach, where there was absolutely no cover.

Essentially, Stella would see her no matter which direction she advanced from.

Carissa decided her best plan was to move in fast and loud. If she took off at a run, screaming at the top of her lungs, hopefully someone in the vicinity would hear her and come to help.

A surprise attack was the best she could do.

When Stella knelt by the chair and began to unfasten Jett's pants, Carissa realized the time was now.

She'd taken just one step forward when a large hand clasped over her mouth and strong arms tugged her back against a muscular chest.

It had never occurred to Carissa that Stella might have an accomplice.

Carissa panicked, kicking out, struggling for freedom, but the arms around her were tight, impenetrable.

Then she heard a "Shhh. I'm here to help you."

It was Phillip's voice.

Carissa stilled, and then turned slowly when Phillip released his grip.

Tears filled her eyes when she saw that he wasn't alone. Flanking him were three members of Eden's security force. For the first time since spying Stella with Jett, Carissa could breathe easy again.

Phillip pulled a gun from a holster under his jacket and the security guards followed suit. Carissa stepped aside as they spread out, surrounding the area.

Carissa silently willed them to go faster when Stella pulled Jett's cock from his pants, stroking it lovingly.

Jett was talking, still trying to reason with the crazy woman. Carissa longed to yell out, to tell him that everything would be okay.

Finally, Phillip gave the signal and the men moved into action.

Stella rose quickly when the first man appeared from the woods.

She lifted the knife defensively as they continued to walk closer. Carissa wished they'd move faster, that Stella wasn't still standing so close to Jett.

Carissa wasn't sure how crazy Stella was, but it would only take the work of seconds for the woman to drive the knife into Jett's chest. That terrifying thought drove all the air from Carissa's chest and she started to step forward.

Phillip noticed her movement and shook his head, but Carissa didn't stop. Someone needed to protect Jett.

All four men moved closer, surrounding Stella. Carissa joined their forces, armed with only her tree branch.

Stella swung around desperately, but they'd tightened the circle. There was no way out. When Stella looked down at Jett, the other members of the security squad pulled out their guns and Carissa leapt forward, employing her original plan of speed and noise.

Startled, Stella made one last ditch attempt to escape. She charged toward Carissa, the knife aimed to kill. She didn't make it more than two steps toward Carissa before Phillip overpowered her, tackling her in the sand.

Stella put up a good fight, but she was no match for the sheer brute strength of the much larger man. One of the security guards jumped in, subduing the woman with ease as he kicked the knife out of reach and cuffed the woman's hands behind her back. The master of the island had staffed his security force well.

Carissa continued running toward the chair, her fingers shaking as she fumbled with the ropes binding Jett.

She sensed he was going to yell at her until he saw her face. She wasn't sure what he saw there, but his eyes softened and she smiled. She wondered how the hell he could look so calm.

The knot defeated her until Jett said, "It's okay, Rissa. I'm okay. Take a breath."

Until he'd spoken, she hadn't been aware of the tears streaming down her face. She was crying. And not some quiet, ladylike tears. She was sobbing, choking.

Phillip stepped next to her and gently pushed her away from the chair, leaning down to free Jett.

Once he was untied, Jett reached for her. She fell to her knees by his side, wrapping her arms around his waist tightly. Jett's grasp was uncharacteristically weak and she realized the drug hadn't fully worked its way out of his system yet.

She refused to release him even as Phillip began to speak to them.

"Your girlfriend came out here by herself and was preparing to rescue you on her own."

"Was she?" Jett asked.

Phillip's tone suggested annoyance. "She just threw herself at that woman without a damn weapon."

"I was t-trying to get to you." Carissa was surprised by the stutter in her voice, her teeth were suddenly chattering.

Jett clearly wasn't as upset by her actions as Phillip. He kissed her lightly on the top of her head. "So brave," he whispered.

Carissa didn't move, didn't acknowledge the compliment. She wasn't ready to let him go yet. Chances were good she'd never be ready. She clung tighter, feeling the need for his warmth. She didn't remember the air being this chilly a few minutes earlier.

"Who are you?" Jett asked.

Carissa had been wondering the same thing since Phillip arrived, gun in hand, swooping in like her savior to save the day.

"I work for the State Department."

"What are you doing here?"

Phillip snorted. "Truthfully, I was on vacation. Then I spotted Gregory at the dungeon. He's been a person of interest for the past few months, suspected of human trafficking, sex slavery, that kind of thing. When I called my superior to tell him Gregory was here, my vacation ended. I was told to run surveillance. Problem was my quarry vanished. I started tailing Stella, thinking she would lead me to him, but she didn't. Then the two of *you* started asking a lot of questions and showing more than casual interest in Gregory and Stella, so I started watching you as well."

"How did you know we would be here?" Carissa asked, finally loosening her grip on Jett enough that she could turn to look at the agent. "Last time I saw you, you were being dragged away by security."

Phillip narrowed his eyes at her, obviously still angry at being set up. "Once I flashed my credentials to the security guards, the master of the island showed up. He told me about the murder. We realized the two of you were in danger. Since we didn't have a clue where you were, we decided the best bet was to return to the scene of the crime. Fortunately, that paid off."

Jett tried to rise, his slow, clumsy movements prompting Carissa to throw his arm over her shoulder, offering her own strength to help him stand.

"I don't know what the hell that woman drugged me with, but it was pretty powerful stuff."

Phillip helped Carissa lead Jett to the golf cart, where a security guard waited to escort them to the castle. They rode to the hotel in silence, the adrenaline of the past hour giving way to exhaustion.

Phillip and the security guard helped Carissa get Jett to the room and into bed. Jett refused when the security guard offered to call Dr. Magdalene to examine him, claiming all he needed was some rest.

Carissa thanked the men for their help and bid them good night. Jett's eyes were drifting closed as she returned. She actually thought he was going to go right to sleep, so she was surprised when he turned his head to watch her as she tugged off her clothes and crawled in next to him.

"Get in bed," he demanded, his voice deep and Dom-like. She'd never noticed that commanding tone at home, never realized her fantasy man had been sitting at the end of her bar for years. "I was afraid you were going into shock out there on the beach."

She turned to him, nestling close to soak up his warmth.

"Yeah. I think I was, but it's okay. I'm only sort of slightly freaked out now instead of in a state of complete and total panic."

Jett chuckled, then sobered up. "You saved my life, Carissa."

She shook her head. "No. I didn't. Phillip did."

"I'm not just talking about tonight." His voice was heavy, his words coming slowly. She wondered if he would even remember this in the morning.

It didn't matter if he didn't. She would. She moved closer and pressed her lips to his.

"You saved mine too," she said.

Jett was asleep within seconds. Carissa thought it would be harder for her, but in the next instant, she drifted off to sleep too.

CHAPTER NINE

J ett nudged his shoulder against Carissa's as they walked along the shore. Dusk was setting in. The two of them had slept in late that morning, and then meandered through the afternoon like a couple of exhausted zombies.

The master of the island had sent a word of thanks to them for their help catching the killer. He'd also invited them to return to Eden for another vacation—free of charge.

Jett liked the idea of coming back here with Carissa for their honeymoon, but he didn't mention that to her. The issue of their relationship and whether or not they even had a future was still up in the air.

"Penny for your thoughts," he urged. She'd been uncharacteristically quiet all day. He'd thought she was merely tired, but as afternoon led to evening, he realized she was troubled.

She paused, using his grip on her hand to stop him as well. "What are we going to do, Jett?"

"I thought we were going to finish up this walk, go back to the castle for a late dinner, then hit the dance club."

She narrowed her eyes. "I'm not talking about tonight."

He knew that. "I'm not sure what you want me to say, Rissa. I think I've made my feelings clear." He grasped her waist and pulled her closer. "I want you and I don't see that changing anytime soon."

"And you don't think we're too different to make it in the long term?"

He tilted his head, shocked by her concern. "Different? No. Not at all."

"I own a seedy little bar, Jett. That's pretty much going to be my life. Forever."

He grinned. "That's the closest you've ever come to admitting you actually like that dive."

She gave him a dirty look. "Dive?"

He chuckled. "So it's okay for you to talk badly about it, but not me."

She lifted one shoulder. "Exactly."

"I love that place, Rissa. And the regulars. And the bartender."

"You could do better."

Now it was his turn to scowl. "What the hell is that supposed to mean?"

She sighed. "I'm saying this so badly."

His temper was piqued. "No. I think you're finally saying exactly what you've been thinking all week. But I'm struggling to decide if you're suffering from low self-esteem issues I've never noticed before or if you're calling me a stuck-up snob."

Carissa put her hands on her hips. "Neither, you jackass. All I'm saying is we sort of exist on two different planes. You read constantly. You know so much worthless crap, it's mind-boggling."

He struggled not to laugh. "Worthless crap?"

"I, on the other hand, have only ever read *your* books. My

idea of relaxing is sitting in front of the TV all day watching a *Dance Moms* marathon."

Jett pretended to wince. He gave her shit for her love of reality shows all the time.

Carissa ignored him. "You aspire to bigger things while, the truth is, I'm pretty happy in my little bar, listening to a bunch of drunk guys talk about sports and their bodily functions."

Jett laughed loudly. "There's nothing wrong with that, Rissa."

"We have nothing in common."

When he wiggled his eyebrows suggestively, she waved him away.

"Besides sex." She paused. "And actually, we can't even confirm that. We haven't had sex yet. It could totally suck."

He sobered up, shaking his head. "It's not gonna suck."

Carissa crossed her arms, her stubbornness and pride coming out in spades. "You say that like you're going to confirm it."

He stepped closer, enjoying how she backed away, her expression leery. With the murder investigation closed, there was nothing else standing in their way. "You're thinking about this too much."

She frowned. "At least I'm thinking."

Lifting his arms, Jett gestured to the beach, the ocean, the beautiful evening surrounding them. "We're in paradise, Rissa. Everything about this place is magic. So we're going to let fate decide this for us.

She rolled her eyes, but he could see she was beginning to give up the fight. Regardless of what she said, Carissa clearly wanted him too. He was simply going to have to teach his no-nonsense best friend how to throw caution to the wind.

"You can't leave something like this up to fate."

He shrugged easily. "Why not?"

"Because it's not practical."

"Love isn't practical, Rissa. That's what I've been trying to tell you."

"So how are we supposed to let fate decide?"

He gave her a wolfish grin. "Easy. You're going to run. If you make it back to our hotel room without being caught, you're right. It's not meant to be. But if I catch you, you're mine."

Jett watched her process his words. He'd asked her their first night on the island what her favorite fantasy was. The answer—a single word—had come quickly and without hesitance.

Capture.

She studied his face and he worried for a moment that she'd refuse, that she'd continue to hide behind this roadblock she'd built between them.

Then she looked over her shoulder at the castle. "Fine."

The word had no more crossed her lips, than she'd taken off in an all-out sprint.

Away from the castle.

Jett waited four, five, six heartbeats, and then he began his pursuit. Carissa was physically fit and no slouch in the running department. She jogged three miles every morning.

He matched her pace and studied their surroundings, not turning on the speed just yet. They were still on the beach and there were too many people around.

He silently rejoiced when she altered course, turning inland toward the tree line. She found a narrow path, then much to his chagrin, increased her pace. She was in better shape than he realized. She'd merely been toying with him.

Jett picked his way along the rough path, struggling not to trip over a branch or lose sight of his quarry. He was impressed with Carissa's surefooted abilities. She had no intention of making this easy for him.

The only thing that set his mind at ease was the fact she was still heading away from the castle. She was setting fate up for a win.

Several hundred yards from the shore, the trees thinned and a glade appeared. Someone had built a gazebo in the middle of a field of tropical flowers. Vines covered the wooden structure, leaving something that looked like it belonged in the middle of a fairy tale. Carissa slowed, obviously surprised by her find as well. Then she headed straight for it.

Jett slowed his pace when he reached the steps to the gazebo. Carissa was inside, waiting for him. The race was over.

"Caught you."

She laughed. "Did you? Or did I lure you here, capturing you in a trap of my own?"

Jett crossed the gazebo, tugging her into his arms. "Does it matter?"

She shook her head. "Not at all."

"Carissa—"

She placed her fingers on his lips. "Shhh. I know you're a writer, Jett. But sometimes words aren't necessary." She reached up on tiptoe, intent on kissing him. Jett met her halfway. He pulled her against him, loving the way her body fit his. The passionate kiss spoke volumes, leaving both of them breathless. Several minutes later, they parted.

There was a pile of plush pillows in the center of the floor. It felt as if someone—maybe fate—had been expecting them. The gazebo was intimate, secluded, romantic.

Jett slowly unbuttoned her blouse, letting his fingers dip beneath as more skin was revealed. Dropping the silky material to the ground, Jett added her bra and his own shirt to the pile.

Carissa ran her hands along his chest reverently. They'd spent the past few days in a mad dash, letting pure driving need overpower the beauty of a slow touch. She leaned closer, drawing her tongue over his nipple, then blowing on the suddenly tight nub.

Jett repeated the same process on her, loving how Carissa held his lips tightly to her chest, the way she threw her head back in utter surrender.

He reached lower, sliding the zipper of her skirt down. When the material cleared her hips, he realized his sexy lover wasn't wearing any panties. He rewarded her naughty behavior by running his finger along her slit, paying special attention to her clit.

Carissa took a tiny step away. "I need to see you. Touch you. All of you."

He unfastened his light summer pants, tugging them and his briefs off. For one spellbound moment, they simply looked their fill. Though they'd seen each other in all sorts of states of undress over the past few days, this was the first time they'd both been completely naked and could relax and enjoy it.

Carissa, quite simply, took his breath away.

Again, words fell to the wayside as they moved together at the exact same moment. He kissed her once more as her breasts rubbed against his chest, his cock tickling her stomach.

They both went to their knees on the soft pillows, then Jett pressed her to her back. As he came over her, Carissa opened her legs. Time seemed to stand still when he placed the head of his cock at her opening.

He paused.

"Nothing between us," she whispered.

He agreed. He was certain she was on birth control, though it didn't matter to him if she wasn't. Jett wanted her forever and that included marriage, babies, a family and a home.

He pressed inside, her tight heat a welcome retreat. She felt as wonderful as he'd imagined. More so.

Carissa lifted her legs, wrapping them around his waist when he reached the hilt. Neither of them moved as he placed his lips against hers, kissing her, relishing this closeness.

Carissa was the first to falter. She raised her hips, seeking sensation, silently urging him to move. He broke off the kiss with a grin.

"Impatient."

She narrowed her eyes. "I think you're forgetting I have a vibrator that I can and will use if you leave me hanging too long."

He lifted his hips, coming back inside her with a fair amount of force. "You use that damn thing without me ever again and I'll flip you over my knee and spank your ass."

She giggled as he thrust in once more. "You really need to work on your threats. That one sucked."

Jett pounded inside three more times, then forgot what they were talking about. He gave up trying to think about anything. It was impossible. All he could see, all he could feel, was her.

Though he'd intended to make love to her, to give her soft and romantic, Carissa refused. Her nails pierced the skin on his back as she arched.

"Harder! God. Please. Fuck me harder."

Her words released him and he took her exactly as she requested. Jett realized this hunger would never be assuaged, the fire never stoked. He thrust in until she came roughly, her pussy squeezing his cock so tightly he winced.

Once that wave had passed, he pulled out and flipped her onto her hands and knees. She cried out as his cock entered her again, assaulting her still quivering pussy.

He gripped her hips tightly as together they fought for more power, more speed. Their bodies matched, mated, fit.

His fingers pressed into her skin when he felt her second climax build, then crash. He was helpless to resist giving in to the same. He exploded—physically, emotionally.

Jett fell to his side, gathering Carissa into his arms, his eyes heavy. Eventually they'd need to make their way back to the castle, but Jett wasn't ready to give up their private paradise just yet.

"I love you," she whispered.

His heart expanded, swelled with her admission. He could write a million books and he'd never, ever find more perfect words than those. "I love you too, Rissa."

She snuggled closer. "I was a fool. Do you forgive me?"

He placed a soft kiss on her head. "There's nothing to forgive. You thought you were protecting us—our friendship, our hearts."

"Can I ask you for something else?"

"Anything."

Something in her tone and the twinkle in her eyes warned him to be on guard. "And you'll give it to me. No questions asked."

"Um...sure."

He tried to prepare himself for her request, but the truth was he knew there was nothing he wouldn't give her. "What do you want, Rissa."

"I want to read your damn book. The rough draft. I'm not waiting until the damn thing is published."

He chuckled, then shrugged. "We'll see."

She narrowed her eyes and started to light into him. He cut off her complaint with a long, deep kiss.

When they parted, he pressed his forehead to hers. "I'll

give you everything, Rissa. My love, my friendship, my body, my words. It's all yours."

She caressed his face and he was surprised to see tears in her eyes. Before this week, he'd never seen Carissa cry—not at funerals or sad movies or even when the Saints lost the Super Bowl.

"Riss—"

"I don't have much, but everything I have is yours as well. I love you, Jett Lewis."

He kissed away the lone tear that slid along her cheek. Then he came over her once more, not even bothering to search for the words to respond. With her, he didn't need them.

EPILOGUE

Carissa wiped the counter at the Royal Lunch. Her small bar was packed to the rafters with regulars, Jett's family and friends, his publisher and his editor. Everyone was in a celebratory mood. His latest book had released and rocketed to number one on the *New York Times* bestseller list during the first week of sales.

Critics and reviewers were calling it his best book ever, raving over the intensity of the criminal investigation while marveling over a new element. Jett's detective had found himself a new female partner. It seemed Riley James had fallen head over heels for a straight-shooting, ball-busting, sexy-as-sin bartender. Longtime female fans of his series were delighted to see the diehard hero reveal his romantic side and they swooned over the sexy scenes Carissa had helped her lover *research* for the story.

Caliph lifted his glass, toasting his baby brother as everyone clinked glasses and drank. Carissa grinned when Jett handed his mother a check for two-hundred dollars, claiming he was paying her back for the loan she'd floated him when he first started writing. Everyone laughed as his brother Justin teasingly remarked that Mama Lewis was letting Jett off easy by not charging him interest.

Carissa walked around the counter to join them. His family had accepted her instantly, Mama Lewis chastising her and Jett for taking so long to see what was clear as day to everyone else.

Jett's sister Chloe mooched a dollar from him, declaring it was time to fire up the jukebox and start dancing. As the sound of Zac Brown's *Chicken Fried* filled the bar, everyone except Justin shifted tables to the walls and started moving to the beat on the tiny makeshift dance floor.

Justin punched Jett's shoulder. "I'm still waiting for you to give me credit for breaking your writer's block. Sort of suspected you to dedicate this last book to me, instead of Carissa."

Jett crossed his arms. "What makes you think you had anything to do with helping me write again?"

Justin gave Carissa a charming wink. "I told you the secret was to get laid."

Carissa and Jett laughed, neither of them bothering to tell Justin sex had nothing to do with it. Jett had confessed shortly after their return from Eden he believed it was love that had set him free.

Carissa had told him that was the corniest thing she'd ever heard, but deep down inside, she loved the idea.

Jett was just reaching for her hand, intent on dragging her out for a dance, when a man entered the bar. Jett stopped when he spotted the stranger.

"Who is it?" Carissa asked.

Jett didn't answer her question. Instead he changed direction, the two of them going to greet the man.

"You found something?" Jett asked.

The stranger nodded and handed Jett a file folder. Jett opened it, scanning the single sheet of paper inside.

Carissa snuck a peek and caught sight of a grainy black-and-white photograph of a pretty blonde woman playing the guitar.

"Is that her?" the man asked Jett.

Jett nodded. Carissa thought for a moment her boyfriend had seen a ghost. His mother didn't miss his shocked expression. She made her way across the room quickly.

"What's wrong, Jett?" Mama Lewis asked.

Jett handed his mother the photograph. "It's Dani, Mama. She's alive and well and in Nashville."

TRIPLE BEAT

TRIPLE BEAT

Dani was 17 years old when she ran from New Orleans like a thief in the night. Together with her best friends, Aiden and Bryson, Dani found success in music. Their band, Closing Time, has just signed with a major label. But Dani can't enjoy any kind of future while constantly looking over her shoulder, waiting for the past to catch up.

Aiden and Bryson have long suspected Dani is hiding some dark secret she refuses to confide. When she leaves Nashville without a word, they follow. What they feel for her...what they want from her...won't allow them to let Dani face her demons alone because they have come to know they're stronger as a trio. And three hearts beat better as one.

This book contains some scenes that may be triggers for readers.

PROLOGUE

He sat at the end of the bar with his baseball cap pulled low over his face. Not that he needed to worry. The Lewis family had never seen him and even if they had, he looked a lot different now than he used to.

He'd grown a long beard to hide the scar he'd gotten in prison when his cellmate took exception to him stealing a cigarette and came at him with a fork in the cafeteria. They'd done a quick, shitty stitch job in the infirmary, and then sent him back to his cell. His attacker had been moved to other accommodations. Even so, he'd wear the reminder of that poor decision on his face for the rest of his life.

For twelve long years, he'd bided his time, looking for *her*. He'd done another stint behind bars for assault and battery after he'd beaten the shit out of the arrogant asshole who'd tried to repossess his car. They'd tacked on a robbery charge after he'd relieved the stupid prick of his wallet. That second time in prison had slowed down his search for her, but he was free again and determined that this time, nothing would stop him.

He took a sip of the beer he'd ordered, keeping his eyes on one man.

Jett Lewis. To the rest of the world, he was a bestselling author. To him, he was a means to an end.

This man was his best chance for finding his missing daughter. For four painstaking months, he'd been following Jett, careful to maintain enough distance that the man never spotted him, while keeping his ears and eyes open for mention of *her*.

Where Jett was, he was. As a result, he'd become a regular at the Royal Lunch. He'd been here often enough that no one seemed to take much notice of him anymore. Jett was fucking the bartender, a sexy little brunette he wouldn't mind sticking it to a time or twenty. Of course, the little money-grubber would never glance his way now that she had her hands on Mr. Big Shot Writer's cock and bank account.

He glanced around the room, wondering if he was taking too big a risk this time. The place was crowded. Most of the Lewis clan was here, celebrating something. While he didn't think anyone would recognize him, it would be stupid to blow his cover.

Besides, their happiness was annoying as shit. It was giving him a headache. He'd almost convinced himself to pay the tab and split when another man came in.

Jett visibly stiffed, which caught his attention.

"Who is it?" he heard the bartender slut ask.

Jett didn't answer her question. Instead, he walked over to greet the man.

His ears perked up when he heard Jett ask, "You found something?"

The stranger nodded and passed over a file folder. Jett opened it, scanning the single sheet of paper inside.

"Is that her?" the stranger asked.

Jett nodded as an old woman—his busybody bitch of a mother—made her way across the room quickly.

"What's wrong?" Mrs. Lewis asked.

Jett handed his mother the photograph. "It's Dani, Mama. She's alive and well and in Nashville."

The man grinned. Jackpot.

He'd found her.

And this time, things would end much differently than they had before.

This time, they were going to finish what they'd started.

CHAPTER ONE

ani Lewis turned onto the highway and settled in for the long, lonely eight-hour drive from Nashville to New Orleans. She hadn't been back to Louisiana since she'd stumbled across the state line in the dead of night twelve years earlier. At the time, she had promised herself she'd never step foot in the Big Easy ever again.

So much for that vow.

She fiddled with the radio, looking for a station actually playing music versus the nonstop barrage of commercials, or deejays who loved the sound of their own voices a little too much. When she found nothing of interest, she switched the damn thing off and let the silence come in.

Unfortunately, with nothing to distract her, memories started to reemerge and form, playing in her mind like a flashback montage in a movie. Good and bad things converged until she was helpless to stop any of it, everything closing in on her at once.

Typically she pushed away thoughts of the past, burying all the horrible stuff deep, even at the expense of happier times.

She couldn't seem to separate the two, so she simply chose to forget it all.

This trip was going to bring it back again. Because of that, Dani would be smart to let the memories come. Force herself to face the tougher things so that she was prepared for what awaited her in New Orleans.

For the four-gazillionth time, she wondered if she should have told Aiden and Bryson where she was going. And just like the three gazillion, nine hundred and ninety-nine times before, she decided she'd been right to keep them in the dark.

If she had told them, she would have had to confess to lying to them about everything from day one. She never wanted to hurt them that way. Never wanted them to think she didn't trust them. She did. There were just some things she'd worked very hard to bury. Dani had no desire to resurrect the victim she'd once been. She was dead and gone and, with any luck, she'd put the final nail in that coffin this weekend.

Of course, even if she had confessed to Aiden and Bryson the truth about her childhood, she didn't doubt for a minute that her wonderful, loving, amazing best friends would have insisted on coming to New Orleans with her. She couldn't let them do that.

Couldn't put them in harm's way.

The highway was quiet this late at night, the endless expanse of asphalt stretching out before her. At the end of the line were two emotions. The first was a fear so powerful and overwhelming, it was almost tangible. But she also felt utter, indescribable joy and excitement over the prospect of being reunited with her beloved foster family.

She'd been shocked when Jett had contacted her two months earlier. Apparently, he had hired a private investigator to find her. The fact that the family had cared so much and gone to such lengths to locate her touched Dani more than words could say.

Hearing Jett's voice on the phone the first time had taken her so much by surprise that she'd had to sit down, her knees too weak to hold her up. She remembered every word they had said.

SHE JUMPED SLIGHTLY as her home phone rang. Most people had her cell number these days, which meant no one called her landline except politicians on the election trail and telemarketers. She'd been meaning to get rid of the landline once and for all, but as a woman living alone, she felt safer with it.

She considered not answering, but reached for the receiver anyway.

"Hello?"

"Dani?"

Dani stood frozen at the kitchen counter. She set down the knife, forgetting about the tomato she had been chopping for her salad the instant she heard her name. She knew the voice, but her head kept telling her she had to be wrong. It couldn't be. "Yes."

"I found you. God. I can't believe it. Your voice is the same. Exactly the same."

"So is yours."

He laughed. "I just started talking, didn't I? Didn't even remember to say what I'd practiced."

Dani laughed as well, despite the fact her heart was racing a million miles an hour. "You practiced?"

She stumbled clumsily to the kitchen table, dropping down into a chair. She couldn't quite wrap her head around the fact she was talking to Jett Lewis. While most of the world heard that name and thought "author", Dani only thought "brother".

"Yep. Wasn't sure if you'd be happy to hear from me or not. I was nervous."

"Jett..." She paused. For two years, he'd been her best friend, her confidante, her savior. If anyone should be nervous, it was her. She was the one who'd run and cut him off without a word...for twelve years. Wasn't he pissed off at her for that?

Somehow, she found enough voice to say, "I'm so happy you called me."

She could almost hear his smile through the phone when he said, "Thank God. I missed you, Dani. So much."

"I missed you too."

THEY'D SPOKEN for almost two hours that night. Dani had tried to explain why she'd left, but in the end, Jett didn't want an explanation. Or an apology. He just wanted to get to know the adult she'd become, to have his sister back.

The Lewis family had opened their home and their arms to her at the lowest point of her life. They'd shown her compassion and what it meant to belong to a loving family. For twenty-three blissful months, she'd been a part of that.

Then she'd run. She thought she'd lost them forever when she left, but Jett had made it perfectly clear she couldn't get rid of them that easily. She'd laughed, grateful he couldn't see the happy tears his words had provoked.

Since then, he had called her at least a dozen times. At first it was just to catch up, and then he started pressuring her to come to New Orleans for a visit. While he had told his family he'd found her in Nashville, he hadn't told them he'd made contact with her. He was keeping that part a secret. Jett, the king of overactive imaginations and lover of pranks, had created this entire scenario where he would throw a surprise reunion at the traditional Lewis family Sunday dinner. He wanted Dani to simply walk in one Sunday and reclaim her seat at the table.

Dani had to admit the plan appealed to her a great deal. There was nothing she wanted more than to sit at Mama Lewis' table again.

At first, she'd put him off. Not because she didn't want to see them, but because her work schedule was insane.

Two things had changed her mind about the reunion in New Orleans.

First, Closing Time, the band she'd formed with Aiden and Bryson, had signed a recording contract with a major label, and there was no way she was going to be able to continue hiding in plain sight. New name or not, her face was the same.

Aiden and Bryson had been dreaming about a deal like this, but Dani wasn't quite as overjoyed. So far, a lot of their performing had taken place in Nashville or smaller cities along the East Coast. She'd managed to keep them out of New Orleans. Hell, they'd avoided the entire state of Louisiana. And she'd taken special pains to make sure she was always in the shadows whenever it came to the media, letting Aiden and Bryson take the lead in interviews for local channels or magazine articles.

The guys had chalked up her reticence to shyness, though she'd seen them struggle with that explanation because she had no problem performing on stage or holding her own in social settings without cameras. She sure as hell couldn't tell them she was lying low, hiding from an abusive father they thought was long dead, so she'd let them find their own explanations for her strange behavior.

Of course, that was a moot point now. And was actually her

second reason for returning to New Orleans. Her father had found her.

It had started a month or so earlier, when she'd opened her mailbox to find a letter addressed to Dani Patton. She'd never experienced such bone-shaking terror as when she opened it to find a single piece of paper written in her dad's scrawl.

All it said was "Gotcha."

Dani had stared at the message until the word blurred, then she'd picked up the phone to call Jett. He'd told her to lock the door and check the windows. He'd even suggested she call the police, but Dani hadn't gone quite that far. The letter had a Louisiana postmark, which had eased her mind a little bit. Plus she'd come home to pack. Mercifully, she, Aiden and Bryson had been headed to Branson, Missouri, for a three-night gig. Jett only calmed down once she told him her bandmates would be there soon and the three of them would be heading out of town.

However, she'd returned home to two more letters. Each letter was ominously threatening and sparse. One had said, "Come home" and the other, "You can't run forever."

She had always known deep inside that her father would never stop looking for her, and for that reason, she'd spent twelve years looking over her shoulder, searching the shadows for the evil man.

Dani recalled the last time she'd seen him. While she'd been able to block out so many bad memories, this was the one that never left her, that caused her to wake up in a cold sweat night after night.

The image of her father's face, the sound of his hateful voice, were emblazoned on her brain and stuck on auto-repeat.

RUSSELL PATTON LOOKED over his shoulder at the social worker and police officer who stood at the end of the room. They were far enough away that they couldn't hear, but close enough to get to Dani should she call out for them. Despite the thick glass between her and her dad, Dani didn't feel safe. He'd clearly put on quite a repentant show to set up this meeting. After his sentencing, she had taken the first real breath she'd had in nearly three years—since before her mother's death.

Dani sat on the edge of the hard metal chair, wishing she were anywhere but here. She clasped her hands together in her lap tightly, surprised by how cold they were. It wasn't particularly cool in the prison visiting room. In fact, it was muggy, humid. None of that heat penetrated the chill that had taken up residence in her bones, ever since she'd heard her father had requested to see her.

The social worker and Mrs. Lewis had assured her the decision was hers, but Dani knew better. Knew there would be hell to pay if she ignored this summons, even if it was wrapped up in a pretty bow of lies. The social worker had bought into her dad's concerned-father act, falling hook, line and sinker for his it-was-the-alcohol and I-love-my-daughter bullshit.

She watched the small bead of sweat that trickled from Dad's receding hairline and along his stubbled jaw.

"You know I got four years." His voice was low, almost a whisper.

She nodded, forcing herself to hold his gaze. She had learned that it was never wise to look afraid in front of her father. He preyed on fear, took pleasure in provoking terror in weaker souls.

"But I'm going to be out in two."

Dani knew that as well. The lawyer had tried to explain something about time served and the judge suspending part of the sentence. None of it made sense. When she'd heard the four-year sentencing, her only thought had been *that's not long enough*. Then she found out it would be two years and she'd had to excuse herself to go to the bathroom to throw up.

"You're going to pay for that, Dani."

She glanced over her shoulder, hoping the others had heard, but they'd begun their own conversation, giving Dani only a cursory glance from time to time.

She started to rise. "I have to go."

"Sit down."

Dani froze, unable to move. Finally her legs made the decision for her as they gave way and she fell back to the chair heavily.

"I'm going to play the game in here, do what I have to do. And when time is up, I'm getting out, and you and I are going to finish what we started. You won't get away from me again. Understand?"

She didn't reply, nor did she try to leave. Fear permeated every crevice, every pore in her body, until she felt as if she were drowning in it, the emotion holding her in place.

"Answer me, girl."

"I understand." Her voice sounded wooden, well-rehearsed. She knew how to respond in such a way that would provoke no further anger. It was a skill she'd had to learn to survive, especially in the last five or six years as her father's alcoholism had destroyed every bit of humanity he possessed.

Once upon a time, when she'd been a foolish little girl, there had been several brief moments of hope when her dad would do something that made her think things would get better, that they could be a normal family. He'd taken her to McDonald's for her seventh birthday and gotten her a Happy Meal and a hot fudge sundae. Once, when she had the flu back in second grade, he'd sat beside her bed and sung her a silly little song that made her laugh.

But those small kindnesses had been few and far between. She was older and wiser now. All her childish dreams had been reduced to ashes, leaving her alone and helpless, captive to a cruel man.

"No one will keep you from me. Not that fucking neighbor or social services. Not the foster family they've got you with or the law. Nobody. You're mine. And you always will be."

SHE'D NEVER TOLD anyone about that conversation. Not the social worker, the police, nor even Mama Lewis. She had been too embarrassed, too ashamed, too frightened. Looking back, she knew those had been the wrong emotions. The fifteen-year-old girl was now a twenty-nine-year-old woman who understood what she should have felt was anger.

Her father had always been a drunken asshole. She couldn't remember a time when he hadn't tipped the bottle up until it was empty, then started slinging the insults and fists, smacking her and her mom around. When her mother passed away, Dani had only been twelve, and she remembered standing at the funeral thinking, *this is it. I'm on my own.*

And for three years, she had been. She'd thrown herself into her schoolwork and joined every damn club the school system offered. She volunteered anywhere and everywhere someone would let her because it kept her out of the house and away from him.

Her dad didn't seem to mind—or maybe he hadn't noticed—her absence. When she was home, she shut herself in her room, putting on her headphones, losing herself in music while living a very silent life.

Occasionally she'd slip up and put herself in the path of her father when he was wasted. He'd yell or hit and she'd work harder to find new ways to disappear.

By the time she turned fifteen, she'd already started the countdown, living for the day when she was eighteen and could get the hell out.

Unfortunately, hormones had kicked in. She'd gotten boobs and for the first time in her life, her father started to actually *see* her. In a way that made her skin crawl.

Dani forced herself to focus on the road, to blink back the tears forming as she recalled the night he'd broken into her room and crawled into bed with her.

SHE WASN'T sure what had woken her up, but as soon as she opened her eyes, she realized she wasn't in bed alone. The strong smell of whiskey told her exactly who was with her.

"Wake up," he demanded.

She stiffened when he shook her roughly.

"Wake up, you little bitch. It's time you started earning your keep around here."

He was drunker than she'd seen him in a very long time. His words were slurred, his dark eyes struggling to find her face.

"I can get a job. Earn money." She prayed to God that was what he meant, though her heart knew it was something else when his hands drifted to her breasts, squeezing them painfully.

She twisted away, but despite his drunkenness, he was stronger than she was.

"I don't want fucking money from you."

Dani tried to push him away when he shoved his hand into her panties.

"No!" she cried out. "Please."

"Shut up. You're gonna like this, Dani."

His rough fingers were thick, callused and cold. She wrapped her hand around his wrist, trying to pull him away. Her touch was ineffective as he burrowed deeper between her legs, touching her where she'd never been touched before.

This wasn't how it was supposed to be.

Why would he do this?

She had never fought her father. Not with words or with fists. Not once.

Dani considered that, feeling slightly shocked by the fact.

Why hadn't she?

Something inside her snapped. His fingers breached the opening to her body, the touch agonizing. It felt as though he was ripping her in two.

Reaching out blindly toward her nightstand, she wrapped her hand around the base of the lamp. She lost her grip as pain ripped through her when he pushed three fingers deep inside her.

She screamed.

"Goddamn. Dry bitch. I'll take care of that. Gonna shove my cock in that tight little hole." He pulled his fingers out and chuckled malevolently when he saw blood on them. "Virgin."

His tone was one of approval, one Dani had never heard him use when talking to her. God, how fucked-up was this? She had to get out of here. *Now.*

He reached for the fastening on his pants, his clumsy fingers fumbling with the zipper.

She took advantage of his distraction. Lifting the lamp, she brought it down on his head, hard. It was wrought iron and made a loud crack when it connected with his skull.

He grunted and fell back on the bed. She spotted the blood

dripping along his scalp, staining her pillow, and for a brief second, Dani wondered if she'd killed him.

Then, he groggily raised his hand to his head. She'd only knocked him out for a second. "What the fu—"

That was all Dani heard as she jumped out of bed and ran from her room. She managed to get out of the apartment, beating on the neighbor's door, begging Ms. Stern to let her in.

Mercifully, the woman did. Dani raced into the apartment, slamming the door closed behind her. Ms. Stern threw the deadbolt and the chain seconds before they heard her dad come out into the hall.

Ms. Stern called 911 as Dad beat on the door, demanding that Dani come out. Dani leaned against the door, praying the locks would hold as he rained a steady stream of insults at her, calling her a slut, a whore, a cock tease.

She didn't realize she was crying until Ms. Stern wiped her eyes with trembling hands.

"It's going to be okay, Dani. The police will be here soon…"

DANI DUG into her purse for a tissue. For a moment, she considered pulling over. Driving and crying didn't mix.

"Get it together, girl," she muttered to herself as she fought back the tears. She blinked several times and then took a steadying breath. She was doing herself no favors with this damn trip down memory lane.

She'd spent her entire adult life recreating herself, working hard to overcome a childhood spent living in fear. She had been helpless and fearful when she was a girl and apparently some of those traits had carried over, despite her best efforts to shed them.

It had to end here. She refused to carry the label of victim for one second longer. She'd go back to New Orleans, face the bastard who'd tried to destroy her and show him he held no more power over her. Then she'd return to Nashville and embrace a very bright future with no regrets or fears, and without the shadow of Russell Patton casting her in never-ending darkness.

Dani Patton had died the night her father crawled into her bed. And Dani Lewis had emerged from the ashes. It was time to dump the baggage.

She made the exit that took her to the next interstate, the last stretch of her trip before she hit Louisiana.

She recalled the last time she'd been on this road so late and grinned. Mercifully, not all of her memories were bad.

Dani had snuck out of the Lewises' house after learning her father had been released from prison. He'd cut his two-year sentence down by a month due to good behavior. Dani had been counting on that extra month because it put her that much closer to her eighteenth birthday.

Mama Lewis had cried when she'd told Dani the court was sending her back to him, but legally, her beloved foster mother's hands had been tied. She had to abide by the rules of the system.

Despite that, Dani had suspected Mama Lewis was preparing to fight the ruling. Dani couldn't let her do it. After all, Mama had taken in two other foster kids, the sweetest little boys on the planet, Zac and Noah. She wouldn't allow Mama Lewis to do anything that might get her in trouble and impact their placement. They'd only been there a few months and had only just begun to feel safe. How could Dani take that security away from them?

So...she ran. Somehow she'd managed to survive on her own for three weeks. When Dani looked back on that time, it all seemed like one giant blur. She had been a homeless runaway with less than a hundred dollars in her pocket and no idea where she was going.

During those few weeks, she had succeeded in putting some serious distance between her and her father. She didn't have a clue how far she'd walked when she had stumbled into an all-night diner just off the highway one night.

DANI WAS RUNNING ON EMPTY, sleeping sporadically and for short periods at a time. She'd eaten the last of the peanut butter and crackers and other food she'd taken from Mama Lewis' house two days earlier. Since then, she'd only had some fruit she had stolen from an orchard. Her stomach ached with emptiness.

She was dirty and tired and she needed somewhere warm to sit down for a little while. She'd only been in the diner a few minutes before she found herself regretting the decision to stop. The waitress was eyeing her suspiciously.

The last thing Dani needed was for the woman to call the cops, so she painted on a friendly smile as she sat down and perused the menu. She quickly scanned the list, looking for the cheapest thing. She didn't dare dip too deeply into her money. There was hardly any in her pocket as it was. As she ordered an egg and toast, her stomach growled loudly.

An older woman turned around in the booth next to hers. Dani was actually surprised when she saw the face. She'd thought it had been a man sitting there at first.

"Is that your stomach making that god-awful racket?" the woman asked, her voice gravelly and deep. Dani pegged her for a two-pack-a-day gal.

Dani nodded and glanced toward the door. She'd been stupid to come out in public. For three weeks, she had avoided main roads and public places, staying hidden as much as possible.

"Egg and toast ain't gonna help that."

To Dani's surprise, the woman rose from her seat, picked up her cup of coffee and shifted over to Dani's booth.

"You alone?" she asked, even as she plopped down across from Dani.

Again, Dani nodded, not sure what to do. She was too tired and hungry and her voice was rusty from lack of use.

The woman chuckled, the sound morphing into a light cough at the end. "Don't talk much, do you? I'm Stella."

She stuck out her hand, so Dani shook it. "Dani."

"Well, Dani. I'm at the end of a cross-country run." Stella pointed her thumb out the window, directing Dani's attention to the tractor-trailer parked outside. "Had only myself for company for weeks. You mind if I join you?"

Dani shook her head, afraid to kick up a fuss about anything in case it caused a scene. Stella reminded her quite a lot of Mama Lewis. Thinking of the dear woman sent a pang of homesickness through her.

Not that it mattered. The judge had believed her father when he said he'd climbed on the wagon, that alcohol had been his downfall, and he had kicked that demon out and seen the error of his ways. He swore he'd been a good and loving father before his wife's death sent him to the bottle. And because he'd had no previous arrests or complaints prior to the night he'd tried to rape her, the judge had decided she'd be better off with the sexual molester rather than the loving woman who'd treated her like a beloved daughter. God bless the court system.

Stella raised her hand to call the waitress back. "You drink coffee?"

"I've never tried it."

Stella's eyebrows rose. "Really? Well, maybe I shouldn't be

the one to start you down that path. Shit is addictive." She looked at the waitress as she pointed to her coffee cup. "I'd like a top-up on the high octane. And get my friend here a Coke. Oh, and add a cheeseburger and fries to that order of hers. You eat meat, right?"

Again Dani nodded, mentally calculating how much money this meal would cost her. "Yes, but—"

Stella winked. "My treat."

Tears sprung to Dani's eyes as the waitress turned back to the kitchen. Mercifully, she didn't see them, but Stella did. She reached across the table and squeezed Dani's hand. "Steady, girl. It's just a burger."

Dani laughed and sniffled. "Thank you."

Stella pointed to the guitar by Dani's seat "You play?"

Grateful for the distraction, Dani shrugged lightly. "A little. I love music."

Actually, she'd played the instrument nonstop since Mama Lewis had given it to her for Christmas the year before last. After so many years spent listening to music as a form of escape, it had felt amazing to Dani to be able to sing out loud. Mama Lewis told her she had the voice of an angel. A compliment she wondered if the kind woman regretted, since it had encouraged Dani to sing even more.

Stella gave her an approving look. "I live in Nashville. That's where I'm heading now. Lots of musicians there. Pretty sure I'm the only person in the city who can't carry a tune in a bucket. Figure the only reason they let me stay there is because I'm out of town more than I'm in it."

Dani found herself envious of Stella's life, her freedom to come and go as she pleased. "You must've seen a lot of the country." This past month was the first time Dani had ever stepped foot out of New Orleans. Her world had been so small for so long.

Stella shrugged. "Seen about as much as you can see from a highway. Don't get many chances to stop and play tourist. Even so, I've seen some pretty cool stuff."

The waitress brought their food and Dani let Stella carry the conversation as she dug into the first real meal she'd had in weeks. Twice, Stella placed her hand over Dani's to encourage her to slow down so she wouldn't get sick.

As they ate, Stella told her about some of the places she'd seen, and then had her cracking up as she told funny stories about other truckers she'd met on the road. Stella was a born storyteller.

Once the waitress had cleared their plates and Stella paid the bill, the conversation winded down. "Where you headed?" Stella asked.

Dani clenched her hands in her lap, hoping Stella wouldn't notice her nervousness. They'd been having so much fun, Dani had almost forgotten about her predicament.

"Um..." She searched for an answer, but the abundance of food had only intensified how exhausted she was. It was all Dani could do not to curl up in a ball on the floor and fall asleep.

"You got anywhere to be, Dani?"

Dani shook her head. She'd probably pay dearly for that honesty, but she could read the concern in Stella's eyes.

Stella didn't talk for a long time. Instead, she simply studied Dani's face. If eyes could plead, Dani's were begging.

Please don't call the cops.

Please don't ask me any questions.

Please don't make me go back.

Finally, Stella said, "Seems like a girl with a guitar belongs in Nashville. Want a ride?"

Dani wiped away another tear as she recalled that night. Stella had given her so much more than a ride. She'd opened her home to Dani, helped her find a job and, when Dani really thought about it, Stella had probably saved her life. She wasn't sure how long she would have survived living on the street before something bad happened. When she looked back now, Dani was shocked she'd made it three weeks on her own.

Stella had been right. Dani *did* belong in Nashville. The city gave her new hope, inspired her, helped her find her voice. She'd needed a fresh start and Music City had given it to her.

Now she was standing at another crossroads, very much like she had been the night she met Stella. If she could make it through the next week, she might have a fighting chance at a real future. One with no roadblocks in her path or cinderblocks weighing her down.

All she had to do was stand up to the devil.

CHAPTER TWO

"Oh, hell no. Are you kidding me?" Dani picked up her guitar, grabbed the handle to drag her rolling suitcase, and made it one whole step away when Aiden followed out of the room and caught her arm and stopped her.

"Wait. Dammit, Dani. Just hold on."

"What are you doing here, Aiden? Why are you in my room?" Then, because she knew he'd be there, she glanced over Aiden's shoulder. Sure enough, Bryson was leaning against a nearby wall. He looked casual and relaxed, but she didn't doubt for a minute he'd chase her down if she got away from Aiden.

"Bryson," she said in cold acknowledgement. The bastard had the temerity to grin and wink.

She took three steps into the room, ready to coldcock the fucker before she realized her mistake. The door closed behind her.

Dani spun angrily. "Open the door or I'm screaming."

Aiden leaned against it and crossed his arms. "Go ahead. We're in the penthouse suite. There's no one else on this floor."

She'd spent the entire night on the road, memory after memory bombarding her. Now she was worn out and on edge. Her nerves were tattered and her emotions riding way to close to the surface. Finding Bryson and Aiden in New Orleans was the last thing she needed. "I don't want you here."

"Tough," Bryson said, approaching them.

"How did you know where to find me?"

"Marco called to see if we'd be joining you in New Orleans this weekend. Lucky for you, I think pretty damn quick on my feet. Said of course we were."

Bryson's smug smile had her fist clenching again.

She'd been a fool to accept Marco's offer of a place to stay in New Orleans. She hadn't meant to tell anyone she was leaving town, but the record producer had called to set up a planning meeting during the time she'd intended to be away. She had asked if they could postpone it a week, as she needed to make a quick trip to Louisiana. Marco had been more than happy to offer her the use of the record company's penthouse apartment for her visit.

She had been tempted to ask Marco to keep her trip a secret, but hadn't wanted to rouse her new boss' suspicions. The ink was still wet on Closing Time's contract. She didn't want the CEO to freak out with news that she had a skeleton in her closet that had decided to poke its head out and wreak havoc.

"What's up, Dani?" Aiden asked. "You've been acting strangely for a few weeks. At first we thought maybe you were just fighting some nerves about the deal and the new album. But it's more than that, isn't it?"

Bryson huffed out a hard, frustrated breath. "You left town without telling us. You never do that. If something is bothering you, just tell us and we'll fix it. I can't stand how you're acting all distant and secretive these days. And now there's this sneaking around crap. What's wrong?"

She smiled sadly. Bryson and Aiden had been her best friends for six years. During that time, she'd gotten closer to them than anyone in a very, very long time.

But Dani hadn't told anyone in Nashville about her past. Not even Stella. She'd walked away from it all and had genuinely believed if she didn't talk about it, it didn't exist.

Then Jett and her dad had found her and doors she'd thought were locked forever flew open.

"It's nothing I can't handle."

Bryson took a quick step toward her, angry at her response. She stiffened her spine. It wouldn't be the first time Bryson had tried to play knight to her damsel. The only problem was she never let him see her distress. "Goddammit, Dani. I thought we were past this."

She knew what he referred to. When they'd first started writing music together, she'd held both men at bay, working hard to remain aloof. It had taken the better part of a year before she'd trusted them enough to share little bits of her life with them. Meanwhile, Bryson and Aiden had been open books from day one. How many times had she wished she could be more like them?

Aiden put a hand on his best friend's shoulder, holding him back. "We didn't come here to fight, Dani."

Dani wasn't sure if Aiden's quiet comment was to reassure her or to remind Bryson. Either way, it worked. Bryson visibly relaxed. She walked over to a couch in the sitting area and sank down tiredly. Then she took a few moments to study her surroundings.

"Swanky place. Awfully nice of the label to let us use it."

Aiden ran his finger along the top of a baby grand that stood in the corner. "I think this is going to be the norm for the next little while. We're their rising stars and as long as we don't blow it, it looks like we get to live the good life."

The idea of the "good life" would have sent her soaring a month ago. Now all she could hear was the "if we don't blow it" part. How would MC Records react if the details of her past came out? She wasn't sure they'd be pleased to hear words like "sexual molestation", "incest" and "runaway" hitting the media about one of their newest artists.

Her chest tightened as she tried to recall if there was something in the contract that would allow them to dissolve it. She was fairly certain there was. What if her father went public, made some sort of big stink, and MCR dumped them? It wasn't just *her* future success she'd be destroying. It was Aiden and Bryson's as well. And the worst part was...they'd be completely blindsided by it.

Bryson sat next to her on the couch, leaning against the soft cushions, his arm resting along the back. She giggled when he tickled the back of her neck. "I could definitely get used to this. Which is why it's upsetting when the third member of our trio splits without saying a word."

"I was going to email you as soon as I got here," she said.

Bryson scowled. "Gee. That's big of you."

Dani rested her head against the cushions, Bryson absent-mindedly playing with her hair. "How did you get here so quickly?"

"We knew you were leaving before you left, so we booked flights," Aiden replied.

She frowned. "When did you find out?"

Bryson stretched out his long legs and crossed his ankles, looking far too pleased with himself. "Marco called about an hour after you picked that damn fight."

Dani didn't respond. She didn't know how. She had felt guilty ever since she'd stormed out of the recording studio a few days earlier. The return trip to New Orleans had been looming before her and she still hadn't figured out how to tell Aiden and Bryson she was leaving.

With her nerves on edge, she'd hit a breaking point as they'd discussed a song list for their first few concert dates. She'd flipped her lid over something really stupid and left the studio. She had wanted to call them immediately to apologize, but she'd decided to use the argument as her out, a reason to give them the silent treatment—something she'd never done—for the few days it took her to travel to New Orleans, clean up her mess and get back to Nashville. She had hoped they'd be none the wiser about her escape.

"I'm sorry about that," she said softly.

Both men grinned and she realized the apology wasn't necessary. Knowing her friends, they'd forgiven her before she'd finished executing her storm-out.

Bryson reached for her hand, squeezing it. "What is it, Dani? Is it the contract? I know you're not comfortable with the limelight, but lately it felt like that had been getting better. I thought this was what we all wanted. What we've been working so hard for."

MC Records had offered them a sweet deal and there had been no question they'd hit the big time. All the hours, writing and rehearsing, performing in clubs and at county fairs had paid off.

The label had huge plans for them, including a three-album deal, a performance on the CMT awards show, and a forty-seven-city tour headlining for Bryan Lucas, the hottest name in country music. It was a dream come true and, according to their agent, James, an unheard-of offer.

Unfortunately all she could think about when they'd been planning their concert playlist was the names of cities for the tour—their kick-off performance was taking place in New Orleans.

Twelve years of repressed fears combined with the stress of returning home had bubbled out and she'd exploded. Irrationally. Insanely. And then she'd raced out of the studio and avoided their calls.

"It's not the deal. Or the playlist. I just have some personal things I need to sort through. Things I need to do. Alone." She had to force herself to add the last word. Now that Aiden and Bryson were here, she was damn happy to see them.

It was ridiculous, considering she didn't want them to know about her past. But the fact remained she was stronger when they were with her.

Bryson snorted. "Yeah. Alone's not an option."

Before she could take exception to the way he dismissed her request out of hand, Aiden stepped closer. "You might want to call Benji and let him know you got here safely."

"Benji knows I'm here too?"

Aiden shrugged. "We stopped by there after Marco's call to see if he knew what you were up to. We figured if you'd confided in anyone, it would be him."

"Shit."

When she'd first arrived in Nashville, she'd found a job bussing the tables and washing the dishes at Benji's bar. From there, she'd graduated to waitressing and then to a performer. For well over a decade, she'd worked for Benji in some manner.

"I'll call him," she muttered, not looking forward to that conversation. Like Aiden and Bryson, her beloved boss was also in the dark about her past. Her two worlds were suddenly colliding and Dani was terrified about the fallout.

"You should have told us what you were doing, Dani," Aiden said.

Dani lifted one shoulder casually, though she didn't feel as relaxed as she was pretending. "You're not my keepers."

Bryson's brows furrowed and she could see the anger in his eyes. She didn't blame him. She'd be pissed as hell if either of them said the same thing to her. They were more than just bandmates. They were her best friends and her family.

"I'm sorry," she added quickly. "You caught me off guard here. I've been driving all night and I'm really tired." Then, she offered them an olive branch. After all, they'd come all this way to be with her because they loved her and they were worried about her. "I'm here to reunite with my foster family."

It wasn't the entire truth, but it was part of it. And given the fact they weren't planning to leave, it was inevitable that they'd meet the Lewises. She'd reunited with Jett and met his fiancée, Carissa, this morning at a late breakfast as soon as she arrived in town. It had been truly wonderful to see him again.

Tomorrow she was going to Mama Lewis' house to reconnect with everyone else. Deep down, she wanted Aiden and Bryson to meet them.

"You were a foster kid?" Aiden asked.

Dani fought hard to stem the tears threatening as she considered the part she couldn't tell them. She'd spent her entire adult life recreating herself. She had been a victim, but Aiden and Bryson had never seen her as such. They saw her as independent, self-sufficient, confident. She didn't want that to change.

"Yes." She didn't offer them more than that. Her short answer annoyed them. She could read it in their faces. It wasn't that she didn't want to confide in them. It was that she couldn't. Her throat was clogged with unshed tears. She swallowed heavily, and then offered them as much as she was able.

"Apparently they've been looking for me for a long time. My foster brother, Jett, called me a couple months ago. We've been talking on the phone quite a lot since then. I thought..." she paused, hating herself for the lie she was about tell. "I thought I'd take this weekend to see them again before our lives go crazy—between the recording studio, the television appearances and the tour, I wasn't sure when I'd have a chance to reunite with them."

"Our first tour stop is New Orleans." Leave it to Aiden to point out the obvious. It was hell trying to lie to him because he was too fucking smart.

"We're going to be busy."

His expression told her he didn't buy that answer, but luckily, he didn't press her on it. "So you're just here to see your foster family?"

She nodded. "Yeah." And again, there was absolutely no reason on earth she couldn't have told the guys that harmless tidbit in Nashville. The confusion on Aiden's face told her he was still trying to find the catch.

"The Lewises," she added stupidly, hoping that by throwing out a name—her last name—they'd find something innocuous to focus on instead of the obvious, which was that she was lying to them.

"You were close to them?" Aiden asked.

Dani swallowed heavily. "Yeah. I was."

She had only suffered one regret by running away, and that was that she'd had to leave the Lewis family. However, the pain she'd felt in leaving them was alleviated by the realization her absence would keep Mama Lewis from doing anything stupid in her attempts to save Dani.

"I thought Stella was your aunt," Bryson said.

She shook her head. That was the lie she and Stella had created when Dani moved in with the oft-absent trucker. Stella had offered her a place to stay for a few weeks. When the weeks turned into months, they decided to make it a permanent arrangement. Stella had never pressed Dani for details about her life before coming to Nashville. She'd simply accepted her presence and they had gone on from there.

Dani had gotten a job at Benji's while Stella continued to make her cross-country runs. Stella said she found it easier to leave knowing someone was looking after her house. It was a lie, but Dani had let herself believe it, so grateful to have a home and a friend.

After a few years, it stopped feeling strange to call Stella her aunt because they'd definitely forged a tiny family—just the two of them. When Stella, a chain smoker, had been diagnosed with lung cancer, it was Dani's name listed as next of kin and she sat beside Stella for weeks in the hospital, holding her hand as she died.

"She wasn't a blood relative, but she was still my aunt." Dani had spent a lifetime perilously short on family. So she'd created her own—adopting Mama Lewis as a mother and Stella as an aunt. Even her cantankerous old boss, Benji, had become family.

After Stella's death, Dani had been devastated, distraught. Benji had stepped in, becoming less employer and more over-protective uncle. He'd helped her deal with Stella's estate, guiding her through the process of planning a funeral, selling the house and settling all of Stella's debts.

Stella had named Dani the beneficiary in her will, and while that hadn't amounted to any great inheritance, it had given Dani enough money for a decent used car, to put down a security deposit on a nice apartment in town, and to tuck a little bit in the bank for a rainy day. Through it all, Benji had held her hand and given her a shoulder to cry on.

She considered Aiden and Bryson family too, though for some reason, she didn't feel the same sisterly fondness for them that she felt for the Lewis kids—Caleb, Justin, Chloe and Jett.

She supposed it was because she'd been a girl when she had met the Lewises and a woman when she'd met Aiden and Bryson. Perhaps her needs in terms of family had changed.

"So you're really only here to reunite with the Lewises? Nothing else?" Aiden asked, his voice still skeptical. She didn't blame him for his doubts.

"Yes," Dani responded quickly, determined to keep the other goal from them. It was her own fault she was in this mess.

For years, she'd covered her tracks—changing her name, setting up residence in Nashville and lying her ass off about her childhood. After so long, she'd actually become complacent and started to feel secure. She should have known her secrets would come back to bite her in the ass eventually.

Dani shuddered to think how Bryson and Aiden would react if she told them about her father and the things he'd done to her. She wasn't sure she'd be able to keep them from killing the man. And while she'd harbored more than a few murderous thoughts toward her dad in the past, that was all they were —thoughts.

Aiden sat down in an oversized chair across from her. "How long has it been since you've seen them?"

"Twelve years."

"Did you live with them for long?"

Aiden was inquisitive by nature. And while he was keeping the conversation light and breezy, she knew he was hurt that she'd lied to him...that she was still lying to him.

As far as Bryson and Aiden knew, Stella had raised Dani after her parents died in a car crash. She'd never mentioned the Lewis family or New Orleans to them. Not once.

She cleared her throat uncomfortably. "Two years."

He nodded slowly, his gaze intent on her face. "And before that?"

Dani couldn't do this. Couldn't give them the answers she

wanted. Exhaustion mixed with fear and shame. She had been so determined to find her father, to call the man a bastard to his face, to tell him he hadn't broken her and he meant nothing to her. To say all those things she'd longed to say when she'd been fifteen.

It had been a much easier prospect in Nashville. However, her courage had begun to waver the second she saw the sign welcoming her to New Orleans.

"I was somewhere else." The vague response had the desired effect, even if it gutted Dani to do it. Aiden looked hurt. And then he looked away.

Bryson wasn't as easy to shake. He cupped her cheek, forcing her to face him. His jaw, covered by that permanent five o'clock shadow he never seemed able to shave away, was tight. "We're not strangers, Dani. I don't know what's going on inside that head of yours, but we're not the enemy and we're not going to hurt you. Why are you shutting us out?"

Dani blinked rapidly, desperate not to cry. Everything he said was true. Neither of them deserved the way she was treating them. They were her friends. The three of them had shared a lifetime of adventures in the past six years as they'd spent hours rehearsing, traveling from one small town to the next, and as they'd written songs that became big hits for one superstar after another to pay the bills.

Then they'd made their own huge breakthrough six months earlier when they had recorded a song they'd written and uploaded it on iTunes. The thing had gone viral and made them a shit ton of money. It had put their little trio, Closing Time, on the map, and from that had come the big record deal.

As far as Dani could see, there was only one thing standing in their way. Her.

Dani wanted to look away, unable to face the hurt on Bryson's face, but he wouldn't let her go, refused to let her escape. "I just need some time to sort things out here. It's nothing you need to worry about. Honest."

"This Lewis family...they're good people?"

Dani smiled. "The best."

"When are you going to see them?" Bryson asked.

"Tomorrow. Sunday dinner. Jett knows I'm coming and he's promised to get the rest of the family there. My arrival is going to be a surprise."

"We're going with you." Bryson's tone told her to save her breath if she was planning to argue. When he made a proclamation like that, it was going to happen, no matter what.

She didn't reject the idea. She wanted them to meet Mama Lewis and Jett and her brothers and sister. There was a large part of her that liked the idea of her two families meeting at last.

The only problem was Jett. He knew what else she intended to do while in town. He wasn't crazy about the idea of her confronting her dad and had insisted on coming with her... as if she'd go by herself. However, even with that concession, he was worried.

She was afraid he'd take one look at her big strong bandmates and decide to recruit them to help.

She'd have to call him later and swear him to secrecy. Then she had to hope that the subject of her father didn't come up during dinner. It was all a long shot, but Dani didn't have enough energy right now to worry about it.

"Okay," she said at last. "You can come with me."

Bryson gently touched her cheek. "Why don't you get some sleep, Dani? You look beat."

She glanced at her watch. It was nearly noon. She'd pulled out of Nashville at three a.m. She had intended to wait until dawn to start the trek, but she'd been too restless, too keyed up to sleep, so she'd just thrown her stuff in the car and hit the road. Once she'd crossed the city limits of New Orleans, she had called Jett, grabbed a quick breakfast then came here.

She looked around. "Where am I sleeping?"

Bryson grasped her hand and they rose from the couch together. He led her to a door on the right as Aiden picked up her suitcase and followed them. "This one. It's got a king-sized bed in it." He pointed across the living room to another door. "That room is a double, two queens. Aiden and I will sleep there."

She smiled appreciatively. "My own room? With a real bed? Wow. A girl could get spoiled by this."

Aiden chuckled. "I think our days of sharing crappy hotel rooms are over, but I have to admit I'm kind of sad about that."

She smirked. "That's because you guys always got the beds while I was relegated to the rollaway."

Aiden set her suitcase on the luggage rack. "You're smaller. They don't make those things big enough for guys over six feet."

She knew that. Which was the only reason she'd always offered to take the cot. In the beginning they had taken turns, but it had simply been too painful to watch Aiden and Bryson struggling to find comfortable positions on a rollaway, tossing and turning all night, then dealing with their grumpiness the next day.

Bryson pulled down the covers. She dropped onto the mattress heavily, flopping onto her back. "Give me your cell."

She fished it out of her pocket and handed it to him.

"I'm turning it off so the damn thing isn't beeping all after-noon." Bryson's own cell tended to be off more than on. He owned one for necessity, but he wasn't a fan of all the pings and dings associated with texts and emails and Facebook.

Bryson shook his head then lifted her feet to tug off her sneakers and her socks. She sighed, her eyes drifting closed.

"Dani," he whispered.

She lifted her lids, though it took some effort. "Hmmm?"

"Clothes?"

"Too sleepy."

He rolled his eyes, and then unfastened her jeans. He pulled them off quickly and efficiently. Shyness had stopped being a thing for them a long time ago. They were broke musicians who spent a lot of time on the road, hence the shared rooms. As a result, they'd seen her in her bra and undies countless times and she'd spent more than a few hours with them as they'd walked around in just their boxers.

Bryson threw the covers over her. It was warm and cozy and despite all the problems facing her, she didn't think sleep was going to be an issue. She was too tired to give a shit about anything right now.

Bryson murmured a quiet good night. Then, to her surprise, he followed it up with a kiss to her forehead. She only had a second to consider how strange that show of affection was when Aiden added his own kiss to her brow.

She sighed contentedly, deciding it didn't matter.

She liked the kisses.

And the bed.

SHE AWOKE to the sound of the penthouse phone ringing. Dani rolled over, reaching toward the nightstand with her eyes closed, desperate to make the noise stop and wondering why Aiden or Bryson didn't answer it.

Then she recalled Bryson coming in earlier to whisper that they were going to do some sightseeing.

She was still worn out and something told her she hadn't been asleep more than a few hours. Finally, she managed to put her hand on the receiver.

"Hello?"

"Welcome home, baby."

Dani's eyes flew open, her blood turning cold as she heard the voice that had tormented her dreams for years. How did he know she was here? Dani was struck dumb, unable to respond.

"I want to see you," her father said.

Panic kicked in as Dani hung up quickly, and then took it off the hook so he couldn't call back. She crawled more deeply under the covers, trying to combat the unexpected chill. She was suddenly freezing, shivering so hard her teeth chattered.

He knew she was in New Orleans. He knew where she was staying. Her heart thudded heavily when she considered he might come to the penthouse to seek her out.

Out in the living room, she heard the sound of the front door opening. Her lips parted to scream, but closed again when she heard Bryson and Aiden talking quietly.

She needed to get them to return to Nashville, out of the line of fire. She'd hoped she would be able to clean up the mess without involving them, but it felt as if there was a ticking time bomb in the room with her.

Dani pretended to be asleep when Aiden popped his head in to check on her, staying under the covers and fighting to calm down. Once she felt as if she had control of her emotions, she reached for her cell and turned it on, her hand trembling when she saw that she'd missed three calls, all from a blocked number.

Did he have her fucking cell number too? How?

She took a deep breath as she found Jett in her contacts and called him, careful to keep her voice down, so Bryson and Aiden didn't overhear.

"Jett," she said when he answered.

Her voice must have given her away. "What happened?"

"He called the penthouse and I think he might have my cell number."

She heard Jett curse. "How does he know you're here?"

"I don't know, but it doesn't matter. He knows."

"Shit. I'll call Blake, but I'm not sure if he's really done enough to warrant getting a restraining order against him." Apparently her foster sister, Chloe, had hooked up with a hot cop from the New Orleans police force. Jett had mentioned bringing him along when Dani faced her father, but Dani had been resistant to have such a humiliating meeting in front of a stranger. She no longer felt that way. Hearing her dad's voice had opened a floodgate, drowning her in a whole sea of terror.

"Okay."

"You at the apartment?" Jett asked. "I'm coming over."

"No. Now isn't a good time."

"Dani, I don't like you staying there alone. I'm going to—"

She cut him off. "I'm not alone."

"I thought you said—"

"Aiden and Bryson followed me. They're here right now."

Jett blew out a relieved breath. "Good. I'm glad you told them."

"I didn't tell them all of it."

"What do you mean?"

"I told them I was here to reunite with my foster family. They don't know about my dad and I'd really like to keep it that way."

"What? Why? I thought these guys were your friends, that you trusted them?"

Dani wasn't sure she could explain. For twelve years, she'd been plain old Dani Lewis. The people in her everyday world saw a waitress, a singer, a songwriter. No one in Nashville had ever looked at her with pity in their eyes; never saw her as a victim or *that poor girl*.

"I do trust them, but I want to take care of this on my own if I can. The fewer people I put in harm's way, the better. I already hate that you're involved and possibly in danger." She didn't doubt for a moment now that her father was a definite threat. His voice was the same, cold and hard.

"You're not doing this on your own, Dani."

"I know I'm not. I have you. And Blake."

"I get that it's not easy for you to let people in, but from what you've told me, Aiden and Bryson are stand-up guys. They'd understand. They wouldn't walk away from you."

Dani knew that. But it didn't make it any easier to say the words. They were too painful, too humiliating.

"Let's just stick with the original plan for now. Until we find my dad and see what I'm up against, it's impossible to know how to proceed."

Jett didn't reply immediately. Dani worried he intended to continue fighting her, but finally he said, "You still coming to Sunday dinner tomorrow? The whole family will be there."

Under better circumstances, the idea of reuniting with that beloved family would have had her turning cartwheels. Now, however, she was too concerned for their safety. "Maybe we should postpone the reunion."

"No. Absolutely not. I'll come get you myself if you force my hand."

"Okay. I'll be there. Aiden and Bryson are planning to tag along. Are you sure we shouldn't clue Mama Lewis in so she knows there will be three extra mouths to feed?"

Jett snorted. "You're joking, right? That woman will have enough food there to feed twelve unexpected guests. She'll be over the moon when she sees you, Dani."

For the first time since hearing her father's voice on the phone, Dani felt warm again. Mama Lewis had always found a way to make her feel safe. Loved. Special.

Regardless of all the shit with her dad, Dani refused to let him take away one moment of her happiness about seeing her family again.

She'd simply focus on that for now. She had managed to push all the bad stuff into the background for twelve years.

One more day wouldn't hurt.

She hoped.

CHAPTER THREE

"I told you I'd get you back, bitch. You're mine. Mine."

Cold, hard hands touched her.

The room was pitch black, but she could tell by the hot, sour-smelling breath he was there. With her.

Dani struggled to fight off his grip but her hands felt heavy, clumsy.

"No," she whispered.

"We're gonna finish what we started, you little slut."

"No!" Dani kicked out, trying to free herself, but she was trapped, held tight. "No! Stop!"

"Time to bleed for Daddy."

"God, please. Let me go!"

Sudden bright light blinded her, but Dani was too focused on the ironclad grip he had on her. She had to get away. She had to run.

"Dani!" The strong arms tightened around her as she punched, scratched and flailed wildly.

"No. Goddammit, no! You won't get me!"

"Jesus, baby. Dani. Wake up. Fucking hell, please wake up!" Aiden's voice broke through the nightmare.

Dani's eyes flew open, blinking against the light. She panted painfully, her breath coming hard and heavy, the air not quite reaching her lungs. She stopped trying to escape when she realized it was Bryson who was holding her. His arms were wrapped around her from behind, her back pressed firmly to his chest.

Aiden was kneeling in front of her, a scratch down his right cheek.

"D-did I do that?"

Aiden reached up to touch the red welt. "It's nothing. What the fuck was *that*?"

She shook her head, trying to force the memory of her father's voice, his hands away. "N-nothing."

Bryson released her as she turned to face him. She saw the slight swelling under his eye.

"Oh my God. Did I hit you?"

He gave her a crooked grin. "You got a lousy right hook. I took harder punches in preschool."

She barked out a loud laugh that morphed too quickly into a cry. "Shit. I'm s-sorry." Tears streamed down her face. Dani was helpless to stop them.

"Aw fuck, I was just kidding." Bryson pulled her into his arms, letting her cry against his chest. "Jesus, Dani. You're tearing my guts out. Please don't cry. I can't take it."

She'd never cried in front of them. That was all she could think as sob after loud sob roared out of her. After a few minutes, Aiden reached for her, tugging her away from Bryson to offer his own comfort.

While Bryson had held her tightly, squeezing her as if his life depended on it, Aiden's embrace was softer as he stroked her back and her hair, repeating a steady stream of "shhh, it's okay" until she managed to calm down and slowly find her breath again.

When she felt steadier, she pulled away from Aiden, sniffling and wiping her face with her hands.

Bryson grabbed a box of tissues from the nightstand. "Here."

She plucked three free and tried to wipe away all evidence of her crying. How the hell was she going to explain this to them?

"Nightmare," she whispered before they could question her.

"Yeah," Bryson said sardonically. "I figured out that much on my own. What was it about?"

She shook her head. "I can't remember."

Bryson narrowed his eyes. "Bullshit."

Aiden grasped her hand and squeezed it gently. "Might help to talk about it."

She knew with a hundred-percent certainty it wouldn't, but instead she just shrugged. "It was nothing."

There was no way in hell she could tell them what she'd dreamed about. Even now, she was still shaken by how real it had seemed. Dani glanced around the room in an effort to convince herself that her father wasn't really there.

Aiden sighed. She'd hurt him again. She was batting a thousand this week and hating herself for it.

"I'm sorry." She knew neither man understood her need to apologize, but they smiled anyway. "I didn't mean to wake you."

"We'd only just crawled into bed," Bryson said.

"What time is it?"

Bryson looked at the alarm clock. "Little after midnight."

She'd woken from her restless napping at six and they'd all gone down to a little restaurant across the street for a quick bite to eat. After that, they'd returned to the room and watched a movie on TV before she'd said good night around ten. She had a big day tomorrow and she wanted to be well rested for it.

Despite that desire, Dani knew she wasn't going back to sleep anytime soon, which meant she had a long night ahead of her.

Aiden ran his hand through her hair kindly. "I guess we'll go back to our room if you're sure you're okay."

They both stood from the bed and that was when she realized they were in their boxers, their hair messy from sleep. They'd lied. She *had* woken them up.

As they headed for the door, panic gripped her, especially when Bryson flicked the lights off.

"Wait!" she called out.

"What is it, Dani?" Aiden asked, stepping back into the room.

"Would you..." She hesitated, hating to show them how afraid she really was.

"Would we what?" Bryson returned to the bed, his brows furrowed with concern. "We'll do anything for you. You know that."

She bit her lower lip. "Would you guys sleep in here tonight?"

"Done," Bryson said. "Scoot over. Into the middle. I'm not sleeping next to Aiden."

She giggled, a mixture of relief and nervousness. Regardless of their past sleeping arrangements, they'd never shared a bed.

Aiden crossed to the opposite side, climbing in as well. The king-size bed had felt enormous when she was sleeping alone, but now that two big guys flanked her, the space shrank considerably.

Once they were beneath the covers, she belatedly remembered their states of relative undress. Both men were shirtless and her legs were completely bare as she was sleeping in her usual—a t-shirt and panties. One of these days she really should invest in proper pajamas.

Neither man seemed concerned by the lack of clothing. Or their unusually close quarters. It had been this way with Bryson and Aiden for as long as she could remember.

Aiden pounded the pillow a bit to fluff it up. "Just warning you now, Dani, if you tell Benji we climbed into this bed with you, we'll both deny it. I'll even swear on a stack of Bibles. I'd rather deal with God himself than Benji if it comes out that we slept together."

Dani started to laugh, then realized Aiden had a valid point. Benji would most likely kill them all if he caught wind of this, regardless of how innocent it was. "I'll never say a word. Because you guys wouldn't be the only ones in mortal peril."

Bryson snorted. "Yeah, right. You're his little girl, the daughter he never had. Everybody in Nashville knows that."

How Dani wished that were true. What would she give to have grown up with Benji as her father? How different would her childhood have been? "I love Benji. And he wouldn't kill you if I pleaded for him to spare you."

Aiden didn't seem appeased. "I don't fancy being maimed either. The man might like to brag about how Closing Time wouldn't exist without him, but I think that would all fade into the background if he thought we took advantage of you. I need my fingers to play the fiddle."

Benji's was a local institution, well known for giving some of the biggest names in music their start. It wasn't unusual for scouts and agents to appear at his weekly Songwriter Night to check out the latest talent.

Benji had long been aware of Dani's interest in music. He'd caught her standing in front of a sink full of bar glasses, singing her heart out enough times to know she had what he called, "some damn good pipes".

After a lot of coercion, he'd finally convinced her to sing one of her songs on Songwriter Night. Though it had been scary as hell to climb onto that tiny stage, once she'd taken her place in front of the mic, something clicked. It had been magic.

For almost a year, she was a staple on Benji's stage and she'd sold a handful of her songs to agents shopping for their clients. She'd enjoyed the extra money, the chance to perform and her continued anonymity.

Then Bryson and Aiden walked in one night and had taken their turn on Benji's stage. Their talent had held Dani spellbound, as they both had amazing voices. Bryson played the guitar and Aiden the fiddle. She hadn't been able to take her eyes off them as they'd performed.

Benji was equally impressed, and then the manipulative man somehow managed to convince the three of them to sing together for that night's grand finale. It had been off-the-cuff, unrehearsed and perfect. Benji had an ear and he'd known exactly how well their three voices would blend.

And so a union was formed. The three of them collaborated on songwriting and continued to sing the final number every Wednesday night at Benji's for three years. That was exactly how long it had taken for Aiden and Bryson to convince her to join them on other stages.

Once they had, Closing Time was formed, the name stemming from their regular spot at Benji's. Her inclusion—taking their duo to a trio—had happened almost effortlessly after they'd decided to give it a try.

For a couple minutes they all lay awkwardly on their backs and she could tell both men were trying to keep a proper distance.

Bryson broke first. "Fuck it. I can't sleep like this." He

turned toward her, twisting her until she faced away from him. He wrapped his arm around her waist, spooning her.

His breath ruffled her hair as he sighed. "That's better.

She laughed quietly. "Never pegged you for a cuddler."

"You don't know everything about me, Dani."

She considered that, and then dismissed it. She knew a whole hell of a lot. From his childhood in Jersey to his lost virginity—under the bleachers at a high school football game during his sophomore year—to the first time he'd picked up a guitar. She'd spent countless hours in cars and hotel rooms with them and they'd filled the time telling stories.

While she'd always brushed over the details of her childhood in New Orleans, she hadn't skimped when it came to talking about her Nashville life. She had shared so much of herself—her dreams and hopes—and in turn, they'd reciprocated.

She knew right down to the day the last time both men in the bed had gotten laid. It had been about six months for Aiden and four for Bryson.

As their popularity had grown, so had the sexual invitations, but she noticed neither man seemed inclined to take advantage of that. She'd been impressed by their restraint. Some of the women making the advances had been quite beautiful. No doubt the crowds of women waiting backstage after their shows would only get bigger once the album released and they started touring.

Dani had received quite a few invites herself, but she was far more discerning about her partners. According to Bryson, she was *too* discerning.

She'd slept with three men in her life. All three had been men she'd entered long-term relationships with. Of course, long-term in her book meant anywhere from four to eight months. And none of them were what she would call serious boyfriends.

Dani had issues when it came to commitment and trust. Of course, she knew exactly why she struggled with forging close sexual relationships. Another thing she could thank her asshole father for.

It was something she'd been trying to deal with, but it was difficult when she didn't have the opportunity to practice. She, Bryson and Aiden were all-in when it came to making it in the music business. They'd dedicated the last few years of their lives to doing whatever it took, making a lot of sacrifices in order to achieve success.

The hard work had paid off, but the price had been steep. None of them had what she would call a personal life, eschewing dating and hanging out with friends and family, in favor of the music.

That commitment—apart from her lacking sex life—hadn't really bothered Dani. It wasn't as if she had any family or friends to hang out with, and while there were plenty of guys who wouldn't mind getting in her pants, they weren't the type of men she'd ever consider dating. So, she'd simply given them all a wide berth and kept strumming her guitar. Her vibrator took the edge off and was a lot less hassle.

Bryson tugged her closer—and that was when Dani felt it.

"Um…Bry?"

He sighed. "Ignore it, Dani. Natural male response when he's in bed with a half-naked woman."

She heard Aiden snort.

"Sort of hard to ignore when it's poking me in the ass," she added.

Aiden laughed louder. "Damn. There's a visual."

She rolled her eyes. "Gross." Even as she said the word, she considered what it would feel like to have sex with Bryson. Or

Aiden. It wasn't the first time that racy thought had crossed her mind. She'd always dismissed it because the band—and their friendship—meant too much to her to risk for sex. No matter how amazing she suspected that sex would be.

She wasn't sure why she was so certain the guys were great in bed. Maybe it was simply a female reaction to the way they made her feel when they sang a love song, or watching their fingers fly with incredible skill over their instruments. She'd spent a little too much time lately considering those fingers strumming *her* instrument.

"I really need to find a guy and get laid," she muttered.

Aiden twisted to his side to face her. The moon provided enough light to allow her to see his expression clearly. "Been telling you that for nearly two years. It's not healthy to go so long without."

"Not sure health has anything to do with it."

She was surprised when Aiden reached out and pushed a strand of hair away from her face. "Feeling better?" He was obviously still worried about her nightmare.

She nodded. "I'm sorry I've been such a pain in the ass this past week. I promise...just a few days more and I'll be back to normal."

Aiden gave her a friendly smile. "Don't set your goals so high, Dani. You were never normal."

She grinned. "Asshole."

"I chalk that up to too many years spent with Bryson. That shit tends to rub off."

"You wish you were as cool as me," Bryson said in his own defense.

Dani glanced over her shoulder. Bryson looked very comfortable, his head resting on the pillow, the longish mass of jet-black hair hiding his dark-brown eyes, his arm wrapped tightly around her waist and his very erect penis pressed firmly to her backside. He was incredibly beautiful, but she was certain he'd scoff if she used that word to describe him.

Then she looked back at Aiden. He wore his light-brown hair shorter and hid his pretty blue eyes behind wire-framed glasses whenever he was working at the computer or reading a new piece of music. Bryson teased him, claiming he just wore them to look smarter, but Aiden never took offense. He just joked back that not even glasses could give Bryson an air of intelligence.

"I'm glad you guys are here." She'd been so wrapped up in her anxieties lately that she'd pushed away the very people she needed the most.

"All you had to do was ask." Aiden placed a soft kiss to her forehead. Then another one.

They weren't overly affectionate friends. Most of their touching typically came in the form of high-fives or roughhousing. Kisses and cuddles weren't part of it.

Dani reached out and cupped Aiden's beloved face. "Thank you."

She wasn't sure who moved first. Maybe they both moved together. But one second she and Aiden were simply smiling at each other, and then they were much closer, their lips touching in a quick, only *somewhat* chaste kiss.

They parted for a moment before they came in for another. This one lingered a second longer than the first.

Bryson's arm tightened around her waist, but he didn't speak, didn't call them out or ask them what the hell they were doing.

Aiden pulled farther away after the second kiss, his brows furrowed, confusion in his eyes. She suspected that expression was mirrored in her face.

And then it cleared. He relaxed, and so did she.

When they moved in for the third kiss, it was as if they were prepared, ready for it.

He stroked her lower lip with his tongue and she opened her mouth on a gasp. Aiden took advantage. This kiss lasted much longer, the two of them taking their time to explore each other's mouths. Aiden's fingers tangled in her hair and he used that grip to gently twist her head this way or that to help him deepen the kiss.

Bryson was silent through it all, but Dani knew he wasn't oblivious to what was happening. He also didn't seem content to merely observe. His hand slipped beneath the hem of her t-shirt, stroking the bare skin of her stomach, and then moving up to her breast.

Dani's breathing became erratic as she tried to keep up with the sensations drowning her. Bryson grasped her breast firmly, his large hand plumping the flesh, his fingers pinching her nipple.

Aiden either didn't notice or he didn't care about Bryson's touches. He tightened his grip on her hair and kissed her harder.

Dani was helpless to resist any of it. She pushed her ass against Bryson's cock, seeking more stimulation. The movement was a blatant invitation. One that Bryson didn't hesitate to accept.

His hand left her breast, traveling to her hip. He gripped it, tugging her back as he pushed forward, letting her feel exactly how much he wanted her.

It was *too* much. Dani broke off the kiss, desperately attempting to suck in some much-needed air. Aiden didn't attempt to resume it, but he didn't let her slow him down either. He ran his fingers along her neck, his gaze following the touch. Then he grasped the comforter covering them and pulled it down, not stopping until the bulk of it rested around her knees.

Regardless of the number of times they'd seen her dressed exactly like this, this was the first time she'd felt exposed, almost naked in front of them. Aiden's gaze traveled over her, studying things he'd never appeared to notice before. Or was it things he'd tried not to see? Had they had lustful thoughts about her as well?

Aiden reached out and ran his fingers over her covered breast, the same one Bryson had just released.

Neither Dani nor Bryson had stopped moving, the humping motion imitating exactly what Dani wanted to do.

With both of them.

The insane thought hovered for only a second before Aiden wiped it away. He lifted her shirt to her neck, hissing with approval as he looked at her bare breasts.

"Jesus," he muttered, just before he leaned down and took one of her tight nipples into his mouth.

Dani reared back, not to escape, but in response to the sheer bliss of it. Bryson was right there behind her, keeping her in place, holding her steady for Aiden's ministrations.

"Oh my God," she said when he increased the suction. "Aiden."

Her mind whirled, trying to land on what exactly was happening, but it felt as if her brain had shut down, taken a vacation. All that was left was a body that made decisions based solely on sensation.

And it liked what was happening.

A lot.

She felt rather than saw Bryson shift, his head lifting from the pillow to watch as Aiden continued to drive her closer to heavenly insanity with his lips on her breast.

"So fucking hot," Bryson said, his voice more breath than

sound. He added his own brand of fuel to the fire when he released her hip, his hand coming around her, lower.

She jerked once more when Bryson's fingers grazed her mound, still covered by her cotton panties. Her face flushed when she considered what he must be feeling.

She was wet. *Really* wet.

Bryson confirmed that fact with an approving moan that he followed with a soft kiss to her ear. "God, Dani. Baby." She wasn't sure she'd ever heard that tone of awe in Bryson's voice. He was a hard man to impress. She liked to tease him, calling him the world's biggest cynic.

"Bryson," she said when his fingers dipped beneath the elastic, grazing her clit.

She saw stars. Instantly.

"Fuck. Me."

Both men froze. Dani could practically feel them trying to work out if she'd just issued an invitation or simply voiced an exclamation. She sort of wondered the same.

Her damn thoughtless, selfish body answered first. "Please."

Aiden lifted his head from her breast, capturing her gaze. Meanwhile, Bryson forged on. He stroked her clit again, harder this time, applying just the right amount of pressure. Dani lost sight of Aiden as her eyelids drifted shut. She was too overwhelmed, too ready for the next adventure to attempt any sort of focus.

Aiden's hand landed on top of Bryson's still buried beneath her panties. She suspected he meant to stop what was happening, but what he'd actually done was push Bryson's fingers deeper. The tips of them grazed the opening to her body. She gasped, her hips flying toward the touch, seeking out more.

Whatever Aiden's original intention, it appeared he'd lost sight of it. "Jesus, Dani. You're so wet."

She would have expected that comment to embarrass her, to leave her blushing. Instead it sent another rush of moisture to her pussy.

Dani was beyond all reason. Her libido had taken complete control. She reached for her shirt and tugged it over her head, hoping it would offer her some air, cool her off. She was on fire.

Aiden and Bryson took action the moment her breasts were bared. Aiden cupped both her breasts in his hands, his mouth moving from nipple to nipple as he sucked, nipped and pinched.

Bryson tugged her panties down, not stopping until they'd cleared her feet. "Put her on her back."

Dani was tempted to remind Bryson she was there and perfectly capable of moving, but as Aiden lightly pushed on her shoulder, shifting her into position, she realized that somewhere along the line, she'd gone boneless along with mindless.

Aiden quickly resumed his place at her breasts, but that touch became secondary to the new one Bryson introduced.

He shifted on the mattress until he was kneeling between her suddenly outstretched legs. Bryson had lost no time pressing them open. It was as if she was made of clay and he was the master sculptor. A streak of electricity ran along her spine as the word *master* took on another meaning.

The men were definitely in control here. That wasn't something she'd ever experienced before, her previous affairs more a game of give and take, tit for tat.

Tonight, she'd relinquished the reins without even realizing it. It didn't appear Bryson or Aiden were in any hurry to give them back.

She hissed when Bryson leaned down, sucking her clit into his mouth. Her back arched off the mattress.

She'd never been the object of such wicked, wonderful attention. It was too damn much and she struggled to hold on.

"Please," she said again. She had no idea what the hell she was asking for, but it didn't matter. Neither man stopped.

Aiden pinched one nipple as he continued to suck on the other. Bryson pressed two thick fingers inside her pussy as he nipped at her clit.

Dani's hands fisted the sheet beneath her but it offered no purchase, no foundation. She was floating, helpless. That idea might have bothered her if she didn't love it so much.

Then Bryson added a third finger to the two already pulsing inside her. It filled her almost to the point of pain. She considered the cock he'd been pressing against her back earlier and suspected his fingers were nothing compared to the size of that.

But that didn't scare her as much as it excited her.

She imagined Bryson shedding his boxers and pushing that thick cock inside her. And then, just like that, she came. Hard. Loud.

Her body trembled as each man continued their sensual assault. Apparently her orgasm wasn't the final act in this show.

Which meant...

"God! Yes!" she yelled, even as her climax began to wane. She wanted more.

Needed it.

Aiden stopped her from saying anything else when he released her breasts and moved up, his lips claiming hers in a kiss so sexy, it stole her breath.

Bryson didn't give up his spot between her legs, his fingers still stroking, though his rhythm had slowed.

After a few moments, Aiden lifted his head and Dani spotted the first traces of doubt, of question in his eyes. "Dani. Are we...can we?"

She knew what he was asking, but she couldn't respond.

She had no idea what came next. Or at least what *should* come next.

She wanted them. Badly. Both of them. That concept alone left her drowning in an ocean full of *what the hells* and *why nots?*

But she wasn't a threesome girl. Wasn't some wild and crazy, throw-caution-to-the-wind kind of woman. She suspected it would take her a good twenty years to sift through what had already happened here and come up with an explanation that made sense to her.

"I...I..." She couldn't tell them to stop. That would kill her. But she couldn't tell them to go on either.

Bryson took the decision away from both of them. He rose from the bed, stripping off his boxers. Dani's gaze raked him from head to...well...cock. Her eyes stopped drifting south once they'd hit pay dirt. She licked her lips.

"It's too late to stop now," Bryson said.

She wasn't sure if that was right or wrong, but she knew what he meant. Dani could never call a halt to this. She wanted it too fucking much.

Aiden slowly raised his hand, pointing to the nightstand. "Check the drawer, Bry. I noticed the nightstand in our room was fully stocked. Apparently the execs at the label believe in safe sex."

Bryson gave his friend a crooked grin, and then opened the drawer. His eyes widened. "Jesus. Talk about variety. Anybody got a color preference?"

Dani giggled, her nerves getting the better of her. Aiden lifted her chin with strong fingers under her jaw. "Bryson was wrong. We can stop. And we will if this isn't what you want. You're in control, Dani. Say no and we go back to our room."

She shook her head, then saw them both freeze, their faces troubled. Her brain finally engaged. "No," she said hastily, sitting up then realizing that answer made it even worse. "I'm not saying no. I don't want to stop."

Bryson released a long breath.

Aiden smiled. "Thank God. I meant what I said, but I'm not going to lie and say it would have been easy to leave this room."

"Blue balls hurt like a son of a bitch," Bryson added.

Dani started to laugh, but the sound died in her throat when she watched him pull out a condom then toss a second to Aiden, who'd risen as well.

She wasn't thinking this through. Two men. Two cocks. One of her.

"How..." She instantly regretted opening her mouth. There was no way she was finishing that question.

Bryson chuckled as he returned to the bed. "We'll take turns, Dani. I don't think you're experienced enough for the other options."

Now that he'd said that, the stubborn, horny part of her that had no sense of self-restraint *really* wanted the other options.

But his words left her with another, more pressing question. One she didn't have a problem voicing. "Have you two done this before?"

Aiden shook his head. "No. Never. Truth is I can't believe we're doing it now."

She was grateful for his honesty. "Well. In for a penny. In for a pound." She picked up the condom Bryson had tossed Aiden's way as he shrugged out of his boxers. Dani bit her lower lip. Neither man was lacking in the penis department.

So much for pennies. She was definitely looking at pounds.

Bryson wrapped his hand around the back of her neck, drawing her attention to him. "Don't look so nervous, bird."

She grinned at his term of endearment. They'd taken to calling her their songbird in the early days of their association, but somewhere along the line that had been shortened to simply *bird*. It comforted her.

She tore open the foil wrapper, her hands shaking as she reached out for Aiden. He gripped her wrists to steady her, and together they slid the condom over his erection.

Aiden glanced at Bryson, who waved his hand, silently giving Aiden the green light to go first.

Aiden guided Dani to her back, coming over her. He kept his motions slow, giving her time to change her mind.

She loved him for that.

Love. That wasn't a new emotion in regards to Aiden and Bryson. They were her best friends. Her love for them had been there for a long time.

But this was different. The feeling had morphed somehow. Changed. It was stronger. More overwhelming. Frightening in a way, where before it had only felt like comfortable old shoes or jeans that had been broken in just right.

Now? Now it felt exciting, exhilarating, dangerous and terrifying. It no longer felt like something she'd never let go of as much as something it would kill her to lose.

If Aiden was experiencing the same, he didn't show it. He knelt between her legs, his face only a few inches above hers.

Her lungs seized when she felt the head of his cock brush against the opening of her body. Aiden held her gaze, his eyes capturing hers, keeping her steady. That was when she saw it—spotted the tiniest speck of fear behind the deep blue. He knew they were on the verge of something big.

"Dani." He leaned down to kiss her softly. "I don't know if this is a mistake or not, but I can't help myself, can't convince myself to stop and think. Right now, it feels right."

She nodded. "It does. So maybe it is."

He closed his eyes then, her words reassuring him. She

wished they'd had the same effect on her. Her heart was racing, pounding.

She wouldn't lose them. She couldn't.

Aiden slowly slid in, his long cock stroking, seeking, finding every hot spot along the way. And then, he was there. Buried deep.

He kissed her cheek and gave her the same playful smile he'd been tossing her way for years. Then he shook his head. "Jesus. What the hell are we doing?" There was no regret in his voice. Instead, he sounded far too pleased with what was most likely very poor judgment.

She grinned. "I'm not an expert, but I'm pretty sure it's called fucking."

Bryson dropped down onto the bed next to them. Though he'd been quietly watching, Dani hadn't forgotten his presence for a second.

Bryson's hand was stroking his own thick erection. "I think the right word is stalling. Christ, man. Get on with it or get out. My cock is aching."

Dani rolled her eyes. "I think I've spotted the mistake. We put the king of impatience second in the line-up."

Aiden laughed, the response sending his cock deeper. They both gasped. "Fuck, Dani."

He'd been trying to resist. Like her, he probably thought his brain would kick in any minute, but Dani could see now that wasn't going to happen.

"Do it," she whispered.

Aiden took the permission granted and drove every remaining cognizant thought from her head. He was known for being the methodical one in the group, the man with a plan who proceeded slowly, with careful forethought. Dani had always thought he'd missed his calling, telling him he was born to be a scientist.

Sometimes that drove her nuts when they were working on a new song or planning their performance schedule because it meant everything took twice as long as details were examined and double-checked. That same annoyance did not carry over into the bedroom.

Aiden was the most attentive lover she'd ever had. He listened to her moans and groans and had her number in less than five minutes. Dani felt the first twinges of her orgasm way too early in the dance. She'd never come so quickly and never without helping the climax along herself. Aiden seemed to know her body better than she did.

When he found a magic little spot inside her that she didn't know existed, she gasped and gripped his upper arms, her body tingling.

He leaned closer and whispered in her ear. "Got you," he teased seductively.

Hook, line and sinker.

He stroked the spot again and Dani shuddered. "Ohmigod."

She had no idea where Aiden was in the process, but she feared there was no way she'd be able to wait for him. He tackled the spot again. Then again. And once more. It was the end of her. She cried out as her orgasm exploded.

Dani was surprised when Aiden stiffened above her, his face twisted, revealing his pleasure.

"So damn good. God, Dani." Their hot breaths mingled, driving the temperature in the overwarm room even higher. The humidity in New Orleans didn't hold a candle to the heat they were producing in this air-conditioned bedroom.

After a few moments, Aiden pushed himself to the side, though leaving her seemed to take some effort. She understood the feeling. She felt empty without him.

Bryson stroked her hair away from her face. "Okay?"

She nodded. He held her gaze, clearly torn. Did he really think she'd let things end here? Lifting her arms, she wrapped them around his neck and tugged him close.

Bryson followed her lead, kissing her. His lips were harder, hungrier than Aiden's had been, but she'd expected that. She'd become accustomed to her polar opposite best friends. Aiden's quiet, thoughtful nature was a direct contrast to Bryson's charge-in-with-guns-blazing-ask-questions-later attitude. She had always thought that was what made them such an amazing team. Aiden was yin to Bryson's yang.

It worked onstage.

And it sure as hell worked in the bedroom.

Bryson slowly rolled to his back, dragging her with him. She straddled his hips as they continued to kiss. His cock brushed against her stomach, clueing her in to two truths. One, he was already sheathed, and two, he was freaking huge.

She pushed herself up, her curiosity getting the best of her as she glanced down.

"Shit," she whispered.

Bryson chuckled. "Thanks for the compliment."

"That was totally not where I was going with that."

Aiden was lying on his stomach, watching them, looking tired but pleased. "Ever heard that expression *hung like a moose?*"

"Haven't you ever heard the guys in the band call me moose?"

Dani had, but she'd had no idea what it was in reference too. "You aren't helping."

Bryson urged her to rise as he gripped his cock, pressing the head to the opening of her body. "Take as much as you can. As much as you want."

She bit her lip, but neither hell nor high water was going to stop her now. She'd already had two mind-blowing orgasms and she was feeling greedy. She'd passed the point of no return, her body demanding more.

Resting her hands on his chest, she slowly slid down on his thick erection. Bryson's hands remained on her hips, but he didn't seek to drive her movement. True to his word, he let her choose the pace.

Both men watched her. Rather than feeling self-conscious about her nudity, she felt beautiful, sexy.

"Halfway there," Bryson murmured.

She giggled, her concentration wavering. She was full, but damn if it didn't feel good. So good, in fact, she got brave and pressed down fast, taking in the rest of him with one swift thrust. She gasped as Bryson moaned.

The sound triggered something primal inside her. She wasted no time moving on to the good stuff. She lifted her hips until just the head of his cock remained, then she pushed down again. Harder this time.

There was the slightest pinch as he filled her, but it only made her want more. She'd never been much for pain—she cried over paper cuts—but there was something about this burn that felt good.

As she set a steady rhythm, bouncing up and down, Bryson's fingers tightened on her hips, giving her subtle signals when she did something he particularly liked. She began to pay attention, wanting him to love this as much as she did.

She glanced to the side when she felt Aiden sit up and shift closer. She stilled when he came behind her, his legs straddling Bryson's, his bare chest rubbing against her back.

Bryson's eyes narrowed, not with wariness as much as curiosity. They'd already confessed this was a new experience for them as well. And while she was feeling overwhelmed and amazed and happier than she'd even been in her life, she didn't have a single clue how they were feeling.

Apart from the obvious, of course.

Which was horny.

Dani started when Aiden's arms came around her, his hands finding her breasts. He cupped them, slowly tightening his grip. Dani struggled to resume her pace, the new stimulation distracting in a wonderful way.

"Pinch her nipples," Bryson said, his eyes locked on the show Aiden was providing.

For the first time since they'd started, Bryson began to direct her motions, his hands lifting her, and then drawing her back down. His hips tilted at the moment of impact, adding a dimension that had her vision going black with pleasure.

"God. I can't..." Speech deserted her. There were simply too many sensations clamoring for dominance, demanding to be felt, experienced, enjoyed. Her mind told her she couldn't take any more. That it was too much, even if it was fan-fucking-tastic. Her body had shut that complaint down quickly.

Aiden began to use his grip on her breasts to move her up and down on Bryson's cock. The men were taking over, using their strength to control her. She loved it.

When Bryson's fingers moved to her pussy, burrowing to find her clit, she gave up trying to hold back her orgasm.

He pressed on the tight nub firmly, stroking it in time with the motion of his cock inside her.

Game over.

She screamed, her body racked as lightning flashed, electricity sparked and stars exploded. She was consumed in a giant mass of white-hot flames.

Her next cognizant thought was that she could hear Bryson's heart beating. She opened her eyes, somewhat surprised to find herself resting on top of him, her head pillowed by his chest, his strong arms embracing her.

Aiden was lying next to them, his head propped up by his

hand. He smiled when her gaze landed on his face. "Welcome back."

"Did I go somewhere?" How long was she lying there?

Bryson's chest shook with silent laughter. "I think you might have passed out."

She lifted her head, frowning. "No way. I've never fainted in my life."

His face was entirely too smug. "What can I say? Aiden and I are good."

If she'd been in her right frame of mind, she would have issued a putdown, simply because it was her job to keep her guys grounded, their feet firmly on the ground. She'd seen too many performers whose fame had gone straight to their head, which made them intolerable, selfish, conceited.

However, in this case, she was letting Bryson's arrogance slide. It was well deserved.

"Wait." She pushed up to her elbows. "You didn't come."

She was lethargic, so bonelessly sated, it hadn't occurred to her until that moment that Bryson was still buried deep, still hard.

"Did you think we were finished?"

She shuddered at the deep timber of his question. His voice was rough and sexy as fuck. Just like that, she was ready for round two. Or three? Or was it four?

Dani tried to push herself upright, but her arms felt like jelly.

Bryson took over. He gently pushed her off, both of them groaning as his hard cock slid out, stroking overly sensitized tissue.

"God," she gasped. Her pussy clenched, greedily attempting to hold him in.

"You're killing me, Dani. It's so goddamn good."

There was no denying this was above and beyond,

universes away from every other sexual encounter she'd ever had. There was no way in hell she'd ever top tonight.

Unless she could convince the guys to sign on for another night or twenty.

She dismissed that thought instantly. This had to be a one-night gig. An encore would be deadly to her heart, her sanity.

Before she could consider if she'd already let things go too far, Bryson had her on her hands and knees in the center of the bed. He knelt behind her, slowly pressing inside once more.

"Breathe, Dani." Aiden lay on his back, watching her face. He cupped her cheek as he issued the reminder.

She released a long, hard breath as Bryson sank the rest of the way in. He was deeper this way. It was bliss.

Bryson's hands gripped her hips as he set a new pace for them and Dani's eyes closed. She gave up trying to think. If she'd learned anything in the past hour, it was pointless to strive for reason. This was beyond the cerebral. Here, together, in this bed it was as if they existed on an entirely different plane. It was physical, animalistic, spiritual. It was a song that didn't need words.

Unlike her more timid rocking, Bryson knew what he wanted. His fingers tightened as he tugged her toward him, her ass slapping out a beat as it struck him.

Deeper, harder.

Where Aiden had offered expertise, Bryson gave her unbridled passion.

Aiden's hand had dropped away from her face, but his attention was still there, still riveted on her expressions. She had no idea what he saw, but it seemed to please him.

"You like it hard," Aiden whispered. "Like your pleasure tinged with pain."

His discovery stirred Bryson on, gave him the permission to take off the kid gloves. Bryson's hand tangled in her hair.

"Pull it," she begged, loving the way his fingertips stroked her scalp, the way his tight grip had her pussy clenching around his huge cock.

Bryson pulled roughly, using his grasp to tug her up. Her back arched as he continued to thrust, her shoulders brushing against his chest. He didn't release his hold on her hair and it added to the sensation of being possessed. Taken.

Her climax struck hard and fast, but this time she didn't go down alone.

Bryson groaned. "So. Fucking. Tight." He punctuated each word with a rough, hard thrust that sent a powerful current thrumming along her slick skin.

"Holy shit," she whispered as she tumbled forward onto the mattress.

Bryson fell too and for several minutes the three of them simply lay there, lifeless, victims of their own avarice.

When Dani finally found enough air to speak, she struggled to find the words. "That was...was..."

Bryson chuckled. "Fucking awesome."

"Yeah. Something like that." And even though she genuinely agreed, now that she had landed, doubt was starting to creep in. "I'm not sure—"

Aiden reached out and clasped her hand in his. "Not tonight, Dani. Let's just savor it for a little while."

She nodded. "Okay. You're right. It was awesome, just like Bryson said. I'm just not sure we should do it again." Even as she spoke the words, she felt the sharp sting of regret. How the hell was she supposed to spend the next several *years* with these men and not want a repeat of that every single damn night of her life?

"Tomorrow," Aiden whispered. "We'll worry about it then."

Though there was no answer in his response, for some

reason, it comforted her. He was right. They had plenty of time to sort through what had happened. For tonight, she was too tired and too damn happy to let anxiety and fear in.

"Tomorrow," she repeated, pleased that Aiden hadn't let go of her hand and even more delighted when Bryson rolled to his side to face her, his hand resting on her stomach.

Her last cognizant thought before sleep came to claim her was, *I could get used to this.*

CHAPTER FOUR

Aiden stumbled to the main room after carefully untangling himself from Dani's sweet embrace. He wasn't sure he'd ever woken up happier to find a naked woman wrapped around him. Typically, his morning-afters consisted of awkward conversations and rapid goodbyes. It had taken more strength than he thought he possessed to leave Dani and that warm bed.

He was drawn out by the realization that Bryson was no longer in the bed with them. That...and the smell of coffee.

Bryson turned as Aiden leaned against the counter that separated the kitchenette from the spacious sitting room. He lifted the pot, a silent question that Aiden answered with a nod.

"Yeah. Thanks."

Bryson poured both of them a cup, handed one to Aiden, then took a quick sip. He pointed to a menu on the counter near Aiden. "Thought we could order some room service for breakfast. I'm starving."

Aiden felt the same hunger. They'd obviously worked up quite an appetite. "Sounds good."

Despite his desire for food, he didn't give the menu a second glance. He knew Bryson too well. Knew it was up to him to start the conversation or it would never be had.

"Are we going to talk about last night?"

Bryson shook his head. "Not interested in doing a bunch of analysis, Aiden. Running through the song, line by line, until you're satisfied we've got every damn word just right."

Aiden rolled his eyes. Bryson would exist in permanent jam-session mode if left to his own devices. "We can't ignore what happened. Can't pretend we both didn't just fuck our best friend last night." Aiden ran his hand through his hair as he spoke the truth aloud. "Jesus."

"It's fine, Aiden. It was good. Shit, it was better than good. But you heard Dani. It was a one-time thing. She's not looking to expand on it."

Aiden frowned. "That's not what she said."

Bryson set his cup down. "Yes, it is. She said we couldn't do it again."

Leave it to Bryson to hear what he was expecting to hear rather than the more subtle truth. "No. What she said was we *shouldn't*. That's different."

Bryson snorted. "Only to you, Mr. Semantics."

Aiden refused to be deterred. "Regardless of what Dani said, what did *you* think about it?"

Bryson looked down at his coffee cup, toying with the rim. Aiden had known this would be a difficult conversation for his friend. Bryson was the visceral one in their trio.

While Dani and Aiden wrote the love songs and broken-heart ballads filled with introspection and self-awareness, Bryson's music and lyrics were simpler, running along the lines of "Friends in Low Places" and "Red Solo Cup". His songs were destined to be feel-good, do-whatever-the-fuck-you-want, barroom staples, while Dani and Aiden wrote music that lent itself to weddings or was most likely to be accompanied by a tub of Ben & Jerry's and a crying woman.

"It was hot."

It was a simple answer. Exactly what Aiden expected for the first pass. "You didn't mind that I was there?"

Bryson let out an exasperated groan and picked up his cup, walking to the couch. "Why do you do that? Why do you always have to go there? Why can't we just say it was fun and move on?"

Aiden took a deep breath, trying to keep a cool head. He'd spent nearly a decade figuring out how to have difficult conversations with Bryson. It required a lot of patience, which Aiden usually had in abundance. This morning, however, he was on edge and struggling to figure out why. "Do you want to move on?"

Bryson narrowed his eyes. "What do you mean?"

"What if we didn't just forget it? What if we expanded on it?"

Bryson didn't reply immediately and Aiden thought he was looking at his own face reflected back at him. The desire to keep going was definitely there. Neither of them wanted last night to be a one-night stand.

"Doesn't matter what we want. Dani doesn't want that."

"And you're okay with that?"

Bryson slammed down his coffee cup, ignoring when it splashed onto the table. Aiden should have expected the response. If he was feeling like a powder keg about to explode, no doubt Bryson was reaching critical mass. "No, I'm not okay with that! But I don't remember us being given a choice. She said it couldn't happen again, so that's it."

"No. That's *not* it. There are three of us with a vested interest in how we proceed from here and we're all capable of voicing our opinions. Neither one of us spoke up last night."

Bryson raised an eyebrow in accusation. "You shut down the conversation. Pretty damn quick."

Aiden dropped down into a chair, leaning back wearily. "We weren't going to solve anything last night. We were still lust drunk."

Bryson's lips tipped up. "That would be a good title for a song. Remind me of that when I'm not still suffering from the condition. That was...just...fuck me." His words were spoken so reverently Aiden almost laughed.

"Yeah. I didn't see that coming."

Bryson tilted his head, curious. "Seriously? I mean...you've never thought about doing it with Dani?"

Aiden lifted one shoulder then confessed, "I've thought about it a lot. Too much. But you were never there with us, bro."

Bryson chuckled. "Ditto." They fell silent for several minutes, sipping their coffee. Aiden wasn't sure what was going through his friend's mind, but he was replaying the previous night. Which was a mistake, as his cock twitched, stirred.

Finally, Bryson shifted, resting his elbows on his knees as he looked at Aiden. "I didn't mind that you were there. It sort of made it better."

Aiden nodded slowly. He felt the same way.

Bryson continued, "It was like being on the same basketball team, passing the ball, the assist, the layup, the rebound. We were working together to score, to win."

"We've always made a pretty good team. Onstage and on the court for those pickup games."

"And apparently in the bedroom," Bryson added quietly.

"Yeah."

Bryson crinkled his nose. "Does this mean we're bisexual or something?"

Aiden laughed loudly. "Jesus Christ, no. Did you want me to touch you sexually?"

Bryson stood up quickly. "Fuck no. I'd have punched the shit out of you if you'd tried."

"Ditto," Aiden said.

Bryson calmed down briefly, but his concerns about his sexuality were clearly not the only thing bothering him. He started pacing across the room. "If Dani doesn't want us, there's not a whole hell of a lot we can do about that." Bryson's fists clenched. "Fuck. Listen to me. *Us*. If she doesn't want *us*! Since when is that even a thing? We don't do threesomes any more than Dani does. I've always been a one-man show when it comes to sex. And no matter how fucking awesome it was, last night was…"

"Was what?" Aiden prodded when it appeared Bryson wouldn't finish his thought.

"A fluke."

Aiden had to admit that word was better than the one he feared Bryson was going to say. He couldn't stand to hear his friend call it a mistake. Because it wasn't. Maybe Bryson and Dani were okay with trying to forget it all, but Aiden couldn't do that. Couldn't give up on the feeling that they'd be wrong to walk away from this.

"No. It wasn't."

Bryson frowned at him. "What are you saying?"

Aiden didn't reply. He wasn't sure Bryson was ready to hear what he was thinking.

"Nothing," he said, as he walked back to the kitchen counter. He picked up the menu. "Beignets and bacon?"

It took Bryson a few seconds to switch gears. For a moment, Aiden thought his friend might press him for an answer. But then, true to form, Bryson's stomach took precedence. "Yeah. Get a lot. I'm starving."

BRYSON HAD JUST TAKEN a seat at the small table set up by the window overlooking the river and loaded his plate with half a dozen slices of bacon when the bedroom door opened.

Dani took a couple steps into the room, and then stopped when she realized he and Aiden were eyeballing her like a seven-course meal. They were going to have to rein this shit in before they spooked her and ran her off for good.

Maybe that would be easier if she didn't look so adorable. Her long blonde hair was tousled, messy in a way that was too sexy for his sanity.

She'd put her t-shirt and panties back on—her standard sleeping outfit. Like her, he and Aiden had opted for the usual and were only wearing their boxers. While he'd pretended to be indifferent to her sleepwear for years, the truth was he'd lie in bed more nights than not with a half-hard cock, resisting the urge to jack-off to that image. Something he'd never been able to do because she had always been just a few feet away, curled up on a rollaway.

Last night had opened a door he wasn't sure he could close again.

Dani glanced back toward her room. "I'll grab a pair of shorts."

"Freeze," Bryson said, louder than he'd intended.

Dani jumped at the sound of his voice.

"Come get some breakfast. You look fine." There was no way in hell he was letting her cover up one more inch of her smooth, silky, lickable skin.

She hesitated until Aiden smiled and held out his hand. "Too late to play the shy card, Dani. We've bared all—all three of us. We don't need to make this awkward. Mainly because it's not."

She considered that, and then shrugged. "I guess it's not. Are those beignets?"

Bryson nodded. "These things are fucking addictive."

She laughed then fairly skipped to the table, her enthusiasm for their meal selection evident. "I swear there wasn't much I missed about New Orleans, but sometimes I wake up in the middle of the night dreaming of these things."

She took a seat, picked up the largest beignet on the plate, dragged it through the mountain of powdered sugar and took a bite.

Bryson tried to ignore the satisfied moan she made as she slowly devoured the sweet treat. Mainly because the sound was a hell of a lot like the one she made when she was coming. Aiden's hand slipped beneath the table, no doubt to adjust his boxers to hide his growing erection. Bryson recognized the action because he needed to do the same.

"What time is Sunday dinner?" Bryson asked, trying to find some topic of conversation that might distract him from the sprinkle of sugar that had landed on Dani's t-shirt. It was as if the powder was drawing him a map to her nipples. They were budded, tight. Which told him she wasn't wearing a bra. She was clearly feeling the lingering effects of last night too. The headlights were on high beam.

The sexual tension in the room was thick enough to cut with a knife.

Bryson forced his gaze back to her face when she replied, "Jett suggested we arrive at two. He wants to make sure everyone is there before us. He's got this grand entrance thing planned. It's sort of silly."

The grin on her face told him she didn't find it silly at all. She looked delighted, excited. Which made Bryson even more confused about her reasons for staying away for so long. Why would she have delayed a reunion she clearly wanted so badly?

She may have been young when she'd left, but there was no reason he could see for her not returning as an adult anytime in the past decade.

Aiden glanced at his cell phone. "It's a little past ten now. Did you want to do anything this morning?"

Dani flushed, her eyes fixated on her plate. Her pink cheeks told them exactly what she'd like to do, and it had nothing to do with the beignets.

Bryson considered Aiden's comment from earlier. His friend believed last night wasn't a fluke. Clearly Aiden refused to accept there wouldn't be a return engagement.

Bryson hoped he was right. Then he decided to test the theory.

Reaching for her chair, Bryson tugged on it until he'd turned it away from the table and toward him. Dani's knees were between his outstretched thighs. The quick movement caught her unaware, so she reached out to steady herself, her hands gripping his upper arms.

"What are you doing?" she asked when he lifted her t-shirt over her head.

Bryson fought to appear nonchalant, casual, as he replied, "Eating breakfast."

He picked up a beignet. However, rather than take a bite, he shook some of the powdered sugar from it, letting the white flakes rain over her breasts. Then he handed it to her. "Here, hold this."

She took the beignet he shoved into her hand. Once again, he moved quickly, not giving her time to guess his intentions or counter them.

Bryson leaned forward and ran his tongue over her breasts, the sweetness of the sugar nothing compared to the salty tang of Dani's skin. They'd worked up quite a sweat the previous night. He liked that there was still evidence, proof that he hadn't imagined it.

Once he'd cleaned off the powder, he leaned back to study her response to his touch. Her cheeks were red, her eyes heavy-lidded.

"Bryson," she whispered. If she wanted to tell him to stop, it didn't look like she could form the words.

That thought made him more determined to keep her speechless. He shifted so that his knees were inside hers, pressing her thighs open.

Aiden had been a quiet observer, but Bryson hadn't worried about his response. His friend wanted this as much as he did.

When Bryson reached for her pussy, Aiden stood, no longer content to be apart. He positioned himself behind her chair, his hands wrapping around to cup her breasts.

"I thought we weren't..." Dani's words faded when Bryson shoved her panties aside and pressed two fingers inside her pussy. Denial was pointless. She was soaking wet.

Her eyes closed as she blew out a long breath. "Ganging. Up. On me," she gasped.

Bryson chuckled. "I want to see you come again, Dani."

Her lids lifted and he gave her a look that said he wouldn't be denied.

She raised one eyebrow, her expression pure smartass. "You don't really expect me to say no to that, do you?"

Aiden laughed softly, then squeezed her breasts. Dani inhaled, her head falling back to rest against Aiden's stomach.

"Do your worst," she dared.

Bryson preferred to give her his best. Hoped that she'd want what he gave her as much as she craved those damn doughnuts. Even twelve years later.

He stroked his thumb against her clit as his fingers

continued to move inside. Aiden had released her breasts, turning his attention to just her nipples. He circled the areolas with his forefingers, and then added his thumbs, pinching the distended tips. Bryson watched as his friend slowly added pressure. They'd both seen traces of Dani's wild side last night.

She wasn't afraid of a little pain and there was definitely a healthy amount of kink behind her inexperience.

As Aiden's pinch tightened, Dani's breathing sped. Bryson sucked in the sweet scent of her breath, however, he resisted leaning in for a taste.

His preference this morning was for something a little stronger, coffee over doughnuts. Sliding off his chair, he dropped to his knees between her legs. Dani's hands flew to his head when he tugged her panties to her ankles, placed his lips around her clit and sucked.

"Holy mother." Dani's fingers tugged at his hair. Not to dislodge him, but to urge him on. He didn't need the provocation. Nothing short of her climax on his tongue would compel him to stop now.

With his head between her legs, he lost sight of what Aiden was doing to her tits, but he could tell from her soft moans, she liked it. A lot.

Adding his own fuel to the fire, Bryson nipped her clit with his teeth, testing some limits of his own.

Dani's grip in his hair became almost painful, but Bryson didn't bother to tug her hands away. She wasn't fighting, wasn't resisting this. That was a pretty heady realization.

Aiden had been right. It wasn't a fluke. And Bryson didn't want this to be all that they got. Somehow, they'd sort this out, find a way to make it work because he wasn't about to give up the heaven to be found in Dani's arms.

For the first time in his life, he felt like writing a damn love song. Even caught the inkling of a tune in his head.

He pulled his fingers from her, enjoying her soft cry of regret and the way her muscles clenched in an attempt to hold him in. She wanted this. *Him.*

Bryson ran his tongue along her drenched flesh from clit to pussy, then pushed it in for a taste. Dani jerked slightly, but clearly Aiden had anticipated her response and held her steady.

Bryson found a rhythm with his tongue, as his thumb played with her clit. He wasn't sure what Aiden was doing above his head, but their combined ministrations had Dani gyrating on the chair, a long string of sighs, moans, and reverent curses flowing from her lips.

Bryson tugged her closer to the edge of the chair so he could thrust his tongue deeper. Then he gathered her juices with his free hand and used that moisture to press one finger into her ass.

Dani jolted as if struck by lightning and came—hard and loud.

Bryson continued to stroke her with his finger and tongue until her aftershocks melted away. Then he lifted his head.

Dani's head was thrown back, resting on Aiden's stomach, her eyes closed. Her chest rose and fell rapidly.

Bryson caught Aiden's gaze. While their lovely songbird was sated, they were both sporting raging hard-ons.

"Shower." Aiden lifted Dani's limp form from the chair. She offered no resistance as she wrapped her hands around his neck.

Bryson rose and followed. Once they entered the master bathroom, Bryson turned on the water. The shower was large, with dual heads on opposite ends. Steam filled the room as Aiden set Dani down and they stripped off what little clothing they wore. Bryson stepped in first and turned to reach for Dani, who accepted his embrace instantly. Aiden was the last to join them.

Bryson gently pushed Dani under the showerhead, running his hands over her slick skin. Then he picked up the soap and made a thick lather on his hands. Aiden reached around, dragging Dani back to the middle. As Bryson washed her body, paying special attention to the fun parts, Aiden shampooed her hair.

Dani giggled.

"What's so funny?" Aiden asked.

"I'm not used to all this pampering. You might want to ease up or I'll get spoiled. Start expecting you guys to carry my luggage and such."

Bryson narrowed his eyes. "I always offer to carry your suitcase and your guitar. You won't let me."

She moved back into the jets and rinsed the suds from her hair and body. "That's because I'm perfectly capable of doing so on my own. Besides," she slipped back to the center once she'd sluiced all the soap away, "sometimes it's nice to be the one doing the spoiling."

She wrapped her hands around both of their erections. He and Aiden gasped in perfect harmony at her unexpected touch. She ran her hands along their flesh as the hot water eased her path.

Then, she went down to her knees. With gentle tugs on their cocks, she pulled them closer, until the heads of their dicks were just an inch or so from her pretty mouth.

He and Aiden were in very close, very naked proximity, standing face-to-face, but Bryson felt no desire to increase the distance. He was briefly surprised by his ease with this. He never would have allowed another man in the bedroom with him and a woman, but now...he wanted Aiden there. Part of him felt like none of this would work without his friend.

Any other thoughts he might have had on that subject vanished the moment Dani opened her mouth and sucked him in.

"Fuck, baby," Bryson said, reaching to touch her wet hair.

Dani took him inside, going deeper with each pass for a minute or two. As she sucked on him, she ran her hand along Aiden's cock. Then she switched, stroking Bryson as she drew Aiden into her mouth.

Back and forth, she moved from one cock to the other. Bryson had one hand on the shower door and one in her hair. When her mouth turned once more to him, he felt his control slip. He thrust his hips toward her, pushing his cock deeper.

"Swallow it, bird. Take it as deep as you can." Bryson used his hand to hold her steady.

She glanced up, her brows creased.

She was inexperienced. He hadn't been around for the first so-called boyfriend, but he'd met the last two. One had been there and gone so quickly he couldn't even remember the man's name or what he'd looked like.

And the last guy was a certified tool, a record executive more interested in landing big names than having sex with Dani. Worst part was the guy wouldn't know true talent if it bit him on the ass...or slept in his bed, which Dani had. For nearly six months. Then he and Aiden convinced her she could do much better.

Though Bryson had to admit this wasn't exactly what he'd been thinking by better.

Dani continued to move, sucking him in. Spots clouded his vision when she did indeed swallow the head.

"Jesus," he whispered.

"Let's up the ante," Aiden said, reaching down to grasp her hips. "Keep Bryson in your mouth."

He shifted back a couple of steps as Dani straightened her

legs and stood, her head still low, Bryson's cock buried between her lips.

Aiden situated himself behind her, Dani's ass perfectly in position to be fucked.

Last night, they'd taken turns, though both had definitely contributed to her orgasms.

Taking her together...

Bryson's cock thickened at the thought. Dani must have noticed, because she moaned around his flesh.

Aiden rubbed his dick along her slit several times before pausing. "Shit. Give me a minute. Condoms are in the bedroom."

He started to slip out of the shower, but Dani shook her head then released Bryson with a pop.

"I'm on birth control. Don't leave."

Aiden hesitated and Bryson could read the indecision on his friend's face. "Are you sure?"

"I know everything about you guys, remember? I spent the better part of an hour during that last road trip to Memphis listening to you two talk about how you'd love to go bareback one day."

Bryson chuckled as she quoted him almost exactly. She had been shocked at the time to learn neither of them had ever had sex without a condom. Then she had confessed she'd never had a man come inside her. Not her mouth or pussy, though Dani hadn't used the word pussy. It had been up to Bryson to fill in that blank as she blushed furiously in the backseat.

"Dani," Aiden said quietly. His tone said it all. She was a dream, a gift, a fantasy come true, all rolled into one.

She wiggled her ass playfully. "Hurry up."

Aiden resumed his spot behind her as Dani wrapped her lips around Bryson's cock. He groaned. "Fuck. I'm not going to last much longer."

Aiden slowly slid into Dani's pussy, his eyes closing in bliss. "I don't think you have to worry about competing with me. Holy shit, this feels good."

Bryson cupped Dani's cheeks and together, he and Aiden found a pace that was so perfect, it was their demise.

Bryson hadn't exaggerated about being close. After only a few minutes, he felt his balls tighten. "Can't stop, Dani." He started to pull free, intent of finishing with his hand.

Dani reached around him, her fingers digging into his ass cheeks to hold him in place. Within a dozen short strokes, he was lost, jet after jet of come exploding into Dani's hot mouth. She swallowed it all, then suckled his softening cock as Aiden continued to pump into her pussy.

Bryson slowly tugged free when he felt her body stiffen, dropping to his knees in front of her. He kissed her, then pulled away to watch her beautiful face as she came. Aiden was right there with her, jerking roughly as he spilled inside.

Bryson had a perfect view of both their faces—and he realized he loved them. Aiden was his best friend and brother. And Dani owned his heart.

He'd tried to convince himself last night had been a fluke because it was too hard to consider he might never have his heart's desire.

Now he understood what Aiden had been alluding to.

This wasn't wrong.

And it wasn't over.

CHAPTER FIVE

ani stood on the porch of the only house that had ever felt like a true home and stared at the door. She could hear laughter inside—loud, boisterous. It had always been that way with the Lewis clan. It had taken her years after leaving here to remember how to have fun.

After she'd run away, her heart had been too heavy, too terrified to summon that emotion. In fact, when she looked back on her life, there had only been two periods where she'd felt secure enough to act like her true self—to be silly and to have fun. With the Lewises. And with Bryson and Aiden.

Following their brief interlude in the shower, Bryson and Aiden had taken catnaps. Dani had intended to do the same until her cell beeped. There was a text from her dad. He definitely had her number, though she couldn't figure out how he'd gotten it. The message, like the ones that had come before, freaked her out enough to have her trembling for several minutes after reading it.

It had said, "Day of reckoning almost here. Ready for it?"

She'd turned off her phone and lain on the couch like a

zombie until Bryson and Aiden had woken up and the three of them had gotten ready to come here.

As she stood on the porch, the hair on the back of her neck stood up as she felt eyes on her. She'd had the same sensation of being watched when she'd met Jett and Carissa for breakfast yesterday, and then again last night in the restaurant.

Dani tried to convince herself it was just her imagination, but she had too strong a sense of self-preservation to discount the feeling completely. She glanced over her shoulder to study the neighborhood behind her. The street was quiet and appeared deserted, but Dani couldn't shake the idea that her dad was there, watching her.

If he was, she'd fucked up royally, as she'd led him to the Lewis home and put Aiden and Bryson on his radar.

"Soooo," Bryson drawled, pulling her from her terrifying thoughts. "Are we knocking anytime this century?"

She grinned at his attempt to ease her nervousness, though she suspected it was a wobbly effort. She was slowly starting to freak out despite the fact Bryson was usually a natural when it came to helping her laugh her cares away.

"We can leave right now, Dani, if you don't want to do this." And in true fashion, Aiden was there to offer her comfort and an escape route if the humor failed.

"I want to see them. It's just...I didn't leave on the best of terms."

"You think they'll be angry?"

Dani shook her head, but even as she did so, she wasn't sure. While Jett had assured her everyone was dying to see her, she felt as though she'd let Mama Lewis down, hurt her by running away.

She'd carried that guilt around for a damn long time.

"Dani?" Aiden stepped closer.

She swallowed her fear and knocked on the door. If she

couldn't handle a reunion as simple as this, there was no way in hell she'd manage to face her asshole of a father.

Jett opened the door, grinning widely. "Everybody is in the dining room. They're going to flip out."

Her beloved foster brother grabbed her hand and tugged her inside as if sensing her desire to bolt. His grip told her she wasn't going anywhere.

Aiden and Bryson followed in their wake as Jett led them to the dining room. They gave her some space, but remained close enough to let her know they were there if she needed them.

The room was much more crowded than it had been in the days when Dani had lived there. Jett had warned her that the family had doubled, as the majority of her foster siblings had found their soul mates.

"Look what I found."

The room erupted.

Chairs scraped along the hardwood floor as everyone began jumping from their seats.

According to Jett, he'd only told his family that he'd found her and he was planning to contact her soon. None of them knew they'd been chatting for two months. Or that she was coming to visit. The shit-eating grin on his face told Dani he was thrilled by the results of his big surprise.

Her foster sister, Chloe, was the first to reach her. For such a tiny woman, she knew how to give one hell of a hug. The two of them laughed when Chloe released her, then slugged Jett in the arm. "I can't believe you didn't tell us she was coming! I would have bought a damn present."

Dani shook her head. "Today is my present. I'm so glad to see you again, Chloe."

Chloe didn't have a chance to respond as Justin grabbed Dani, and then Caleb took his turn. Both men gave her gigantic bear hugs. They'd been older when Dani came to live with the

Lewis family, Justin in his early twenties, and Caleb a big, bad senior in high school. They'd both instantly assumed the role of overprotective brothers, making Dani feel safe and cared for.

"I think you guys got bigger," she said, attempting to catch her breath. "I didn't think that was possible."

"We missed you, Dani," Justin said.

Caleb crossed his tattooed arms, drawing her attention to his muscular chest. Most people would probably take one look at Caleb and head in the opposite direction, but Dani knew he was a giant teddy bear under the fearsome exterior. "Never again, Dani. Don't you dare disappear on us again."

She'd run because she'd been afraid, felt helpless. She had been too scared to consider what her actions had done to the family she'd left behind and the pain she'd cause them.

"I promise. No more running away." She'd never meant anything more. Despite the threat of her father looming over her head, she refused to hide from the people she loved ever again.

"Remember us?"

Dani looked over, her eyes widening. "Zac? Noah? Oh my God. You were just annoying little kids the last time I saw you! You guys grew up. And got hot."

They all laughed as the two boys stepped closer to add their hugs to the pile. They'd only been with Mama Lewis a few months before Dani ran. Their mother, a drug-addict, had come to the realization she couldn't raise the boys. As such, she'd placed her two young sons in the Lewis house to give them a shot at a good life.

During all the welcomes, Dani had been very aware of the woman standing at the end of the table, patiently waiting her turn. Once the crowd around Dani cleared, she stood, feeling somewhat nervous, as she faced Mama Lewis.

Then Mama Lewis lifted her arms and Dani ran into them,

feeling for the first time since she'd stepped foot in Louisiana that she had indeed come home.

Dani clung to the dear woman and was thrilled that Mama Lewis clung back. Dani was crying and she couldn't stop.

Mama Lewis rocked her gently. "It's okay, baby girl. You're home. I've got you."

When Dani finally composed herself enough to speak, she pulled away to look at Mama Lewis. "I missed you."

Mama Lewis had tears in her eyes as well. "Oh, Dani. I prayed every single night that you were safe and that you'd find your way back to us." Mama Lewis cupped her cheeks, wiping away the tears on Dani's face. "You're a sight for sore eyes."

Dani laughed and sniffled. Then she remembered Aiden and Bryson. She turned around and found them both hovering just inside the doorway of the dining room, taking it all in. They'd given her the time she needed to reunite with her family. She smiled when she saw Aiden's happy, crooked grin and laughed when Bryson winked at her.

"So," Bryson said, "I assume this is the Lewis family, or are we in the wrong house?"

Dani rolled her eyes and giggled. "Mama, I'd like to introduce you to Aiden and Bryson. They're my b—" Dani stumbled for a split second then recovered. "Bandmates." She'd been perilously close to saying boyfriends.

Mama Lewis walked over and gave them both hugs. "I'm so glad to meet you. You boys keeping an eye on our girl? Keeping her out of trouble?"

Aiden graced Mama Lewis with a charming grin. "We do the best we can, but she's a wild one."

Mama Lewis laughed. "That she is. Come in here and meet the rest of the family."

Dani stood next to Aiden and Bryson as Mama Lewis introduced them to the significant others who had joined the family over the past few years.

Caleb had married a very nice woman named Jennifer. Apparently, they'd met at his tattoo parlor, Midnight Ink, when she went in for a tattoo. Dani marveled at her tattoo, and the several new ones Caleb was sporting. He'd always been an amazing artist and it looked like he'd found the perfect medium for his talent. Bryson started asking him a lot of questions, describing a design he'd always wanted inked on his shoulder. Dani glanced at Aiden, who gave her an exasperated eye-roll. It looked like there was going to be a tattoo in Bryson's near future.

Chloe interrupted the discussion when she pointed to the handsome man next to her. "This is my fiancé, Blake."

Dani recognized the name immediately. Jett intended for the two of them to pull Blake aside at some point today to talk to him about her issues with her father.

"Nice to meet you," Dani said, shaking Blake's hand. She could see why Chloe had fallen for the guy. He had "sexy bad boy" written all over him.

Carissa, Jett's girlfriend, stepped forward, her arm wrapped around Jett's waist. "It's good to see you again, Dani. I've heard a lot about you guys," Carissa said to Aiden and Bryson. "Dani told me about your record deal yesterday at breakfast. Congratulations."

"Thanks," Aiden said.

"And last but not least," Justin said, "these are my partners, Ned and Bella."

Dani struggled for a moment to understand the meaning of "partners". The issue was cleared up when Ned and Justin each took one of Bella's hands, lifting them for a kiss.

Through her peripheral vision, she saw Aiden's eyes widen and his grin grow.

Great. She'd spent the better part of the morning trying to convince herself that a ménage a trois was fantasy fodder, not real life.

Now she was face-to-face with a real-life threesome.

"How long have you been together?" Bryson asked.

Aaaand now Bryson was gathering ammunition. She'd gotten a sense that neither man was interested in halting what they'd begun the night before. Dani was going to have to be the voice of reason. But that was going to be hard to do. Mainly because she wanted very badly to throw caution to the wind.

"A couple of years," Ned answered. "Gets better every day. We work together at Lewis and Kinnaman, the marketing firm Justin and I started. Bella is our graphic artist. She can't stand to spend one minute away from us because we're so damn irresistible."

Bella grinned at his joke. "I work for you because of the awesome health insurance."

They all laughed, then Mama Lewis asked Zac and Noah to grab some more chairs. After a bit of plate shifting, they were all squeezed around the huge dining room table, multiple conversations going at once. It was as loud as a rock concert and every bit as much fun.

Dani soaked it all in as she took another bite of Mama Lewis' homemade scalloped potatoes. Sunday dinners had been her favorite part about living here. With so many kids, most of them teenagers who were constantly in and out, Mama Lewis made only one demand of them. On Sunday afternoon, come hell or high water, they would all have their butts in a chair at the table to come together for a meal. It was the only day of the week where they were all home at the same time to talk, catch up, settle arguments and discuss the chore schedule.

Though she'd been away a long time, sitting there at that table, Dani felt as though she'd never left.

Once they'd put a fairly substantial dent in the mountain of food, they slowly started rising, most of the guys heading for the living room to watch baseball, while the women cleared the table.

Dani had begun to help, but was interrupted when Jett came into the dining room and gave her a quick head jerk toward the front door. She followed him out onto the porch, where Blake was sitting on an old wicker rocking chair. Jett and Dani claimed the porch swing as Dani glanced toward the house.

"Aiden and Bryson are watching the game with the others," Jett said, clearly aware of her concern.

Blake leaned forward. "What's going on, Dani? Jett said you were having some trouble with your dad."

Quickly and quietly, Dani filled Blake in on the letters, text message and phone call from her father.

Blake listened intently until she'd finished. "So you haven't seen him at all?"

Dani shook her head. "No, but I've sort of felt like someone's been watching me since I've gotten back in town."

"What?" Jett asked, obviously upset to just be learning that tidbit.

"It's probably paranoia. Right, Blake?" Dani hoped the police officer would set her mind at ease about it.

Blake tilted his head. "Maybe, but I think you'd be smart to listen to that voice and make sure you're never alone in public. At least until you see what your father wants with you."

"What he wants?" Jett asked hotly. "The guy is threatening her."

Blake shrugged. "We don't know that, Jett. I'm not sure the law would recognize his contact as such. The only thing he's said is he wants to see you again. Finish things right. And while that day of reckoning comment is definitely ominous when you consider the past, there are some who might read it as your dad wanting to make amends, to set things right."

Dani shook her head. "No. That's not what he wants."

Blake raised his hand quickly. "I agree with you. But I'm playing devil's advocate. I'm not sure you have enough to request a restraining order. In fact, there's not enough here for you to take any sort of legal action right now."

It wasn't the news Dani wanted to hear, even though it was exactly what she'd expected. She'd learned at fifteen, she was on her own when it came to issues with her dad. "So the plan remains the same. I contact him, set up a meeting in public and find out what the bastard wants."

She didn't want to return to Nashville with the shadow of her dad still looming over her. She wanted the terrifying calls and the messages to stop.

Blake rocked slowly in the chair. "Before you proceed with that, let me do some background checks on your dad. See if I can find a current address, place of employment, previous records, stuff like that. We need to know exactly what we're up against before we seek the man out."

"We?" she asked.

Blake grinned. "There's not a snowball's chance in hell you're meeting that guy without reinforcements. Jett and me. Wouldn't hurt to have those two giant bandmates of yours along as well. Intimidation might be enough to scare the guy off. Especially when he sees how many bad-ass protectors have your back."

Dani laughed, looking down in an attempt to hide the tears that filled her eyes. She was touched by Blake's kindness.

Blake rubbed his chin. "You said he's been in jail again since you left?"

Dani nodded. "I found something on the Internet when I

Googled his name. An article about his arrest for assault and battery."

Blake ran a hand through his short, dark hair. "Well, if he's been in prison twice for felonies, he's facing the *three strikes, you're out* law."

"What's that mean?" Dani asked.

"It means if he steps over the line again and commits a serious crime, he's facing life in prison. It'll be game over."

Dani got the feeling Blake meant that information to be comforting. Like all she had to do was wish for dear old Dad to fuck up again. Unfortunately, that idea wasn't reassuring. She didn't think her dad gave a shit about the possibility of spending the rest of his life in jail. Right now, he seemed wholly focused on her. And until it all played out, Dani wasn't safe.

Their conversation was interrupted when Chloe stepped out on the porch. "There you guys are. What's up?"

Blake smiled as he stood and joined his fiancée. "Getting some fresh air. We didn't miss dessert, did we?"

Dani was grateful to Blake for dodging the question, protecting her secret. So far no one had mentioned her father. Probably because they knew it was such a painful subject for her. Bryson and Aiden had return flights back to Nashville tomorrow. She'd simply say she wanted to spend more time with Mama Lewis, bid them farewell at the airport and make plans to see them at home again next weekend.

Hopefully by then, she would have gotten Russell off her back and out of her life.

Chloe started back into the house with Blake, then glanced over her shoulder. "Mama's looking for you, Dani. She's in the kitchen."

Dani rose from the porch swing. "I'll go see what she needs. It was nice talking to you, Blake."

He nodded once. With any luck, he'd discover something about her dad that she could use.

As Dani passed by the living room, she peeked in. Aiden and Bryson were kicked back on the large sectional with Caleb and Justin, beers in hand, bitching about some call the umpire had made. They were settled in for the duration of the game.

Dani continued to the kitchen, surprised to find Mama Lewis alone, sitting at the kitchen table with a cup of coffee.

"Where did everyone else go?" Dani asked.

"The girls are out back, soaking up the sunshine and a bottle of wine while looking at bride magazines. Chloe is planning an October wedding."

"That's a nice time for a wedding."

Mama Lewis nodded, then gestured to an empty chair at the table. "Care to join me?"

Dani grabbed her own cup of coffee, and then took the seat as she glanced around the room. "You got new cabinets."

Mama Lewis smiled. "Yeah. The boys put them in for me a couple of years ago. I like the white. They brighten the room."

She agreed.

"How are you, Dani? Are you happy?"

Dani smiled. "I am. Very much so." For nearly a half an hour, she filled Mama Lewis in on everything she'd done since leaving New Orleans, telling her about the people she'd met who had helped her along the way.

"I'm so sorry I never got the chance to meet Stella. Sounds like she was a wonderful person."

Dani dashed away a tear. "She was. In a lot of ways she reminded me of you. I think the two of you would have loved each other."

"I love her for finding you and keeping you safe. Benji too, though I'll admit he sounds like a character."

Dani laughed. "Oh my God. You have no idea. You'll have

to come visit me in Nashville sometime and I'll take you to the club."

Mama Lewis reached over to take her hand. "I'd like that very much."

"So would I." Suddenly Dani regretted letting her fear keep her away for so long. So many wasted years.

"Aiden and Bryson are very nice. Have the three of you been performing together for long?"

"Three years," Dani replied. "But we've been writing music together for six."

"How long have you been in love with them?"

Dani blushed. "That obvious?"

Mama Lewis squeezed her hand gently. "I've had a bit of practice reading the signs lately. You noticed the family has grown quite a bit in your absence."

"Justin's relationship is—" Dani started before stopping suddenly. What the hell was it? Besides extremely unusual and infinitely fascinating.

"Is what?" Mama Lewis prodded.

"Different."

"That it is. But it works. Ned and Bella were made for my Justin. But it's not *his* relationship you're worried about, is it?"

Dani shook her head. "Aiden, Bryson and I are sort of new to this. So new, in fact, I'm not sure it's even a thing."

Mama Lewis released her hand and picked up her cup of coffee, taking a tiny sip before saying, "Oh, that's wonderful. There's nothing more exciting than the beginning of a new love affair."

Dani agreed it was exhilarating. And terrifying. "You don't think it's strange? I mean, despite Justin's relationship, three people together isn't exactly a normal thing."

"If it feels right to you doesn't that make it normal?"

Before she realized it, every fear Dani had experienced

since she'd woken up this morning came pouring out. "The thing is, I'm not sure it's smart to start something like this. We just signed a contract that is going to tie the three of us together for the next several years. What if it doesn't work out? What if it goes bad? We'd be stuck, forced to work in very close proximity, living together on a tour bus."

"That's definitely something worth thinking about. But every relationship in the world comes with risks. Have you talked to Bryson and Aiden about it?"

"No. We haven't talked about anything. It just happened. Last night."

Mama Lewis smiled. "Wow. That *is* new. I assume by *it*, you mean sex?"

Dani's cheeks went hot, but she nodded. "Yeah."

"But the friendship, the love, that's not new. And that's a very good foundation, Dani. Many successful couples have started with much less. Strangers meeting in a tattoo parlor. An employee going on a date with her bosses."

Dani laughed as Mama Lewis described how Caleb and Justin met their lovers.

"Or you could have faced what Chloe and Blake did. Finding each other after years apart and having to overcome the betrayal and broken hearts that accompanied their first time around."

"What about Jett and Carissa?" Dani asked.

"You and Jett were always such kindred spirits. Like you, he fell in love with his best friend. All I'm saying, Dani, is every relationship starts out with barriers, problems that feel like good reasons to walk away. You could certainly take the easy road, play it safe and break things off. But you've never been a quitter."

Dani appreciated Mama Lewis' compliment, but at the moment, she felt very much like a coward. For so many reasons.

"I've never told them about my dad. Bryson and Aiden think my parents died when I was young."

Mama Lewis' brows creased. "Why haven't you told them?"

Dani swallowed heavily. "When I left New Orleans, I never intended to come back."

Dani caught Mama Lewis' hurt expression and she reached out to hold the woman's hand. "I wanted to see you again so badly. I love you, Mama. But when I left here, I was Dani Patton and nothing more than a helpless victim. In my head, all those things are tied to this city because he's still here. No one knows about my past. When I'm in Nashville, I'm Dani Lewis, a singer and songwriter, a strong, independent woman. I like that Aiden and Bryson see that woman instead of the weak one."

"You took our name."

Dani could see the pleasure that gave Mama Lewis. She nodded. "I loved you all so much. I hated leaving, so I decided to keep a part of you with me."

Mama Lewis smiled. Dani saw the sheen of tears in her eyes. "Thank you, darling."

Dani swallowed heavily, unable to speak for a moment.

Mama Lewis was the first to break the silence. "You realize you're not one person or the other, Dani. You can't separate who you are into two parts and call them different people. All of those traits have combined to make you the person you are. The woman Bryson and Aiden love."

"Maybe so, but I can't make any commitments right now. Not until I sort out my past." Dani bit her lower lip, and then told Mama Lewis the rest. "He's found me."

"Your father?"

Dani nodded. "He's sent me messages, called. He wants to see me."

The troubled look in Mama Lewis' eyes seemed to mirror Dani's own fears. "Are you going to?"

"Yes. Jett has suggested I invite him to meet at the Royal Lunch. Jett plans to be there and Blake will be close by as well. I don't know what he wants, but I refuse to spend the rest of my life wondering, hiding."

"You need to be careful, Dani. Are you sure you don't want Aiden and Bryson there as well? There's strength in numbers."

Dani shook her head. "No. I can handle this on my own. I'm already putting two people I care about at risk. I don't plan to add Bryson and Aiden to that list. I'll just take care of unfinished business and then...with any luck, everything else will fall into place."

"I hope it's as simple as that."

"But you don't think it will be?"

Mama Lewis gave her a sad smile. "I think old habits die hard. You're used to taking care of yourself, Dani. But you don't have to do that anymore. Things are easier with the ones you love by your side."

Dani jumped when she heard a deep voice behind her.

"Sorry," Bryson said, stepping into the kitchen. "Hope I'm not interrupting. I lost rock, paper, scissors."

Mama Lewis laughed. "So you're here to grab the next round of beers?"

Bryson nodded, but he wasn't smiling. He was looking at Dani. "Everything okay, bird?"

"Yeah," she said, striving for a breezy, lighthearted sound. She failed miserably. She got the feeling he'd overheard some of their conversation. Problem was she didn't know how much.

Bryson grabbed the beers, stopping by her chair on his way back out. "You sure?"

She nodded slowly.

He accepted her answer, returning to the living room.

Mama Lewis reached out to hold her hand. "Talk to them, Dani. Open your heart and let them in."

Bryson returned to the living room, unaware he was scowling until Aiden snickered. "Jesus, man. Never realized you were such a sore loser."

Bryson worked to lighten his expression as he handed Aiden, Caleb and Justin their beers. Ned, Zac and Noah had gone outside to shoot hoops earlier, so Bryson claimed the recliner Ned had vacated. His interest in the game had vanished as he considered what he'd just heard. Mama Lewis was accusing Dani of falling back into old habits. What had prompted that comment? Had Dani told her foster mother about them? Had she said she wanted to break things off?

Or had they been discussing something else? Perhaps Dani's real reason for returning home? After meeting the Lewises, there had to be something else, something bad to keep Dani from the family she loved so much.

Before he could ponder that idea further, Justin muted the TV when a commercial break began. "Now might be a good time for us to discuss your intentions toward our sister."

Suddenly Bryson understood why the room had cleared out. They'd been set up.

Aiden chuckled. "Seriously?"

Justin's lip tipped up in an amused grin, but Caleb's serious expression still warned them to proceed with caution.

If Aiden sensed any peril, he didn't let on. "I know you guys had Dani first, but we've been the ones looking out for her the past six years. I appreciate that you want to protect her, but believe me, she's not in danger from us."

Caleb's frown deepened. "It's not a case of who met her first. Dani was our little sister for two years. She was a lonely, terrified girl, so we made sure she felt safe, knew she was loved. As brothers," he stressed. "I'm not getting a brotherly vibe from you two."

Bryson wanted to be annoyed by the fifth degree, but part of him was glad to know Dani had these men in her life. For so long, she'd been alone. The idea that she had a family that cared for her warmed him. She deserved this. "You're right. We don't love Dani like brothers and we sure as hell don't see her as our little sister. But I'd cut out my own heart before I ever hurt her or let someone else cause her pain. I promise you that."

"I can't speak for Bryson, but I'm in love with her, and if she'll have me..." Aiden paused and looked at Bryson before correcting himself. "If she'll have us, we want to spend the rest of our lives making her happy."

It was the first time Bryson had heard his own hopes for the future spoken aloud. It was amazing to him to think that this time yesterday, they were still foolishly living in just-friends mode and thinking that was okay. That was normal.

Caleb's expression cleared and he smiled. "Yeah. That's the vibe I was getting. Glad to have it confirmed."

"It took her a long time to relax when she lived here and even then, I'm not sure she ever fully dropped her guard," Justin said. "When she was sitting with you two at the table earlier, it felt like the first time I'd ever seen her without the shields in place."

Bryson knew Justin's comments should please him, but he couldn't help but focus on the negative parts. *Lonely, terrified girl. Living her life on guard.*

What the hell had happened to bring her to the Lewis house to begin with? Bryson was tempted to ask, but he didn't want to hear Dani's story from anyone except her. It felt too much like cheating. Maybe it was a silly test and maybe he'd pay for it, but Bryson couldn't shake the feeling that the three of them couldn't have a future until Dani trusted them enough to tell them everything.

The words he'd overheard Mama Lewis say came floating back to him.

Old habits die hard.

Dani wasn't finished fighting her demons from the past.

Which left Bryson and Aiden struggling to defeat an unknown foe.

CHAPTER SIX

Bryson tapped his hand on his knee restlessly as he leaned his head back against the couch. It had been three days since their dinner with the Lewis family. Dani had tried to convince them to use their return flights to Nashville on Monday, but they'd canceled instead. Bryson had thought she'd appreciate the company on the long drive back, but she became uncharacteristically quiet—sullen—after they'd told her what they had done.

Since then, she'd been distant. He and Aiden had tried to cajole her out of her mood—offering to do some sightseeing or take her out for nice dinners. While she'd been polite, she'd refused every invitation, refusing to leave the apartment. And despite the fact she was in the same room with them, it almost felt as if she was somewhere else.

Worst of all was the sleeping situation. They'd returned to their own beds. Whatever magic had pushed them together had vanished. Aiden had tried to initiate a conversation about it several times, but Dani had brushed him off, claiming headaches or exhaustion or by simply saying it was over and they needed to move on.

It was frustrating, infuriating, maddening, but Bryson couldn't figure out how to make things better. Aiden was better at dealing with emotions and talking and shit like that.

So now it was midday on Wednesday and they were stuck in limbo. None of them had suggested leaving the room today. In fact, no one had said anything in the past hour. Aiden was sitting at the counter, poring over lyrics for a new song he was working on. Dani was in her bedroom, strumming her guitar, though he hadn't heard her sing a note. And he was sitting in the living room, brooding.

While he hadn't caught the entire conversation between Dani and Mama Lewis, Bryson was more and more convinced that Dani wasn't in New Orleans for the reason she'd given them. He was starting to suspect her annoyance with them was based on the fact they were keeping her from doing whatever it was she wanted to do. Which left Bryson with an uneasy feeling.

He glanced up when the door to Dani's room opened and she stepped out.

Aiden gave her a tentative smile. "Hey."

She pointed toward the kitchen area. "I'm just getting a bottle of water. Don't let me interrupt you."

"You're not." Aiden's voice was careful.

Bryson rolled his eyes. They were tiptoeing around her as if she were an injured dog they were trying not to spook. His patience was gone. "Why are you really in New Orleans, Dani?"

Dani's brows creased but not before Bryson caught the glimmer of fear in her eyes. "I told you."

He nodded. "Yeah, you came to reconnect with your foster

family. But the reunion already happened. So why are we still here?"

Dani's temper sparked. "I told you guys to leave on Monday. You didn't have to hang around on my account."

Bryson stood up and walked toward her. "That's not an answer."

She scowled. "It's the only one you're going to get. So why don't you just leave me alone?"

Aiden rose at the hostility in her voice. "Dani. What's going on?"

She closed her eyes. "I'm sorry. I didn't mean to snap. Being back is stirring up some things. Things I need to figure out and deal with. I can't do that with you guys here."

Bryson snorted. "And there's another non-answer."

Dani lifted her chin angrily. "Why can't you just listen to what I'm saying? I need to be alone."

Bryson stepped in front of her when she started back toward her room. He cupped her face and saw the sadness in her eyes. "That's the last thing you need, bird."

Before she could respond, he kissed her. He didn't bother to keep it gentle, to try to cajole her or ease her into this. He wanted her, and not just physically. He loved her and he knew she felt the same, but something was holding her back, keeping her from reaching out for what was right there in front of them all.

Dani pressed against his chest, but the shove was short-lived. Within seconds, her attempts at pushing him away faded, her hands rising until she wrapped them around his neck. He moved two steps forward until he had her pressed against the wall. It allowed him to lean closer. He wanted her to feel what she did to him. His cock was hard, throbbing.

He forced her lips open with his, demanding entrance. He couldn't let her pull away from him—from them—again.

"Dammit, Dani," he whispered against her cheek. "Can't you see that this is right?"

Dani's teeth scraped his jaw and neck as they continued to cling, marking each other like wild animals.

Bryson wasn't sure how long they touched, tasted, scratched and bit. He suspected he could have stood there with her in his arms for years.

They broke apart when a hard fist pounded the wall by their heads.

Aiden stood next to them, his eyes dark with desire, his nostrils flaring as he sucked in air. "Get in the bedroom."

"Yes," Dani hissed. "God. Yes."

Bryson bent and picked her up, carrying her into her room as Aiden led the way.

Bryson dropped her onto the mattress, following her down before she could attempt to rise. He felt a dip in the bed as Aiden joined them.

Dani gripped his shirt, tearing at the material in her attempt to get him naked. He felt the same sense of urgency.

For three days, they'd been swimming in a thick brew of unrequited lust and sexual hunger. They'd fasted when they should have been feasting.

"Make me forget," Dani pleaded. "Make it all go away."

Bryson hesitated, torn between continuing and demanding that she explain her request. Aiden didn't share that need. He stripped out of his clothes, tossing them to the floor, before dragging Dani's shirt over her head.

Bryson was left to rise and catch up as Aiden fell next to Dani on the bed. The two of them rolled around on the mattress, kissing, clinging, desperate.

Once he was also naked, Bryson didn't bother to join them. Instead, he watched for several minutes as he ran his hand over his raging erection. He was in pain, but unwilling to rush this.

Every time he thought they were taking a step forward, Dani found some way to shove them back.

What they shared was still too tenuous, too fragile. If Dani kept resisting this—refusing them—he needed to make this time count because he was afraid it may be the last.

Aiden and Dani broke apart briefly and he realized they were both looking for him. He grinned, and then joined them.

She wanted to forget, but Bryson wanted to remember... every minute, every second.

Bryson turned to lie on his back. "Climb on, bird."

Dani straddled his hips enthusiastically. He hoped that excitement didn't waver when he told her what he wanted to do next. This interlude wasn't going to be like the last. Though he wanted to go slow, time wasn't on his side. He just couldn't shake the feeling that it was now or never.

She lifted until he was poised at the entrance to her hot pussy. The past few days had obviously been difficult for all of them. Dani was wet and ready. She sank down faster than the last time, her trepidation over his size gone. Now that she knew he fit, her anxiety had given way to eagerness.

Once he was seated to the hilt, she started to rise again. He gripped her upper thighs tightly, holding her down. "No. Lean forward, Dani."

She gave him a quizzical look, but their wild lady had yet to refuse them. While the previous requests had been tame, this time he was going to push her limits.

Bryson glanced at Aiden, kneeling next to them as Dani lowered until her breasts rested against his chest. He wrapped his arms around her shoulders and held her. He'd release her if she asked, but at the same time, he wanted her to feel captured.

Aiden's gaze drifted to Dani's ass, then back to Bryson's face. Words weren't necessary. They wanted the same thing.

"Can you take us both?" Aiden asked as he caressed her ass.

Dani stiffened, but she didn't seek to escape. She knew exactly what Aiden was asking. Neither man sought to rush her. This had to be her decision and they knew it.

Even so, Bryson felt compelled to comfort her. Reassure her. He placed a soft kiss on the top of her head. "You can say no, Dani. At any time. Now or later...if it hurts or if you don't like it. The call is yours."

"I want to try," she whispered. "So much." Her inner muscles clenched around his cock, confirming her words. Fear wasn't going to stop her from taking what she wanted.

Aiden released a long sigh, not bothering to hide his joy at her answer.

Bryson grinned. "There's lube in that nightstand."

Aiden shifted to grab the tube from the drawer as Bryson and Dani held each other. Bryson was fighting every instinct in his body that cried out for him to move, to thrust. He'd never been great at restraint.

That was Aiden's forte, and the bastard was proving it as he took his sweet time preparing Dani for his cock in her ass.

Dani's escalated breathing tickled his chest. Her soft cries and the way her pussy quivered against Bryson's hard flesh told him she was enjoying Aiden's ministrations. So far he'd slowly worked the lube in with a single finger.

"Think you can take two?" Aiden asked.

Dani nodded.

Bryson lifted his head when he felt the second digit claim her ass. "Jesus. I can feel that too. Holy fuck, that's hot."

"Three," Dani pleaded. "Give me three. And then I want you."

Aiden added a third finger as he stretched her ass. Bryson and Dani groaned in unison.

"I don't think I can wait any longer, Dani," Aiden murmured.

She twisted to look at their lover over her shoulder. "Then don't."

Aiden quickly covered his cock with lubrication and then... they all held their breath as he moved into position. He pressed the head of his dick in slowly—too fucking slowly. None of the sensations Dani experienced were lost on Bryson. He felt what she did. It was incredible.

"Aiden," Bryson said through gritted teeth, hoping his friend got the message to pick up the pace. Bryson didn't have enough air in his lungs to say anything more.

"Don't. Want. To hurt her," Aiden said, his own words coming out stilted.

Dani lifted up to her elbows, the tips of her breasts rubbing against Bryson's chest. "I love it, but I need more, Aiden. Please."

Aiden gripped her hips and gave in to their pleas. He thrust forward until he was buried and all three of them gasped.

"I can't believe we're doing this," Dani said as she started moving. Both men reached out to stop her, to slow her down, but she was a woman who wouldn't be denied.

She leaned down and bit Bryson's pec. Hard.

"Ow!" he cried. "Fuck, Dani. That hurt."

She lifted her head and gave him the sexiest grin he'd ever seen.

Then Bryson pressed her mouth back down. "Do it again," he demanded, his voice husky with need.

She marked the other pec just as Aiden retreated.

Dani and Bryson hissed.

"It's like you're fucking us both," Bryson said. Then he frowned as he caught Aiden's eye.

Aiden chuckled. "Still not bisexual, you jackass."

Dani giggled, but the sound morphed into something much more animalistic when Aiden thrust in roughly.

After that, words were lost and time stood still.

Selfish, grasping need took over as they moved, each of them reaching for more and amazed when they found it.

Bryson had never felt like this, never felt as if his cock would explode, like he would lose consciousness, like he'd have a heart attack. It didn't seem possible his body could withstand this fucking much pleasure.

Dani fell first, her body trembling with her orgasm. Her pussy muscles clamped down so hard on his cock, Bryson saw stars as he came.

Aiden was only a split second behind them, his rough jerks shifting them all as he filled her ass with his come.

As the last vestiges of mind-blowing pleasure faded away, they fell to the bed like Jenga tiles, tumbling heedlessly to the mattress.

The only sounds in the room were those of the three of them gasping, struggling to catch their breath.

"Mother of God. I thought I was going to die," Aiden confessed, prompting Bryson to chuckle. They lay together in quiet contentment for only a few minutes before Bryson caught the sound of light snoring. He lifted his head to look over Dani's pretty body. Aiden was down for the count.

Bryson suspected he wouldn't be far behind. He was lethargic, exhausted. Happy as fuck.

"I want to do that again," Dani said quietly.

Bryson looked at her, trying to decide if it was the sex hang-over talking.

She smiled at him. "I tried to resist you guys. I made it three days."

Bryson moved toward her, kissing her softly. "We'll figure it out, Dani."

"Okay. I want to talk to you both about something else later too. About my past. When Aiden's awake."

She trusted them. She was going to let them in. If he hadn't been so freaking tired, he would have done a bit of Gronking that would have put Rob Gronkowski to shame.

"And just so you know," he added, though his drowsy voice was betraying how tired he was, "we're definitely doing that again." He placed his head on the pillow, trying to stay awake and failing.

Dani's smile was the last thing he saw before he drifted off.

———

Dani rose from the bed and stretched. There was a definite tenseness in muscles she felt certain had never been used. Not that she minded the workout. It was one she'd have no problem committing to, unlike her weak attempts at visiting the gym with any semblance of regularity.

She smiled as she studied Bryson and Aiden lying on the bed. They were both sprawled out facedown, which gave her the perfect opportunity to admire their firm butts, muscular backs and strong shoulders. Dani resisted the urge to pinch herself. There was simply no way these two hot guys could be in her bed.

She'd only managed a brief catnap, wondering what it was about sex that put her men to sleep, yet made her feel energetic, wide awake.

She plodded toward the bathroom to brush her teeth and considered a shower. They'd worked up quite a sweat.

A text flashed on the screen of her phone as she passed the nightstand. She reached for it, her blood running cold when she read it.

"How long are you going to make me wait? You can change your name, but that doesn't make you one of them. It's time you were reunited with your real family."

He knew she'd gone to see the Lewises. He *had* been watching her.

Dani picked up her clothes from the floor and tiptoed to the main room. Dressing quickly, she grabbed a room key and her purse and snuck out, closing the door quietly behind her.

She blinked against the bright sunlight as she left the apartment building, then waved down a taxi as she pulled out her cell and called Jett. "Where are you?"

"Royal Lunch. Why?"

She climbed into the back of the cab. "I'll be there in ten minutes."

Dani actually got there in eight. As she walked into the bar, she had that same sense of being watched. She glanced over her shoulder, scanning the area. There were quite a few people on the street, everyone walking with purpose, with a definite direction. No one seemed to notice her.

She needed to deal with her father once and for all. Otherwise, she feared she'd never feel truly safe.

Jett rose when she entered the bar. She accepted the brotherly hug he offered and felt so grateful to have him back in her life. Though she loved all the Lewis kids dearly, there had always been a special bond between her and Jett. One that didn't appear to have weakened after all the years they'd spent apart.

"What's going on?" he asked. "You sounded upset on the phone."

"My dad texted. Said he wasn't going to wait much longer for *his* reunion. He knows I was at Mama Lewis' house on Sunday and I'm worried about her safety. I think he's following me."

Jett frowned. "I'll see if Caleb can stop by Mama's house to check on her before his shift at the tattoo parlor. And I'll call Blake. See what he's found out about Russell."

She smiled when Carissa walked over to say hello. "Want something to drink?"

Dani gestured to Jett's glass. "I'll have whatever he's having."

Carissa poured her a beer from the tap, and then went over to serve another customer.

"Where are Aiden and Bryson?" Jett asked.

Dani took a drink. "Back at the penthouse."

"Have you told them about your dad?"

She shook her head, knowing her response would annoy Jett. "Not yet."

"Dammit, Dani. They're decent guys and it's pretty obvious they'd do anything for you."

Aiden and Bryson had made a good impression on her foster brother. She was glad that Jett liked them, though she wondered how he'd feel if he knew she'd been having sex with both of them.

Then she considered Justin's relationship with Ned and Bella and realized Jett would probably just welcome them both to the family.

"I've tried, Jett. I've opened my mouth to say it at least a million times over the last six years, but I can't seem to get the words out."

"Why not?"

She looked at the beer mug, uncomfortable and unable to face Jett. "I'm embarrassed. And ashamed."

Jett reached out for her, turning her head toward him, forcing her to meet his gaze. "No. Don't say that. God, don't *feel* that. Dani, you didn't do anything wrong. You know that, right?"

She nodded slowly, swallowing hard to dislodge the lump in her throat. "Knowing it doesn't seem to help. I don't want them to look at me differently."

"They won't."

She smiled sadly. "You can't know that."

Jett didn't waver. "Yeah. I can. I saw the way they looked at you at the dinner table, Dani. They couldn't take their eyes off of you. They're in love with you."

She bit her lower lip. "You really think so?"

He chuckled. "Do you seriously doubt that?"

She shook her head. She didn't. Not for a minute. She trusted their feelings for her, knew they were just as strong as what she felt for them. For the first time in her life, she wasn't second-guessing a relationship or looking for the exit. "It's just so new."

Jett tilted his head. "How new?"

"Four days."

Jett laughed. "Yeah, I thought so. You had that nice, new car smell on Sunday."

She laughed. "God. You're an idiot."

They both took a sip of their beer.

"Are you in love with them?"

She nodded. "So much."

"Then tell them. Everything. Let them help you through this next part. Aren't you tired of doing everything alone?"

Dani wasn't sure how to respond. She'd spent so much of her life making her own way, being self-sufficient. And while she'd had lots of help—from the Lewises, Stella and Benji—she'd never been very good about opening up and letting people in. Jett was the first person she'd ever given that glance inside, but it had been brief and ended too quickly. Aiden and Bryson had gotten the closest to breaking through her shell completely. If she confided in them, told them about her past, they'd have it all. Every tatty piece to her puzzle.

Jett's question rang in her ears. She was tired. And she was desperately lonely. How amazing would it feel to let someone else carry her along for a little while? Just until she found her footing, her own strength again. Because God knew right now, she was running on empty. She was terrified of what her father wanted. There was no way she could—or would—face him alone. And until she faced him, she was trapped in this hell of uncertainty. She couldn't take it anymore.

"I'll talk to them."

Jett smiled. "Good. In the meantime, I'll confer with Blake. See what he thinks our next step should be. Showdown. Restraining order. Murder."

"That's quite a list."

He shrugged. "I like to keep our options open."

Dani rose from the stool and placed a friendly kiss on Jett's cheek. "Thanks. For listening. And for talking me off the ledge."

He rose as well. "That's what big brothers are for."

Dani picked up on the old joke instantly, a game they had played many times before when they were teenagers. "By big, I have to assume you mean larger because as you well know, I'm two months older than you. Which makes me the big sister."

Jett walked to the door of the bar with her. "Want a ride home?"

She shook her head, pointing to a cab that was parked outside. "Nope. I'll just grab that cab and I'll text Bryson on the way back. Ask him to meet me out front. I'll be fine, promise."

He walked her to the car and opened the door for her. "Love you, Dani."

Dani suspected he could say that to her a million more times and she'd never, ever, get tired of hearing it. Brother. Family. Love. It felt as if everything she'd ever wished for was in her grasp. All she had to do was reach out and grab it.

"Back atcha."

He kissed her on the cheek, and then closed the car door

after she'd climbed in. She gave the driver the address for the apartment building. She was much calmer now than she'd been on her way to the bar. As always, Jett found a way to calm her down, help her see things that would have been obvious if she weren't acting like a ninny.

She fired off a quick text to Bryson, then sighed as she considered the conversation that was facing her when she returned to the penthouse. She knew her guys would be supportive, understanding, wonderful. She didn't doubt that for a minute. All she had to do was find a way to get the words out without falling apart completely.

Afternoon was giving way to evening and the sun had dropped down behind the buildings. Unfortunately that disappearance hadn't helped with the humidity. While Nashville was no stranger to hot summer days, it felt like Siberia compared to New Orleans.

She swiped at the tiny drop of sweat sliding down her neck and tugged at her t-shirt, wishing the driver would turn up the air-conditioning.

She tapped her thigh as she watched the streets roll by. She was anxious to get back to the penthouse to talk to Aiden and Bryson. She frowned when she realized nothing looked familiar.

"This isn't the way to the apartment."

"Shortcut," was the driver's very brusque response. For the first time since entering the cab, Dani felt uneasy. She couldn't see the driver's face except in profile. Even then, his bushy beard and the ball cap he had tugged to his eyebrows obscured it.

She remained quiet for a few minutes more. When the man turned down a road that looked more likely to lead to hell than the fancy apartment where she was staying, she spoke up again. "I think you're going the wrong way."

Her heart started to race when he pulled over to the curb and turned the car off. When he twisted in the seat, Dani felt all the blood drain from her face.

Her father lifted the gun, allowing her to see it. "Actually, I have you exactly where I want you."

JETT HAD JUST HUNG up after asking Caleb to check on Mama when his cell rang. "Blake," he said as he answered. "I was just about to call you. Dani's dad texted her again. He's definitely following her. What did you find out about him?"

"Got an address and place of employment. Hold tight. I'm going to text you a recent photo of Russell right now."

"Cool." Jett flicked the speaker function as the picture flashed on the screen.

Carissa walked by as the text came through, glancing at his phone. "Russ?"

Jett looked at her quizzically. "You know him?"

She nodded. "Yeah. You should too." Carissa pointed to a seat at the other end of the bar. "Guy sits there every time he comes in."

Jett's blood ran cold as he recognized the face. "Fuck."

"What's wrong?" Blake asked.

"I know how Dani's father found her. Bastard's been spying on me."

"Well, Dani was right. Guy's been in jail since she left town, but since his release, he's kept his nose clean. Got a job driving a taxi."

Jett jerked from his seat. "What?"

"He drives a cab."

"Give me the address, Blake. I need to call Dani."

"Why?"

Jett swallowed heavily, a very bad feeling settling in his gut. "Because I think he got her."

DANI REACHED FOR THE DOOR, hoping to jump out and run, but it wouldn't open.

"Child lock. Here's what's going to happen. I'm going to come open the door and you're going to get out of this car and walk inside with me. If you scream, I'll not only kill you, but I'll take down anyone who comes to help. You got it?"

She nodded as she looked around the street. She saw two older ladies talking at the corner, a young mother pushing a baby stroller and three middle-school-aged boys roughhousing and laughing. None of them deserved to die.

"Good girl."

Her father quickly climbed from the car and she watched helplessly as he crossed in front of it to her side of the vehicle. She clenched her hands into fists, trying to hide how badly they were shaking when he opened her door.

"Now, we're going to take a little walk together." He reached in and pulled her out of the cab. His hand wrapped painfully tight around her upper arm as he directed her toward a rundown building. New Orleans had always possessed an abundance of dark alleys and sketchy streets. This area certainly ranked right up there on the scary-as-shit scale.

Dani's mind whirled over her options. Running was the smart thing to do, but her dad was too strong. Though she struggled as he dragged her toward the building, she couldn't break free of his grip. Her attempts infuriated him as he shoved her against a wall just inside the building. The back of her head slammed into the cinderblock painfully.

"Stop fucking around. You're not getting away from me this

time. You wanna walk on your own or should I shoot you here?"

"Where are you taking me?"

He gave her a grin that was nothing short of malevolent. "Home. You and me got loose ends to tie up."

She stiffened, and then found a brazenness she didn't know she possessed. "Shoot me here."

He laughed, though the sound was cold. "Let me put this another way. I'll shoot you. Then I'll go over to that fancy apartment of yours and put a couple bullets in those men you're fucking. Always knew you were a slut."

"You wouldn't make it there. The cops would catch you first."

"Look around, Dani. You think a gunshot is going to draw much attention around here?"

The sound of doors slamming outside, babies crying and people shouting filled the air. And while she didn't think a gun going off would be unnoticed, she couldn't be sure anyone would dare to investigate it too closely. The hallway of the apartment building was filled with garbage, and dimly lit. She wasn't even sure anyone would see her body amidst the filth.

And if they did find her body, would they find it before her dad made it to the apartment? It wouldn't take him long to get there. Aiden and Bryson didn't even know there was a threat or that they were in danger.

She'd been a coward, guarding her heart instead of opening up and letting them in. Now they would never know how much she loved them.

Her cell rang, but Dani made no move to pull it from her pocket.

Once the ringing stopped, her father held out his hand. "Give it to me."

She hoped to distract him from taking it. "How did you get my cell number?"

"You gave it to me, you stupid bitch. Didn't see me sitting at the bar when you had breakfast with that arrogant, little prick of a writer, did you?"

Dani thought back to the morning she'd reconnected with Jett upon arriving in New Orleans. They'd laughed when they realized he only had her home number. Then she'd rattled off the number for him as he plugged it into his cell.

Her father had been that close to her and she hadn't realized? Granted she'd been super tired that morning, after driving all night, and stressed to the max. And her dad looked a lot different nowadays, his face covered in a bushy beard streaked with gray. His face was puffy. No doubt he was still a drinker and there were defined lines, deep wrinkles around his eyes and grooved into his forehead. She could just make out a scar cutting a jagged red line across his cheek, before disappearing beneath the beard.

He hadn't aged well. The face that had haunted her dreams for years looked much younger than this one. Of course, his eyes were still the same. Cold and angry.

"Give me the fucking phone. Now!"

Dani reluctantly withdrew it, knowing she was losing her last hope for being saved. He grabbed the phone from her, smashing it against the brick wall.

Prison had made him stronger.

Dani tried to fight down the panic threatening to consume her. She needed to keep her wits, to keep calm. If she gave in to the terror, she was lost.

"You finished fighting me?"

She didn't respond.

"I know their names, Dani. First and last. And I've got their address in Nashville. You give me what I want and I'll spare

Aiden and Bryson. Keep resisting and I'll make their lives a living hell."

He was more than capable of carrying out his threat. She knew that well enough.

While she was helpless to defend herself, there was at least one thing she could do. Protect the men she loved.

"I'll come quietly," she said at last.

Her father smiled evilly, and then dragged her up the stairs.

CHAPTER SEVEN

Aiden sat on the couch, watching as Bryson made his twenty-eighth trip across the room, pacing from the baby grand to the kitchen and back again.

"Where the hell is she?" Bryson asked.

They'd woken up half an hour earlier to discover the sun setting and Dani gone. Aiden had called her cell half a dozen times, but she must have turned it off. It kept going to voicemail.

"You think we came on too strong?"

It wasn't the first time Bryson had asked that question.

Aiden's answer didn't change. "No, Bry. She liked it. She wasn't afraid of us or what we did. Something's been upsetting her. We both know it's not us. It's whatever brought her back to New Orleans."

"She was going to tell us."

Aiden lifted his head. "What?"

"You passed out right after you came. Dani told me she wanted to talk to us later, that she had something to tell us about her past. She's ready to open up to us."

Aiden prayed that was true. Dani's uncharacteristic moodiness, the distance she'd put between them the past few days, had eaten at him like a cancer.

They both jumped when the penthouse phone rang. Aiden got to it first.

"Dani?" he said as he answered.

"What? No. It's Jett."

"Oh, shit. Sorry, Jett." Aiden sighed. He'd really hoped it was Dani.

"Dani's not there?" There was no mistaking the concern in the man's voice, which sent a chill through him.

"No. We've been trying to call her but she's not picking up."

"Fuck," Jett muttered. "I've tried too. I was hoping her cell was dead. That's why I called the apartment complex. Manager was only too happy to patch me through to your penthouse."

"Why would that be a problem? What's going on, Jett?" It was apparent from the man's tone he was worried and that he knew something.

"I think her dad took her."

"Her dad?"

Bryson scowled. "I thought her parents were dead."

Aiden raised his hand as he repeated the same query to Jett.

"No. Her mother died when she was twelve but her dad's still around. Listen, he's bad fucking news. If he's got her..."

Jett paused and Aiden sensed he didn't want to finish his statement, didn't want to admit how bad it might be.

"Where can we find him?"

"I got his address from Blake. You got a pen?"

Aiden gestured for Bryson to bring him a pen and paper. Once he did, Aiden wrote down the address Jett provided.

"I'm on my way there, but you guys are closer. Blake's on his way too, but he was on the other side of the city when we talked. It's going to take him time. If you get there before me, be careful. Her dad's been in prison a couple times. He's mean as a snake."

Aiden forced himself to ask the most important question despite his desire to get to Dani immediately. "What does he want with Dani?"

"Revenge," Jett said. "She was the reason he went to jail the first time. He tried to rape her when she was fifteen."

Aiden slammed down the phone and dashed for the door. He didn't even have to tell Bryson to follow. Once they were in the elevator, Aiden related everything Jett had said. Bryson's expression morphed from fear to murderous rage within seconds.

"We have to get to her," his friend said before the elevator doors opened and they ran through the apartment lobby. Mercifully, there was a taxi parked by the curb. They gave the man the address and promised him an extra fifty if he could get them there in five minutes.

The driver accepted the challenge. Aiden held on as the man made one sharp, fast turn after another. Fear of a car accident was nothing compared to the terror he felt for Dani.

"We'll get her," Bryson said, his voice deep, determined.

It calmed him. Aiden wouldn't be any good to Dani if he gave in to panic. He shut down the part of his brain that kept replaying Jett's words.

He tried to rape her. Her father tried to rape her.

Suddenly he understood Dani's reticence about coming back to New Orleans, but something must have compelled her to return. Something she hadn't told him and Bryson. Once they got her back—please God, let them get her back—they were going to sit down and have a long talk.

He'd never said, "I love you." That regret would burn in his gut forever if anything happened to her before they could get to her.

THE FIRST THING Dani noticed when her father opened the door to his apartment was the stench. She saw a rat scurry across the floor when he turned on the light and she had to swallow down bile. Then she wondered if vomiting all over the floor would disgust him enough to keep him away from her.

Given his willingness to live in this filthy apartment, she ventured to guess it wouldn't bother him at all. In her mind, she tried to decide how long it would be until someone missed her. If Bryson and Aiden had woken up, they'd probably tried to call. But she was notoriously bad about charging her phone, so they wouldn't immediately worry if she didn't answer. They also didn't have any phone contacts for Jett or any of the Lewises.

She had promised to call Jett later, but he was expecting her to have a long chat with the guys. And if she didn't phone, he'd most likely assume they were having sex. Chances were good he wouldn't try to contact her until tomorrow at the earliest.

Which meant she could be on her own for quite a while.

Her father took off his jacket and tossed it on a chair, well away from her. He'd put the gun in the pocket of it when he'd gotten out of the cab. She felt a weird sense of relief now that it was out of reach.

"Take a seat. Make yourself comfortable."

Now that he had her where he wanted, her father was smug, looming in front of her looking far too pleased with himself.

She looked at the shabby, stained couch. "I'm fine standing." She didn't pretend for a moment this was a social visit as she glanced toward the door, searching for some way to escape.

"Sit down, Dani. Now."

In the past, she'd responded to his demands instantly because that was the path of least resistance, the best way to avoid getting slapped.

However, pain was a given. She wasn't going to get out of here unscathed no matter what she did. The child she'd been—the one who always cowered—had grown up and developed a backbone. Maybe it was the height of foolishness, but she refused to tremble before him ever again. Even if it did mean he'd hurt her.

"No."

He didn't move for a moment and it looked as if he was trying to decide if he'd heard what he thought he had.

"Did you tell me no?" His deep voice promised retribution.

She decided for diversion. "What do you want from me?"

The abrupt change of subject worked. Briefly. "You've changed, baby girl. I don't like it. Go sit down."

Again, she refused to acknowledge his demand. "Money? Is that what you're after?" She threw the offer out, hoping he'd take the bone. It was obvious from his living conditions he needed cash. Maybe she could buy her way out of this place.

"You know what I want, Dani."

She laughed mirthlessly. "Seriously? After all this time. What's the matter, Russell? Run out of women in New Orleans to rough up?"

She'd gone too far. The second she called him by his real name rather than Dad, she knew it was over the line. It just felt too good to face down the bully, to call him out for his cruelty rather than hide in the corner.

His hand connected with her right cheek before she even

realized he'd raised his arm. The fucker still packed a wallop. Her vision went black for several seconds as her head twisted sharply with the impact.

The pain wasn't new. It had been years since she'd been slapped like this, yet the sensation was as familiar to her as if it had only been yesterday.

But the blow didn't have the same effect it used to, didn't do what her father expected. If he'd thought the slap would snap her out of it, make her the properly fearful girl she'd been in her teens, he was destined for disappointment. She wasn't going down without a fight.

Once she found a way to shake off the pain, to beat down the flames erupting along the side of her face, she straightened up and looked him in the eye again.

He didn't like her lack of tears or pleas. And he sure as fuck did *not* like that she wasn't afraid. "Think you're tough, don't you, Dani?"

She snorted, the sound catching him unaware. "You made sure of that, didn't you, Russell?"

He reached up, his hand gripping her tightly around the neck. "Call me by my name again and I'll break your fucking neck."

She didn't respond. Couldn't answer. He was cutting off her air supply. She struggled to pull his hand away, but it was abundantly clear that her only weapon in this fight was bravado. All the physical strength was on his side. For a moment, pure, unadulterated panic clawed at her chest. She was in way over her head.

Dani pushed the fear away. Maybe she couldn't win. But at least she could lose with dignity. She went limp, refusing to continue the struggle.

Her father released her and took a step away. Fury filled his eyes, but she noticed something new as well. Confusion.

He was a professional bully who chose targets who wouldn't fight back. Regardless of her lack of strength, she was messing with his head. Hope reemerged, combined with even more determination.

"Sit down," he repeated. He was hung up on the first command.

She didn't move and he didn't bother to give the order again. He grabbed her and shoved her roughly down onto the threadbare cushions. A spring poking through the armrest scratched her wrist.

Dani glanced down at the welt, the blood welling there. Great. It looked like she could add tetanus to the list of horrible things she was about to endure.

"You were stupid to run from me, girl. I told you in the jail I was coming back for you. Did you really think you could hide from me forever?"

She didn't reply. Mainly because she felt more vulnerable sitting, which had probably been her father's goal all along.

He towered over her. Now that he had his audience in place, he unleashed twelve years' worth of pent-up anger. "You ruined my life, you little whore! Called the cops, got me thrown in jail. I lost my job, my apartment. Meanwhile, you're living it up in that big house with that annoying bitch and all her kids."

He reached down and grabbed a handful of hair, pulling it painfully so that she had no choice but to look up at him. "You think I didn't know you hated me? The way you were never home, always hiding in your room. Thought you were better than me. Thought you deserved a better life. You got me arrested because you were a selfish *cunt*. You thought you got away with it too, didn't you?"

The man was clearly unhinged. He'd had too many years to make her the villain in his life story, to blame her for everything bad that happened to him.

Her eyes watered as he increased the pressure on her scalp. "Now it's time to pay."

Dani was out of options. Her attempts at stalling had gotten her to this point, but they wouldn't buy her more time. Which left her with only two more choices. Fight or flight.

She glanced around, recalling how she'd escaped the last time. If she could just manage to get her hands on something heavy...

Surprisingly, there was nothing. No lamps, cups, pictures. Nothing. It was as if the room had been cleared.

Her father chuckled. "What's wrong, Dani? No weapons to use against me?"

He released her hair, his hands going to his jeans.

She reacted without thought, leaning back as she swung her foot up hard, right between his legs. Jackpot.

Her dad doubled over from her kick to his crotch, a loud "ugh" flying from his lips.

"I wouldn't say I have no weapons." She tried to use his momentary pain to run. She leapt from the couch, trying to dodge his hand as he reached out to catch her.

She was a second too slow as he caught her by her hair, yanking her backwards with enough force to knock her to her back on the floor.

"You fucking bitch." He kicked her ribs, the blow sending sharp shards of pain along her side.

She rolled away from him as he swung his foot again, his boot connecting hard against her mid-back, propelling her face first toward the couch.

Despite the waves of pain and the strong urge to vomit, she needed to fucking move. Get up. One more goddamn kick like that and he'd break her in half.

She used the couch for support to lift herself, clearing the floor mere seconds before his foot flew again. He kicked the frame of the couch, but the sturdiness of his freaking boots—Jesus, were they made of steel?—protected him from any pain from the ill-aimed blow.

"Goddamn cunt!" he bellowed as he unbuttoned his jeans. Unlike the last time, there was no fumbling. His purpose was clear.

"You realize you won't get away with this," she said, fighting like the devil to keep her tone calm. "Regardless of what you do right now, you'll be arrested, and this time, they'll throw away the key. Three strikes, you're out. Did you like prison that much?"

His brows were furrowed with a fury so intense she had to look away lest she lose her nerve. "Who the fuck do you think you're talking to? All you had to do was spread your skinny fucking legs!"

"Don't pretend this is about sex. You and I both know it's a fucking power trip with you. A way for you to lord yourself over me. Well, guess what Daddy Dearest, I'm not fucking impressed or scared. You're a weak, stupid, small man who only feels big when he's terrorizing women and children."

Her dad's eyes nearly bugged out of his head, his breath was coming in loud, harsh pants. She'd propelled him from merely angry to raging, fiery fury. "Shut your fucking mouth!"

He bent down as she struggled to stand and slapped her again. And this one hurt. Bad. Her teeth rattled and her neck jerked so hard to the left she thought she heard a snap. Stars exploded behind her eyes, blinding her momentarily.

She couldn't shake off the pain, couldn't find her way back from the agony. Her legs started to give way and she feared she was going down. If she fell, if she hit the floor, she was done for. She locked her knees.

"I don't give a fuck if I go back to jail. All I care about is that the trip there is worth it. I didn't get to finish last time. This time, I will. I'm gonna make you hurt, Dani. I'm gonna fuck you up good."

The fear she'd managed to hold at bay responded to his threat. There wasn't much fight left in her. Her arms felt like rubber, her brain was still rattling from the last blow and her legs were only holding her up by the grace of God.

"Why do you hate me so much?" She hadn't meant to voice the question, even though it was one she'd carried around inside her for most of her life. He was her father. She'd seen the other girls in school with their daddies. She knew what that relationship was supposed to look like.

He laughed. He'd taken delight in her question, in knowing that he'd hurt her.

"I know how to shut you up, whore." It was the only answer she got as his fist flew, punching her in the stomach so hard, she lurched forward, gagging.

His fingers found her hair once more as he shoved her to her knees in front of him. With one hand, he slid the zipper down.

Her chest went tight, a wave of dizziness swamping her. There was a sudden roaring in her ears that drowned out the rest of her father's hateful, terrifying words.

The sound of a siren pierced the night. Hope emerged.

"Don't get excited. Cops don't come here."

Regardless of her father's confidence, Dani couldn't help but notice the siren was getting louder, coming closer.

That was when she heard heavy footsteps pounding, racing up the stairs.

Her dad's conviction wavered, but there was something in his twisted mind that refused to let go of the goal at hand. Even in the face of arrest.

If he'd been thinking clearly, he would have gone for the gun, would have attempted to get away before the inevitable.

Instead, he was determined to finish what he'd started when she was just a girl.

He shoved her back down on the couch, pushing her into the stained cushions. His fingers clawed at her shirt even as she tried to shove them away, fighting to get up. He ignored the sound of car brakes squealing, the siren right outside the window.

She screamed, praying the cops were there for her. If they weren't, by fucking God, they would be.

Her father tried to cover her mouth, but she bit his fingers, screaming again.

A loud bang accompanied the front door flying open. Bryson and Aiden rushed into the room. They took one look at her on the couch, bruised and disheveled, and the fear she witnessed briefly in their eyes turned to cold, hard rage.

Dani lay on the couch, every ounce of strength draining from her body as the world began to move in slow motion. She was acutely aware of every single movement in the room. While her body failed her, her senses seemed to take over.

Bryson grabbed her father by the back of his shirt, yanking him away from her. Aiden moved in front of Russell, his fist flying fast and hard. Her dad's neck flew back as blood spurted from his mouth. Dani could have sworn she could count how many drops were shed.

Then Bryson moved in for his vengeance, using his elbow against her dad's shoulder in a way that knocked Russell to his knees, "oomphing" loudly, the sound racked with pain.

If she'd had the strength, she would have laughed at her dad crawling on his hands and knees, attempting to escape her beautiful men as they rained down a rapid succession of punches and kicks.

She wasn't sure if they would have quit. They'd seen her in danger and gone into warrior-mode. Part of her wondered if they would have been able to stem their anger, to regain control or if the bloodlust would have raged on, but the point was moot when Jett and Blake ran into the room. Blake had his gun drawn and they both looked equally intimidating.

Dani was instantly struck by how much her life had changed. That night so long ago when her father attacked, she'd had to find her own way out and her protector had been an equally terrified, gray-haired neighbor. This time, men who would lay down their lives for her surrounded her.

For the first time since she'd stepped into the apartment, tears fell. How strange was it that she cried now? When she was safe?

Aiden came to her, drawing her up from the couch and into his warm embrace. Like he had after her nightmare, he gently rocked her, stroking her back and telling her everything was okay. Unlike the last time, the tears didn't turn into sobs. Instead they were quiet creatures that slid slowly down her cheeks as each emotion—fear, love, relief, gratitude—found its way to the forefront.

Blake handcuffed her father and read him his rights, giving her time to pull herself together.

"Dani?" Blake asked after a few minutes. "You okay?"

She nodded.

"Do you need to go to the hospital?"

"No."

Bryson scowled, his gaze raking her face. She had no idea what he saw there, but she could tell her eye and lip were puffy from her dad's rough slaps. "Dammit, Dani. I think you should—"

"I'm fine, Bryson. Honest. He only hit me twice. And believe it or not, I've had worse." He didn't need to know how badly she'd been hurt. There was enough terror in his eyes. All that mattered was that he was here and they were all safe.

Bryson winced as he digested that information, his face hard, his jaw chiseled in stone. If Blake weren't there, she didn't doubt for a moment, Bryson would make her father pay for those past abuses. And pay dearly.

"Did you come here on your own?" Jett asked.

Dani tilted her head. "Are you insane? Of course not. He was driving the cab. There's a gun in the pocket of that jacket," she said, pointing to the coat.

Blake retrieved the gun. "I'll be sure to let your parole officer know you've violated that condition. Though that's a drop in the bucket as far as what we're going to charge you with. Kidnapping, assault, attempted rape."

Russell didn't reply. Since the arrival of the other men, he'd gone uncharacteristically quiet. It was then Dani realized her father truly was a bully. Only brave when the cards were stacked in his favor, only a tough guy when he was surrounded by people weaker than he was.

Blake grasped her father's arm, intent on taking him out. "I'm going to need you to come by the station and make a statement, Dani."

Dani nodded, her gaze locked on her father's face. "I should be happy you're going back to jail."

Russell scowled at her words, but he remained silent.

"But it occurs to me, I don't care *where* you are. You're nothing to me. In fact, you're nothing, period."

"Watch it, girl," her father said, though his tone had lost some of its menace.

Aiden and Bryson stepped closer, flanking her, but she raised her hand to hold them back.

"You can't break me, Russell. God knows you've tried, but there aren't enough punches and cruel words in the world to erase the amazing life I've led. You can't take away the support I've been given by my foster family and my friends, the kindnesses shown to me from strangers who owed me nothing, yet gave me so damn much. You can't diminish or ruin the love I've known either." She looked at Bryson and Aiden and smiled. "My life has been one giant blessing despite everything you've tried to do. You're an utter failure. Be sure to think about that while you spend the rest of your life behind bars."

Russell snapped forward, trying to break Blake's grip in an attempt to get to her. Blake held tight, then twisted him toward the door, shoving him to the hall as he chuckled. "She summed that up pretty good."

Jett kissed Dani on the cheek, his smile so big Dani thought it must physically hurt his face. "You are so fucking cool. Love you, sis. I'm going to help Blake, leave my car here and see if I can't finagle a ride in the police car. I wanna turn on the lights and blare the siren."

Dani laughed. "What are you? Twelve?"

"Hey," Jett protested. "It's research. For my next book. I'll call you later."

Aiden reached out to place a hand on Jett's shoulder. "Thanks for everything, man."

Jett shrugged. "You guys did the heavy lifting. Wish I could have punched the fuck out of that asshole. Sort of jealous." He looked at Bryson. "You kick the door in?"

Bryson nodded.

Jett shook his head in obvious awe. "I'm putting that move in my next book too."

Bryson rolled his eyes. "Do me a favor. Call Dani tomorrow. We're putting her to bed as soon as we get back to the penthouse."

Jett winked at her, then bid his goodbyes.

"I want to go home," she said, the adrenaline of the last few hours giving way to exhaustion.

"Okay. I'll call Blake and see if the statement can wait until morning. We asked the taxi driver to wait," Aiden said. "We can be back at the penthouse in fifteen minutes."

Dani shook her head. "No. Home. Nashville. With you guys."

Bryson kissed her on the cheek. "That sounds damn good to me."

CHAPTER EIGHT

Dani opened her eyes, blinking in the darkness, struggling to figure out where she was.

"You okay, bird?"

She looked to her left to find Bryson lying next to her. "What time is it?"

Bryson glanced toward the nightstand. "A little after one. You fell asleep in the cab on the way back from the police station."

Dani hadn't wanted to wait until morning to talk to Blake because it would simply slow down her return home. Now that she had Nashville in her sights, she was anxious to get there.

"How did I get up here?"

Aiden's arm snaked around her waist as he spooned her. "Bryson carried you."

She grinned. "Damn. Sorry I missed that. Sounds kinda hot."

Bryson patted her hip playfully. "For you, maybe. You may want to cut back on those beignets for a while."

She laughed at his joke, punching him lightly on the arm. "Asshole."

Aiden didn't join in the laughter. Instead, he tightened his grip on her. Dani sensed he was still struggling with some latent fear over what they'd faced. She felt the same way.

"You ready to talk about it?" Aiden asked.

Dani was confused. "You guys were in the room when I gave my statement. You know what happened."

"I mean before. When you were a girl. Why didn't you ever tell us, Dani?"

Dani bit her lip. She'd kept quiet about it because she'd been ashamed. Jett had told her that was the wrong emotion to feel, but that didn't make it go away.

However, now, after confronting her father, her fears and the words came much easier. The whole story tumbled out. Every single sordid second of it. From her mother's death to her father's drinking problem, the abuse and the details of the first night he'd tried to rape her and his threats at the prison.

And then she talked about life at the Lewis house and when she'd come downstairs to find her guitar under the Christmas tree. She told them about her father's release and how she'd run away, how Stella had saved her.

Bryson and Aiden listened as she talked, asking questions, laughing with her. Once, she even saw Bryson trying to covertly wipe a tear.

"I'm sorry I never told you any of this," she said at last.

"Why didn't you?" Aiden asked.

"I was embarrassed. Ashamed. I know it's stupid, but for a long time, I felt like maybe I'd done something wrong. I knew he was dangerous. I should have locked my bedroom door. Should have asked for help. Should have done...something."

Aiden clasped her face tightly in his hands, forcing her to hold his gaze. "You were fifteen years old. He was the adult.

Your father, for God's sake. It was his job to protect you. You didn't do a damn thing wrong. You got it?"

"I do now. Honest. I was young when I left. The emotions tied up in all of this..." she struggled for a word to describe it, then settled on the only one that worked, "*shit* were immature. The fears and reasoning of a teenage girl. I know they weren't rational, but they were all I could remember."

Bryson had been holding her hand throughout her tale. He lifted it, his lips brushing her knuckles. "You were incredible in that apartment today, Dani. The way you confronted him, told him off. Jesus. I never saw anything so brave, so fucking awesome."

She laughed quietly. "It's weird. I've spent most of my life living in terror, hiding in shadows, looking over my shoulder. The memory of my dad was way worse than the reality."

Bryson lifted a disbelieving eyebrow.

"I'm not going to say he wasn't scary, but...I don't know...it's hard to explain. I'd built him up as some horrible, all-mighty monster who couldn't be defeated. Today, I realized he was just a really mean, twisted, abusive bully."

"He could have seriously hurt you, Dani. Fuck," Aiden muttered, his tone telling her exactly what kind of toll the day's events were taking on him. "He could have killed you."

"Don't," she said quickly. "Don't think about that. We're here. You saved me. That's all that matters."

Aiden blew out a long, tired sigh. "It might take me a little while to get there. I don't think I've ever been that scared in my fucking life. When Jett called to say your dad had you...that he'd tried to rape you before..."

"We didn't know where you were," Bryson added, his own fears finding their way out. "We woke up and you were gone."

"I texted you from the taxi, but that was before I realized my dad was driving it."

Aiden flashed an annoyed look at Bryson. "Your phone was off, wasn't it?"

Bryson glanced at the nightstand, picking up his cell, flicking it on. "Damn. Yeah. Thing has been here since the last time the three of us were in this bed. Sorry. I didn't even think about it. She wasn't answering your calls. It didn't occur to me to check *my* phone." He looked at Dani. "Why in the hell did you text me? You know my phone's always off."

She laughed, then admitted. "That was really stupid of me."

Bryson grinned and kissed her on the cheek, but Aiden wasn't finished. "Dani, I, God, I don't ever want to feel that way again."

She kissed Aiden softly on the mouth. "I'm sorry."

He shook his head. "No. No apologies. Just give me a promise."

She nodded. "Okay. Anything."

"No more secrets."

Dani smiled. It was an easy thing to give. "Done."

Bryson sat up slowly. "Since we're putting all the cards on the table, I think it's time we talked about us, where we're going."

Aiden raised his eyebrows. "Holy shit. Are you suggesting we have a serious conversation about feelings and crap like that?"

Dani laughed as Bryson shot his friend a dirty look.

"Yeah, smartass," Bryson said. "I am. And then, if Dani's interested, I'd like to expand on some of the dirty, kinky sex we've been having lately."

Dani sat up as well, tugging her t-shirt over her head. The guys must have taken off her bra, pants, shoes and socks after carrying her up. "Who undressed me?"

Aiden ran a gentle finger along her side. "There's a bruise here."

She suspected there was one on her back too, but she didn't want to point that out. She'd only just managed to talk them off the ledge, their fear and worry starting to lessen.

"I'm fine."

Bryson cupped her face, his thumb stroking her upper cheek. "You have a black eye."

Her fingers flew to her eye. "Dammit. How am I supposed to explain that to people? Benji will freak the fuck out."

Bryson kissed the cheek as if to heal it with his lips. "We'll think of something."

"Or you can give Benji the truth," Aiden suggested. "He loves Dani."

Dani nodded. "Yeah. I think I might like to talk to him."

Aiden smiled as he reached out to cup one of her breasts. He was clearly a boob guy. "And by the way, we both undressed you. But we didn't look. Much."

"Well then," she said, gesturing at their boxers. "Fair is fair. My turn for a peek. But don't worry. I won't look. Much."

Bryson stood to strip off his boxers, while Aiden simply lay on the bed and lifted his ass to toss them away. Dani giggled at their haste, then reached for Bryson's hard cock as he returned to the bed.

He grasped her wrist, keeping her from her prize. "Talk first. Sex second."

She narrowed her eyes. "Who are you and what have you done with Bryson?"

He dropped back down to the mattress, releasing her hand. "I'm serious, bird. If this was like every other relationship I'd ever had, I would be perfectly fine with skipping straight to the good part, but this feels different. *I* feel different. I can't keep riding in limbo where one minute you want us and the next you're pushing us away."

"Damn," Dani whispered. "I *have* been doing that. I'm sorry."

Bryson winced and shook his head. "No. I'm not saying that to make you feel bad. You've been dealing with some heavy shit this past month. And then, on top of all the stuff with your dad, signing the biggest deal of our careers and finding your foster family, Aiden and I both hop in bed with you. Sort of crazy when you think about it."

She hadn't considered how much stress she had been under until Bryson's list. "Yeah. I guess it was. But you guys were the best part of all of it. You got me through all the crap. I'd be a quivering mass of goo on the floor right now if it weren't for you two. It's just..." Dani had promised them honesty and no more secrets. "I'm scared."

"Of us?" Aiden asked.

"Yes and no. I love you both so much, but we're standing at the starting line of something really big. We've basically committed to being in each other's faces twenty-four-seven for the next few years. What if..."

"What if this doesn't work out?" Aiden finished for her.

She nodded.

Aiden ran his hand through her hair. "You think I haven't considered that?" He looked at Bryson. "We both have. But Dani, I'm not sure we can turn back now, go back to the way things were."

She frowned. "What are you saying?"

"I'm saying I'm in love with you and I can't turn that off. I'd walk through fire to make this work, to keep you and Bryson in my life, in my bed."

Bryson turned her face to him. "We didn't get where we are by playing it safe, bird. We took a lot of chances in order to make something of Closing Time. Some things are worth the risk because the payoff is huge. And sure, this might be the biggest risk of all, but I'm willing to go for it because at the end we'll have each other. Forever."

Dani smiled tremulously, her eyes filling with tears. She couldn't believe she had any left. She'd gone years without crying, but in the past few days, she didn't seem able to stop. "Forever sounds amazing."

"We'll make it work," Aiden said assuredly, turning her face to him. "We've been together for six years and even though we've had fights, at the end of the day, we always found a way to fix things and move on. This will be the same. I promise."

Aiden leaned closer to seal that vow with the sweetest kiss she'd ever had.

Then Bryson shifted them until his cock was nestled against her ass. It looked like the talking part was over.

And then, as she'd done every single time before, she put herself into their very capable, very loving hands.

Aiden continued to kiss her, cupping and plumping her breasts as Bryson reached around to touch her clit. The calluses on his fingertips from years spent playing the guitar worked the sensitive nub until Dani was gasping, overwhelmed by pure pleasure.

She tried to offer something to them as well, her hands stroking Aiden's shoulders, his upper back as she wiggled her ass against Bryson's cock.

"God, Dani," Aiden murmured against her lips. "Need you."

Hallelujah. She shoved roughly at his shoulders, pushing him onto his back on the mattress as she climbed over him.

Bryson released a low whistle. "Oh hell yeah, baby. Take him. Take him hard."

She wasn't sure if Bryson's words were a suggestion, a

command or a dare. It didn't matter. She didn't need any instructions.

They were all-in, all aware of the risks and ready to do what it took to make this trio last—onstage and in the bedroom. With that uncertainty off the table and her father safely behind bars, Dani had nothing holding her back.

Aiden and Bryson wouldn't know what hit them.

She lifted her hips, placed Aiden's cock at the opening of her body and slammed down. She was wet and ready, so he slid in easily. He groaned as she gave him no time to adjust. Instead, she moved over him, a staccato rhythm, played triple beat. It was a fast, wild ride that ended far too quickly when Aiden added his own bass line, a steady pounding as he lifted his hips each time she banged back down.

Sweat formed at her brow, her body slick. She crash-landed first, crying out loudly. Or was she yelling? The roaring in her ears soaked up the sound as she fell forward, her head landing on Aiden's chest. Her body jerked with aftershocks when he erupted, filling her with hot come. His heart was thudding loudly, comforting her.

She wasn't sure how long they lay there. It couldn't have been more than a few minutes. That was all the time it took for her to remember Bryson was still there, still watching. Still hard.

Dani lifted her head, searching for him in the darkened room. She was surprised to find he was no longer beside her, but sitting in an easy chair that faced the bed.

"Bryson?" she asked quietly. Her question roused Aiden, who lifted his head, seeking out his friend as well.

"Why are you over there?" Aiden asked.

"Better view." Bryson leaned forward. "That was the hottest thing I've ever seen. I love being a part of it, don't get me wrong.

But goddamn, there's just something about watching you two fuck. I want to watch you do it everywhere—in the dressing room, onstage after everyone is gone, in the back of a limo, outside under the stars. I'm not going to get enough of that. Ever."

Bryson's imagination had taken flight and his fantasies ignited a few of her own. She lifted her hand. "Come back to bed."

He shook his head. "No. It's Aiden's turn for a show. Come here."

Bryson had this deep, commanding voice in the bedroom that twisted Dani's insides, made her want to crawl on his lap and give him the world.

Instead, she pretended to be annoyed by it, calling him out. "Trying to boss me around?"

His nostrils flared and she expected him to come claim her. She was surprised when he capitulated. "You want to direct the show?"

Did she? Until he asked, she'd thought she liked how her men were always in control. Now that he'd offered, she realized she wanted a chance to bring them to their knees.

She nodded slowly.

Bryson lifted his palms upward in surrender. "Do your worst."

She rose, pleased by the strength in her legs after her killer orgasm. Bryson stood as she approached. She glanced down and licked her lips at the sight of his thick cock.

He captured her face in his large hands and kissed her. It was surprisingly gentle for Bryson, whose past kisses had been so potent, so hungry.

It was also brief. He released her lips with a soft smile. "What now?"

She didn't reply. Instead, Dani dropped to her knees, the

soft, plush carpeting in the room providing a comfortable cushion, as a low groan of approval rumbled from Bryson.

Dani wasted no time as she ran her tongue along the base of his cock from balls to tip.

Bryson hissed, his fingers grasping her hair. Despite his grip, he didn't seek to direct her motions, content to let her hold the reins. She wondered how long that would last. Bryson had proven to be a less-than-passive lover. While he might offer her brief moments of control, he'd never been able to restrain the dominant for long.

She stroked him with her tongue twice more before opening her lips to take in his large head. Dani captured the tiniest taste of tangy precome, licking it away before taking his cock deeper.

Bryson's hands tightened, but still he held strong, letting her move at her own pace.

While she enjoyed the opportunity to explore, to discover his hot spots and what turned him on, she missed his dominance. She seriously got off on Bryson's control. So she decided to force his hand.

She released his cock, and then shifted back a few inches so he could see her face. She licked her own finger before sucking it into her mouth. His gaze was locked onto her face and she could sense Aiden's rapt attention as well. Both men were focused solely on her actions. Once her finger was wet, she pressed Bryson's legs farther apart and reached between, seeking out some new terrain.

When she found his anus, she wiggled her wet digit at the opening.

His eyes narrowed. "What are you doing?"

She ignored the question, countering with her own. "Do you like it?"

His jaw twitched when she pressed her finger deeper, one

knuckle, and then two, thrusting past the tight ring of flesh.

"Fuck me! Jesus, Dani. I can't...I'm trying, but..."

His resistance was wavering. She decided to ring the bell on the end of this round as she pushed her finger in the rest of the way. Bryson jerked, his patience in tatters.

He wrapped his hand around her wrist as he tugged her finger from his ass. Before she could complain, he grasped her upper arms, pulled her from the floor, twisted her and had her bent over, her hands on the cushion of his armchair.

"You like playing with fire, bird?"

She was sucking in deep, harsh breaths, too turned-on to think straight.

Bryson smacked her ass, just one quick, sharp slap.

She gasped, and then moaned.

She heard footsteps approach, sensing rather than seeing Aiden's presence at her side. Her eyes were clenched shut as she fought against coming. What the fuck was that about? A few brusque moves, a smack on the butt and the idea of being wholly dominated by her guys had her ready to blow like the lid on a shaken bottle of soda.

"Please." Her voice was hoarse with need.

Bryson didn't ask for clarification. He knew what she wanted. Though the sexual relationship was new, the foundation had been laid years earlier. They knew each other inside and out, which meant there was no hesitance, no need to constantly ask permission.

Bryson smacked her again. She half expected Aiden to join in as well, but he seemed content to simply watch as Bryson peppered her ass with quick taps and harder slaps. She'd just started to become accustomed to his rhythm when he stopped and thrust two fingers inside her. Over and over, he fucked her with his fingers. It was rough, beautiful.

"Oh God." She was seconds from coming. Just a little bit...

"Wait."

She scowled at Aiden as she glanced over her shoulder and spotted his hand on Bryson's wrist, halting his thrusts. "Don't wait," she demanded.

Aiden moved closer, lifting her hands from the seat of the chair so that he could claim it. He was naked, his cock at half-mast, still not fully recovered from their previous interlude. "I want to see your face when he takes you, Dani. I want to watch you come."

He positioned her hands on his thighs. And then, as if he couldn't resist, he reached up to pinch one turgid nipple.

She bit her lip to hold back the moan, but it escaped anyway when Bryson's cock brushed her pussy. He ran the thick flesh along her slit several times before pressing the head of it inside.

After the rough motions of his fingers, this slower, gentler pace was driving her insane. And not in a good way. She wanted him to take her. Hard. She'd held back so much of herself for so long, living in a constant state of self-preservation.

She was finished hiding the true Dani, the woman she'd always longed to be. Her fingers tightened on Aiden's thighs as she looked at his beloved face.

Aiden smiled at her. "Take what you want, Dani. There's nothing we won't give you."

The words were spoken so softly Dani was sure Bryson hadn't heard. It didn't matter. *She* had, and they'd soaked right through her skin and traveled straight to her heart.

She used her grip to move. Dani pounded back, forcing Bryson's cock deeper than it had ever been.

Bryson's hands flew to her hips, but all bets were off. He used his hold to drive them, thrusting so hard, so fast, she saw stars. She came quickly, not bothering to hide one iota of her pleasure from Aiden, who watched her, who called her beautiful.

Bryson, ever the master, continued to plunge inside, unwilling to let the song end yet. She had only a moment to recover from her first orgasm before the second struck. It was more intense as her inner muscles were overstimulated, sensitive, raw. This time, she didn't just yell. She screamed.

Bryson came just as her orgasm started to wane, filling her, as he shouted words of love, of forever.

They were beautiful lyrics, and she couldn't wait to set them to music.

EPILOGUE

Aiden and Bryson each claimed one of Dani's hands, the three of them bowing as thunderous applause shook the arena. They'd just completed their second encore at the kick-off to their first concert tour.

Dani's face hurt from smiling as she glanced out and spotted her family standing front row and center, clapping and screaming her name. She'd gotten them the tickets, wanting them to be there as she started this next amazing, incredible part of her life.

Dani woke up every morning to find herself actually living in a dream. She was part of a successful band, a loving relationship and a family. It was almost too much to take in.

The three of them exited stage left as the concert crew quickly worked to break down their set to prepare for the main act. While they knew everyone in the crowd had come to see Lucas Bryan, Dani felt like Closing Time had definitely made an impression.

"I would like to go on record as saying this was the best night of my life."

Neither man laughed. In fact, she could see from their expressions they agreed wholeheartedly.

"I swear to God, I think that was our most solid performance ever." Leave it to Aiden to start analyzing immediately.

"How fucking hot was it out there?" Bryson was grinning from ear to ear and dripping with sweat. They all were.

"I don't know," Dani said. "Somewhere between a hundred and fifty degrees and the surface of the sun?"

Bryson held out his arm. "Yeah, well you can stick a fork in me because I am well done." And as usual, Bryson focused on the simple stuff.

She laughed and tugged at her shirt. "Come on. Let's take advantage of those showers in our dressing rooms."

Aiden grasped her hand. "I think we can make do with just one. I'll scrub your back if you scrub mine."

Bryson walked beside them, shaking his head. "Part of me still can't believe we're here."

Dani understood that sense of wonder and amazement. She wasn't sure she'd ever get used to it. "It's incredible, isn't it?"

They walked into Dani's dressing room and slowly peeled off their damp clothing. Aiden handed them each a bottle of water. "Better hydrate."

She laughed as the three of them—naked as the day they were born—chugged the water like they were dying of thirst.

"Race you to the shower," she said, as she sprinted toward the shower. She bent over to turn on the water as Bryson strolled in behind her, stroking her ass, his fingers dipping into the slit between her legs to do a little exploring. They were approaching their six-month anniversary. Maybe it was juvenile to count the time in months, but it was a step up from her initial celebrations...of days, then weeks.

With every day that passed she fell more in love with them and the anxiety she'd felt at the beginning faded, even started to feel ridiculous. How could she have ever doubted this?

They'd only just stepped beneath the water of the dual showerheads, when there was a knock at the dressing room door.

"Ignore it," Aiden murmured, kissing the side of her neck. "Maybe they'll go away."

Dani didn't have any problem with that suggestion until she heard Jett's voice through the door.

"Dani? You all in there?" Jett yelled. There was the sound of other voices, all chattering away in the hallway. She recognized every voice, every laugh.

There were only a handful of people she wouldn't ignore in lieu of a shower with her guys. And they were apparently standing right outside the dressing room.

"Give me a minute," Dani yelled back. "Changing my clothes."

Neither Bryson nor Aiden called her to task for answering. In fact, Bryson had immediately started doing a quick clean—hair and body, sluicing off the soap and stepping out.

She and Aiden followed suit, showering off the sweat quickly, before turning off the water and drying off.

Bryson had always been the quickest to get ready. The man could, as he liked to say, "shit, shower, shave and be out the door in five minutes."

Crude, but accurate, Dani decided as Bryson threw on a clean t-shirt and shorts. He left her and Aiden drying off in the bathroom, closing the door behind them so he could let their guests in.

Bryson had become particularly close to Caleb when her foster brother had given him the ink he'd always wanted on his left pec. Dani had to admit. The new tat was hot.

Dani dressed quicker when she heard Mama Lewis talking

to Bryson about the show. She was dying to hear what she thought of it.

Loud cheers greeted her when she stepped into the room.

"What are you guys doing in here?" Dani asked. "You're going to miss the main act. Lucas Bryan is terrific."

Justin shrugged, unconcerned that they'd just vacated front row seats at a sold out concert. "We already saw the good stuff. The three of you were amazing. Twenty bucks says Lucas What's-His-Name is opening for you within a year."

Aiden grinned and slapped her brother on the back. "Man, I wouldn't mind that."

"You're our star, Dani," Mama said, walking over to hug her. "My God. You were just incredible."

Chloe came up next to give Dani a hug. "Mama cried when you dedicated that song to her."

"I didn't cry, Chloe," Mama Lewis said. "I just had something in my eye."

Dani giggled, knowing it was a lie. Even as she spoke, Mama Lewis had tears in her eyes.

"It was a beautiful song, baby girl."

She sensed Mama Lewis wanted to say more, but couldn't. Dani felt a lump form in her own throat. She'd written the song shortly after returning to Nashville. The lyrics had practically fallen out of her. It was a song about being lost, then found again and the undying love of a mother. As soon as it was finished, she'd sung it for the guys and Benji and they'd all insisted that it needed to be included on their first album. The music company agreed.

Given the response of tonight's audience, Dani suspected the song would begin to see some airplay soon.

"I wouldn't be here tonight if it weren't for you," Dani said.

Mama Lewis shook her head and started to disagree, but Dani wouldn't let her lessen the importance of her role. She'd taken Dani out of a terrifying, loveless home and given her a safe place to stay, unconditional love and the courage to reveal parts of herself that might never have seen the light of day.

"You told me I could sing. You were the first person to ever tell me my voice was beautiful. Then you bought me that guitar and encouraged me to explore, to let my talent grow. The guitar was the greatest gift I've ever gotten."

Mama Lewis smiled, not bothering to hide her tears any longer. She opened her arms and Dani walked toward her as the two of them embraced for several moments.

"I love you so much, Dani. And I'm so very proud of the woman you've become."

When they broke apart, Jett was there, wrapping his arm around her shoulders. "What do you say we go out and celebrate? Take Bourbon Street by storm."

Aiden chuckled. "Jesus. Is that even possible? That place is wilder than a Midwest tornado and that's on a weeknight."

Carissa took Jett's hands. "We can kick off the bar crawl at the Royal Lunch. Hurricanes are on the house."

Bryson walked over, lifting her hand to kiss her knuckles. "What do you say, bird? Want to hit the town? Show the Big Easy how we do it back in Nashville."

"I'm in." She took Bryson and Aiden's hands as they followed her family out of the arena.

And when she crawled into bed with them six hours later—six hours!—she realized it had indeed been the very best day of her life.

WINNER TAKES ALL
BIG EASY, BOOK 6

WINNER TAKES ALL

When Noah enters Food Fight, a new cooking competition show airing on the Food Network, he makes it to the finals and scores a trip to Vegas to compete. Problem is fellow finalist Hollie has captured his attention—in and out of the kitchen.

As the competition heats up, so does the sexual tension between Hollie and Noah. One night in Vegas, the simmering need explodes into full boil. But in this contest, it's winner takes all. Will they choose fame over forever? Or will they claim an even bigger prize?

PROLOGUE

ight One — Finale Script

Tom: Good Evening, and welcome to the special two-night finale of *Food Fight*, coming to you live from Sin City itself, Las Vegas! I'm Tom Federico and sitting beside me, as always, is the very lovely Angelica Stone. Angelica, I know I've said it before, but it bears repeating. What a season!

Angelica (light laughter): Oh Tom, that is so true. *Food Fight* is in its tenth season and this show just keeps getting hotter, with ratings that are through the roof. However, I don't think anyone could have foreseen exactly *how* exciting this season would be.

Tom: Well, I think we can attribute that success to the contestants. Have you ever seen a stronger field of competitors?

Angelica: No, Tom, I haven't. The judges have had their work cut out for them since the very first episode. Everyone seems to agree that this year's crop of wannabe chefs are the most talented and creative the show has ever seen.

Tom: Indeed they are. Why don't we do a quick recap of

the season for those viewers who may be joining us for the first time tonight?

Angelica: Great idea, Tom. The show started with sixteen cooks, all vying for the title of *Food Fight* Champion. They were quite a diverse group, coming from all areas of the United States.

Tom: Who could forget Seth Gilbert from Juneau, Alaska? He emerged as an early favorite, with some judges predicting he had the chops to go all the way.

Angelica: Yes, they did. America was stunned when he was eliminated in show seven after that fiasco with the undercooked venison.

Tom: And then there was Jillian Cohen, the little spitfire from New Jersey. She caused quite a spectacle in the kitchen, continually launching into her now-famous temper tantrums. How many times have you seen that picture of her waving the frying pan and cursing at judge Robert Conover?

Angelica: Too many. It came as little surprise when she was given the boot in the ninth round. Other strong competitors who ultimately didn't make the cut include Mark Pollis, a barbeque master from Little Rock, Arkansas, and Ava Emerson, the single mom from Chicago, who was cut in the very last episode. Her departure was simply heartbreaking.

Tom: Yes, it was. Which brings us to the big three. The last men standing, so to speak.

Angelica: Last men, plus one woman.

(Laugh together)

Tom: And what a woman!

Angelica: Now, behave yourself, Tom. Judge Jessica Rodriguez called Hollie Mills one of the most creative cooks she's ever met. The lovely vegetarian grew up in Carlisle, Pennsylvania. She's the only girl in a family of eight siblings who all work on the family's farm. And for the first time tonight, her family is in the audience. Hollie explained early in the season how difficult it was for her parents and brothers to leave their large farm for any length of time. I know she's delighted to have them all here. I caught a glimpse of her brothers, Tom, and let me just say, this born-and-bred city girl is considering a move to the country.

Tom: Angelica!

Angelica (giggle): I suspect most of the single women in America will share my sentiment after tonight. Hollie is an advocate of organic foods and has a huge fan following.

Tom: Including me, Angelica. I had the opportunity to try her stuffed Italian peppers with the vegetable risotto after that last show and I'm still dreaming about them. Hollie definitely has the talent to win this entire competition.

Angelica: Well now, don't get ahead of yourself, Tom, because she's facing some serious competition in Manny Walsh and Noah Lewis.

Tom: That she is. I'm not sure anyone expected Manny Walsh to make it this far. A weak performer at the beginning of the season, he was in the bottom three during the first four shows, only remaining by the skin of his teeth.

Angelica: And then, boom!

Tom: Boom, indeed. He's dubbed himself the hungry hippie and he certainly fits the part. He has thirty years on the other finalists and has the distinction of being the oldest cook to ever participate in the show. At fifty-six, the Californian has become well known for his tatty t-shirts and shaggy gray hair. According to behind-the-scenes reports, the other participants have started calling him Dad.

Angelica: He's definitely made this season fun with his quick wit and one-liners.

Tom: The entire country has enjoyed his humor, evident by

the fact that Manny has quite a few entertaining memes circulating on social media.

Angelica: But let's not forget Noah Lewis. This hot tamale hails from New Orleans and I think it's safe to say that in addition to melting butter, he's melted the hearts—and panties—of every woman in America.

Tom (chuckle): Be careful, Angelica. We're on live TV.

(Laugh together)

Angelica: We first heard Noah's personal story during the tenth show, when it was revealed he grew up in a foster home due to his real mother's addiction to drugs and inability to care for him.

Tom: Members of Noah's foster family, including Mama Lewis, have been staples in the studio audience, cheering Noah on from the very beginning. Their support of him has been truly touching. Now the entire family has flown to Vegas to watch Noah in the live finals. According to Noah, it's Mama Lewis's first time in the city and she's become quite a fan of the slot machines. He joked earlier that he was worried she wouldn't go back to New Orleans with them.

Angelica: I have to admit, I think I've developed a bit of a crush on his foster brother, Caliph. There's just something about a man with tattoos...

Tom: Down girl.

(Laugh together)

Angelica: There has also been speculation swirling since the fifth show—the partners cook-off—that Noah and Hollie are secretly dating, though both have adamantly denied the rumors.

Tom: It comes as no surprise those stories started. Hollie and Noah were partnered up for that unique challenge and the chemistry between them—according to judge Billy Oxford— was off the charts. It was during that show that viewers took notice and the two contestants have been fan favorites ever since. Their faces consistently grace the covers of tabloids and the media has declared them the most perfect "not a couple" couple, even going so far as to dub them "Nollie" in true Hollywood style.

Angelica: It looks like the contestants are about to take the stage. Tonight we'll see one of the three leave us. Then tomorrow night, we will return for the ultimate face-off between the final two competitors.

Tom: Who will be the next champion? Let's find out. Let the *Food Fight* begin!

CHAPTER ONE

"I'm so proud of you," Mama Lewis said, hugging Noah for the fiftieth time in less than an hour.

"I haven't won yet, Mama. I'm only in the finals."

Mama Lewis waved off his words as if they were pure nonsense. "You're going to win. You're too talented not to."

His brother Jett's wife, Carissa, walked up and linked her arm in his. "And if you don't, to hell with those judges. That just means we get to keep you to ourselves."

"We? Or you?" Noah teased. He'd been the head cook at Carissa's bar for the past three years. The Royal Lunch had been a hole-in-the-wall pub for nearly three decades, but it became a favorite restaurant of the locals after Noah took over in the kitchen. Now it was known for its delicious, reasonably priced Cajun fare.

"I'm not going to lie. Business is booming since you started taking the world by storm on *Food Fight*. I'm making enough money that I don't even mind the fact my beloved bar is now filled with blonde bimbos all hoping to win the heart of sex god Noah Lewis."

He shook his head, grinning, as his family laughed. They'd had a great deal of fun at his expense, now that he was apparently some sort of heartthrob. That whole part of the *Food Fight* gig was starting to wear thin.

He'd entered the competition on a lark. The show had held auditions in New Orleans and his brother Justin had talked him into trying out. After all, the prize was five hundred thousand dollars that the winner could use to start up their own restaurant.

Nine months ago, that much money had seemed like a pipe dream. Now, he was twenty-four hours and one rival away from possibly winning it all.

If only that rival wasn't Hollie.

He sighed. Noah hadn't been able to stop thinking about the woman since the first day she'd walked onto the set and blown him away with her sexy legs and butternut squash soup.

"Are you sure you don't want to come with us to see Cirque du Soleil?" Dani asked.

He shook his head as he smiled at his foster sister. They'd taken him out for a celebratory dinner after tonight's airing of *Food Fight*. He'd been really sad to see Manny cut from the competition. Dad, as he and Hollie affectionately referred to him, had always found a way to relieve the tension and make them laugh.

Noah had never appreciated that more than this evening. The previous shows had all been recorded in a studio. There was something about cooking on stage in front of a sold-out audience—as well as the millions of people watching live at home—that had him struggling to concentrate. "No, I'm heading back to the hotel. Calling it a night. Believe me, I'll be ready to paint the town red tomorrow with y'all once all this shit is over with."

Zac slapped him on the back. "I'd hardly call fame, fortune, and a smokin'-hot pretend girlfriend 'shit', bro."

His brother had been trying to talk Noah into dropping the pretend part of his so-called relationship with Hollie for months. Noah had considered it, but they were competitors, both vying for the same title.

Of course, winning the money had dropped down to number two on his list of desires lately, coming in way after taking Hollie to his bed and keeping her there for a decade or three.

Problem was this damn show. If he'd met her in a bar, he would have started a conversation and he would have asked her for a date. And then another. And then...

She was everything he'd ever wanted in a woman. Funny, smart, and an amazing cook. Plus she was completely dedicated to her family.

Family meant the world to Noah. Growing up as he and Zac had—with their mom constantly strung out and screwing strangers for drug money, rather than for food for her two young sons—he'd learned to appreciate what it meant to have people who cared about him. Mama Lewis had saved his life, taught him the meaning of unconditional love, and shown him that with a family at your back, you can take on the world.

Hollie talked about her brothers the same way he talked about his siblings. In her gorgeous blue eyes, the sun rose and set on their shoulders. He respected that. Understood it.

He glanced down the Strip, his vision assaulted by the flashing neon. "I'm going to head back to the Nyte. I have some sort of photo shoot in the morning and then interviews and sound tests right after lunch. I probably won't have a chance to see y'all until after the show tomorrow."

Mama Lewis gave him hug number fifty-one. "We'll be

right there in the front row. I'm so proud of you, Noah. Win or lose, you will always be my champion."

He tightened his arms around her. "Thank you for everything, Mama Lewis." He had taken the Lewis name the summer he'd turned eighteen. He'd gotten his first job as a lifeguard at a local pool, and had saved up every paycheck until he had enough to legally change his name. He hadn't told Mama Lewis what he'd planned until after it was official. She'd cried and hugged him and said no matter what his last name was, he would always be her son.

Noah said goodbye to the rest of his family and walked toward the Nyte. One of the perks of being a finalist in the top-rated *Food Fight* was his all-expenses-paid week at one of Las Vegas's most exclusive and luxurious resorts. When he'd told his sister Chloe where he was staying, she'd immediately Googled the place and the pictures had blown them both away. Then they'd checked out the room rates and *really* been blown away.

As he entered the hotel, he couldn't resist doing the same thing he had done since he'd arrived in Vegas three days earlier. He paused just over the threshold and looked around, taking in the sheer splendor. The Nyte was a sixty-story architectural wonder of gold, silver, crystal and glass. For a kid who'd grown up in the slums of New Orleans in a rat-infested hellhole, it felt as if he'd stepped out of Dorothy's black-and-white shack and straight into Oz.

One of the coolest aspects of the hotel was its themed suites that catered to specialty fantasies. The producer of *Food Fight* had pulled him aside after he was announced a finalist tonight to tell him that the owner of the hotel, Mr. Nyte, had offered to upgrade his and Hollie's rooms for the remainder of their stay.

They were both being given their choice of the fantasy suites and he'd known immediately which room he'd choose.

After all, he and Chloe had spent nearly an hour studying the Nyte's website, exploring all the options.

His sister had recently become engaged to her boyfriend, Blake, and she'd gone into great detail—his family had *no* boundaries—about the fantasy she would indulge in if she were rich enough to afford a room at the hotel. It had involved a bubble bath, champagne, massages and some pretty serious bondage. Noah had remained silent during Chloe's description, trying to block out the image of his sister having sex and fighting a growing erection as he imagined he and Hollie enacting the exact same fantasy.

His visual tour of the place was interrupted when a large, boisterous group entered the hotel behind him. He turned to find Hollie, surrounded by seven huge, hulking men.

He knew her bio by heart, knew she was the only girl in a family of eight. It was something else they had in common—large families. Mama Lewis had four biological kids, plus three fosters—him, Zac and Dani.

The Mills clan spotted him within seconds and Noah was treated to Hollie's smiling eyes along with fourteen narrowed, suspicious ones. God, it would be a miracle if Hollie had ever had a boyfriend. The Mills boys were an intimidating force.

Hollie waved. "Hey, Noah. Congratulations."

"Same to you," Noah said. Immediately after the show had ended, they had both been engulfed in the swarms that were their families. He hadn't had a chance to talk to her since they'd made the cut.

Hollie had introduced him to her brothers this afternoon as they'd checked out their kitchen stations, but Noah couldn't remember a single one of their names. He'd been too focused on Hollie.

"Thanks for walking me back, guys," Hollie said, clearly dismissing her brothers. He suspected she felt the same way he did. Overwhelmed and longing for some peace and quiet. It had been a whirlwind few days and Noah was grateful the producers had agreed to give them the night off to mentally prepare and rest up for the finale.

Each of her brothers gave her a good-night hug, while treating Noah to a warning glare. He struggled not to laugh at their obvious intimidation tactics. He'd spent the last decade of his life in a house full of alpha males and the trait had rubbed off. It would take more than the evil eye to scare him.

Hollie waved as her brothers reluctantly left her alone with him. She sighed once they left and he noticed her shoulders begin to relax.

"I love my brothers," she said, "but they tend to be a bit overprotective."

"I'm not going to fault them for that." Noah was pleased to have a few minutes alone with her. Those moments were too few and far between. When they'd been filming the original televised shows, the other contestants had constantly surrounded them. Hollie had joked once it felt as if they were all summer camp counselors, always traveling around in a big pack. For three months they'd stayed in a cheap hotel on the outskirts of Hollywood and they had done everything with the cast and crew, enjoying their anonymity and obscurity. He'd said goodbye to Hollie at LAX after the last recorded show was filmed—and then gone back to New Orleans and had his life turned on its head.

Once the show began airing, his relatively peaceful life had vanished. As each subsequent episode aired, the number of paparazzi stalking him doubled. He'd appeared on talk shows, been invited to red carpet movie premieres and even done an interview last week with Jimmy Fallon on *The Tonight Show*. Hollie had been there through all of it, the two of them feeling more like a team than adversaries. His five minutes of fame was just about over and, while Noah had enjoyed every minute of the journey, he wouldn't mind returning to a calmer existence.

"Last night," he said, more for himself than her. For nine months, they'd been tied together by a show, by a common goal. After tomorrow, one of them would take home the title and the money, while the other would just go home.

He was going to miss her. More than he cared to admit.

"I know. I can't believe it. I'm trying to decide if I'm relieved or disappointed that it's almost over."

He grinned. As always, she summed up his feelings perfectly.

And then, as if on cue, the paparazzi swarmed, reminding them why the end wasn't necessarily a bad thing.

Noah put his arm around her shoulders as the cameramen pushed closer, asking them a bunch of personal questions that had him seeing red.

Fortunately, the Nyte was more than prepared for this type of onslaught. Within minutes, two security guards pushed their way through the crowd, a petite spitfire hot on their heels, telling the paparazzi in no uncertain terms to disperse.

Noah was slightly amazed to see so many grown men almost cower before the tiny woman. The entire ordeal lasted less than five minutes.

"I'm Lucy Pine, head of security. I'm sorry about that. We'd given the press access for a brief interview with Manny Walsh. We did *not* give them access to you."

At that moment, another hotel employee arrived. "Mr. Lewis. Ms. Mills. I'm Laird Beckett, the resort manager. I hope you're both okay."

"We're fine," Hollie said as Noah struggled to contain the jealous beast that didn't like the way Laird Beckett was smiling at her. The man was good looking and he knew it. He oozed charm in a way that probably would have had his sisters Chloe and Dani swooning. He didn't enjoy seeing that superpower unleashed on Hollie.

Noah hadn't released Hollie after the cameramen descended and the alpha male inside him couldn't resist tightening his hold. When Beckett's gaze caught his, he knew the man understood the subtle warning to back off.

Beckett raised his hand, gesturing for the valet. "This is Tripp Ross. Tripp, did you move Mr. Lewis's and Ms. Mills's luggage to their new rooms?"

Tripp hesitated briefly, looking slightly confused before nodding. "Um, yes sir."

"Very good. As you know, it's a keyless entry. Your thumbprint will open the door. I believe you received your new room numbers via text?"

Noah and Hollie nodded. He'd gotten the text during dinner with his family. He'd debated inviting Chloe back to see the room he'd selected, but something had held him back. Probably embarrassment. He didn't need his big sister to know how deeply her fantasy had resonated with him.

"There are voice-activated controls in the rooms, full wet bars, and we offer butler and maid services as well if you so desire."

"Wow," Hollie murmured. "I could get used to this place."

Mr. Beckett grinned. "I don't expect you'll have any more trouble, but Lucy will escort you to the elevator just in case. Please let me know if you need anything and enjoy the rest of your stay."

Mr. Beckett left and Noah felt like grinning when Hollie ignored the man's departure, her attention remaining on him.

"If you'll follow me." Lucy turned, walking briskly toward the elevator. Once they were there, she pushed the up button and waited until the doors slid open.

"If you have any more trouble with the press during your stay, call me. I'll take care of it."

With that, she was gone, and Noah was once again alone with Hollie.

As they stepped into the empty elevator, Noah asked, "What floor?"

"Fifteen."

Hollie was on the same floor he was. Noah pressed the button, deciding then and there it was fate kicking him in the ass, telling him to do what he'd dreamed of doing for the past nine months.

Without a word, he turned to Hollie, grasped the back of her neck and kissed her.

CHAPTER TWO

Hollie didn't have time to move as Noah leaned toward her, his lips crushing hers in what was undoubtedly the greatest kiss of her life. She didn't bother to question her sanity or give herself a single second to succumb to common sense. She'd wanted to kiss Noah since the first day she'd seen him on the set. She had taken one look at his smoldering chocolate-brown eyes, a taste of his red beans and rice, and fallen head over heels in lust.

Those feelings had only continued to grow as the months passed. But her desires stopped being based on "oh my God, he's hot" and more on "Wow, he's such a nice guy".

Right now, she wasn't thinking about his looks *or* his personality. She was too wrapped up in the heat pooling between her thighs. She wondered what would happen if she hit the emergency stop button on the elevator. How long would that give them to take care of business?

Because she had lots of unfinished business with Noah Lewis. Months; worth of pent-up horniness and two million and twelve raunchy fantasies.

He forced her mouth open, his tongue diving in to explore. She never would have pegged him as such an aggressive kisser. Her lady parts liked it. A lot.

Just then, the elevator slowed to a stop. Though she tried to hold him close, Noah managed to break free of her grip just before the doors slid open. She was flushed, breathing heavily and considering ripping off her bra, simply because it was rubbing against her hard nipples.

Fortunately, unlike her, Noah had retained some small shred of control. Which was very lucky when Isaac Thornton, *Food Fight's* producer, stepped into the elevator.

"There are my superstars," he said with a smile as the doors closed. She glanced at the number panel. They'd only gone up seven flights. Noah had kissed her so senseless, she'd expected to discover they'd ridden all the way up to the penthouse, smashed through the glass ceiling and were currently doing a Willy Wonka-style tour of the city.

Isaac glanced at his watch. "Early night?"

Noah nodded. "Yeah. I just ran into Hollie in the lobby. Apparently she had the same plan. Big day tomorrow."

Isaac was clearly pleased to hear they weren't intending to party their asses off all night and show up for the live finale hungover. "This is why you two are still in the game. You take the competition seriously."

Finally, after a lifetime, the doors slid open on the fifteenth floor. She and Noah both stepped off after saying good night. If Isaac thought it was weird they were staying on the same floor, he had the good grace not to say so.

"You're on the fifteenth floor too?" Hollie asked.

"Yep."

Hollie wondered what that meant. Did all the rooms on this floor have a similar theme? When she found out she could choose a fantasy suite for the rest of the week, she hadn't hesitated to select the one that spoke to her soul. The one that so closely matched her dreams.

She was shocked when Noah took her hand and led her to room 1503.

"How did you know this was my room?" she asked.

Noah frowned then tugged his cell phone from his pocket. "I was actually taking you to *my* room." He flicked open his messages and showed her the text he'd received from the hotel's front desk clerk.

She dug her phone out of her purse and did the same.

CHAPTER THREE

They'd been given the same room.

Had the Nyte made a mistake?

If they had, Noah didn't seem to be in any hurry to correct it. "Open the door," he said, his voice deep, almost demanding.

Her body reacted as if she'd been struck by lightning.

What if the front desk clerk had made a mistake and sent Noah her room number instead of his own? What would Noah say when he discovered her secret fantasy?

Then again, what if *she* was standing outside Noah's room? She was dying to know what he'd selected for the remainder of his stay.

He leaned closer, placing a kiss on her cheek, his hot breath causing her stomach to flip-flop in anticipation.

"Open it, Hollie."

She placed her thumb against the keypad and the locks clicked. It was her room. Her fantasy.

She opened the door. Noah caught her wrist before she could enter, holding her back, and together they looked inside.

The harem room was more decadent, more scandalously sensual than she'd imagined.

"Oh my God," she whispered breathlessly.

What was she doing? This room revealed far too much about her desires to a man she'd never even kissed until ten minutes ago.

"If you step over that threshold, we're playing the fantasy out."

Hollie had never heard Noah use that voice, that deep, rich, dark-chocolate tone that had her two seconds away from stripping naked in the hallway and kneeling at his feet.

"Okay."

He grinned at her quick capitulation. "Jesus. I expected *you* to be the voice of reason."

She frowned, confused. "What?"

Noah shook his head. "Oh no. If you're not going to stand here and tell me we're idiots to start this, the night before the final show, then *I'm* sure as hell not going to say it."

She giggled. "Um, hate to break it to you, but I think you just did."

Hollie expected Noah to laugh, but his face suddenly became too serious, too intense.

"I've wanted you from day one," he confessed.

"Same with me."

"It's only one more night. We could—"

She shook her head, cutting him off before he could finish the thought. "No. Please. I don't want to wait any longer."

"Tomorrow is going to be a big enough head game as it is, Holl. I don't want to mess things up for you. You deserve to walk onto that stage with your eyes on the prize and nothing else."

She tilted her head. "And you don't deserve the same?"

"I haven't been looking at anything except you since the fifth show."

She smiled. "The partner round."

"Working with you in that kitchen was the highlight of my year. You're such a good freaking cook."

Hollie took his hand in hers and squeezed. "I feel the same way about you. There have been so many shows since then when I was losing my shit, stressing out. I'd look at you, watch you work with such confidence, and then you'd give me that wink and secret smile that said you believed in me, and all the anxiety just vanished. Truth is...right now? I'm Team Noah."

"Great. We're both fucked. Because I'm currently president of your fan club."

"Tonight isn't about the contest, is it?"

Noah shook his head. "No. Not for me."

She reached up and cupped his cheek affectionately. "It's not for me either."

He gave her a sultry look that set her panties on fire. "So... are you going in? Are you going to be my harem girl? I won't lie. I have some pretty serious plans for you if you walk through that door."

Hollie bit her lip as she considered his offer. Noah was clearly warning her, giving her an out. Her previous sexual experiences had been so vanilla, she was embarrassed to claim them. She'd grown up in a fairly small town with seven brothers. Who the hell was going to do anything even remotely interesting with her *or* to her in that scenario?

"I want to be yours, want to belong to you."

"Do you know what a safe word is?" he asked.

She shook her head, prompting a big smile from him. He placed his forehead against hers. "You're so fucking perfect."

Hollie had no idea what she'd done to provoke that

comment, but she'd never felt more cherished, more special in her life. Her heart beat a little bit faster.

"If I do anything you hate, just say no or stop and I will."

She had a feeling there was more to his so-called safe word than that. After all, those words were pretty universal for "get your hands off me", but she didn't question him. This was Noah.

Over the past nine months, he'd become her friend, a kindred spirit, someone she could rely on and trust. Her brothers would go mad if they knew what she was about to do. They would yell, rant and rave, and tell her he was trying to sabotage her chances at the championship. But she knew...deep down in her heart...nothing could be further from the truth.

With her decision made, Hollie gave Noah a sultry come-hither glance and stepped into the room.

She couldn't hold back her giddy laughter when Noah followed her inside and shut the door. The sound, however, was cut short when he pushed her against the wall and kissed her as if his life depended on it. She honestly wouldn't mind if all he wanted to do was this and nothing more tonight. She'd show up tomorrow on the set with swollen, chapped lips and never regret it for a second.

Hollie wrapped her arms around his shoulders, desperate to keep him close. For so many months she'd dreamt of this moment. She should have known Noah would take her expectations and blow them out of the water.

His tongue tangled with hers. He tasted like red wine and tiramisu. He was delicious, her new favorite treat.

When he broke the contact of their lips, he gave her that charming grin that had captured her attention during the very first show. So many of their competitors had been cutthroat, aggressive, and their wolfish smiles were definitely meant to intimidate. Then Hollie had glanced across the kitchen and seen Noah. He'd caught her eye and given her that sweet, silly grin that seemed to say "Get a load of these clowns". She'd actually giggled, even though he'd been on the other side of the room and hadn't said a word.

"While I realize I run the risk of sounding like a complete tool, I have to admit I would give up cooking forever if I could have just one of your kisses every single day for the rest of my life."

Hollie wasn't sure anyone had ever said anything so romantic to her. Most of the guys she'd dated were total duds, clueless wonders who talked about sports with more emotion than their relationship.

"Just one kiss a day?" she asked.

"Greedy woman. I like your style." Noah kissed her again, but he didn't let his lips linger this time.

They both turned to study the room. It was unlike anything she'd ever seen. Utter decadence, sensual elegance. Though it was a suite, it had an open floor plan. Everything was in one large room, with the exception of a closed door that she assumed led to the bathroom.

To the right was the sitting area decorated in rich hues of gold and burgundy; large pillows covered the floor and surrounded a rounded, plush couch that Hollie was dying to sink into. The left side of the room contained a giant king-size four-poster bed, with a sheer canopy that reminded her of that old Indiana Jones movie—the one with the blonde actress.

She tried to soak in the beauty of it, but her gaze couldn't focus on more than the four silk scarves tied to each post, clearly there to bind a willful slave.

Noah certainly fit the bill looking far-too-much like the exotic sheik of her dreams with his dark eyes, black hair, and tanned skin. His jaw was covered with just a hint of that five o'clock shadow she'd always found so damn sexy on men.

Her pussy fluttered in nervous, excited, yes-please antic-ipation.

The corner nearest the door held the kitchenette, complete with a cozy, intimate table for two, decorated with a rich red tablecloth and a vase of white roses. A bottle of champagne rested in a chiller full of ice, with a dish of the ripest, most luscious-looking strawberries sitting next to it.

Between the sitting area and the bed, near the floor-to-ceiling window was the largest, most inviting hot tub she'd ever seen. It was heart-shaped, surrounded by rose petals and illuminated by candles. The steam rising from it called to her. The entire suite invited indulgence and screamed of carnal pleasure.

"Wow," she whispered.

"It's incredible," Noah agreed.

"How did they know when we would return?"

Noah shrugged. "Beckett said these rooms had maid and butler service. Maybe he called someone to get this set up when he spotted us in the lobby."

"That makes sense."

Then he gestured to their suitcases, sitting next to each other on stands by the bed. "Why do I feel like the hotel put us here together on purpose?"

"This was your fantasy too?"

Noah nodded.

Hollie wasn't sure how to respond. He wanted this. He'd chosen it.

It was clear someone had set the scene for seduction and romance. But who? And why?

Noah walked over to an open closet and pulled out a colorful outfit. His eyes darkened hungrily as she took in the harem slave attire. The gold lamé bra with halter ties was adorned with gold coins. The matching thong had an attached sheer purple skirt—if she could call the two pieces that draped over the front and back a skirt—that didn't leave much to the imagination.

The outfit was sexy and revealing and nothing Hollie would ever have imagined herself wearing. However, her gaze was locked on the lone accessory also hanging from the hanger.

A gold chain was attached to a collar.

"I'd love to see you in this."

Noah hadn't needed to speak that desire, it was apparent in this gaze.

Hollie nodded slowly. She wanted to wear it for him. All of it. She glanced at the scarves on the bed once more as her fantasies took shape, molding themselves to everything this room invited, promised.

"I think we need to discuss that safe-word thing again," she said, slightly shocked at what she was about to confess. She knew how she wanted this night to play out and she knew—deep down inside—he was the man to give her exactly what she wanted.

Noah's brows furrowed. "Okay. What do you mean?"

She gave him a sexy smile. "I don't intend to be a good little slave." She stepped closer as her voice lowered, the sound little more than a whisper. "You've captured me, but you haven't claimed me. Not yet. I won't surrender willingly."

Noah's eyes narrowed with a hunger that was almost palpable. "You're going to fight me?" His question was spoken in a deep voice that sent shivers along her spine.

She nodded.

He reached out and gripped her wrist, shackling it tightly, letting her feel exactly what she was inviting. "Your safe word is risotto. Say that and it ends. That's the only word that will make me stop. Do you understand?"

Hollie licked her lips, her mouth suddenly going dry. His

dark words provoked the exact reaction she wanted to feel—fear laced with heart-pumping, pussy-throbbing desire. She wanted to belong to him, but by God, he had to prove he was worthy of her submission.

She was so overwhelmed, she failed to respond.

Noah hadn't missed that fact. "Say it, Hollie. Say the word. Let me hear it."

"Risotto," she whispered. The word reminded her of the night the two of them had been paired up for the partner challenge. There had been given five ingredients hidden on the table in front of them. Each team had a different grain and was told to create a delicious side dish. She and Noah had received risotto and that was the night that her star—and his—began to rise. People began to recognize her when she went out in public and her face first appeared on the cover of a tabloid, the article mistakenly linking her and Noah romantically, claiming they were engaged in a scandalous, secret affair.

"Take off your clothes."

She reared back, surprised when he returned the harem girl outfit to the closet.

"What?"

He returned and captured both of her wrists with one of his hands, shackling them in front of her as he led her toward the hot tub. Her affable, good-natured friend had vanished. What remained was this demanding, imperious, sexy-as-fuck stranger. "My slaves only wear clothing when it pleases me. And I don't repeat myself. *Ever.*"

She had told him she'd fight him. That was certainly what she'd planned, but there was something about his tone, the way he looked at her, that had her fingers itching to tear off every scrap of material hiding her body from his view.

Hollie pushed that desire away. Noah was offering her something she'd never had the guts to ask for before. She wasn't going to let this opportunity slip away. She tugged her hands out of his grasp. Clearly he thought she was going to comply. Otherwise, he would never have let her go so easily.

She took a step away as she reached for the first button on her blouse. He watched with avid attention, not noticing at first when she continued to back away. She recognized the exact second he realized she didn't plan to obey his command.

He took a predatory step closer, stalking her slowly, keeping his motions steady.

Her heart raced, her breathing growing more rapid, shallow.

"Hollie."

The way he used her name threw her off-guard. In her mind, she'd always been someone else in her fantasy, someone adventurous, exotic, a hell of a lot more interesting than plain old Hollie Mills from Carlisle, Pennsylvania.

She jerked when she backed herself against one of the tall posts at the bottom of the bed. She started to twist toward the left, intent on running away, but Noah anticipated her move before she made it.

He gripped her arms with a strength that should have terrified her. Instead, her traitorous body reacted instantly. Her nipples budded, her panties went wet and a flash of pure electricity shot straight to her pussy, leaving her breathless and on the verge of begging.

While Hollie struggled to regain control of her overwhelming need, Noah made short work of securing her hands behind her back, around the post of the bed. She tugged and expected the silk to give way, but Noah wasn't playing around. Apparently he knew his stuff when it came to knots.

Without hesitance, his fingers worked free the buttons of her blouse until it hung open, revealing her simple white bra. She wished she'd realized her night was going to take such an amazing turn. She would have gone for Hootchie Mama over Catholic Schoolgirl. Her plain white panties were worse than the bra. They weren't exactly granny style, but they were damn close.

Of course, given the way Noah studied her breasts, his gaze practically stroking her cleavage, it appeared he didn't mind.

She bumped against the post roughly when his hands reached for the fastening of her skirt. For the past nine months, she had lived in a constant state of horniness, but now that she was here, the moment of truth at hand, everything was going too fast.

"Noah," she gasped.

His hands left her skirt, his fingers tangling in her hair, tugging it with a force that had her scalp tingling and her eyes watering. It also had her so fucking turned on, she wasn't completely sure she hadn't just had a mini-orgasm.

"Master," he said gruffly. "You will only call me Master."

In every other instance of her life, that demand would have had her scoffing. Refusing. This was clearly the one exception.

God, Hollie. You're supposed to be fighting him.

"I'll never call you that." The words sounded breathy and every bit like the lie they were.

The smile he gave her looked dangerous and sexy and—oh God—her body trembled again. What the hell was going on? She was in physical, aching pain. If he didn't fuck her soon, she was pretty sure she'd die.

Noah released her hair. She missed the rough touch instantly. Until his hands returned to her skirt, making short work of the zipper. The material slid to the floor with little effort.

He peeled her panties away next and once again she wanted to ask him to slow down. Which was ridiculous because what she really needed was for him to hurry up.

"Kick them off," he demanded when her panties joined her skirt on the floor. "Toe off those sandals as well."

She considered refusing, but she was too excited to see what came next. She did as he asked. Once more, Noah wasted no time taking what he wanted. He nudged at the inside of her ankles.

"Spread your legs apart."

Her mouth opened as she prepared to say no. Noah didn't give her a chance. His lips captured hers in a hard kiss that was more possessive than caring.

When he released her, his eyes were narrowed. "There are consequences to challenging me. Be very sure you're willing to pay the price."

Holy shit. Could he be any fucking sexier? Part of her wanted to ask what the consequences were, but he pressed against her ankle again.

Her legs parted of their own volition. She expected him to touch her. God knew that was what she wanted—needed—him to do.

She was shocked when instead he knelt before her. With his thumbs, he tugged her mons apart, his face so close to her pussy she could feel the heat of his breath. He looked at her so closely, she blushed. Hollie had never been the subject of such intense scrutiny. She understood his intention. She was to be his slave, his possession. She was his to look at, to play with, and —if he so desired—to give away to someone else.

That thought sparked something, a dirty desire she'd kept buried deep. He'd tapped into her needs and he was flushing them out, driving them into the bright light and forcing her to face them, acknowledge them.

"My servants will shave you; keep you bare for my touch, my kisses." He spoke in a matter-of-fact voice that had her not only believing those servants existed, but certain she wanted them to do exactly what he'd said.

He tugged on her pubic hair as he spoke, sparking more of those confusing pleasurably painful sensations.

Hollie shook her head as if to resist his words, wishing she had the breath to speak.

"Do you want me to touch you, Hollie? Do you want me to fuck your virgin pussy and ass with my big cock?"

Hollie's face flamed with heat—the perfect melding of shock, embarrassment and desire.

"Noah," she whispered, her eyelids drifting shut as she tried to hide her reactions. He didn't allow her the escape.

He pulled her pubic hair again, harder this time.

She gasped as her eyes flew open, his gaze capturing hers.

"Master," he corrected. He waited for her to say it, but she pursed her lips. Refused. He seemed to enjoy that refusal. She had no doubt he'd pull that title out of her before the night was over. And what was more, he'd enjoy doing so.

"It will hurt the first time," he continued. "But soon you'll come to love it, to want it more than your next breath. Soon, you'll be begging me to take you. Over and over."

She was on the verge of doing that right now.

So lame, Hollie. Fight him. This is your fantasy. Stop fucking it up.

"Never," she said, proud of the strength in her voice.

When he stood up without touching her, she had to bite her lower lip to take back her denial. To stop herself from giving in and starting the pleading right now. That desire grew stronger when he untied her hands.

She didn't want to be free. Not yet.

Not ever.

That thought took her aback. This was her first night with

Noah and already her heart was hoping for more. So much more.

Which was dangerous, considering the outcome of tomorrow night's show would change everything for them. One of them would be crowned the champion and awarded a huge sum of money that would allow them to make all their dreams come true. The other would leave with nothing.

While she tried to tell herself she could handle it—one way or the other—she wasn't sure that was the truth.

How would Noah react if she won? Would he get pissed off? Walk away from her?

And what happened if *he* won? Would he return to New Orleans? Open his restaurant there? He was a Big Easy boy—born and bred in the city—while she was a country-bumpkin farm girl from PA. There were one thousand, one hundred and forty miles between them. She knew because she'd looked it up one night.

Regardless of what happened tonight, tomorrow was going to change everything.

She just didn't know how.

CHAPTER FOUR

Once he untied her hands, Noah pushed her blouse over her shoulders. He was anxious to peel that damn bra away so he could see her breasts. He'd jacked off no less than a hundred times as he imagined her naked. As her popularity on the show had grown, the producers had decided to cash in on her beauty. Her clothing had become more revealing with each subsequent appearance and tonight's attire had been no different. Though she'd worn an apron during the actual cooking, he'd caught more than a few peeks of her sexy cleavage as she worked. It had distracted him so much, he'd almost forgotten to add the honey to his Mrouzia.

He added the bra to the pile of clothing on the floor.

Finally, she was naked. Noah took a step back, treating himself to a long, hard look at her. She was the most beautiful woman he'd ever seen. His cock thickened at the sight, the constriction of his jeans almost unbearably painful.

Despite his discomfort, he didn't seek to shed the denim. If he took off his pants right now, it was game over. He'd shove her down on that bed and fuck her, fantasy be damned.

And while he didn't think Hollie would complain, he wasn't about to let the night end so soon. Her reactions to his commands were heady. She wasn't holding anything back.

"Get into the tub. I prefer my slaves be freshly cleaned before coming to me."

She glanced at the hot tub, then back at him. He wondered how far she'd allow him to go with this role-play before she balked.

Given the way she obeyed, stepping into the water, it appeared he had quite a bit more leeway.

She sank into the tub until only her head and the tops of her shoulders broke the surface. He suspected she was trying to hide from him.

Time to up the ante.

He reached for the hem of his shirt and tugged it over his head. His efforts at the gym were rewarded when she treated him to a soft appreciative inhalation.

Noah took a steadying breath before unfastening his jeans and pushing them, his boxers and his shoes off. He'd vowed to take his time, but the way her auburn hair curled in the steam had him longing to run his fingers through it once more. Had him itching to grab a handful of it as he directed her mouth toward his cock, using that grip to hold her still as he fucked her—

Jesus, Noah. Take it easy, buddy.

He needed to concentrate on the here and now. Too many more visions like that and he'd blow before he ever touched her.

Hollie's eyes remained locked on his cock, which wasn't helping his control, either. He stepped into the tub and sank down onto the seat. A jet hit his lower back and he groaned aloud at the relaxing sensation.

"It's nice, isn't it?"

He nodded. She was breaking character, but he let her.

This was their first time, and, God willing, it wouldn't be their last. Noah wanted her to want *him* as much as she seemed to enjoy this dominant sheik. "Long day."

She smiled. "Tomorrow will be longer."

He shifted on the seat as he reached for her. He didn't like the distance between them. Noah was surprised when she moved toward him easily, without resistance. He turned her so her back rested against his chest, allowing him to wrap his arms around her waist.

She sighed contentedly.

"Would you prefer to call it a night? Turn in early to rest?" If she said yes, Noah would kick his own ass for asking the question, but there was a part of him that was still worried about what would happen tomorrow.

Noah wanted to say it didn't matter. Win or lose, his feelings would remain the same. But at heart, they were both serious competitors—that was evident by the fact they were in the finals—and the prize was something that would definitely change one of their lives forever. Five hundred grand and the opportunity to open their own restaurant were huge—for him and for Hollie.

Then it occurred to him he'd never asked about her plans for the money. Until today, he hadn't thought about much more than getting to this point, to making the finals. Now, the idea that he could win it all was a very real possibility. All he had to do was shatter Hollie's dreams.

He wasn't aware that he'd tightened his grip on her until he felt her hands on his wrists. She glanced over her shoulder at him.

"Are you okay?"

He nodded, and then pushed his fears away. He wasn't going to let his worries ruin what was shaping up to be one of the best nights of his life. There was time to deal with the fallout tomorrow. For now, he wanted her.

Time to put them back on track. Reaching toward the ledge, he grabbed the bottle of bath gel. Squeezing some onto his palm, he rubbed his hands together and worked up a lather on her breasts.

Hollie's head rested on his shoulder, her quiet mews and stillness led him to believe she'd fall asleep if he continued this way. But sleep wasn't on the agenda. Not for a few more hours anyway.

He gripped her nipples between his forefingers and thumbs and began to increase the pressure. Hollie's spine stiffened and she started to pull away. He held fast, keeping her trapped against him.

"Noah," she cried out as he pinched the tight nubs harder.

He released her then gently rubbed away the pain. He half expected to hear her use her safe word, so he was surprised when she sighed as if confused.

"I don't understand...why..."

"Why what?"

"That hurt."

He didn't interrupt her. Instead, he gave her time to gather her thoughts, to choose her words. She obviously had more to say.

"But I loved it. It makes me ache for more."

In that moment, Noah understood exactly how fucked he was. Hollie was truly the most perfect woman in the world. He'd never found anyone he connected with on every single level. But with her, there was no denying she was the yin to his yang, the salt to his pepper.

He nipped her shoulder, just a tiny, quick bite that he then soothed with his tongue. "Your body knows exactly who its Master is. Even if your head isn't ready to admit it yet."

She narrowed her eyes as she glanced at him over her shoulder. She was attempting for a rebellious look, but falling short. Her face was flushed and her breathing too unsteady.

"I'll never be yours. I'm a free woman."

He chuckled darkly and the sound had the desired effect. It pulled her back into the fantasy.

She tried to escape his grip. He let her manage to put a couple of feet between them before he grasped her upper arm and twisted her until they were facing each other. Reaching for the body gel, he gently squeezed her arm.

"Put out your palm."

She shook her head defiantly. Noah grabbed her wrist, amused when she kept her hand clenched in a tight fist.

"Open it now, Hollie, or I'll be forced to punish you."

"Punish me how?"

Her question was too curious, without an ounce of fear behind it. She liked the idea. But how was she playing it out in her mind? He wondered what she would think of his response.

"I'll yank you out of this tub, turn you over my knee and spank your bare, wet ass until it's as red as those strawberries over there on the counter."

She bit her lower lip, clearly letting that image play out in her mind. Then she threw her head back haughtily. "You wouldn't dare."

Noah loved the way she challenged him. "You've earned yourself ten smacks when we're finished in here. Open your hand *now* or the number increases."

Her fingers slowly loosened. "There," she said once her palm was flat. "Now you don't have to spank me."

He kept his expression stern despite his desire to kiss the tip of her cute little nose. "The punishment stands. I told you. I don't repeat myself."

"But—"

He cut off her argument with a hard kiss as he dropped the shower gel. He intended to keep it quick, but the second his lips touched hers, he couldn't resist lingering. With one hand, Noah kept a tight grip on her wrist while he wrapped the other around the back of her neck, holding her to him.

His tongue touched hers and he tried to recall if he'd ever tasted anything sweeter than Hollie. Nothing came to mind. And he had a sweet tooth.

After several heated minutes, he finally managed to pull away. It took him a few seconds to remember his plan. The sight of her open palm reminded him.

Retrieving the bath gel once more, he placed a dollop in her hand. "Scrub me, pet."

She hesitated for only a moment, and then reached toward his chest.

He shook his head. "Lower."

Interestingly enough, she didn't balk at the order. Her hand encircled his cock tightly, the soap allowing her fingers to glide smoothly.

Noah clenched his teeth, praying for control. The idea of her with her lips wrapped around his dick returned.

He grasped her wrist and slowed her strokes. The first time he came, he was going to be inside her. His time with her was limited—perhaps to just this one night—so every orgasm was going to count.

"Very good," he murmured. He pulled her hand away from him, noticing her attempt to cling tighter. "Now it's your turn. Open your legs."

She glanced around the room. Noah wondered if she'd try to escape. He knew she was determined to put up at least a token resistance, but the clever woman wasn't about to let this opportunity pass her by. He loved that her sex drive matched his so perfectly.

She parted her legs.

He leaned closer and placed a soft kiss on her cheek before whispering in her ear. "You're mine, little pet. Mine to play with, to take however I want."

As he spoke, he stroked the inside of her thighs. Noah felt her tremble. Hollie never held anything back in the kitchen, putting it all on the line, every time. Obviously the same held true in the bedroom. Her commitment to the fantasy was pulling him in as well. He wanted to possess her, to keep her his captive. Like the most doting sheik, he'd pamper and cherish her. Give her jewels and clothing, a soft bed and long, wet kisses.

Hollie's hands gripped his shoulders. "Noah."

"Master," he murmured again. "You will call me that before the night is over."

Her fingers tightened, but she didn't deny his assertion again.

He stroked her clit, just a brief, barely there touch.

She released her breath loudly. "Please. God."

"What, angel? What do you want?"

"Touch me. Harder."

Noah rubbed her clit once more, adding only a tiny bit of pressure. She white-knuckled his shoulders, her nails digging into his skin. It burned, but like her, Noah didn't mind a little pain with his pleasure.

"More. I can't take this. I need more." Her pleading was almost his undoing. Almost.

He ran a single finger from her clit to her anus, one quick journey, and then he pulled away again.

"God. Enough, Noah!"

She leaned forward and bit him, right on the pec.

Noah reared back in shock...and arousal.

Any semblance of control he'd maintained fell away. When

he touched her again, he drove two fingers deep into her pussy. Her inner muscles fluttered against him, clenched. She was already there, right on the verge of coming.

Noah considered giving her the push she needed, but changed his mind. He slid his fingers out slowly and when he pressed in the second time, it was with less force, more gently.

It pissed off his wild cat.

Hollie reached out and grabbed his cock, intent on dragging him to the spot she wanted him. He would have laughed if her hand wasn't dragging him closer to that point of no return, where she was already languishing.

He tried to pry her hand away, but her grip was tenacious. "In me. Now."

Her demanding tone helped center him. There was only one person running this show and it was him.

"Let go, Hollie." Something in his voice must have warned her she was on thin ice. She released him instantly.

"Please," she whispered.

Noah couldn't have refused her if his life depended on it. He thrust three fingers into her pussy, fucking her rapidly and with a strength he'd never used before with his previous lovers.

Hollie exploded instantly. Her body trembled, her fists slammed against his chest and she cried out his name. Her inner muscles flexed violently against his fingers, the climax stretching out longer than he would have imagined.

When it finally started to wane, he slowly withdrew, loving the way Hollie sank into his embrace. She clung to him as she struggled to regain her breath.

He held her, swaying slowly.

After a few minutes, she lifted her head, her gaze finding his. "That was unbelievable."

Noah grinned. "That was just the first course."

She laughed lightly. "Bon appétit."

CHAPTER FIVE

ollie stepped out of the tub as Noah held open a large white towel for her. When he wrapped her in the soft cotton, she sighed happily, trying to recall a time she'd ever been so coddled or cared for.

After all, she was smack-dab in the middle of eight kids. She and her twin brother were siblings four and five. As such, by the time they'd come along, her parents already had their hands full.

While she'd always been loved, she had learned at a very young age to fend for herself when it came to taking what she wanted. She had seven huge, hungry, boisterous brothers who, though overprotective when it came to strangers, had no compunction stealing her food, her toys and her spot on the couch when she stood up to go to the bathroom.

She couldn't remember ever being spoiled or taken care of like Noah was doing right now. A girl could get used to this.

Hollie squealed in surprise when Noah lifted her into his arms and carried her to the huge harem bed. He placed her on the mattress as if she were made of precious porcelain.

"Noah," she said, her arms wrapped tightly around his neck. "Kiss me."

His lips were on hers before she finished the request. The kiss was hard and hungry, almost brutal in its intensity, a direct contrast to the gentleness he'd just shown her.

Tonight was increasingly eye-opening for her as more and more layers of Noah were revealed. For months, she'd been witness to his affable, good-natured, easygoing persona. She'd also seen his competitive side, the way he never held back, cut corners, or lost his shit in the kitchen. He'd come to the game to win and she'd never seen him waver in his conviction that he could take home the prize. She recognized that part of him best because she shared a similar play-to-win nature. She respected that side of him, even as she dreaded coming face-to-face with it tomorrow.

What she hadn't seen before tonight was this sex-on-a-stick dominant, possessive, demanding, amazing man. The one who had her wanting him to do all sorts of dirty things to her. She had expected him to be a gentle, easy lover.

This man...

Whoo-boy.

When he pulled away, Noah, her friend, had vanished again. The sheik was back. And ready to stake a serious claim.

Her attempts at resisting, at fighting him as part of the fantasy, had vanished as well.

"Are you forgetting something, pet?"

She licked her lips, feigning nervousness. What she really felt was a throbbing need to be fucked. Hard.

So yeah. She was finding it hard to remember her name, let alone whatever it was Noah was referring to.

She frowned. "Um..."

He chuckled darkly. "Let me remind you."

Before she could puzzle out his actions, Noah was sitting

on the edge of the bed and she was sprawled out facedown over his lap.

"Oh, hell no," she cried out as she attempted to rise.

Noah halted her escape with one hard slap on her ass. "Say your safe word or hold still."

Hollie stopped squirming as her mind raced over what to do. Noah was offering her an out. But that damn competitive nature of hers didn't want to cry defeat.

His hand struck again.

"Ow!"

"This is a punishment, Hollie. I warned you what would happen if you disobeyed me." He punctuated his statement with two more slaps.

He wasn't holding anything back, wasn't trying to take it easy on her.

Then she realized she would resent him if he did. Noah knew her too well.

She tensed up when his hand moved again, but this time, Noah didn't hit. Instead, his talented fingers dipped into her pussy. She was slightly embarrassed and surprised by how wet she was.

He stroked in and out just long enough for her to relax, to feel safe.

Then he withdrew and placed two more holy-fuck-me-that-hurts smacks on her already sore bottom. Once again, she considered saying her safe word, and once again, she dismissed the thought as soon as it passed through her brain.

Of course, that consideration was completely driven out when Noah's fingers returned to play with her clit. Stars flashed behind her closed eyelids as she fought to find her release. Noah read her intentions and stopped just before the lightning struck.

"Fucker!" she yelled, her anger building when he merely laughed.

After that, he forgot to count, giving her way more than the promised ten, his hand rising and falling on her ass. The spanking was broken up by those wicked fingers that continued to drive her right to the brink, and then leave her there.

Hollie began to lose all sense of time and place. Nothing mattered to her except the orgasm.

"Please," she gasped when she seriously felt as though she would explode if he didn't let her come.

Noah pushed two fingers deep inside her pussy, curling them and hitting her G-spot. Her own personal self-destruct button. She splintered and screamed.

When she finally managed to recall where she was, Noah was cradling her on his lap, rocking her gently. He'd done the same thing in the hot tub. So far, he'd given her two mind-blowing orgasms, and he'd yet to come himself.

She slid to her knees in front of him.

"Hollie," he said, when she pressed his thighs apart and took his cock in her hand. She sucked the head into her mouth, provoking a deep groan from him that pleased her.

She'd never really wanted to give a man a blow job. It had usually been something she just did for the guy. But right now, taking Noah into her mouth was as much for her as him. She loved the way he cupped her cheek affectionately, the way his softly spoken words of praise soaked into her skin like warm sunshine.

When he took a handful of her hair in his hand and tugged, Hollie felt a spark of the arousal he was an expert at provoking.

She took him deeper, the head of his cock brushing the back of her throat.

Noah grunted, and then, to her surprise, he withdrew.

"No," she protested.

"Not that way, Hollie. Not the first time. I want to be inside you."

Despite the bone-rattling orgasm she'd just had, his words had her raring to go, ready for more.

She rose from the floor and climbed onto the bed. As she lay on her back, Noah crawled over her body, caging her beneath him as he kissed her.

Her legs open, she reached down, trying to draw him inside.

Noah broke the kiss and shook his head. "Not yet, pet. Your training isn't over. I'm still waiting to hear you call me Master."

It took Hollie a few moments to shake the cobwebs from her hormone-fuzzy brain to understand the fantasy wasn't over.

"Noah," she whispered.

"See?"

He moved away from her, even though she attempted to hold him close. "Wait—"

"No. This doesn't end until you're mine. Your body, your mind, your soul." As he spoke, he lifted her right arm, securing her wrist to the bedpost. Then he repeated the same process with the left.

She struggled not to complain when he left the bed completely to do the same to her ankles. She squirmed slightly, testing the bondage as Noah stood at the foot of the bed and surveyed his work. She was naked and tied spread-eagle, everything she possessed on display. The Hollie she had been before she'd walked into this hotel room tonight would have been mortified. This new Hollie, the one Noah had uncovered, felt freer than ever—which was completely ironic given her trussed-up state.

"Please come back to bed."

He stood akimbo, his hands resting on his hips. He was the very picture of a powerful sheik. Then she recalled the outfit hanging in the closet. She wanted to wear it for him, wanted that collar with its fancy gold leash around her neck.

"You're very beautiful."

No lover had ever said those words to her. Not once. She'd actually never considered her looks much before the competition. Before the tabloids started discussing them. Before the show plopped her in the makeup chair and went mad with foundation, then gave her a stylish haircut and highlights. She lived and worked on a farm. Her beauty regime included getting a shower and getting the hell out of the bathroom so someone else could take a turn. That was it.

Right now, she looked like the Hollie from home. She'd scrubbed off her makeup after the show and brushed out all the damn hairspray. She didn't doubt for a second the steam from the hot tub had turned her curls to frizz.

Yet Noah said she was beautiful. And the look in his eyes told her he was sincere.

When he returned to the bed, she expected him to resume his place above her. She was surprised when he knelt between her outstretched legs and leaned closer.

She gasped when he ran his tongue around her clit.

"Oh my God," she said as he used his lips and tongue to drive her insane. The man sure as hell knew his way around a woman's body. He'd found all her hot buttons. After too many years of having to draw a freaking map for previous lovers, she now began to fear that old adage was coming true. Noah was ruining her for all other men. That expression had always struck her as clichéd and unlikely. Now...she was in serious danger of living it out.

When Noah added his fingers to the play, she stopped

worrying about the future. The here and now was too fucking awesome to miss.

Her hips lifted when he pressed two fingers inside, trying to seek more. She'd never considered herself a greedy lover, but with Noah, she was as selfish as they came. He offered and she took. Without regret or guilt.

Two fingers became three as he wrapped his lips around her clit, sucking the sensitive nub into this mouth. Once again, she was a goner.

She came loudly.

Her orgasm had only just begun to wane when Noah's fingers moved lower. She jerked when he slowly thrust one wet finger into her ass.

"I...oh, shit." She'd never indulged in anal play. She'd never even been tempted. It always felt like one of those porn moves, one that someone had to pay a woman a lot of freaking money to pretend to enjoy.

"I'm going to take you here, pet. Going to press my cock deep and fuck your ass."

Hello, Mr. Dirty Talk. Where have you been all my life?

"I..." Hollie tried to speak, but he'd robbed all the air from her body. He continued to move his finger in and out of her tight ass and while the sensation was unusual, she didn't dislike it at all. Quite the contrary. It felt naughty and hot and...

"Okay," she whispered.

Noah froze, his eyes drifting closed. "You're killing me, Hollie."

She was killing *him?*

She'd barely touched him. Meanwhile, he'd driven her to mind-blowing orgasm time and time again.

"I need you, Noah."

He slowly pulled his finger from her ass and she realized—finally!—he was going to fuck her.

Noah climbed over her—then paused. When he looked over his shoulder, searching the room for something, she understood what he was doing.

"I'm on the Pill."

He glanced back at her, his brows furrowed. "I have a condom in my pants, Holl, if you'd rather I—"

"I don't. Don't want you to use one if you don't have a reason to."

"I'm clean," he said.

"So am I."

He blew out a long sigh. "I've never...God...I really want..."

"Untie me, Noah. I want to touch you."

The fantasy had been incredible. Something she wanted to revisit with him about a million times in the future if he'd agree to it. But right now, this time, their first time, she wanted it to be just them.

Hollie and Noah.

Nollie, she thought, with a grin.

Noah missed her smile as he leaned forward, releasing the ties on her arms, then reached lower to tug the knots at her ankles loose.

Once she was free, she wrapped her arms around his neck and her legs around his waist. Noah wasted no time placing his cock at the entrance to her body and sliding home.

He filled her perfectly.

Noah moved slowly at first, taking the time to kiss her.

Hollie squeezed her eyes closed to hold back the tears threatening. She'd never once shed tears of happiness, but right now, it took a great deal of effort not to dissolve into sobs. Which was ridiculous.

Then she realized *why* she was so moved.

She was in love with Noah.

The emotion crashed into her like a tidal wave. She'd never

been in love before. She'd been in lust, in fondness, in genuine like with other guys, but not once had she given her heart away.

When Noah released her lips and gave her a sweet smile, she returned it, trying to ignore the part of her that worried about tomorrow.

"Okay?" he asked.

She wondered if she had revealed something in her expression, then realized he meant physically. She took mental stock and giggled.

"My ass is on fire, my nipples are sore and my insides feel slightly bruised. I've never been better."

He laughed loudly. "Wanna go for broke?"

"Meaning?"

"I'm trying to be a gentleman when all I want to do right now is take you hard, deep and fast."

Her pussy clenched in response. "Oh, hell yeah. It's Vegas, baby. Let it ride."

She expected him to laugh at her joke. Instead, it appeared her words released the beast.

Noah knelt, grasping the backs of her knees and tucking them into the crooks of his elbows. The position lifted her ass off the mattress slightly and left her wide open for what he had in mind.

Which was exactly what he'd asked for.

Noah pounded inside her, free of restraint, taking her with more force, more passion than she'd ever dreamed possible.

It was incredible. She came within a dozen thrusts but this time, Noah didn't pause, didn't seek to comfort or rock her. Instead, he kept moving, claiming.

Her second orgasm came right on the heels of the first, but Noah still wasn't finished.

Hollie's head thrashed wildly on the pillow as she gripped his muscular arms, holding on for dear life.

"Can't take it," she said, though that was a lie. In just a few short hours, she'd come to know there was nothing this man could dish out that she wouldn't scarf down like a starving person.

"Hollie," Noah said, his voice tight. He was there. At last.

And she was with him. God. She didn't know she had this many orgasms in her.

He thrust deep one last time and held steady as he came. Hollie's back arched as she joined him.

Considering the noise they'd just been making, Hollie was struck by the sudden silence in the room. All she could hear was their labored breathing as Noah slowly withdrew and dropped next to her on the bed.

She turned to face him, neither of them speaking.

He ran the back of his fingers along her cheek, staring at her with...

Love.

Hollie was certain of it.

She smiled and he returned it. It was on the tip of her tongue to tell him how she felt, but something held her back.

Tomorrow loomed like a black, scary shadow, casting her happy ending in darkness.

Noah leaned toward her and kissed her gently. "Shut it down for the night, Hollie. There's plenty of time to figure this out later. Okay?"

She narrowed her eyes. "Are you a mind reader?"

He shook his head, clearly amused by her question. "I don't think it takes any special skill to know what's on your mind. Especially since it's the same thing that's on mine."

Hollie loved how open and honest Noah was. What you saw was what you got with him.

"Later," she said with a sigh. "We'll talk later."

He wrapped his arm around her waist. Hollie expected

stress and worry over the show and what would happen between them to keep her awake, but the moment she closed her eyes, physical exhaustion won the day.

CHAPTER SIX

Noah glanced at the clock. It was just a few minutes before three a.m. He was surprised to realize he'd only slept a few hours. When he had tugged Hollie into his arms, he'd been dog-tired and a bit afraid about missing his alarm and oversleeping come morning.

Today was the most important day of his life. When he thought about it, it wasn't exactly surprising that he couldn't sleep. Everything was about to change.

For better. Or for worse.

Unable to relax, Noah slowly disentangled himself from Hollie. He sat on the edge of the bed for a few minutes, turning to look at her.

She was so gorgeous. Her shoulder-length red hair fanned around her on the crisp white silk sheets. Even in the candle-light, he could make out the light smattering of freckles on her nose and cheeks. In his mind, she was the image of the All-American girl, wholesome, healthy—perfect.

God. That word kept weaving into his thoughts. Hollie was

perfect for him in every way. The more time he spent with her, the more it felt as if she'd been made just for him.

He stood up and walked over to where he'd shed his clothing earlier. Noah had never been a great sleeper. He suspected his inability to maintain any sort of deep slumber stemmed from his childhood.

His mother had been a drug addict and it wasn't unusual for her to support that habit by prostitution. He and his brother, Zac, had gotten pretty good at hiding themselves when they were younger, after they'd had a couple run-ins with johns who'd thought it was fun to beat on little kids. Then there had been the guy who'd offered his mom money to let him fuck them. She'd gone nuts on the asshole and kicked him out, but after that, he and Zac had spent too many restless nights with one eye open, prepared to defend themselves if necessary.

When Mama Lewis had taken them in, Noah had been surprised that sleep was the one thing that still seemed to evade him. The Lewises had given him a warm, safe home, but some habits and fears never left you. For Noah, he'd learned early on that sleep made you vulnerable, and as a result, he was no stranger to midnight walks or late-night TV.

Once he'd dressed and put his shoes on, he left a note for Hollie on his pillow. God forbid she woke up and thought he'd left her. He needed some time to think, so he decided to head down to the hotel bar. Lucky for him, he was in a city that never slept. He felt the need for a beer and a chance to figure out what he should do next.

There were a lot more people in the elegant bar than he would have expected, given the late hour. He considered claiming a stool at the long counter, but the bartender looked like the type who liked to chat and there were two women sitting there eyeing him with appreciative, inviting smiles.

He hadn't come here looking for company. If he had

wanted that, he would have simply rolled over and woken up the angel in his bed.

Glancing around, he spotted a small table near the corner. The lighting there was very dim. So dark, in fact, he wondered if that section of the bar was closed. He hesitated.

A waitress walked by and stopped. "Can I help you?"

He pointed to the table. "Do you mind if I sit over there?"

She shook her head. "Not at all. You can sit anywhere you want. Want a drink?"

Noah grinned, said he liked craft beer on draft and told her to surprise him. She winked and promised to bring one over.

Noah sank into the comfortable chair, releasing a long, weary breath. He'd been an idiot to get out of bed. He needed the rest, needed a clear head and his wits if he was going to make it through the finale and the aftermath.

The waitress set down a dark milk stout, claiming it was her favorite beer. He took a sip and complimented her taste. She said she'd check on him later and left him alone.

Noah played over the events of the evening, starting with the moment he'd realized the hotel had screwed up, placing him and Hollie in the same room. Not that he intended to complain about that mistake.

Then he recalled the feeling he'd had that they had been set up. He couldn't imagine the producer would do such a thing. The man didn't appear to see anything more than the ratings and money from the sponsors. It seemed unlikely he would purposely try to drive his last two competitors into each other's arms the night before the finale.

Which brought him back to the hotel staff. Perhaps they'd believed the tabloids, seen that they'd chosen the same fantasy, and assumed they wanted to be together. It felt far-fetched, but Noah was lacking any other explanation.

Of course, the more he considered everything he'd done

with Hollie tonight, the harder it was for him to think any of it had been a mistake. Maybe it had been ill advised to take Hollie to bed the night before they both had to take the stage to compete against each other in front of millions of viewers. But try as he may, he couldn't find an ounce of regret over that action.

He took another longer swig of his beer, and then rubbed his eyes. He needed rest, but he didn't foresee getting any. He couldn't get his brain to shut down.

"Shit," he murmured.

"That's a heavy look," a deep voice said.

Noah jerked slightly at the unexpected sound. Squinting, he could just make out the silhouette of a man at the next table. The guy was sitting in a corner seat in a dark shadow. Noah wouldn't have known he was there if the man hadn't spoken.

He smiled and lifted one shoulder casually. "I'm in a bar at three a.m. nursing a beer. Isn't that supposed to be the standard look?"

The guy chuckled. "Given the fact you're competing for half a million dollars in about twelve hours, I guess I expected you'd be in bed."

Noah wasn't surprised that the man knew who he was. He was slowly getting accustomed to complete strangers calling out his name or coming up to him on the street, starting conversations as if they knew him. Apparently that was part and parcel of becoming a celebrity.

"Yeah. Bed is where I should be, but..."

"Nervous?"

Noah figured he should just tell the guy yeah, finish his beer and go back upstairs. After all, he'd come to the bar to be alone.

But Noah never did what he should do. As was apparent by the fact Hollie was naked in his hotel room.

"Not really. I'll sort of be glad when the whole thing is over. I didn't anticipate how much the show would change my life. Auditioned as a lark. Then, well...things snowballed."

"So you aren't enjoying your newfound celebrity status?"

"It's okay." Noah chuckled. "There are definitely some perks attached." It felt good to be able to talk about some of this. While he couldn't make out the man's face, he could make out was seemed a very expensive suit. When the man lifted his glass, he caught a shimmer of an expensive watch on his wrist and heard the clinking of ice in his glass.

"Scotch?" Noah asked.

"Macallan."

"Never heard of it."

The man raised his hand and the waitress appeared as if she'd been hovering nearby. He ordered another glass for himself, and then asked her to bring one to Noah.

"Thank you," Noah said. "You didn't have to do that. I was fine with the beer."

"Life is better with scotch, and Macallan is one of the best."

Noah nodded his thanks when the waitress set the glass in front of him. The man had excellent taste. It was clearly expensive stuff. "Wow. I need to write down the name of that scotch. It's amazing."

"At ten grand a bottle, it should be."

Noah set the glass down, mentally trying to calculate what that single drink cost. He debated asking the man his name, but considering the way the stranger was sitting alone in the dim corner, hiding in the shadows, he clearly preferred his anonymity.

Before Noah could thank the man again for what was probably the most expensive drink he'd ever have in his life, the stranger returned to the previous conversation.

"So if it's not nervousness or depression over the end of the show, what is it that's driven you to a bar alone in the middle of the night?"

"A woman." The response slipped out before Noah could even consider the wisdom of sharing something so personal with a stranger.

"Ah, the best and worst kind of problem in the world. Are you trying to get rid of this woman or has she just broken things off with you?"

"Neither. I'm in love with her and I think she might feel the same way."

The man had picked up his glass for another drink, but put it back down at Noah's response. "That doesn't seem like a problem at all."

"It's Hollie." The guy had already proved he knew enough about *Food Fight* to recognize him. He probably knew Hollie too.

"Ah. I see."

"Yeah. If you'd asked me nine, even six months ago if I cared about winning or losing the competition, I would have said it didn't make a difference to me."

"But now you're on the verge of winning a lot of money—"

"It's more than the money," Noah interjected. "It's a dream come true. My own restaurant. I've wanted that for longer than I can even remember."

"You can still open a restaurant. Even if you lose."

Noah kept telling himself that. It was true. But it would take a hell of a lot longer. And even then, he wasn't sure he'd manage to launch his dream restaurant. Half a million dollars was huge. Something a boy raised on the wrong side of the Big Easy had never expected to see in his lifetime.

"Yeah," he said. "I could."

"I guess it all boils down to what's more important to you. Money or love?"

It was a simple question. A choice between two things. And deep down inside, Noah knew what the answer should be. It was what Mama Lewis had been telling him since the first day he met her.

He'd only been twelve years old. The social worker had shown up that morning and taken him away from his mom. He'd cried and screamed and begged his mother not to let him go, but she'd only shrugged and told him it was probably better if he and his older brother went somewhere else to live. He'd been devastated. And then he'd been pissed off.

So angry in fact, he hadn't been able to summon up much fear when the social worker dropped him off at the Lewis house. He'd followed behind Mama Lewis as she showed him and Zac to their bedroom and he'd stayed there all day, through dinner and straight on 'til bedtime.

That's when Mama Lewis came to the room and sat on the edge of his bed. She'd told him it was okay to be afraid in a new home with strangers. And he'd exploded.

A day's worth of pure white-hot rage spewed out as he told her he didn't give a shit where he was. He claimed to hate her, her house, his brother and his mother. His voice broke when he spoke the last. Mama Lewis hadn't missed that sound.

She'd told him hate took energy. A lot of it. And it made life really hard. She said love was always the most important thing. If you kept hold of that, everything else would simply fall into place. Life would be easy and fun and good things would come your way.

He hadn't believed her right away. In fact, he'd been a real pain in the ass the first few months. But Mama Lewis led by example. He saw and felt all the love she had for her kids—biological and foster—and he came to understand how important it was.

What was more, he'd come to understand why his mother

had let him go without a fight. She'd wanted to give him a chance at something better. And she had.

"I'd rather be poor with Hollie than have all the money in the world." The second he said the words, all the tension he felt melted away.

"Good answer. But you know if she feels the same way as you, one of you is still walking away with that money. I don't think a pauper's life is in either of your futures."

Noah nodded slowly. "Yeah, but I can't throw the competition. Hollie would know it if I did and it would piss her off. She'd kill me."

"And you're afraid that if *you* win, she'll walk? Does that sound like someone you should be pursuing?"

Hollie wouldn't walk away from him if he won any more than he would leave her if *she* did. Noah grinned. "I'm an idiot. Worrying about stuff that won't happen, that doesn't matter."

The man lifted his glass and Noah followed suit. "Here's to a happy life for you and your Hollie."

Noah took the last sip of the scotch and let the smooth liquor warm him all the way down. "That's damn fine stuff. I should probably get back up to the room."

Noah rose and started to walk away. He'd only gone two steps when the man called out, "If I may make a suggestion about the competition?"

Noah turned, wishing he could see the guy's face. "Sure."

"If I don't like the rules of a game, I change them."

"Okay. Thanks."

Noah let those words sink in as he glanced around for the waitress. When he found her, he reached for his wallet, intent on paying for his beer. She waved him away. "Mr. Nyte already paid your tab."

"Mr. Nyte?" Noah asked. "The owner of the hotel?"

"Yes."

He turned back toward the table he'd just left. The shadow was gone.

Now he was *really* sorry he hadn't seen the man's face. Mr. Nyte was a legend and a mystery, as very few people had ever seen him.

He was halfway across the lobby when Mr. Beckett stopped him. "Mr. Lewis? Is everything okay?"

Noah nodded. "Yeah."

"Is your room to your liking?"

Noah didn't bother to restrain his grin. "Oh yeah. Funny thing, Hollie and I were given the same room."

Mr. Beckett's lack of surprise answered the question of who put them together. Just not the why.

"Was there any certain reason we were put together?"

"That directive came from Mr. Nyte after you and Ms. Mills both selected the same fantasy room."

Interesting. Noah regretted once more not knowing who the stranger in the shadows had been. If he had, he would have thanked the man for setting up what was the best night of his life.

"You'll have to pass along my thanks."

Mr. Beckett nodded. "I'll do that." The man reached into the pocket of his suit jacket. "Actually, I'm glad I ran into you. Mr. Nyte asked me to pass this along to you."

Noah took the small piece of paper, embossed with the Nyte logo.

"If you'll excuse me."

Noah glanced at the man. "Of course. Good night."

The message inscribed was short, but it packed a punch. It simply said, "Call me if you and Hollie ever decide to work in Vegas."

Holy shit. Had Mr. Nyte seriously just offered him a job in one of his restaurants? Until the seed had been planted, Noah had seen himself returning to New Orleans. Now though? What if he and Hollie stayed here? He let himself imagine for a few moments the two of them as co-executive chefs in one of the Nyte hotel's five star restaurants. It was more appealing than he could say.

He pushed the dream out of his mind...for the time being. He still had too many hurdles to clear before the night was over.

As Noah walked toward the elevators, he considered Mr. Nyte's advice.

Change the rules.

An idea emerged. Noah stepped into the elevator, his excitement growing as it slid past floor after floor.

Change the rules.

He rushed down the hallway, pressing his thumb against the keypad for entry. He knew exactly how tomorrow was going to play out.

Time to wake Hollie. They had a plan to make.

When he entered the room, he didn't have to wake Hollie. She was already up.

And wearing the harem girl outfit.

"Mother of God." His mouth went dry and his cock went stiff. She was the sexiest thing he'd ever laid eyes on.

She tilted her head. "You left."

"I put a note on the pillow."

"I saw it. Everything okay?"

"It is now."

Hollie walked toward him. That was when he noticed she had something in her hands.

The collar and leash.

"Hollie," he began, wondering if she knew what she was inviting. If she knew how much he wanted what she was offering.

Once she stood in front of him, she dropped down to her knees. "I missed you," she paused briefly before adding, "Master."

She lifted the collar to him.

He took it, and then lifted her back to her feet. He had something he needed to say before they got swept away in the fantasy again. Noah had every intention of continuing the game, but before they did that, he wanted them to move forward without questions or anxiety.

"I love you."

She blinked a couple times in confusion at his abrupt declaration.

"I mean," he clarified, "I'm in love with you. Completely. Head over heels in an insane, moving-way-too-fast sort of way."

Her smile grew as he rambled, which was why he kept going when he should have shut up. "I look at you and see a future, Hollie. A forever future. And maybe you'll think it's too soon for me to start talking about—"

"It's not too soon," she interrupted. "I feel the exact same way."

"My feelings aren't going to change tomorrow night, regardless of the outcome of the show."

She paused and he realized she'd had the same concerns as him. When she spoke, he heard the things he'd considered fall from her lips. "We're both pretty competitive. I was afraid..."

"That I'd be a sore loser?"

She shrugged lightly. "Or that I would. A half a million dollars is a lot of money. I genuinely believe I can lose gracefully, but..."

"But it will still hurt. To think you're second best."

She nodded. "And as always, you get me. It's kind of scary. You're sure there's no ESP at play?"

He chuckled. "I have a plan. A way for both of us to win. The game. The money. And each other."

She reached out to cup his cheek affectionately. "You've already won my heart."

"Ditto," he said, leaning down to give her a kiss.

"So what's the plan?"

He raised the collar. "Lift your hair and turn around."

She did so without hesitation, trembling slightly as Noah fastened the collar around her neck. Once it was secured, he placed a light kiss against her nape then he turned her to face him again.

"How does it feel?" he asked.

"Perfect."

It was their word. Now that he had a plan, he was determined to make all their dreams come true.

"So about the competition?"

"We're going to change the rules."

She smiled. "I like the sound of that."

"But first, we're going to move on to the second course."

EPILOGUE

Tom: Hello, and welcome back to the live finale of *Food Fight*. Our contestants have spent the last hour racing around, cooking the meal that will make or break their futures. What do you think of this final challenge, Angelica?

Angelica: I think it's inspired, Tom. Just inspired. It's really going to give our contestants one last chance to show the judges exactly what they're made of, to prove they have what it takes to open and operate their own restaurant.

Tom: I couldn't agree more, and I'm dying to know what each contestant considers their signature dish.

Angelica: Well, we can see that Hollie has remained true to her roots, using a wide variety of organic vegetables in her preparation.

Tom: While Noah isn't holding back with the spices. But rumor has it that just prior to the show, both Noah and Hollie changed a few items in their recipes. Do you think those changes were brought on due to nervousness or a mutual desire to take their competitor by surprise?

Angelica: Maybe a bit of both, Tom. As you can see, there are two plates on that table at center stage. They'll each put their dishes on one of those for presentation to the judges. And in a competition like this, appearance is as important as taste.

Tom: And the clock is just about to run out. Looks like Noah is the first to finish his meal. There he is, headed to the center table.

Angelica: Um...what's he doing?

Tom: I'm not sure... He appears to have stacked the two plates. Does he understand that one is for Hollie's dish?

Angelica: The judges are trying to catch his attention, but either he doesn't hear them or he's ignoring them. He's plating his food. I have to admit it looks lovely. I hope Hollie doesn't mess up his presentation when she tries to grab her plate from under his.

Tom: Here comes Hollie with her food.

Angelica: Wait. What's going on? Is she putting her dish on the *same* serving platter as Noah!? Can she do that?

Tom: The judges appear to be looking off stage for the producer. It's clear they're as confused by this unusual turn of events as the rest of us.

Angelica: Tom, look—Noah and Hollie are now combining their food, putting it together on the plate to create *one dish*.

Tom: And there's the buzzer to end the competition! I have to admit, I've never seen anything like this in ten years with the show. Like the rest of America, I can't wait to see how this turns out. The judges are approaching the table.

Angelica: It appears the producer has given them the green light to proceed with the judging. They're sampling the food. Which I have to say looks absolutely amazing.

Tom: If the look on Billy Oxford's face is any indication, Angelica, I'd say you're correct. I think that expression is called bliss.

Angelica (laughing lightly): It is indeed, Tom. And given their expressions, I think it's obvious Noah and Hollie have created something very special together. But I'm not sure how they can award a winner.

Tom: I agree. I'm concerned their actions may disqualify them.

Angelica: It appears, after conferring with the producer, the judges have reached a decision.

Tom: And the winner is—it's a tie. *A tie!* How about that? Ladies and gentlemen, tonight we're witnessing *Food Fight* history as Noah Lewis and Hollie Mills are both crowned champion. It looks like they'll have to split the prize money!

Angelica: Or maybe not, Tom.

Tom: Is he...? Are they...? Can they—?

Angelica: Kissing. They're kissing, Tom. And yes, they can do that on live TV.

GOING TOO FAST

BIG EASY, BOOK 7

GOING TOO FAST

Zac is about to embark on his five-year residency to become an orthopedic surgeon. Before it starts, he decides to borrows an old RV from a friend and head west with no definite direction. Fate puts him in Sapphire Falls during festival week.

Forced to quit playing soccer due to injury, Tacy is left to figure out "what now?" She decides a relaxing trip to Sapphire Falls might be just the ticket. However, the easy pace she was looking for evaporates once she lays eyes on Zac.

One minute Tacy and Zac are playfully arguing over who gets the last caramel apple, the next they're doing the naked mambo in his RV. Neither one of them has a clue where they're headed, but they know they're going too fast.

*This story is dedicated to Erin Nicholas.
Not only has she created a beautiful world called Sapphire Falls,
she's made my world brighter as well through her friendship and
support.*

CHAPTER ONE

"It's about time you got your ass to Sapphire Falls."

Tacy Bradford grinned over her cup of coffee and resisted the urge to roll her eyes. Her friend and former babysitter, Lauren Davis—Bennett, now that she was married—had been going on and on about her new hometown of Sapphire Falls for years, begging Tacy to come for a visit.

Unfortunately, Tacy's crazy travel schedule with the U.S. women's national soccer team had kept her too busy to ever squeeze in a stopover. Of course, all that changed when she blew out her knee during practice three months earlier. Now she'd been forced into early retirement and possessed only a skeletal plan of what the hell she was going to do with her life from this point on.

Actually, the entire plan included just one goal, this trip to Sapphire Falls for their annual festival. After that, she had no more direction than a feather in a tornado. She figured she might be more upset about that fact if she weren't with Lauren. It was sort of hard to be down in the dumps with Lauren around.

She'd checked into the Rise & Shine Bed & Breakfast shortly after her dawn arrival in town. Tacy had taken a red-eye flight from L.A. to Omaha, rented a car and pulled into Sapphire Falls at first light. She suspected the sleepy town would have been more...well...*sleepy* if it had been a regular week, but this was festival week and the place was jumping. Even at eight a.m. on a Sunday.

So far Lauren had introduced her to her husband, Travis, and adorable baby girl—all three of whom had been waiting at the B&B to welcome her—and at least ten more people since they'd sat down to breakfast.

After Tacy stowed her luggage in her room, Travis took the baby back to the farm and Lauren took charge, dragging her to Dottie's Diner, where she'd met so many people her head was spinning. She hoped there wasn't a quiz later because apart from recalling that the redhead was Phoebe, and Mason was Lauren's business partner, she couldn't remember anyone else's name or what they did.

Tacy wiped her mouth with her napkin, fairly certain she'd never eaten better home fries. The grease-to-potato ratio was spot on. Flying made her hungry, so she'd splurged, ordering a western omelet, home fries, wheat toast and orange juice. "So what happened to your big-city lifestyle? I thought Chicago was supposedly your paradise? Or was it D.C.?"

Lauren grimaced, though she didn't look all that upset. "I guess you can take the girl out of the small town, but you can't take the small town out of the girl. Mason moved a big chunk of IAS to Sapphire Falls and I fell in love."

"With the town?"

"And Travis," Lauren added with a grin. She and Mason owned a world-renowned agricultural engineering company that had broken ground on so many scientific advances, Tacy had lost count. Not that Tacy had been surprised by her former babysitter's success. Lauren had always been super smart and creative. Plus she had an inner drive and go-getter personality that basically made it clear to everyone she met that she was a force to be reckoned with.

"How are your folks?" Lauren asked.

Tacy shrugged. "The same."

Lauren chuckled. "In other words, they're driving you insane."

"Yeah. Since the whole knee thing, they're scrambling, trying to figure out the next way I can find fame, fortune, glory and—Oh my God. It never ends with them."

"I assume you aren't planning to settle down back at home."

Tacy snorted. "Hell would freeze over first before I made Longview my permanent address. My stuff is there for now, but I'm keeping the visits short. It's been easy to get away with that, considering my doctor and the rehab are all happening in Los Angeles. Of course, that's winding down now."

"All better?"

Tacy nodded. "Yeah. Pretty much. Which means it's time to make a move. And I have only one requirement for my new life. There must be no less than eight hundred miles between me and my parents." She added a sinister tone to her voice when she referred to her *parents*.

"You're an adult now, Tace. And the world is your oyster. You don't have to do everything your parents tell you to."

When Tacy looked back on her childhood, there was no denying the times she'd spent with Lauren were some of her happiest moments growing up. The only child of two overzealous, extremely strict parents, Tacy's life was one long string of violin and dance lessons, soccer practices and games, cotillion classes, and study hours as they pushed Tacy to succeed in everything. When it became apparent she had a talent for soccer, the other interests fell away and her parents focused most of their time, energy and money on making her the world's greatest player.

The only times Tacy broke free of the structured, rigid routine were when Lauren came to babysit. Those were the nights she got to stay up late, stuff her face with too much pizza and watch R-rated movies. Lauren was the coolest teenager ever, and for some strange reason, she thought Tacy was cool too. It went without saying Tacy had always adored her. They'd remained in touch through email and phone calls over the years, but they hadn't managed an actual face-to-face visit in nearly six years. If Tacy had to find a bright spot to the whole career-ending knee injury, seeing Lauren again was definitely one.

"Oh, I know that. And believe me, I've stressed that fact to them too. The problem is I don't really have any idea what I want to do now, so dear old Mom and Dad feel like they need to figure it out for me. Their current plan is for me to pursue a job in coaching. If my dad has his way, I'll be the head coach of the next World Cup champs."

"But you prefer no more soccer?"

Tacy wrinkled her nose. "Not if I can't play."

"So pick something else."

Tacy sighed but didn't reply. She *had* been thinking of something lately, but when she'd mentioned it to her parents, they'd looked at her like she had spouted a second head. While she knew Lauren would be more supportive, she still felt funny talking about what she really wanted to do.

She should have realized Lauren wouldn't let the subject drop.

"You have no aspirations? Dreams? Hopes? I find that hard to believe," Lauren pressed.

"I'm only twenty-six. I thought I'd have at least five more years with the team. Hell, Hope Solo is thirty-four and still going strong, and Abby Wambach made it to thirty-five before she retired."

"Stop dodging. There's something rattling around in that pretty head of yours, I can tell. So pretend you're thirty-five, my age. What was your plan for life after soccer?"

Tacy stopped hesitating. She needed to talk to someone about her aspirations. Someone who wasn't her parents. "I want to go back to school to study landscape design."

Lauren's brows rose. "Still like playing in the dirt?"

It was Lauren who had introduced her to gardening. While Tacy had never admitted it to anyone, the times she was outside, digging up weeds, planting flowers, creating beautiful, colorful beds, were the times she was most at peace. "I love it."

Lauren was clearly pleased that she'd been able to share her love of something with Tacy. "I'll hire you to work for IAS. You can plant in Haiti."

Tacy appreciated the offer, but she wasn't tempted. "Thanks, but I'm more interested in creating flowerbeds, not growing food. And I'm finished with travel. The next roots I put in the ground are going to be mine."

"Did you tell your folks about wanting to go back to school?"

Tacy grimaced. "I did. My dad said it was a waste of my God-given talents and abilities."

Lauren tilted her head. "What did I just say about—"

Tacy raised her hand to cut her off. "I know. I know. I'm not giving up on the dream because of that."

"Then what's holding you back?"

Nothing. Not really. Except the fear of failure. Going back to school after so many years was sort of terrifying. Plus, aside from the tinkering she'd done in the flowerbeds in her parents' backyard, Tacy didn't know if landscaping was more hobby than talent. She'd been raised on the precept that you only pursued something if you could be the best. "Me, I guess. What if I start the classes and can't do it?"

Lauren's eyes filled with sympathy. Her former babysitter was probably one of the few people who had ever really seen what Tacy's childhood had been like. "Then you'll pick something else. This is your time, Tace. Try a bunch of different things. Fail, succeed, quit, try again, do whatever feels right to you. You know, all those things that make you human."

"Human." This was why Tacy loved Lauren so. She walked through life without fear of making mistakes. Tacy wished she had even a quarter of her friend's courage and self-confidence.

"Can you afford to go to school?"

Tacy had saved nearly every penny she'd made playing soccer, plus there had been some nice-size royalties from endorsements. It would take all her money, but she could swing it. If she could find the nerve to take that risk. "Yeah. I could."

Lauren lifted her hands as if all Tacy's problems were solved. "So there you go. Just do it."

"Just do it? Go to college. Anywhere in particular?" Tacy joked, amused by Lauren's Nike philosophy.

"You get a map and you circle the spot where your parents' house is in Longview, Nebraska. Then you measure out eight hundred miles in every direction. Any school outside of the circle is fair game."

Tacy laughed. "I think it speaks to my present state of mind when I say that actually sounds like a pretty solid idea."

"Glad I could help."

Tacy leaned back and sighed, feeling more carefree and happy than she had in months. She wasn't sure her life was as settled as Lauren seemed to believe, but Tacy was willing to pretend they'd sorted out her future for a little while. She was tired of stressing out about it. She'd come to Sapphire

Falls because she needed a break from her anxieties, her waning self-confidence, and her folks—not necessarily in that order.

"To be honest, my aspirations for this week aren't much bigger than overindulging on caramel apples, kettle corn and deep-fried Oreos. Tell me about this festival of yours. Given the number of booths already set up in the town square, it appears to be a pretty big deal."

"Oh, around these parts, it's huge. There's all kinds of stuff going on—rides, a kissing booth, a haunted house."

"Haunted house? In June."

Lauren nodded. "Yeah. It's weird, but whatever. Just embrace the crazy and you'll get along fine this week."

Tacy giggled, but Lauren lifted a finger in warning. "And don't accept any invitation to that haunted house from the local boys."

"Why not?"

"Lots of dark corners. Fellas around here have learned how to take advantage of that with their girlfriends."

"Would you happen to be one of those girlfriends?"

Lauren flipped her hair over her shoulder and shrugged. "No comment."

"Which is all the answer I need."

They both grinned as Lauren continued her list of festivities. "There's also a dunk tank, petting zoo, beer garden—"

"Beer garden?" Tacy interjected.

"With craft beer, Tace. Not that cheap-ass shit you drink."

Tacy took another bite of her omelet, silently deciding to eat breakfast at this diner every morning she was here. The food really was incredible.

Lauren continued her list. "There's a 5K mud run too."

"That sounds fun."

"Can you do that with your knee?"

Tacy shrugged. "Maybe. If I take it easy. Might actually be good for me to give it a little workout."

"And there's a dance auction tonight to kick things off. I was hoping you'd let me sign you up for that."

"Me?" Tacy asked. "Why?"

"Because I can list at least a dozen guys in town who would love to dance with a World Cup champion."

Tacy narrowed her eyes. "I thought we agreed you were going to be low-key about my past profession."

Lauren looked completely unrepentant as she confessed to breaking that deal. "It's a festival. We like celebrities and you definitely qualify."

"Seriously?"

As if on cue, they were approached by a tall, beautiful blonde who claimed a seat at their table without invitation. "Hey, Lauren," she said, her gaze locked on Tacy.

Lauren grinned. "Perfect timing, Hailey. Feels almost like you were eavesdropping on us."

Hailey rolled her eyes. "Even if I was, it took you long enough to get to the point." The woman extended her hand toward Tacy. "I'm Hailey Bennett, Director of Business Development and Tourism in Sapphire Falls."

"Bennett?" Tacy asked, looking at Lauren.

"For better or worse, Hailey is my sister-in-law. She married Travis' brother, Ty."

"Ah." Then Tacy recalled the rest of Hailey's introduction. "Director of Tourism?"

Hailey nodded. "There are a lot of wonderful things about Sapphire Falls that we hope will draw tourists, and the annual festival is certainly one of the biggest events. Folks who grew up here, but moved away as adults, often return to visit at this time of the year. Lots of people from surrounding towns take part in all the fun stuff we have going on—it's sort of a nice kickoff to summer. And let's face it, all of that is good for the local businesses because it increases sales in the shops, fills the rooms in the B&B, and sends lots of patrons to the bars and restaurants."

Tacy looked at Lauren. "Is there a reason she's telling me all this?"

Lauren laughed loudly. "Not really. Hailey's just fond of the sound of her own voice."

Hailey didn't appear offended. "Bite me, Lauren."

Lauren took a sip of her juice and then lowered the boom. "Some marketing may have gone out, advertising the fact that World Cup Soccer Champion Tacy Bradford would be attending the festival, in addition to Chase Hamilton and her husband, Ty, of course."

"Ty?"

Lauren pointed her thumb at Hailey. "Ty won a silver in the Olympics, and Chase grew up here then became a famous actor."

"Wow. That's awesome. Those guys seem like much bigger celebrities than me."

Lauren grinned mischievously. "Yeah, but Chase is trying to be incognito—like that will work—and Ty's old news around here."

Hailey snorted. "I'm going to tell him you said that."

Lauren didn't look worried as she continued speaking to Tacy. "You'd be the new celebrity this year."

"And what exactly would that entail?" Tacy didn't like the idea of riding around on some float and looking like a fool doing the queen's wave. Lauren hadn't mentioned a parade, had she?

"Oh, don't worry," Hailey said in a tone that didn't reassure her. "Lauren said you were here for a relaxing vacation, so we didn't fill your schedule with too many events."

"My schedule?"

Hailey pulled a piece of paper from her handbag. "It's pretty much the stuff Lauren already mentioned to you." Hailey's comment revealed she *had* been eavesdropping on their conversation, as she continued to explain their plans. "We were hoping you'd take a go in the dunk tank one afternoon, be one of the judges in the apple pie baking contest, pose for some pictures with people at the photo booth and participate in the dance auction. Other than that, you can just mill around and enjoy yourself."

Lauren added to Hailey's list. "I'll warn you that there are quite a few people hoping to get your autograph. Would you be okay with that?"

Tacy nodded. She hadn't been a star player on the team, so while she had signed the occasional autograph, she hadn't spent much time in the limelight. Part of her was sort of pleased that anyone would even consider her a celebrity. She certainly didn't see herself that way. "Sure. Why not? It sounds like fun."

"Wonderful." Hailey rose. "Hate to dash off, but there are a million things to do to get ready for the festival kickoff. It was nice to meet you, Tacy. I'm looking forward to hanging out with you this week."

Hailey was gone before Tacy could respond.

"Is she always like that?"

"A whirlwind?" Lauren asked. "Oh yeah. Hailey has one speed—fast-forward. She's actually pretty great. I think you'll like her."

Lauren looked around the diner. "In fact, chances are good you'll like everyone here. Come to think of it..." Lauren pulled her phone from her purse and started tapping away in search of something.

"What are you doing?"

"I'm trying to see how far it is from here to Longview. It's gotta be eight hundred miles. You can do online classes and stay here with us forever."

Tacy laughed. "Forget it. You may have given up on your big-city aspirations, but I have not. Wherever I settle, it's going to be a place with countless malls, restaurants, bars and an airport within spitting distance. Might help if it has a warm climate year-round so I don't have to curtail my dirt-digging activities because of snow and ice. I don't know how you can stand living so far away from civilization after making your break from Longview."

"I'm not worried about your rejection. I swore I'd never move to Sapphire Falls too and look at me now. I have a whole week to change your mind."

Tacy started to assure her friend that wouldn't happen when the front door to the diner opened, and the hottest guy she'd ever laid eyes on walked in. "On second thought..."

Lauren followed her gaze as the man walked to the counter and claimed a stool near the end.

"If all the guys in Sapphire Falls are as hot as that, I might be convinced to stick around."

Lauren turned back to face her. "Sadly, we can't claim him. I've never seen that guy before. Wonder if he's here visiting relatives for the week."

Before Tacy could respond, the man shifted on the stool, letting his gaze travel around the room. She licked her lips as she took in his thick dark hair and chocolate-brown eyes. He had laugh lines around his eyes and mouth that said he was no stranger to smiling, and he had the slightest shadow of a beard that told her he hadn't shaved this morning. God, she was a sucker for a five o'clock shadow. His muscular arms were show-cased in a T-shirt that fit him just right. Tacy hated guys who wore their shirts a size too small in hopes of showing off their physique. This man didn't play that game. Hell, he didn't need to. He was built perfectly.

She didn't realize she was staring until his eyes met hers. Tacy knew she should look away, but she couldn't. It was as if something came over them when their gazes locked and neither of them pretended to do anything other than what they were doing. Which was the most blatant checking-each-other-out in the history of flirting. He smiled and she returned it. Her cheeks flushed slightly when he winked.

Tacy was no stranger to attraction, but this felt different somehow. It was as though she'd been struck by a serious, almost crippling case of lust at first sight. Her nipples tightened, her pussy clenched, and she was suddenly very, *very* warm. If she'd been wearing more than a T-shirt and jean shorts, she would have been tempted to strip off a layer to seek some cooler air. Sadly, there was only one layer between her and her panties and bra.

Not that she minded showing him those. They were baby-blue silk with tiny white flowers and really cute.

Regrettably, the idea of taking off her clothing only added to her horny state, and she was overwhelmed by the desire to drag the man off the stool and back to her room at the B&B. Which was a ridiculous response.

The man was a stranger. A completely hot-as-hell, sex-on-a-stick, ohmigod, I-want-to-lick-him-from-top-to-bottom stranger.

Tacy wasn't sure how long they would have continued the silent dalliance, but it ended when the waitress behind the counter asked the man if he wanted a cup of coffee. He turned to respond and Tacy was forced back to the present.

To Lauren, looking at her with an all-too-knowing smirk.

"I think maybe we should add something else to your schedule for this week," Lauren said.

"Oh yeah?"

"There's no cure on earth for whatever ails you like a good hard workout between the sheets, and something tells me that man would know his way around a woman's body."

"Are you suggesting I go pick up that guy for a one-night stand?" Tacy tried to feign shock or offense or something. She failed at all three, of course. Mainly because she was hoping Lauren would give her the green light to do just that.

Maybe like right now.

Damn. She needed to get a grip. Tacy rubbed her eyes and tried to shake off the lingering lust that had her heart beating just a smidge too fast. This was why she should have sprung for the more expensive ticket instead of saving money with the red-eye. She was overtired and not thinking clearly. If she didn't manage to get in a nap at some point today, God only knew what sort of trouble she'd get into.

Problem was Lauren didn't seem amenable to letting her escape. Her comment when Tacy put her bags in her room and mentioned lying down for a little while was simply to say, "You can sleep when you get back home. It's festival time."

Lauren glanced over her shoulder. The man hadn't turned back around since getting his coffee. "I'm not sure I'd limit myself to just one night with him."

"You're a married woman."

Lauren laughed. "Maybe so, but I can appreciate fine physiques. And that guy has it going on in all the right places. It's something worth considering. After all, you're only here for a week and it's not like you're looking for anything long-term. You said you wanted to let your hair down and relax. I don't see why you can't add hot sex with a stranger to that sugar-and-grease overload you've got planned. Just do it."

The Nike advice again.

The old Tacy would have dismissed the suggestion out of

hand, not because she didn't like sex, but because there had never been time. Her focus had always been on the game.

Now her entire life had been flipped upside down in just a few months. It was obvious she was going to have to step out of her comfort zone and try some new things. It was the only way she could hope to forge a future that might bring her some level of happiness and contentment.

Maybe she could test those wings here.

In Sapphire Falls.

With him.

CHAPTER TWO

Zac Lewis sat on the steps of a gazebo in the middle of Sapphire Falls and chatted with his foster brother, Justin, on the phone as he watched the world go by. He tried to lie to himself, tried to pretend he wasn't looking for the smokin'-hot blonde he had seen in the diner this morning, and was instead taking in the scenery.

"Zac?"

"I'm still here." Zac forced himself to forget about the woman and focus on the conversation with his brother. Ever since he'd borrowed the old RV Justin's business—and life—partner Ned had inherited from his great uncle and taken off in search of the West Coast, his siblings had taken turns calling to check up on him. Apparently it was Justin's day to make sure he hadn't driven the hunk of junk he was calling home for six weeks off a cliff.

"Where are you again?"

"Sapphire Falls," Zac repeated.

"Where the hell is that?"

Zac chuckled. "Bumfuck, Nebraska."

"Jesus. How'd you end up there?"

"Just where the nose of the RV happened to be pointing today." While that was true of most of his trip so far, his sojourn to Sapphire Falls had actually been a bit more intentional. He'd stopped for gas on the highway about fifty miles back and spotted a flyer promoting a festival, and decided to check it out.

He was a week and a half into what he was calling his six-week walkabout. Only he wasn't walking, but driving.

Born and bred in New Orleans, Zac's only venture out of the southern city was a few months ago when his brother, Noah, had been a finalist in a cooking show, and the family had scored a brief trip to Las Vegas. Touring the desert during that long weekend, Zac realized there was a big world out there, and at twenty-nine, he'd seen precious little of it.

Not that there'd been much help for that. Zac had come up with a life plan when he was sixteen and he'd never looked back. After graduating as valedictorian of his class in high school, he'd gotten enough scholarship money and financial aid to attend college. From there, he had been accepted to medical school. He'd just finished up his classes, passed the licensing exam, and was about to embark on a five-year residency at New Orleans East.

As such, he'd spent the majority of his life with his nose buried in a book. When he finally lifted his head and looked around, he realized there was a world outside the medical library. With a month and a half hiatus before beginning his residency, he decided to take advantage of the time—and the RV—and head west. He'd always had a desire to see the Pacific Ocean and Big Sur.

Because his life had been regimented for so long, he decided against mapping a course. Instead, he was rambling his way across the country, taking off-the-beaten-track highways, stopping whenever a place looked interesting, eating when he got hungry, sleeping when he got tired, and refusing to come up with a schedule or deadlines. Only ten days in and he was having the time of this life.

"Still loving the trip?" Justin asked.

"More than I can say."

His brother chuckled. "Gotta admit, I'm jealous. Wish I'd done the same thing when I was younger."

Zac rolled his eyes. "You're not that damn old."

"I'm pushing forty. I've got a business, a mortgage and a pregnant wife who probably wouldn't enjoy spending her last trimester in a rickety RV with me and Ned."

Zac was exceptionally fond of Justin and Ned's wife, Bella. While she was only legally wed to Justin, those closest to the couple knew their lifelong vows had included Ned. "Yeah. I think you're smart to stay put for now. At least until my little niece comes along."

The trio was expecting their first child in July. Neither man knew who the biological father was, and they'd confided to Zac that unless it became medically necessary to know, they would never seek that knowledge. The baby belonged to all three of them. It was a beautiful union, and Zac couldn't wait to hold the newest little Lewis.

"Just got back from Sunday supper at Mama's house. You were missed, bro."

The family had a standing date for dinner at Mama Lewis' house every week. Zac had only missed a handful of times in the past, and now he'd missed two in a row. "Not going to pretend I'm not dreaming about Mama's cooking. There's only so much fast food, sandwiches and cereal one man can take."

Although he had to admit he'd enjoyed his meal at Dottie's Diner this morning. He'd been trying to save money by eating breakfast and lunch in the RV, then finding local places for dinner. However, sometimes if he was still on the highway and starving, he'd slide through a fast-food drive-thru simply for convenience's sake.

"You'll have plenty of time to catch up when you get back. Enjoy your time in Emerald City."

"Sapphire Falls," Zac corrected with a laugh. "And I will. Talk to you soon, Justin."

"Later."

They disconnected the call and Zac glanced around. He'd spent most of the day just roaming around the streets, checking out the booths and picking up some handmade jewelry for his sisters, Chloe and Dani, as well as Mama Lewis. All that was left was to find the caramel apple he'd been craving all day before returning to the RV for the night. While the festival was fun, he planned to hop back onto the highway tomorrow morning to see what else the Midwest had to offer.

As he walked to the booth with all the sweet treats, he searched the crowd once more for the blonde. He wasn't sure what it was about her that had captured his attention, but the attraction he'd felt toward her had been instant and powerful. He'd eaten his entire breakfast in a half-hard state, and he'd been perfectly aware when she had risen and left the diner. She'd glanced back at him when she reached the door and he'd given her a subtle goodbye nod. They hadn't spoken a single word to each other, yet it seemed as if they'd said volumes.

There were two people ahead of him in line so he filed into place and studied the menu. The booth was dedicated to all things sugar—kettle corn, cotton candy, funnel cakes, and caramel apples. Then he noticed there was just one more caramel apple on the woman's pan. He hoped the people in front of him steered clear. His major reason for turning the RV toward Sapphire Falls had been in hopes of finding his favorite carnival fare.

Fortunately, the two customers before him chose other temptations.

"I'll have a caramel apple," Zac said when the woman asked for his order.

"You got the last one," she confirmed as she took his money, and then went to grab the apple.

"Damn," someone muttered behind him.

Zac turned, surprised to find the blonde standing right behind him. Her eyes widened when she realized it was him.

"It's you," she said.

He nodded. "Yep. And it's you."

The smile she gave him sent too much blood traveling south again. What the hell was it about this woman?

"Don't suppose I could talk you into changing your order to a candy apple?"

Zac shook his head. "Nowhere near as good."

She shot him a wry look that said she agreed wholeheartedly. "Probably best that I missed out. I've eaten more junk food today than I have in the past three years put together."

He laughed. "That's what's great about a fair. Health concerns fly out the window."

She tilted her head. "I love your southern accent. Where are you from?"

"New Orleans," he replied.

"Oh! I love that city. I've only been once for a tournament and I didn't get to spend nearly enough time there. It's on the top of my list of places to go back to one day."

"For a tournament?" Zac asked.

"Soccer."

His mind flashed back to the flyer he'd seen advertising the festival. "You're Tacy Bradford."

She nodded. "Guilty."

"Damn. I watched the final of that World Cup game. Y'all kicked ass."

Tacy laughed, clearly pleased by his compliment. "Thanks."

"Are you still playing?"

Her smiled faded briefly before she managed to paste on a sunny expression that didn't fool him a bit. "Unfortunately no. I blew out my knee in practice a few months ago."

"ACL?"

"Meniscus. Big tear. Second one in four years. The doctor suggested I not risk a third."

"Probably good advice." Zac glanced down. "You've had surgery to repair it?"

"Yeah," she replied. "There was a lot of scar tissue from the first surgery, so my recovery took a bit longer. I just got rid of the brace a week ago. Still have some rehab to do, but it feels a lot better. Unfortunately, I've been dealing with pain in the other knee because it's been supporting all my weight the past three months. I had arthroscopic surgery on it about six years ago. Basically, my knees are jacked."

"Soccer's a tough sport on knees. And ankles."

"You seem to know a lot about it. You play?"

"No," Zac replied, grinning. "Just finished up med school. About to start my residency to become an orthopedic surgeon."

"No kidding," she said. "Wow. What are the chances? I'm a regular customer when it comes to orthopedics."

"Well, in that case, let me give you my card." He stuck out his hand. "Zac Lewis."

She accepted his handshake, but the moment her hand touched his, Zac felt a jolt of...something he couldn't describe or understand. All he knew was he was overwhelmed by the desire to keep hold of her hand.

He wondered if she felt the same way because he noticed

she didn't seek to pull away from him. They stared at each other and her expression held the same curiosity that he felt.

Finally, he released her hand.

Tacy shoved her hands in the pockets of her shorts. "You have relatives in Sapphire Falls, Zac?"

Zac shook his head. "No. I actually just happened to be driving by, saw a flyer for the festival and decided to check it out. How about you? You from here?"

"No. I'm just passing through like you. I have a friend who lives in town and she invited me to visit. Are you planning to stay for the entire week?"

Zac had been ready to leave, but now... "Actually no. I intended to get back on the road tomorrow morning. However..."

"However?"

He thought perhaps there was a bit of hope in her expression.

"However, I'm rethinking that."

Her smile grew. "Good."

Zac was suddenly grateful his schedule wasn't set in stone. Suddenly glad he'd made this detour to Sapphire Falls. Suddenly scrambling for a way to keep talking to her.

"Listen, Tacy—" He was about to ask her if she'd like to join him for a drink at the bar he'd just walked by, the Come Again, but his request was cut off when they were joined by another woman.

"There you are." It was the same brunette he'd seen Tacy sitting with in the diner this morning.

"Hey, Lauren." Tacy pointed to him. "This is—"

"It's you!" Lauren said when she glanced in his direction. "The guy from the diner."

Zac chuckled, secretly pleased Tacy's friend recognized

him. Maybe that meant the two of them had talked about him over breakfast. "Zac Lewis."

"Lauren Bennett. Are you in town visiting relatives?"

He shook his head. "Nope. Saw a flyer for the festival at a gas station, somewhere near York. Thought I'd come check it out."

Lauren's brows rose. "Really? Wonderful. I'll have to tell Hailey her advertising was effective. That's a really cool southern accent."

"New Orleans."

"You're a long way from home," Lauren said.

Zac got a sense Lauren was checking him out for her friend. Not that he minded. He was hoping to convince Tacy to spend some time with him. At least until he could figure out what is was about her that had him as smitten as a kitten.

"I have six weeks before I start my residency."

"He's going to be an orthopedic surgeon," Tacy added.

Lauren snorted. "That's convenient."

Zac agreed. "I've always wanted to see the Pacific Ocean, so I borrowed a friend's RV and I'm ten days into a rambling trip cross-country."

Lauren seemed interested in his journey. "And you ended up in Sapphire Falls. Amazing. We're not that easy to find." Lauren glanced at her watch and quietly cursed. "Damn. I really hate to break this up, but the dance is about to begin. You're the third person up for auction."

"Auction?" Zac asked.

Tacy grimaced good-naturedly. "I got drafted."

Lauren gave a more detailed explanation. "The first night of the festival, we hold a dance auction. We have a few local celebrities—and this year Tacy—who agreed to dance with the highest bidder. Were you planning to join the party?"

"I...am now." Zac did a mental calculation, trying to recall how much money he had left in his wallet. He was determined to be the high bidder for Tacy's dance.

"Good." Lauren turned and led the way as the three of them set off toward the dance. Along the way, Lauren gave them an insider's look at Sapphire Falls, pointing out the blue lampposts with speakers in them, the photo booth on the edge of the square, and Borcher's Booze.

Zac made plans to check out the liquor store tomorrow. Lauren had piqued his interest in trying the strawberry Booze. Sounded a bit like moonshine. If it was as good as she proclaimed, he'd take a couple jars back to New Orleans to share with his brothers.

When they arrived at the dance, he waved goodbye as Lauren dragged Tacy toward the stage. The auction appeared to be underway, an auctioneer calling out prices and hopefuls raising their hands to join the bidding.

It was a good thing Lauren had found them when she had, because Tacy was onstage within minutes of their arrival. He watched as several men entered the bidding early. Zac studied his competition, biding his time.

The auctioneer had been just about to seal the deal, selling Tacy's dance to some muscle-bound farm-boy type. There was no way Zac was going to let that guy win. He raised his hand at the last minute, adding twenty bucks and a caramel apple for the lady to the last bid.

Several folks around him laughed at his extra incentive.

The farm boy looked surprised as he considered his opponent. Zac held his gaze, letting him know he had no intention of losing. After just a moment, the man good-naturedly nodded his head in defeat, and then looked back to the auctioneer. He shook his head and Zac was declared the winner.

Zac had been struck over and over today by how nice everyone in this town was. He hadn't passed a single person who hadn't said hello or welcomed him to Sapphire Falls. He'd run into some lively cast of characters who called themselves the Blue Brigade earlier. They had given him a card that told him to shake hands with and introduce himself to a stranger.

The random guy who had been walking by at that time—Travis—was clearly a local. He caught a glimpse of the card in Zac's hand and took the impromptu introduction in stride.

Zac couldn't imagine such a thing flying in New Orleans. Not that there weren't friendly people in his hometown. It was simply that there were a lot of eccentric, offbeat, and even sketchy, stay-the-hell-away types, and as a whole, locals were more guarded until they knew a person.

Tacy grinned widely as she left the stage and joined him. "You realize I would have danced with you later for free?"

Zac handed her the caramel apple. "Call me greedy, but I want all your dances tonight."

Tacy didn't seem to mind his forwardness, but she still teased him. "And you think one little old caramel apple will guarantee that?"

"Will it?"

She nodded. "Oh heck yeah."

The music began—an old Elvis tune—and Zac grasped Tacy's hand.

"Hang on a second." She pulled away to place her apple on the table where Lauren was sitting with a little girl on her lap, and then she returned.

The moment her hands landed on his shoulders, Zac realized that even if he danced every single dance with her tonight, it still wouldn't be enough. He pulled her closer thinking that—odd as it seemed—he felt the same way as Elvis, as if he couldn't help falling in love with this woman.

Tacy didn't appear unaffected either. A fact she confirmed when she spoke. "Is it weird that I feel like I know you?"

He shook his head. "No. I feel the same way. Maybe we knew each other in a previous life."

He'd meant his words as a joke, but Tacy didn't laugh. Instead, she seemed to consider the supposition. "I like that idea. Makes it sound like we're soul mates and we've managed to cross generations, worlds, lifetimes to find each other."

"Are you looking for a soul mate, darlin'?"

"Isn't everyone?"

Until that moment, Zac hadn't been. It wasn't that he wasn't interested in romance, love, sex, marriage and kids. Eventually. All of those things were certainly on his list, under the heading Someday.

He'd been so focused, so intent on becoming a doctor, everything else had taken a backseat. Zac had dated. And he'd indulged in more than a few sexual affairs. He was only human, after all, and a man had needs. But he'd kept serious emotion out of it. Because there hadn't been time.

"You went quiet." Tacy was looking at him, still waiting for an answer. "Didn't mean to freak you out or anything."

He *was* freaked out. Not by her question, but by what it revealed. This trip had opened his eyes to how many places, how many adventures and opportunities he'd let pass him by as he kept his eyes on just one prize. Now he was forced to add love to the list. Until holding Tacy, he hadn't realized how much he'd wanted someone to share his life with.

Zac placed his cheek against the top of her head as they continued to dance. "We must have been soul mates in another life because now that you're here, I realize how much I've missed you."

She leaned back a few inches, looking up at his face. "That's the most romantic thing anyone's ever said to me."

"You caught me on a good night," he joked, trying to find a way to lighten the moment, to put them back on steadier ground. He never acted like this on first dates. Hell, this wasn't even a first date, was it?

Regardless, he never came on this strong. Must be all the fresh air, rich food and lack of deadlines. He was acting loopy with all this relaxation and freedom.

Tacy rested her head against his chest as he tightened his grip, molding their bodies together. She didn't resist the closeness, despite the fact they were virtual strangers.

Or maybe they weren't. If they weren't soul mates, there was no denying they were kindred spirits. There was something in her eyes that told him she was just now recognizing the same deep-seated loneliness he'd found within himself.

She felt good in his arms. Zac couldn't remember the last time he'd danced with a woman. God, now that he considered it, he was pretty sure it was senior prom.

The song came to an end, a faster tune taking its place. He and Tacy simply continued to sway, finding their own rhythm through the next three songs.

Tacy was the first to step away. "Getting kind of warm in here. Want to go for a walk?"

Zac nodded. He was feeling the heat as well, but it had nothing to do with the actual temperature at the dance and everything to do with the effect she was having on his libido. "Yeah. I'd like that."

He stood near the exit as Tacy said goodbye to Lauren, who was slow dancing with the man he'd met earlier on the street, Travis. The couple glanced his way. Lauren winked, while Travis offered him a friendly smile. Both responses surprised him.

In the Lewis clan, the men were far too protective of the females. His sisters, Chloe and Dani, had been forced to endure as their older brothers, Caliph, Justin and Jett, subjected their dates to some serious third degrees. He and

Noah had been younger than the others, so they'd mainly just watched. And learned.

While *he* knew he was a decent guy, he couldn't believe Lauren and Travis would let her leave the dance with a complete stranger. Then again, he couldn't imagine Sapphire Falls had much crime. Knowing this idyllic, modern-day Mayberry, the law probably never dealt with anything more serious than someone keeping a fish that was too small or hunting out of season.

"You ready?" She had retrieved her caramel apple and held out her free hand to him.

He took it, enjoying the warmth of it as they stepped out into the crisp night air. Zac glanced up at the stars. "Never see a sky like that in the city."

Tacy looked up as well. "It's beautiful here. First time in Nebraska?"

He nodded. "With the exception of Vegas, this trip is my first time anywhere."

"Really?" She seemed fascinated by that information, and he figured he was a bit of an anomaly to someone like her, who'd traveled all over the world. Her next comment confirmed that. "Sometimes I feel like I've been everywhere. And nowhere. Despite all the places I've traveled to, I didn't see much more than the hotels and the stadiums. Kind of a waste, now that I think about it."

"You're still young. Start over. Maybe my friend will let you borrow his RV and you can take your own hobo adventure."

She laughed. "I love what you're doing. It's so cool."

He lifted one shoulder casually. "The trip is just my way of making up for lost time. Doing things I never had the chance to do."

Tacy studied his face as they walked. He liked the way she wasn't shy around him. She didn't demur or avoid his eyes.

Instead, she looked him straight in the face and didn't bother to hide her thoughts. "Like what?"

"I've lived a fairly single-minded existence for the past decade or so. Focusing on achieving my career goals. Now I'm at a place where I find I have some regrets about the things I've missed."

Tacy blew out a long sigh. "I can relate to that."

"How so?"

"Soccer has been my life since, well, forever. Without it, I'm sort of stuck, trying to figure out who I am, what my purpose is now."

"Sounds like we've both been walking the straight and narrow for a while. I've spent the last week wondering if there's more to me than just medicine. Talking to you has made me realize exactly how much I've missed."

"What do you mean?"

"With the exception of you, I haven't danced with a woman since high school prom."

Her eyes widened. "No way."

"What can I say? I'm a pretty boring guy."

"I don't buy that for a minute. The fact that you had the guts to hop in an RV and head west with no real aim tells me you're far from dull. I wish I had your sense of adventure."

"Don't sell yourself so short, Tacy. None of us are just one thing. Something tells me you could do anything you set your mind to. Soccer was one passion. You'll find a new one soon enough."

He probably shouldn't have used the word passion while talking to her because it sent his mind straight to the bedroom. Zac was struggling to keep his cock under control after holding her so closely during the dance. He didn't want to scare the poor woman away this soon in the game.

She smiled appreciatively. "You're going to be a great doctor, Zac. You have an amazing bedside manner."

Great. That didn't help either.

Zac considered himself a gentleman, but right now, he was having a hard time keeping all his thoughts about Tacy pure. She was truly beautiful, with long trim legs, a slender build, a bright smile and the most expressive eyes he'd ever seen. Plus she smelled like sugar.

Time to deflect, to distract himself. "So tell me about yourself."

He and Tacy meandered around the town square no less than a dozen times, talking until the wee hours. She reminisced about winning the gold in the World Cup, about the parties, parades and celebrations that followed.

Then her stories turned to her childhood. The dance had ended hours ago, the rides and booths closed down. Even the lampposts were silent, the music shut off.

And still they walked. She told him about her parents, their ambitious goals for her, the pressure to constantly succeed. He'd been outraged on her behalf, upset for the little girl she'd been, the one who hadn't gotten a carefree childhood.

"God. I feel like I'm the only one talking. How about you? What do your folks do?" she asked.

Zac sucked in a deep breath. As a rule, he didn't talk about his childhood. Not the earlier stuff anyway. However, he loved talking about the Lewises. "I was in the foster system."

Her forehead creased with concern. "Oh, I'm sorry."

"Don't be. My experience was positive. My brother and I were taken in by the most amazing woman on the face of the earth. Mama Lewis took us away from a bad situation and provided a wonderful home."

Tacy smiled. "She sounds great."

"You have no idea. Before her, I didn't have a clue what it

meant to feel secure, safe. She gave me and Noah a home, a family, unconditional love. It was because of her I had enough confidence to follow my dreams and study medicine."

He hadn't meant to reveal so much, but Tacy was easy to talk to. Words he'd never spoken aloud just seemed to fall out around her.

"How old were you when you moved in with her?"

They were entering forbidden territory. Zac hadn't talked about his mom to anyone in years, with the exception of Mama Lewis, and even that hadn't been much.

Unlike his brother, Noah, he'd remained in touch with their real mother. He knew it was ridiculous, but there'd always been a part of him that believed he could save her. As the years passed, he'd realized that was more and more unlikely. Regardless, he checked in on her monthly. He never gave her actual cash, but he took her food. He'd learned the hard way that no matter how hungry she might be, any money he gave her would go to feed her addiction, not her stomach.

"When I was fifteen."

"It must have been tough for you before that."

He couldn't go into those details. That was a time he refused to revisit, even in his own mind. He just shut it out. "I lived."

Tacy looked as if she wanted to ask more, but mercifully she let it drop. She glanced at the B&B. They'd walked past it three times already on their rambling stroll around town. Each time, they'd stopped, kept talking, and before they knew it, they were taking another lap around the square.

"This is my stop."

"Yeah." Zac looked at his watch and winced. "Damn. Three a.m. Didn't mean to keep you out so late."

They had run into her friends, Lauren and Travis, when

they were leaving the dance. He'd overheard them making plans to meet for breakfast at Dottie's Diner at eight a.m.

Tacy shrugged. "I'm used to getting up early. Most of our workouts started at the crack of dawn. Are you still planning to leave tomorrow?"

He shook his head. Zac wasn't sure what was going on between them, but he wanted more time to explore it. "No. I think I'm going to stay a little longer." Maybe the whole week. It would cut into his West Coast time, but he didn't doubt it would be worth it.

"Good."

The genuine pleasure on her face was more than he could resist. Zac reached out, cupped her cheek and kissed her.

He'd kissed his fair share of girls, but none of them—not one—impacted him like Tacy.

She wrapped her arms around his neck, her breasts pressing against his chest. He tightened his hold on her, moving his hands to grip her hips, to pull her more firmly against him.

She tasted like apples and sugar, remnants of the caramel apple they'd shared. His tongue swiped against hers, exploring the warmth of her mouth.

Tacy ran her fingers through his hair, turning her head so that he could deepen the kiss. Zac didn't have a clue how long they stood there. It didn't matter. He didn't want this to end. Ever.

She was the first to pull away, to suck in a deep breath. "Wow. Not sure, but I think I might have seen some fireworks there."

He chuckled, her openness and humor inviting. "Me too. It's been a while since I've actually kissed anyone. Was afraid I might be a little rusty."

"I think it's like riding a bike." She looked over her shoulder at the inn, and he thought he saw something like regret on her face. Was she sorry to leave him? To see the night end? He knew *he* was.

"Well," she started.

"What's on the celebrity's agenda for tomorrow?" he asked. "Need an escort?"

Her face brightened. "There's a softball game, but I'm not playing in it. Not sure my knee is ready for that. So I'm free. I was hoping we could ride the Ferris wheel and check out the haunted house. And maybe after..."

She flushed as her words faded away.

"After..." he prompted.

"I was hoping you'd give me a tour of your RV. My parents weren't campers—tent, RV or otherwise. Always wanted to see the inside of one of those."

The idea of having Tacy alone in his RV was going to wreak havoc on his self-control. Even now he was rock hard and hurting.

But he'd only met her a few hours ago. And Tacy wasn't the sort of woman you had a one-night stand with. She was too sweet, too nice...too special.

Unfortunately, they were living on borrowed time—approximately seven days' worth—and then they were heading in different directions to places unknown. He needed to make every second of it count.

Maybe he was going too fast. But the way he saw it, they didn't have any other choice.

So it was going to be life in the fast lane this week. After so many years of plodding along in slow motion, he liked the idea of a whirlwind.

With Tacy.

In Sapphire Falls.

CHAPTER THREE

Tacy didn't even bother to dim her smile as she and Zac sat side by side atop the Ferris wheel. The sky was bright blue without a single cloud to mar the vivid color. The late afternoon sun was shining but not blazing too hot, and there was a slight breeze that had their seat swaying gently.

Up here, she could see forever, could take in the beauty of this quaint little town, nestled in the midst of the sea of green farms that surrounded it. The carnival was hopping, loads of people milling around below them, playing the games, eating junk food, laughing and talking. The soft strains of Frank Sinatra singing in the background of all the normal fair sounds simply added to the ambiance, the sheer magic of the moment.

Of course, the fact she was sitting next to the sexiest southern doctor she'd ever met didn't hurt either.

Tacy had felt like a teenager on her very first date last night as she and Zac spent hours just walking and talking. He'd been completely engaged, interested in hearing what she had to say, and when he spoke, she found herself equally enthralled.

So much so, she'd woken up excited and energetic, despite the fact she hadn't managed more than a few hours' sleep. And she'd been thrilled to discover he was awake and thinking of her too when he texted to see when she wanted to meet.

Zac had joined her and Lauren for breakfast and they'd been together every moment since then. The more she learned about him, the more her infatuation, her attraction grew.

He was a fascinating man, to have achieved so much when he'd clearly come from such a rough beginning.

And when he'd kissed her...

Oh man. That kiss last night had knocked her socks off. Perfect amount of pressure, tongue, and his hands gripped her in just the right places. She'd had good kisses and she'd suffered through some shitty ones. Zac's was, by far, the best ever.

In fact...

She turned to face him at the same time he looked at her. Her gaze landed on his lips, and she noticed his stare was in the exact same place.

"I'm going to kiss you, darlin'."

She licked her lips as she grinned. "That's funny. I thought *I* was going to kiss *you*."

They moved toward each other without another word. And just like that, Tacy was blown away. Again.

She was vaguely aware of when the Ferris wheel began to move again. She sort of thought she heard some catcalls and whistles when they whizzed by, closest to the ground, but none of that mattered. Not the view. Not the public display of affection. Nothing.

She was Tacy Bradford, former soccer player. A woman with no job, no home, no clue. And she didn't give a damn because she was kissing Dr. Zac Lewis at a carnival.

The kiss might have gone on forever if not for the interruption of someone clearing their throat nearby. She and Zac both turned their heads in unison, surprised to find themselves face-to-face with the carnie running the ride. He was amused and patiently waiting for them to debark.

"Sorry 'bout that," Zac said in a tone that was far from sorry.

The man lifted the bar securing them inside the car and they got out. Tacy giggled as Zac warned the man they would be back later with double the tickets. He wanted a longer ride.

The man chuckled as he tipped his head, drawing her attention to his dusty ball cap emblazoned with the words Midway Magic Carnival Supplies on it. "I'll be waiting."

Zac took her hand as the two of them debated their next move.

"We could grab something to eat from a booth now," he suggested. "Or head over to the haunted house first, and then hit the diner for a sit-down supper."

She grinned at his twang as he rolled his eyes. Tacy found it hard to resist mimicking some of his more southern sounds. Zac didn't take offense. Instead, he turned it up a notch for her entertainment. "We can see if Dottie will whip us up some shrimp and grits."

"Hey, there you are." Lauren walked up with her daughter, Whitney. "Heard you two just put on quite a show on the Ferris wheel."

Tacy laughed. "Dear God. There's no way you could have heard that already. It literally just happened."

Lauren shrugged. "News travels at a normal pace in Sapphire Falls. Gossip flies at the speed of light. Softball game is about to start. I'm heading over to watch. Wanna join me?"

Zac looked at Tacy, clearly leaving the decision up to her. She loved how considerate he was. "Maybe we'll meet up with you later. Right now, we're going to check out the haunted house."

Lauren's eyes narrowed as she studied Zac more closely. "Ferris wheel *and* haunted house? You sure you're not a local boy, Zac?"

Confused by her question, he asked, "This accent doesn't prove that?"

Tacy giggled. "Apparently the local guys have learned how to incorporate the Ferris wheel and haunted house into their seduction routines."

Zac wrapped his arm around Tacy's shoulders. "Thanks for the tip, Lauren."

Lauren rolled her eyes as she waved. "Go have fun. But be warned. You get too carried away and I'll know about it before you manage to get to the ball game."

"We'll behave," Tacy promised.

"Don't write checks you can't cash, sweet pea," he teased Tacy, before looking at Lauren again. "We'll be discreet," Zac amended as Lauren's loud laughter caught the attention of several people walking by.

"Text me later, Tace. Let me know if you two want to meet up for dinner with me and Travis."

They waved goodbye, Lauren heading for the game as they took off for the haunted house.

Zac claimed her hand. She loved the feel of his fingers looped through hers. It made her feel safe, protected, cared for. Probably strange emotions considering she wasn't in danger, but after a lifetime of fending for herself, this one simple act—holding hands with Zac—had her longing for so much more.

"Am I the only one who thinks a haunted house in June is strange?"

Tacy paused as they passed one of the craft booths. "Oh, I love that scarf. Remind me to come back," she said as they continued walking. "Lauren says they all know it's weird to have a haunted house this time of year, but I think they keep it going because the local boys don't want to have to find some other way to get a girl they like alone in a dark room. Guess they're fans of the tried and true."

"Well, when you put it that way, it's not so weird after all."

Zac handed the man at the door their tickets to enter, then grinned when Tacy wrapped her arm around his waist, clinging to him tightly.

"Scared already? We haven't even walked in."

"I'm going to warn you right now. Stuff like this gets to me. People jumping out of dark corners. Loud, unexpected noises. Every horror movie ever made. I'm the girl who closes her eyes, screams and startles easily. I'm probably going to look like a lunatic."

"Then why are we here?"

Tacy gave him a flirtatious smile. "I'm hoping you'll take advantage of my irrational fears."

"Challenge accepted."

They walked in together as Zac wrapped his arm around her shoulders. "Not going to lie. I like playing the role of protector. I haven't been in a haunted house since I was a teenager."

"Man, you really *have* been in a rut."

"Yeah. Just needed to find a pretty girl to help me break free." He looked around the dark room with the scary music playing. "Oh yeah. This place is great."

"Figures you'd like it. I bet you're the type who loves horror movies too."

Before he could reply, a zombie seemed to detach itself from what Tacy had thought was a blank wall, approaching them with a loud groan.

She jumped at least five feet in the air and screamed.

Zac laughed as he quickly guided her away from the horrible creature and into another room.

While she'd feared how she would react, she had actually

believed she could control it better. After all, she knew none of this was real. "Shit. That was embarrassing."

"It was ador—"

Before Zac could finish, a spider dropped from the ceiling right in front of her. Even though her brain said fake, the rest of her reacted instinctively.

"Oh my God! Motherfucker!" She dodged behind Zac, gripping his shirt so tightly she was in danger of tearing it right off him.

Zac batted the plastic thing away and pulled her farther along, not bothering to loosen her grip on his shirt. "Maybe we should walk faster. Get this over with. I'm starting to worry about you, darlin'."

"I thought I could handle—"

The sound of a witch cackling loudly filled the room and Tacy screamed in outright terror.

"That's it." Zac reached out to open a closed door nearby. He pushed her inside, following quickly before shutting them in.

Tacy gazed around the dim room. "Um, Zac. I think this is a closet."

"Yeah. I thought you might like a breather before we go back out there and try to find the exit."

Her heart was still racing, her hands shaking, but now that she knew nothing was going to come at her, she was beginning to relax. "Thanks. I appreciate that."

She released a long breath just before Zac stepped closer.

"Besides, I seem to recall a challenge being laid down earlier."

Tacy laughed softly. Obviously she stood corrected. There was something coming at her in here too. And it made her heart race even faster.

The difference was this time she wasn't afraid. Not even a little.

She lifted her arms to his shoulders as he bent to kiss her. Three kisses in, and every time, he took her breath away. Zac kissed her as if she mattered, as though she was special.

There was no denying the intensity of the kiss, but there was also a gentleness behind it. She appreciated that care as much as it drove her nuts. She felt as if he was holding back.

This time when their lips parted, she decided to test the waters. She nipped at his lower lip, slowly increasing the pressure until Zac pulled away.

There was a tiny, frosted window in the far wall, but there appeared to be a large tree blocking the sunlight from streaming in. As such, the room was painted in a dim gray that left her and Zac in shadows. Nevertheless, she could still make out his hungry expression.

She'd surprised him. And aroused him.

"You wanna play rough?" His voice was deep, husky, that gorgeous southern accent adding even more wetness to her already-damp panties. Tacy hadn't had sex in one year, two months, three days and a handful of hours. And sadly, it hadn't been much to write home about.

Zac set her body on fire. Her nipples were tight, her pussy clenching. She feared one touch from him in the right spot and she'd spontaneously combust.

God. She was so tired of finding her own lukewarm orgasms. Tired of being alone. Tired of feeling out of control.

Everything she'd known, planned, and expected in life had been blown to bits in one stupid fall.

Maybe she didn't know where she was going in the future, but she knew exactly what she wanted right now. And it was Zac.

"Yeah," she replied. "Rough is good."

Zac closed his eyes at her response. She wasn't sure if he was turned on, praying or overwhelmed. All three ideas described her current state of mind fairly well. She liked the idea that he might feel the same.

When his lids lifted, she was treated to the sexiest, horniest look ever cast her way.

"We've only known each other a day. I was trying to be a gentleman."

Zac wasn't saying anything that hadn't crossed her mind every second since they'd struck up that conversation over caramel apples. Perhaps if they'd met under normal circumstances, they would have moved at a steadier, slower pace. Gone on a few dates, spent several weeks talking on the phone and texting, taken the time to get to know each other before jumping into something sexual.

But this wasn't a normal situation. Zac was only here for a few more days and then he was on the road again to Big Sur, and then his future as a doctor in New Orleans.

As for her, her life was one big question mark. All her belongings were packed in boxes in her parents' garage in Longview as she tried to figure out what came next. Maybe if she weren't in such a state of flux, of utter confusion, she'd be better able to figure out what it was about Zac that was pushing all the right buttons and making her act so out of character.

Her gut told her it was vacation brain. Both of them were taking a break from real life and stress and...common sense. People did things on vacation they would never do in their everyday lives. Scuba diving, zip lines, luaus on the beach, making out with a sexy doctor in the closet of a haunted house in June.

"Zac?"

"Yeah."

"I don't care how long we've known each other. And I don't

mind that it's moving way too fast. I just really, *really* want to be with you."

He didn't reply, didn't smile. As far as she could tell, he didn't even take a breath. Instead, he pressed his lips to hers firmly and gave her the kiss she'd been waiting for. The one that told her everything she needed to know. Zac might be a sweet, patient, funny, easygoing doctor on the surface, but underneath, he was a bad boy.

His hands gripped her head, turning it so that he could take the kiss from scorching to hotter than the surface of the sun instantly.

Tacy dug her fingers into the muscles of his upper arms, searching for something to hold on to, something to keep her from dissolving into a puddle of goo at his feet.

As they kissed, Zac pressed her back three steps until he had her caged against the wall. It was a move worthy of Hollywood, and it drove the temperature in the tiny space up another twenty degrees.

Zac kept one hand on her head, using it to direct the kiss as the other slid lower, skimming over all the parts of her body that desperately wanted to be touched. He palmed one of her breasts, squeezing the flesh, pinching the nipple.

She kept trying to break free of the kiss in search of some much-needed air. She was light-headed, dizzy. Zac granted her no reprieve, his mouth taking hers relentlessly, beautifully.

Tacy moaned when his hand moved lower, reaching down to grip the hem of her miniskirt. She'd thrown the thing into her suitcase at the last minute, not really expecting to wear it. She was a jeans-and-shorts kind of girl. This morning, she'd been grateful to have something pretty...and sexy to wear for him.

His fingers traveled beneath the material, tickling the tops of her thighs, journeying closer. God. So close to the place she really needed to be touched.

Finally, Zac released her lips. "Open your legs, darlin'."

It was the third time he'd used that term of endearment and when spoken with that accent of his, it was deadly to her libido. No one had ever bothered with a sweet nickname for her like that. Always a tomboy and a jock, she wasn't viewed by guys as the type of girl worthy of something so cute, so panty-melting adorable.

Her thighs parted almost of their own volition and Zac took immediate advantage. He tugged her panties aside, his fingers sliding along her slit.

His eyes met hers and she blushed. She was soaking wet. She might be more embarrassed by that if Zac wasn't looking at her as if she was the pot of gold at the end of the rainbow.

"You're the sexiest woman I've ever met."

She smiled. "I'd be more flattered if you hadn't admitted to spending the majority of the past eight years in the library."

Zac chuckled. "I think librarians are hot."

"Zac?"

"Yeah?"

"Start with two fingers."

"Fuck me," Zac muttered. Then, he granted her request, driving two fingers inside her as deep as they would go.

Tacy's head flew back, her eyes drifting shut, as he thrust the fingers in and out. He took her with the roughness she'd always dreamed about, but had never managed to find. Her hips moved in time as she sought more stimulation, more...

"God, more."

Zac's thumb found her clit, stroking it firmly as his fingers still moved inside her.

And then she stiffened, her back arching as the unexpected orgasm struck her like lightning.

"Holy shit," she whispered as her body trembled so hard her bones rattled. "Fuck."

Zac's fingers remained buried deep inside her, but he no longer moved. Instead, he gave her time to find her bearings, to recover.

What the hell had just happened?

One minute she was enjoying the festival with a stranger, the next she was in a dark closet with a guy's hand up her skirt.

"I've never come so quickly," she admitted, not bothering to hide her amazement. Orgasms had never been all that easy for her to achieve. They typically took a bit of work on the part of both her and her lover.

Zac slowly withdrew his fingers, kissing her as he did so.

She shivered, the final traces of her climax rumbling through her. "I—"

Tacy wasn't sure what to do next. She wasn't a selfish lover, but the truth was, while Zac had rocked her world, she hadn't done the same for him.

A scream outside the door caused them both to jerk slightly. God. They were in a haunted house. In a closet with an unlocked door. Anyone could open it and catch them.

Though she hadn't spoken her concerns, Zac seemed to have an inside track on her thoughts. "This probably isn't the best place for us to continue. What do you say we try to make our way out of this haunted house without you having a heart attack and get something to eat?"

She glanced down. Even in the dim light, she could see the outline of his erection pressing against his jeans. "What about—"

He kissed her before she could finish her question. "And after supper, I'll give you that tour of my RV. If you're still interested."

She loved the way he was giving her a choice. Even after what they'd just done, he was giving her a way out if she wanted one.

Tacy was familiar with the concept of a southern gentleman—thanks to *Gone With the Wind*—but she'd always believed that ideal had disappeared right after the Civil War.

"I still want the tour."

Zac sighed. "Not gonna pretend I'm not glad to hear that." Then he paused. "Wait, do you just want to see the camper or..."

He let her fill in the blanks, which she did with a laugh. "I want the full tour. And maybe a sleepover after."

Zac cupped her cheek. "Just so you know, keep saying stuff like that and I'm not going to have any choice but to fall in love with you."

Her heart literally skipped a beat at his sweet confession. She was fairly certain she was halfway to falling for him too. "You won't hear an argument from me."

"Let's get out of here." Zac took her hand and led her from the closet. A group of three teens were making their way through the haunted house and the entire group jumped back and screamed at their sudden appearance. Obviously they thought she and Zac were part of the entertainment.

Tacy jumped as well, and Zac laughed. "Sorry 'bout that," he said to the kids before guiding her from the room. She managed to make it through the rest of the scary tour without screaming, but it was a close call.

Once they made it back out onto the main street, Tacy's phone beeped. She glanced at the text. "Lauren wants to know if we want to meet up with her and Travis at the diner for dinner."

"It's up to you. I know you're here to visit your friend and I've been monopolizing your time."

Tacy was touched by his thoughtfulness, and torn. She *had* come to Sapphire Falls to catch up with her old friend, but her body was still thrumming from the orgasm she'd just had, and the greedy, selfish, ohmigodgimmemore side of her was having a hard time deciding.

Her phone beeped again and she laughed.

Zac glanced over her shoulder and chuckled as well. "I like Lauren."

Lauren had texted *Unless you've had a better offer. If so, we can meet for breakfast. No. Zac is hot. Make that lunch.*

Tacy texted back, not bothering to hide her response from Zac, who clearly approved. "Diner for lunch."

Lauren's reply was one word. *Squeeeeeeeeeee!*

Zac reclaimed her hand and they walked through town to the campground just across the highway. "I have some snacks in the RV that might tide us over until tomorrow. And if not, we can come back later and grab a late meal."

They meandered along the park's path, past quite a few RVs, all tricked out and clearly here for the week's festivities.

When they reached Zac's, he turned to her. "This is me."

Zac didn't have the camper's awning rolled out, no beach chairs or card tables with food, or wood in the fire pit. It actually looked as though he was ready to fire the thing up and roll out of town. Which reminded her that he had only remained in Sapphire Falls in order to spend today with her.

What were his plans for tomorrow? And the day after that? Tacy knew he was looking forward to seeing the West Coast and his vacation time was limited. Could she really ask him to stay the entire week?

Once again, she was struck by the fact that she'd only known this man twenty-four hours. It seemed like longer.

"Zac," she said softly.

"If you've changed your mind, we can turn around right now and I'll walk you back to your friends."

He'd misunderstood her reticence.

Tacy shook her head. "No. That's not what I want. At all."

"What's wrong, Tacy?"

She let go of her inhibitions. She was here to live in the moment, to let go of the anxiety that hadn't left her since she'd given up her place on the team. Worrying about the future wouldn't keep it from coming, so she couldn't let those fears ruin right now. Because right now was pretty damn awesome.

"Nothing's wrong, Zac. Can we go in?"

CHAPTER FOUR

Zac sensed something was bothering Tacy, but whatever it was, she didn't seem inclined to share. He walked to the camper door, unlocked it and waited as she stepped inside.

"Hey. This is really great." Tacy spun around slowly, taking in his temporary home as he remained by the door and watched her.

"Yeah. It's not bad, is it?"

"Nice of your friend to let you borrow it."

Zac shrugged. "Ned is actually more like family. He and my brother, Justin, are partners in a marketing firm and best friends. They're also..." He paused, wondering what Tacy would think of his brother's marital dynamics. They didn't really broadcast the unorthodox relationship to strangers, but everyone in their close circle of friends knew that Justin was in a committed ménage relationship.

"Also?" she prompted. Then her face cleared. "Oh, are they dating too?"

Zac shook his head. "Not exactly."

Her confusion was adorable and he couldn't resist tapping her crinkled-up nose as she waited for him to explain.

"They're both married to the same woman."

Her frown deepened. "That's not legal."

He lifted his hands, palms toward her. "Bella is legally married to Justin, but committed to both him and Ned."

Tacy looked intrigued. "And it works? They're all happy?"

"Yeah. Expecting their first kid in a month or so. Truth is, my foster sister, Dani, is in the same type of relationship."

"Ménages run in the family?"

Zac chuckled. "Not for all of us."

"Not you?"

"No. Not me." Zac had seen Justin with his partners, and Dani with hers, and he'd been fascinated by the dynamics and happy that his siblings had found not one, but two people to spend the rest of their lives with. However, Zac had always known he was destined for coupledom, not a threesome. "Why? You interested in trying something like that?"

Tacy was quick to shake her head. "Good God, no. Not that there's anything wrong with it for them. I'm just...well...I'll be lucky to find one person willing to put up with my crap for a lifetime. Can't imagine there are two such patient souls roaming the earth."

Zac knew she meant her words as a joke, but something told him there was a thread of truth buried in the comment as well. Did she really believe herself difficult? Unlovable? Because he hadn't found a single flaw in her yet.

Granted, it had only been a day, but he'd spent far less time with other women and found plenty to keep him from pursing another date with them.

"Wait. Did you say Dani? You don't mean Dani Lewis, the singer?"

Zac nodded. "Yep. That's her. For the record, I'm also

related to Jett Lewis, the writer and my other brother, Noah, just won the grand prize on the TV show *Food Fight*. That was why I traveled to Vegas. The whole family went to see him in the finale."

Tacy's mouth hung open for just a second before she managed to close it. "That's incredible. And your other siblings?"

"Chloe's a photographer and Caliph is one of the best tattoo artists in New Orleans. A family full of creative types. Until you get to me."

She grinned. "No artistic ability?"

"Can't draw stick figures, and I seem to be the only person on the planet who can't get a clear shot with a basic camera phone."

Her delight grew as she continued to tease. "Can't sing? Play an instrument?"

"Nope. And before you ask, I can't write or cook up a storm in the kitchen either."

She sighed heavily. "Such a shame. Well, looks like barring all that, you really had no choice but to settle for a boring career in medicine and becoming a surgeon."

He reached out to grab her, wrapping her in a playful hug as he messed up her hair, much in the same way he would his sisters whenever they teased him. "Yeah. I'm a real disappointment to my family."

She wrestled her way out of his grip, laughing loudly. "I bet you are. Probably just a matter of time before they start cropping you out of the family photos. No one wants to admit they have an orthopedic surgeon in the family."

Tacy escaped his next attempt to pull her close for a tickle. Instead she began backing away from him down the narrow hallway. Zac continued to chase her, pleased with her direction. She was headed straight for the bedroom.

She didn't stop moving or giggling until her knees hit the edge of his bed unexpectedly and she tumbled to her back. The laughter ended with a gasp when she realized where she was. And that he was standing above her.

Tacy looked around the room, and then pushed herself up to a sitting position. "Big bed for an RV."

"Yeah. Didn't appreciate that fact until just this minute."

He sat down next to her, but didn't touch her. He wanted to give her a chance to decide if this was really what she wanted. She had said as much in town and even just outside the RV a few minutes ago. But he also understood feelings could change when faced with the moment of truth.

When she didn't balk at his closeness, he decided to test the waters, reaching out to run his fingers through her thick blonde hair. "You're so beautiful, Tacy."

She smiled shyly. "So are you. I mean…"

He enjoyed her flushed cheeks. Zac knew she wasn't inexperienced, yet there was an innocence to her responses that triggered his desire to care for her, to take things slow, to protect her.

"Are you leaving tomorrow?"

Her abrupt question took him off guard. Then he understood her reticence outside. He shook his head. "Hadn't planned on it. I'm not sure what's going on between us. I mean, I'm as sensible and boring as they come, and I know deep inside we're moving too fast and in the end, we'll be heading in different directions. Regardless, I can't make myself leave. I want to spend the rest of this week with you."

"You do?" Her tone was the perfect blend of surprise and pleasure.

"What do you say we throw caution to the wind?"

She tilted her head. "Whirlwind romance?"

Zac had never pictured himself as the romantic type, but

he'd been forced to endure enough chick flicks with his sisters and Mama Lewis that he figured he could pull it off. "Sounds good to me."

He thought his response would please her, but instead she bit her lip nervously. "Zac, I'm not sure when I'm going to get the chance to..." She glanced behind her at the bed.

"Chance to?"

"It's been a long time since I've had a long-term boyfriend. And even when I did date a guy for longer than a few months, the relationships were long-distance, which meant they always felt more like a string of first dates. I've never had a chance to..."

Again the pause. "Spit it out, darlin'. You're not going to scare me away, no matter what you say."

"I've never had a chance to experiment in bed." Her words came out in a rush, so quickly he almost didn't understand what she said.

When he finally puzzled them out and let them soak in, he fought not to readjust his pants. His cock had gone from merely stiff to rock-hard concrete in two-point-one seconds.

"Experiment how?"

Tacy's gaze was averted, her attention seemingly focused on her hands, which were clenched in her lap. "Nothing too wild."

"Give me an example."

Her cheeks moved out of the pink range into flaming red. Even so, he liked that—despite such a short acquaintance—she trusted him enough to ask.

"No one's ever made me come so quickly. Or even, you know, on their own. I've always had to help my orgasms along. But you..."

She was obviously recalling their time in the closet.

"You seem to know how to. I mean, you're really good at..." Tacy released a frustrated sigh. "I don't want just missionary.

And I don't want you constantly asking for permission or if I'm okay. And I sort of like the idea of being taken...hard. Roughly."

He frowned, his assumptions about her innocence confirmed. Then he felt annoyance at her past lovers. What kind of man could look at Tacy and not want to possess her, claim her? "Christ. What kind of guys have you been sleeping with?"

Tacy looked at him curiously. "What do you mean?"

"You're not exactly asking for anything weird here, Tace. I was expecting you to start listing kinky stuff when you said you wanted to experiment."

"What do you mean by kinky?" She looked way too interested in that explanation. His cock thickened even more. Fucking jeans were killing him.

"We'll get there. Eventually. For now, I want you to stand up and take your clothes off for me."

She looked surprised by his request. "You're not going to undress me?"

Tacy was used to mild lovers, sweet guys. It dawned on him she didn't want romance. She wanted the complete opposite. Which was a lucky break for him. Romance would have been a challenge. Domination, meanwhile, fit him like a glove.

"I'm not going to ask again." He kept his voice low, making sure to lace it with just enough threat.

Zac kept his eyes on her face, making sure that she really *did* want what she'd just asked for. The change in her expression was almost instant. Her embarrassment, her discomfort faded and her eyes softened. He held his breath for one, two, three beats, and then Tacy rose from the bed, reached for the hem of her shirt and pulled it over her head.

Zac sucked in a deep breath. She truly was gorgeous. He forced himself to remain on the bed, praying for the patience to let her finish the task on her own. Right now, he wanted nothing more than to run his hands and lips over every inch of her.

Tacy shimmied her skirt down, kicking it and her shoes off. Her bra and panties matched. God, he loved matching sets.

Tacy's underwear was surprising girlie. Pale pink, silky. The bra was one of those push-up types that showcased her breasts perfectly.

She hesitated for only a moment, until he captured her gaze. "Keep going," he said, his voice gentler. He didn't want to scare her. Couldn't stand the thought of her changing her mind now. He wanted her more than he'd ever wanted a woman.

Her bra fastened in front and with one quick flick, it was open. She slid the straps over her shoulders and dropped the silk to the floor. Then she took a deep breath and shed the panties as well.

Zac had slept with some lovely women, but Tacy put them all to shame. Her body was trim and toned. He studied her knee, evidence of her recent surgery catching his attention. She had clearly gone to a good surgeon. She wouldn't have much of a scar.

"Playing doctor?" she teased.

He chuckled. "Shit. Yeah."

She laughed and he was struck by how easy it was to be with her. Tacy wasn't hard work. He didn't have to put on airs or try to impress her.

"Now what?" she asked breathlessly.

And just like that, the air in the room thickened as he considered what Tacy wanted. What *he* wanted.

Zac stood and reached out, pulling her toward him. His hands skimmed along her arms, then her sides and her hips. Tacy shivered, though not with cold. Her skin felt too warm for her to be chilled.

He cupped her breasts, weighing the firm flesh with his palms before tightening his grip.

Tacy sighed, her eyes drifted closed.

Zac couldn't resist a taste. Bending forward, he captured one nipple between his lips and sucked hard. Tacy's hands flew to his hair.

He continued to increase the pressure until she cried out, the sound a beautiful blend of pleasure and pain.

"If I do anything you don't like, tell me to stop."

Tacy nodded. "Okay."

"I'm going to test your limits, darlin'. Gonna take you. Rough and hard." He repeated her request.

Her fingers tightened in his hair. "Please," she whispered.

It was all he needed to hear. Zac twisted her toward the bed, pushing her onto her back on the mattress. He came over her, kissing her with all the strength, all the desire he'd kept tamped down.

Tacy responded to everything. Her tongue stroked his. She nipped at his lower lip, pulled his hair, and her nails scored his skin through the thin cotton of his T-shirt.

Zac held her face in his hands, turning it so that he could deepen the kiss. Tacy's legs parted and she wrapped them around his hips, gyrating against him.

Zac pressed into her, letting her feel his cock, still trapped inside the denim.

"Take off your clothes," she murmured against his lips, unwilling to break the kiss as she spoke.

He reached down with one hand, working the button and zipper on his jeans free as Tacy struggled to get him out of his T-shirt. Through it all, they continued kissing, neither willing to part for even a second.

They fought with his clothing for several minutes before they finally broke for air. Zac knelt above her and finished tugging off the shirt she'd only managed to get halfway up his chest.

"How do you get a body like that in the library?"

Zac chuckled. "Did I mention the gym was next door? Made it convenient for study breaks."

He was tempted to begin the kissing again, but the pain of keeping his cock contained was becoming too much to bear. The problem was Zac knew the second he freed it, he would be hard-pressed to keep himself from taking her.

It was apparent her past experiences had come up lacking. He didn't want to add his name to the list of lackluster lovers who'd spent time in her bed.

Regardless, something had to give. He shoved his jeans down, but kept his boxers on. Then he did a mental eye roll. Yeah. That wasn't going to help.

Fuck it.

He pulled off his boxers, and then joined her on the bed once again. Tacy added fuel to the fire when she immediately reached for his dick, encircling the flesh and stroking.

"God, Tace. You keep doing that and this will be over way too fast."

She didn't relent or respond. Zac let himself enjoy her touch for a minute more, and then he grasped her wrist and pulled her hand away.

"Put your hands above your head, darlin'."

She looked as if she'd complain, so he shot her a serious look that told her he wasn't kidding. "You can put them there of your own accord or I can tie them to the headboard."

Tacy licked her lips. "Is that what you mean by kinky?"

"You like the idea of bondage?"

She nodded. "I think..." She slowly lifted her arms, placing them on the mattress by her head.

The idea of bondage turned her on, but that took trust.

This thing between them was still too new. He was glad to see her exercising caution. Maybe they'd revisit the idea at the end of the week.

Zac tried to ignore the way his chest tightened when he considered how short their time together was.

"Good girl," he whispered, kissing her quickly. He straddled her waist, grabbed her wrists and dragged them higher. While she wasn't ready for real bondage, he sensed the idea of being held captive turned her on. And her quick intake of breath when he held her hands to the bed proved it.

When he bent lower, she lifted her face, clearly expecting him to kiss her again. Instead, Zac ran his lips along her cheek before sucking her earlobe into his mouth. Her breathing grew heavier and she struggled slightly to move her hands. She was used to touching. It would be hard for her to lose the use of her hands. He squeezed her wrists as a warning to hold still.

Zac dragged his mouth along the side of her neck, licking her soft skin. Tacy tried to move her lower body, clearly ready to advance the game. He reached back and lightly tapped her upper thigh as a warning.

"Stop trying to control things, Tacy."

She blinked rapidly, her eyes seeming to lose focus. God, she really did like the idea of being dominated in bed.

Zac's sexual preferences and hers were in perfect harmony. There was no bigger turn-on than taking a strong, independent woman to bed and finding a sweet submissive lingering beneath the surface.

He scooted lower, caging her knees between his thighs as he released her hands. She started to lift them, but he shook his head.

"Leave your hands there."

She studied his face, clearly trying to decide if she should test his limits.

He held her gaze and decided to test a limit or two of his own. "Disobey me and I won't hesitate to flip you over and spank that pretty little ass of yours."

Her eyes widened, then that same heavy-lidded look returned as his words soaked in. "New fan of dirty talk. Just sayin'."

Zac grinned. "I'll take that under advisement."

He moved farther down then shifted until he was kneeling between her ankles. Tacy jerked slightly when he ran his tongue along her slit.

"Oh my God."

Finding her clit with his thumb, he tasted her once more.

Tacy's hips lifted from the mattress, seeking more. He dipped his tongue into her opening and applied more pressure on the tight nub of her clit. She came apart. Just like that.

He found it difficult to believe her assertions that her orgasms were hard to achieve. Every time he touched her, she went off like a bottle rocket. He glanced up her body to see her hands balled into fists, but still resting where he told her to keep them. Her face was flushed, her eyes closed, and her chest rose and fell rapidly.

Slow and steady be damned. He was staying the rest of the week and if he had his way, he'd spend every fucking minute of it right here. In this bed. Naked. Sweaty. Buried deep inside her.

He moved quickly, grasping a condom from the small nightstand drawer. Ned had pulled him aside when he'd handed him the keys for the RV and confided he'd stocked the drawer. At the time, Zac figured that nicety a waste of money. Now, he was grateful for the kindness.

Zac donned the condom as Tacy slowly stirred, as she returned from wherever her orgasm had sent her. "Ready for another?"

She blinked rapidly, and then nodded. "Does that make me greedy?"

He kissed her and placed the head of his cock at her opening. "No, darlin'. Not a bit."

He pressed in with one steady, relentless push, not stopping until he was buried to the hilt. Tacy wrapped her legs around his waist, the position allowing him to go even deeper.

They groaned in unison and then, he gave up all semblance of control. He withdrew and returned, gaining speed with each thrust.

Tacy had asked that it be hard, rough. Thank God. Zac wasn't sure he could have given her anything else. He wanted her too much. She was warm and wet, and she made the most adorable little sex squeaks he'd ever heard.

Over and over, he moved inside, until he felt her inner muscles clench, tighten, grip his dick almost painfully. Her orgasm triggered his own. He jerked roughly as he filled the condom.

Tacy's cries filled the room as she said his name. "God. Zac. Yes. Holy shit."

He held himself above her on his elbows, trying to keep his weight off her, as he fought to catch his breath.

"We're doing that again," he announced several minutes later.

Tacy's laughed turned to a groan—her pussy clenching—when he slid out and fell to her side. "Amen."

They lay side by side for several moments, both of them staring at the ceiling. He reached over to find her hand, linking her fingers with his.

He turned to look at her. "Stay the night."

She nodded. "Okay."

"Stay here with me all week."

Tacy smiled. "Okay."

CHAPTER FIVE

"**G**otta say, Tace. When I suggested you hook up with Zac, the hot doctor, I had no idea you'd take me so literally."

Tacy rolled her eyes as she sat on the tailgate of Travis' truck, watching Zac and several locals from Sapphire Falls pass a bottle of Borcher's Booze around the bonfire.

She'd spent the last three nights in Zac's bed. Tacy had lost count of how many orgasms she'd had. They'd indulged in missionary, doggy, and 69, as well as sex against the wall, on the kitchen table, and even outside under the stars.

It was absolute insanity. She had known the man four days. Just four damn days, and he'd turned her world upside down.

"Earth to Tacy."

Tacy looked over at Lauren and gave her a sheepish grin. "Sorry. Drifted."

"Yeah. Lost in a haze of good sex seems to be your standard state these days."

"I've been a terrible guest, haven't I?"

Lauren laughed good-naturedly. "I wanted you to come to

Sapphire Falls to relax and enjoy yourself. To shrug off that anxiety that's been following you around lately. I'd say you've done just that. So you'll hear no complaints from me."

"He's amazing." Tacy sounded like a lovestruck teenage girl with stars in her eyes, but she didn't care.

"I hate to be the wet blanket, but you realize it's Thursday, right? Time is sort of running out on," Lauren waved her hands around, "whatever this is."

Tacy couldn't find a word to define the whatever, so she left it alone. "I know."

"Do you think you'll see him again?"

Tacy shrugged. "He lives in New Orleans. And I'm essentially homeless at the moment. Besides, we don't really..." She was embarrassed to finish her thought. They'd connected that first night, sharing a little bit about their childhoods, but since then...well. Uncomfortable confessing that apart from some surface-y type conversations and a shit-ton of rocking-the-camper sex, she and Zac didn't know each other as well as they should, given the way she was starting to feel about him.

"Talk?" Lauren supplied with an amused grin.

Tacy nodded. "I can't really explain it. We have a great time, walking around, taking in all the festival events, but the second we're alone, the clothes are on the floor and we're going at it like he's been away to war for ten years."

Lauren handed Tacy her cup and she took a small sip of the Booze, the alcohol burning all the way down. She wasn't sure how the locals could stomach the stuff. It packed a punch.

"So maybe the two of you should spend a little time getting to know each other—in a nonphysical way. You've clearly established you've got the sex thing in common. Might be a good idea to see if you're compatible in other ways. Find out who he's voting for in the next presidential election. Shit like that tells you a lot about a person."

Tacy made a face. "Oh man. You're not kidding."

"I think he's proven he's worth the effort."

He had, which prompted Tacy to speak her main concern. "I'm sure he is, but to what end? What am I working toward here?" Tacy worried part of her reason for not pushing to learn more about Zac was because she feared what would happen at the end of the week. What if she fell hard for the guy, but he wasn't interested in more?

Neither of them discussed future plans. Why would they? They'd gone into this treating it like some fun weeklong summer fling. He hadn't asked her for more than this week. And she hadn't offered more. Now, she was starting to fear she might want more. She just wasn't sure how much.

"If it's just a shits-and-giggles thing, then by all means, ignore my advice and just keep having fun. But I'd hate to see you hold back from a really great guy simply because of geography. The last thing I ever planned to do was settle in a small town. Travis changed my mind about that. Like you said, you're free as a bird. And New Orleans is an awesome city. I wouldn't mind having a friend to stay with there come Mardi Gras and Jazz Fest time."

Tacy took another sip of the Booze, tipsiness be damned. "I'll keep your future happiness in mind as I debate following some guy I just met halfway across the country."

Lauren winked. "You're a good friend. If it were me and the sex was that damn good, I'd be taking a closer look at the whole package. You don't want to let a few years go by and find yourself constantly wondering if he was the one and you let him slip away."

Tacy could totally see that happening. Maybe she did owe it to herself to see if this instant attraction had the possibility to lead to something more. "Great. As if I didn't have enough questions to sort through in my life."

After that first night, they'd sort of managed to talk about everything except themselves. And for Tacy, that holding back had been intentional. She thought it would protect her heart, but that clearly hadn't happened. At all.

Lauren patted her knee sympathetically. "Look on the bright side. You could start talking and realize he's a complete tool. That would make things really easy."

Zac Lewis was not a tool. In fact, Tacy was fairly certain he had all the characteristics to be her Mr. Right. Which would really suck if he didn't feel the same way about her. Regardless, Lauren was right about regrets. Tacy didn't want any. Not with Zac. "Okay. So tonight, before happy naked time, I'll initiate a conversation, get to know him on a deeper level."

"You can start now." Lauren hopped off the tailgate of the truck as Travis approached her. The party was starting to break up.

The river party was taking place on Lauren's friend Phoebe's property. When Phoebe had issued the invitation to Zac and Tacy to join them, she'd told Zac to just drive his RV out and park it in the field for the night, so they could enjoy the Booze and not have to worry about driving.

Since Tacy had given up her room at the B&B two days earlier, her suitcase was parked next to Zac's bed. She was surprised how much she loved staying in the camper.

Zac was only a few steps behind Travis. "I told Phoebe we'd put the fire out before heading back to the RV. Thought maybe you'd like to hang out a little longer."

She would. There was something very peaceful and romantic about sitting next to a bonfire. Even one that was dying down.

Add in the babbling of the river, the singing of the crickets and the gentle breeze rustling the leaves, and Tacy was fairly certain she'd found heaven.

"Sounds great."

She and Zac bid Lauren, Travis and their friends goodbye, then reclaimed the two beach chairs they'd carried down from the RV.

"This place is incredible," Zac said, mimicking her thoughts exactly.

"It is." She paused, wondering how she should initiate the get-to-know-you conversation. Would he think it weird if she started asking a bunch of personal questions? Before she could chicken out, she just dove in.

"Tell me about your family."

Zac tilted his head, his forehead creased in confusion. "The Lewises? What do you want to know?"

"You always talk about Mama Lewis. Was there a Papa Lewis?"

He nodded and his instant smile told her he adored the dad as much as the mom. "Yeah. Huge giant of a guy. He'd been a boxer in his younger days. Toughest man I've ever known. He was away from home most of the year. Worked on an oil rig for months at a time. Died of a massive heart attack about six, seven years ago. Damn. Can't believe it's been that long. It was a rough time for all of us, losing him so unexpectedly."

"You said you went to live with Mama Lewis when you were fifteen?"

"Yeah."

"Were you in the foster care system before that or with your parents?"

Zac fell silent. Tacy bit her lip, suddenly sorry for starting this conversation. The problem was she felt extraordinarily close to Zac. It was preposterous, considering their short acquaintance and how little she truly knew about him. Regardless, she felt like—deep down—she really did know him.

"I haven't talked about my mom to anyone in years. Except for Mama Lewis."

"I'm sorry. I didn't mean to—"

"No," Zac cut her off mid-sentence. "Don't apologize. I'd like to tell you about it. We haven't talked much about personal stuff, have we?" He gave her a wicked grin that let her know he was perfectly aware of exactly what had kept them virtual— and intimate—strangers.

"I guess I'm curious. I find myself wanting to know everything about you."

Zac gave her a smile so genuine she felt tears sting her eyes. "I want the same. I'm fascinated by you, darlin'."

She closed her eyes to stem the happy, touched tears. God, she was not the weepy type. Ever. She'd sat through *P.S. I Love You* and *The Notebook* without shedding a tear. Her teammates had teasingly called her a heartless bitch. Truth was tears had always been treated as weakness in her family. If she got a stitch in her side or a cramp in her leg, her father had scolded her for getting weepy and told her to play through the pain. After a while, she'd sort of forgotten how to cry.

"I'm hardly fascinating."

Zac scoffed. "You're kidding me, right? You're interesting, funny, cute, and sexy as hell. If that doesn't make you fascinating, Tacy Bradford, I don't know what else would."

"Damn," she whispered.

"What's wrong?"

"I really want to talk to you, learn more about you, but when you say stuff like that, it's very difficult for me not to jump on board and fuck your brains out."

Zac's loud laughter filled the quiet night. "Standing invitation to hop on anytime, darlin'."

"I like the way you call me darlin'. No one's ever really given me a pet name."

"I'm sort of glad to be your first on that...and the other thing."

Zac still marveled at the fact she'd struggled to have orgasms with her past lovers. Probably because he only had to call her that sweet nickname with that sexy southern accent of his, blow in her ear twice and she was coming hard enough to shake the ground more than a stampede of cattle.

They fell silent for a few moments, both staring into the dying fire.

"My mom was a drug addict, crack, heroin, shit like that," he started.

She had just decided she wouldn't push him for the story, not wanting to make him uncomfortable or sad.

"Oh." It was a lame response, but really...what else could she say to that? No child deserved to grow up around something like that.

"I only have a vague memory of our lives before she got addicted. It was just her and me for three years. Then my brother, Noah, came along. She's never told either one of us who our dad is. Or I guess I should say dads. I'm pretty sure we don't have the same one. She wasn't always hooked on drugs. At first, she worked in a liquor store. A neighbor in the apartment next door looked after us. But then Mom lost the job and the woman who took care of us died. Someone introduced her to coke. After that, most of the years I can remember are of her strung out. Prostituting for money that she would spend on drugs. I learned to grab as much of the cash as I could without her noticing after she and the johns passed out. Used that to feed me and Noah."

"Jesus. Zac." She failed to keep the tears at bay. Her heart shattered as she considered how hard his life had been. It made it even more incredible to see the man he'd become today.

"Hey, it didn't kill me, so no tears, okay?" He stood up,

reaching out for her and Tacy went to him. He sat down in the sand and tugged her in between his legs so that she could rest her back against his chest. He wrapped his arms around her tightly. "That's better. I missed touching you."

"Was that really your life until you were fifteen?"

Zac shook his head. "No. Not exactly. The state stepped in when I was twelve and Noah nine. Teacher spotted a nasty bruise on Noah's side. He'd gotten hit by one of my mom's boyfriends for breaking a glass in the kitchen."

Tacy bit her lip, trying not to cry any more. "What an asshole."

He chuckled, but the sound wasn't a happy one. "Yeah. There were a lot of assholes in and out of our apartment. We got put in the system. First home they sent us to was almost as bad as the one they'd pulled us out of. I grabbed Noah after three months there and ran. Cops found us, put us back in foster care. That was when we met Mama Lewis. She was one of the few foster parents willing to take both of us. I'd made it pretty clear to the social worker that Noah and I were not getting split up."

"But I thought you said you went to live with Mama Lewis at fifteen?"

"We stayed with Mama Lewis off and on for two years. My mom was trying to get straight, doing everything the court asked. It looked like she was going to pull herself out, get off the drugs. I'm no different from any other kid, I guess. I wanted to be with my mom, and I resented the hell out of the system and Mama Lewis for keeping me away from her."

"What changed your mind?"

"My mom managed to convince the court to give us back. She stayed clean for exactly eight weeks."

"Shit," she murmured.

"Yeah. And when she fell off the wagon, she fell off hard.

That was when she started doing heroin. The johns were back in her bed, the cabinets were empty and I stopped believing in...well...basically everything. I was an angry little prick blaming the world for all the shit in my life. Started smoking pot, stealing, drinking, doing everything wrong."

"I can't imagine you like that. Not even for a second."

"It didn't last long. We'd only been back with my mom about six months. She'd passed out after a party with some random guy. Always the same routine. Stoned and sex. I was feeling like a badass and thought I'd rob the guy. He woke up. Beat the shit out of me."

"Oh my God. Bad?"

Zac's arms tightened around her, but the response seemed to be unconscious. He was reliving a bad time in his mind. "Pretty bad. Noah ran to the neighbor's house and called Mama Lewis. She showed up with Justin, Caliph and Jett, the police and an ambulance not two steps behind her."

"Hooray for Mama Lewis."

Zac kissed the back of her head. "You can say that again. Spent a couple days in the hospital and then I went home."

"Home?"

"Mama Lewis' house became home to me from that day on. She saved my life. Saved *me*. I straightened my ass out, stopped being such a punk, started studying, started believing in family and love and second chances."

"And your mom?"

Zac blew out a long sigh. "Still alive. Still in New Orleans. I see her about once a month. Take her food. She's...well...she hasn't changed at all."

Tacy wasn't sure how to reply. He took his drug-addicted mother food every month? Even after the hell she'd put him through growing up?

This was why she didn't want to get to know Zac. Because

just like that, she fell completely, spectacularly, head over heels in love with him.

And it only took four days.

She twisted around, cupped his cheek in one hand and kissed him. Zac deepened the embrace, the two of them kissing as if their lips had never touched before.

When they broke apart, she gave him a soft smile. "I'm never complaining about my parents again."

Zac laughed softly. "It's not a contest, Tace."

"I'll admit I'm jealous of your siblings. Sort of sucks being an only child. Always thought life would have been a lot more fun with a brother or a sister."

"I'll share mine. I've got plenty of them."

"I guess I used to believe maybe my parents wouldn't have put so much pressure on me to constantly succeed if there had been another kid in the house. They were living vicariously through me—exclusively through me. Would have been nice to have someone to share that load with."

"Why do you think your folks felt the need to do that to you?"

Tacy shrugged. "My dad had always dreamed of playing baseball in the major leagues, but he never made it beyond college ball. Said he wished he'd had more support from his parents."

"Is that what they call it? Support? Because it sounds like it was a lot of pressure."

She sighed. "I'll be honest. I've seen some amazing places and done some incredible things. I wouldn't have had those opportunities if it hadn't been for my parents pushing me so hard."

"Why do I feel like there's a 'but' coming?"

"But sometimes I wonder if this is the life I would have

chosen for myself. Growing up, I wasn't really given options. And now..."

"Now you have to decide for yourself what you want."

Tacy ran her hand through her hair, pulling it away from her face. "I don't have a lot of experience with making my own decisions. What if I mess up?"

Zac reached for the strand of hair she'd just moved and twirled it around his finger. "You won't."

It was a simple assertion, but somehow, knowing he believed in her went a long way toward setting her mind at ease.

"What do you want to do?"

She didn't hesitate to share her dream with him. She told him about Lauren introducing her to gardening, how much she loved creating beauty from the things she planted in the ground. About her desire to go back to school and her fear of failing.

Zac listened intently and, like Lauren, he offered words of encouragement, bolstered her with his belief that she could do anything she set her mind to. He was good for her, managing to help her overcome her wavering confidence. She'd never had a problem believing in herself until the fall. Since then, her self-assurance had taken a hit. Zac and Lauren had helped her find her footing again, and suddenly she wasn't as worried about going back to college.

"So see?" he said. "You're a hobo at heart too. You've already planned your next adventure. You'll go back to college and hook up with a frat boy."

She laughed. "There will be no frat boys. Wait. God, you weren't in a fraternity, were you?"

He shrugged. "Boring guy, remember? Besides, I was working two part-time jobs just to ensure I wouldn't be in debt for the rest of my life. Wasn't much money or time left over for the fun stuff."

His words provoked that same pang in her heart, the one that ached for how hard he'd had to work to accomplish all he had. The same pain that told her she didn't want to say goodbye to him in a few days.

It was on the tip of her tongue to mention that end date. To ask him what he thought would happen next, but he spoke before she could find the nerve to voice her concerns.

"Wanna head back to the RV?" he asked.

She nodded, taking the coward's way out. He'd mentioned her hooking up with a frat boy, and while she knew that comment was a joke, she was struck by the impression he wasn't too bothered by that idea.

Together, they dumped river water on what was left of the bonfire, making sure it was out completely. Then they returned to the RV, hand in hand. Neither of them spoke, both lost in their thoughts.

Tacy's mind was racing over a million different things. Zac's painful childhood, Mama Lewis saving him, his drug-addicted mom, the fact it was already Thursday. Her heart was beating fast, not so much in anticipation of sleeping with Zac, but because her emotions were all over the place.

She'd come to Sapphire Falls intent on mapping out a plan, considering her next move. She thought that would simply involve deciding what she wanted to do for a living and where she wanted to live.

Now she was trying to figure out *how*—God, *if*—Zac could fit into that plan.

When they entered the RV, they walked straight to the bedroom. Though they'd only spent a few nights together, they'd established some patterns, eased into comfortable routines.

Tacy turned to face him as they stood at the foot of the bed. Her chest was tight—with anticipation and fear. There were so many things she wanted to say to him, but how could she? This whole thing was going way too fast. What if she told him she had feelings for him—serious feelings—and he looked at her like she was crazy? Telling someone you loved him after only a few days *was* insane. Wasn't it?

If Zac was feeling any reticence, it didn't show. Instead, he acted like he had every other night. He tugged her T-shirt over her head in one fell swoop. She'd eschewed a bra and worn her bikini top underneath. He made short work of that as well, untying the laces holding it on and dropping it to the floor.

After that, she stopped worrying about everything. When she was with Zac, like this, the whole world disappeared. It was just the two of them, living in the moment. And nothing—not one damn thing—mattered right now except this.

She added his shirt to the pile of discarded clothing, and then they each stripped off their own bottoms. Within seconds they were naked. And in one second more, they were on the bed, Zac caging her beneath him as he kissed her lips, her neck, her breasts. He didn't stop until his mouth hovered just above her clit, his hot breath tickling the sensitive skin there.

He ran his tongue along her slit, and then pressed it against her clit as he pushed two fingers deep inside her. As always, his rough touches triggered her arousal, every nerve tingling as she lifted her hips to grasp more.

Zac added a third finger, increased his pace, and just like that...she was flying. When she returned to earth, he was laying next to her. She expected him to have a condom in hand, ready to go. Instead, he was looking at her, studying her face.

"That was amazing."

His grin told her he was pleased. "Our time is running out."

And then, her peaceful, easy feeling was shattered. "I

know." She wondered if he'd mention what happened next. Would they simply say goodbye on Saturday or would he want to see her again?

"I think we should make the most of it."

She nodded slowly, trying to ignore the pain in her chest. Dammit, she was going to leave this town with a broken heart. She just knew it. "Okay."

"You said you wanted to explore sexually. Test some limits."

Tacy *had* said that. And they'd already broken through more than a few barriers. "The kinky ones?" She ignored the voice that said she was a fool to stay here, to fall deeper and deeper under his spell, but there was also the impractical, horny Tacy who wanted to put her body in his oh-so-capable hands and steal a few thousand more of those incredible orgasms. After all, she'd need as many memories as she could make to keep her warm through the lonely nights to come.

He kissed her cheek gently. "Yeah. The kinky ones."

"What did you have in mind?"

"Thought we could start easy. Two options. I'd like to spank you. Or I'd like to tie you up."

"So...it's an *or*? Not an *and*?"

Zac groaned, a deep-throated growl that sent shivers of need along her spine. "It can be an and."

She bit her lip as she considered his request. She wanted both things. Badly. Then she remembered what he'd said. "And these are the easy kinky things?"

He chuckled. "You're adorable. This week is going too damn fast."

Tacy wished he'd stop saying that, stop pointing out the inevitable ending. "I know," she whispered.

Zac leaned close and kissed her. "If you hate it, you say stop."

"Okay," she agreed, knowing she wouldn't want to. No matter what they did in bed, Zac had a way of making her toes curl with delight. He was a thorough, attentive, talented lover. He knew what to say, where to touch her, how to drive her out of her mind. It was addictive.

Zac left the bed briefly, rifling through the small closet. She sat up and watched as he tossed two neckties onto the bed.

"Ties? On vacation?"

He shrugged. "Wanted to be prepared."

"For bondage?" she asked without thinking.

He laughed. "God, no. I wasn't sure if I'd find a nice restaurant to try or a church to attend."

"Oh."

"The bondage option just turned out to be a lucky circumstance."

She rolled her eyes, grinning widely at his humor. "So how does this work? I just let you do all these naughty things to me?"

He studied her as she sat on the bed. "No one said you had to be complacent."

Her interests in his offer piqued even more. "So I can fight you?"

Something in her tone must have given her away because Zac's eyes darkened with lust, his face suddenly dangerously seductive. "Oh yeah. You could definitely try."

The man had her number, knew exactly how to spark her competitive nature. "I don't try, Zac. I succeed. Remember?" She gave him back just enough cheek to make sure he felt the same need to win that she did.

"You've never come against an opponent like me, darlin'. So here are the rules. You're welcome to fight me as much as you want. Give it everything you've got. And *when*," he stressed the word, "I subdue you, you're mine. Completely. To do whatever I want."

She bit her lip as she considered the offer. She wanted that. Truly. But there was something sort of terrifying about that "whatever I want" taunt.

He must have noticed her sudden reticence. "How do you stop me, Tacy? Truly stop me."

"By asking."

He nodded. "I'm not going to hurt you in any way you're not going to love."

She suspected—no, she knew—that was true. He'd proven his skills every single time they'd been together. "Not much room to move around in here."

"We can take it back outside if you want. I can even give you a head start."

She laughed nervously at the offer to run around naked in a field with Zac chasing her.

Tacy shook her head. "Here is fine. I prefer being able to see the bad boy coming."

"We're going to have to work on your fear of haunted houses and horror films."

Tacy moved away from him, rising so that the bed was between them. "Ready?"

"Set," he answered.

Her gaze flew around the room. She hadn't been kidding about the tight space. She figured she had a fifty-fifty shot at making it to the kitchen area. And then what?

She laughed as she shouted, "Go!" Who was she fooling? She wanted him to catch her.

Tacy darted for the narrow corridor and made it a couple steps in front of Zac. She had no doubt he'd let her have that victory. He obviously understood as well as she did how quickly this chase was going to end.

She made it to the front of the RV, and then twisted. Zac blocked her path back to the bedroom. Which left her two options—flight through the door and out to the field. Or to stand and fight. It didn't matter how strong she was. Zac had half a foot and about fifty pounds of sheer muscle on her.

So she went with the element of surprise. Darting out the door.

There was a full moon to light her way, and she ran with absolute, unbridled delight through the field. She was barefoot, but the grass was green and soft. She'd never in her life imagined doing anything so scandalous. She felt wild, reckless, free. She was halfway back to the river when Zac caught up to her. His large hand wrapped around her upper arm, twisting her toward him. She started to stumble and feared this chase was going to end painfully, but Zac turned at the last minute, tugging her onto his chest as he took the brunt of the fall.

"Are you okay?" she asked breathlessly.

"Caught you."

Tacy tried to break free of his grip, but as she suspected, he'd captured her. And he had no intention of letting her go.

Zac managed to smoothly pull himself—and her—up from the ground. She dug in her feet when he started back toward the RV. She gasped when he lifted and tossed her over his shoulder as if she weighed no more than a sack of potatoes.

She couldn't help it. She giggled. Zac hesitated for a moment then his laughter mingled with hers. He was going for some sexy capture fantasy, and she was ruining it with the happiness she couldn't contain no matter how hard she tried.

Once they returned to the RV, Zac set her back on her feet, but kept hold of her, guiding her to the bedroom again.

She tried to twist out of his grasp, but the man was nothing if not determined. She expected him to push her to the mattress and tie her up. The mere thought of that had her pussy clenching in excitement. So she was surprised when he sat down first and pulled her facedown over his lap.

Shit. The spanking. She'd forgotten that part. Her horny mind had latched onto the sight of those two ties on the mattress and the rest had faded away. He'd promised to stop if it hurt and she knew he'd stand by that.

Tacy jerked when his hand caressed her bare ass gently.

"Nervous?" he asked, though he clearly knew she was, given her reaction.

"I was the queen of vanilla when you met me. What do you think?"

"I think you were made for this."

She didn't have time to consider that assertion before his hand rose, coming down harder this time. While it stung, she suspected he was holding back, letting her test the water first.

And there went another little piece of her heart.

Tacy decided to reward his kindness. Glancing up at him over her shoulder, she feigned a bored expression. "Is that the best you've got?"

Like her, Zac seemed hard-pressed to resist a dare. Probably a result of growing up in a house full of siblings.

He spanked her again, and this time, he put some force behind it.

"Ow," she yelled.

Zac landed two more without pausing. She started to take him to task, to tell him he was hurting her, but then she remembered the word. All she had to do was say stop.

She never even considered it. Not when he added another hard smack to her upper thigh. Actually, that was the moment when things stopped hurting and went a bit fuzzy. Her inner muscles clenched, the spasm more painful than the spanking. God, she needed him to fuck her. Like yesterday.

And hard.

Tacy fought to rise from his lap, determined to straddle it and sink down on the hard cock pressing against her hip.

Zac held her down firmly.

"Dammit, Zac. Let me up. I need you. Need you to fuck me." Her demands came out in harsh breaths.

He didn't give way. He landed half a dozen more smacks, varying the strengths and locations. They only drove her arousal higher.

Her body was on fire—her ass from the spanking, the rest from sheer, unadulterated horniness.

"Please. God. Please." If she had any pride left, she sure as hell couldn't find it. Didn't want to.

Zac finally relented. He lifted her from her lap, but rather than move them onto the bed, he cuddled her, kissing her cheeks gently. "You're perfect, Tacy."

No one had ever told her that. Not once. And the crazy thing was, when she thought about it, that was all she'd ever tried to be. The perfect daughter. The perfect player.

Zac was the only one to make no demands other than for her to be herself, to be happy, and that was what he found perfect.

She swallowed down the lump forming in her throat and silently prayed tonight would never end. Mercifully, he didn't see her expression, didn't notice the impact he'd just had on her.

Instead, he moved her slowly to the center of the bed. He grabbed one of the ties and bound her hands together above her head. Zac didn't bother to restrain her to the headboard, didn't use the other tie.

Once he had her hands where he wanted them, he caged her beneath him, kissing her as if his life depended on it. She understood the passion, that overwhelming desire to take as much as she could grab.

His fingers tightened in her hair, pulling it until her scalp stung as he kept kissing her. She pretended it was the stinging that sent tears to her eyes, but she knew better. Knew exactly why she was crying.

She blinked them away, refusing to let him see.

"Tacy," Zac murmured against her cheek. "God, darlin'. I need you so much."

She listened as he pulled on the condom, parting her legs so that he could come inside.

He thrust in with one hard motion that sent stars whirring behind her closed eyelids. Zac didn't hesitate to take what they both wanted. Over and over, he pushed. Then, just before she came, he withdrew and flipped her to her stomach. Tacy went up on her knees, her head and hands still pressed to the pillow as he pounded into her from behind.

She urged him to go faster. Harder.

He wrapped his arms around her, gripped her breasts, squeezed them roughly as she shoved her ass against him with all the force she could muster. It still wasn't enough.

Zac withdrew again, flipping her onto her back once more. "Want to see you. See your face."

He kissed her as he returned to her body. She wrapped her ankles around his waist, but it wasn't enough. Lifting her bound hands, she placed them around his neck, tying herself to him.

Zac didn't take her to task for moving them. She wasn't even sure he'd realized she had. He keep thrusting in, going deeper than she'd thought possible.

Then he lifted her knees, threw them over her shoulders and showed her exactly how deep he could go.

She screamed when her orgasm came, but Zac didn't stop moving. He pounded harder and she took it. Needed it. If this was all she could have, she would steal every ounce of pleasure and pain and hoard it in her memories for the rest of her life.

Her climax had only started to wane when the second overtook her. God, could orgasms lap each other?

She trembled roughly, her body on system overload. Zac couldn't resist this time. He fell too.

"Tacy. Jesus. Darlin'." Every word came out with a rough grunt, punctuated by one, two, three more hard thrusts into her body before he stilled.

He kissed her, neither of them seeking to part despite the undeniable heat in the room. It was steamy, humid, almost sweltering, but she didn't care. Didn't want him to leave her.

Zac broke the kiss, his hands holding her cheeks as he looked deeply into her eyes. "Soul mates," he whispered.

She didn't bother to hide her tears at that. She let them fill her eyes and she let him kiss them away.

He *was* her soul mate. There wasn't a doubt in her mind she would have spent centuries searching for this man again.

She was in love with him. God. Love.

And she thought the haunted house had been terrifying.

CHAPTER SIX

Zac knew Tacy wasn't in the bed before he even opened his eyes. Hell, he could tell she wasn't in the RV at all. It was too still, too quiet. He couldn't quite explain it to himself, but there was an energy in the air whenever she was around. It was a silly thought, but it was the only way he could describe it. His body seemed to know whenever she was within a fifty-foot radius, and it responded.

He'd never experienced anything like it before, but he liked it. A lot.

He liked Tacy a lot. Maybe more than like. When he'd told her about his childhood last night and she'd looked at him with those compassionate eyes, he'd lost his heart to her. The whole damn thing fell out of his hands and into hers. Which was crazy.

God, he could imagine Tacy's response if he took her hands in his and told her he loved her. She'd think he was a nutjob. Who fell in love in less than a week?

He knew. Those clinging guys who could never hold on to

a girlfriend because they were making plans to introduce her to the parents and proposing within forty-eight hours.

Yet that was what Zac wanted to do with Tacy. He wanted to take her home to Mama Lewis. Wanted to invite her to Sunday supper and introduce her to his big crazy family. God. They'd love her.

Caliph and his girlfriend, Jennifer, would show her their ink. Chloe would want to get a picture of the two of them together. Noah and Mama Lewis would compete to impress her with their gumbo, teasingly forcing her to tell them whose was the best. After dinner, Dani and her boyfriends, Aiden and Bryson, would pull out their guitars and they'd all sing along to every song they'd ever loved. And then they'd sink deeper into the well-worn couches in front of the big screen as Justin, Ned and Jett cussed out whichever team or ref was currently pissing them off. He wanted to see her there, wanted her to be a part of his family.

Dammit. He pushed the insanity deep inside and opened his eyes. His vision confirmed what he already knew. He was alone.

Glancing at his phone, he discovered he'd slept late. It was nearly noon. Perhaps she'd decided to let him sleep in and had gone to breakfast with Lauren. Apparently there was a mud run today, though he and Tacy had decided to skip it. Originally she had planned to do it, but he wasn't sure her knee was up to it, and the only kind of dirty he planned to get was with her, between the sheets.

He started to text her when he spotted a piece of paper on her pillow.

Zac,

Have to cut trip short. Heading back home today. Unex-
pected emergency. Had a wonderful week. I'll text you later.
Xo,
Tacy

WHAT THE FUCK WAS THAT?

Did she seriously just cut and run, say goodbye in a damn note?

Hell no. Hell fucking no.

Zac rose and quickly tugged on a pair of khaki shorts and a T-shirt. There was no way he was letting Tacy leave without saying goodbye. In person. Jesus. After all they'd done together, she owed him *at least* that much.

No. Now she owed him more than that. He wanted an explanation for the note. She wasn't callous or thoughtless, so clearly something had spooked her. Scared her.

But what?

It sure as shit wasn't the sex. Last night had been incredible. Hotter than hell. And Tacy had felt that too. She'd loved every single second she was tied up and she'd begged him to spank her harder.

His mind raced over everything they'd said and done, but nothing triggered any alarms. If anything, he turned a corner last night. The attraction he'd felt for her changing into genuine emotions—friendship, attraction...love.

Love. Zac sank down on the edge of the bed. He'd fallen for Tacy over the course of this week, but last night was the first time he had admitted it to himself. What if Tacy had made the same discovery?

Her life was in a major state of flux right now and he'd just added another wrench to the works.

He needed to find her, to talk to her. He fired off a text,

asking where she was, but that act proved futile when he heard her phone beep. She'd left the thing on the nightstand next to her side of the bed.

While that find made him happy—surely she wouldn't leave town without her phone—it didn't help him find her in the meantime. He didn't have Lauren's number, or anyone else's in town for that matter.

Zac grabbed the keys to the RV from the table and started the vehicle. They were parked in a field in the middle of nowhere. The nearest house was Phoebe's, so he'd start there. He had no idea how much of a head start she had on him, but he prayed she was still in Sapphire Falls.

He parked the camper in front of Phoebe's house, not bothering to shut off the engine. After knocking on the door several minutes and glancing around back, he had to admit no one was home.

His next stop was Lauren's house. Once again, the place was deserted. Clearly everyone was at the mud run. He returned to the town limits and reclaimed his same spot at the campsite before jogging toward the square. He had absolutely no idea where the mud run was supposed to happen. He consulted with one member of the Blue Brigade and learned the run was over, and most folks were cleaning up by floating down the river in tubes.

The river he'd just been parked beside. He sighed in frustration.

Tacy hadn't planned to do the run, but Lauren's husband, Travis, had. He did a quick sweep of the booths and rides just to confirm Tacy wasn't there, and then decided to drive back to the river.

Panic set in when he returned and realized he didn't have a clue where these tubers got in and out. He forced himself to sit on the bank and calm down. He needed to think rationally. Driving all over Kingdom Come was getting him nowhere.

He took a deep breath and considered everything they'd said last night, the confidences they'd shared. When he found her, Zac needed to have a plan. He grinned when he considered what he would say to her.

Then he flipped on his phone and started doing a Google search. He had quite a few things to say to Tacy Bradford. If she'd left town, he'd follow her. To hell with Big Sur and the Pacific Ocean. His rambling trip suddenly had a purpose, a set-in-stone schedule.

Once he found what he was looking for, his gaze swept over his surroundings.

He'd just wasted two hours searching for Tacy, and he was in the exact same place he'd started. What he needed to do was stop moving around. He clearly wasn't going to find her out here, so it was best to head back into town and ask around.

He'd start at the Come Again because he needed a drink. Big time.

***

"Oh my God, I'm such a freaking idiot," Tacy repeated, her head in her hands.

Lauren was kicked back in her chair at the Come Again, watching her over the rim of the giant margarita she'd just ordered. Tacy's sat untouched in front of her on the table, though getting drunk certainly seemed like a good idea at the moment.

"So what did the note say again?"

Tacy crinkled up her face. "Stupid shit. Something about an emergency and leaving early and thanks for the week. Why did I do that?"

"Panic."

Lauren's answer was succinct and there was no question in her tone. Her friend was right. She'd panicked. In spectacular fashion. Then she'd acted like an idiot, leaving him a note. A note, for God's sake!

"He must hate me." Tacy could only imagine how Zac would have felt waking up to find the bed empty and that horrible note on her pillow. "It was a terrible thing to do. Who says goodbye like that? And after such an amazing week?"

"He doesn't hate you."

Tacy didn't acknowledge Lauren's comment. Instead, she just buried her head deeper in her hands. "To make it worse, I left my phone in the RV. That's why I couldn't call you."

After leaving the RV this morning at the crack of dawn, Tacy had walked the almost-five miles to Lauren's house. And she'd cursed herself for being an absolute idiot the entire way. Upon arriving at Lauren's, she'd discovered her friend gone and recalled the mud run.

Fortunately, Travis' parents had passed her as she'd begun the trek to town. Her knee had started to hurt from so much walking and she'd been limping. The lovely couple had picked her up and driven her to town. Once there, she discovered she'd missed the mud run. Her first instinct had been to sit down and have a good old-fashioned cry right in the middle of the festival. Instead, she'd headed straight for the haunted house. She'd find some dark corner for her breakdown and if she was terrified out of her mind, it served her right for acting like such an idiot. She'd remained there for a long, terrifying hour, letting the tears fall without bothering to hide them, before daring to return to the carnival.

Mercifully, she'd found Lauren almost immediately. Her friend had taken one look at her stressed-out, freaked-out, tear-stained face and dragged her directly to the Come Again for drinks.

"Do you think you left your phone there subconsciously? Looking for a reason to go back?" Lauren asked.

She shook her head. "No. Believe me, I wasn't thinking that clearly. Left my favorite T-shirt and a pair of flip-flops too. What am I going to do, Lauren? I have no excuse for my behavior."

"Of course you do."

For the first time since sitting down, Tacy looked up and faced her friend, blowing out an exasperated breath. "I have no excuse. I'm going to *tell* him. Good God, how do you look at a guy you've known a handful of days and say, 'hey, by the way, I'm totally in love with you'? He'll think I'm a lunatic."

Lauren grinned and Tacy realized her friend wasn't looking at her, but over her shoulder.

"Why don't you turn around and test that lunatic theory?"

Tacy winced at the sound of Zac's voice. She didn't move, didn't take her eyes off Lauren's face. "How long has he been behind me?"

Lauren scrunched up her face and pretended to consider her question. "I think you were saying something about being a freaking idiot. Was that it, Zac? Freaking idiot?"

"Yep. Freaking idiot," he repeated.

The humor in his tone was the only thing that gave her the courage to stand up, turn around and face him. That, and the fact he and Lauren were having a lot of fun at her expense. "You're both assholes."

Zac laughed and there wasn't a trace of anger on his face.

Every ounce of regret and fear that had consumed her today vanished.

He reached for her. "I owed you a little payback for

running out on me this morning. I've driven all over this damn town looking for you."

She walked over to him, taking the hand he offered, loving how warm and strong it was. "I was hiding in the haunted house."

Zac tugged her toward him, wrapping her up in a tight hug. "Damn. That was a serious panic attack. You're limping."

"Sort of overdid it on the walking today."

He shook his head, his eyes concerned. "Tacy."

"I'm so sorry, Zac. I don't usually overreact like this."

He took a small step away and cupped her cheek. "I don't understand why. You've been in love before, right?"

She nodded. "Yeah, but it's never felt quite this intense. Or happened so quickly." She paused and then narrowed her eyes. "Why aren't you bothered by what I'm saying and trying to escape?"

He placed a soft kiss on her cheek. "Because I'm in love with you too. I've been in my own state of sheer panic all day, afraid I wouldn't be able to find you."

"So we're both crazy?" she asked, suddenly feeling about a thousand pounds lighter.

"Apparently."

"What do we do now?"

He shrugged. "You hop in the RV and come see Big Sur with me."

She laughed. "That really *would* be insane."

"You don't have anywhere to be for the next few weeks, do you?"

She shook her head. She didn't have one single plan. And his sounded awesome. "Nope. Nowhere to be."

"So it's settled." Zac seemed to subscribe to Lauren's life motto. Just do it.

"Okay. Then what?"

"If things go the way I'm hoping, I'm going to convince you to come back to New Orleans with me to meet Mama Lewis."

"I'd like to meet your family. A lot."

"They're gonna love you, darlin'."

"And then?"

He didn't hesitate to reply, and it occurred to her she hadn't been the only one thinking—and dreaming about the future. "I've got this little apartment a few blocks away from the French Quarter. I was thinking maybe you'd like to stay there with me for a while."

"A while?"

"As long as you want."

"Do you know if there are any schools in New Orleans that offer a landscape design degree?"

He grinned. "I just happen to know for a fact there are. Did a bit of Internet research this afternoon."

She sucked in a breath, relieved, thrilled, amazed that he'd actually been planning for a future with her. "That sounds awesome. If you don't mind putting up with an out-of-work, stressed-out college student for a while."

He shrugged good-naturedly. "I don't mind that if *you* don't mind I'm buried in a mountain of college debt and my hours at the hospital are bound to be long."

"I don't mind."

"I figure once you've tasted the beignets, I'll have you twisted up in my web forever."

"You're going to win me over with doughnuts?"

"And powdered sugar."

She laughed. "You realize you had me at caramel apple, right?"

Zac kissed her, a quick, hard, passionate one that made her heart race. The good kind of racing, though. "I love you, Tacy.

And maybe folks will say we're being reckless or crazy or going too fast, but I don't care."

She wrapped her arms around his neck and returned his kiss...with interest. "Fast, slow, standing still. I don't mind which way we go, as long as it's together."

ABOUT THE AUTHOR

Virginia native Mari Carr is a New York Times and USA TODAY bestseller of contemporary erotic romance novels. With over two million copies of her books sold, Mari was the winner of the Romance Writers of America's Passionate Plume award for her novella, Erotic Research. She has over a hundred published works, including her popular Wild Irish and Compass books, along with the Trinity Masters series she writes with Lila Dubois.

Follow Mari:
www.maricarr.com
mari@maricarr.com

Join her newsletter so you don't miss new releases and for exclusive subscriber-only content.